THE HERITAGE OF
SHANNARA
BOOKS I AND II
THE SCIONS OF SHANNARA
THE DRUID OF SHANNARA

TERRY BROOKS

THE HERITAGE OF
SHANNARA
BOOKS I AND II

THE SCIONS OF SHANNARA
THE DRUID OF SHANNARA

WINGS BOOKS
NEW YORK

Originally published in two separate volumes by Del Ray under the titles:

The Scions of Shannara copyright © 1990 by Terry Brooks
The Druid of Shannara copyright © 1991 by Terry Brooks

This edition contains the complete and unabridged texts of the original editions.

This 2006 edition is published by Wings Books, an imprint of
Random House Value Publishing, by arrangement with Del Ray,
divisions of Random House, Inc., New York.

Wings Books is a registered trademark and the colophon is
a trademark of Random House, Inc.

Random House
New York • Toronto • London • Sydney • Auckland
www.randomhouse.com

Map by Shelly Shapiro

Printed and bound in the United States of America.

A catalog record for this title is available from the Library of Congress.

ISBN-13: 978-0-517-22852-4
ISBN-10: 0-517-22852-1

10 9 8 7 6 5 4 3 2 1

Contents

THE SCIONS OF SHANNARA

FOR JUDINE
WHO MAKES ALL THE MAGIC POSSIBLE

THE SCIONS OF SHANNARA

CHAPTER

1

THE OLD MAN SAT ALONE in the shadow of the Dragon's Teeth and watched the coming darkness chase the daylight west. The day had been cool, unusually so for midsummer, and the night promised to be chill. Scattered clouds masked the sky, casting their silhouettes upon the earth, drifting in the manner of aimless beasts between moon and stars. A hush filled the emptiness left by the fading light like a voice waiting to speak.

It was a hush that whispered of magic, the old man thought.

A fire burned before him, small still, just the beginning of what was needed. After all, he would be gone for several hours. He studied the fire with a mixture of expectation and uneasiness before reaching down to add the larger chunks of deadwood that brought the flames up quickly. He poked at it with a stick, then stepped away, driven back by the heat. He stood at the edge of the light, caught between the fire and the growing dark, a creature who might have belonged to neither or both.

His eyes glittered as he looked off into the distance. The peaks of the Dragon's Teeth jutted skyward like bones the earth could not contain. There was a hush to the mountains, a secrecy that clung like mist on a frosty morning and hid all the dreams of the ages.

The fire sparked sharply and the old man brushed at a stray bit of glowing ash that threatened to settle on him. He was just a bundle of sticks, loosely tied together, that might crumble into dust if a strong wind were to blow. Gray robes and a forest

3

cloak hung on him as they would have on a scarecrow. His skin was leathery and brown and had shrunken close against his bones. White hair and beard wreathed his head, thin and fine, like wisps of gauze against the firelight. He was so wrinkled and hunched down that he looked to be a hundred years old.

He was, in fact, almost a thousand.

Strange, he thought suddenly, remembering his years. Paranor, the Councils of the Races, even the Druids—gone. Strange that he should have outlasted them all.

He shook his head. It was so long ago, so far back in time that it was a part of his life he only barely recognized. He had thought that part finished, gone forever. He had thought himself free. But he had never been that, he guessed. It wasn't possible to be free of something that, at the very least, was responsible for the fact that he was still alive.

How else, after all, save for the Druid Sleep, could he still be standing there?

He shivered against the descending night, darkness all about him now as the last of the sunlight slipped below the horizon. It was time. The dreams had told him it must be now, and he believed the dreams because he understood them. That, too, was a part of his old life that would not let him go—dreams, visions of worlds beyond worlds, of warnings and truths, of things that could and sometimes must be.

He stepped away from the fire and started up the narrow pathway into the rocks. Shadows closed about him, their touch chill. He walked for a long time, winding through narrow defiles, scrambling past massive boulders, angling along craggy drops and jagged splits in the rock. When he emerged again into the light, he stood within a shallow, rock-strewn valley dominated by a lake whose glassy surface reflected back at him with a harsh, greenish cast.

The lake was the resting place for the shades of Druids come and gone. It was to the Hadeshorn that he had been summoned.

"Might as well get on with it," he growled softly.

He walked slowly, cautiously downward into the valley, his steps uneasy, his heart pounding in his ears. He had been away a long time. The waters before him did not stir; the shades lay sleeping. It was best that way, he thought. It was best that they not be disturbed.

He reached the lake's edge and stopped. All was silent. He took a deep breath, the air rattling from his chest as he exhaled like dry leaves blown across stone. He fumbled at his waist for a pouch and loosened its drawstrings. Carefully he reached within and drew out a handful of black powder laced with silver sparkle. He hesitated, then threw it into the air over the lake.

The powder exploded skyward with a strange light that brightened the air about him as if it were day again. There was no heat, only light. It shimmered and danced against the night-time like a living thing. The old man watched, robes and forest cloak pulled close, eyes bright with the reflected glow. He rocked back and forth slightly and for a moment felt young again.

Then a shadow appeared suddenly in the light, lifting out of it like a wraith, a black form that might have been something strayed from the darkness beyond. But the old man knew better. This was nothing strayed; this was something called. The shadow tightened and took shape. It was the shade of a man cloaked all in black, a tall and forbidding apparition that anyone who had ever seen before would have recognized at once.

"So, Allanon," the old man whispered.

The hooded face tilted back so that the light revealed the dark, harsh features clearly—the angular bearded face, the long thin nose and mouth, the fierce brow that might have been cast of iron, the eyes beneath that seemed to look directly into the soul. The eyes found the old man and held him fast.

—I need you—

The voice was a whisper in the old man's mind, a hiss of dissatisfaction and urgency. The shade communicated by using thoughts alone. The old man shrank back momentarily, wishing that the thing he had called would instead be gone. Then he recovered himself and stood firm before his fears.

"I am no longer one of you!" he snapped, his own eyes narrowing dangerously, forgetting that it was not necessary to speak aloud. "You cannot command me!"

—I do not command. I request. Listen to me. You are all

that is left, the last that may be until my successor is found. Do you understand—

The old man laughed nervously. "Understand? Ha! Who understands better than me?"

—A part of you will always be what once you would not have questioned. The magic stays within you. Always. Help me. I send the dreams and the Shannara children do not respond. Someone must go to them. Someone must make them see. You—

"Not me! I have lived apart from the races for years now. I wish nothing more to do with their troubles!" The old man straightened his stick form and frowned. "I shed myself of such nonsense long ago."

The shade seemed to rise and broaden suddenly before him, and he felt himself lifted free of the earth. He soared skyward, far into the night. He did not struggle, but held himself firm, though he could feel the other's anger rushing through him like a black river. The shade's voice was the sound of bones grating.

—Watch—

The Four Lands appeared, spread out before him, a panorama of grasslands, mountains, hills, lakes, forests, and rivers, bright swatches of earth colored by sunlight. He caught his breath to see it so clearly and from so far up in the sky, even knowing that it was only a vision. But the sunlight began to fade almost at once, the color to wash. Darkness closed about, filled with dull gray mist and sulfurous ash that rose from burned-out craters. The land lost its character and became barren and lifeless. He felt himself drift closer, repulsed as he descended by the sights and smells of it. Humans wandered the devastation in packs, more animals than men. They rent and tore at each other; they howled and shrieked. Dark shapes flitted among them, shadows that lacked substance yet had eyes of fire. The shadows moved through the humans, joining with them, becoming them, leaving them again. They moved in a dance that was macabre, yet purposeful. The shadows were devouring the humans, he saw. The shadows were feeding on them.

—Watch—

The vision shifted. He saw himself then, a skeletal, ragged beggar facing a cauldron of strange white fire that bubbled and swirled and whispered his name. Vapors lifted from the cauldron

6

and snaked their way down to where he stood, wrapping about him, caressing him as if he were their child. Shadows flitted all about, passing by at first, then entering him as if he were a hollow casing in which they might play as they chose. He could feel their touch; he wanted to scream.

—Watch—

The vision shifted once more. There was a huge forest and in the middle of the forest a great mountain. Atop the mountain sat a castle, old and weathered, towers and parapets rising up against the dark of the land. Paranor, he thought! It was Paranor come again! He felt something bright and hopeful well up within him, and he wanted to shout his elation. But the vapors were already coiling about the castle. The shadows were already flitting close. The ancient fortress began to crack and crumble, stone and mortar giving way as if caught in a vise. The earth shuddered and screams lifted from the humans become animals. Fire erupted out of the earth, splitting apart the mountain on which Paranor sat and then the castle itself. Wailing filled the air, the sound of one bereft of the only hope that had remained to him. The old man recognized the wailing as his own.

Then the images were gone. He stood again before the Hadeshorn, in the shadow of the Dragon's Teeth, alone with the shade of Allanon. In spite of his resolve, he was shaking.

The shade pointed at him.

—It will be as I have shown you if the dreams are ignored. It will be so if you fail to act. You must help. Go to them—the boy, the girl, and the Dark Uncle. Tell them the dreams are real. Tell them to come to me here on the first night of the new moon when the present cycle is complete. I will speak with them then—

The old man frowned and muttered and worried his lower lip. His fingers once more drew tight the drawstrings to the pouch, and he shoved it back into his belt. "I will do so because there is no one else!" he said finally, spitting out the words in distaste. "But do not expect . . . !"

—Only go to them. Nothing more is required. Nothing more will be asked. Go—

The shade of Allanon shimmered brightly and disappeared. The light faded, and the valley was empty again. The old man stood looking out over the still waters of the lake for a moment, then turned away.

The fire he had left behind still burned on his return, but it was small now and frail-looking against the night. The old man stared absently at the flames, then hunkered down before them. He stirred at the ashes already forming and listened to the silence of his thoughts.

The boy, the girl, and the Dark Uncle—he knew them. They were the Shannara children, the ones who could save them all, the ones who could bring back the magic. He shook his grizzled head. How was he to convince them? If they would not heed Allanon, what chance that they would heed him?

He saw again in his mind the frightening visions. He had best find a way to make them listen, he thought. Because, as he was fond of reminding himself, he knew something of visions, and there was a truth to these that even one such as he, one who had foresworn the Druids and their magic, could recognize.

If the Shannara children failed to listen, these visions would come to pass.

CHAPTER

2

PAR OHMSFORD STOOD in the rear doorway of the Blue Whisker Ale House and stared down the darkened tunnel of the narrow street that ran between the adjoining buildings into the glimmer of Varfleet's lights. The Blue Whisker was a ramshackle, sprawling old building with weathered board walls and a wood shingle roof and looked for all the world as if once it had been someone's barn. It had sleeping rooms upstairs over the serving hall and storerooms in the back. It sat at the base of a block of buildings that formed a somewhat lopsided U, situated on a hill at the western edge of the city.

Par breathed deeply the night air, savoring its flavors. City smells, smells of life, stews with meats and vegetables laced with spice, sharp-flavored liquors and pungent ales, perfumes that scented rooms and bodies, leather harness, iron from forges still red with coals kept perpetually bright, the sweat of animals and men in close quarters, the taste of stone and wood and dust, mingling and mixing, each occasionally breaking free—they were all there. Down the alleyway, beyond the slat-boarded, graffiti-marked backs of the shops and businesses, the hill dropped away to where the central part of the city lay east. An ugly, colorless gathering of buildings in daylight, a maze of stone walls and streets, wooden siding and pitch-sealed roofs, the city took on a different look at night. The buildings faded into the darkness and the lights appeared, thousands of them, stretching away as far as the eye could see like a swarm of fireflies. They dotted the masked landscape, flickering in the black, trailing lines of

9

gold across the liquid skin of the Mermidon as it passed south. Varfleet was beautiful now, the scrubwoman become a fairy queen, transformed as if by magic.

Par liked the idea of the city being magic. He liked the city in any case, liked its sprawl and its meld of people and things, its rich mix of life. It was far different from his home of Shady Vale, nothing like the forested hamlet that he had grown up in. It lacked the purity of the trees and streams, the solitude, the sense of timeless ease that graced life in the Vale. It knew nothing of that life and couldn't have cared less. But that didn't matter to Par. He liked the city anyway. There was nothing to say that he had to choose between the two, after all. There wasn't any reason he couldn't appreciate both.

Coll, of course, didn't agree. Coll saw it quite differently. He saw Varfleet as nothing more than an outlaw city at the edge of Federation rule, a den of miscreants, a place where one could get away with anything. In all of Callahorn, in all of the entire Southland for that matter, there was no place worse. Coll hated the city.

Voices and the clink of glasses drifted out of the darkness behind him, the sounds of the ale house breaking free of the front room momentarily as a door was opened, then disappearing again as it was closed. Par turned. His brother moved carefully down the hallway, nearly faceless in the gloom.

"It's almost time," Coll said when he reached his brother.

Par nodded. He looked small and slender next to Coll, who was a big, strong youth with blunt features and mud-colored hair. A stranger would not have thought them brothers. Coll looked a typical Valeman, tanned and rough, with enormous hands and feet. The feet were an ongoing joke. Par was fond of comparing them to a duck's. Par was slight and fair, his own features unmistakably Elven from the sharply pointed ears and brows to the high, narrow bones of his face. There was a time when the Elven blood had been all but bred out of the line, the result of generations of Ohmsfords living in the Vale. But four generations back (so his father had told him) his great-great-grandfather had returned to the Westland and the Elves, married an Elven girl, and produced a son and a daughter. The son had married another Elven girl, and for reasons never made clear the young couple who would become Par's great-grandparents had returned to the Vale, thereby infusing a fresh supply of Elven blood back into the Ohmsford line. Even then, many members of the family showed nothing of their mixed heritage; Coll and his parents Jaralan and Mirianna were examples. Par's bloodlines, on the other hand, were immediately evident.

Being recognizable in this way, unfortunately, was not necessarily desirable. While in Varfleet, Par disguised his features, plucking his brows, wearing his hair long to hide his ears, shading his face with darkener. He didn't have much choice. It wasn't wise to draw attention to one's Elven lineage these days.

"She has her gown nicely in place tonight, doesn't she?" Coll said, glancing off down the alleyway to the city beyond. "Black velvet and sparkles, not a thread left hanging. Clever girl, this city. Even the sky is her friend."

Par smiled. My brother, the poet. The sky was clear and filled with the brightness of a tiny crescent moon and stars. "You might come to like her if you gave her half a chance."

"Me?" Coll snorted. "Not likely. I'm here because you're here. I wouldn't stay another minute if I didn't have to."

"You could go if you wanted."

Coll bristled. "Let's not start again, Par. We've been all through that. You were the one who thought we ought to come north to the cities. I didn't like the idea then, and I don't like it any better now. But that doesn't change the fact that we agreed to do this together, you and me. A fine brother I'd be if I left you here and went back to the Vale now! In any case, I don't think you could manage without me."

"All right, all right, I was just . . ." Par tried to interrupt.

"Attempting to have a little fun at my expense!" Coll finished heatedly. "You have done that on more than one occasion of late. You seem to take some delight in it."

"That is not so."

Coll ignored him, gazing off into the dark.

"I would never pick on anyone with duck feet."

Coll grinned in spite of himself. "Fine talk from a little fellow with pointed ears. You should be grateful I choose to stay and look after you!"

Par shoved him playfully, and they both laughed. Then they

went quiet, staring at each other in the dark, listening to the sounds of the ale house and the streets beyond. Par sighed. It was a warm, lazy midsummer night that made the cool, sharp days of the past few weeks seem a distant memory. It was the kind of night when troubles scatter and dreams come out to play.

"There are rumors of Seekers in the city," Coll informed him suddenly, spoiling his contentment.

"There are always rumors," he replied.

"And the rumors are often true. Talk has it that they plan to snatch up all the magic-makers, put them out of business and close down the ale houses." Coll was staring intently at him. "Seekers, Par. Not simple soldiers. Seekers."

Par knew what they were. Seekers—Federation secret police, the enforcement arm of the Coalition Council's Lawmakers. He knew.

They had arrived in Varfleet two weeks earlier, Coll and he. They journeyed north from Shady Vale, left the security and familiarity and protective confines of their family home and came into the Borderlands of Callahorn. They did so because Par had decided they must, that it was time for them to tell their stories elsewhere, that it was necessary to see to it that others besides the Vale people knew. They came to Varfleet because Varfleet was an open city, free of Federation rule, a haven for outlaws and refugees but also for ideas, a place where people still listened with open minds, a place where magic was still tolerated—even courted. He had the magic and, with Coll in tow, he took it to Varfleet to share its wonder. There was already magic aplenty being practiced by others, but his was of a far different sort. His was real.

They found the Blue Whisker the first day they arrived, one of the biggest and best known ale houses in the city. Par persuaded the owner to hire them in the first sitting. He had expected as much. After all, he could persuade anyone to do just about anything with the wishsong.

Real magic. He mouthed the words without speaking them.

There wasn't much real magic left in the Four Lands, not outside the remote wilderness areas where Federation rule did not yet extend. The wishsong was the last of the Ohmsford magic. It had been passed down through ten generations to reach him, the gift skipping some members of his family altogether, picking and choosing on a whim. Coll didn't have it. His parents didn't. In fact, no one in the Ohmsford family had had it since his great-grandparents had returned from the Westland. But the magic of the wishsong had been his from the time he was born, the same magic that had come into existence almost three hundred years ago with his ancestor Jair. The stories told him this, the legends. Wish for it, sing for it. He could create images so lifelike in the minds of his listeners that they appeared to be real. He could create substance out of air.

That was what had brought him to Varfleet. For three centuries the Ohmsford family had handed down stories of the Elven house of Shannara. The practice had begun with Jair. In truth, it had begun long before that, when the stories were not of the magic because it had not yet been discovered but of the old world before its destruction in the Great Wars and the tellers were the few who had survived that frightening holocaust. But Jair was the first to have use of the wishsong to aid in the telling, to give substance to the images created from his words, to make his tales come alive in the minds of those who heard them. The tales were of the old days: of the legends of the Elven house of Shannara; of the Druids and their Keep at Paranor; of Elves and Dwarves; and of the magic that ruled their lives. The tales were of Shea Ohmsford and his brother Flick and their search to find the Sword of Shannara; of Wil Ohmsford and the beautiful, tragic Elven girl Amberle and their struggle to banish the Demon hordes back into the Forbidding; of Jair Ohmsford and his sister Brin and their journey into the fortress of Graymark and confrontation with the Mord Wraiths and the Ildatch; of the Druids Allanon and Bremen; of the Elven King Eventine Elessedil; of warriors such as Balinor Buckhannah and Stee Jans; of heroes many and varied. Those who had command of the wishsong made use of its magic. Those who did not relied on simple words. Ohmsfords had come and gone, many carrying the stories with them to distant lands. Yet for three generations now, no member of the family had told the stories outside the Vale. No one had wanted to risk being caught.

It was a considerable risk. The practice of magic in any form was outlawed in the Four Lands—or at least anywhere the Federation governed, which was practically the same thing. It had been so for the past hundred years. In all that time no Ohmsford had left the Vale. Par was the first. He had grown tired of telling the same stories to the same few listeners over and over. Others needed to hear the stories as well, to know the truth about the Druids and the magic, about the struggle that preceded the age in which they now lived. His fear of being caught was outweighed by the calling he felt. He made his decision despite the objections of his parents and Coll. Coll, ultimately, decided to come with him—just as he always did whenever he thought Par needed looking after. Varfleet was to be the beginning, a city where magic was still practiced in minor forms, an open secret defying intervention by the Federation. Such magic as was found in Varfleet was small stuff really and scarcely worth the trouble. Callahorn was only a protectorate of the Federation, and Varfleet so distant as to be almost into the free territories. It was not yet army occupied. The Federation so far had disdained to bother with it.

But Seekers? Par shook his head. Seekers were another matter altogether. Seekers only appeared when there was a serious intent on the part of the Federation to stamp out a practice of magic. No one wanted any part of them.

"It grows too dangerous for us here," Coll said, as if reading Par's mind. "We will be discovered."

Par shook his head. "We are but one of a hundred practicing the art," he replied. "Just one in a city of many."

Coll looked at him. "One in a hundred, yes. But the only one using real magic."

Par looked back. It was good money the ale house paid them, the best they had ever seen. They needed it to help with the taxes the Federation demanded. They needed it for their family and the Vale. He hated to give up because of a rumor.

His jaw tightened. He hated to give up even more because it meant the stories must be returned to the Vale and kept hidden there, untold to those who needed to hear. It meant that the repression of ideas and practices that clamped down about the Four Lands like a vise had tightened one turn more.

"We have to go," Coll said, interrupting his thoughts.

Par felt a sudden rush of anger before realizing his brother was not saying they must go from the city, but from the doorway of the ale house to the performing stage inside. The crowd would be waiting. He let his anger slip away and felt a sadness take its place.

"I wish we lived in another age," he said softly. He paused, watching the way Coll tensed. "I wish there were Elves and Druids again. And heroes. I wish there could be heroes again—even one."

He trailed off, thinking suddenly of something else.

Coll shoved away from the doorjamb, clapped one big hand to his brother's shoulder, turned him about and started him back down the darkened hallway. "If you keep singing about it, who knows? Maybe there will be."

Par let himself be led away like a child. He was no longer thinking about heroes though, or Elves or Druids, or even about Seekers.

He was thinking about the dreams.

THEY TOLD THE STORY of the Elven stand at Halys Cut, how Eventine Elessedil and the Elves and Stee Jans and the Legion Free Corps fought to hold the Breakline against the onslaught of the Demon hordes. It was one of Par's favorite stories, the first of the great Elven battles in that terrible Westland war. They stood on a low platform at one end of the main serving room, Par in the forefront, Coll a step back and aside, the lights dimmed against a sea of tightly packed bodies and watchful eyes. While Coll narrated the story, Par sang to provide the accompanying images, and the ale house came alive with the magic of his voice. He invoked in the hundred or more gathered the feelings of fear, anger, and determination that had infused the defenders of the Cut. He let them see the fury of the Demons; he let them hear their battle cries. He drew them in and would not let them go. They stood in the pathway of the Demon assault. They saw the wounding of Eventine and the emergence of his son Ander as leader of the Elves. They watched the Druid

Allanon stand virtually alone against the Demon magic and turn it aside. They experienced life and death with an intimacy that was almost terrifying.

When Coll and he were finished, there was stunned silence, then a wild thumping of ale glasses and cheers and shouts of elation unmatched in any performance that had gone before. It seemed for a moment that those gathered might bring the rafters of the ale house down about their ears, so vehement were they in their appreciation. Par was damp with his own sweat, aware for the first time how much he had given to the telling. Yet his mind was curiously detached as they left the platform for the brief rest they were permitted between tellings, thinking still of the dreams.

Coll stopped for a glass of ale by an open storage room and Par continued down the hallway a short distance before coming to an empty barrel turned upright by the cellar doors. He slumped down wearily, his thoughts tight.

He had been having the dreams for almost a month now, and he still didn't know why.

The dreams occurred with a frequency that was unsettling. They always began with a black-cloaked figure that rose from a lake, a figure that might be Allanon, a lake that might be the Hadeshorn. There was a shimmering of images in his dreams, an ethereal quality to the visions that made them difficult to decipher. The figure always spoke to him, always with the same words. "Come to me; you are needed. The Four Lands are in gravest danger; the magic is almost lost. Come now, Shannara child."

There was more, although the rest varied. Sometimes there were images of a world born of some unspeakable nightmare. Sometimes there were images of the lost talismans—the Sword of Shannara and the Elfstones. Sometimes there was a call for Wren as well, little Wren, and sometimes a call for his uncle Walker Boh. They were to come as well. They were needed, too.

He had decided quite deliberately after the first night that the dreams were a side effect of his prolonged use of the wish-song. He sang the old stories of the Warlock Lord and the Skull Bearers, of Demons and Mord Wraiths, of Allanon and a world threatened by evil, and it was natural that something of those stories and their images would carry over into his sleep. He had tried to combat the effect by using the wishsong on lighter tellings, but it hadn't helped. The dreams persisted. He had refrained from telling Coll, who would have simply used that as a new excuse to advise him to stop invoking the magic of the wishsong and return to the Vale.

Then, three nights ago, the dreams had stopped coming as suddenly as they had started. Now he was wondering why. He was wondering if perhaps he had mistaken their origin. He was considering the possibility that instead of being self-induced, they might have been sent.

But who would have sent them?

Allanon? Truly Allanon, who was three hundred years dead? Someone else?

Some*thing* else? Something that had a reason of its own and meant him no good?

He shivered at the prospect, brushed the matter from his mind, and went quickly back up the hallway to find Coll.

THE CROWD WAS even larger for the second telling, the walls lined with standing men who could not find chairs or benches to sit upon. The Blue Whisker was a large house, the front serving room over a hundred feet across and open to the rafters above a stringing of oil lamps and fish netting that lent a sort of veiled appearance that was apparently designed to suggest intimacy. Par couldn't have tolerated much more intimacy, so close were the patrons of the ale house as they pressed up against the platform, some actually sitting on it now as they drank. This was a different group than earlier, although the Valeman was hard-pressed to say why. It had a different feel to it, as if there was something foreign in its makeup. Coll must have felt it, too. He glanced over at Par several times as they prepared to perform, and there was uneasiness mirrored in his dark eyes.

A tall, black-bearded man wrapped in a dun-colored forest cloak waded through the crowd to the platform's edge and eased himself down between two other men. The two looked up as if they intended to say something, then caught a close glimpse of the other's face and apparently thought better of it. Par watched momentarily and looked away. Everything felt wrong.

Coll leaned over as a rhythmic clapping began. The crowd was growing restless. "Par, I don't like this. There's something . . ."

He didn't finish. The owner of the ale house came up and told them in no uncertain terms to begin before the crowd got out of hand and started breaking things. Coll stepped away wordlessly. The lights dimmed, and Par started to sing. The story was the one about Allanon and the battle with the Jachyra. Coll began to speak, setting the stage, telling those gathered what sort of day it was, what the glen was like into which the Druid came with Brin Ohmsford and Rone Leah, how everything suddenly grew hushed. Par created the images in the minds of his listeners, instilling in them a sense of anxiety and expectation, trying unsuccessfully not to experience the same feelings himself.

At the rear of the room, men were moving to block the doors and windows, men suddenly shed of cloaks and dressed all in black. Weapons glittered. There were patches of white on sleeves and breasts, insignia of some sort. Par squinted, Elven vision sharp.

A wolf's head.

The men in black were Seekers.

Par's voice faltered and the images shimmered and lost their hold. Men began to grumble and look about. Coll stopped his narration. There was movement everywhere. There was someone in the darkness behind them. There was someone all about.

Coll edged closer protectively.

Then the lights rose again, and a wedge of the black-garbed Seekers pushed forward from the front door. There were shouts and groans of protest, but the men making them were quick to move out of the way. The owner of the Blue Whisker tried to intervene, but was shoved aside.

The wedge of men came to a stop directly in front of the platform. Another group blocked the exits. They wore black from head to toe, their faces covered above their mouths, their wolf-head insignia gleaming. They were armed with short swords, daggers, and truncheons, and their weapons were held ready. They were a mixed bunch, big and small, stiff and bent, but there was a feral look to all of them, as much in the way they held themselves as in their eyes.

Their leader was a huge, rangy man with tremendously long arms and a powerful frame. There was a craggy cast to his face where the mask ended, and a half-beard of coarse reddish hair covered his chin. His left arm was gloved to the elbow.

"Your names?" he asked. His voice was soft, almost a whisper.

Par hesitated. "What is it that we have done?"

"Is your name Ohmsford?" The speaker was studying him intently.

Par nodded. "Yes. But we haven't . . ."

"You are under arrest for violating Federation Supreme Law," the soft voice announced. There was a grumbling sound from the patrons. "You have used magic in defiance of . . ."

"They was just telling stories!" a man called out from a few feet away. One of the Seekers lashed out swiftly with his truncheon and the man collapsed in a heap.

"You have used magic in defiance of Federation dictates and thereby endangered the public." The speaker did not even bother to glance at the fallen man. "You will be taken . . ."

He never finished. An oil lamp dropped suddenly from the center of the ceiling to the crowded ale house floor and exploded in a shower of flames. Men sprang to their feet, howling. The speaker and his companions turned in surprise. At the same moment the tall, bearded man who had taken a seat on the platform's edge earlier came to his feet with a lunge, vaulted several other astonished patrons, and slammed into the knot of Seekers, spilling them to the floor. The tall man leaped onto the stage in front of Par and Coll and threw off his shabby cloak to reveal a fully armed hunter dressed in forest green. One arm lifted, the hand clenched in a fist.

"Free-born!" he shouted into the confusion.

It seemed that everything happened at once after that. The decorative netting, somehow loosened, followed the oil lamp to the floor, and practically everyone gathered at the Blue Whisker was suddenly entangled. Yells and curses rose from those trapped. At the doors, green-clad men pounced on the bewildered Seekers and hammered them to the floor. Oil lamps were smashed, and the room was plunged into darkness.

The tall man moved past Par and Coll with a quickness they would not have believed possible. He caught the first of the Seekers blocking the back entrance with a sweep of one boot, snapping the man's head back. A short sword and dagger appeared, and the remaining two went down as well.

"This way, quick now!" he called back to Par and Coll.

They came at once. A dark shape clawed at them as they rushed past, but Coll knocked the man from his feet into the mass of struggling bodies. He reached back to be certain he had not lost his brother, his big hand closing on Par's slender shoulder. Par yelled in spite of himself. Coll always forgot how strong he was.

They cleared the stage and reached the back hallway, the tall stranger several paces ahead. Someone tried to stop them, but the stranger ran right over him. The din from the room behind them was deafening, and flames were scattered everywhere now, licking hungrily at the flooring and walls. The stranger led them quickly down the hall and through the rear door into the alleyway. Two more of the green-clad men waited. Wordlessly, they surrounded the brothers and rushed them clear of the ale house. Par glanced back. The flames were already leaping from the windows and crawling up toward the roof. The Blue Whisker had seen its last night.

They slipped down the alleyway past startled faces and wide eyes, turned into a passageway Par would have sworn he had never seen before despite his many excursions out that way, passed through a scattering of doors and anterooms and finally emerged into a new street entirely. No one spoke. When at last they were beyond the sound of the shouting and the glow of the fire, the stranger slowed, motioned his two companions to take up watch and pulled Par and Coll into a shadowed alcove.

All were breathing heavily from the run. The stranger looked at them in turn, grinning. "A little exercise is good for the digestion, they say. What do you think? Are you all right?"

The brothers both nodded. "Who are you?" asked Par.

The grin broadened. "Why, practically one of the family, lad. Don't you recognize me? Ah, you don't, do you? But, then, why should you? After all, you and I have never met. But the songs should remind you." He closed his left hand into a fist, then thrust a single finger sharply at Par's nose. "Remember now?"

Mystified, Par looked at Coll, but his brother appeared as confused as he was. "I don't think . . ." he started.

"Well, well, it doesn't matter just at the moment. All in good time." He bent close. "This is no longer safe country for you, lad. Certainly not here in Varfleet and probably not in all of Callahorn. Maybe not anywhere. Do you know who that was back there? The ugly one with the whisper?"

Par tried to place the rangy speaker with the soft voice. He couldn't. He shook his head slowly.

"Rimmer Dall," the stranger said, the smile gone now. "First Seeker, the high mucky-muck himself. Sits on the Coalition Council when he's not out swatting flies. But you, he's taken a special interest if he's come all the way to Varfleet to arrest you. That's not part of his ordinary fly-swatting. That's hunting bear. He thinks you are dangerous, lad—very dangerous, indeed, or he wouldn't have bothered coming all the way here. Good thing I was looking out for you. I was, you know. Heard Rimmer Dall was going to come for you and came to make sure he didn't get the job done. Mind now, he won't give up. You slipped his grasp this time, but that will make him just that much more determined. He'll keep coming for you."

He paused, gauging the effect of what he was saying. Par was staring at him speechlessly, so he went on. "That magic of yours, the singing, that's real magic, isn't it? I've seen enough of the other kind to know. You could put that magic to good use, lad, if you had a mind to. It's wasted in these ale houses and backstreets."

"What do you mean?" Coll asked, suddenly suspicious.

The stranger smiled, charming and guileless. "The Movement has need of such magic," he said softly.

Coll snorted. "You're one of the outlaws!"

The stranger executed a quick bow. "Yes, lad, I am proud

to say I am. More important, I am free-born and I do not accept Federation rule. No right-thinking man does." He bent close. "You don't accept it yourself now, do you? Admit it."

"Hardly," Coll answered defensively. "But I question whether the outlaws are any better."

"Harsh words, lad!" the other exclaimed. "A good thing for you I do not take offense easily." He grinned roguishly.

"What is it you want?" Par interrupted quickly, his mind clear again. He had been thinking of Rimmer Dall. He knew the man's reputation and he was frightened of the prospect of being hunted by him. "You want us to join you, is that it?"

The stranger nodded. "You would find it worth your time, I think."

But Par shook his head. It was one thing to accept the stranger's help in fleeing the Seekers. It was another to join the Movement. The matter needed a great deal more thought. "I think we had better decline for now," he said evenly. "That is, if we're being given a choice."

"Of course you are being given a choice!" The stranger seemed offended.

"Then we have to say no. But we thank you for the offer and especially for your help back there."

The stranger studied him a moment, solemn again. "You are quite welcome, believe me. I wish only the best for you, Par Ohmsford. Here, take this." He removed from one hand a ring that was cast in silver and bore the insigne of a hawk. "My friends know me by this. If you need a favor—or if you change your mind—take this to Kiltan Forge at Reaver's End at the north edge of the city and ask for the Archer. Can you remember that?"

Par hesitated, then took the ring, nodding. "But why . . . ?"

"Because there is much between us, lad," the other said softly, anticipating his question. One hand reached out to rest on his shoulder. The eyes took in Coll as well. "There is history that binds us, a bond of such strength that it requires I be there for you if I can. More, it requires that we stand together against what is threatening this land. Remember that, too. One day, we will do so, I think—if we all manage to stay alive until then."

He grinned at the brothers and they stared back silently.

The stranger's hand dropped away. "Time to go now. Quickly, too. The street runs east to the river. You can go where you wish from there. But watch yourselves. Keep your backs well guarded. This matter isn't finished."

"I know," Par said and extended his hand. "Are you certain you will not tell us your name?"

The stranger hesitated. "Another day," he said.

He gripped Par's hand tightly, then Coll's, then whistled his companions to him. He waved once, then melted into the shadows and was gone.

Par stared down momentarily at the ring, then glanced questioningly at Coll. Somewhere close at hand, the sound of shouting started up.

"I think the questions will have to wait," said Coll.

Par jammed the ring into his pocket. Wordlessly, they disappeared into the night.

3

IT WAS NEARING MIDNIGHT by the time Par and Coll reached the waterfront section of Varfleet, and it was there that they first realized how ill-prepared they were to make their escape from Rimmer Dall and his Federation Seekers. Neither had expected that flight would prove necessary, so neither had brought anything that a lengthy journey might require. They had no food, no blankets, no weapons save for the standard long knives all Valemen wore, no camping gear or foul-weather equipment, and worst of all, no money. The ale house keeper hadn't paid them in a month. What money they had managed to save from the month before had been lost in the fire along with everything else they owned. They had only the clothes on their backs and a growing fear that perhaps they should have stuck with the nameless stranger a bit longer.

The waterfront was a ramshackle mass of boathouses, piers, mending shops, and storage sheds. Lights burned along its length, and dockworkers and fishermen drank and joked in the light of oil lamps and pipes. Smoke rose out of tin stoves and barrels, and the smell of fish hung over everything.

"Maybe they've given up on us for the night," Par suggested at one point. "The Seekers, I mean. Maybe they won't bother looking anymore until morning—or maybe not at all."

Coll glanced at him and arched one eyebrow meaningfully. "Maybe cows can fly too." He looked away. "We should have insisted we be paid more promptly for our work. Then we wouldn't be in this fix."

Par shrugged. "It wouldn't have made any difference."

"It wouldn't? We'd at least have some money!"

"Only if we'd thought to carry it with us to the performance. How likely is that?"

Coll hunched his shoulders and screwed up his face. "That ale house keeper owes us."

They walked all the way to the south end of the docks without speaking further, stopped finally as the lighted waterfront gave way to darkness, and stood looking at each other. The night was cooler now and their clothes were too thin to protect them. They were shivering, their hands jammed down in their pockets, their arms clamped tightly against their sides. Insects buzzed about them annoyingly.

Coll sighed. "Do you have any idea where we're going, Par? Do you have some kind of plan in mind?"

Par took out his hands and rubbed them briskly. "I do. But it requires a boat to get there."

"South, then—down the Mermidon?"

"All the way."

Coll smiled, misunderstanding. He thought they were headed back to Shady Vale. Par decided it was best to leave him with that impression.

"Wait here," Coll said suddenly and disappeared before Par could object.

Par stood alone in the dark at the end of the docks for what seemed like an hour, but was probably closer to half that. He walked over to a bench by a fishing shack and sat down, hunched up against the night air. He was feeling a mix of things. He was angry, mostly—at the stranger for spiriting them away and then abandoning them—all right, so Par had asked to have it that way, that didn't make him feel any better—at the Federation for chasing them out from the city like common thieves, and at himself for being stupid enough to think he could get away with using real magic when it was absolutely forbidden to do so. It was one thing to play around with the magics of sleight of hand and quick change; it was another altogether to employ the magic of the wishsong. It was too obviously the real thing, and he should have known that sooner or later word of its use would get back to the authorities.

25

He put his legs out in front of him and crossed his boots. Well, there was nothing to be done about it now. Coll and he would simply have to start over again. It never occurred to him to quit. The stories were too important for that; it was his responsibility to see to it that they were not forgotten. He was convinced that the magic was a gift he had received expressly for that purpose. It didn't matter what the Federation said—that magic was outlawed and that it was a source of great harm to the land and its people. What did the Federation know of magic? Those on the Coalition Council lacked any practical experience. They had simply decided that something needed to be done to address the concerns of those who claimed parts of the Four Lands were sickening and men were being turned into something like the dark creatures of Jair Ohmsford's time, creatures from some nether existence that defied understanding, beings that drew their power from the night and from magics lost since the time of the Druids.

They even had names, these creatures. They were called Shadowen.

Suddenly, unpleasantly, Par thought again of the dreams and of the dark thing within them that had summoned him.

He was aware then that the night had gone still; the voices of the fishermen and dockworkers, the buzz of the insects, and even the rustle of the night wind had disappeared. He could hear the sound of his own pulse in his ears, and a whisper of something else . . .

Then a splash of water brought him to his feet with a start. Coll appeared, clambering out of the Mermidon at the river's edge a dozen feet away, shedding water as he came. He was naked. Par recovered his composure and stared at him in disbelief.

"Shades, you frightened me! What were you doing?"

"What does it look like I was doing?" Coll grinned. "I was out swimming!"

What he was really doing, Par discovered after applying a bit more pressure, was appropriating a fishing skiff owned by the keeper of the Blue Whisker. The keeper had mentioned it to Coll once or twice when bragging about his fishing skills. Coll had remembered it when Par had mentioned needing a boat, remembered as well the description of the boat shed where the man said it was kept, and gone off to find it. He'd simply swum up to where it was stored, snapped the lock on the shed, slipped the mooring lines and towed it away.

"It's the least he owes us after the kind of business we brought in," he said defensively as he brushed himself dry and dressed.

Par didn't argue the point. They needed a boat worse than the ale house keeper, and this was probably their only chance to find one. Assuming the Seekers were still scouring the city for them, their only other alternative was to strike out on foot into the Runne Mountains—an undertaking that would require more than a week. A ride down the Mermidon was a journey of only a few days. It wasn't as if they were stealing the boat, after all. He caught himself. Well, maybe it was. But they would return it or provide proper compensation when they could.

The skiff was only a dozen feet in length, but it was equipped with oars, fishing gear, some cooking and camping equipment, a pair of blankets, and a canvas tarp. They boarded and pushed off into the night, letting the current carry them out from the shore and sweep them away.

They rode the river south for the remainder of the night, using the oars to keep it in mid-channel, listening to the night sounds, watching the shoreline, and trying to stay awake. As they traveled, Coll offered his theory on what they should do next. It was impossible, of course, to go back into Callahorn any time in the immediate future. The Federation would be looking for them. It would be dangerous, in fact, to travel to any of the major Southland cities because the Federation authorities stationed there would be alerted as well. It was best that they simply return to the Vale. They could still tell the stories—not right away perhaps, but in a month or so after the Federation had stopped looking for them. Then, later, they could travel to some of the smaller hamlets, the more isolated communities, places the Federation seldom visited. It would all work out fine.

Par let him ramble. He was willing to bet that Coll didn't believe a word of it; and even if he did, there was no point in arguing about it now.

They pulled into shore at sunrise and made camp in a grove

of shade trees at the base of a windswept bluff, sleeping until noon, then rising to catch and eat fish. They were back on the river by early afternoon and continued on until well after sunset. Again they pulled into shore and made camp. It was starting to rain, and they put up the canvas to provide shelter. They made a small fire, pulled the blankets close, and sat silently facing the river, watching the raindrops swell its flow and form intricate patterns on its shimmering surface.

They spoke then for a while about how things had changed in the Four Lands since the time of Jair Ohmsford.

Three hundred years ago, the Federation governed only the deep Southland cities, adopting a strict policy of isolationism. The Coalition Council provided its leadership even then, a body of men selected by the cities as representatives to its government. But it was the Federation armies that gradually came to dominate the Council, and in time the policy of isolationism gave way to one of expansion. It was time to extend its sphere of influence, the Federation determined—to push back its frontiers and offer a choice of leadership to the remainder of the Southland. It was logical that the Southland should be united under a single government, and who better to do that than the Federation?

That was the way it started. The Federation began a push north, gobbling up bits and pieces of the Southland as it went. A hundred years after the death of Jair Ohmsford, everything south of Callahorn was Federation governed. The other races, the Elves, the Trolls, the Dwarves, and even the Gnomes cast nervous glances south. Before long, Callahorn agreed to become a protectorate, its Kings long dead, its cities feuding and divided, and the last buffer between the Federation and the other lands disappeared.

It was about this same time that the rumors of the Shadowen began to surface. It was said that the magic of the old days was at fault, magic that had taken seed in the earth and nurtured there for decades and was now coming to life. The magic took many forms, sometimes as nothing more than a cold wind, sometimes as something vaguely human. It was labeled, in any case, as Shadowen. The Shadowen sickened the land and its life, turning pockets of it into quagmires of decay and lifelessness. They attacked mortal creatures, man or beast, and, when they were sufficiently weakened, took them over completely, stealing into their bodies and residing there, hidden wraiths. They needed the life of others for their own sustenance. That was how they survived.

The Federation lent credibility to those rumors by proclaiming that such creatures might indeed exist and only it was strong enough to protect against them.

No one argued that the magic might not be at fault or that the Shadowen or whatever it was that was causing the problem had nothing to do with magic at all. It was easier simply to accept the explanation offered. After all, there hadn't been any magic in the land since the passing of the Druids. The Ohmsfords told their stories, of course, but only a few heard and fewer still believed. Most thought the Druids just a legend. When Callahorn agreed to become a protectorate and the city of Tyrsis was occupied, the Sword of Shannara disappeared. No one thought much of it. No one knew how it happened, and no one much cared. The Sword hadn't even been seen for over two hundred years. There was only the vault that was said to contain it, the blade set in a block of Tre-Stone, there in the center of the People's Park—and then one day that was gone as well.

The Elfstones disappeared not long after. There was no record of what became of them. Not even the Ohmsfords knew.

Then the Elves began to disappear as well, entire communities, whole cities at a time, until even Arborlon was gone. Finally, there were no more Elves at all; it was as if they had never been. The Westland was deserted, save for a few hunters and trappers from the other lands and the wandering bands of Rovers. The Rovers, unwelcome anyplace else, had always been there, but even the Rovers claimed to know nothing of what had become of the Elves. The Federation quickly took advantage of the situation. The Westland, it declared, was the seeding ground for the magic that was at the root of the problems in the Four Lands. It was the Elves, after all, who introduced magic into the Lands years earlier. It was the Elves who first practiced it. The magic had consumed them—an object lesson on what would happen to all those who tried to do likewise.

The Federation emphasized the point by forbidding the

practice of magic in any form. The Westland was made a protectorate, albeit an unoccupied one since the Federation lacked enough soldiers to patrol so vast a territory unaided, but one that would be cleansed eventually, it was promised, of the ill effects of any lingering magic.

Shortly after that, the Federation declared war on the Dwarves. It did so ostensibly because the Dwarves had provoked it, although it was never made clear in what way. The result was practically a forgone conclusion. The Federation had the largest, most thoroughly equipped and best trained army in the Four Lands by this time, and the Dwarves had no standing army at all. The Dwarves no longer had the Elves as allies, as they had all those years previous, and the Gnomes and Trolls had never been friends. Nevertheless, the war lasted nearly five years. The Dwarves knew the mountainous Eastland far better than the Federation, and even though Culhaven fell almost immediately, the Dwarves continued to fight in the high country until eventually they were starved into submission. They were brought down out of the mountains and sent south to the Federation mines. Most died there. After seeing what happened to the Dwarves, the Gnome tribes fell quickly into line. The Federation declared the Eastland a protectorate as well.

There remained a few pockets of isolated resistance. There were still a handful of Dwarves and a scattering of Gnome tribes that refused to recognize Federation rule and continued to fight from the deep wilderness areas north and east. But they were too few to make any difference.

To mark its unification of the greater portion of the Four Lands and to honor those who had worked to achieve it, the Federation constructed a monument at the north edge of the Rainbow Lake where the Mermidon poured through the Runne. The monument was constructed entirely of black granite, broad and square at its base, curved inward as it rose over two hundred feet above the cliffs, a monolithic tower that could be seen for miles in all directions. The tower was called Southwatch.

That was almost a hundred years ago, and now only the Trolls remained a free people, still entrenched deep within the mountains of the Northland, the Charnals, and the Kershalt. That was dangerous, hostile country, a natural fortress, and no one from the Federation wanted much to do with it. The decision was made to leave it alone as long as the Trolls did not interfere with the other lands. The Trolls, very much a reclusive people for the whole of their history, were happy to oblige.

"It's all so different now," Par concluded wistfully as they continued to sit within their shelter and watch the rain fall into the Mermidon. "No more Druids, no Paranor, no magic—except the fake kind and the little we know. No Elves. Whatever happened to them do you think?" He paused, but Coll didn't have anything to say. "No monarchies, no Leah, no Buckhannahs, no Legion Free Corps, no Callahorn for all intents and purposes."

"No freedom," Coll finished darkly.

"No freedom," Par echoed.

He rocked back, drawing his legs tight against his chest. "I wish I knew how the Elfstones disappeared. And the Sword. What happened to the Sword of Shannara?"

Coll shrugged. "Same thing that happens to everything eventually. It got lost."

"What do you mean? How could they let it get lost?"

"No one was taking care of it."

Par thought about that. It made sense. No one bothered much with the magic after Allanon died, after the Druids were gone. The magic was simply ignored, a relic from another time, a thing feared and misunderstood for the most part. It was easier to forget about it, and so they did. They all did. He had to include the Ohmsfords as well—otherwise they would still have the Elfstones. All that was left of their magic was the wishsong.

"We know the stories, the tales of what it was like; we have all that history, and we still don't know anything," he said softly.

"We know the Federation doesn't want us talking about it," Coll offered archly. "We know that."

"There are times that I wonder what difference it makes anyway." Par's face twisted into a grimace. "After all, people come to hear us and the day after, who remembers? Anyone besides us? And what if they do? It's all ancient history—not even that to some. To some, it's legend and myth, a lot of nonsense."

"Not to everyone," Coll said quietly.

"What's the use of having the wishsong, if the telling of the stories isn't going to make any difference? Maybe the stranger was right. Maybe there are better uses for the magic."

"Like aiding the outlaws in their fight against the Federation? Like getting yourself killed?" Coll shook his head. "That's as pointless as not using it at all."

There was a sudden splash from somewhere out in the river, and the brothers turned as one to seek out its source. But there was only the churning of rain-swollen waters and nothing else.

"Everything seems pointless." Par kicked at the earth in front of him. "What are we doing, Coll? Chased out of Varfleet as much as if we were outlaws ourselves, forced to take that boat like thieves, made to run for home like dogs with our tails between our legs." He paused, looking over at his brother. "Why do you think we still have use of the magic?"

Coll's blocky face shifted slightly toward Par's. "What do you mean?"

"Why do we have it? Why hasn't it disappeared along with everything else? Do you think there's a reason?"

There was a long silence. "I don't know," Coll said finally. He hesitated. "I don't know what it's like to have the magic."

Par stared at him, realizing suddenly what he had asked and ashamed he had done so.

"Not that I'd want it, you understand," Coll added hastily, aware of his brother's discomfort. "One of us with the magic is enough." He grinned.

Par grinned back. "I expect so." He looked at Coll appreciatively for a moment, then yawned. "You want to go to sleep?"

Coll shook his head and eased his big frame back into the shadows a bit. "No, I want to talk some more. It's a good night for talking."

Nevertheless, he was silent then, as if he had nothing to say after all. Par studied him for a few moments, then they both looked back out over the Mermidon, watching as a massive tree limb washed past, apparently knocked down by the storm. The wind, which had blown hard at first, was quiet now, and the rain was falling straight down, a steady, gentle sound as it passed through the trees.

Par found himself thinking about the stranger who had rescued them from the Federation Seekers. He had puzzled over the man's identity for the better part of the day, and he still hadn't a clue as to who he was. There was something familiar about him, though—something in the way he talked, an assurance, a confidence. It reminded him of someone from one of the stories he told, but he couldn't decide who. There were so many tales and many of them were about men like that one, heroes in the days of magic and Druids, heroes Par had thought were missing from this age. Maybe he had been wrong. The stranger at the Blue Whisker had been impressive in his rescue of them. He seemed prepared to stand up to the Federation. Perhaps there was hope for the Four Lands yet.

He leaned forward and fed another few sticks of deadwood into the little fire, watching the smoke curl out from beneath the canvas shelter into the night. Lightning flashed suddenly farther east, and a long peal of thunder followed.

"Some dry clothes would be good right now," he muttered. "Mine are damp just from the air."

Coll nodded. "Some hot stew and bread, too."

"A bath and a warm bed."

"Maybe the smell of fresh spices."

"And rose water."

Coll sighed. "At this point, I'd just settle for an end to this confounded rain." He glanced out into the dark. "I could almost believe in Shadowen on a night like this, I think."

Par decided suddenly to tell Coll about the dreams. He wanted to talk about them, and there no longer seemed to be any reason not to. He debated only a moment, then said, "I haven't said anything before, but I've been having these dreams, the same dream actually, over and over." Quickly he described it, focusing on his confusion about the dark-robed figure who spoke to him. "I don't see him clearly enough to be certain who he is," he explained carefully. "But he might be Allanon."

Coll shrugged. "He might be anybody. It's a dream, Par. Dreams are always murky."

"But I've had this same dream a dozen, maybe two dozen times. I thought at first it was just the magic working on me, but . . ." He stopped, biting his lip. "What if . . . ?" He stopped again.

"What if what?"

"What if it isn't just the magic? What if it's an attempt by Allanon—or someone—to send me a message of some sort?"

"A message to do what? To go traipsing off to the Hadeshorn or somewhere equally dangerous?" Coll shook his head. "I wouldn't worry about it if I were you. And I certainly wouldn't consider going." He frowned. "You aren't, are you? Considering going?"

"No," Par answered at once. *Not until I think about it, at least,* he amended silently, surprised at the admission.

"That's a relief. We have enough problems as it is without going off in search of dead Druids." Coll obviously considered the matter settled.

Par didn't reply, choosing instead to poke at the fire with a stray stick, nudging the embers this way and that. He was indeed thinking about going, he realized. He hadn't considered it seriously before, but all of a sudden he had a need to know what the dreams meant. It didn't matter if they came from Allanon or not. Some small voice inside him, some tiny bit of recognition, hinted that finding the source of the dreams might allow him to discover something about himself and his use of the magic. It bothered him that he was thinking like this, that he was suddenly contemplating doing exactly what he had told himself he must not do right from the time the dreams had first come to him. But that was no longer enough to deter him. There was a history of dreams in the Ohmsford family and almost always the dreams had a message.

"I just wish I was sure," he murmured.

Coll was stretched out on his back now, eyes closed against the firelight. "Sure about what?"

"The dreams," he hedged. "About whether or not they were sent."

Coll snorted. "I'm sure enough for the both of us. There aren't any Druids. There aren't any Shadowen either. There aren't any dark wraiths trying to send you messages in your sleep. There's just you, overworked and under-rested, dreaming bits and pieces of the stories you sing about."

Par lay back as well, pulling his blanket up about him. "I suppose so," he agreed, inwardly not agreeing at all.

Coll rolled over on his side, yawning. "Tonight, you'll probably dream about floods and fishes, damp as it is."

Par said nothing. He listened for a time to the sound of the rain, staring up at the dark expanse of the canvas, catching the flicker of the firelight against its damp surface.

"Maybe I'll choose my own dream," he said softly.

Then he was asleep.

HE DID DREAM THAT NIGHT, the first time in almost two weeks. It was the dream he wanted, the dream of the dark-robed figure, and it was as if he were able to reach out and bring it to him. It seemed to come at once, to slip from the depths of his subconscious the moment sleep came. He was shocked at its suddenness, but didn't wake. He saw the dark figure rise from the lake, watched it come for him, vague yet faceless, so menacing that he would have fled if he could. But the dream was master now and would not let him. He heard himself asking why the dream had been absent for so long, but there was no answer given. The dark figure simply approached in silence, not speaking, not giving any indication of its purpose.

Then it came to a stop directly before him, a being that could have been anything or anyone, good or evil, life or death.

Speak to me, he thought, frightened.

But the figure merely stood there, draped in shadow, silent and immobile. It seemed to be waiting.

Then Par stepped forward and pushed back the cowl that hid the other, emboldened by some inner strength he did not know he possessed. He drew the cowl free and the face beneath was as sharp as if etched in bright sunlight. He knew it instantly. He had sung of it a thousand times. It was as familiar to him as his own.

The face was Allanon's.

CHAPTER

4

WHEN HE CAME AWAKE the next morning, Par decided not to say anything to Coll about his dream. In the first place, he didn't know what to say. He couldn't be sure if the dream had occurred on its own or because he had been thinking so hard about having it—and even then he had no way of knowing if it was the real thing. In the second place, telling Coll would just start him off again on how foolish it was for Par to keep thinking about something he obviously wasn't going to do anything about. Was he? Then, if Par was honest with him, they would fight about the advisability of going off into the Dragon's Teeth in search of the Hadeshorn and a three-hundred-year-dead Druid. Better just to let the matter rest.

They ate a cold breakfast of wild berries and some stream water, lucky to have that. The rains had stopped, but the sky was overcast, and the day was gray and threatening. The wind had returned, rather strong out of the northwest, and tree limbs bent and leaves rustled wildly against its thrust. They packed up their gear, boarded the skiff, and pushed off onto the river.

The Mermidon was heavily swollen, and the skiff tossed and twisted roughly as it carried them south. Debris choked the waters, and they kept the oars at hand to push off any large pieces that threatened damage to the boat. The cliffs of the Runne loomed darkly on either side, wrapped in trailers of mist and low-hanging clouds. It was cold in their shadow, and the brothers felt their hands and feet grow quickly numb.

They pulled into shore and rested when they could, but it accomplished little. There was nothing to eat and no way to get warm without taking time to build a fire. By early afternoon, it was raining again. It grew quickly colder in the rainfall, the wind picked up, and it became dangerous to continue on the river. When they found a small cove in the shelter of a stand of old pine, they quickly maneuvered the skiff ashore and set camp for the night.

They managed a fire, ate the fish Coll caught and tried their best to dry out beneath the canvas with rain blowing in from every side. They slept poorly, cold and uncomfortable, the wind blowing down the canyon of the mountains and the river churning against its banks. That night, Par didn't dream at all.

Morning brought a much-needed change in the weather. The storm moved east, the skies cleared and filled with bright sunlight, and the air warmed once more. The brothers dried out their clothing as their craft bore them south, and by midday it was balmy enough to strip off tunics and boots and enjoy the feel of the sun on their skin.

"As the saying goes, things always get better after a storm," Coll declared in satisfaction. "There'll be good weather now, Par—you watch. Another three days and we'll be home."

Par smiled and said nothing.

The day wore on, turning lazy, and the summer smells of trees and flowers began to fill the air again.

They sailed beneath Southwatch, its black granite bulk jutting skyward out of the mountain rock at the edge of the river, silent and inscrutable. Even from as far away as it was, the tower looked forbidding, its stone grainy and opaque, so dark that it seemed to absorb the light. There were all sorts of rumors about Southwatch. Some said it was alive, that it fed upon the earth in order to live. Some said it could move. Almost everyone agreed that it seemed to keep getting bigger through some form of ongoing construction. It appeared to be deserted. It always appeared that way. An elite unit of Federation soldiers were supposed to be in service to the tower, but no one ever saw them. Just as well, Par thought as they drifted past undisturbed.

By late afternoon, they reached the mouth of the river where it opened into the Rainbow Lake. The lake spread away before

them, a broad expanse of silver-tipped blue water turned golden
at its western edge by the sun as it slipped toward the horizon.
The rainbow from which it took its name arched overhead, faint
now in the blaze of sunlight, the blues and purples almost invisible, the reds and yellows washed of their color. Cranes glided
silently in the distance, long graceful bodies extended against
the light.

The Ohmsfords pulled their boat to the shore's edge and
beached it where a stand of shade trees fronted a low bluff.
They set their camp, hanging the canvas in the event of a change
back in the weather, and Coll fished while Par went off to gather
wood for an evening fire.

Par wandered the shoreline east for a ways, enjoying the
bright glaze of the lake's waters and the colors in the air. After
a time, he moved back up into the woods and began picking up
pieces of dry wood. He had gone only a short distance when
the woods turned dank and filled with a decaying smell. He
noticed that many of the trees seemed to be dying here, leaves
wilted and brown, limbs broken off, bark peeling. The ground
cover looked unwell, too. He poked and scraped at it with his
boot and looked about curiously. There didn't appear to be
anything living here; there were no small animals scurrying about
and no birds calling from the trees. The forest was deserted.

He decided to give up looking for firewood in this direction
and was working his way back toward the shoreline when he
caught sight of the house. It was a cottage, really, and scarcely
that. It was badly overgrown with weeds, vines, and scrub.
Boards hung loosely from its walls, shutters lay on the ground,
and the roof was caving in. The glass in the windows was broken
out, and the front door stood open. It sat at the edge of a cove
that ran far back into the trees from the lake, and the water of
the cove was still and greenish with stagnation. The smell that
it gave off was sickening.

Par would have thought it deserted if not for the tiny column of smoke that curled up from the crumbling chimney.

He hesitated, wondering why anyone would live in such
surroundings. He wondered if there really was someone there
or if the smoke was merely a residue. Then he wondered if
whoever was there needed help.

He almost went over to see, but there was something so odious about the cottage and its surroundings that he could not make himself do so. Instead, he called out, asking if anyone was home. He waited a moment, then called out again. When there was no reply, he turned away almost gratefully and continued on his way.

Coll was waiting with the fish by the time he returned, so they hastily built a fire and cooked dinner. They were both a little tired of fish, but it was better than nothing and they were more hungry than either would have imagined. When the dinner was consumed, they sat watching as the sun dipped into the horizon and the Rainbow Lake turned to silver. The skies darkened and filled with stars, and the sounds of the night rose out of dusk's stillness. Shadows from the forest trees lengthened and joined and became dark pools that enveloped the last of the daylight.

Par was in the process of trying to figure out a way to tell Coll that he didn't think they should return to Shady Vale when the woodswoman appeared.

She came out of the trees behind them, shambling from the dark as if one of its shadows, all bent over and hunched down against the fire's faint light. She was clothed in rags, layers of them, all of which appeared to have been wrapped about her at some time in the distant past and left there. Her head was bare, and her rough, hard face peered out through long wisps of dense, colorless hair. She might have been any age, Par thought; she was so gnarled it was impossible to tell.

She edged out of the forest cautiously and stopped just beyond the circle of the fire's yellow light, leaning heavily on a walking stick worn with sweat and handling. One rough arm raised as she pointed at Par. "You the one called me?" she asked, her voice cracking like brittle wood.

Par stared at her in spite of himself. She looked like something brought out of the earth, something that had no right to be alive and walking about. There was dirt and debris hanging from her as if it had settled and taken root while she slept.

"Was it?" she pressed.

He finally figured out what she was talking about. "At the cottage? Yes, that was me."

The woodswoman smiled, her face twisting with the effort, her mouth nearly empty of teeth. "You ought to have come in, not just stood out there," she whined. "Door was open."

"I didn't want . . ."

"Keep it that way to be certain no one goes past without a welcome. Fire's always on."

"I saw your smoke, but . . ."

"Gathering wood, were you? Come down out of Callahorn?" Her eyes shifted as she glanced past them to where the boat sat beached. "Come a long way, have you?" The eyes shifted back. "Running from something, maybe?"

Par went instantly still. He exchanged a quick look with Coll.

The woman approached, the walking stick probing the ground in front of her. "Lots run this way. All sorts. Come down out of the outlaw country looking for something or other." She stopped. "That you? Oh, there's those who'd have no part of you, but I'm not one. No, not me!"

"We're not running," Coll spoke up suddenly.

"No? That why you're so well fitted out?" She swept the air with the walking stick. "What's your names?"

"What do you want?" Par asked abruptly. He was liking this less and less.

The woodswoman edged forward another step. There was something wrong with her, something that Par hadn't seen before. She didn't seem to be quite solid, shimmering a bit as if she were walking through smoke or out of a mass of heated air. Her body didn't move right either, and it was more than her age. It was as if she were fastened together like one of the marionettes they used in shows at the fairs, pinned at the joints and pulled by strings.

The smell of the cove and the crumbling cottage clung to the woodswoman even here. She sniffed the air suddenly as if aware of it. "What's that?" She fixed her eyes on Par. "Do I smell magic?"

Par went suddenly cold. Whoever this woman was, she was no one they wanted anything to do with.

"Magic! Yes! Clean and pure and strong with life!" The

woodswoman's tongue licked out at the night air experimentally. "Sweet as blood to wolves!"

That was enough for Coll. "You had better find your way back to wherever you came from," he told her, not bothering to disguise his antagonism. "You have no business here. Move along."

But the woodswoman stayed where she was. Her mouth curled into a snarl and her eyes suddenly turned as red as the fire's coals.

"Come over here to me!" she whispered with a hiss. "You, boy!" She pointed at Par. "Come over to me!"

She reached out with one hand. Par and Coll both moved back guardedly, away from the fire. The woman came forward several steps more, edging past the light, backing them further toward the dark.

"Sweet boy!" she muttered, half to herself. "Let me taste you, boy!"

The brothers held their ground against her now, refusing to move any further from the light. The woodswoman saw the determination in their eyes, and her smile was wicked. She came forward, one step, another step . . .

Coll launched himself at her while she was watching Par, trying to grasp her and pin her arms. But she was much quicker than he, the walking stick slashing at him and catching him alongside the head with a vicious whack that sent him sprawling to the earth. Instantly, she was after him, howling like a maddened beast. But Par was quicker. He used the wishsong, almost without thinking, sending forth a string of terrifying images. She fell back, surprised, trying to fend the images off with her hands and the stick. Par used the opportunity to reach Coll and haul him to his feet. Hastily he pulled his brother back from where his attacker clawed at the air.

The woodswoman stopped suddenly, letting the images play about her, turning toward Par with a smile that froze his blood. Par sent an image of a Demon wraith to frighten her, but this time the woman reached out for the image, opened her mouth and sucked in the air about her. The image evaporated. The woman licked her lips and whined.

Par sent an armored warrior. The woodswoman devoured it greedily. She was edging closer again, no longer slowed by the images, actually anxious that he send more. She seemed to relish the taste of the magic; she seemed eager to consume it. Par tried to steady Coll, but his brother was sagging in his arms, still stunned. "Coll, wake up!" he whispered urgently.

"Come, boy," the woodswoman repeated softly. She beckoned and moved closer. "Come feed me!"

Then the fire exploded in a flash of light, and the clearing was turned as bright as day. The woodswoman shrank away from the brightness, and her sudden cry ended in a snarl of rage. Par blinked and peered through the glow.

An old man emerged from the trees, white-haired and gray-robed, with skin as brown as seasoned wood. He stepped from the darkness into the light like a ghost come into being. There was a fierce smile on his mouth and a strange brightness in his eyes. Par wheeled about guardedly, fumbling for the long knife at his belt. Two of them, he thought desperately, and again he shook Coll in an effort to rouse him.

But the old man paid him no notice. He concentrated instead on the woodswoman. "I know you," he said softly. "You frighten no one. Begone from here or you shall deal with me!"

The woodswoman hissed at him like a snake and crouched as if to spring. But she saw something in the old man's face that kept her from attacking. Slowly, she began to edge back around the fire.

"Go back into the dark," whispered the old man.

The woodswoman hissed a final time, then turned and disappeared into the trees without a sound. Her smell lingered on a moment longer, then faded. The old man waved almost absently at the fire, and it returned to normal. The night filled again with comforting sounds, and everything was as before.

The old man snorted and came forward into the firelight. "Bah. One of nighttime's little horrors come out to play," he muttered in disgust. He looked at Par quizzically. "You all right, young Ohmsford? And this one? Coll, is it? That was a nasty blow he took."

Par eased Coll to the ground, nodding. "Yes, thanks. Could you hand me that cloth and a little water?"

The old man did as he was asked, and Par wiped the side of Coll's head where an ugly bruise was already beginning to form. Coll winced, sat forward, and put his head down between his legs, waiting for the throbbing to ease off. Par looked up. It dawned on him suddenly that the old man had used Coll's name.

"How do you know who we are?" he asked, his tone guarded.

The old man kept his gaze steady. "Well, now. I know who you are because I've come looking for you. But I'm not your enemy, if that's what you're thinking."

Par shook his head. "Not really. Not after helping us the way you did. Thank you."

"No need for thanks."

Par nodded again. "That woman, or whatever she was—she seemed frightened of you." He didn't make it a question, he made it a statement of fact.

The old man shrugged. "Perhaps."

"Do you know her?"

"I know of her."

Par hesitated, uncertain whether to press the matter or not. He decided to let it drop. "So. Why are you looking for us?"

"Oh, that's rather a long story, I'm afraid," the old man answered, sounding very much as if the effort required to tell it was entirely beyond him. "I don't suppose we might sit down while we talk about it? The fire's warmth provides some relief for these ageing bones. And you wouldn't happen to have a touch of ale, would you? No? Pity. Well, I suppose there was no chance to procure such amenities, the way you were hustled out of Varfleet. Lucky to escape with your skins under the circumstances."

He ambled in close and lowered himself gingerly to the grass, folding his legs before him, draping his gray robes carefully about. "Thought I'd catch up with you there, you know. But then that disruption by the Federation occurred, and you were on your way south before I could stop you."

He reached for a cup and dipped it into the water bucket, drinking deeply. Coll was sitting up now, watching, the damp cloth still held to the side of his head. Par sat down next to him.

The old man finished his water and wiped his mouth on his sleeve. "Allanon sent me," he declared perfunctorily.

There was a long silence as the Ohmsford brothers stared first at him, then at each other, then back again at him.

"Allanon?" Par repeated.

"Allanon has been dead for three hundred years," Coll interjected bluntly.

The old man nodded. "Indeed. I misspoke: It was actually Allanon's ghost, his shade—but Allanon, still, for all intents and purposes."

"Allanon's shade?" Coll took the cloth from the side of his head, his injury forgotten. He did not bother to hide his disbelief.

The old man rubbed his bearded chin. "Now, now, you will have to be patient for a moment or two until I've had a chance to explain. Much of what I am going to tell you will be hard for you to accept, but you must try. Believe me when I tell you that it is very important."

He rubbed his hands briskly in the direction of the fire. "Think of me as a messenger for the moment, will you? Think of me as a messenger sent by Allanon, for that's all I am to you just now. You, Par. Why have you been ignoring the dreams?"

Par stiffened. "You know about that?"

"The dreams were sent by Allanon to bring you to him. Don't you understand? That was his voice speaking to you, his shade come to address you. He summons you to the Hadeshorn—you, your cousin Wren, and . . ."

"Wren?" Coll interrupted, incredulous.

The old man looked perturbed. "That's what I said, didn't I? Am I going to have to repeat everything? Your cousin, Wren Ohmsford. And Walker Boh as well."

"Uncle Walker," Par said softly. "I remember."

Coll glanced at his brother, then shook his head in disgust. "This is ridiculous. No one knows where either of them is!" he snapped. "Wren lives somewhere in the Westland with the Rovers. She lives out of the back of a wagon! And Walker Boh hasn't been seen by anyone for almost ten years. He might be dead, for all we know!"

"He might, but he isn't," the old man said testily. He gave Coll a meaningful stare, then returned his gaze to Par. "All of you are to come to the Hadeshorn by the close of the present moon's cycle. On the first night of the new moon, Allanon will speak with you there."

Par felt a chill go through him. "About magic?"

Coll seized his brother's shoulders. "About Shadowen?" he mimicked, widening his eyes.

The old man bent forward suddenly, his face gone hard. "About what he chooses! Yes, about magic! And about Shadowen! About creatures like the one that knocked you aside just now as if you were a baby! But mostly, I think, young Coll, about this!"

He threw a dash of dark powder into the fire with a suddenness that caused Par and Coll to jerk back sharply. The fire flared as it had when the old man had first appeared, but this time the light was drawn out of the air and everything went dark.

Then an image formed in the blackness, growing in size until it seemed to be all around them. It was an image of the Four Lands, the countryside barren and empty, stripped of life and left ruined. Darkness and a haze of ash-filled smoke hung over everything. Rivers were filled with debris, the waters poisoned. Trees were bent and blasted, shorn of life. Nothing but scrub grew anywhere. Men crept about like animals, and animals fled at their coming. There were shadows with strange red eyes circling everywhere, dipping and playing within those humans who crept, twisting and turning them until they lost their shape and became unrecognizable.

It was a nightmare of such fury and terror that it seemed to Par and Coll Ohmsford as if it were happening to them, and that the screams emanating from the mouths of the tortured humans were their own.

Then the image was gone, and they were back again about the fire, the old man sitting there, watching them with hawk's eyes.

"That was a part of my dream," Par whispered.

"That was the future," the old man said.

"Or a trick," a shaken Coll muttered, stiffening against his own fear.

The old man glared. "The future is an ever-shifting maze

of possibilities until it becomes the present. The future I have shown you tonight is not yet fixed. But it is more likely to become so with the passing of every day because nothing is being done to turn it aside. If you would change it, do as I have told you. Go to Allanon! Listen to what he will say!"

Coll said nothing, his dark eyes uneasy with doubt.

"Tell us who you are," Par said softly.

The old man turned to him, studied him for a moment, then looked away from them both, staring out into the darkness as if there were worlds and lives hidden there that only he could see. Finally, he looked back again, nodding.

"Very well, though I can't see what difference it makes. I have a name, a name you should both recognize quickly enough. My name is Cogline."

For an instant, neither Par nor Coll said anything. Then both began speaking at once.

"Cogline, the same Cogline who lived in the Eastland with . . . ?"

"You mean the same man Kimber Boh . . . ?"

He cut them short irritably. "Yes, yes! How many Coglines can there possibly be!" He frowned as he saw the looks on their faces. "You don't believe me, do you?"

Par took a deep breath. "Cogline was an old man in the time of Brin Ohmsford. That was three hundred years ago."

Unexpectedly, the other laughed. "An old man! Ha! And what do you know of old men, Par Ohmsford? Fact is, you don't know a whisker's worth!" He laughed, then shook his head helplessly. "Listen. Allanon was alive five hundred years before he died! You don't question that, do you? I think not, since you tell the story so readily! Is it so astonishing then that I have been alive for a mere three hundred years?" He paused, and there was a surprisingly mischievous look in his eye. "Goodness, what would you have said if I had told you I had been alive longer even than that?"

Then he waved his hand dismissively. "No, no, don't bother to answer. Answer me this instead. What do you know about me? About the Cogline of your stories? Tell me."

Par shook his head, confused. "That he was a hermit, living off in the Wilderun with his granddaughter, Kimber Boh. That my ancestor, Brin Ohmsford, and her companion, Rone Leah, found him there when they . . ."

"Yes, yes, but what about the *man*? Think now of what you've seen of me!"

Par shrugged. "That he . . ." He stopped. "That he used powders that exploded. That he knew something of the old sciences, that he'd studied them somewhere." He was remembering the specifics of the tales of Cogline now, and in remembering found himself thinking that maybe this old man's claim wasn't so far-fetched. "He employed different forms of power, the sorts that the Druids had discarded in their rebuilding of the old world. Shades! If you are Cogline, you must still have such power. Do you? Is it magic like my own?"

Coll looked suddenly worried. "Par!"

"Like your own?" the old man asked quickly. "Magic like the wishsong? Hah! Never! Never so unpredictable as that! That was always the trouble with the Druids and their Elven magics—too unpredictable! The power I wield is grounded in sciences proven and tested through the years by reliable study! It doesn't act of its own accord; it doesn't evolve like something alive!" He stopped, a fierce smile creasing his aged face. "But then, too, Par Ohmsford, my power doesn't sing either!"

"Are you really Cogline?" Par asked softly, his amazement at it being possible apparent in his voice.

"Yes," the old man whispered back. "Yes, Par." He swung quickly then to face Coll, who was about to interrupt, placing a narrow, bony finger to his lips. "Shhhh, young Ohmsford, I know you still disbelieve, and your brother as well, but just listen for a moment. You are children of the Elven house of Shannara. There have not been many and always much has been expected of them. It will be so with you as well, I think. More so, perhaps. I am not permitted to see. I am just a messenger, as I have told you—a poor messenger at best. An unwilling messenger, truth is. But I am all that Allanon has."

"But why you?" Par managed to interject, his lean face troubled now and intense.

The old man paused, his gnarled, wrinkled face tightening even further as if the question demanded too much of him. When he spoke finally, it was in a stillness that was palpable.

"Because I was a Druid once, so long ago I can scarcely remember what it felt like. I studied the ways of the magic and the ways of the discarded sciences and chose the latter, forsaking thereby any claim to the former and the right to continue with the others. Allanon knew me, or if you prefer, he knew about me, and he remembered what I was. But, wait. I embellish a bit by claiming I actually was a Druid. I wasn't; I was simply a student of the ways. But Allanon remembered in any case. When he came to me, it was as one Druid to another, though he did not say as much. He lacks anyone but myself to do what is needed now, to come after you and the others, to advise them of the legitimacy of their dreams. All have had them by now, you understand—Wren and Walker Boh as well as you. All have been given a vision of the danger the future holds. No one responds. So he sends me."

The sharp eyes blinked away the memory. "I was a Druid once, in spirit if not in practice, and I practice still many of the Druid ways. No one knew. Not my grandchild Kimber, not your ancestors, no one. I have lived many different lives, you see. When I went with Brin Ohmsford into the country of the Maelmord, it was as Cogline the hermit, half-crazed, half-able, carrying magic powders filled with strange notions. That was who I was then. That was the person I had become. It took me years afterward, long after Kimber had gone, to recover myself, to act and talk like myself again."

He sighed. "It was the Druid Sleep that kept me alive for so long. I knew its secret; I had carried it with me when I left them. I thought many times not to bother, to give myself over to death and not cling so. But something kept me from giving way, and I think now that perhaps it was Allanon, reaching back from his death to assure that the Druids might have at least one spokesman after he was gone."

He saw the beginning of the question in Par's eyes, anticipated its wording, and quickly shook his head. "No, no, not me! I am not the spokesman he needs! I barely have time enough left me to carry the message I have been given. Allanon knows that. He knew better than to come to me to ask that I accept a life I once rejected. He must ask that of someone else."

"Me?" asked Par at once.

The old man paused. "Perhaps. Why don't you ask him yourself?"

No one said anything, hunched forward toward the firelight as the darkness pressed close all about. The cries of the night birds echoed faintly across the waters of the Rainbow Lake, a haunting sound that somehow seemed to measure the depth of the uncertainty Par felt.

"I want to ask him," he said finally. "I need to, I think."

The old man pursed his thin lips. "Then you must."

Coll started to say something, then thought better of it. "This whole business needs some careful thought," he said finally.

"There is little time for that," the old man grumbled.

"Then we shouldn't squander what we have," Coll replied simply. He was no longer abrasive as he spoke, merely insistent.

Par looked at his brother a moment, then nodded. "Coll is right. I will have to think about this."

The old man shrugged as if to indicate that he realized there was nothing more he could do and came to his feet. "I have given you the message I was sent to give, so I must be on my way. There are others to be visited."

Par and Coll rose with him, surprised. "You're leaving now, tonight?" Par asked quickly. Somehow he had expected the old man to stay on, to keep trying to persuade him of the purpose of the dreams.

"Seems best. The quicker I get on with my journey, the quicker it ends. I told you, I came first to you."

"But how will you find Wren or Walker?" Coll wanted to know.

"Same way I found you." The old man snapped his fingers and there was a brief flash of silver light. He grinned, his face skeletal in the firelight. "Magic!"

He reached out his bony hand. Par took it first and found the old man's grip like iron. Coll found the same. They glanced at each other.

"Let me offer you some advice," the old man said abruptly. "Not that you'll necessarily take it, of course—but maybe. You tell these stories, these tales of Druids and magic and your ancestors, all of it a kind of litany of what's been and gone. That's fine, but you don't want to lose sight of the fact that what's happening here and now is what counts. All the telling in the world won't mean a whisker if that vision I showed you comes to pass. You have to live in this world—not in some other. Magic serves a lot of purposes, but you don't use it any way but one. You have to see what else it can do. And you can't do that until you understand it. I suggest you don't understand it at all, either one of you."

He studied them a moment, then turned and shambled off into the dark. "Don't forget, first night of the new moon!" He stopped when he was just a shadow and glanced back. "Something else you'd better remember and that's to watch yourselves." His voice had a new edge to it. "The Shadowen aren't just rumors and old wives' tales. They're as real as you and I. You may not have thought so before tonight, but now you know different. They'll be out there, everywhere you're likely to go. That woman, she was one of them. She came sniffing around because she could sense you have the magic. Others will do the same."

He started moving away again. "Lots of things are going to be hunting you," he warned softly.

He mumbled something further to himself that neither of them could hear as he disappeared slowly into the darkness.

Then he was gone.

5

AR AND COLL OHMSFORD did not get much sleep that night. They stayed awake long after the old man was gone, talking and sometimes arguing, worrying without always saying as much, eyes constantly scanning the darkness against the promise that *things*, Shadowen or otherwise, were likely to be hunting them. Even after that, when there was nothing left to say, when they had rolled themselves wearily into their blankets and closed their eyes against their fears, they did not sleep well. They rolled and tossed in their slumber, waking themselves and each other with distressing regularity until dawn.

They rose then, dragged themselves from the warmth of their coverings, washed in the chilling waters of the lake, and promptly began talking and arguing all over again. They continued through breakfast, which was just as well because once again there wasn't much to eat and it took their minds off their stomachs. The talk, and more often now the arguments, centered around the old man who claimed to be Cogline and the dreams that might or might not have been sent and if sent might or might not have been sent by Allanon, but included such peripheral topics as Shadowen, Federation Seekers, the stranger who had rescued them in Varfleet, and whether there was sense to the world anymore or not. They had established their positions on these subjects fairly well by this time, positions that, for the most part, weren't within a week's walk of each other. That being the case, they were reduced to communicating with each other across vast stretches of intractability.

Before their day was even an hour old, they were already thoroughly fed up with each other.

"You cannot deny that the possibility exists that the old man really is Cogline!" Par insisted for what must have been the hundredth time as they carried the canvas tarp down to the skiff for stowing.

Coll managed a quick shrug. "I'm not denying it."

"And if he really is Cogline, then you cannot deny the possibility that everything he told us is the truth!"

"I'm not denying that either."

"What about the woodswoman? What was she if not a Shadowen, a night thing with magic stronger than our own?"

"Your own."

Par fumed. "Sorry. My own. The point is, she *was* a Shadowen! She had to be! That makes at least part of what the old man told us the truth, no matter how you view it!"

"Wait a minute." Coll dropped his end of the tarp and stood there with his hands on his hips, regarding his brother with studied dismay. "You do this all the time when we argue. You make these ridiculous leaps in logic and act as if they make perfect sense. How does it follow that, if that woman was a Shadowen, the old man was telling the truth?"

"Well, because, if . . ."

"I won't even question your assumption that she *was* a Shadowen," Coll interrupted pointedly. "Even though we haven't the faintest idea what a Shadowen is. Even though she might just as easily have been something else altogether."

"Something else? What sort of . . . ?"

"Like a companion to the old man, for instance. Like a decoy to give his tale validity."

Par was incensed. "That's ridiculous! What would be the purpose of that?"

Coll pursed his lips thoughtfully. "To persuade you to go with him to the Hadeshorn, naturally. To bring you back into Callahorn. Think about it. Maybe the old man is interested in the magic, too—just like the Federation."

Par shook his head vehemently. "I don't believe it."

"That's because you never like to believe anything that you haven't thought of first," Coll declared pointedly, picking up his end of the tarp again. "You decide something and that's the end of it. Well, this time you had better not make your decision too quickly. There are other possibilities to consider, and I've just given you one of them."

They walked down to the shoreline in silence and deposited the tarp in the bottom of the skiff. The sun was barely above the eastern horizon, and already the day was beginning to feel warm. The Rainbow Lake was smooth, the air windless and filled with the scent of wildflowers and long grass.

Coll turned. "You know, it's not that I mind you being decisive about things. It's just that you then assume I ought simply to agree. I shouldn't argue, I should acquiesce. Well, I am not going to do that. If you want to strike out for the Hadeshorn and the Dragon's Teeth—fine, you go right ahead. But quit acting as if I ought to jump at the chance to go along."

Par didn't say anything back right away. Instead, he thought about what it had been like for them growing up. Par was the older by two years and while physically smaller than Coll, he had always been the leader. He had the magic, after all, and that had always set him apart. It was true, he was decisive; it had been necessary to be decisive when faced with the temptation to use the magic to solve every situation. He had not been as even-tempered as he should have; he wasn't any better now. Coll had always been the more controlled of the two— slower to anger, thoughtful and deliberate, a born peacemaker in the neighborhood fights and squabbles because no one else had the physical and emotional presence. Or was as well liked, he added—because Coll was always that, the sort of fellow that everyone takes to instantly. He spent his time looking after everyone, smoothing over hard feelings, restoring injured pride. Par was always charging around, oblivious to such things, busy searching for new places to explore, new challenges to engage, new ideas to develop. He was visionary, but he lacked Coll's sensitivity. He foresaw so clearly life's possibilities, but Coll was the one who understood best its sacrifices.

There had been a good many times when they had covered for each other's mistakes. But Par had the magic to fall back on and covering up for Coll had seldom cost him anything. It hadn't been like that for Coll. Covering up for Par had sometimes cost him a great deal. Yet Par was his brother, whom he loved, and he never complained. Sometimes, thinking back on those days, Par was ashamed of how much he had let his brother do for him.

He brushed the memories aside. Coll was looking at him, waiting for his response. Par shifted his feet impatiently and thought about what that response ought to be. Then he said simply, "All right. What do you think we should do?"

"Shades, I don't know what we should do!" Coll said at once. "I just know that there are a lot of unanswered questions, and I don't think we should commit ourselves to anything until we've had a chance to answer some of them!"

Par nodded stoically. "Before the time of the new moon, you mean."

"That's better than three weeks away and you know it!"

Par's jaw tightened. "That's not as much time as you make it seem! How are we supposed to answer all the questions we have before then?"

Coll stared at him. "You are impossible, you know that?"

He turned and walked back from the shoreline to where the blankets and cooking gear were stacked and began carrying them down to the skiff. He didn't look at Par. Par stood where he was and watched his brother in silence. He was remembering how Coll had pulled him half-drowned from the Rappahalladran when he had fallen in the rapids on a camping trip. He had gone under and Coll had been forced to dive down for him. He became sick afterward and Coll had carried him home on his back, shaking with fever and half-delirious. Coll was always looking out for him, it seemed. Why was that, he wondered suddenly, when he was the one with the magic?

Coll finished packing the skiff, and Par walked over to him. "I'm sorry," he said and waited.

Coll looked down at him solemnly a moment, then grinned. "No, you're not. You're just saying that."

Par grinned back in spite of himself. "I am not!"

"Yes, you are. You just want to put me off my guard so you can start in again with your confounded decision-making once we're out in the middle of that lake where I can't walk away from you!" His brother was laughing openly now.

Par did his best to look mortified. "Okay, it's true. I'm not sorry."

"I knew it!" Coll was triumphant.

"But you're wrong about the reason for the apology. It has nothing to do with getting you out in the middle of the lake. I'm just trying to shed the burden of guilt I've always felt at being the older brother."

"Don't worry!" Coll was doubled over. "You've always been a terrible older brother!"

Par shoved him, Coll shoved back, and for the moment their differences were forgotten. They laughed, took a final look about the campsite and pushed the skiff out onto the lake, clambering aboard as it reached deeper water. Coll took up the oars without asking and began to row.

They followed the shoreline west, listening contentedly as the distant sounds of birds rose out of the trees and rushes, letting the day grow pleasantly warm about them. They didn't talk for a while, satisfied with the renewed feeling of closeness they had found on setting out, anxious to avoid arguing again right away.

Nevertheless, Par found himself rehashing matters in his mind—much the same as he was certain Coll was doing. His brother was right about one thing—there were a lot of unanswered questions. Reflecting on the events of the previous evening, Par found himself wishing he had thought to ask the old man for a bit more information. Did the old man know, for instance, who the stranger was who had rescued them in Varfleet? The old man had known about their trouble there and must have had some idea how they escaped. The old man had managed to track them, first to Varfleet, then down the Mermidon, and he had frightened off the woodswoman—Shadowen or whatever—without much effort. He had some form of power at his command, possibly Druid magic, possibly old world science—but he had never said what it was or what it did. Exactly what was his relationship with Allanon? Or was that simply a claim without any basis in fact? And why was it that he had given up on Par so easily when Par had said he must think over the matter of going off to the Hadeshorn for a meeting with Allanon? Shouldn't he have worked harder at persuading Par to go?

But the most disturbing question was one that Par could not bring himself to discuss with Coll at all—because it concerned Coll himself. The dreams had told Par that he was needed and that his cousin Wren and his uncle Walker Boh were needed as well. The old man had said the same—that Par, Wren, and Walker had been called.

Why was there no mention of Coll?

It was a question for which he had no answer at all. He had thought at first that it was because he had the magic and Coll didn't, that the summons had something to do with the wish-song. But then why was Wren needed? Wren had no magic either. Walker Boh was different, of course, since it had always been rumored that he knew something of magic that none of the others did. But not Wren. And not Coll. Yet Wren had been specifically named and Coll hadn't.

It was this more than anything that made him question what he should do. He wanted to know the reason for the dreams; if the old man was right about Allanon, Par wanted to know what the Druid had to say. But he did not want to know any of it if it meant separating from Coll. Coll was more than his brother; he was his closest friend, his most trusted companion, practically his other self. Par did not intend to become involved in something where both were not wanted. He simply wasn't going to do it.

Yet the old man had not forbidden Coll to come. Nor had the dreams. Neither had warned against it.

They had simply ignored him.

Why would that be?

The morning lengthened, and a wind came up. The brothers rigged a sail and mast using the canvas tarp and one of the oars, and soon they were speeding across the Rainbow Lake, the waters slapping and foaming about them. Several times they almost went over, but they stayed alert to sudden shifts in the wind and used their body weight to avoid capsizing. They set a southwest course and by early afternoon had reached the mouth of the Rappahalladran.

There they beached the skiff in a small cove, covered it with rushes and boughs, left everything within but the blankets and cooking gear, and began hiking upriver toward the Duln forests. It soon became expedient to cut across country to save time, and they left the river, moving up into the Highlands of Leah. They hadn't spoken about where they were going since the previous evening, when the tacit understanding had been that they would debate the matter later. They hadn't, of course. Neither had brought the subject up again, Coll because they were moving in the direction he wanted to go anyway, and Par because he had decided that Coll was right that some thinking needed to be done before any trip back north into Callahorn was undertaken. Shady Vale was as good a place as any to complete that thinking.

Oddly enough, though they hadn't talked about the dreams or the old man or any of the rest of it since early that morning, they had begun separately to rethink their respective positions and to move closer together—each inwardly conceding that maybe the other made some sense after all.

By the time they began discussing matters again, they were no longer arguing. It was midafternoon, the summer day hot and sticky now, the sun a blinding white sphere before them as they walked, forcing them to shield their eyes protectively. The country was a mass of rolling hills, a carpet of grasses and wildflowers dotted with stands of broad-leafed trees and patches of scrub and rock. The mists that blanketed the Highlands year-round had retreated to the higher elevations in the face of the sun's brightness and clung to the tips of the ridgelines and bluffs like scattered strips of linen.

"I think that woodswoman was genuinely afraid of the old man," Par was saying as they climbed a long, gradual slope into a stand of ash. "I don't think she was pretending. No one's that good an actor."

Coll nodded. "I think you're right. I just said all that earlier about the two of them being in league to make you think. I can't help wondering, though, if the old man is telling us everything he knows. What I mostly remember about Allanon in the stories is that he was decidedly circumspect in his dealings with the Ohmsfords."

"He never told them everything, that's true."

"So maybe the old man is the same way."

They crested the hill, moved into the shade of the ash trees, dropped their rolled-up blankets wearily and stood looking out at the Highlands. Both were sweating freely, their tunics damp against their backs.

"We won't make Shady Vale tonight," Par said, settling to the ground against one of the trees.

"No, it doesn't look like it." Coll joined him, stretching until his bones cracked.

"I was thinking."

"Good for you."

"I was thinking about where we might spend the night. It would be nice to sleep in a bed for a change."

Coll laughed. "You won't get any argument out of me. Got any idea where we can find a bed out here in the middle of nowhere?"

Par turned slowly and looked at him. "Matter-of-fact, I do. Morgan's hunting lodge is just a few miles south. I bet we could borrow it for the night."

Coll frowned thoughtfully. "Yes, I bet we could."

Morgan Leah was the eldest son in a family whose ancestors had once been Kings of Leah. But the monarchy had been overthrown almost two hundred years ago when the Federation had expanded northward and simply consumed the Highlands in a single bite. There had been no Leah kings since, and the family had survived as gentlemen farmers and craftsmen over the years. The current head of the family, Kyle Leah, was a landholder living south of the city who bred beef cattle. Morgan, his oldest son, Par and Coll's closest friend, bred mostly mischief.

"You don't think Morgan will be around, do you?" Coll asked, grinning at the possibility.

Par grinned back. The hunting lodge was really a family possession, but Morgan was the one who used it the most. The last time the Ohmsford brothers had come into the Highlands they had stayed for a week at the lodge as Morgan's guests. They had camped, hunted and fished, but mostly they had spent their time recounting tales of Morgan's ongoing efforts to cause distress to the members of the Federation government-in-residence at Leah. Morgan Leah had the quickest mind and the fastest pair of hands in the Southland, and he harbored an abiding dislike for the army that occupied his land. Unlike Shady Vale, Leah was a major city and required watching. The Federation, after abolishing the monarchy, had installed the provisional governor and cabinet and stationed a garrison of soldiers to insure order. Morgan regarded that as a personal challenge. He took every opportunity that presented itself, and a few that didn't, to make life miserable for the officials that now lodged comfortably and without regard for proper right of ownership in his ancestral home. It was never a contest. Morgan was a positive genius at disruption and much too sharp to allow the Federation officials to suspect he was the thorn in their collective sides that they could not even find, let alone remove. On the last go-around, Morgan had trapped the governor and vice-governor in a private bathing court with a herd of carefully muddied pigs and jammed all the locks on the doors. It was a very small court and a whole lot of pigs. It took two hours to free them all, and Morgan insisted solemnly that by then it was hard to tell who was who.

The brothers regained their feet, hoisted their packs in place, and set off once more. The afternoon slipped away as the sun followed its path westward, but the air stayed quiet and the heat grew even more oppressive. The land at this elevation at midsummer was so dry that the grass crackled where they walked, the once-green blades dried to a brownish gray crust. Dust curled up in small puffs beneath their boots, and their mouths grew dry.

It was nearing sunset by the time they caught sight of the hunting lodge, a stone and timber building set back in a grouping of pines on a rise that overlooked the country west. Hot and sweating, they dumped their gear by the front door and went directly to the bathing springs nestled in the trees a hundred yards back. When they reached the springs, a cluster of clear blue pools that filled from beneath and emptied out into a sluggish little stream, they began stripping off their clothes immediately, heedless of anything but their by now overwhelming need to sink down into the inviting water.

Which was why they didn't see the mud creature until it was almost on top of them.

It rose up from the bushes next to them, vaguely manlike, encrusted in mud and roaring with a ferocity that shattered the stillness like glass. Coll gave a howl, sprang backward, lost his balance and tumbled headfirst into the springs. Par jerked away, tripped and rolled, and the creature was on top of him.

"Ahhhh! A tasty Valeman!" the creature rasped in a voice that was suddenly very familiar.

"Shades, Morgan!" Par twisted and turned and shoved the other away. "You scared me to death, confound it!"

Coll pulled himself out of the springs, still wearing boots and pants halfway off, and said calmly, "I thought it was only the Federation you intended to drive out of Leah, not your friends." He heaved himself up and brushed the water from his eyes.

Morgan Leah was laughing merrily from within his mud cocoon. "I apologize, I really do. But it was an opportunity no man could resist. Surely you can understand that!"

Par tried to wipe the mud from his clothes and finally gave up, stripping bare and carrying everything into the springs with him. He gave a sigh of relief, then glanced back at Morgan. "What in the world are you doing anyway?"

"Oh, the mud? Good for your skin." Morgan walked to the springs and lowered himself into the water gingerly. "There are mud baths about a mile back. I found them the other day quite by accident. Never knew they were here. I can tell you honestly that there is nothing like mud on your body on a hot day to cool you down. Better even than the springs. So I rolled about quite piglike, then hiked back here to wash off. That was when I heard you coming and decided to give you a proper Highlands greeting."

He ducked down beneath the water; when he surfaced, the mud monster had been replaced by a lean, sinewy youth approximately their own age with skin so sun-browned it was almost the color of chocolate, shoulder-length reddish hair, and clear gray eyes that looked out of a face that was at once both clever and guileless. "Behold!" he exclaimed and grinned.

"Marvelous," Par replied tonelessly.

"Oh, come now! Not every trick can be earth-shattering. Which reminds me." Morgan bent forward questioningly. He spent much of his time wearing an expression that suggested he was secretly amused about something, and he showed it to them now. "Aren't you two supposed to be up in Callahorn somewhere dazzling the natives? Wasn't that the last I heard of your plans? What are you doing here?"

"What are *you* doing here?" Coll shot back.

"Me? Oh, just another little misunderstanding involving the governor—or more accurately, I'm afraid, the governor's wife. They don't suspect me, of course—they never do. Still, it seemed a good time for a vacation." Morgan's grin widened. "But come on now, I asked you first. What's going on?"

He was not to be put off and there had never been any unshared secrets among the three in any case, so Par, with considerable help from Coll, told him what had happened to them since that night in Varfleet when Rimmer Dall and the Federation Seekers had come looking for them. He told him of the dreams that might have been sent by Allanon, of their encounter with the frightening woodswoman who might have been one of the Shadowen, and of the old man who had saved them and might have been Cogline.

"There are a good number of 'might have beens' in that story," the Highlander observed archly when they were finished. "Are you certain you're not making this all up? It would be a fine joke at my expense."

"I just wish we were," Coll replied ruefully.

"Anyway, we thought we'd spend the night here in a bed, then go on to the Vale tomorrow," Par explained.

Morgan trailed one finger through the water in front of him and shook his head. "I don't think I'd do that if I were you."

Par and Coll looked at each other.

"If the Federation wanted you badly enough to send Rimmer Dall all the way to Varfleet," Morgan continued, his eyes coming up suddenly to meet their own, "then don't you think it likely they might send him to Shady Vale as well?"

There was a long silence before Par finally said, "I admit, I hadn't thought of that."

Morgan stroked over to the edge of the springs, heaved himself out, and began wiping the water from his body. "Well, thinking has never been your strong point, my boy. Good thing you've got me for a friend. Let's walk back up to the lodge and I'll fix you something to eat—something besides fish for a change—and we'll talk about it."

They dried, washed out their clothes and returned to the lodge where Morgan set about preparing dinner. He cooked a wonderful stew filled with meat, carrots, potatoes, onions, and broth, and served it with hot bread and cold ale. They sat out under the pines at a table and benches and consumed the better part of their food and drink, the day finally beginning to cool as night approached and an evening breeze rustled down out of the hills. Morgan brought out pears and cheese for dessert, and they nibbled contentedly as the sky turned red, then deep purple, and finally darkened and filled with stars.

"I love the Highlands," Morgan said after they had been silent for a time. They were seated on the stone steps of the lodge now. "I could learn to love the city as well I expect, but not while it belongs to the Federation. I sometimes find myself wondering what it would have been like to live in the old home, before they took it from us. That was a long time ago, of course—six generations ago. No one remembers what it was like anymore. My father won't even talk about it. But here—well, this is still ours, this land. The Federation hasn't been able to take that away yet. There's just too much of it. Maybe that's why I love it so much—because it's the last thing my family has left from the old days."

"Besides the sword," Par reminded.

"Do you still carry that battered old relic?" Coll asked. "I keep thinking you will discard it in favor of something newer and better made."

Morgan glanced over. "Do you remember the stories that said the Sword of Leah was once magic?"

"Allanon himself was supposed to have made it so," Par confirmed.

"Yes, in the time of Rone Leah." Morgan furrowed his brow. "Sometimes I think it still is magic. Not as it once was, not as a weapon that could withstand Mord Wraiths and such, but in a different way. The scabbard has been replaced half-a-dozen times over the years, the hilt once or twice at least, and both are worn again. But the blade—ah, that blade! It is still as sharp and true as ever, almost as if it cannot age. Doesn't that require magic of a sort?"

The brothers nodded solemnly. "Magic sometimes changes in the way it works," Par said. "It grows and evolves. Perhaps that has happened with the Sword of Leah." He was thinking as he said it how the old man had told him he did not understand the magic at all and wondering if that were true.

"Well, truth is, no one wants the weapon in any case, not anymore." Morgan stretched like a cat and sighed. "No one wants anything that belongs to the old days, it seems. The reminders are too painful, I think. My father didn't say a word when I asked for the blade. He just gave it to me."

Coll reached over and gave the other a friendly shove. "Well, your father ought to be more careful to whom he hands out his weapons."

Morgan managed to look put upon. "Am I the one being asked to join the Movement?" he demanded. They laughed. "By the way. You mentioned the stranger gave you a ring. Mind if I take a look?"

Par reached into his tunic, fished out the ring with the hawk insigne and passed it over. Morgan took it and examined it carefully, then shrugged and handed it back. "I don't recognize it. But that doesn't necessarily mean anything. I hear there are a dozen outlaw bands within the Movement and they all change their markings regularly to confuse the Federation."

He took a long drink from his ale glass and leaned back again. "Sometimes I think I ought to go north and join them—quit wasting time here playing games with those fools who live in my house and govern my land and don't even know the history." He shook his head sadly and for a moment looked old.

Then he brightened. "But now about you." He swung his legs around and sat forward. "You can't risk going back until you're certain it's safe. So you'll stay here for a day or so and let me go ahead. I'll make certain the Federation hasn't gotten there before you. Fair enough?"

"More than fair," Par said at once. "Thanks, Morgan. But you have to promise to be careful."

"Careful? Of those Federation fools? Ha!" The Highlander grinned ear to ear. "I could step up and spit in their collective eye and it would still take them days to work it out! I haven't anything to fear from them!"

Par wasn't laughing. "Not in Leah, perhaps. But there may be Seekers in Shady Vale."

Morgan quit grinning. "Your point is well-taken. I'll be careful."

He drained the last of his ale and stood up. "Time for bed. I'll want to leave early."

Par and Coll stood up with him. Coll said, "What was it exactly that you did to the governor's wife?"

Morgan shrugged. "Oh, that? Nothing much. Someone said she didn't care for the Highlands air, that it made her queasy. So I sent her a perfume to sweeten her sense of smell. It was contained in a small vial of very delicate glass. I had it placed in her bed, a surprise for her. She accidently broke it when she lay on it."

His eyes twinkled. "Unfortunately, I somehow got the perfume mixed up with skunk oil."

The three of them looked at each other in the darkness and grinned like fools.

THE OHMSFORDS SLEPT WELL that night, wrapped in the comfort and warmth of real beds with clean blankets and pillows. They could easily have slept until noon, but Morgan had them awake at dawn as he prepared to set out for Shady Vale. He brought out the Sword of Leah and showed it to them, its hilt and scabbard badly worn, but its blade as bright and new as the Highlander had claimed. Grinning in satisfaction at the looks on their faces, he strapped the weapon across one shoulder, stuck a long knife in the top of one boot, a hunting knife in his belt, and strapped an ash bow to his back.

He winked. "Never hurts to be prepared."

They saw him out the door and down the hill west for a short distance where he bade them goodbye. They were still sleepy-eyed and their own goodbyes were mixed with yawns.

"Go on back to bed," Morgan advised. "Sleep as long as you like. Relax and don't worry. I'll be back in a couple of days."

He waved as he moved off, a tall, lean figure silhouetted against the still-dark horizon, brimming with his usual self-confidence.

"Be careful!" Par called after him.

Morgan laughed. "Be careful yourself!"

The brothers took the Highlander's advice and went back to bed, slept until afternoon, then wasted the remainder of the day just lying about. They did better the second day, rising early, bathing in the springs, exploring the countryside in a futile effort to find the mud baths, cleaning out the hunting lodge, and preparing and eating a dinner of wild fowl and rice. They talked a long time that night about the old man and the dreams, the magic and the Seekers, and what they should do with their immediate future. They did not argue, but they did not reach any decisions either.

The third day turned cloudy and by nightfall it was raining. They sat before the fire they had built in the great stone hearth and practiced the storytelling for a long time, working on some of the more obscure tales, trying to make the images of Par's song and the words of Coll's story mesh. There was no sign of Morgan Leah. In spite of their unspoken mutual resolve not to do so, they began to worry.

On the fourth day, Morgan returned. It was late afternoon when he appeared, and the brothers were seated on the floor in front of the fire repairing the bindings on one of the dinner table chairs when the door opened suddenly and he was there. It had been raining steadily all day, and the Highlander was soaked through, dripping water everywhere as he lowered his backpack and weapons to the floor and shoved the door closed behind him.

"Bad news," he said at once. His rust-colored hair was plastered against his head, and the bones of his chiseled features glistened with rainwater. He seemed heedless of his condition as he crossed the room to confront them.

Par and Coll rose slowly from where they had been working. "You can't go back to the Vale," Morgan said quietly. "There are Federation soldiers everywhere. I can't be certain if there are Seekers as well, but I wouldn't be surprised. The village is under 'Federation Protection'—that's the euphemism they use for armed occupation. They're definitely waiting for you. I asked a few questions and found out right away; no one's making any secret of it. Your parents are under house arrest. I think they're okay, but I couldn't risk trying to talk to them. I'm sorry. There would have been too many questions."

He took a deep breath. "Someone wants you very badly, my friends."

Par and Coll looked at each other, and there was no attempt by either to disguise the fear. "What are we going to do?" Par asked softly.

"I've been thinking about that the whole way back," Morgan said. He reached over and put a hand on his friend's slim shoulder. "So I'll tell you what we're going to do—and I do mean 'we' because I figure I'm in this thing with you now."

His hand tightened. "We're going east to look for Walker Boh."

CHAPTER

6

ORGAN LEAH COULD BE very persuasive when he chose, and he proved it that night in the rain-shrouded Highlands to Par and Coll.

He obviously had given the matter a great deal of thought, just as he claimed he had, and his reasoning was quite thorough. Simply stated, it was all a matter of choices. He took just enough time to strip away his wet clothing and dry off before seating the brothers cross-legged before the warmth of the fireplace with glasses of ale and hot bread in hand to hear his explanation.

He started with what they knew. They knew they could not go back to Shady Vale—not now and maybe not for a long time. They could not go back to Callahorn either. Matter of fact, they could not go much of anywhere they might be expected to go because, if the Federation had expended this much time and effort to find them so far, they were hardly likely to stop now. Rimmer Dall was known to be a tenacious enforcer. He had personally involved himself in this hunt, and he would not give it up easily. The Seekers would be looking for the brothers everywhere Federation rule extended—and that was a long, long way. Par and Coll could consider themselves, for all intents and purposes, to be outlaws.

So what were they to do? Since they could not go anyplace where they were expected, they must go someplace they were not expected. The trick, of course, was not to go just anywhere, but to go where they might accomplish something useful.

"After all, you could stay here if you chose, and you might not be discovered for who-knows-how-long because the Federation wouldn't know enough to look for you in the Highlands." He shrugged. "It might even be fun for a while. But what would it accomplish? Two months, four months, whatever, you would still be outlaws, you would still be unable to go home, and nothing would have changed. Doesn't make sense, does it? What you need to do is to take control of things. Don't wait for events to catch up with you; go out and meet them head-on!"

What he meant was that they should attempt to solve the riddle of the dreams. There was nothing they could do about the fact that the Federation was hunting them, that soldiers occupied Shady Vale, or that they were perceived to be outlaws. One day, all that might change—but not in the immediate future. The dreams, on the other hand, were something with which they might be able to come to grips. If the dreams were the real thing, they were worth knowing more about. The old man had told them to come to the Hadeshorn on the first night of the new moon. They hadn't wanted to do that before for two very sound reasons. First, they didn't know enough about the dreams to be certain they were real, and second, there were only the two of them and they might be placing themselves in real danger by going.

"So why not do something that might ease those concerns," the Highlander finished. "Why not go east and find Walker Boh. You said the old man told you the dreams had been sent to Walker as well. Doesn't it make sense to find out what he thinks about all this? Is he planning on going? The old man was going to talk to him, too. Whether that's happened or not, Walker is certain to have an opinion on whether the dreams are real or not. I always thought your uncle was a strange bird, I'll admit, but I never thought he was stupid. And we all know the stories about him. If he has the use of any part of the Shannara magic, now might be a good time to find out."

He took a long drink and leaned forward, jabbing his finger at them. "If Walker believes in the dreams and decides to go to the Hadeshorn, then you might be more inclined to go as well. There would be four of us then. Anything out there that might cause trouble would have to think twice."

He shrugged. "Even if you decide not to go, you'll have satisfied yourselves better than you would have by just hiding out here or somewhere like here. Shades, the Federation won't think to look for you in the Anar! That's just about the last place they'll think to look for you!"

He took another drink, bit off a piece of fresh bread and sat back, eyes questioning. He had that look on his face again, that expression that suggested he knew something they didn't and it amused him no end. "Well?" he said finally.

The brothers were silent. Par was thinking about his uncle, remembering the whispered stories about Walker Boh. His uncle was a self-professed student of life who claimed he had visions; he insisted he could see and feel things others could not. There were rumors that he practiced magic of a sort different from any known. Eventually, he had gone away from them, leaving the Vale for the Eastland. That had been almost ten years ago. Par and Coll had been very young, but Par still remembered.

Coll cleared his throat suddenly, eased himself forward and shook his head. Par was certain his brother was going to tell Morgan how ridiculous his idea was, but instead he asked, "How do we go about finding Walker?"

Par looked at Morgan and Morgan looked at Par, and there was an instant of shared astonishment. Both had anticipated that Coll would prove intractable, that he would set himself squarely in the path of such an outrageous plan, and that he would dismiss it as foolhardy. Neither had expected this.

Coll caught the look that passed between them and said, "I wouldn't say what I was thinking, if I were you. Neither of you knows me as well as he thinks. Now how about an answer to my question?"

Morgan quickly masked the flicker of guilt that passed across his eyes. "We'll go first to Culhaven. I have a friend there who will know where Walker is."

"Culhaven?" Coll frowned. "Culhaven is Federation-occupied."

"But safe enough for us," Morgan insisted. "The Federation won't be looking for you there, and we need only stay a day or two. Anyway, we won't be out in the open much."

"And our families? Won't they wonder what's happened to us?"

"Not mine. My father is used to not seeing me for weeks at a time. He's already made up his mind that I'm undependable. And Jaralan and Mirianna are better off not knowing what you're about. They're undoubtedly worried enough as it is."

"What about Wren?" Par asked.

Morgan shook his head. "I don't know how to find Wren. If she's still with the Rovers, she could be anywhere." He paused. "Besides, I don't know how much help Wren would be to us. She was only a girl when she left the Vale, Par. We don't have time to find both. Walker Boh seems a better bet."

Par nodded slowly. He looked uncertainly at Coll and Coll looked back. "What do you think?" he asked.

Coll sighed. "I think we should have stayed in Shady Vale in the first place. I think we should have stayed in bed."

"Oh, come now, Coll Ohmsford!" Morgan exclaimed cheerfully. "Think of the adventure! I'll look out for you, I promise!"

Coll glanced at Par. "Should I feel comforted by that?"

Par took a deep breath. "I say we go."

Coll studied him intently, then nodded. "I say what have we got to lose?"

So the issue was decided. Thinking it over later, Par guessed he was not surprised. After all, it was indeed a matter of choices, and any way you looked at it the other choices available had little to recommend them.

They slept that night at the lodge and spent the following morning outfitting themselves with foodstuffs stored in the cold lockers and provisions from the closets. There were weapons, blankets, travel cloaks, and extra clothing (some of it not a bad fit) for the brothers. There were cured meats, vegetables and fruits, and cheese and nuts. There were cooking implements, water pouches and medications. They took what they needed, since the lodge was well-stocked, and by noon they were ready to set out.

The day was gray and clouded when they stepped through the front door and secured it behind them; the rain had turned to drizzle, the ground beneath their feet no longer hard and dusty, but as damp and yielding as a sponge. They made their

way north again toward the Rainbow Lake, intent on reaching
its shores by nightfall. Morgan's plan for making the first leg of
their journey was simple. They would retrieve the skiff the
brothers had concealed earlier at the mouth of the Rappahalladran and this time follow the southern shoreline, staying well
clear of the Lowlands of Clete, the Black Oaks, and the Mist
Marsh, all of which were filled with dangers best avoided. When
they reached the far shore, they would locate the Silver River
and follow it east to Culhaven.

It was a good plan, but not without its problems. Morgan
would have preferred to navigate the Rainbow Lake at night
when they would be less conspicuous, using the moon and stars
to guide them. But it quickly became apparent as the day drew
to a close and the lake came in sight that there would be no
moon or stars that night and as a result no light at all to show
them the way. If they tried to cross in this weather, there was
a very real possibility of them drifting too far south and becoming entangled in the dangers they had hoped to avoid.

So, after relocating the skiff and assuring themselves that she
was still seaworthy, they spent their first night out in a chill,
sodden campsite set close back against the shoreline of the lake,
dreaming of warmer, more agreeable times. Morning brought a
slight change in the weather. It stopped raining entirely and
grew warm, but the clouds lingered, mixing with a mist that
shrouded everything from one end of the lake to the other.

Par and Coll studied the morass dubiously.

"It will burn off," Morgan assured them, anxious to be off.

They shoved the skiff out onto the water, rowed until they
found a breeze, and hoisted their makeshift sail. The clouds
lifted a few feet and the skies brightened a shade, but the mist
continued to cling to the surface of the lake like sheep's wool
and blanketed everything in an impenetrable haze. Noon came
and went with little change, and finally even Morgan admitted
he had no idea where they were.

By nightfall, they were still on the lake and the light was
gone completely. The wind died and they sat unmoving in the
stillness. They ate a little food, mostly because it was necessary
and not so much because anyone was particularly hungry, then
they took turns trying to sleep.

"Remember the stories about Shea Ohmsford and a thing that lived in the Mist Marsh?" Coll whispered to Par at one point. "I fully expect to discover firsthand whether or not they were true!"

The night crept by, filled with silence, blackness, and a sense of impending doom. But morning arrived without incident, the mist lifted, the skies brightened, and the friends found that they were safely in the middle of the lake pointing north. Relaxed now, they joked about their own and the others' fears, turned the boat east again, and took turns rowing while they waited for a breeze to come up. After a time, the mist burned away altogether, the clouds broke up, and they caught sight of the south shore. A northeasterly breeze sprang up around noon, and they stowed the oars and set sail.

Time drifted, and the skiff sped east. Daylight was disappearing into nightfall when they finally reached the far shore and beached their craft in a wooded cove close to the mouth of the Silver River. They shoved the skiff into a reed-choked inlet, carefully secured it with stays, and began their walk inland. It was nearing sunset by now, and the skies turned a peculiar pinkish color as the fading light reflected off a new mix of low-hanging clouds and trailers of mist. It was still quiet in the forest, the night sounds waiting expectantly for the day to end before beginning their symphony. The river churned beside them sluggishly as they walked, choked with rainwater and debris. Shadows reached out to them, the trees seemed to draw closer together and the light faded. Before long, they were enveloped in darkness.

They talked briefly of the King of the Silver River.

"Gone like all the rest of the magic," Par declared, picking his way carefully along the rain-slicked trail. They could see better this night, though not as well as they might have liked; the moon and stars were playing hide-and-seek with the clouds. "Gone like the Druids, the Elves—everything but the stories."

"Maybe, maybe not," Morgan philosophized. "Travelers still claim they see him from time to time, an old man with a lantern, lending guidance and protection. They admit his reach is not what it was, though. He claims only the river and a small part of the land about it. The rest belongs to us."

"The rest belongs to the Federation, like everything else!" Coll snorted.

Morgan kicked at a piece of deadwood and sent it spinning into the dark. "I know a man who claims to have spoken to the King of the Silver River—a drummer who sells fancy goods between the Highlands and the Anar. He comes through this country all the time, and he said that once he lost his way in the Battlemound and this old man appeared with his lantern and took him clear." Morgan shook his head. "I never knew whether to believe the man or not. Drummers make better storytellers than truth-sayers."

"I think he's gone," Par said, filled with a sense of sadness at his own certainty. "The magic doesn't last when it isn't practiced or believed in. The King of the Silver River hasn't had the benefit of either. He's just a story now, just another legend that no one but you and I and Coll and maybe a handful of others believe was ever real."

"We Ohmsfords always believe," Coll finished softly.

They walked on in silence, listening to the night sounds, following the trail as it wound eastward. They would not reach Culhaven that night, but they were not yet ready to stop either, so they simply kept on without bothering to discuss it. The woods thickened as they moved farther inland, deeper into the lower Anar, and the pathway narrowed as scrub began to inch closer from the darkness. The river turned angry as it passed through a series of rapids, and the land grew rough, a maze of gullies and hillocks peppered with stray boulders and stumps.

"The road to Culhaven isn't what it once was," Morgan muttered at one point. Par and Coll had no idea if that was so or not since neither had ever been to the Anar. They glanced at each other, but gave no reply.

Then the trail ended abruptly, blocked by a series of fallen trees. A secondary pathway swung away from the river and ran off into the deep woods. Morgan hesitated, then took it. The trees closed about overhead, their branches shutting out all but a trickle of moonlight, and the three friends were forced to grope their way ahead. Morgan was muttering again, inaudibly this time, although the tone of his voice was unmistakable. Vines and overhanging brush were slapping at them as they passed, and they were forced to duck their heads. The woods began to smell oddly fetid, as if the undergrowth was decaying. Par tried to hold his breath against the stench, irritated by its pervasiveness. He wanted to move faster, but Morgan was in the lead and already moving as fast as he could.

"It's as if something died in here," Coll whispered from behind him.

Something triggered in Par's memory. He remembered the smell that had emanated from the cottage of the woodswoman the old man had warned them was a Shadowen. The smell here was exactly the same.

In the next instant, they emerged from the tangle of the forest into a clearing that was ringed by the lifeless husks of trees and carpeted with mulch, deadwood and scattered bones. A single stagnant pool of water bubbled at its center in the fashion of a cauldron heated by fire. Gimlet-eyed scavengers peered out at them from the shadows.

The companions came to an uncertain halt. "Morgan, this is just like it was . . ." Par began and then stopped.

The Shadowen stepped noiselessly from the trees and faced them. Par never questioned what it was; he knew instinctively. Skepticism and disbelief were erased in an instant's time, the discarded trappings of years of certainty that Shadowen were what practical men said they were—rumors and fireside tales. Perhaps it was the old man's warning whispering in his ear that triggered his conversion. Perhaps it was simply the look of the thing. Whatever it was, the truth that was left him was chilling and unforgettable.

This Shadowen was entirely different than the last. It was a huge, shambling thing, manlike but twice the size of a normal man, its body covered in coarse, shaggy hair, its massive limbs ending in paws that were splayed and clawed, its body hunched over at the shoulders like a gorilla. There was a face amid all that hair, but it could scarcely be called human. It was wrinkled and twisted about a mouth from which teeth protruded like stunted bones, and it hid within leathery folds eyes that peered out with insistent dislike and burned like fire. It stood looking at them, studying them in the manner of a slow-witted brute.

"Oh-oh," Morgan said softly.

The Shadowen came forward a step, a hitching movement that suggested a stalking cat. "Why are you here?" it rasped from some deep, empty well within.

"We took a wrong . . ." Morgan began.

"You trespass on what is mine!" the other cut him short, teeth snapping wickedly. "You cause me to be angered!"

Morgan glanced back at Par and the Valeman quickly mouthed the word "Shadowen" and glanced in turn at Coll. Coll was pale and tense. Like Par, he was no longer questioning.

"I will have one of you in payment!" the Shadowen growled. "Give me one of you! Give me!"

The three friends looked at each other once more. They knew there was only one way out of this. There was no old man to come to their aid this time. There was no one but themselves.

Morgan reached back and slid the Sword of Leah from its scabbard. The blade reflected brightly in the eyes of the monster. "Either you let us pass safely . . ." he began.

He never finished. The Shadowen launched itself at him with a shriek, bounding across the little clearing with frightening swiftness. He was on top of Morgan almost at once, claws ripping. Even so, the Highlander managed to bring the flat of the blade about in time to deflect the blow and knock the creature off-balance, driving it sideways so that its attack missed. Coll slashed at it with the short sword he was carrying as he leaped past toward the pool, and Par struck at it with the magic of the wishsong, clouding its vision with a swarm of buzzing insects.

The Shadowen surged back to its feet with a roar of anger, flailed madly at the air, then rushed them once more. It caught Morgan a stinging blow as the Highlander jumped aside and knocked him sprawling. The Shadowen turned, and Coll struck it so hard with the short sword that he severed one arm above the elbow. The Shadowen reeled away, then darted back, snatched up its severed limb and retreated again. Carefully, it placed its arm back against its shoulder. There was sudden movement, an entwining of sinew and muscle and bone, like snakes moving. The limb had reattached itself.

The Shadowen hissed in delight.

Then it came at them. Par tried to slow it with images of wolves, but the Shadowen barely saw them. It slammed into Morgan, shoving past the blade of his sword, throwing the Highlander back. He might have been lost then if not for the Ohmsfords, who flung themselves on the beast and bore it to the ground. They held it there for only an instant. It heaved upward, freed itself, and sent them flying. One great arm caught Par across the face, snapping his head back, causing flashes to cloud his vision as he tumbled away. He could hear the thing coming for him, and he threw out every image he could muster, rolling and crawling to regain his feet. He could hear Coll's cry of warning and a series of grunts. He pushed himself upright, forcing his vision to clear.

The Shadowen was right in front of him, clawed forelimbs spread wide to embrace him. Coll lay slumped against a tree a dozen paces to his left. There was no sign of Morgan. Par backed away slowly, searching for an escape. There was no time for the magic now. The creature was too close. He felt the rough bark of a tree trunk jammed against his back.

Then Morgan was there, launching himself from the darkness, crying out "Leah, Leah" as he hammered into the Shadowen. There was blood on his face and clothing, and his eyes were bright with anger and determination. Down came the Sword of Leah, an arc of glittering metal—and something wondrous happened. The sword struck the Shadowen full on and burst into fire.

Par flinched and threw one arm across his face protectively. No, he thought in amazement, it wasn't fire he was seeing, it was magic!

The magic happened all at once, without warning, and it seemed to freeze the combatants in the circle of its light. The Shadowen stiffened and screamed, a shriek of agony and disbelief. The magic spread from the Sword of Leah into the creature's body, ripping through it like a razor through cloth. The Shadowen shuddered, seemed to sag inward against itself, lost definition, and began to disintegrate. Quickly Par dropped under the thing and rolled free. He saw it heave upward desperately, then flare as brightly as the weapon that was killing it and disappear into ash.

The Sword of Leah winked instantly into darkness. The air was a blanket of sudden silence. Smoke floated in a cloud across the little clearing, its smell thick and pungent. The stagnant pool bubbled once and went still.

Morgan Leah dropped to one knee, the sword falling to the ground before him, striking the little mound of ash and flaring once. He flinched and then shuddered. "Shades!" he whispered, his voice choked with astonishment. "The power I felt, it was . . . I never thought it possible . . ."

Par came to him at once, knelt beside him and saw the other's face, cut and bruised and drained of blood. He took the Highlander in his arms and held him.

"It still has the magic, Morgan!" he whispered, excited that such a thing could be. "All these years, and no one has known it, but it still has the magic!" Morgan looked at him uncomprehendingly. "Don't you see? The magic has been sleeping since the time of Allanon! There's been no need for it! It took another magic to bring it awake! It took a creature like the Shadowen! That's why nothing happened until the magics touched . . ."

He trailed off as Coll stumbled over to them and dropped down as well. One arm hung limply. "Think I broke it," he muttered.

He hadn't, but he had bruised it severely enough that Par felt it wise to bind it against his body in a cradle for a day or so. They used their drinking water to wash themselves, bandaged their cuts and scrapes, picked up their weapons, and stood looking at each other. "The old man said there would be lots of things hunting us," Par whispered.

"I don't know if that thing was hunting us or if we were just unlucky enough to stumble on it." Coll's voice was ragged. "I do know I don't want to run across any more like it."

"But if we do," Morgan Leah said quietly and stopped. "If we do, we have the means now to deal with them." And he fingered the blade of the Sword of Leah as he might have the soft curve of a woman's face.

Par would never forget what he felt at that moment. The memory of it would overshadow even that of their battle with the Shadowen, a tiny piece of time preserved in perfect still life. What he felt was jealousy. Before, he had been the one who had possessed real magic. Now it was Morgan Leah. He still had the wishsong, of course, but its magic paled in comparison to that of the Highlander's sword. It was the sword that had destroyed the Shadowen. Par's best images had proven to be little more than an irritation.

It made him wonder if the wishsong had any real use at all.

CHAPTER

7

PAR REMEMBERED SOMETHING LATER that night that forced him to come to grips with what he was feeling toward Morgan. They had continued on to Culhaven, anxious to complete their journey, willing to walk all night and another day if need be rather than attempt one moment's sleep in those woods. They had worked their way back to the main pathway where it ran parallel to the Silver River and pushed eastward. As they trudged on, nudged forward by apprehension one step, dragged backward by weariness the next, buffeted and tossed, their thoughts strayed like grazing cattle to sweeter pastures, and Par Ohmsford found himself thinking of the songs.

That was when he remembered that the legends had it that the power of the Sword of Leah was literally two-edged. The sword had been made magic by Allanon in the time of Brin Ohmsford while the Druid was journeying east with the Valegirl and her would-be protector, Morgan's ancestor, Rone Leah. The Druid had dipped the sword's blade into the forbidden waters of the Hadeshorn and changed forever its character. It became more than a simple blade; it became a talisman that could withstand even the Mord Wraiths. But the magic was like all the magics of old; it was both blessing and curse. Its power was addictive, causing the user to become increasingly dependent. Brin Ohmsford had recognized the danger, but her warnings to Rone Leah had gone unheeded. In their final confrontation with the dark magic, it was her own power and Jair's that had saved them and put an end to further need for the magic of the sword. There was no record of what had become of the weapon after— only that it was not required and therefore not used again.

Until now. And now it seemed it might be Par's obligation to warn Morgan of the danger of further use of the sword's magic. But how was he to do that? Shades, Morgan Leah was his best friend next to Coll, and this newfound magic Par envied so had just saved their lives! He was knotted up with guilt and frustration at the jealousy he was feeling. How was he supposed to tell Morgan that he shouldn't use it? It didn't matter that there might be good reason to do so; it still sounded impossibly grudging. Besides, they would need the magic of the Sword of Leah if they encountered any further Shadowen. And there was every reason to expect that they might.

He struggled with his dilemma only briefly. He simply could not ignore his discomfort and the vivid memory of that creature breathing over him. He decided to keep quiet. Perhaps there would be no need to speak out. If there was, he would do so then. He put the matter aside.

They talked little that night, and when they did it was mostly about the Shadowen. There was no longer any doubt in their minds that these beings were real. Even Coll did not equivocate when speaking of what it was that had attacked them. But acceptance did not bring enlightenment. The Shadowen remained a mystery to them. They did not know where they had come from or why. They did not even know what they were. They had no idea as to the source of their power, though it seemed it must derive from some form of magic. If these creatures were hunting them, they did not know what they could do about it. They knew only that the old man had been right when he had warned them to be careful.

It was just after dawn when they reached Culhaven, emerging aching and sleepy-eyed from the fading night shadows of the forest into the half-light of the new day. Clouds hung across the Eastland skies, scraping the treetops as they eased past, lending the Dwarf village beneath a gray and wintry cast. The companions stumbled to a halt, stretched, yawned, and looked about. The trees had thinned before them and there was a gathering of cottages with smoke curling out of stone chimneys, sheds filled with tools and wagons, and small yards with animals staked and penned. Vegetable gardens the size of thumbprints fought to control tiny patches of earth as weeds attacked from everywhere. Everything seemed crammed together, the cottages and sheds, the animals, the gardens and the forest, each on top of the other. Nothing looked cared for; paint was peeling and chipped, mortar and stone were cracked, fences broken and sagging, animals shaggy and unkempt, and gardens and the weeds grown so much into each other as to be almost indistinguishable.

Women drifted through doors and past windows, old mostly, some with laundry to hang, some with cooking to tend, all with the same ragged, disheveled look. Children played in the yards, on the pathways, and in the roads, as shabby and wild as mountain sheep.

Morgan caught Par and Coll staring and said, "I forgot—the Culhaven you're familiar with is the one you tell about in your stories. Well, all that's in the past. I know you're tired, but, now that you're here, there are things you need to see."

He took them down a pathway that led into the village. The housing grew quickly worse, the cottages replaced by shacks, the gardens and animals disappearing entirely. The path became a roadway, rutted and pocked from lack of repair, filled with refuse and stones. There were more children here, playing as the others had, and there were more women working at household chores, exchanging a few words now and then with each other and the children, but withdrawn mostly into themselves. They watched guardedly as the three strangers walked past, suspicion and fear mirrored in their eyes.

"Culhaven, the most beautiful city in the Eastland, the heart and soul of the Dwarf nation," Morgan mused quietly. He didn't look at them. "I know the stories. It was a sanctuary, an oasis, a haven of gentle souls, a monument to what pride and hard work could accomplish." He shook his head. "Well, this is the way it is now."

A few of the children came up to them and begged for coins. Morgan shook his head gently, patted one or two, and moved past.

They turned off into a lane that led down to a stream clogged with trash and sewage. Children walked the banks, poking idly at what floated past. A walkway took them across to the far bank. The air was fetid with the smell of rotting things.

"Where are all the men?" Par asked.

Morgan looked over. "The lucky ones are dead. The rest are in the mines or in work camps. That's why everything looks the way it does. There's no one left in this city but children, old people, and a few women." He stopped walking. "That's how it has been for fifty years. That's how the Federation wants it. Come this way."

He led them down a narrow pathway behind a series of cottages that seemed better tended. These homes were freshly painted, the stone scrubbed, the mortar intact, the gardens and lawns immaculate. Dwarves worked the yards and rooms here as well, younger women mostly, the tasks the same, but the results as different from before as night is to day. Everything here was bright and new and clean.

Morgan took them up a rise to a small park, easing carefully into a stand of fir. "See those?" he pointed to the well-tended cottages. Par and Coll nodded. "That's where the Federation soldiers and officials garrisoned here live. The younger, stronger Dwarf women are forced to work for them. Most are forced to live with them as well." He glanced at them meaningfully.

They walked from the park down a hillside that led toward the center of the community. Shops and businesses replaced homes, and the foot traffic grew thick. The Dwarves they saw here were engaged in selling and buying, but again they were mostly old and few in number. The streets were clogged with outlanders come to trade. Federation soldiers patrolled everywhere.

Morgan steered the brothers down byways where they wouldn't be noticed, pointing out this, indicating that, his voice at once both bitter and ironic. "Over there. That's the silver exchange. The Dwarves are forced to extract the silver from the mines, kept underground most of the time—you know what that means—then compelled to sell it at Federation prices and turn the better part of the proceeds over to their keepers in the form of taxes. And the animals belong to the Federation as well—on loan, supposedly. The Dwarves are strictly rationed. Down there, that's the market. All the vegetables and fruits are grown and sold by the Dwarves, and the profits of sale disposed of in the same manner as everything else. That's what it's like here now. That's what being a 'protectorate' means for these people."

He stopped them at the far end of the street, well back from a ring of onlookers crowded about a platform on which young Dwarf men and women chained and bound were being offered for sale. They stood looking for a moment and Morgan said, "They sell off the ones they don't need to do the work."

He took them from the business district to a hillside that rose above the city in a broad sweep. The hillside was blackened and stripped of life, a vast smudge against a treeless skyline. It had been terraced once, and what was left of the buttressing poked out of the earth like gravestones.

"Do you know what this is?" he asked them softly. They shook their heads. "This is what is left of the Meade Gardens. You know the story. The Dwarves built the Gardens with special earth hauled in from the farmlands, earth as black as coal. Every flower known to the races was planted and tended. My father said it was the most beautiful thing he had ever seen. He was here once, when he was a boy."

Morgan was quiet a moment as they surveyed the ruin, then said, "The Federation burned the Gardens when the city fell. They burn them anew every year so that nothing will ever grow again."

As they walked away, veering back toward the outskirts of the village, Par asked, "How do you know all this, Morgan? Your father?"

Morgan shook his head. "My father hasn't been back since that first visit. I think he prefers not to see what it looks like now, but to remember it as it was. No, I have friends here who tell me what life for the Dwarves is like—that part of life I can't see for myself whenever I come over. I haven't told you much about that, have I? Well, it's only been recently, the last half year or so. I'll tell you about it later."

They retraced their steps to the poorer section of the village, following a new roadway that was nevertheless as worn and rutted as the others. After a short walk, they turned into a walkway that led up to a rambling stone and wood structure that looked as if once it might have been an inn of some sort. It rose three stories and was wrapped by a covered porch filled with swings and rockers. The yard was bare, but clear of debris and filled with children playing.

"A school?" Par guessed aloud.

Morgan shook his head. "An orphanage."

He led them through the groups of children, onto the porch and around to a side door settled well back in the shadows of an alcove. He knocked on the door and waited. When the door opened a crack, he said, "Can you spare a poor man some food?"

"Morgan!" The door flew open. An elderly Dwarf woman stood in the opening, gray-haired and aproned, her face bluff and squarish, her smile working its way past lines of weariness and disappointment. "Morgan Leah, what a pleasant surprise! How are you, youngster?"

"I am my father's pride and joy, as always," Morgan replied with a grin. "May we come in?"

"Of course. Since when have you needed to ask?" The woman stepped aside and ushered them past, hugging Morgan and beaming at Par and Coll, who smiled back uncertainly. She shut the door behind them and said, "So you would like something to eat, would you?"

"We would gladly give our lives for the opportunity," Morgan declared with a laugh. "Granny Elise, these are my friends, Par and Coll Ohmsford of Shady Vale. They are temporarily . . . homeless," he finished.

"Aren't we all," Granny Elise replied gruffly. She extended a callused hand to the brothers, who each gripped it in his own. She examined them critically. "Been wrestling with bears, have you, Morgan?"

Morgan touched his face experimentally, tracing the cuts and scrapes. "Something worse than that, I'm afraid. The road to Culhaven is not what it once was."

"Nor is Culhaven. Have a seat, child—you and your friends. I'll bring you a plate of muffins and fruit."

There were several long tables with benches in the center of the rather considerable kitchen and the three friends chose the nearest and sat. The kitchen was large but rather dark, and the furnishings were poor. Granny Elise bustled about industriously, providing the promised breakfast and glasses of some sort of extracted juice. "I'd offer you milk, but I have to ration what I have for the children," she apologized.

They were eating hungrily when a second woman appeared, a Dwarf as well and older still, small and wizened, with a sharp face and quick, birdlike movements that never seemed to cease. She crossed the room matter-of-factly on seeing Morgan, who rose at once and gave her a small peck on the cheek.

"Auntie Jilt," Morgan introduced her.

"Most pleased," she announced in a way that suggested they might need convincing. She seated herself next to Granny Elise and immediately began work on some needlepoint she had brought with her into the room, fingers flying.

"These ladies are mothers to the world," Morgan explained as he returned to his meal. "Me included, though I'm not an orphan like their other charges. They adopted me because I'm irresistibly charming."

"You begged like the rest of them the first time we saw you, Morgan Leah!" Auntie Jilt snapped, never looking up from her work. "That is the only reason we took you in—the only reason we take any of them in."

"Sisters, though you'd never know it," Morgan quickly went on. "Granny Elise is like a goose-down comforter, all soft and warm. But Auntie Jilt—well, Auntie Jilt is more like a stone pallet!"

Auntie Jilt sniffed. "Stone lasts a good deal longer than goose down in these times. And both longer still than Highland syrup!"

Morgan and Granny Elise laughed, Auntie Jilt joined in after a moment, and Par and Coll found themselves smiling as well. It seemed odd to do so, their thoughts still filled with images of the village and its people, the sounds of the orphaned children playing outside a pointed reminder of how things really stood. But there was something indomitable about these old women, something that transcended the misery and poverty, something that whispered of promise and hope.

When breakfast was finished, Granny Elise busied herself at the sink and Auntie Jilt departed to check on the children. Morgan whispered, "These ladies have been operating the orphanage for almost thirty years. The Federation lets them alone because they help keep the children out from underfoot. Nice, huh?

There are hundreds of children with no parents, so the orphanage is always full. When the children are old enough, they are smuggled out. If they are allowed to stay too long, the Federation sends them to the work camps or sells them. Every so often, the ladies guess wrong." He shook his head. "I don't know how they stand it. I would have gone mad long ago."

Granny Elise came back and sat with them. "Has Morgan told you how we met?" she asked the Ohmsfords. "Oh, well, it was quite something. He brought us food and clothes for the children, he gave us money to buy what we could, and he helped guide a dozen children north to be placed with families in the free territories."

"Oh, for goodness sake, Granny!" Morgan interjected, embarrassed.

"Exactly! And he works around the house now and then when he visits, too," she added, ignoring him. "We have become his own private little charity, haven't we, Morgan?"

"That reminds me—here." Morgan reached into his tunic and extracted a small pouch. The contents jingled as he passed it over. "I won a wager a week or so back about some perfume." He winked at the Valemen.

"Bless you, Morgan." Granny Elise rose and came around to kiss him on the cheek. "You seem quite exhausted—all of you. There are spare beds in the back and plenty of blankets. You can sleep until dinnertime."

She ushered them from the kitchen to a small room at the rear of the big house where there were several beds, a wash basin, blankets, and towels. Par glanced around, noticing at once that the windows were shuttered and the curtains carefully drawn.

Granny Elise noticed the look that the Valeman exchanged with his brother. "Sometimes, my guests don't wish to draw attention to themselves," she said quietly. Her eyes were sharp. "Isn't that the case with you?"

Morgan went over and kissed her gently. "Perceptive as always, old mother. We'll need a meeting with Steff. Can you take care of it?"

Granny Elise looked at him a moment, then nodded wordlessly, kissed him back and slipped from the room.

IT WAS TWILIGHT when they woke, the shuttered room filled with shadows and silence. Granny Elise appeared, her bluff face gentle and reassuring, slipping through the room on cat's feet as she touched each and whispered that it was time, before disappearing back the way she had come. Morgan Leah and the Ohmsfords rose to find their clothes clean and fresh-smelling again. Granny Elise had been busy while they slept.

While they were dressing, Morgan said, "We'll meet with Steff tonight. He's part of the Dwarf Resistance, and the Resistance has eyes and ears everywhere. If Walker Boh still lives in the Eastland, even in the deepest part of the Anar, Steff will know."

He finished pulling on his boots and stood up. "Steff was one of the orphans Granny took in. He's like a son to her. Other than Auntie Jilt, he's the only family she has left."

They went out from the sleeping room and down the hall to the kitchen. The children had already finished dinner and retired to their rooms on the upper two stories, save for a handful of tiny ones that Auntie Jilt was in the process of feeding, patiently spooning soup to first one mouth, then the next and so on until it was time to begin the cycle all over again. She looked up as they entered and nodded wordlessly.

Granny Elise sat them down at one of the long tables and brought them plates of food and glasses of harsh ale. From overhead came the sounds of thumping and yelling as the children played. "It is hard to supervise so many when there is only the two of us," she apologized, serving Coll a second helping of meat stew. "But the women we hire to help out never seem to stay very long."

"Were you able to get a message to Steff?" Morgan asked quietly.

Granny Elise nodded, her smile suddenly sad. "I wish I could see more of that child, Morgan. I worry so about him."

They finished their meal and sat quietly in the evening shadows as Granny Elise and Auntie Jilt finished with the children and saw them all off to bed. A pair of candles burned on the table where the three sat, but the remainder of the room was left dark. The voices upstairs faded away one by one, and the silence deepened.

Auntie Jilt came back into the kitchen after a time and sat with them. She didn't speak, her sharp face lowered as she concentrated on her needlepoint, her head bobbing slightly. Outside, somewhere, a bell rang three times and went still. Auntie Jilt looked up briefly. "Federation curfew," she muttered. "No one is allowed out after it sounds."

The room went silent again. Granny Elise appeared and worked quietly at the sink. One of the children upstairs began to cry and she went out again. The Ohmsfords and Morgan Leah looked at each other and the room and waited.

Then, suddenly, there was a soft tapping at the kitchen door. Three taps. Auntie Jilt looked up, her fingers stilled, and waited. The seconds slipped away. Then the tapping came again, three times, a pause, three times again.

Auntie Jilt rose quickly, walked to the door, unlatched it and peeked out. Then she opened the door wide for an instant and a shadowy figure slipped into the room. Auntie Jilt pushed the door closed again. Granny Elise appeared at the same instant from the hall, motioned Morgan and the Ohmsford brothers to their feet and led them over to where the stranger stood.

"This is Teel," said Granny Elise. "She will take you to Steff."

It was hard to tell much of anything about Teel. She was a Dwarf, but smaller than most, rather slight, clothed in dark, nondescript forest clothing including a short cloak and hood. Her features were hidden by a strange leather mask that wrapped the whole of her face, save for her right jaw and her mouth. A glimmer of dusky blond hair was visible within the covering of the hood.

Granny Elise reached up and hugged Morgan. "Be careful, youngster," she cautioned. She smiled, patted Par and Coll gently on the shoulder, and hastened to the door. She peeked through the curtains for a moment, then nodded. Teel went out through the door without a word. The Ohmsfords and Morgan Leah went with her.

Outside, they slipped silently along the side of the old house and through a back fence onto a narrow pathway. They followed the pathway to an empty road, then turned right. The mix of cottages and shacks that lined the roadway were dark, their silhouettes ragged and broken against the sky. Teel moved them down the road quickly and into a patch of fir. She stopped then and dropped into a crouch, motioning them down with her. Moments later, a Federation patrol of five appeared. They joked and talked among themselves as they passed, unconcerned with any who might hear them. Then their voices faded and they were gone. Teel stood up, and they were off again.

They stayed on the road for another hundred yards, then turned into the forest. They were on the very edge of the village now, almost due north, and the sounds of insects began to break through the stillness. They slipped along silently through the trees, Teel pausing now and then to listen before continuing on. The smell of wildflowers filled the air, sweet and strong against the reek of garbage.

Then Teel stopped at a line of thick brush, pushed the branches aside, reached down to grip a hidden iron ring and pulled. A trapdoor lifted clear of the earth to reveal a stairway. They felt their way along its walls until they were completely inside and crouched there in the dark. Teel secured the trapdoor behind them, lit a candle and took the lead once more. The company started down.

It was a short descent. The stairs ended after two dozen steps and became a tunnel, the walls and ceiling shored by thick wooden beams and pinned by iron bolts. Teel offered no explanation for the tunnel, but simply moved ahead into it. Twice the tunnel branched in several directions, and each time she made her choice without hesitating. It occurred to Par that if they had to find their way out again without Teel, they probably couldn't do it.

The tunnel ended minutes later at an iron door. Teel struck the door sharply with the hilt of her dagger, paused, then struck it twice more. The locks on the other side snapped free and the door swung open.

The Dwarf who stood there was no older than they, a stout, muscular fellow with a shading of beard and long hair the color of cinnamon, a face that was scarred all over, and the biggest mace Par had ever seen strapped across his back. He had the top half of one ear missing and a gold ring dangling from the remainder.

"Morgan!" he greeted and embraced the Highlander warmly.

His smile brightened his fierce countenance as he pulled the other inside and looked past him to where Par and Coll stood nervously waiting. "Friends?"

"The best," Morgan answered at once. "Steff, this is Par and Coll Ohmsford from Shady Vale."

The Dwarf nodded. "You are welcome here, Valemen." He broke away from Morgan and reached out to grip their hands. "Come take a seat, tell me what brought you."

They were in an underground room filled with stores, boxed, crated and wrapped, that surrounded a long table with benches. Steff motioned them onto the benches, then poured each a cup of ale and joined them. Teel took up a position by the door, settling carefully onto a small stool.

"Is this where you live now?" Morgan asked, glancing about. "It needs work."

Steff's smile wrinkled his rough face. "I live a lot of places, Morgan, and they all need work. This one is better than most. Underground, though, like the others. We Dwarves all live underground these days, either here or in the mines or in our graves. Sad."

He hoisted his mug. "Good health to us and misfortune to our enemies," he toasted. They all drank but Teel, who sat watching. Steff placed his mug back on the table. "Is your father well?" he asked Morgan.

The Highlander nodded. "I brought Granny Elise a little something to buy bread with. She worries about you. How long since you've been to see her?"

The Dwarf's smile dropped away. "It's too dangerous to go just now. See my face?" He pointed, tracing the scars with his finger. "The Federation caught me three months back." He glanced at Par and Coll conspiratorially. "Morgan wouldn't know, you see. He hasn't been to see me of late. When he comes to Culhaven, he prefers the company of old ladies and children."

Morgan ignored him. "What happened, Steff?"

The Dwarf shrugged. "I got away—parts of me, at least." He held up his left hand. The last two fingers were missing, sheared off. "Enough of that, Highlander. Leave off. Instead, tell me what brings you east."

Morgan started to speak, then took a long look at Teel and

stopped. Steff saw the direction his gaze had taken, glanced briefly over his shoulder and said, "Oh, yes. Teel. Guess I'll have to talk about it after all."

He looked back at Morgan. "I was taken by the Federation while raiding their weapons stores in the main compound in Culhaven. They put me in their prisons to discover what I could tell them. That was where they did this." He touched his face. "Teel was a prisoner in the cell next to mine. What they did to me is nothing compared to what they did to her. They destroyed most of her face and much of her back punishing her for killing the favorite dog of one of the members of the provisional government quartered in Culhaven. She killed the dog for food. We talked through the walls and came to know each other. One night, less than two weeks after I was taken, when it became apparent that the Federation had no further interest in me and I was to be killed, Teel managed to lure the jailor on watch into her cell. She killed him, stole his keys, freed me, and we escaped. We have been together ever since."

He paused, his eyes as hard as flint. "Highlander, I think much of you, and you must make your own decision in this matter. But Teel and I share everything."

There was a long silence. Morgan glanced briefly at Par and Coll. Par had been watching Teel closely during Steff's narration. She never moved. There was no expression on her face, nothing mirrored in her eyes. She might have been made of stone.

"I think we must rely on Steff's judgment in this matter," Par said quietly, looking to Coll for approval. Coll nodded wordlessly.

Morgan stretched his legs beneath the table, reached for his ale mug and took a long drink. He was clearly making up his own mind. "Very well," he said finally. "But nothing I say must leave this room."

"You haven't said anything as yet worth taking out," Steff declared pointedly and waited.

Morgan smiled, then placed the ale mug carefully back on the table. "Steff, we need you to help us find someone, a man we think is living somewhere in the deep Anar. His name is Walker Boh."

Steff blinked. "Walker Boh," he repeated quietly, and the way he spoke the name indicated he recognized it.

"My friends, Par and Coll, are his nephews."

Steff looked at the Valemen as if he were seeing them for the first time. "Well, now. Tell me the rest of it."

Quickly, Morgan related the story of the journey that had brought them to Culhaven, beginning with the Ohmsford brothers' flight from Varfleet and ending with their battle with the Shadowen at the edge of the Anar. He told of the old man and his warnings, of the dreams that had come to Par that summoned him to the Hadeshorn, and of his own discovery of the dormant magic of the Sword of Leah. Steff listened to it all without comment. He sat unmoving, his ale forgotten, his face an expressionless mask.

When Morgan was finished, Steff grunted and shook his head. "Druids and magic and creatures of the night. Highlander, you constantly surprise me." He rose, walked around the table, and stood looking at Teel momentarily, his rough face creased in thought. Then he said, "I know of Walker Boh." He shook his head.

"And?" Morgan pressed.

He wheeled back slowly. "And the man scares me." He looked at Par and Coll. "Your uncle, is he? And how long since you've seen him—ten years? Well, listen close to me, then. The Walker Boh I know may not be the uncle you remember. This Walker Boh is more whispered rumor than truth, and very real all the same—someone that even the things that live out in the darker parts of the land and prey on travelers, wayfarers, strays, and such are said to avoid."

He sat down again, took up the ale mug and drank. Morgan Leah and the Ohmsfords looked at one another in silence. At last, Par said, "I think we are decided on the matter. Whoever or whatever Walker Boh is now, we share a common bond beyond our kinship—our dreams of Allanon. I have to know what my uncle intends to do. Will you help us find him?"

Steff smiled faintly, unexpectedly. "Direct. I like that." He looked at Morgan. "I assume he speaks for his brother. Does he speak for you as well?" Morgan nodded. "I see." He studied them for long moments, lost in thought. "Then I will help," he said finally. He paused, judging their reaction. "I will take you to Walker Boh—if he can be found. But I will do so for some reasons of my own, and you'd best know what they are."

His face lowered momentarily into shadow, and the scars seemed like strands of iron mesh pressed against his skin. "The Federation has taken your homes from you, from all of you, taken them and made them their own. Well, the Federation has taken more than that from me. It has taken everything—my home, my family, my past, even my present. The Federation has destroyed everything that was and is and left me only what might be. It is the enemy of my life, and I would do anything to see it destroyed. Nothing I do here will accomplish that end in my lifetime. What I do here merely serves to keep me alive and to give me some small reason to stay that way. I have had enough of that. I want something more."

His face lifted, and his eyes were fierce. "If there is magic that can be freed from time's chains, if there are Druids yet, ghosts or otherwise, able to wield it, then perhaps there are ways of freeing my homeland and my people—ways that have been kept from us all. If we discover those ways, if the knowledge of them passes into our hands, they must be used to help my people and my homeland." He paused. "I'll want your promise on this."

There was a long moment of silence as his listeners looked at one another.

Then Par said softly, "I am ashamed for the Southland when I see what has happened here. I don't begin to understand it. There is nothing that could justify it. If we discover anything that will give the Dwarves back their freedom, we will put it to use."

"We will," Coll echoed, and Morgan Leah nodded his agreement as well.

Steff took a deep breath. "The possibility of being free—just the possibility—is more than the Dwarves dare hope for in these times." He placed his thick hands firmly on the table. "Then we have a bargain. I will take you to find Walker Boh—Teel and I, for she goes where I go." He glanced at each of them quickly for any sign of disapproval and found none. "It will take a day or so to gather up what we need and to make an inquiry or two.

I need not remind you, but I will anyway, how difficult and dangerous this journey is likely to be. Go back to Granny's and rest. Teel will take you. When all is in place, I will send word."

They rose, and the Dwarf embraced Morgan, then smiled unexpectedly and slapped him on the back. "You and I, Highlander—let the worst that's out there be wary!" He laughed and the room rang with the sound of it.

Teel stood apart from them and watched with eyes like chips of ice.

CHAPTER

8

TWO DAYS PASSED, and they did not hear from Steff. Par and Coll Ohmsford and Morgan Leah passed the time at the orphanage completing some much-needed repairs on the old home and helping Granny Elise and Auntie Jilt with the children. The days were warm, lazy ones, filled with the sounds of small voices at play. It was a different world within the confines of the rambling house and the shaded grounds, a world quite apart from the one that crouched begging a dozen yards in any direction beyond the enclosing fence. There was food here, warm beds, comfort and love. There was a sense of security and future. There wasn't a lot of anything, but there was some of everything. The remainder of the city faded into a series of unpleasant memories—the shacks, the broken old people, the ragged children, the missing mothers and fathers, the grime and the wear, the desperate and defeated looks, and the sense that there was no hope. Several times, Par thought to leave the orphanage and walk again through the city of Culhaven, unwilling to leave without seeing once more sights he felt he should never forget. But the old ladies discouraged it. It was dangerous for him to walk about. He might unwittingly draw attention to himself. Better to stay where he was, let the world outside stay where it was, and the both of them get on the best they could.

"There is nothing to be done for the misery of the Dwarves," Auntie Jilt declared bitterly. "It's a misery that's put down deep roots."

Par did as he was told, feeling at once both unhappy and relieved. The ambiguity bothered him. He couldn't pretend he didn't know what was happening to the people of the city—didn't want to, in fact—but at the same time it was a difficult knowledge to face. He could do as the old ladies said and let the world without get along as best as it could, but he couldn't forget that it was there, pressed up against the gate like some starving beast waiting for food.

On the third day of waiting, the beast snapped at them. It was early morning, and a squad of Federation soldiers marched up the roadway and into the yard. A Seeker was leading them. Granny Elise sent the Valemen and the Highlander to the attic and with Auntie Jilt in tow went out to confront their visitors. From the attic, the three in hiding watched what happened next. The children were forced to line up in front of the porch. They were all too small to be of any use, but three were selected anyway. The old women argued, but there was nothing they could do. In the end, they were forced to stand there helplessly while the three were led away.

Everyone was subdued after that, even the most active among the children. Auntie Jilt retired to a windowseat overlooking the front yard where she could sit and watch the children and work on her needlepoint, and she didn't say a word to anyone. Granny Elise spent most of her time in the kitchen baking. Her words were few, and she hardly smiled at all. The Ohmsfords and Morgan went about their work as unobtrusively as they could, feeling as if they should be somewhere else, secretly wishing that they were.

Late that afternoon, Par could stand his discomfort no longer and went down to the kitchen to talk to Granny Elise. He found her sitting at one of the long tables, sipping absently at a cup of amber tea, and he asked her quite directly why it was that the Dwarves were being treated so badly, why it was that soldiers of the Federation—Southlanders like himself, after all—could be a part of such cruelty.

Granny Elise smiled sadly, took his hand and pulled him down next to her. "Par," she said, speaking his name softly. She had begun using his name the past day or so, a clear indication that she now considered him another of her children. "Par, there are some things that cannot ever be explained—not properly, not so as we might understand them the way we need to. I think sometimes that there must be a reason for what's happening and other times that there cannot be because it lacks any semblance of logic. It has been so long since it all started, you see. The war was fought over a hundred years ago. I don't know that anyone can remember the beginning of it anymore, and if you cannot remember how it began, how can you determine *why* it began?"

She shook her squarish head and hugged him impulsively. "I'm sorry, Par, but I don't have any better answer to give you. I suppose I gave up trying to find one a long time ago. All my energy these days is given over to caring for the children. I guess I don't believe questions are important anymore, so I don't look for answers. Someone else will have to do that. All that matters to me is saving the life of one more child, and one more after that, and another, and another, until the need to save them doesn't exist anymore."

Par nodded silently and hugged her back, but the answer didn't satisfy him. There was a reason for everything that happened, even if the reason wasn't immediately apparent. The Dwarves had lost the war to the Federation; they were a threat to no one. Why, then, were they being systematically ground down? It would have made better sense to heal the wounds that the war had opened than to throw salt into them. It almost seemed as if the Dwarves were being intentionally provoked, as if a cause for them to resist was being provided. Why would that be?

"Perhaps the Federation wants an excuse to exterminate them altogether," Coll suggested blackly when Par asked his opinion that night after dinner.

"You mean you think the Federation believes the Dwarves are of no further use, even in the mines?" Par was incredulous. "Or that they're too much trouble to supervise or too dangerous, so they ought to simply be done away with? The entire nation?"

Coll's blocky face was impassive. "I mean, I know what I've seen here—what we've both seen. It seems pretty clear to me what's happening!"

Par wasn't so sure. He let the matter drop because for the moment he didn't have any better answer. But he promised himself that one day he would.

He slept poorly that night and was already awake when Granny Elise slipped into the sleeping room before dawn to whisper that Teel had come for them. He rose quickly and dragged the covers from Coll and Morgan. They dressed, strapped on their weapons and went down the hall to the kitchen where Teel was waiting, a shadow by the door, masked and wrapped in a drab forest cloak that gave her the look of a beggar. Granny Elise gave them hot tea and cakes and kissed each of them, Auntie Jilt warned them sternly to keep safe from whatever dangers might lie in wait for them, and Teel led them out into the night.

It was dark still, the dawn not yet even a small glimmer in the distant trees, and they slipped silently through the sleeping village, four ghosts in search of a haunt. The morning air was chill, and they could see their breath cloud the air before them in small puffs. Teel took them down back pathways and through dense groves of trees and gatherings of brush, keeping to the shadows, staying away from the roads and lights. They moved north out of the village without seeing anyone. When they reached the Silver River, Teel took them downstream to a shallows, avoiding the bridges. They crossed water like ice as it lapped at their legs. They were barely into the trees again when Steff appeared out of the shadows to join them. He wore a brace of long knives at his waist, and the giant mace was slung across his back. He said nothing, taking the lead from Teel and guiding them ahead. A few faint streaks of daylight appeared in the east, and the sky began to brighten. The stars winked out and the moon disappeared. Frost glimmered on leaves and grasses like scattered bits of crystal.

A bit farther on, they reached a clearing dominated by a massive old willow, and Steff brought them to a halt. Backpacks, rolled blankets, foul-weather gear, cooking implements, water bags, and forest cloaks for each of them were concealed in an old hollow tree trunk that had fallen into the brush. They strapped everything in place without speaking and were off again.

They walked the remainder of the day at a leisurely pace,

bearing directly north. There was little discussion, none what-
soever as to where they were going. Steff offered no explanation, and neither the Valemen nor the Highlander were inclined
to ask. When the Dwarf was ready to tell them, he would. The
day passed quickly and by midafternoon they had reached the
foothills south of the Wolfsktaag. They continued on for what
was perhaps another hour, following the forestline upward to
where it began to thin before the wall of the mountains, then
Steff called a halt in a pine-sheltered clearing close to a small
stream that trickled down out of the rocks. He led them over
to a fallen log and seated himself comfortably, facing them.

"If the rumors are to be believed—and in this case, rumors
are all we have—Walker Boh will be found in Darklin Reach.
To get there, we will travel north through the Wolfsktaag—in
through the Pass of Noose, out through the Pass of Jade, and
from there east into the Reach."

He paused, considering what he saw in their faces. "There
are other ways, of course—safer ways, some might argue—but I
disagree. We could skirt the Wolfsktaag to the east or west, but
either way we risk an almost certain encounter with Federation
soldiers or Gnomes. There will be neither in the Wolfsktaag.
Too many spirits and things of old magic live in the mountains;
the Gnomes are superstitious about such and stay away. The
Federation used to send patrols in, but most of them never came
out. Truth is, most of them just got lost up there because they
didn't know the way. I do."

His listeners remained silent. Finally Coll said, "I seem to
remember that a couple of our ancestors got into a good bit of
trouble when they took this same route some years back."

Steff shrugged. "I wouldn't know about that. I do know that
I have been through these mountains dozens of times and know
what to look for. The trick is to stay on the ridgelines and out
of the deep forests. What lives in the Wolfsktaag prefers the
dark. And there's nothing magic about most of it."

Coll shook his head and looked at Par. "I don't like it."

"Well, the choice is between the devil we know and the one
we suspect," Steff declared bluntly. "Federation soldiers and their
Gnome allies, which we know are out there, or spirits and
wraiths, which we don't."

"Shadowen," Par said softly.

There was a moment of silence. Steff smiled grimly. "Haven't you heard, Valeman—there aren't any Shadowen. That's all a rumor. Besides, you have the magic to protect us, don't you? You and the Highlander here? What would dare challenge that?"

He looked about, sharp eyes darting from one face to the next. "Come now. No one ever suggested that this journey would be a safe one. Let us have a decision. But you have heard my warning about the choices left us if we forgo the mountains. Pay heed."

There wasn't much any of them could say after that, and they left it to the Dwarf's best judgment. This was his country after all, not theirs, and he was the one who knew it. They were relying on him to find Walker Boh, and it seemed foolish to second-guess the way he thought best to go about it.

They spent the night in the clearing of pines, smelling needles and wildflowers and the crispness of air, sleeping undisturbed and dreamless in a silence that stretched far beyond where they could see. At dawn, Steff took them up into the Wolfsktaag. They slipped into the Pass of Noose, where Gnomes had once tried to trap Shea and Flick Ohmsford, crossed the rope walkway that bridged the chasm at its center, wound their way steadily upward through the ragged, blunted peaks of slab-sided stone and forested slopes, and watched the sun work its way across the cloudless summer sky. Morning passed into afternoon, and they reached the ridgelines running north and began following their twists and bends. Travel was easy, the sun warm and reassuring, and the fears and doubts of the night before began to fade. They watched for movement in the shadows of rock and wood, but saw nothing. Birds sang in the trees, small animals scampered through the brush, and the forests here seemed very much the same as forests everywhere in the Four Lands. The Valemen and the Highlander found themselves smiling at one another; Steff hummed tonelessly to himself, and only Teel showed nothing of what she was feeling.

When nightfall approached, they made camp in a small meadow nestled between two ridgelines cropped with fir and cedar. There was little wind, and the day's warmth lingered in the sheltered valley long after the sun was gone. Stars glimmered faintly in the darkening skies, and the moon hung full against the western horizon. Par recalled again the old man's admonition to them—that they were to be at the Hadeshorn on the first day of the new moon. Time was slipping past.

But it wasn't of the old man or Allanon that Par found himself thinking that night as the little company gathered around the fire Steff had permitted them and washed down their dinner with long draughts of spring water. It was of Walker Boh. Par hadn't seen his uncle in almost ten years, but what he remembered of him was strangely clear. He had been just a boy then, and his uncle had seemed rather mysterious—a tall, lean man with dark features and eyes that could see right through you. The eyes—that was what Par remembered most, though he remembered them more for how remarkable they had seemed than for any discomfort they might have caused him. In fact, his uncle had been very kind to him, but always rather introspective or perhaps just withdrawn, sort of there but at the same time somewhere else.

There were stories about Walker Boh even then, but Par could recall few of them. It was said he used magic, although it was never made clear exactly what sort of magic. He was a direct descendent of Brin Ohmsford, but he had not had use of the wishsong. No one on his side of the family had, not in ten generations. The magic had died with Brin. It had worked differently for her than for her brother Jair, of course. Where Jair had only been able to use the wishsong to create images, his sister had been able to use it to create reality. Her magic had been by far the stronger of the two. Nevertheless, hers had disappeared with her passing, and only Jair's had survived.

Yet there had always been stories of Walker Boh and the magic. Par remembered how sometimes his uncle could tell him things that were happening at other places, things he could not possibly have known yet somehow did. There were times when his uncle could make things move by looking at them, even people. Sometimes he could tell what you were thinking, too. He would look at you and tell you not to worry, that this or that would happen, and it would turn out that it was exactly what you were thinking about.

Of course, it was possible that his uncle had simply been

astute enough to reason out what he was thinking, and that it had simply appeared that the older man could read his thoughts.

But there was the way he could turn aside trouble, too— make it disappear almost as fast as it came. Anything threatening always seemed to give way when it encountered him. That seemed a sort of magic.

And he was always encouraging to Par when he saw the boy attempting to use the wishsong. He had warned Par to learn to control the images, to be cautious about their use, to be selective in the ways in which he exposed the magic to others. Walker Boh had been one of the few people in his life who had not been afraid of its power.

So as he sat there with the others in the silence of the mountain night, the memories of his uncle skipping through his mind, his curiosity to know more was piqued anew, and finally he gave in to it and asked Steff what tales the other had heard of Walker Boh.

Steff looked thoughtful. "Most of them come from woodsmen, hunters, trackers and such—a few from Dwarves who fight in the Resistance like myself and who pass far enough north to hear of the man. They say the Gnome tribes are scared to death of him. They say they think of Walker Boh in the same way they think of spirits. Some of them believe that he's been alive for hundreds of years, that he's the same as the Druids of legend." He winked. "Guess that's just talk, though, if he's your uncle."

Par nodded. "I don't remember anyone ever suggesting he hadn't lived the same number of years as any normal man."

"One fellow swore to me that your uncle talked with animals and that the animals understood. He said he saw it happen, that he watched your uncle walk right up to a moor cat the size of a plains bull and speak with it the same way I'm speaking with you."

"It was said that Cogline could do that," Coll interjected, suddenly interested. "He had a cat called Whisper that followed him. The cat protected his niece, Kimber. Her name was Boh as well, wasn't it, Par?"

Par nodded, remembering that his uncle had taken the name Boh from his mother's side of the family. Strange, now that he thought about it, but he could never remember his uncle using the Ohmsford name.

"There was one story," Steff said, pausing then to mull the details over in his mind. "I heard it from a tracker who knew the deep Anar better than most and, I think, knew Walker Boh as well, though he'd never admit to it. He told me that something born in the days of the old magic wandered down out of Ravenshorn into Darklin Reach two years back and started living off the life it found there. Walker Boh went out to find it, confronted it, and the creature turned around and went back to wherever it had come from—just like that." Steff shook his head and rubbed his chin slowly. "It makes you think, doesn't it?"

He stretched his hands toward the fire. "That's why he scares me—because there doesn't appear to be much of anything that scares him. He comes and goes like a ghost, they say—here one minute, gone the next, just a shadow out of night. I wonder if even the Shadowen frighten him. I'd guess not."

"Maybe we should ask him," Coll offered with a sly grin.

Steff brightened. "Well, now, maybe we should," he agreed. "I suggest you be the one to do it!" He laughed. "That reminds me, has the Highlander told you yet how we happened on each other that first time?"

The Ohmsford brothers shook their heads no, and despite some loud grumbling from Morgan, Steff proceeded to tell the tale. Morgan was fishing the eastern end of the Rainbow Lake at the mouth of the Silver River some ten months earlier when a squall capsized his craft, washed away his gear, and left him to make his way ashore as best he could. He was drenched and freezing and trying without success to start a fire when Steff came across him and dried him out.

"He would have died of exposure, I expect, if I hadn't taken pity on him," Steff finished. "We talked, exchanged information. Before you know it, he was on his way to Culhaven to see whether life in the homeland of the Dwarves was as grim as I had described it." Steff cast an amused look at the chagrined Highlander. "He kept coming back after that—each time with a little something to help out Granny and Auntie and the Resistance as well. His conscience won't allow him to stay away, I suppose."

"Oh, for goodness sake!" Morgan huffed, embarrassed.

Steff laughed, his voice booming out through the stillness, filling up the night. "Enough, then, proud Highland Prince! We will talk of someone else!" He shifted his weight and looked at Par. "That stranger, the one who gave you the ring—let's talk about him. I know something of the outlaw bands that serve in the Movement. A rather worthless bunch, for the most part; they lack leadership and discipline. The Dwarves have offered to work with them, but the offer hasn't been accepted as yet. The problem is that the whole Movement has been too fragmented. In any case, that ring you were given—does it bear the emblem of a hawk?"

Par sat bolt upright. "It does, Steff. Do you know whose it is?"

Steff smiled. "I do and I don't, Valeman. As I said, the Southland outlaws have been a fragmented bunch in the past—but that may be changing. There are rumors of one among them who seems to be taking control, uniting the bands together, giving them the leadership they have been lacking. He doesn't use his name to identify himself; he uses the symbol of a hawk."

"It must be the same man," Par declared firmly. "He was reluctant to give his name to us as well."

Steff shrugged. "Names are often kept secret in these times. But the way in which he managed your escape from the Seekers—well, that sounds like the man I have been hearing about. They say he would dare anything where the Federation is concerned."

"He was certainly bold enough that night," Par agreed, smiling.

They talked a bit longer of the stranger, the outlaw bands in both Southland and Eastland, and the way in which the Four Lands festered like an open sore under Federation rule. They never did get back to the subject of Walker Boh, but Par was content with where they had left it. He had his mind made up where his uncle was concerned. It did not matter how frightening Walker Boh appeared to others, to Steff or anyone else; he would remain for Par the same man he had been when the Valeman was a boy until something happened to change his mind—and he had a curious feeling that nothing would.

Their talk dwindled finally, interrupted by frequent yawns and distracted looks, and one by one they began to roll into their blankets. Par offered to build the fire up one final time before they went to sleep and walked to the edge of the trees in search of deadwood. He was in the process of gathering some pieces of an old cedar that had been blown down by the winds last winter when he suddenly found himself face-to-face with Teel. She seemed to materialize right in front of him, her masked face intent, her eyes quite steady as she looked at him.

"Can you make the magic for me?" she asked quietly.

Par stared. He had never heard her speak, not once, not a single time since he had encountered her that first night in Granny Elise's kitchen. As far as he had been able to determine, she couldn't. She had traveled with them as if she were Steff's faithful dog, obedient to him, watchful of them, unquestioning and aloof. She had sat there all evening listening and not speaking, keeping what she knew and what she thought carefully to herself. Now, this.

"Can you make the images?" she pressed. Her voice was low and rough. "Just one or two, so I can see them? I would like it very much if you could."

He saw her eyes then, where he hadn't seen them before. They were a curious azure, the way the sky had been that day so high up in the mountains, clear and depthless. He was startled by how bright they were, and he remembered suddenly that her hair was a honey color beneath the covering hood, behind the concealing mask. She had seemed rather unpleasant before in the way in which she chose to distance herself from them, but now, standing here amid the silence and shadows, she just seemed small.

"What images would you like to see?" he asked her.

She thought for a moment. "I would like to see what Culhaven was like in the days of Allanon."

He started to tell her he wasn't sure what Culhaven had been like that long ago, then caught himself and nodded. "I can try," he said.

He sang softly to her, alone in the trees, reaching out with the magic of the wishsong to fill her mind with images of the village as it might have looked three hundred years ago. He sang of the Silver River, of the Meade Gardens, of the cottages and homes all carefully tended and kept, of life in the home city of the Dwarves before the war with the Federation. When he was finished, she studied him expressionlessly for a moment, then turned without a word and disappeared back into the night.

Par stared after her in confusion for a moment, then shrugged, finished picking up the deadwood and went off to sleep.

THEY STRUCK OUT AGAIN at dawn, working their way along the upper stretches of the Wolfsktaag where the forests thinned and the sky hovered close. It was another warm, bright day filled with good smells and a sense of endless possibilities. Breezes blew gently against their faces, the woods and rocks were filled with tiny creatures that darted and flew, and the mountains were at peace.

Despite all of that, Par was uneasy. He hadn't felt that way the previous two days, but he did so on this one. He tried to dispel the uneasiness, telling himself it lacked any discernible cause, that it was probably the result of needing something to worry about when it appeared that Steff had been right about this being the safest way after all. He tried studying the faces of the others to see if they were experiencing any discomfort, but the others seemed quite content. Even Teel, who seldom showed anything, walked with an air of total unconcern.

The morning slipped away into afternoon, and the uneasiness grew into a certainty that something was following them. Par found himself glancing back on any number of occasions, not knowing what it was he was looking for, but knowing nevertheless that it was back there. He hunted through the distant trees and across the rocks and there was nothing to be seen. Above, to their right, the ridgeline rose into the cliffs and defiles where the rock was too barren and dangerous to traverse. Below, to their left, the forest was thick with shadows that gathered in pools amid a tangle of heavy brush and close-set black trunks.

Several times, the trail branched downward into the murk.

Steff, who was in the lead with Teel, motioned that way once and said, "That is what might have happened to those missing Federation parties. You don't want to wander into the dark places in these mountains."

It was Par's hope that this was the source of his discomfort. Identifying the source should allow him to dismiss it, he told himself. But just as he was prepared to believe that the matter had resolved itself, he glanced over his shoulder one final time and saw something move in the rocks.

He stopped where he was. The others walked on a few steps, then turned and looked at him. "What is it?" Steff asked at once.

"There's something back there," Par said quietly, not shifting his eyes from where he had last seen the movement.

Steff walked back to him. "There, in the rocks," Par said and pointed.

They stood together and looked for a long time and saw nothing. The afternoon was waning, and the shadows were lengthening in the mountains as the sun dropped low against the western horizon, so it was difficult to discern much of anything in the mix of half-light. Par shook his head finally, frustrated. "Maybe I was mistaken," he admitted.

"Maybe you weren't," Steff said.

Ignoring the surprised look Par gave him, he started them walking again with Teel in the lead and himself trailing with Par. Once or twice, he told Par to glance back, and once or twice he did so himself. Par never saw anything, although he still had a sense of something being back there. They crossed a ridgeline that ran from east to west and started down. The far side was cloaked in shadow, the sun's fading light blocked away entirely, and the trail below wound its way through a maze of rocks and scrub that were clustered on the mountainside like huddled sheep. The wind was at their backs now, and the sound of Steff's voice, when he spoke, carried ahead to them.

"Whatever's back there is tracking us, waiting for dark or at least twilight before showing itself. I don't know what it is, but it's big. We have to find a place where we can defend ourselves."

No one said anything. Par experienced a sudden chill. Coll glanced at him, then at Morgan. Teel never turned.

They were through the maze of rocks and brush and back on an open trail leading up again when the thing finally emerged from the shadows and let them see what it was. Steff saw it first, called out sharply and brought them all about. The creature was still more than a hundred yards back, crouched on a flat rock where a narrow shaft of sunlight sliced across its blunted face like a lance. It looked like some sort of monstrous dog or wolf with a massive chest and neck thick with fur and a face that was all misshapen. It had oddly fat legs, a barrel body, small ears and tail, and the look of something that had no friends. Its jaws parted once, the biggest jaws Par had ever seen on anything, and spittle drooled out. The jaws snapped shut, and it started toward them in a slow amble.

"Keep moving," Steff said quietly, and they did. They walked ahead steadily, following the weave of the trail, trying not to look back.

"What is it?" Morgan asked, his voice low.

"They call it a Gnawl," Steff answered calmly. "It lives east in the deepest part of the Anar, beyond the Ravenshorn. Very dangerous." He paused. "I never heard of one being seen in the central Anar, though—let alone in the Wolfsktaag."

"Until now, you mean," muttered Coll.

They made their way through a broad split in the mountains where the trail began to dip sharply downward into a hollows. The sun was gone, and gray twilight hung over everything like a shroud. It was getting hard to see. The thing behind them appeared and disappeared in fits and starts, causing Par to wonder what would happen when they lost sight of it altogether.

"I never heard of one stalking men either," Steff declared suddenly from just behind him.

The strange hunt continued, the Gnawl trailing them at a distance of about a hundred yards, apparently content to wait for darkness to descend completely. Steff urged them on, searching for a spot where they could make a stand.

"Why don't you simply let me go after it!" Morgan snapped back at him at one point.

"Because you would be dead quicker than I could say your name, Highlander," the Dwarf answered, his voice cold. "Don't be fooled. This creature is more than a match for the five of us if it catches us unprepared. All the magic in the world won't make a difference if that happens!"

Par froze, wondering suddenly if the magic in Morgan's sword was of any use against this beast. Wasn't the sword's magic triggered only by an encounter with similar magic? Wasn't it simply a common sword when otherwise employed? Wasn't that what Allanon had intended when he had given the blade its power? He struggled to remember the particulars of the story and failed. But the other magics, those of the Sword of Shannara and of the Elfstones, had been effective only against things of magic—he remembered that well enough. It was very likely the same with . . .

"Ahead, down by that hollows," Steff said abruptly, ending his speculation. "That's where we will . . ."

He never finished. The Gnawl came at them, hurtling through the darkness, a huge, black shape bounding across the broken rock and scrub with a speed that was astonishing. "Go!" Steff shouted at them, pointed hurriedly down the trail and turned to face the beast.

They went without thinking, all but Morgan who wrenched free the Sword of Leah and rushed to stand with his friend. Teel, Coll, and Par dashed ahead, glancing back just as the Gnawl reached their companions. The creature lunged at Steff, but the Dwarf was waiting, the huge mace held ready. He caught the beast full against the side of its head with a blow that would have dropped anything else. But the Gnawl shrugged the blow aside and came at the Dwarf again. Steff hammered it a second time, then broke past it, pulling the Highlander after him. They came down the trail in a spring, quickly catching the fleeing Valemen and Teel.

"Down the slope!" Steff yelled, literally shoving them off the trail. They rushed into the scrub and rocks, skidding and sliding. Par went down, tumbled head-over-heels, and came back to his feet all in the same motion. He was disoriented, and there was blood in his eyes. Steff jerked him about and dragged him forward, down the slide, the sound of labored breathing and shouting all about him.

Then he was aware of the Gnawl. He heard it before he saw it, its heavy body churning up the ground behind them, scattering rocks and dirt as it came, its cry an ugly whine of hunger. The magic, Par thought, distracted—I have to use the magic. The wishsong will work, confuse it, at least . . .

Steff pulled him onto a flat rock, and he felt the others bunch around him. "Stay together!" the Dwarf ordered. "Don't leave the rock!"

He stepped out to meet the Gnawl's rush.

Par would never forget what happened next. Steff took the Gnawl's charge on the slope just to the left of the rock. He let the creature come right up against him, then suddenly fell back, mace jamming upward into the Gnawl's throat, booted feet thrusting against its massive chest. Steff went down, and the Gnawl went right over him, the momentum of its lunge carrying it past. The Gnawl could not catch itself. It tumbled past Steff, rolled wildly down the slope into the hollows below, right up against the fringe of the trees. It came to its feet instantly, growling and snarling. But then something huge shot out of the trees, snapped up the Gnawl in a single bite and pulled back again into the murk. There was a sharp cry, a crunching of bones, and silence.

Steff came to his feet, put a finger to his lips, and beckoned them to follow. Silently, or as nearly so as they could keep it, they climbed back up to the trail and stood looking downward into the impenetrable dark.

"In the Wolfsktaag, you have to learn what to look out for," Steff whispered with a grim smile. "Even if you're a Gnawl."

They brushed themselves off and straightened their packs. Their cuts and bruises were slight. The Pass of Jade, which would take them clear of the mountains, was no more than another hour or two ahead, Steff advised.

They decided to keep walking.

CHAPTER

9

T TOOK LONGER than Steff had estimated to reach the Pass of Jade, and it was almost midnight when the little company finally broke clear of the Wolfsktaag. They slept in a narrow canyon screened by a tangle of fir and ancient spruce, so exhausted that they did not bother with either food or fire, but simply rolled into their blankets and dropped off to sleep. Par dreamed that night, but not about Allanon or the Hadeshorn. He dreamed instead of the Gnawl. It tracked him relentlessly through the landscape of his mind, chasing him from one dark corner to the next, a vaguely distinguishable shadow whose identity was nevertheless as certain as his own. It came for him and he ran from it, and the terror he felt was palpable. Finally it cornered him, backing him into a shallow niche of rock and forest, and just as he was about to attempt to spring past it, something monstrous lunged from the dark behind him and took him into its maw, dragging him from sight as he screamed for the help that wouldn't come.

He came awake with a start.

It was dark, though the sky was beginning to lighten in the east, and his companions still slept. The scream was only in his mind, it seemed. There was sweat on his face and body, and his breathing was quick and ragged. He lay back quietly, but did not sleep again.

They walked east that morning into the central Anar, winding through a maze of forested hills and ravines, five pairs of eyes searching the shadows and dark places about them as they went. There was little talking, the encounter of the previous day having left them uneasy and watchful. The day was clouded and gray, and the forests about them seemed more secretive somehow. By noon, they came upon the falls of the Chard Rush, and they followed the river in until nightfall.

It rained the next day, and the land was washed in mist and damp. Travel slowed, and the warmth and brightness of the previous few days faded into memory. They passed the Rooker Line Trading Center, a tiny waystation for hunters and traders in the days of Jair Ohmsford that had built itself into a thriving fur exchange until the war between the Dwarves and the Federation disrupted and finally put an end altogether to Eastland commerce north of Culhaven. Now it stood empty, its doors and windows gone, its roof rotted and sagging, its shadows filled with ghosts from another time.

At lunch, huddled beneath the canopy of a massive old willow that overhung the banks of the river, Steff talked uneasily of the Gnawl, insisting again that one had never before been seen west of the Ravenshorn. Where did this one come from? How did it happen to be here? Why had it chosen to track them? There were answers to his questions, of course, but none that any of them cared to explore. Chance, they all agreed outwardly, and inwardly thought just the opposite.

The rain slowed with the approach of nightfall, but continued in a steady drizzle until morning, when it changed to a heavy mist. The company pushed on, following the Chard Rush as it wound its way down into Darklin Reach. Travel grew increasingly difficult, the forests thick with brush and fallen timber, the pathways almost nonexistent. When they left the river at midday, the terrain transformed itself into a series of gullies and ravines, and it became almost impossible to determine their direction. They slogged through the mud and debris, Steff in the lead, grunting and huffing rhythmically. The Dwarf was like a tireless machine when he traveled, tough and seemingly inexhaustible. Only Teel was his equal, smaller than Steff but more agile, never slowing or complaining, always keeping pace. It was the Valemen and the Highlander who grew tired, their muscles stiffened, their wind spent. They welcomed every chance to rest that the Dwarf offered them, and when it was time to start up again it was all they could do to comply. The dreariness of their travel was beginning to affect them as well, especially the Valemen. Par and Coll had been running either from or toward something for weeks now, had spent much of that time in hiding, and had endured three very frightening encounters with creatures best left to one's imagination. They were tired of keeping constant watch, and the darkness, mist, and damp just served to exhaust them further. Neither said anything to the other, and neither would have admitted it if the other had asked, but both were starting to wonder if they really knew what they were doing.

It was late afternoon when the rain finally stopped, and the clouds suddenly broke apart to let through a smattering of sunlight. They crested a ridge and came upon a shallow, forested valley dominated by a strange rock formation shaped like a chimney. It rose out of the trees as if a sentinel set at watch, black and still against the distant skyline. Steff brought the others to a halt and pointed down.

"There," he said quietly. "If Walker Boh's to be found, this is the place he's said to be."

Par shoved aside his exhaustion and despondency, staring in disbelief. "I know this place!" he exclaimed. "This is Hearthstone! I recognize it from the stories! This is Cogline's home!"

"Was," Coll corrected wearily.

"Was, is, what's the difference?" Par was animated as he confronted them. "The point is, what is Walker Boh doing here? I mean, it makes sense that he would be here because this was once the home of the Bohs, but it was Cogline's home as well. If Walker lives here, then why didn't the old man tell us? Unless maybe the old man isn't Cogline after all or unless for some reason he doesn't know Walker is here, or unless Walker . . ." He stopped suddenly, confused to the point of distraction. "Are you sure this is where my uncle is supposed to live?" he demanded of Steff.

The Dwarf had been watching him during all this the same way he might have watched a three-headed dog. Now he simply shrugged. "Valeman, I am sure of very little and admit to less. I was told this was where the man makes his home. So if you're all done talking about it, why don't we simply go down there and see?"

Par shut his mouth, and they began their descent. When they reached the valley floor, they found the forest surprisingly clear of scrub and deadwood. The trees opened into clearings that were crisscrossed with streams and laced with tiny wild-flowers colored white, blue, and deep violet. The day grew still, the wind calmed, and the lengthening shadows that draped the way forward seemed soft and unthreatening. Par forgot about the dangers and hardships of his journey, put aside his weariness and discomfort, and concentrated instead on thinking further about the man he had come to find. He was admittedly con-fused, but at least he understood the reason. When Brin Ohms-ford had come into Darklin Reach three hundred years earlier, Hearthstone had been the home of Cogline and the child he claimed as his granddaughter, Kimber Boh. The old man and the little girl had guided Brin into the Maelmord where she had confronted the Ildatch. They had remained friends afterward, and that friendship had endured for ten generations. Walker Boh's father had been an Ohmsford and his mother a Boh. He could trace his father's side of the family directly back to Brin and his mother's side to Kimber. It was logical that he would choose to come back here—yet illogical that the old man, the man who claimed to be Cogline, the very same Cogline of three hundred years earlier, would know nothing about it.

Or say nothing, if in fact he knew.

Par frowned. What *had* the old man said about Walker Boh when they had talked with him? His frown deepened. Only that he knew Walker was alive, he answered himself. That and noth-ing else.

But was there more between them than what the old man had revealed? Par was certain of it. And he meant to discover what it was.

The brief flurry of late sunlight faded and twilight cloaked the valley in darkening shades of gray. The sky remained clear and began to fill with stars, and the three-quarter moon, waning now toward the end of its cycle, bathed the forest in milky light. The little company walked cautiously ahead, working its way steadily in the direction of the chimney-shaped rock formation, crossing the dozens of little streams and weaving through the maze of clearings. The forest was still, but its silence did not feel ominous. Coll nudged Par at one point when he caught sight of a gray squirrel sitting up on its hind legs and regarding them solemnly. There were night sounds, but they seemed distant and far removed from the valley.

"It feels sort of . . . protected here, don't you think?" Par asked his brother quietly, and Coll nodded.

They continued on for almost an hour without encountering anyone. They had reached the approximate center of the valley when a sudden glimmer of light winked at them through the forest trees. Steff slowed, signaled for caution, then led them forward. The light drew closer, flickering brightly through the dark, changing from a single pinprick of brightness to a cluster. *Lamps*, Par thought. He pushed ahead to reach Steff, his sharp Elven senses picking out the source. "It's a cottage," he whispered to the Dwarf.

They broke clear of the trees and stepped into a broad, grassy clearing. There was indeed a cottage. It stood before them, precisely at the center of the clearing, a well-kept stone and timber structure with front and rear porches, stone walkways, gardens, and flowering shrubs. Spruce and pine clustered about it like miniature watchtowers. Light streamed forth from its windows and mingled with moonglow to brighten the clearing as if it were midday.

The front door stood open.

Par started forward at once, but Steff quickly yanked him back. "A little caution might be in order, Valeman," he lectured.

He said something to Teel, then left them all to go on alone, sprinting across the open spaces between the spruce and pine, keeping carefully to the shadows between, eyes fixed on the open door. The others watched him make his way forward, crouched down now at Teel's insistence at the edge of the forest. Steff reached the porch, hunkered down close to it for a long time, then darted up the steps and through the front door. There was a moment of silence, then he reappeared and waved them forward.

When they reached him, he said, "No one is here. But it appears we are expected."

They discovered his meaning when they went inside. A pair of chimneys bracketed the central room, one for a seating area in which chairs and benches were drawn up, the other for a cooking grill and oven. Fires burned brightly in both. A kettle of stew simmered over the grill and hot bread cooled on a cutting board. A long trestle table was carefully set with plates and cups for five. Par stepped forward for a closer look. Cold ale had been poured into all five cups.

The members of the little company looked at each other silently for a moment, then glanced once more about the room. The wood of the walls and beams was polished and waxed. Silver, crystal, carved wooden pieces, and clothwork hangings gleamed in the light of oil lamps and hearth flames. There was a vase of fresh flowers on the trestle table, others in the sitting area. A hall led back into the sleeping rooms. The cottage was bright and cheerful and very empty.

"Is this Walker's?" Morgan asked doubtfully of Par. Somehow it didn't fit the image he had formed of the man.

Par shook his head. "I don't know. There isn't anything here I recognize."

Morgan moved silently to the back hall, disappeared from sight for a moment and returned. "Nothing," he reported, sounding disappointed.

Coll walked over to stand with Par, sniffed the stew experimentally, and shrugged. "Well, obviously our coming here isn't such a surprise after all. I don't know about the rest of you, but that stew smells awfully good. Since someone has gone to the trouble of making it—Walker Boh or whoever—I think the least we can do is sit down and eat it."

Par and Morgan quickly agreed, and even Teel seemed interested. Steff was again inclined to be cautious, but since it was apparent Coll was probably right in his analysis of the situation he quickly gave in. Nevertheless, he insisted on checking first to make certain neither food nor drink was tainted in any way. When he had pronounced the meal fit, they seated themselves and eagerly consumed it.

When dinner was over, they cleared and washed the dishes

and put them carefully away in a cabinet built to contain them. Then they searched the cottage a second time, the grounds around it, and finally everything for a quarter-mile in every direction. They found nothing.

They sat around the fire after that until midnight, waiting. No one came. There were two small bedrooms in back with two beds in each. The beds were turned down and the linens and blankets fresh. They took turns sleeping, one keeping watch for the others. They slept the night undisturbed, the forest and the valley at peace about them. Dawn brought them awake feeling much refreshed. Still no one came.

That day, they searched the entire valley from one end to the other, from the cottage to the odd, chimney-shaped rock, from north wall to south, from east to west. The day was warm and bright, filled with sunshine and gentle breezes and the smell of growing things. They took their time, wandering along the streams, following the pathways, exploring the few dens that burrowed the valley slopes like pockets. They found scattered prints, all of them made by animals, and nothing else. Birds flew overhead, sudden flashes of color in the trees, tiny woods creatures watched with darting eyes, and insects buzzed and hummed. Once a badger lumbered into view as Par and Coll hunted the west wall by the rock tower, refusing to give way to them. Other than that, none of them saw anything.

They had to fix their own meal that night, but there was fresh meat and cheese in a cold locker, day-old bread from the previous evening, and vegetables in the garden. The Valemen helped themselves, forcing the others to partake as well despite Steff's continued misgivings, convinced that this was what was expected of them. The day faded into a warm and pleasant night, and they began to grow comfortable with their surroundings. Steff sat with Teel before the gathering fire and smoked a long-stemmed pipe, Par worked in the kitchen with Coll cleaning the dishes, and Morgan took up watch on the front steps.

"Someone has put a lot of effort into keeping up this cottage," Par observed to his brother as they finished their task. "It doesn't seem reasonable that they would just go off and leave it."

"Especially after taking time to make us that stew," Coll

added. His broad face furrowed. "Do you think it belongs to Walker?"

"I don't know. I wish I did."

"None of this really seems like him though, does it? Not like the Walker I remember. Certainly not like the one Steff tells us about."

Par wiped the last few droplets of dishwater from a dinner plate and carefully put it away. "Maybe that's how he wants it to appear," he said softly.

It was several hours after midnight when he took the watch from Teel, yawning and stretching as he came out onto the front porch to look for her. The Dwarf was nowhere to be seen at first, and it wasn't until he had come thoroughly awake that she appeared from behind a spruce some several dozen yards out. She slipped noiselessly through the shadows to reach him and disappeared into the cottage without a word. Par glanced after her curiously, then sat down on the front steps, propped his chin in his hands, and stared off into the dark.

He had been sitting there for almost an hour when he heard the sound.

It was a strange sound, a sort of buzzing like a swarm of bees might make, but deep and rough. It was there and then just as quickly gone again. He thought at first he must have made it up, that he had heard it only in his mind. But then it came again, for just an instant, before disappearing once more.

He stood up, looked around tentatively, then walked out onto the pathway. The night was brilliantly clear and the sky filled with stars and bright. The woods about him were empty. He felt reassured and walked slowly around the house and out back. There was an old willow tree there, far back in the shadows, and beneath it a pair of worn benches. Par walked over to them and stopped, listening once again for the noise and hearing nothing. He sat down on the nearest bench. The bench had been carved to the shape of his body, and he felt cradled by it. He sat there for a time, staring out through the veil of the willow's drooping branches, daydreaming in the darkness, listening to the night's silence. He wondered about his parents—if they were well, if they worried for him. Shady Vale was a distant memory.

He closed his eyes momentarily to rest them against the weariness he was feeling. When he opened them again, the moor cat was standing there.

Par's shock was so great that at first he couldn't move. The cat was right in front of him, its whiskered face level with his own, its eyes a luminous gold in the night. It was the biggest animal that Par had ever seen, bigger even than the Gnawl. It was solid black from head to tail except for the eyes, which stared at him unblinkingly.

Then the cat began to purr, and he recognized it as the sound he had heard earlier. The cat turned and walked away a few paces and looked back, waiting. When Par continued to stare at it, it returned momentarily, started away again, stopped and waited.

It wanted him to follow, Par realized.

He rose mechanically, unable to make his body respond in the way he wanted it to, trying to decide if he should do as the cat expected or attempt to break away. He discarded any thought of the latter almost immediately. This was no time to be trying anything foolish. Besides, if the cat wanted to harm him, it could have done so earlier.

He took a few steps forward, and the cat turned away again, moving off into the trees.

They wound through the darkened forest for long minutes, moving silently, steadily into the night. Moonlight flooded the open spaces, and Par had little trouble following. He watched the cat move effortlessly ahead of him, barely disturbing the forest about him, a creature that seemed to have the substance of a shadow. His shock was fading now, replaced by curiosity. Someone had sent the cat to him, and he thought he knew who.

Finally, they reached a clearing in which several streams emptied through a series of tiny rapids into a wide, moonlit pool. The trees here were very old and broad, and their limbs cast an intricate pattern of shadows over everything. The cat walked over to the pool, drank deeply for a moment, then sat back and looked at him. Par came forward a few steps and stopped.

"Hello, Par," someone greeted.

The Valeman searched the clearing for a moment before

finding the speaker, who sat well back in the dark on a burled stump, barely distinguishable from the shadows about him, When Par hesitated, he rose and stepped into the light.

"Hello, Walker," Par replied softly.

His uncle was very much as he remembered him—and at the same time completely different. He was still tall and slight, his Elven features apparent though not as pronounced as Par's, his skin a shocking white hue that provided a marked contrast to the shoulder-length black hair and close-cropped beard. His eyes hadn't changed either; they still looked right through you, even when shadowed as they were now. What was different was more difficult to define. It was mostly in the way Walker Boh carried himself and the way he made Par feel when he spoke, even though he had said almost nothing. It was as if there were an invisible wall about him that nothing could penetrate.

Walker Boh came forward and took Par's hands in his own. He was dressed in loose-fitting forest clothing—pants, tunic, a short cloak, and soft boots, all colored like the earth and trees. "Have you been comfortable at the cottage?" he asked.

Par seemed to remember himself then. "Walker, I don't understand. What are you doing out here? Why didn't you meet us when we arrived? Obviously, you knew we were coming."

His uncle released his hands and stepped away. "Come sit with me, Par," he invited, and moved back again into the shadows without waiting for his nephew's response. Par followed, and the two seated themselves on the stump from which Walker had first risen.

Walker looked him over carefully. "I will only be speaking with you," he said quietly. "And only this once."

Par waited, saying nothing. "There have been many changes in my life," his uncle went on after a moment. "I expect you remember little of me from your childhood, and most of what you remember no longer has much to do with who I am now in any case. I gave up my Vale life, any claim to being a Southlander, and came here to begin again. I left behind me the madness of men whose lives are governed by the baser instincts. I separated myself from men of all races, from their greed and their prejudice, their wars and their politics, and their monstrous conception of betterment. I came here, Par, so that I could live alone. I was always alone, of course; I was made to feel alone. The difference now is that I am alone, not because others choose it for me, but because I choose it for myself. I am free to be exactly what I am—and not to feel strange because of it."

He smiled faintly. "It is the time we live in and who we are that make it difficult for both of us, you know. Do you understand me, Par? You have the magic, too—a very tangible magic in your case. It will not win you friends; it will set you apart. We are not permitted to be Ohmsfords these days because Ohmsfords have the magic of their Elven forebears and neither magic nor Elves are appreciated or understood. I grew tired of finding it so, of being set apart, of being constantly looked at with suspicion and mistrust. I grew tired of being thought different. It will happen to you as well, if it hasn't done so already. It is the nature of things."

"I don't let it bother me," Par said defensively. "The magic is a gift."

"Oh? Is it now? How so? A gift is not something you hide as you would a loathsome disease. It is not something of which you are ashamed or cautious or even frightened. It is not something that might kill you."

The words were spoken with such bitterness that Par felt chilled. Then his uncle's mood seemed to change instantly; he grew calm again, quiet. He shook his head in self-reproach. "I forget myself sometimes when speaking of the past. I apologize. I brought you here to talk with you of other things. But only with you, Par. I leave the cottage for your companions to use during their stay. But I will not come there to be with them. I am only interested in you."

"But what about Coll?" Par asked, confused. "Why speak with me and not with him?"

His uncle's smile was ironic. "Think, Par. I was never close with him the way I was with you."

Par stared at him silently. That was true, he supposed. It was the magic that had drawn Walker to him, and Coll had never been able to share in that. The time he had spent with his uncle, the time that had made him feel close to the man, had always been time away from Coll.

"Besides," the other continued softly, "what we need to talk about concerns only us."

Par understood then. "The dreams." His uncle nodded. "Then you have experienced them as well—the figure in black, the one who appears to be Allanon, standing before the Hadeshorn, warning us, telling us to come?" Par was breathless. "What about the old man? Has he come to you also?" Again, his uncle nodded. "Then you do know him, don't you? Is it true, Walker? Is he really Cogline?"

Walker Boh's face emptied of expression. "Yes, Par, he is."

Par flushed with excitement, and rubbed his hands together briskly. "I cannot believe it! How old is he? Hundreds of years, I suppose—just as he claimed. And once a Druid. I knew I was right! Does he live here still, Walker—with you?"

"He visits, sometimes. And sometimes stays a bit. The cat was his before he gave it to me. You remember that there was always a moor cat. The one before was called Whisper. That was in the time of Brin Ohmsford. This one is called Rumor. The old man named it. He said it was a good name for a cat—especially one who would belong to me."

He stopped, and something Par couldn't read crossed his face briefly and was gone. The Valeman glanced over to where the cat had been resting, but it had disappeared.

"Rumor comes and goes in the manner of all moor cats," Walker Boh said as if reading his thoughts.

Par nodded absently, then looked back at him. "What are you going to do, Walker?"

"About the dreams?" The strange eyes went flat. "Nothing."

Par hesitated. "But the old man must have . . ."

"Listen to me," the other said, cutting him short. "I am decided on this. I know what the dreams have asked of me; I know who sent them. The old man has come to me, and we have talked. He left not a week past. None of that matters. I am no longer an Ohmsford; I am a Boh. If I could strip away my past, with all its legacy of magic and all its glorious Elven history, I would do so in an instant. I want none of it. I came into the Eastland to find this valley, to live as my ancestors once lived, to be just once where everything is fresh and clean and untroubled by the presence of others. I have learned to keep my life in perfect order and to order the life around me. You have seen this valley; my mother's people made it that way and I have learned to keep it. I have Rumor for company and occasionally the old man. Once in a while, I even visit with those from the outside. Darklin Reach has become a haven for me and Hearthstone my home."

He bent forward, his face intense. "I have the magic, Par—different from yours, but real nevertheless. I can tell what others are thinking sometimes, even when they are far away. I can communicate with life in ways that others cannot. All forms of life. I can disappear sometimes, just like the moor cat. I can even summon power!" He snapped his fingers suddenly, and a brief spurt of blue fire appeared on his fingers. He snuffed it out. "I lack the magic of the wishsong, but apparently some of its power has taken root inside me. Some of what I know is innate; some is self-taught; some was taught to me by others. But I have all I need, and I wish no more. I am comfortable here and will never leave. Let the world get on as best it can without me. It always did so before."

Par struggled to respond. "But what if the dream is right, Walker?" he asked finally.

Walker Boh laughed derisively. "Par! The dreams are never right! Have you not paid heed to your own stories? Whether they manifest themselves as they have this time or as they did when Allanon was alive, one fact remains unchanged—the Ohmsfords are never told everything, only what the Druids deem necessary!"

"You think that we are being used." Par made it a statement of fact.

"I think I would be a fool to believe anything else! I do not trust what I am being told." The other's eyes were as hard as stone. "The magic you insist on regarding as a gift has always been little more than a useful tool to the Druids. I do not intend to let myself be put to whatever new task they have discovered. If the world needs saving as these dreams suggest, let Allanon or the old man go out and save it!"

There was a long moment of silence as the two measured

each other. Par shook his head slowly. "You surprise me, Walker. I don't remember the bitterness or the anger from before."

Walker Boh smiled sadly. "It was there, Par. It was always there. You just didn't bother to look for it."

"Shouldn't it be gone by now?"

His uncle kept silent.

"So you are decided on this matter, are you?"

"Yes, Par. I am."

Par took a deep breath. "What will you do, Walker, if the things in the dream come to pass? What will become of your home then? What will happen if the evil the dream showed us decides to come looking for you?"

His uncle said nothing, but the steady gaze never wavered. Par nodded slowly. "I have a different view of matters from yours, Walker," he said softly. "I have always believed that the magic was a gift, and that it was given to me for a reason. It appeared for a long time that it was meant to be used to tell the stories, to keep them from being forgotten completely. I have changed my mind about that. I think now that the magic is meant for something more."

He shifted, straightening himself because he was feeling suddenly small in the presence of the other. "Coll and I cannot go back to the Vale because the Federation has found out about the magic and is hunting for us. The old man, Cogline, says there may be other things hunting us as well—perhaps even Shadowen. Have you see the Shadowen? I have. Coll and I are scared to death, Walker, though we don't talk about it much. The funny thing is, I think the things hunting us are scared, too. It's the magic that scares them." He paused. "I don't know why that is, but I mean to find out."

There was a flicker of surprise in Walker Boh's eyes. Par nodded. "Yes, Walker, I have decided to do as the dreams have asked. I believe they were sent by Allanon, and I believe they should be heeded. I will go to the Hadeshorn. I think I made the decision just now; I think listening to you helped me decide. I haven't told Coll. I don't really know what he will do. Maybe I will end up going alone. But I will go. If for no other reason, I will go because I think Allanon can tell me what the magic is intended to do."

He shook his head sadly. "I can't be like you, Walker. I can't live apart from the rest of the world. I want to be able to go back to Shady Vale. I don't want to go away and start life over. I came this way through Culhaven. The Dwarves who brought us are from there. All of the prejudice and greed, the politics and wars, all of the madness you speak about is very much in evidence there. But unlike you I don't want to escape it; I want to find a way to end it! How can that happen if I simply pretend it doesn't exist!"

His hands tightened into fists. "You see, I keep thinking, what if Allanon knows something that can change the way things are? What if he can tell me something that will put an end to the madness?"

They faced each other in the dark for a long time without speaking, and Par thought he saw things in his uncle's dark eyes that he hadn't seen since his childhood—things that whispered of caring and need and sacrifice. Then the eyes were flat again, expressionless, empty. Walker Boh came to his feet.

"Will you reconsider?" Par asked him quietly.

Walker regarded him silently, then walked to the pool at the center of the clearing and stood looking down. When his fingers snapped, Rumor materialized from out of nowhere and came over to him.

He turned momentarily and looked back. "Good luck, Par," was all he said.

Then he turned, the cat beside him, and disappeared into the night.

CHAPTER

10

PAR WAITED UNTIL MORNING to tell the others of his meeting with Walker Boh. There did not seem to be any reason to hurry it. Walker had made clear his intentions, and there was nothing any of them could do about it in any case. So Par made his way back to the cottage, surprising himself at how easily he was able to retrace his steps, resumed his watch without disturbing the others, lost himself in his thoughts, and waited for dawn.

Reactions were mixed when he finally related his story. There was some initial doubt as to whether he was mistaken about what happened, but that dissipated almost at once. They made him tell the story twice more after that, interjecting comments and questions in equal measure as he went. Morgan was outraged that Walker should treat them like this, declaring that they deserved at the very least the courtesy of a direct confrontation. He insisted that they search the valley again, convinced that the man must be close by and should be found and made to face them all. Steff was more pragmatic. He was of the opinion that Walker Boh was no different from most, preferring to stay out of trouble when he could, avoiding situations in which trouble would most probably result.

"It seems to me that his behavior, however irritating you might find it, is certainly not out of character," the Dwarf declared with a shrug. "After all, you said yourselves that he came here to escape involvement with the Races. By refusing to go to the Hadeshorn, he is simply doing what he said he would do."

Teel, as usual, had nothing to say. Coll only said, "I wish I could have spoken with him," and dropped the matter.

There was no reason now to stay longer at Hearthstone, but they decided to postpone leaving for at least another day. The moon was still more than half full, and they had at least another ten days left to them before they were required to be at the Hadeshorn—if, indeed, they were going at all. The subject of what was to happen next was being carefully avoided. Par had made up his own mind, but had not yet told the others. They, of course, were waiting to hear from him. While they played at this game of cat-and-mouse, they finished breakfast and decided to go along with Morgan's suggestion and scout the valley one more time. It gave them something to do while they considered the implications of Walker Boh's decision. Tomorrow morning would be time enough to make any decisions of their own.

So they went back to the clearing where Par had met with Walker and the moor cat the previous night and began a second search, agreeing to meet back at the cottage by late afternoon. Steff and Teel formed one group, Par and Coll a second, and Morgan went alone. The day was warm and filled with sunshine, and a light breeze blew down out of the distant mountains. Steff scoured the clearing for signs of any sort and found nothing— not even the tracks of the cat. Par had a feeling that it was going to be a long day.

He walked east with Coll after parting from the others, his mind crowding with thoughts of what he should say to his brother. A mix of emotions worked their way through him, and he found it difficult to sort them out. He ambled along half-heartedly, conscious of Coll watching him from time to time, but avoiding his gaze. After they had wandered through several dozen clearings and forded half that many streams without coming on even a trace of Walker Boh, Par called a halt.

"This is a waste of time," he announced, a hint of exasperation creeping into his voice. "We're not going to find anything."

"I don't imagine we are," Coll replied.

Par turned to him, and they faced each other silently for a moment. "I have decided to go on to the Hadeshorn, Coll. It doesn't matter what Walker does; it only matters what I do. I have to go."

Coll nodded. "I know." Then he smiled. "Par, I haven't been your brother all these years without learning something about the way you think. The moment you told me that Walker had said he would have nothing to do with the matter, I knew you'd decided you would. That's the way it is with you. You're like a dog with a bone in its teeth—you can't let go."

"I suppose that's the way it seems sometimes, doesn't it?" Par shook his head wearily and moved over to a patch of shade beneath an old hickory. He turned his back to the trunk and slid to the ground. Coll joined him. They sat staring out at the empty woodlands. "I admit that I made the decision pretty much the way you describe it. I just couldn't accept Walker's position. Truth is, Coll, I couldn't even understand it. I was so upset, I didn't even think to ask him whether he believed the dreams were real or not."

"Not consciously, perhaps—but you thought about it. And you decided at some point it wasn't necessary. Walker said that he'd had the same dreams as you. He told you the old man had come to him just as he did to us. He admitted the old man was Cogline. He didn't dispute any of it. He simply said he didn't want to become involved. The implication is that he believes the dreams are real—otherwise, there wouldn't be anything to get involved with."

Par's jaw tightened. "I don't understand it, Coll. That was Walker I spoke with last night; I know it was. But he didn't talk like Walker. All that business about not becoming involved, about his decision to separate himself from the Races, and to live out here like a hermit. Something's not right; I can feel it! He wasn't telling me everything. He kept talking about how the Druids kept secrets from the Ohmsfords, but he was doing the same thing with me! He was hiding something!"

Coll looked unconvinced. "Why would he do that?"

Par shook his head. "I don't know. I just sense it." He looked at his brother sharply. "Walker never backed down from anything in his entire life; we both know that. He was never afraid to stand up and be counted when he was needed. Now he talks as if he can scarcely bear the thought of getting up in the morning! He talks as if the only important thing in life is to look out for himself!" The Valeman leaned back wearily against the hickory trunk. "He made me feel embarrassed for him. He made me feel ashamed!"

"I think you might be reading too much into this." Coll scuffed the ground with the heel of his boot. "It may be just the way he says it is. He's lived alone out here for a long time, Par. Maybe he simply isn't comfortable with people anymore."

"Even you?" Par was incensed. "For goodness sake, Coll—he wouldn't even speak with you!"

Coll shook his head and held his gaze steady. "The truth is, Par, we never spoke much as it was. You were the one he cared about, because you were the one with the magic."

Par looked at him and said nothing. Walker's exact words, he thought. He was just fooling himself when he tried to equate Coll's relationship with their uncle to his own. It had never been the same.

He frowned. "There is still the matter of the dreams. Why doesn't he share my curiosity about them? Doesn't he want to know what Allanon has to say?"

Coll shrugged. "Maybe he already knows. He seems to know what everyone is thinking most of the time."

Par hesitated. He hadn't considered that. Was it possible his uncle had already determined what the Druid would tell them at the Hadeshorn? Could he read the mind of a shade, a man three hundred years dead?

He shook his head. "No, I don't think so. He would have said something more than he did about the reason for the dreams. He spent all of his time dismissing the matter as one more instance when the Ohmsfords would be used by the Druids; he didn't care what the reason was."

"Then perhaps he is relying on you to tell him."

Par nodded slowly. "That makes better sense. I told him I was going; maybe he thinks that one of us going is enough."

Coll stretched his big frame full length on the ground and stared up into the trees. "But you don't believe that either, do you?"

His brother smiled faintly. "No."

"You still think that it's something else."

"Yes."

They didn't speak for a time, staring off into the woods,

thinking their separate thoughts. Slender streams of sunlight played along their bodies through chinks in the limbs canopied overhead, and the songs of birds filtered through the stillness. "I like it here," Par said finally.

Coll had his eyes closed. "Where do you think he's hiding?"

"Walker? I don't know. Under a rock, I suppose."

"You're too quick to judge him, Par. You don't have the right to do that."

Par bit off what he was going to say next and contented himself with watching a ray of sunlight work its way across Coll's face until it was in his eyes, causing him to blink and shift his body. Coll sat up, his squarish face a mask of contentment. Not much of anything ruffled him; he always managed to keep his sense of balance. Par admired him for that. Coll always understood the relative importance of events in the greater scheme of things.

Par was aware suddenly of how much he loved his brother.

"Are you coming with me, Coll?" he asked then. "To the Hadeshorn?"

Coll looked at him and blinked. "Isn't it odd," he replied, "that you and Walker and even Wren have the dreams and I don't, that all of you are mentioned in them, but never me, and that all of you are called, but not me?" There was no rancor in his voice, only puzzlement. "Why do you think that is? We've never talked about it, you and I, have we? Not once. I think we have both been very careful to avoid talking about it"

Par stared at him and didn't know what to say. Coll saw his discomfort and smiled. "Awkward, isn't it? Don't look so miserable, Par. It isn't as if the matter is any fault of yours." He leaned close. "Maybe it has something to do with the magic— something none of us knows yet. Maybe that's it."

Par shook his head and sighed. "I'd be lying if I said that the whole business of me having dreams and you not having them doesn't make me very uncomfortable. I don't know what to say. I keep expecting you to involve yourself in something that doesn't really concern you. I shouldn't even ask—but I guess I can't help it. You're my brother, and I want you with me."

Coll reached out and put a hand on Par's shoulder. His smile was warm. "Now and then, Par, you do manage to say the right thing." He tightened his grip. "I go where you go. That's the way it is with us. I'm not saying I always agree with the way you reason things out, but that doesn't change how I feel about you. So if you believe you must go to the Hadeshorn to resolve this matter of the dreams, then I am going with you."

Par put his arms around his brother and hugged him, thinking of all the times Coll had stood by him when he was asked, warmed by the feeling it gave him to know that Coll would be with him again now. "I knew I could depend on you," was all he said.

It WAS LATE AFTERNOON by the time they started back. They had intended to return earlier, but had become preoccupied with talking about the dreams and Allanon and had wandered all the way to the east wall of the valley before realizing how late it had become. Now, with the sun already inching toward the rim of the western horizon, they began to retrace their steps.

"It looks as if we might get our feet wet," Coll announced as they worked their way back through the trees.

Par glanced skyward. A mass of heavy rain clouds had appeared at the northern edge of the valley, darkening the whole of the skyline. The sun was already beginning to disappear, enveloped in the growing darkness. The air was warm and sticky, and the forest was hushed.

They made their way more quickly now, anxious to avoid a drenching. A stiff breeze sprang up, heralding the approach of the storm, whipping the leafy branches of the trees about them in frantic dances. The temperature began to drop, and the forest grew dark and shadowed.

Par muttered to himself as he felt a flurry of scattered raindrops strike his face. It was bad enough that they were out there looking for someone who wasn't about to be found in the first place. Now they were going to get soaked for their efforts.

Then he saw something move in the trees.

He blinked and looked again. This time he didn't see anything. He slowed without realizing it, and Coll, who was trailing a step or so behind, asked what was wrong. Par shook his head and picked up the pace again.

The wind whipped into his face, forcing him to lower his head against its sting. He glanced right, then left. There were flashes of movement to either side.

Something was tracking them.

Par felt the hair on the back of his neck prickle, but he forced himself to keep moving. Whatever was out there didn't have the look or the movement of either Walker Boh or the cat. Too quick, too agile. He tried to gather his thoughts. How far were they from the cottage—a mile, maybe less? He kept his head up as he walked, trying to follow the movement out of the corner of his eye. Movements, he corrected himself. There was clearly more than one of them.

"Par!" Coll said as they brushed close passing through a narrow winding of trees. "There's something . . ."

"I know!" Par cut him short. "Keep moving!"

They made their way through a broad stand of fir, and the rain began to fall in earnest. The sun, the walls of the valley, even the dark pinnacle of Hearthstone had disappeared. Par felt his breathing quicken. Their pursuers were all around them now, shadows that had taken on vaguely human form as they flitted through the trees.

They're closing in on us, Par thought frantically. How much farther was the cottage?

Coll cried out suddenly as they pushed through a stand of red maple into a small, empty clearing. "Par, run for it! They're too close . . . !"

He grunted sharply and pitched forward. Par wheeled instinctively and caught him. There was blood on Coll's forehead, and he was unconscious.

Par never had time to figure out what had happened. He looked up, and the shadows were on top of him. They broke from the concealment of the trees all around him, bounding into view in a flurry of motion. Par caught a brief glimpse of bent, crooked forms covered with coarse, black hair and of glinting, ferret eyes, and then they were all over him. He flung them away as he struggled to escape, feeling tough, wiry limbs grapple at him. For a moment, he kept his feet. He cried out frantically, summoning the magic of the wishsong, sending forth a scattering of frightful images in an effort to protect himself. There were howls of fear, and his attackers shrank from him.

This time, he got a good look at them. He saw the strange, insectlike forms with their vaguely human faces, all twisted and hairy.

Spider Gnomes, he thought in disbelief!

Then they were on him once more, bearing him down by the sheer weight of their numbers. He was enveloped in a mass of sinew and hair and thrown to the ground. He could no longer summon the magic. His arms were being forced back, and he was being choked. He struggled desperately, but there were too many.

He had only a moment more to try to call out for help, and then everything went dark.

CHAPTER

11

HEN HE CAME AWAKE AGAIN, Par Ohmsford found himself in the middle of a nightmare. He was bound hand and foot and hanging from a pole. He was being carried through a forest thick with mist and shadows, the dark crease of a deep ravine visible to his left, the jagged edge of a ridgeline sharp against the night sky to his right. Scrub and the dense tangle of grasses and weeds slapped at his back and head as he swung helplessly from the pole, and the air was thick, humid, and still.

There were Spider Gnomes all around him, creeping soundlessly through the half-light on crooked legs.

Par closed his eyes momentarily to shut out the images, then opened them again. The skies were dark and overcast, but a scattering of stars shone through creases in the clouds and there was a faint hint of brightness beyond the drop of the ravine. Night had come and gone, he realized. It was almost morning.

He remembered then what had happened to him, how the Spider Gnomes had chased him, seized him, and taken him away. Coll! What had happened to Coll? He craned his neck in an effort to see if his brother had been brought as well, but there was no sign of him. He clenched his jaw in rage, remembering Coll falling, then sprawled on the ground with blood on his face . . .

He wiped the image quickly from his mind. It was useless to dwell on it. He must find a way to get free and return for his brother. He worked momentarily against the ropes that bound him, testing their strength, but there was no give. Hanging as he was, he could not find the leverage necessary to loosen them. He would have to wait. He wondered then where he was being taken—why he had been taken in the first place, for that matter. What did the Spider Gnomes want of him?

Insects buzzed in his face, flying at his eyes and mouth. He buried his face into his arms and left it there.

When he brought it out again, he tried to determine where he was. The light was to his left, the beginnings of the new day. East, then, he decided—the Spider Gnomes were traveling north. That made sense. The Spider Gnomes had made their home on Toffer Ridge in Brin Ohmsford's time. That was probably where he was. He swallowed against the dryness in his mouth and throat. Thirst and fear, he thought. He tried to recall what he could of Spider Gnomes from the stories of the old days, but he was unable to focus his thoughts. Brin had encountered them when she, Rone Leah, Cogline, Kimber Boh, and the moor cat Whisper had gone after the missing Sword of Leah. There was something else, something about a wasteland and the terrifying creatures that lived within it . . .

Then he remembered. *Werebeasts.* The name whispered in his mind like a curse.

The Spider Gnomes turned down a narrow defile, filling it with their hairy forms like a dark stain, chittering now in what appeared to be anticipation. The brightness in the east disappeared, and shadows and mist closed about them like a wall. His wrists and ankles ached, and his body felt stretched beyond help. The Gnomes were small and carried him close to the ground so that he bumped and scraped himself at every turn. He watched from his upside down position as the defile broadened into a shelf that opened out over a vast, mist-shrouded stretch of emptiness that seemed to run on forever. The shelf became a corridor through a series of boulders that dotted the side of Toffer Ridge like knots on the back of a boar. Firelight flickered in the distance, pinpricks of brightness playing hide-and-seek among the rocks. A handful of Spider Gnomes bounded ahead, skittering effortlessly over the rocks.

Par took a deep breath. Wherever it was they were going, they were almost there.

A moment later, they emerged from the rocks and came to a halt on a low bluff that ran back to a series of burrows and caves tunneled into the side of the ridge. Fires burned all about, and hundreds of Spider Gnomes hoved into view. Par was dumped unceremoniously, the bonds that secured him cut and the pole removed. He lay there on his back for a moment, rubbing his wrists and ankles, finding creases so deep that he bled, conscious all the time of the eyes watching him. Then he was hauled to his feet and dragged toward the caves and burrows. They bypassed the latter in favor of the former, the gnarled hands of the Gnomes fastened on him at every conceivable point, the stink of their bodies filling his nostrils. They chittered at each other in their own language, their talk incessant now and meaningless to him. He did not resist; he could barely stand upright. They took him through the largest of the cave openings, propelled him past a small fire that burned at its mouth and stopped. There was some discussion, a few moments' worth at best, and then he was thrust forward. He saw they were in a smallish cave that ran back only twenty yards or so and was no more than eight feet at its highest point. A pair of iron rings had been hammered into the rock wall at the cave's deepest point, and the Spider Gnomes lashed him to those. Then they left him, all but two who remained behind to take up watch by the fire at the cave entrance.

Par let his mind clear, listening to the silence, waiting to see what would happen next. When nothing did, he took a careful look about. He had been left spread-eagle against the rock wall, one arm secured to each of the iron rings. He was forced to remain standing because the rings were fastened too high up on the rock to allow him to sit. He tested his bonds. They were leather and secured so tightly that his wrists could not slip within them even the smallest amount.

He sagged back momentarily in despair, forcing down the panic that threatened to overwhelm him. The others would be looking for him by now—Morgan, Steff, Teel. They would already have found Coll. They would track the Spider Gnomes and come for him. They would find him and rescue him.

He shook his head. He was just kidding himself, he knew. It was almost dark when the Gnomes had taken him and the rain had been a hard one. There would have been no time for a search and no real chance of finding a trail. The best he could hope for was that Coll had been found or revived himself and gone to the others to tell them what had happened:

He swallowed again against the dryness. He was so thirsty!

Time slipped away, turning seconds to minutes, minutes to hours. The darkness outside brightened minimally, bringing a barely penetrable daylight, choked with heat and mist. The faint sounds of the Spider Gnomes disappeared altogether, and he would have thought them gone completely if not for the two who sat hunkered down by the cave's entrance. The fire went out, smoking for a time, then turning to ash. The day slipped away. Once, one of the guards rose and brought him a cup of water. He drank it greedily from the hands that held it up to his mouth, spilling most of it, soaking his shirt front. He grew hungry as well, but no food was offered.

When the day began to fade to darkness again, the guards rebuilt the fire at the mouth of the cave, then disappeared.

Par waited expectantly, forgetting for the first time the ache of his body, the hunger and the fear. Something was going to happen now. He could feel it.

What happened was altogether unexpected. He was working again at his bonds, his sweat loosening them now, mingling with traces of his blood from the cuts the ties had made, when a figure appeared from the shadows. It came past the fire and into the light and stopped.

It was a child.

Par blinked. The child was a girl, perhaps a dozen years of age, rather tall and skinny with dark, lank hair and deepset eyes. She was not a Gnome, but of the Race of Man, a Southlander, with a tattered dress, worn boots, and a small silver locket about her neck. She looked at him curiously, studied him as she might a stray dog or cat, then came slowly forward. She stopped when she reached him, then lifted one hand to brush back his hair and touch his ear.

"Elf," she said quietly, fingering the ear's tip.

Par stared. What was a child doing out here among the Spider Gnomes? He wet his lips. "Untie me," he begged.

She looked at him some more, saying nothing. "Untie me!"

Par said again, more insistent this time. He waited, but the child just looked at him. He felt the beginnings of doubt creep through him. Something was not right.

"Hug you," the child said suddenly.

She came to him almost anxiously, wrapping her arms about him, fastening herself to him like a leech. She clung to him, burying herself in his body, murmuring over and over again something he could not understand. What was the matter with this child, he wondered in dismay? She seemed lost, frightened perhaps, needing to hold him as much as he . . .

The thought died away as he felt her stirring against him, moving within her clothes, against his clothes, then against his skin. Her fingers had tightened into him, and he could feel her pressing, pressing. Shock flooded through him. She was right against him, against his skin, as if they wore no clothes at all, as if all their garments had been shed. She was burrowing, coming against him, then coming into him, merging somehow with him, making herself a part of him.

Shades! What was happening?

Repulsion filled him with a suddenness that was terrifying. He screamed, shook himself in horror, kicked out desperately and at last flung her away. She fell in a crouch, her child's face transformed into something hideous, smiling like a beast at feeding, eyes sharp and glinting with pinpricks of red light.

"Give me the magic, boy!" she rasped in a voice that sounded nothing of a child's.

Then he knew. "Oh, no, oh, no," he whispered over and over, bracing himself as she came slowly back to her feet.

This child was a Shadowen!

"Give it to me!" she repeated, her voice demanding. "Let me come into you and taste it!"

She came toward him, a spindly little thing, a bit of nothing, if her face had not betrayed her. She reached for him and he kicked out at her desperately. She smiled wickedly and stepped back.

"You are mine," she said softly. "The Gnomes have given you to me. I will have your magic, boy. Give yourself to me. See what I can feel like!"

She came at him like a cat at its prey, avoiding his kick,

fastening herself to him with a howl. He could feel her moving almost immediately—not the child herself, but something within the child. He forced himself to look down and could see the faintest whisper of a dark outline shimmering within the child's body, trying to move into his own. He could feel its presence, like a chill on a summer's day, like fly's feet against his skin. The Shadowen was touching, seeking. He threw back his head, clenched his jaw, made his body as rigid as iron, and fought it. The thing, the Shadowen, was trying to come into him. It was trying to merge with him. Oh, Shades! He must not let it! He must not!

Then, unexpectedly, he cried out, releasing the magic of the wishsong in a howl of mingled rage and anguish. It took no form, for he had already determined that even his most frightening images were of no use against these creatures. It came of its own volition, breaking free from some dark corner of his being to take on a shape he did not recognize. It was a dark, unrecognizable thing, and it whipped about him like webbing from a spider about its prey. The Shadowen hissed and tore itself away, spitting and clawing at the air. It dropped again into a crouch, the child's body contorted and shivering from something unseen. Par's cry died into silence at the sight of it, and he sagged back weakly against the cave wall.

"Stay back from me!" he warned, gasping for breath. "Don't touch me again!"

He didn't know what he had done or how he had done it, but the Shadowen hunched down against the firelight and glared at him in defeat. The hint of the being within the child's body shimmered briefly and was gone. The glint of red in the eyes disappeared. The child rose slowly and straightened, a child in truth once more, frail and lost. Dark eyes studied him for long moments and she said faintly once more, "Hug me."

Then she called into the gathering darkness without, and the Spider Gnomes reappeared, several dozen strong, bowing and scraping to the child as they entered. She spoke to them in their own language while they knelt before her, and Par remembered how superstitious these creatures were, believing in gods and spirits of all sorts. And now they were in the thrall of a Shadowen. He wanted to scream.

The Spider Gnomes came for him, loosened the bonds that

secured him, seized his arms and legs, and pulled him forward. The child blocked their way. "Hug me?" She looked almost forlorn.

He shook his head, trying to break free of the dozens of hands that held him. He was dragged outside in the twilight haze where the smoke of the fires and the mist of the lowlands mingled and swirled like dreams in sleep. He was stopped at the bluff's edge, staring down into a pit of emptiness.

The child was beside him, her voice soft, insidious. "Olden Moor," she whispered. "Werebeasts live there. Do you know Werebeasts, Elf-boy?" He stiffened. "They shall have you now if you do not hug me. Feed on you despite your magic."

He broke free then, flinging his captors from him. The Shadowen hissed and shrank away, and the Spider Gnomes scattered. He lunged, trying to break through, but they blocked his way and bore him back. He whirled, buffeted first this way, then that. Hands reached for him, gnarled and hairy and grasping. He lost himself in a whirl of coarse bodies and chittering voices, hearing only his own voice screaming from somewhere inside not to be taken again, not to be held.

He was suddenly at the edge of the bluff. He summoned the magic of the wishsong, striking out with images at the Spider Gnomes who beset him, desperately trying to force a path through their midst. The Shadowen had disappeared, lost somewhere in the smoke and shadows.

Then he felt his feet go out from under him, the edge of the bluff giving way beneath the weight of his attackers. He grappled for them, for a handhold anywhere, and found nothing. He toppled clear of the bluff, falling into the abyss, tumbling into the swirl of mist. The Shadowen, the Spider Gnomes, the fires, caves, and burrows all disappeared behind him. Down he fell, head-over-heels, tumbling through scrub brush and grasses, across slides and between boulders. Miraculously, he missed the rocks that might have killed or crippled him, falling clear finally in a long, agonizing drop that ended in jarring blackness.

HE WAS UNCONSCIOUS for a time; he didn't know how long. When he came awake again, he found himself in a crushed bed of damp marsh grasses. The grasses, he realized, must have broken his fall and probably saved his life. He lay there, the breath knocked from his body, listening to the sound of his heart pumping in his breast. When his strength returned and his vision cleared, he climbed gingerly to his feet and checked himself. His entire body was a mass of cuts and bruises, but there appeared to be nothing broken. He stood without moving then and listened. From somewhere far above, he could hear the voice of the Spider Gnomes.

They would be coming for him, he knew. He had to get out of there.

He looked about. Mist and shadows chased each other through a twilight world of gathering darkness, night descending quickly now. Small, almost invisible things skipped and jumped through the tall grasses. Ooze sucked and bubbled all about, hidden quagmires surrounding islands of solid earth. Stunted trees and brush defined the landscape, frozen in grotesque poses. Sounds were distant and directionless. Everything seemed and looked the same, a maze without end.

Par took a deep breath to steady himself. He could guess where he was. He had been on Toffer Ridge. His fall had taken him down off the ridge and right into Olden Moor. In his efforts to escape his fate, he had only managed to find it sooner. He had put himself exactly where the Shadowen had threatened to send him—into the domain of the Werebeasts.

He set his jaw and started moving. He was only at the edge of the moor, he told himself—not fully into it yet, not lost. He still had the ridge behind him to serve as a guide. If he could follow it far enough south, he could escape. But he had to be quick.

He could almost feel the Werebeasts watching him.

The stories of the Werebeasts came back to him now, jarred free by the realization of where he was and sharpened by his fear. They were an old magic, monsters who preyed off strayed and lost creatures who wandered into the moor or were sent there, stealing away their strength and spirit and feeding on their lives. The Spider Gnomes were their principal food; the Spider Gnomes believed the Werebeasts were spirits that required appeasement, and they sacrificed themselves accordingly. Par went cold at the thought. That was what the Shadowen had intended for him.

Fatigue slowed him and made him unsteady. He stumbled several times, and once he stepped hip-deep into a quagmire before quickly pulling free. His vision was blurred, and sweat ran down his back. The moor's heat was stultifying, even at night. He glanced skyward and realized that the last of the light was fading. Soon it would be completely black.

Then he would not be able to see at all.

A massive pool of sludge barred his passage, the wall of the ridge eaten away so that it was impossible to climb past. His only choice was to go around, deeper into the moor. He moved quickly, following the line of the swamp, listening for sounds of pursuit. There were none. The moor was still and empty. He swung back toward the bluff, encountered a maze of gullies with masses of things moving through them, and swung wide again. Steadily, he went on, exhausted, but unable to rest. The darkness deepened. He found the end of the maze and started back again toward the bluff. He walked a long way, circling quagmires and sinkholes, peering expectantly through the gloom.

He could not find Toffer Ridge.

He walked more quickly now, anxious, fighting down the fear that threatened to overwhelm him. He was lost, he realized—but he refused to accept it. He kept searching, unable to believe that he could have mistaken his direction so completely. The base of the ridge had been right there! How could he have become so turned about?

At last he stopped, unable to continue with the charade. There was no point in going on, because the truth of the matter was he had no idea where he was going. He would simply continue to wander about endlessly until either the swamp or the Werebeasts claimed him. It was better that he stand and fight.

It was an odd decision, one brought about less by sound reasoning than by fatigue. After all, what hope was there for him if he didn't escape the moor and how could he escape the moor if he stopped moving? But he was tired and he didn't like the idea of running about blindly. And he kept thinking of that child, that Shadowen—shrinking from him, driven back by some shading of his magic that he hadn't even known existed. He still didn't understand what it was, but if he could somehow summon it again and master it in even the smallest way, then he had a chance against the Werebeasts and anything else the swamp might send against him.

He glanced about momentarily, then walked to a broad hillock with quagmire on two sides, jutting rocks on a third, and only one way in. Only one way out, as well, he reminded himself as he ascended the rise, but then he wasn't going anywhere, was he? He found a flat rock and seated himself, facing out into the mist and night. Until it grew light again, this was where he would make his stand.

The minutes slipped away. Night descended, the mist thickened, but there was still light, a sort of curious phosphorescence given off by the sparse vegetation. Its glow was faint and deceptive, but it gave Par the means to distinguish what lay about him and the belief that he could catch sight of anything sneaking up.

Nevertheless, he didn't see the Shadowen until it was almost on top of him. It was the child again, tall, thin, wasted. She appeared seemingly out of nowhere, no more than a few yards in front of him, and he started with the suddenness of her coming.

"Get back from me!" he warned, coming quickly to his feet. "If you try to touch me . . ."

The Shadowen shimmered into mist and disappeared.

Par took a deep breath. It hadn't been a Shadowen after all, he thought, but a Werebeast—and not so tough, if he could send it packing with just a threat!

He wanted to laugh. He was near exhaustion, both physically and emotionally, and he knew he was no longer entirely rational. He hadn't chased anything away. That Werebeast had simply come in for a look. They were toying with him, the way they did with their prey—taking on familiar forms, waiting for the right opportunity, for fatigue or fright or foolishness to give them an opening. He thought again about the stories, about the inevitability of the stalking, then pushed it all from his mind.

Somewhere in the distance, far from where he sat, something cried out once, a quick shriek of dismay. Then everything was still again.

He stared into the mist, watching. He found himself thinking of the circumstances that had brought him here—of his flight from the Federation, of his dreams, his meeting with the old man, and his search for Walker Boh. He had come a long way because of those circumstances and he still wasn't anywhere. He felt a pang of disappointment that he hadn't accomplished more, that he hadn't learned anything useful. He thought again of his conversation with Walker. Walker had told him the wishsong's magic was not a gift, despite his insistence that it was, and that there wasn't anything worthwhile to discover about its use. He shook his head. Well, perhaps there wasn't. Perhaps he had just been kidding himself all along.

But something about it had frightened that Shadowen. Something.

Yet only that child, not any of the others that he had encountered.

What had been different?

There was movement again at the edge of the mists, and a figure detached itself and moved toward him. It was the second Shadowen, the great, shambling creature they had encountered at the edge of the Anar. It slouched toward him, grunting, carrying a monstrous club. For a moment, he forgot what he was facing. He panicked, remembering that the wishsong had been ineffective against this Shadowen, that he had been helpless. He started to back away, then caught himself, thrust away his confusion and shook clear his mind. Impulsively, he used the wishsong, its magic creating an identical image of the creature facing him, an image that he used to cloak himself. Shadowen faced Shadowen. Then the Werebeast shimmered and faded back into the mist.

Par went still and let the image concealing him dissolve. He sat down again. How long could he keep this up?

He wondered if Coll was all right. He saw his brother stretched upon the earth bleeding and he remembered how helpless he had felt at that moment. He thought about how much he depended on his brother.

Coll.

His mind wandered, shifted. There was a use for his magic, he told himself sternly. It was not as Walker had said. There was a purpose in his having it; it was indeed a gift. He would find the answers at the Hadeshorn. He would find them when he spoke to Allanon. He must simply get free of this moor and . . .

A gathering of shadowy forms emerged from the mists before him, dark and forbidding bits of ethereal motion in the night. The Werebeasts had decided to wait no longer. He jerked to his feet, facing them. They eased gradually closer, first one, then another, none with any discernible shape, all shifting and changing as rapidly as the mists.

Then he saw Coll, pulled from the darkness behind the shadows, gripped in substanceless hands, his face ashen and bloodied. Par went cold. *Help me,* he heard his brother call out, though the sound of the voice was only in his mind. *Help me, Par.*

Par screamed something with the magic of the wishsong, but it dissipated into the dank air of Olden Moor in a scattering of broken sounds. Par shook as if chilled. Shades! That really was Coll! His brother struggled, fighting to break free, calling out repeatedly, *Par, Par!*

He went to his brother's aid almost without thinking. He attacked the Werebeasts with a fury that was entirely unexpected. He cried out, the wishsong's magic thrusting at the creatures, hammering them back. He reached Coll and seized him, pulling him free. Hands groped for him, touching. He felt pain, freezing and burning both at once. Coll gripped him, and the pain intensified. Poison flooded into him, bitter and harsh. His strength almost gave out, but he managed to keep his feet, hauling his brother clear of the shadows, pulling him onto the rise.

Below, the shadows clustered and shifted watchfully. Par howled down at them, knowing he was infected, feeling the poison work its way through his body. Coll stood next to him, not speaking. Par's thoughts scattered, and his sense of what he was about drifted away.

The Werebeasts began to close.

Then there was fresh movement on the rocks to his right, and something huge appeared. Par tried to move away, but the effort brought him to his knees. Great, luminous yellow eyes blinked into the night, and a massive black shadow bounded to his side.

"Rumor!" he whispered in disbelief.

The moor cat edged carefully past him to face Coll. The huge cat growled, a low, dangerous warning cough that seemed to break through the mist and fill the darkness with shards of sound. "Coll?" Par called out to his brother and started forward, but the moor cat quickly blocked his way, shoving him back. The shadows were moving closer, taking on form now, becoming lumbering things, bodies covered with scales and hair, faces that showed demon eyes and jaws split wide in hunger. Rumor spat at them and lunged, bringing them up short to hiss back at him.

Then he whirled with claws and teeth bared and tore Coll to pieces.

Coll—what had appeared to be Coll—turned into a thing of indescribable horror, bloodied and shredded, then shimmered and disappeared—another deception. Par cried out in anguish and fury. Tricked! Ignoring the pain and the sudden nausea, he sent the magic of the wishsong hurtling at the Werebeasts, daggers and arrows of fury, images of things that could rend and tear. The Werebeasts shimmered and the magic passed harmlessly by.

Re-forming, the Werebeasts attacked.

Rumor caught the closest a dozen paces off, hammering it away with a single breathtaking swipe of one great paw. Another lunged, but the cat caught it as well and sent it spinning. Others were appearing now from the shadows and mist behind those already creeping forward. Too many, thought Par frantically! He was too weak to stand, the poison from the Werebeasts' touch seeping through him rapidly now, threatening to drop him into that familiar black abyss that had begun to open within.

Then he felt a hand on his shoulder, firm and instantly comforting, reassuring him and at the same time holding him in place, and he heard a voice call sharply, "Rumor!"

The moor cat edged back, never turning to look, responding to the sound of the voice alone. Par lifted his face. Walker Boh was beside him, wrapped in black robes and mist, his narrow, chiseled face set in a look that turned Par cold, his skin so white it might have been drawn in chalk.

"Keep still, Par," he said.

He moved forward to face the Werebeasts. There were more than a dozen now, crouched down at the edge of the rise, drifting in and out of the mist and night. They hesitated at Walker Boh's approach, almost as if they knew him. Par's uncle came directly down to them, stopping when he was less than a dozen yards from the nearest.

"Leave," he said simply and pointed off into the night. The Werebeasts held their ground. Walker came forward another step, and this time his voice was so hard that it seemed to shiver the air. "Leave!"

One of them lunged at him, a monstrous thing, jaws snapping as it reached for the black-robed figure. Walker Boh's hand shot out, dust scattering into the beast. Fire erupted into the night with an explosion that rocked the bottomland, and the Werebeast simply disappeared.

Walker's extended hand swept the circle of those that remained, threatening. An instant later, the Werebeasts had faded back into the night and were gone.

Walker turned and came back up the rise, kneeling next to Par. "This is my fault," he said quietly.

Par struggled to speak and felt his strength give out. He was sick. Consciousness slipped away. For the third time in less than two days, he tumbled into the abyss. He remembered thinking as he fell that this time he was not sure he would be able to climb out again.

CHAPTER

12

AR OHMSFORD DRIFTED through a landscape of dreams. He was both within himself and without as he journeyed, a participant and a viewer. There was constant motion, sometimes as charged as a voyage across a stormy sea, sometimes as gentle as the summer wind through the trees. He spoke to himself alternately in the dark silence of his mind and from within a mirrored self-image. His voice was a disembodied whisper and a thunderous shout. Colors appeared and faded to black and white. Sounds came and departed. He was all things on his journey, and he was none.

The dreams were his reality.

He dreamed in the beginning that he was falling, tumbling downward into a pit as black as night and as endless as the cycle of the seasons. There were pain and fear in him; he could not find himself. Sometimes there were voices, calling to him in warning, in comfort, or in horror. He convulsed within himself. He knew somehow that if he did not stop falling, he would be forever lost.

He did stop finally. He slowed and leveled, and his convulsions ceased. He was in a field of wildflowers as wondrous as a rainbow. Birds and butterflies scattered at his approach, filling the air with new brightness, and the smells of the field were soft and fragrant. There was no sound. He tried to speak so that there might be, but found himself voiceless. Nor did he have touch. He could feel nothing of himself, nothing of the world about him. There was warmth, soothing and extended, but that was all.

He drifted and a voice somewhere deep within him whispered that he was dead.

The voice, he thought, belonged to Walker Boh.

Then the world of sweet smells and sights disappeared, and he was in a world of darkness and stench. Fire erupted from the earth and spat at an angry, smudge-colored sky. Shadowen flitted and leaped, red eyes glinting as they whipped about him, hovering one moment, ducking away the next. Clouds rolled overhead, filled with lightning, borne on a wind that howled in fury. He felt himself buffeted and tossed, thrown like a dried leaf across the earth, and he sensed it was the end of all things. Touch and voice returned, and he felt his pain once more and cried out with it.

"Par?"

The voice came once and was gone again—Coll's voice. But he saw Coll in his dream then, stretched against a gathering of rocks, lifeless and bloodied, eyes open in accusation. "You left me. You abandoned me." He screamed and the magic of the wishsong threw images everywhere. But the images turned into monsters that wheeled back to devour him. He could feel their teeth and claws. He could feel their touch . . .

He came awake.

Rain fell into his face, and his eyes opened. There was darkness all about, the sense of others close at hand, a feeling of motion, and the coppery taste of blood. There was shouting, voices that called to one another against the fury of a storm. He rose up, choking, spitting. Hands bore him back again, slipping against his body and face.

". . . awake again, hold him . . ."

". . . too strong, like he's ten instead of . . ."

"Walker! Hurry!"

Trees thrashed in the background, long-limbed giants lifting into the roiling black, the wind howling all about them. They threw shadows against cliffs that blocked their passage and threatened to pen them up. Par heard himself scream.

Lightning crashed and thunder rolled, filling the dark with echoes of madness. A wash of red screened his vision.

Then Allanon was there—Allanon! He came from nowhere, all in black robes, a figure out of legend and time. He bent close to Par, his voice a whisper that somehow managed to rise above the chaos. Sleep, Par, he soothed. One weathered hand reached out and touched the Valeman, and the chaos dissipated and was replaced by a profound sense of peace.

Par drifted away again, far down into himself, fighting now because he sensed that he would live if he could just will it to be so. Some part of him remembered what had happened—that the Werebeasts had seized him, that their touch had poisoned him, that the poison had made him sick, and that the sickness had dropped him into that black abyss. Walker had come for him, found him somehow, and saved him from those creatures. He saw Rumor's yellow lamp eyes, blinking in warning, lidding and going out. He saw Coll and Morgan. He saw Steff, his smile sardonic, and Teel, enigmatic and silent.

He saw the Shadowen girl-child, begging again to be hugged, trying to enter his body. He felt himself resist, saw her thrown back, watched as she disappeared. Shades! She had tried to enter him, to come into him, to put herself within his skin and become him! That was what they were, he thought in a burst of understanding—shadows that lacked substance of their own and took the bodies of men. And women. And children.

But can shadows have life?

His thoughts jumbled around unanswerable questions, and he slipped from reason to confusion. His mind slept, and his journey through the land of dreams wore on. He climbed mountains filled with creatures like the Gnawl, crossed rivers and lakes of mist and hidden dangers, traversed forests where daylight never penetrated, and swept on into moors where mist stirred in an airless, empty cauldron of silence.

Help me, he begged. But there was no one to hear.

Time suspended then. The journey ended and the dreams faded into nothingness. There was a moment's pause at their end, and then waking. He knew he had slept, but not for how long. He knew only that there had been a passage of time when the dreams had ended and dreamless sleep had begun.

More important, he knew that he was alive.

He stirred gingerly, barely more than a twitch, feeling the softness of sheets and a bed beneath him, aware that he was stretched out full-length and that he was warm and snug. He did not want to move yet, frightened that he might still be dreaming. He let the feel of the sheets soak through him. He listened to the sound of his own breathing in his ears. He tasted the dryness of the air.

Then he let his eyes slip open. He was in a small, sparsely furnished room lit by a single lamp set on a table at his bedside. The walls of the room were bare, the ceiling beams uncovered. A comforter wrapped him and pillows cradled his head. A break in the curtains that covered the windows opposite where he lay told him it was night.

Morgan Leah dozed in a chair just inside the circle of light given off by the lamp, his chin resting on his chest, his arms folded loosely. "Morgan?" he called, his voice sounding fuzzy.

The Highlander's eyes snapped open, his hawk face instantly alert. He blinked, then jumped to his feet. "Par! Par, are you awake? Good heavens, we've been worried sick!" He rushed over as if to hug his friend, then thought better of it. He ran the fingers of one hand through his rust-colored hair distractedly. "How do you feel? Are you all right?"

Par grinned weakly. "I don't know yet. I'm still waking up. What happened?"

"What *didn't* happen is more like it!" the other replied heatedly. "You almost died, do you realize that?"

Par nodded. "I guessed it. What about Coll, Morgan?"

"Sleeping, waiting for you to come around. I packed him off several hours ago when he fell out of his chair. You know Coll. Wait here, I'll get him." He grinned. "Wait here, I tell you—as if you were going anywhere. Pretty funny."

Par had a dozen things he wanted to say, questions he wanted to ask, but the Highlander was already out the door and gone. It didn't matter, he guessed. He lay back quietly, flooded with relief. All that mattered was that Coll was all right.

Morgan returned almost immediately, Coll beside him, and Coll, unlike Morgan, did not hesitate as he reached down and practically squeezed the life out of Par in his enthusiasm at finding him awake. Par hugged him back, albeit weakly, and the three laughed as if they had just enjoyed the biggest joke of their lives.

"Shades, we thought we'd lost you!" Coll exclaimed softly. He wore a bandage taped to his forehead, and his face seemed pale. "You were very sick, Par."

Par smiled and nodded. He'd heard enough of that. "Will someone tell me what happened?" His eyes shifted from one face to the other. "Where are we anyway?"

"Storlock," Morgan announced. One eyebrow arched. "Walker Boh brought you here."

"Walker?"

Morgan grinned with satisfaction. "Thought you'd be surprised to learn that—Walker Boh coming out of the Wilderun, Walker Boh appearing in the first place for that matter." He sighed. "Well, it's a long story, so I guess we'd better start at the beginning."

He did, telling the story with considerable help from Coll, the two of them stepping on each other's words in their eagerness to make certain that nothing was overlooked. Par listened in growing surprise as the tale unfolded.

Coll, it seemed, had been felled by a Gnome sling when the Spider Gnomes attacked them in that clearing at the eastern end of the valley at Hearthstone. He had only been stunned, but, by the time he had recovered consciousness, Par and their attackers were gone. It was raining buckets by then, the trail disappearing back into the earth as quickly as it was made, and Coll was too weak to give chase in any case. So he stumbled back to the cottage where he found the others and told them what had occurred. It was already dark by then and still raining, but Coll demanded they go back out anyway and search for his brother. They did, Morgan, Steff, Teel, and himself, groping about blindly for hours and finding nothing. When it became impossible to see anything, Steff insisted they give it up for the night, get some rest and start out again fresh in the morning. That was what they did, and that was how Coll encountered Walker Boh.

"We split up, trying to cover as much ground as possible, working the north valley, because I knew from the stories of

Brin and Jair Ohmsford that the Spider Gnomes made their homes on Toffer Ridge and it was likely they had come from there. At least, I hoped so, because that was all we had to go on. We agreed that if we didn't find you right away we would just keep on going until we reached the Ridge." He shook his head. "We were pretty desperate."

"We were," Morgan agreed.

"Anyway, I was all the way to the northeast edge of the valley when, all of a sudden, there was Walker and that giant cat, big as a house! He said that he'd sensed something. He asked me what had happened, what was wrong. I was so surprised to see him that I didn't even think to ask what he was doing there or why he had decided to appear after hiding all that time. I just told him what he wanted to know."

"Do you know what he said then?" Morgan interrupted, gray eyes finding Par's, a hint of the mischievousness in them.

"He said," Coll took control again of the conversation, " 'Wait here, this is no task for you; I will bring him back'—as if we were children playing at a grown-up's game!"

"But he was as good as his word," Morgan noted.

Coll sighed. "Well, true enough," he admitted grudgingly.

Walker Boh was gone a full day and night, but when he returned to Hearthstone, where Coll and his companions were indeed waiting, he had Par with him. Par had been infected by the touch of the Werebeasts and was near death. The only hope for him, Walker insisted, lay at Storlock, the community of Gnome healers. The Stors had experience in dealing with afflictions of the mind and spirit and could combat the Werebeasts' poison.

They set out at once, the six of them less the cat, who had been left behind. They pushed west out of Hearthstone and the Wilderun, following the Chard Rush upriver to the Wolfsktaag, crossing through the Pass of Jade, and finally reaching the village of the Stors. It had taken them two days, traveling almost constantly. Par would have died if not for Walker, who had used an odd sort of magic that none of them had understood to prevent the poison from spreading and to keep Par sleeping and calm. At times, Par had thrashed and cried out, waking feverish and spitting blood—once in the middle of a ferocious storm they had encountered in the Pass of Jade—but Walker had been there to soothe him, to touch him, to say something that let him sleep once more.

"Even so, we've been in Storlock for almost three days and this is the first time you've been awake," Coll finished. He paused, eyes lowering. "It was very close, Par."

Par nodded, saying nothing. Even without being able to remember anything clearly, he had a definite sense of just how close it had been. "Where is Walker?" he asked finally.

"We don't know," Morgan answered with a shrug. "We haven't seen him since we arrived. He just disappeared."

"Gone back to the Wilderun, I suppose," Coll added, a touch of bitterness in his voice.

"Now, Coll," Morgan soothed.

Coll held up his hands. "I know, Morgan—I shouldn't judge. He was there to help when we needed him. He saved Par's life. I'm grateful for that."

"Besides, I think he's still around," Morgan said quietly. When the other two looked inquiringly at him, he simply shrugged.

Par told them what had befallen him after his capture by the Spider Gnomes. He was still reasoning out a good part of it, so he hesitated from time to time in his telling. He was convinced that the Spider Gnomes had been sent specifically to find him, otherwise they would have taken Coll as well. The Shadowen had sent them, that girl-child. Yet how had it known who he was or where he could be found?

The little room was silent as they thought. "The magic," Morgan suggested finally. "They all seem interested in the magic. This one must have sensed it as well."

"All the way from Toffer Ridge?" Par shook his head doubtfully.

"And why not go after Morgan as well?" Coll asked suddenly. "After all, he commands the magic of the Sword of Leah."

"No, no, that's not the sort of magic they care about," Morgan replied quickly. "It's Par's sort of magic that interests them, draws them—magic that's part of the body or spirit."

"Or maybe it's simply Par," Coll finished darkly.

They let the thought hang a moment in the silence. "The

Shadowen tried to come into me," Par said finally, then explained it to them in more detail. "It wanted to merge with me, to be a part of me. It kept saying, 'hug me, hug me'—as if it were a lost child or something."

"Hardly that," Coll disputed quickly.

"More leech than lost child," Morgan agreed.

"But what are they?" Par pressed, bits and pieces of his dreams coming back to him, flashes of insight that lacked meaning. "Where is it that they come from and what is it that they want?"

"Us," Morgan said quietly.

"You," Coll said.

They talked a bit longer, mulling over what little they knew of Shadowen and their interest in magic, then Coll and Morgan rose. Time for Par to rest again, they insisted. He was still sick, still weak, and he needed to get his strength back.

The Hadeshorn, Par remembered suddenly! How much time did they have before the new moon?

Coll sighed. "Four days—if you still insist on going."

Morgan grinned from behind him. "We'll be close by if you need us. Good to see you well again, Par."

He slipped out the door. "It is good," Coll agreed and gripped his brother's hand tightly.

When they were gone, Par lay with his eyes open for a time, letting his thoughts nudge and push one another. Questions whispered at him, asking for answers he didn't have. He had been chased and harried from Varfleet to the Rainbow Lake, from Culhaven to Hearthstone, by the Federation and the Shadowen, by things that he had only heard about and some he hadn't even known existed. He was tired and confused; he had almost lost his life. Everything centered on his magic, and yet his magic had been virtually useless to him. He was constantly running from one thing and toward another without really understanding much of either. He felt helpless.

And despite the presence of his brother and his friends, he felt oddly alone.

His last thought before he fell asleep was that, in a way he didn't yet comprehend, he was.

HE SLEPT FITFULLY, but without dreaming, waking often amid stirrings of dissatisfaction and wariness that darted through the corridors of his mind like harried rats. Each time he came awake it was still night, until the last time when it was almost dawn, the sky beyond the curtained window brightening faintly, the room in which he lay still and gauzy. A white-robed Stor passed briefly through the room, appearing from out of the shadows like a ghost to pause at his bedside and touch his wrist and forehead with hands that were surprisingly warm before turning and disappearing back the way he had come. Par slept soundly after that, drifting far down within himself and floating undisturbed in a sea of black warmth.

When he woke again, it was raining. His eyes blinked open and he stared fixedly into the grayness of his room. He could hear the sound of the raindrops beating on the windows and roof, a steady drip and splash in the stillness. There was daylight yet; he could see it through the part in the curtains. Thunder rolled in the distance, echoing in long, uneven peals.

Gingerly, he hoisted himself up on one elbow. He saw a fire burning in a small stove that he hadn't even noticed the previous night, tucked back in the shadows. It gave a solid warmth to the room that wrapped and cradled him and made him feel secure. There was tea by his bedside and tiny cakes. He pushed himself up the rest of the way, propping himself against the headboard of his bed with his pillows and pulling the cakes and tea to him. He was famished, and he devoured the cakes in seconds. Then he drank a small portion of the tea, which had gone cold in the sitting, but was wonderful in any case.

He was midway through his third cup when the door opened soundlessly and Walker Boh appeared. His uncle paused momentarily on seeing him awake, then closed the door softly and came over to stand at his bedside. He was dressed in forest green—tunic and pants belted tight, soft leather boots unlaced and muddied, long travel cloak spotted with rain. There was rain on his bearded face as well, and his dark hair was damp against his skin.

He pushed the travel cloak back across his shoulders. "Feeling better?" he asked quietly.

Par nodded. "Much." He set his cup aside. "I understand I

have you to thank for that. You saved me from the Werebeasts. You brought me back to Hearthstone. It was your idea to bring me to Storlock. Coll and Morgan tell me that you even used magic to see to it that I stayed alive long enough to complete the journey."

"Magic." Walker repeated the word softly, his voice distracted. "Words and touching in combination, a sort of variation on the workings of the wishsong. My legacy from Brin Ohmsford. I haven't the curse of the fullness of her powers—only the annoyance of its shadings. Still, now and again, it does become the gift you insist it must be. I can interact with another living thing, feel its life force, sometimes find a way to strengthen it." He paused. "I don't know if I would call it magic, though."

"And what you did to the Werebeasts in Olden Moor when you stood up for me—was that not magic?"

His uncle's eyes shifted away from him. "I was taught that," he said finally.

Par waited a moment, but when nothing more was forthcoming he said, "I'm grateful for all of it in any case. Thank you."

The other man shook his head slowly. "I don't deserve your thanks. It was my fault that it happened in the first place."

Par readjusted himself carefully against his pillows. "I seem to remember you saying that before."

Walker moved to the far end of the bed and sat down on its edge. "If I had watched over you the way I should have, the Spider Gnomes would never have even gotten into the valley. Because I chose to distance myself from you, they did. You risked a fair amount in coming to find me in the first place; the least I could have done was to make certain that once you reached me, you would be safe. I failed to do that."

"I don't blame you for what happened," Par said quickly.

"But I do." Walker rose, as restless as a cat, stalking to the windows and peering out into the rain. "I live apart because I choose to. Other men in other times made me decide that it was best. But I forget sometimes that there is a difference between disassociating and hiding. There are limits to the distances we can place between ourselves and others—because the dictates of our world don't allow for absolutes." He looked back, his skin pale against the grayness of the day. "I was hiding myself when you came to find me. That was why you went unprotected."

Par did not fully understand what Walker was trying to say, but he chose not to interrupt, anxious to hear more. Walker turned from the window after a moment and came back. "I haven't been to see you since you were brought here," he said, coming to a stop at Par's bedside. "Did you know that?"

Par nodded, again keeping silent. "It wasn't that I was ignoring you. But I knew you were safe, that you would be well, and I wanted time to think. I went out into the woodlands by myself. I returned for the first time this morning. The Stors told me that you were awake, that the poison was dispelled, and I decided to come to see you."

He broke off, his gaze shifting. When he spoke again, he chose his words carefully. "I have been thinking about the dreams."

There was another brief silence. Par shifted uncomfortably in the bed, already beginning to feel tired. His strength would be awhile returning. Walker seemed to recognize the problem and said, "I won't be staying much longer."

He sat down again slowly. "I anticipated that you might come to me after the dreams began. You were always impulsive. I thought about the possibility, about what I would say to you." He paused. "We are close in ways you do not entirely understand, Par. We share the legacy of the magic; but more than that, we share a preordained future that may preclude our right to any meaningful form of self-determination." He paused again, smiling faintly. "What I mean, Par, is that we are the children of Brin and Jair Ohmsford, heirs to the magic of the Elven house of Shannara, keepers of a trust. Remember now? It was Allanon who gave us that trust, who said to Brin when he lay dying that the Ohmsfords would safeguard the magic for generations to come until it was again needed."

Par nodded slowly, beginning to understand now. "You believe we might be the ones for whom the trust was intended."

"I believe it—and I am frightened by the possibility as I have never been frightened of anything in my life!" Walker's voice was a low hiss. "I am terrified of it! I want no part of the Druids and their mysteries! I want nothing to do with the Elven magic, with its demands and its treacheries! I wish only to be left alone, to live out my life in a way I believe useful and fulfilling—and that is all I wish!"

Par let his eyes drop protectively against the fury of the other man's words. Then he smiled sadly. "Sometimes the choice isn't ours, Walker."

Walker Boh's reply was unexpected. "That was what I decided." His lean face was hard as Par looked up again. "While I waited for you to wake, while I kept myself apart from the others, out there in the forests beyond Storlock, that was what I decided." He shook his head. "Events and circumstances sometimes conspire against us; if we insist on inflexibility for the purpose of maintaining our beliefs, we end up compromising ourselves nevertheless. We salvage one set of principles only to forsake another. My staying hidden within the Wilderun almost cost you your life once. It could do so again. And what would that, in turn, cost me?"

Par shook his head. "You cannot hold yourself responsible for the risks I choose to take, Walker. No man can hold himself up to that standard of responsibility."

"Oh, but he can, Par. And he must when he has the means to do so. Don't you see? If I have the means, I have the responsibility to employ them." He shook his head sadly. "I might wish it otherwise, but it doesn't change the fact of its being."

He straightened. "Well, I came to tell you something, and I still haven't done so. Best that I get it over with so you can rest." He rose, pulling the damp forest cloak about him as if to ward off a chill. "I am going with you," he said simply.

Par stiffened in surprise. "To the Hadeshorn?"

Walker Boh nodded. "To meet with Allanon's shade—if indeed it is Allanon's shade who summons us—and to hear what it will say. I make no promises beyond that, Par. Nor do I make any further concessions to your view of matters—other than to say that I think you were right in one respect. We cannot pretend that the world begins and ends at the boundaries we might make for it. Sometimes, we must acknowledge that it extends itself into our lives in ways we might prefer it wouldn't, and we must face up to the challenges it offers."

His face was lined with emotions Par could only begin to

imagine." "I, too, would like to know something of what is intended for me," he whispered.

He reached down, his pale, lean hand fastening briefly on one of Par's. "Rest now. We have another journey ahead and only a day or two to prepare for it. Let that preparation be my responsibility. I will tell the others and come for you all when it is time to depart."

He started away, then hesitated and smiled. "Try to think better of me after this."

Then he was out the door and gone, and the smile belonged now to Par.

WALKER BOH PROVED as good as his word. Two days later he was back, appearing shortly after sunrise with horses and provisions. Par had been out of bed and walking about for the past day and a half now, and he was much recovered from his experience in Olden Moor. He was dressed and waiting on the porch of his compound with Steff and Teel when his uncle walked out of the forest shadows with his pack train in tow into a morning clouded by fog and half-light.

"There's a strange one," Steff murmured. "Haven't seen him for more than five minutes for the entire time we've been here. Now, back he comes, just like that. More ghost than man." His smile was rueful and his eyes sharp.

"Walker Boh is real enough," Par replied without looking at the Dwarf. "And haunted by ghosts of his own."

"Brave ghosts, I am inclined to think."

Par glanced over now. "He still frightens you, doesn't he?"

"Frightens me?" Steff's voice was gruff as he laughed. "Hear him, Teel? He probes my armor for chinks!" He turned his scarred face briefly. "No, Valeman, he doesn't frighten me anymore. He only makes me wonder."

Coll and Morgan appeared, and the little company prepared to depart. Stors came out to see them off, ghosts of another sort, dressed in white robes and cloaked in self-imposed silence, a perpetually anxious look on their pale faces. They gathered in groups, watchful, curious, a few coming forward to help as the members of the company mounted. Walker spoke with one or two of them, his words so quiet they could be heard by no one else. Then he was aboard with the others and facing briefly back to them.

"Good fortune to us, my friends," he said and turned his horse west toward the plains.

Good fortune, indeed, Par Ohmsford prayed silently.

CHAPTER

13

SUNLIGHT SPRAYED THE STILL SURFACE of the Myrian Lake through breaks in the distant trees, coloring the water a brilliant red-gold and causing Wren Ohmsford to squint against its glare. Farther west, the Irrybis Mountains were a jagged black tear across the horizon that separated earth and sky and cast the first of night's shadows across the vast sprawl of the Tirfing.

Another hour, maybe a bit more, and it would be dark, she thought.

She paused at the edge of the lake and, for just a moment, let the solitude of the approaching dusk settle through her. All about, the Westland stretched away into the shimmering heat of the dying summer's day with the lazy complacency of a sleeping cat, endlessly patient as it waited for the coming of night and the cool it would bring.

She was running out of time.

She cast about momentarily for the signs she had lost some hundred yards back and found nothing. He might as well have vanished into thin air. He was working hard at this cat-and-mouse game, she decided. Perhaps she was the cause.

The thought buoyed her as she pressed ahead, slipping silently through the trees along the lake front, scanning the foliage and the earth with renewed determination. She was small and slight of build, but wiry and strong. Her skin was nut-brown from weather and sun, and her ash-blond hair was almost boyish, cut short and tightly curled against her head. Her features were Elven, sharply so, the eyebrows full and deeply slanted, the ears small and pointed, the bones of her face lending it a narrow and high-cheeked look. She had hazel eyes, and they shifted restlessly as she moved, hunting.

She found his first mistake a hundred feet or so farther on, a tiny bit of broken scrub, and his second, a boot indentation against a gathering of stones, just after. She smiled in spite of herself, her confidence growing, and she hefted the smooth quarterstaff she carried in anticipation. She would have him yet, she promised.

The lake cut into the trees ahead forming a deep cove, and she was forced to swing back to her left through a thick stand of pine. She slowed, moving more cautiously. Her eyes darted. The pines gave way to a mass of thick brush that grew close against a grove of cedar. She skirted the brush, catching sight of a fresh scrape against a tree root. He's getting careless, she thought—or wants me to think so.

She found the snare at the last moment, just as she was about to put her foot into it. Its lines ran from a carefully concealed noose back into a mass of brush and from there to a stout sapling, bent and tied. Had she not seen it, she would have been yanked from her feet and left dangling.

She found the second snare immediately after, better concealed and designed to catch her avoiding the first. She avoided that one, too, and now became even more cautious.

Even so, she almost missed seeing him in time when he swung down out of the maple not more than fifty yards farther on. Tired of trying to lose her in the woods, he had decided to finish matters in a quicker manner. He dropped silently as she slipped beneath the old shade tree, and it was only her instincts that saved her. She sprang aside as he landed, bringing the quarterstaff about and catching him alongside his great shoulders with an audible thwack. Her attacker shrugged off the blow, coming to his feet with a grunt. He was huge, a man of formidable size who appeared massive in the confines of the tiny forest clearing. He leaped at Wren, and she used the quarterstaff to vault quickly away from him. She slipped on landing, and he was on top of her with a swiftness that was astonishing. She rolled, using the staff to block him, came up underneath with the makeshift dagger and jammed the flat of its blade against his belly.

The sun-browned, bearded face shifted to find her own, and the deepset eyes glanced downward. "You're dead, Garth," she told him, smiling. Then her fingers came up to make the signs.

The giant Rover collapsed in mock submission before rolling over and climbing to his feet. Then he smiled, too. They brushed themselves off and stood grinning at each other in the fading light. "I'm getting better, aren't I?" Wren asked, signing with her hands as she spoke the words.

Garth replied soundlessly, his fingers moving rapidly in the language he had taught her. "Better, but not yet good enough," she translated. Her smile broadened as she reached out to clasp his arm. "Never good enough for you, I suspect. Otherwise, you would be out of a job!"

She picked up the quarterstaff and made a mock feint that caused the other to jump back in alarm. They fenced for a moment, then broke it off and started back toward the lakeshore. There was a small clearing just beyond the cove, not more than half an hour away, that offered an ideal campsite for the night. Wren had noticed it during the hunt and made for it now.

"I'm tired and I ache and I have never felt better," the girl said cheerfully as they walked, enjoying the last of the day's sunlight on her back, breathing in the smells of the forest, feeling alive and at peace. She sang a bit, humming some songs of the Rovers and the free life, of the ways that were and the ways that would be. Garth trailed along, a silent shadow at her back.

They found the campsite, built a fire, prepared and ate their dinner, and began trading drinks from a large leather aleskin. The night was warm and comforting, and Wren Ohmsford's thoughts wandered contentedly. They had another five days allotted to them before they were expected back. She enjoyed her outings with Garth; they were exciting and challenging. The big Rover was the best of teachers—one who let his students learn from experience. No one knew more than he did about tracking, concealment, snares, traps, and tricks of all sorts in the fine art of staying alive. He had been her mentor from the first. She had never questioned why he chose her; she had simply felt grateful that he had.

She listened momentarily to the sounds of the forest, trying to visualize out of habit what she heard moving in the dark. It was a strenuous, demanding life she led, but she could no longer imagine leading any other. She had been born a Rover girl and lived with them for all but the very early years of her youth when she had resided in the Southland hamlet of Shady Vale with her cousins, the Ohmsfords. She had been back in the Westland for years now, traveling with Garth and the others, the ones who had claimed her after her parents died, taught her their ways, and showed her their life. All of the Westland belonged to the Rovers, from the Kershalt to the Irrybis, from the Valley of Rhenn to the Blue Divide. Once, it had belonged to the Elves as well. But the Elves were all gone now, disappeared. They had passed back into legend, the Rovers said. They had lost interest in the world of mortal beings and gone back into faerie.

Some disputed it. Some said that the Elves were still there, hidden. She didn't know about the truth of that. She only knew that what they had abandoned was a wilderness paradise.

Garth passed her the aleskin and she drank deeply, then handed it back again. She was growing sleepy. Normally, she drank little. But she was feeling especially proud of herself tonight. It wasn't often that she got the best of Garth.

She studied him momentarily, thinking of how much he had come to mean to her. Her time in Shady Vale seemed long ago and far away, although she remembered it well enough. And the Ohmsfords, especially Par and Coll—she still thought about them. They had been her only family once. But it felt as if all that might have happened in another life. Garth was her family now, her father, mother, and brother all rolled into one, the only real family she knew anymore. She was tied to him in ways she had never been tied to anyone else. She loved him fiercely.

Nevertheless, she admitted, she sometimes felt detached from everyone, even him—orphaned and homeless, a stray shunted from one family to the next without belonging to anyone, having no idea at all who she really was. It bothered her that she didn't know more about herself and that no one else seemed to know either. She had asked often enough, but the explanations were always vague. Her father had been an Ohmsford. Her mother had been a Rover. It was unclear how they had died. It was uncertain what had become of any other members of her immediate family. It was unknown who her ancestors had been.

She possessed, in fact, but one item that offered any clue at all as to who she was. It was a small leather bag she wore tied about her neck that contained three perfectly formed stones. Elfstones, one might have thought—until one looked more closely and saw that they were just common rocks painted blue. But they had been found on her as a baby and they were all she had to suggest the heritage that might be hers.

Garth knew something about the matter, she suspected. He had told her that he didn't when she had asked once, but there was something in the way he had made his disavowal that convinced her he was hedging. Garth kept secrets better than most, but she knew him too well to be fooled completely. Sometimes, when she thought about it, she wanted to shake an answer out of him, angry and frustrated at his refusal to be as open with her in this as he was in everything else. But she kept her anger and her frustration to herself. You didn't push Garth. When he was ready to tell her, he would.

She shrugged as she always ended up doing whenever she considered the matter of her family history. What difference did it make? She was who she was, whatever her lineage. She was a Rover girl with a life that most would envy, if they bothered to be honest about it. The whole world belonged to her, because she was tied to no part of it. She could go where she wanted and do what she pleased, and that was more than most could say. Besides, many of her fellow Rovers were of dubious parentage, and you never heard them complain. They reveled in their freedom, in their ability to lay claim to anything and anyone that caught their fancy. Wasn't that good enough for her as well?

She stirred the dirt in front of her with her boot. Of course, none of them were Elven, were they? None of them had the Ohmsford-Shannara blood, with its history of Elven magic. None of them were plagued by the dreams . . .

Her hazel eyes shifted abruptly as she became aware of Garth looking at her. She signed some innocuous response, thinking as she did so that none of the other Rovers had been as thoroughly trained to survive as she had and wondering why.

They drank a little more of the ale, built the fire up again, and rolled into their blankets. Wren lay awake longer than she wished to, caught up in the unanswered questions and unresolved puzzles that marked her life. When she did sleep, she tossed restlessly beneath her blankets, teased by fragments of dreams that slipped from her like raindrops through her fingers in a summer storm and were forgotten as quickly.

It was dawn when she came awake, and the old man was sitting across from her, poking idly at the ashes of the fire with a long stick. "It's about time," he snorted.

She blinked in disbelief, then started sharply out of her blankets. Garth was still sleeping, but awoke with the suddenness of her movement. She reached for the quarterstaff at her side, her thoughts scattering into questions. Where had this old man come from? How had he managed to get so close without waking them?

The old man lifted one sticklike arm reassuringly, saying, "Don't be getting yourself all upset. Just be grateful I let you sleep."

Garth was on his feet as well now, crouched, but to Wren's astonishment the old man began speaking to the Rover in his own language, signing, telling him what he had already told Wren, and adding that he meant no harm. Garth hesitated, obviously surprised, then sat back watchfully.

"How did you know to do that?" Wren demanded. She had never seen anyone outside the Rover camp master Garth's language.

"Oh, I know a thing or two about communication," the old man replied gruffly, a self-satisfied smile appearing. His skin was weather-browned and seamed, his white hair and beard wispy, his lank frame scarecrow-thin. A gathering of dusty gray robes hung loosely about him. "For instance," he said, "I know that messages may be sent by writing on paper, by word of mouth, by use of hands . . ." He paused. "Even by dreams."

Wren caught her breath sharply. "Who are you?"

"Well, now," the old man said, "that seems to be everyone's favorite question. My name doesn't matter. What matters is that I have been sent to tell you that you can no longer afford to ignore your dreams. Those dreams, Rover girl, come from Allanon."

As he spoke he signed to Garth, repeating his words with the language of his fingers, as dexterous at the skill as if he had known it all his life. Wren was aware of the big Rover looking at her, but she couldn't take her eyes off the old man. "How do you know of the dreams?" she asked him softly.

He told her who he was then, that he was Cogline, a former Druid pressed back into service because the real Druids were gone from the Four Lands and there was no other who could go to the members of the Ohmsford family and warn them that the dreams were real. He told her that Allanon's ghost had sent him to convince her of the purpose of the dreams, to persuade her that they spoke the truth, that the Four Lands were in gravest danger, that the magic was almost lost, that only the Ohmsfords could restore it, and that they must come to him on the first night of the new moon to discover what must be done. He finished by saying that he had gone first to Par Ohmsford, then to Walker Boh—recipients of the dreams as well—and now finally he had come to her.

When he was done, she sat thinking for a moment before speaking. "The dreams have troubled me for some time now," she confessed. "I thought them dreams like any other and nothing more. The Ohmsford magic has never been a part of my life . . ."

"And you question whether or not you are an Ohmsford at all," the old man interrupted. "You are not certain, are you? If you are not an Ohmsford, then the magic has no part in your life—which might be just as well as far as you're concerned, mightn't it?"

Wren stared at him. "How do you know all this, Cogline?" She didn't question that he was who he claimed; she accepted it because she believed that it didn't really matter one way or the other. "How do you know so much about me?" She leaned forward, suddenly anxious. "Do you know the truth of who I really am?"

The old man shrugged. "It is not nearly so important to know who you are as who you might be," he answered enigmatically. "If you wish to learn something of that, then do as the dreams have asked. Come to the Hadeshorn and speak to Allanon."

She eased away slowly, glancing momentarily at Garth before looking back. "You're playing with me," she told the old man.

"Perhaps."

"Why?"

"Oh, quite simple, really. If you are intrigued enough by what I say, you might agree to do as I ask and come with me. I chose to chastise and berate the other members of your family. I thought I might try a new approach with you. Time grows short, and I am just an old man. The new moon is only six days distant now. Even on horseback, it will require at least four days to reach the Hadeshorn—five, if I am to make the journey."

He was signing everything he said, and now Garth made a quick response. The old man laughed. "Will I choose to make the journey? Yes, by golly, I think I will. I have gone about a shades's business for some weeks now. I believe I am entitled to know what the culmination of that business might be." He paused, thoughtful. "Besides, I am not altogether sure I have been given a choice . . ." He trailed off.

Wren glanced eastward to where the sun was a pale white ball of fire resting atop the horizon, screened by clouds and haze, its warmth still distant. Gulls swooped across the mirrored waters of the Myrian, fishing. The stillness of the early morning let her thoughts whisper undisturbed within her.

"What did my cousin . . . ?" she began, then caught herself. The word didn't sound right when she spoke it. It distanced her from him in a way she didn't care for. "What did Par say that he was going to do?" she finished.

"He said he was going to think the matter over," the old man replied. "He and his brother. They were together when I found them."

"And my uncle?"

The other shrugged. "The same."

But there was something in his eyes that said otherwise.

Wren shook her head. "You are playing with me again. What did they say?"

The old man's eyes narrowed. "Rover girl, you try my patience. I haven't the energy to sit about and repeat entire conversations just so you can use that as an excuse for making your decision in this matter. Haven't you a mind of your own? If they go, they will do so for their own reasons and not for any you might provide. Shouldn't you do likewise?"

Wren Ohmsford was a rock. "What did they say?" she repeated once again, measuring each word carefully before she spoke it.

"What they chose!" the other snapped, his fingers flicking his responses angrily now at Garth, though his eyes never left Wren's. "Am I a parrot to repeat the phrases of others for your amusement?"

He glared at her a moment, then threw up his hands. "Very well! Here is the whole of it, then! Young Par, his brother with him, has been chased from Varfleet by the Federation for making use of the magic to tell stories of their family history and the Druids. He thought to go home when I last saw him, to think about the dreams a bit. He will have discovered by now that he cannot do so, that his home is in Federation hands and his parents—your own of sorts, once upon a time—are prisoners!"

Wren started in surprise, but the old man ignored her. "Walker Boh is another matter. He thinks himself severed from the Ohmsford family. He lives alone and prefers it that way. He wants nothing to do with his family and the world at large and Druids in particular. He thinks that only he knows the proper uses of magic, that the rest of us who possess some small skill are incapable of reason! He forgets who taught him what! He . . ."

"You," Wren interjected.

". . . charges about on some self-proclaimed mission of . . ." He stopped short. "What? What did you say?"

"You," she repeated, her eyes locking on his. "You were his teacher once, weren't you?"

There was a moment of silence as the sharp old eyes studied

her appraisingly. "Yes, girl. I was. Are you satisfied now? Is that the revelation you sought? Or do you require something more?"

He had forgotten to sign what he was saying, but Garth seemed to have read his lips in any case. He caught Wren's attention, nodding in approval. Always try to learn something of your adversary that he doesn't want you to know, he had taught her. It gives you an edge.

"So he isn't going then, is he?" she pressed. "Walker, I mean."

"Ha!" the old man exclaimed in satisfaction. "Just when I conclude what a smart girl you are, you prove me wrong!" He cocked an eyebrow on his seamed face. "Walker Boh says he isn't going, and he thinks he isn't going. But he is! The young one, too—Par. That's the way it will be. Things work out the way we least expect them to sometimes. Or maybe that's just the Druid magic at work, twisting those promises and oaths we so recklessly take, steering us where we didn't think we could ever be made to go." He shook his head in amusement. "Always was a baffling trick."

He drew his robes about him and bent forward. "Now what is it to be with you, little Wren? Brave bird or timid flyaway— which will you be?"

She smiled in spite of herself. "Why not both, depending on what is needed?" she asked.

He grunted impatiently. "Because the situation calls for one or the other. Choose."

Wren let her eyes shift briefly to Garth, then off into the woods, slipping deep into the shadows where the still distant sunlight had not yet penetrated. Her thoughts and questions of the previous night came back to her, darting through her mind with harrying insistence. Well, she could go if she chose, she knew. The Rovers wouldn't stop her, not even Garth—though he would insist on going as well. She could confront the shade of Allanon. She could speak with the shade of a legend, a man many said never existed at all. She could ask the questions of him she had carried about with her for so many years now, perhaps learn some of the answers, possibly come to an understanding about herself that she had lacked before. A rather ambitious task, she thought. An intriguing one.

She felt sunlight slipping across the bridge of her nose, tick-ling her. It would mean a reunion with Par and Coll and Walker Boh—her other family that maybe wasn't really family at all. She pursed her lips thoughtfully. She might enjoy that.

But it would also mean confronting the reality of her dreams—or at least a shade's version of that reality. And that could mean a change in the course of her life, a life with which she was perfectly content. It could mean disruption of that life, an involvement in matters that she might better avoid.

Her mind raced. She could feel the presence of the little bag with the painted stones pressing against her breast as if to remind her of what might be. She knew the stories of the Ohmsfords and the Druids, too, and she was wary.

Then, unexpectedly, she found herself smiling. Since when had being wary ever stopped her from doing anything? Shades! This was an unlocked door that begged to be opened! How could she live with herself if she passed it up?

The old man interrupted her thoughts. "Rover girl, I grow weary. These ageing bones require movement to keep from locking up. Let me have your decision. Or do you, like the others in your family, require untold amounts of time to puzzle this matter through?"

Wren glanced over at Garth, cocking one eyebrow. The giant Rover's nod was barely perceptible.

She looked back at Cogline. "You are so testy, old grandfa-ther!" she chided. "Where is your patience?"

"Gone with my youth, child," he said, his voice unexpect-edly soft. His hands folded before him. "Now what's it to be?"

She smiled. "The Hadeshorn and Allanon," she answered. "What did you expect?"

But the old man did not reply.

CHAPTER

14

FIVE DAYS LATER, with the sun exploding streamers of
violet and red fire all across the western horizon in the
kind of day's-end fireworks display that only summer
provides, Wren, Garth, and the old man who said
he was Cogline reached the base of the Dragon's Teeth and the
beginning of the winding, narrow rock trail that led into the
Valley of Shale and the Hadeshorn.

Par Ohmsford was the first to see them. He had gone up
the trail a few hundred yards to a rock shelf where he could sit
and look out over the sweep of Callahorn south and be by
himself. He had arrived with Coll, Morgan, Walker, Steff, and
Teel one day earlier, and his patience at waiting for the arrival
of the first night of the new moon had begun to wear a little
thin. He was immersed mostly in his admiration for the majesty
of the sunset when he caught sight of the odd trio as they rode
their horses out of the westward glare from a screen of poplar
trees and started toward him. He came to his feet slowly, refusing to trust his eyes at first. Then, having determined that he
was not mistaken, he leaped from his perch and charged back
down the trail to alert the others of his little company who were
camped immediately below.

Wren got there almost before he did. Her sharp Elven eyes
caught sight of him at about the same time he saw her. Acting
on impulse and leaving her companions to follow as best they
could, she spurred her horse ahead recklessly, came charging
into camp, vaulted from the saddle before her mount was fully

checked, rushed up to Par with a wild yell, and hugged him with such enthusiasm that he was almost knocked from his feet. When she was done with him, she gave the same reception to an astonished, but delighted Coll. Walker got a more reserved kiss on the cheek and Morgan, whom she barely remembered from her childhood, a handshake and a nod.

While the three Ohmsford siblings—for they seemed such, despite the fact that Wren wasn't a true sister—traded hugs and words of greeting, those with them stood around uncomfortably and sized up one another with wary glances. Most of the sizing up was reserved for Garth, who was twice as big as any of the rest of them. He was dressed in the brightly colored clothing common to the Rovers, and the garishness of his garb made him seem larger still. He met the stares of the others without discomfort, his gaze steady and implacable. Wren remembered him after a moment and began the required series of introductions. Par followed with Steff and Teel. Cogline hung back from the others; since everyone seemed to know who he was, in any case, no formal introduction was attempted. There were nods and handshakes all around, courtesies observed as expected, but the wariness in the faces of most did not subside. When they all moved over to the fire that formed the center of the little campsite to partake of the dinner that the Dwarves had been in the process of preparing when Wren and her companions had appeared, the newly formed company of nine quickly fragmented into groups. Steff and Teel turned their attention to the completion of the meal, mute as they hovered over the pots and cooking fire, Walker withdrew to a patch of shade under a scrawny pine, and Cogline disappeared into the rocks without a word to anyone. He was so quiet about it that he was gone almost before they realized it. But Cogline was not really considered a part of the company, so no one much bothered about it. Par, Coll, Wren, and Morgan clustered together by the horses, unsaddling them and rubbing them down, and talked about old times, old friends, the places they had been, the things they had seen, and the vicissitudes of life.

"You are much grown, Wren," Coll marveled. "Not at all the broomstick little girl I remember when you left us."

"A rider of horses, wild as the wind! No boundaries for you!" Par laughed, throwing up his hands in a gesture meant to encompass the whole of the land.

Wren grinned back. "I live a better life than the lot of you, resting on your backsides, singing old tales and rousting tired dogs. The Westland's a good country for free-spirited things, you know." Then her grin faded. "The old man, Cogline, told me of what's happened in the Vale. Jaralan and Mirianna were my parents for a time, too, and I care for them still. Prisoners, he said. Have you heard anything of them?"

Par shook his head. "We have been running ever since Varfleet."

"I am sorry, Par." There was genuine discomfort in her eyes. "The Federation does its best to make all of our lives miserable. Even the Westland has its share of soldiers and administrative lackeys, though it's country they mostly ignore. The Rovers know how to avoid them in any case. If need be, you would be welcome to join us."

Par gave her another quick hug. "Best that we see how this business of the dreams turns out first," he whispered.

They ate a dinner of fried meats, fresh-baked hard bread, stewed vegetables, cheese, and nuts, and washed it all down with ale and water while they watched the sun disappear beneath the horizon. The food was good, and everyone said so, much to Steff's pleasure, for he had prepared the better part of it. Cogline remained absent, but the others began talking a bit more freely among themselves, all but Teel, who never seemed to want to speak. As far as Par knew, he was the only one besides Steff to whom the Dwarf girl had ever said anything.

When the dinner was complete, Steff and Teel took charge of cleaning the dishes, and the others drifted away in ones and twos as the dusk settled slowly into the night. While Coll and Morgan went down to a spring a quarter-mile off to draw fresh water, Par found himself ambling back up the trail that led into the mountains and the Valley of Shale in the company of Wren and the giant Garth.

"Have you been back there yet?" Wren asked as they walked, nodding in the direction of the Hadeshorn.

Par shook his head. "It's several hours in and no one's much wanted to hurry matters along. Even Walker has refused to go there before the scheduled time." He glanced skyward where clusters of stars dotted the heavens in intricate patterns and a small, almost invisible crescent moon hung low against the horizon north. "Tomorrow night," he said.

Wren didn't reply. They walked on in silence until they reached the shelf of rock that Par had occupied earlier that day. There they stopped, looking back over the country south.

"You've had the dreams, too?" Wren asked him then and went on to describe her own. When he nodded, she said, "What do you think?"

Par eased himself down on the rock, the other two sitting with him. "I think that ten generations of Ohmsfords have lived their lives since the time of Brin and Jair, waiting for this to happen. I think that the magic of the Elven house of Shannara, Ohmsford magic now, is something more than we realize. I think Allanon—or his shade, at least—will tell us what that something is." He paused. "I think it may turn out to be something wondrous—and something terrible."

He was aware of her staring at him with those intense hazel eyes, and he shrugged apologetically. "I don't mean to be overdramatic. That's just the sense I have of things."

She translated his comments automatically for Garth, who gave no indication of what he thought. "You and Walker have some use of the magic," she said quietly. "I have none. What of that?"

He shook his head. "I'm not sure. Morgan's magic is stronger than mine these days and he wasn't called." He went on to tell her about their confrontation with the Shadowen and the Highlander's discovery of the magic that had lain dormant in the Sword of Leah. "I find myself wondering why the dreams didn't command him to appear instead of me, for all the use the wishsong has been."

"But you don't know for certain how strong your magic is, Par," she said quietly. "You should remember from the stories that none of the Ohmsfords, from Shea on down, fully understood when they began their quests the uses of the Elven magic. Might it not be the same with you?"

It might, he realized with a shiver. He cocked his head. "Or you, Wren. What of you?"

"No, no, Par Ohmsford. I am a simple Rover girl with none of the blood that carries the magic from generation to generation in me." She laughed. "I'm afraid I must make do with a bag filled with make-believe Elfstones!"

He laughed as well, remembering the little leather bag with the painted rocks that she had guarded so carefully as a child. They traded life stories for a time, telling each other what they had been doing, where they had been, and whom they had encountered on their journeys. They were relaxed, much as if their separation had been but a few weeks rather than years. Wren was responsible for that, Par decided. She had put him immediately at ease. He was struck by the inordinate amount of confidence that she exhibited in herself, such a wild, free girl, obviously content with her Rover life, seemingly unshackled by demands or constraints that might hold her back. She was strong both inwardly and outwardly, and he admired her greatly for it. He found himself wishing that he could display but a fraction of her pluck.

"How do you find Walker?" she asked him after a time.

"Distant," he said at once. "Still haunted by demons that I cannot begin to understand. He talks about his mistrust of the Elven magic and the Druids, yet seems to have magic of his own that he uses freely enough. I don't really understand him."

Wren relayed his comments to Garth, and the giant Rover responded with a brief signing. Wren looked at him sharply, then said to Par, "Garth says that Walker is frightened."

Par looked surprised. "How does he know that?"

"He just does. Because he is deaf, he works harder at using his other senses. He detects other people's feelings more quickly than you or I would—even those that are kept hidden."

Par nodded. "Well, he happens to be exactly right in this instance. Walker is frightened. He told me so himself. He says he's frightened of what this business with Allanon might mean. Odd, isn't it? I have trouble imagining anything frightening Walker Boh."

Wren signed to Garth, but the giant merely shrugged. They sat back in silence for a time, thinking separate thoughts. Then

Wren said, "Did you know that the old man, Cogline, was once Walker's teacher?"

Par looked at her sharply. "Did he tell you that?"

"I tricked it from him, mostly."

"Teacher of what, Wren? Of the magic?"

"Of something." Her dark features turned introspective momentarily, her gaze distant. "There is much between those two that, like Walker's fear, is kept hidden, I think."

Par, though he didn't say so, was inclined to agree.

THE MEMBERS OF the little company slept undisturbed that night in the shadow of the Dragon's Teeth, but by dawn they were awake again and restless. Tonight was the first night of the new moon, the night they were to meet with the shade of Allanon. Impatiently, they went about their business. They ate their meals without tasting them. They spoke little to one another, moving about uneasily, finding small tasks that would distract them from thinking further on what lay ahead. It was a clear, cloudless day filled with warm summer smells and lazy sunshine, the kind of day that, under other circumstances, might have been enjoyed, but which on this occasion simply seemed endless.

Cogline reappeared about midday, wandering down out of the mountains like some tattered prophet of doom. He looked dusty and unkempt as he came up to them, his hair wild, his eyes shadowed from lack of sleep. He told them that all was in readiness—whatever that meant—and that he would come for them after nightfall. Be ready, he advised. He refused to say anything more, though pressed by the Ohmsfords to do so, and disappeared back the way he had come.

"What do you suppose he is doing up there?" Coll muttered to the others as the ragged figure dwindled into a tiny black speck in the distance and then into nothing at all.

The sun worked its way westward as if dragging chains in its wake, and the members of the little company retreated further into themselves. The enormity of what was about to happen began to emerge in their unspoken thoughts, a specter of such size that it was frightening to contemplate. Even Walker

Boh, who might have been assumed to be more at home with the prospect of encountering shades and spirits, withdrew into himself like a badger into its hole and became unapproachable.

Nevertheless, when it was nearing midafternoon, Par happened on his uncle while wandering the cooler stretches of the hills surrounding the springs. They slowed on coming together, then stopped and stood looking at each other awkwardly.

"Do you think he will really come?" Par asked finally.

Walker's pale features were shadowed beneath the protective hood of his cloak, making his face difficult to read. "He will come," his uncle said.

Par thought a moment, then said, "I don't know what to expect."

Walker shook his head. "It doesn't matter, Par. Whatever you choose to expect, it won't be enough. This meeting won't be like anything you might envision, I promise you. The Druids have always been very good at surprises."

"You suspect the worst, don't you?"

"I suspect . . ." He trailed off without finishing.

"Magic," said Par.

The other frowned.

"Druid magic—that's what you think we will see tonight, don't you? I hope you are right. I hope that it sweeps and resounds and that it opens all the doors that have been closed to us and lets us see what magic can really do!"

Walker Boh's smile, when it finally overcame his astonishment, was ironic. "Some doors are better left closed," he said softly. "You would do well to remember that."

He put his hand on his nephew's arm for a moment, then continued silently on his way.

The afternoon crawled toward evening. When the sun at last completed its long journey west and began to slip beneath the horizon, the members of the little company filtered back to the campsite for the evening meal. Morgan was garrulous, an obvious sign of nerves with him, and talked incessantly of magic and swords and all sorts of wild happenings that Par hoped would never be. The others were mostly silent, eating without comment and casting watchful glances northward toward the mountains. Teel wouldn't eat at all, sitting off by herself in a gathering of shadows, the mask that covered her face like a wall that separated her from everyone. Even Steff let her alone.

Darkness descended and the stars began to flicker into view, a scattering here and there at first, and then the sky was filled with them. No moon showed itself; it was the promised time when the sun's pale sister wore black. Daylight's sounds faded and night's remained hushed. The cooking fire crackled and snapped in the silence as conversation lagged. One or two smoked, and the air was filled with the pungent smell. Morgan took out the bright length of the Sword of Leah and began to polish it absently. Wren and Garth fed and curried the horses. Walker moved up the trail a short distance and stood staring into the mountains. Others sat lost in thought.

Everyone waited.

It WAS MIDNIGHT when Cogline returned for them. The old man appeared out of the shadows like a ghost, materializing so suddenly that they all started. No one, not even Walker, had seen him coming.

"It is time," he announced.

They came to their feet voicelessly and followed him. He took them up the trail from their campsite into the gradually thickening shadows of the Dragon's Teeth. Although the stars shone brightly overhead when they started out, the mountains soon began to close about, leaving the little company shrouded in blackness. Cogline did not slow; he seemed to possess cat's eyes. His charges struggled to keep pace. Par, Coll, and Morgan were closest to the old man, Wren and Garth came next, Steff and Teel behind them, and Walker Boh brought up the rear. The trail steepened quickly after they reached the beginning peaks, and they moved through a narrow defile that opened like a pocket into the mountains. It was silent here, so still that they could hear one another breathe as they labored upward.

The minutes slipped away. Boulders and cliff walls hindered their passage, and the trail wound about like a snake. Loose rock carpeted the whole of the mountains, and the climbers had to scramble over it. Still Cogline pressed on. Par stumbled and scraped his knees, finding the loose rock as sharp as glass. Much of it was a strange, mirrorlike black that reminded him of coal. He scooped up a small piece out of curiosity and stuck it in his pocket.

Then abruptly the mountains split apart before them, and they stepped out onto the rim of the Valley of Shale. It was little more than a broad, shallow depression strewn with crushed stone that glistened with the same mirrored blackness as the rock Par had pocketed. Nothing grew in the valley; it was stripped of life. There was a lake at its center, its greenish black waters moving in sluggish swirls in the windless expanse.

Cogline stopped momentarily and looked back at them. "The Hadeshorn," he whispered. "Home for the spirits of the ages, for the Druids of the past." His weathered old face had an almost reverent look to it. Then he turned away and started them down into the valley.

Except for the huff of their breathing and the rasp of their boots on the loose rock, the valley, too, was wrapped in silence. Echoes of their movements played in the stillness like children in the slow heat of a midsummer's day. Eyes darted watchfully, seeking ghosts where there were none to find, imagining life in every shadow. It was strangely warm here, the heat of the day captured and held in the airless bowl through the cool of the night. Par felt a trickle of sweat begin to run down his back.

Then they were on the valley floor, closely bunched as they made their way toward the lake. They could see the movement of the waters more clearly now, the way the swirls worked against each other, haphazard, unbidden. They could hear the rippling of tiny waves as they lapped. There was the pungent scent of things ageing and decayed.

They were still several dozen yards from the water's edge when Cogline brought them to a halt, both hands lifting in caution. "Stand fast, now. Come no closer. The waters of the Hadeshorn are death to mortals, poison to the touch!" He crouched down and put a finger to his lips as if hushing a child.

They did as they were bidden, children indeed before the power they sensed sleeping there. They could feel it, all of them, a palpable thing that hung in the air like wood smoke from a fire. They remained where they were, alert, anxious, filled with a mix of wonder and hesitancy. No one spoke. The star-filled sky stretched away endlessly overhead, canopied from horizon to horizon, and it seemed as if the whole of the heavens was focused on the valley, that lake, and the nine of them who kept watch.

At last Cogline lifted from his crouch and came back to them, beckoning with birdlike movements of his hands to draw them close about him. When they were gathered in a knot that locked them shoulder to shoulder, he spoke.

"Allanon will come just before dawn." The sharp old eyes regarded them solemnly. "He wishes me to speak with you first. He is no longer what he was in life. He is just a shade now. His purchase in this world is but the blink of an eye. Each time he crosses over from the spirit world, it requires tremendous effort. He can stay only a little while. What time he is allotted he must use wisely. He will use that time to tell you of the need he has of you. He has left it to me to explain to you why that need exists. I am to tell you of the Shadowen."

"You've spoken to him?" asked Walker Boh quickly.

Cogline said nothing.

"Why wait until now to tell us about the Shadowen?" Par was suddenly irritated. "Why now, Cogline, when you could have done so before?"

The old man shook his head, his face both reproving and sympathetic. "It was not permitted, youngster. Not until all of you had been brought together."

"Games!" Walker muttered and shook his head in disgust.

The old man ignored him. "Think what you like, only listen. This is what Allanon would have me tell you of the Shadowen. They are an evil beyond all imagining. They are not the rumors or the tall tales that men would have them be, but creatures as real as you and I. They are born of a circumstance that Allanon in all his wisdom and planning did not foresee. When he passed from the world of mortal men, Allanon believed the age of magic at an end and a new age begun. The Warlock Lord was no more. The Demons of the old world of faerie were again imprisoned within the Forbidding. The Ildatch was destroyed. Paranor was gone into history and the last of the Druids were about to go with it. It seemed the need for magic was past."

"The need is never past," Walker said quietly.

Again, the old man ignored him. "The Shadowen are an aberration. They are a magic that grew out of the use of other magics, a residue of what has gone before. They began as a seeding that lay dormant within the Four Lands, undetected during the time of Allanon, a seeding that came to life only after the Druids and their protective powers were gone. No one could have known they were there, not even Allanon. They were the leavings of magic come and gone, and they were as invisible as dust on a pathway."

"Wait a minute!" Par interjected. "What are you saying, Cogline? That the Shadowen are just bits and pieces of some stray magic?"

Cogline took a deep breath, his hands locking before him. "Valeman, I told you once before that for all the use you have of magic, you still know little about it. Magic is as much a force of nature as the fire at the earth's core, the tidal waves that sweep out of the ocean, the winds that flatten forests or the famine that starves nations. It does not happen and then disappear without effect! Think! What of Wil Ohmsford and his use of the Elfstones when his Elven blood no longer permitted such use? It left as its residue the wishsong that found life in your ancestors! Was that an inconsequential magic? All uses of the magic have effects beyond the immediate. And all are significant."

"Which magic was it that created the Shadowen?" asked Coll, his blocky face impassive.

The old man shook his wispy head. "Allanon does not know. There is no way of being certain. It could have happened at any time during the lives of Shea Ohmsford and his descendents. There was always magic in use in those times, much of it evil. The Shadowen could have been born of any part of it."

He paused. "The Shadowen were nothing at first. They were the debris of magic spent. Somehow they survived, their presence unknown. It was not until Allanon and Paranor were gone that they emerged into the Four Lands and began to gain strength. There was a vacuum in the order of things by then. A void must be filled in all events, and the Shadowen were quick to fill this one."

"I don't understand," Par said quickly. "What sort of vacuum do you mean?"

"And why didn't Allanon foresee it happening?" added Wren.

The old man held up his fingers and began crooking them downward one by one as he spoke. "Life has always been cyclical. Power comes and goes; it takes different forms. Once, it was science that gave mankind power. Of late, it has been magic. Allanon foresaw the return of science as a means to progress—especially with the passing of the Druids and Paranor. That was the age that would be. But the development of science failed to materialize quickly enough to fill the vacuum. Partly this was because of the Federation. The Federation kept the old ways intact; it proscribed the use of any form of power but its own—and its own was primitive and military. It expanded its influence throughout the Four Lands until all were subject to its dictates. The Elves had an effect on matters as well; for reasons we still don't know they disappeared. They were a balancing force, the last people of the faerie world of old. Their presence was necessary, if the transition from magic to science was to be made faultlessly."

He shook his head. "Yet even had the Elves remained in the world of men and the Federation been less a presence, the Shadowen might have come alive. The vacuum was there the moment the Druids passed away. There was no help for it." He sighed. "Allanon did not foresee as he should have. He did not anticipate an aberration on the order of the Shadowen. He did what he could to keep the Four Lands safe while he was alive—and he kept himself alive for as long as was possible."

"Too little of each, it seems," Walker said pointedly.

Cogline looked at him, and the anger in his voice was palpable. "Well, Walker Boh. Perhaps one day you will have an opportunity to demonstrate that you can do it better."

There was a strained moment of silence as the two faced each other in the blackness. Then Cogline looked away. "You need to understand what the Shadowen are. The Shadowen are parasites. They live off mortal creatures. They are a magic that feeds on living things. They enter them, absorb them, become them. But for some reason the results are not always the same. Young Par, think of the woodswoman that you and Coll encountered at the time of our first meeting. She was a Shadowen of the more obvious sort, a once-mortal creature infected, a ravaged thing that could no more help herself than an animal made mad. But the little girl on Toffer Ridge, do you remember her?"

His fingers brushed Par's cheek lightly. Instantly, the Valeman was filled with the memory of that monster to whom the Spider Gnomes had given him. He could feel her stealing against him, begging him, "hug me, hug me," desperate to make him embrace her. He flinched, shaken by the impact of the memory.

Cogline's hand closed firmly about his arm. "That, too, was a Shadowen, but one that could not be so easily detected. They appear to varying extents as we do, hidden within human form. Some become grotesque in appearance and behavior; those you can readily identify. Others are more difficult to recognize."

"But why are there some of one kind and some of the other?" Par asked uncertainly.

Cogline's brow furrowed. "Once again, Allanon does not know. The Shadowen have kept their secret even from him."

The old man looked away for a long moment, then back again. His face was a mask of despair. "This is like a plague. The sickness is spread until the number infected multiplies impossibly. Any of the Shadowen can transmit the disease. Their magic gives them the means to overcome almost any defense. The more of them there are, the stronger they become. What would you to do to stop a plague where the source was unknown, the symptoms undetectable until after they had taken root, and the cure a mystery?"

The members of the little company glanced at one another uneasily in the silence that followed.

Finally, Wren said, "Do they have a purpose in what they do, Cogline? A purpose beyond simply infecting living things? Do they think as you and I or are they . . . mindless?"

Par stared at the girl in undisguised admiration. It was the best question any of them had asked. He should have been the one to ask it.

Cogline was rubbing his hands together slowly. "They think as you and I, Rover girl, and they most certainly do have a purpose in what they do. But that purpose remains unclear."

"They would subvert us," Morgan offered sharply. "Surely that's purpose enough."

But Cogline shook his head. "They would do more still, I think."

And abruptly Par found himself recalling the dreams that Allanon had sent, the visions of a nightmarish world in which everything was blackened and withered and life was reduced to something barely recognizable. Reddened eyes blinked like bits of fire, and shadow forms flitted through a haze of ash and smoke.

This is what the Shadowen would do, he realized.

But how could they bring such a vision to pass?

He glanced without thinking at Wren and found his question mirrored in her eyes. He recognized what she was thinking instinctively. He saw it reflected in Walker Boh's eyes as well. They had shared the dreams and those dreams bound them, so much so that for an instant their thinking was the same.

Cogline's face lifted slightly, pulling free of the darkness that shaded it. "Something guides the Shadowen," he whispered. "There is power here that transcends anything we have ever known . . ."

He let the sentence trail off, ragged and unfinished, as if unable to give voice to any ending. His listeners looked at one another.

"What are we to do?" Wren asked finally.

The old man rose wearily. "Why, what we came here to do, Rover girl—listen to what Allanon would tell us."

He moved stiffly away, and no one called after him.

CHAPTER

15

THEY MOVED APART from each other after that, drifting away one by one, finding patches of solitude in which to think their separate thoughts. Eyes wandered restlessly across the valley's glistening carpet of black rock, always returning to the Hadeshorn, carefully searching the sluggishly churning waters for signs of some new movement.

There was none.

Perhaps nothing is going to happen, Par thought. Perhaps it was all a lie after all.

He felt his chest constrict with mixed feelings of disappointment and relief and he forced his thoughts elsewhere. Coll was less than a dozen paces away, but he refused to look at him. He wanted to be alone. There were things that needed thinking through, and Coll would only distract him.

Funny how much effort he had put into distancing himself from his brother since this journey had begun, he thought suddenly. Perhaps it was because he was afraid for him . . .

Once again, this time angrily, he forced his thoughts elsewhere. Cogline. Now there was an enigma of no small size. Who was this old man who seemed to know so much about everything? A failed Druid, he claimed. Allanon's messenger, he said. But those brief descriptions didn't seem nearly complete enough. Par was certain that there was more to him than what he claimed. There was a history of events behind his relationships with Allanon and Walker Boh that was hidden from the rest of them. Allanon would not have gone to a failed Druid for assistance, not even in the most desperate of circumstances. There was a reason for Cogline's involvement with this gathering beyond what any of them knew.

He glanced warily at the old man who stood an uncomfortable number of feet closer than the rest of them to the waters of the Hadeshorn. He knew all about the Shadowen, somehow. He had spoken more than once with Allanon, somehow again. He was the only living human being to have done so since the Druid's death three hundred years ago. Par thought a moment about the stories of Cogline in the time of Brin Ohmsford—a half-crazed old man then, wielding magic against the Mord Wraiths like some sort of broom against dust—that's the picture the tales conjured up. Well, he wasn't like that now. He was controlled. Cranky and eccentric, yes—but mostly controlled. He knew what he was about—enough so that he didn't seem particularly pleased with any of it. He hadn't said that, of course. But Par wasn't blind.

There was a flash of light from somewhere far off in the night skies, a momentary brightness that winked away instantly and was gone. A life ended, a new life begun, his mother used to say. He sighed. He hadn't thought of his parents much since the flight out of Varfleet. He felt a twinge of guilt. He wondered if they were all right. He wondered if he would see them again.

His jaw tightened with determination. Of course he would see them again! Things would work out. Allanon would have answers to give him—about the uses of the magic of the wishsong, the reasons for the dreams, what to do about the Shadowen and the Federation . . . all of it.

Allanon would know.

Time slipped away, minutes into hours, the night steadily working its way toward dawn. Par moved over to talk with Coll, needing now to be close to his brother. The others shifted, stretched, and moved about uneasily. Eyes grew heavy and senses dulled.

Far east, the first twinges of the coming dawn appeared against the dark line of the horizon.

He's not coming, Par thought dismally.

And as if in answer the waters of the Hadeshorn heaved

upward, and the valley shuddered as if something beneath it had come awake. Rock shifted and grated with the movement, and the members of the little company went into a protective crouch. The lake began to boil, the waters to thrash, and spray shot skyward with a sharp hiss. Voices cried out, inhuman and filled with longing. They rose out of the earth, straining against bonds that were invisible to the nine gathered in the valley, but which they could all too readily imagine. Walker's arms flung wide against the sound, scattering bits of silver dust that flared in a protective curtain. The others cupped their ears protectively, but nothing could shut the sound away.

Then the earth began to rumble, thunder that rolled out of its depth and eclipsed even the cries. Cogline's stick-thin arm lifted, pointing rigidly to the lake. The Hadeshorn exploded into a whirlpool, waters churning madly, and from out of the depths rose . . .

"Allanon!" Par cried out excitedly against the fury of sounds.

It was the Druid. They knew him instantly, all of them. They remembered him from the tales of three centuries gone; they recognized him in their heart of hearts, that secret innermost whisper of certainty. He rose into the night air, light flaring about him, released somehow from the waters of the Hadeshorn. He lifted free of the lake to stand upon its surface, a shade from some netherworld, cast in transparent gray, shimmering faintly against the dark. He was cloaked and cowled from head to foot, a tall and powerful image of the man that once was, his long, sharp-featured, bearded face turned toward them, his penetrating eyes sweeping clear their defenses, laying bare their lives for examination and judgment.

Par Ohmsford shivered.

The churning of the waters subsided, the rumbling ceased, the wails died into a hush that hung suspended across the expanse of the valley. The shade moved toward them, seemingly without haste, as if to discredit Cogline's word that it could stay only briefly in the world of men. Its eyes never left their own. Par had never been so frightened. He wanted to run. He wanted to flee for his life, but he stood rooted to the spot on which he stood, unable to move.

The shade came to the water's edge and stopped. From somewhere deep within their minds, the members of the little company heard it speak.

—I am Allanon that was—

A murmur of voices filled the air, voices of things no longer living, echoing the shade's words.

—I have called you to me in your dreams—Par, Wren, and Walker. Children of Shannara, you have been summoned to me. The wheel of time comes around again—for rebirthing of the magic, for honoring the trust that was given you, for beginning and ending many things—

The voice, deep and sonorous within them, grew rough with feelings that scraped the bone.

—The Shadowen come. They come with a promise of destruction, sweeping over the Four Lands with the certainty of day after night—

There was a pause as the shade's lean hands wove a vision of his words through the fabric of the night air, a tapestry that hung momentarily in brilliant colors against the misted black. The dreams he had sent them came alive, sketches of nightmarish madness. Then they faded and were gone. The voice whispered soundlessly.

—It shall be so, if you do not heed—

Par felt the words reverberate through his body like a rumble from the earth. He wanted to look at the others, wanted to see what was on their faces, but the voice of the shade held him spellbound.

Not so Walker Boh. His uncle's voice was as chilling as the shade's. "Tell us what you would, Allanon! Be done with it!"

Allanon's flat gaze shifted to the dark figure and settled on him. Walker Boh staggered back a step in spite of himself. The shade pointed.

—Destroy the Shadowen! They subvert the people of the Races, creeping into their bodies, taking their forms as they choose, becoming them, using them, turning them into the misshapen giant and maddened woodswoman you have already encountered—and into things worse still. No one prevents it. No one will, if not you—

"But what are we supposed to do?" Par asked at once, almost without thinking.

The shade had been substantial when it had first appeared, a ghost that had taken on again the fullness of life. But already the lines and shadings were beginning to pale, and he who was once Allanon shimmered with the translucent and ephemeral inconsistency of smoke.

—Shannara child. There are balances to be restored if the Shadowen are to be destroyed—not for a time, not in this age only, but forever. Magic is needed. Magic to put an end to the misuse of life. Magic to restore the fabric of man's existence in the mortal world. That magic is your heritage—yours, Wren's, and Walker's. You must acknowledge it and embrace it—

The Hadeshorn was beginning to roil again, and the members of the little company fell back before its hiss and spray—all but Cogline who stood rock-still before the others, his head bowed upon his frail chest.

The shade of Allanon seemed to swell suddenly against the night, rising up before them. The robes spread wide. The shade's eyes fixed on Par, and the Valeman felt the stab of an invisible finger penetrate his breast.

—Par Ohmsford, bearer of the wishsong's promise, I charge you with recovering the Sword of Shannara. Only through the Sword can truth be revealed and only through truth shall the Shadowen be overcome. Take up the Sword, Par; wield it according to the dictates of your heart—the truth of the Shadowen shall be yours to discover—

The eyes shifted.

—Wren, child of hidden, forgotten lives, yours is a charge of equal importance. There can be no healing of the Lands or of their people without the Elves of faerie. Find them and return them to the world of men. Find them, Rover girl. Only then can the sickness end—

The Hadeshorn erupted with a booming cough.

—And Walker Boh, you of no belief, seek that belief—and the understanding necessary to sustain it. Search out the last of the curatives that is needed to give life back to the Lands. Search out disappeared Paranor and restore the Druids—

There was astonishment mirrored in the faces of all, and for an instant it smothered the shouts of disbelief that struggled to surface. Then everyone was yelling at once, the words tumbling over one another as each sought to make himself heard above the tumult. But the cries disappeared instantly as the shade's arms came up in a sweep that caused the earth to rumble anew.

—Cease—

The waters of the Hadeshorn spit and hissed behind him as he faced them. It was growing lighter now in the east; dawn was threatening to break.

The shade's voice was again a whisper.

—You would know more. I wish that it could be so. But I have told you what I can. I cannot tell you more. I lack the power in death that I possessed in life. I am permitted to see only bits and pieces of the world that was or the future that will be. I cannot find what is hidden from you for I am sealed away in a world where substance has small meaning. Each day, the memory of it slips further from me. I sense what is and what is possible; that must suffice. Therefore, pay heed to me. I cannot come with you. I cannot guide you. I cannot answer the questions you bring with you—not of magic or family or self-worth. All that you must do for yourselves. My time in the Four Lands is gone, children of Shannara. As it once was for Bremen, so it is now for me. I am not chained by shackles of failure as was he, but I am chained nevertheless. Death limits both time and being. I am the past. The future of the Four Lands belongs to you and to you alone—

"But you ask impossible things of us!" Wren snapped desperately.

"Worse! You ask things that should never be!" Walker raged. "Druids come again? Paranor restored?"

The shade's reply came softly.

—I ask for what must be. You have the skills, the heart, the right, and the need to do what I have asked. Believe what I have told you. Do as I have said. Then will the Shadowen be destroyed—

Par felt his throat tighten in desperation. Allanon was beginning to fade.

"Where shall we look?" he cried out frantically. "Where do we begin our search? Allanon, you have to tell us!"

There was no answer. The shade withdrew further.

"No! You cannot go!" Walker Boh howled suddenly.

The shade began to sink into the waters of the Hadeshorn.

"Druid, I forbid it!" Walker screamed in fury, throwing off sparks of his own magic as he flung his arms out as if to hold the other back.

The whole of the valley seemed to explode in response, the earth shaking until rocks bounced and rattled ferociously, the air filling with a wind that whipped down out of the mountains as if summoned, the Hadeshorn churning in a maelstrom of rage, the dead crying out—and the shade of Allanon bursting into flame. The members of the little company were thrown flat as the forces about them collided, and everything was caught up in a whirlwind of light and sound.

At last it was still and dark again. They lifted their heads cautiously and looked about. The valley was empty of shades and spirits and all that accompanied them. The earth was at rest once more and the Hadeshorn a silent, placid stretch of luminescence that reflected the sun's brilliant image from where it lifted out of the darkness in the east.

Par Ohmsford climbed slowly to his feet. He felt that he might have awakened from a dream.

CHAPTER

16

WHEN THEY RECOVERED THEIR COMPOSURE, the members of the little company discovered that Cogline was missing. At first they thought such a thing impossible, certain that they must be mistaken, and they cast about for him expectantly, searching the lingering nighttime shadows. But the valley offered few places to hide, and the old man was nowhere to be found.

"Perhaps Allanon's shade whisked him away," Morgan suggested in an attempt to make a joke of it.

Nobody laughed. Nobody even smiled. They were already sufficiently distressed by everything else that had happened that night, and the strange disappearance of the old man only served to unsettle them further. It was one thing for the shades of Druids dead and gone to appear and vanish without warning; it was something else again when it was a flesh-and-blood person. Besides, Cogline had been their last link to the meaning behind the dreams and the reason for their journey here. With the apparent severing of that link, they were all too painfully aware that they were now on their own.

They stood around uncertainly a moment or two longer. Then Walker muttered something about wasting his time. He started back the way he had come, the others of the little company trailing after him. The sun was above the horizon now, golden in a sky that was cloudless and blue, and the warmth of the day was already settling over the barren peaks of the Dragon's Teeth. Par glanced over his shoulder as they reached the valley rim. The Hadeshorn stared back at him, sullen and unresponsive.

The walk back was a silent one. They were all thinking about what the Druid had said, sifting and measuring the revelations and charges, and none of them were ready yet to talk. Certainly Par wasn't. He was so confounded by what he had been told that he was having trouble accepting that he had actually heard it. He trailed the others with Coll, watching their backs as they wound single file through the breaks in the rocks, following the pathway that led down through the cliff pocket to the foothills and their campsite, thinking mostly that Walker had been right after all, that whatever he might have imagined this meeting with the shade of Allanon would be like, he would have imagined wrong. Coll asked him at one point if he were all right and he nodded without replying, wondering inwardly if indeed he would ever be all right again.

Recover the Sword of Shannara, the shade had commanded him. Sticks and stones, how in the world was he supposed to do that?

The seeming impossibility of the task was daunting. He had no idea where to begin. No one, to the best of his knowledge, had even seen the Sword since the occupation of Tyrsis by the Federation—well over a hundred years ago. And it might have disappeared before that. Certainly no one had seen it since. Like most things connected with the time of the Druids and the magic, the Sword was part of a legend that was all but forgotten. There weren't any Druids, there weren't any Elves, and there wasn't any magic—not anymore, not in the world of men. How often had he heard that?

His jaw tightened. Just exactly what was he supposed to do? What were any of them supposed to do? Allanon had given them nothing to work with beyond the bare charging of their respective quests and his assurance that what he asked of them was both possible and necessary.

He felt a hot streak race through him. There had been no mention of his own magic, of the uses of the wishsong that he believed were hidden from him. Nothing had been said about the ways in which it might be employed. He hadn't even been given a chance to ask questions. He didn't know one thing more about the magic than he had before.

Par was angry and disappointed and a dozen other things too confusing to sort out. Recover the Sword of Shannara, indeed! And then what? What was he supposed to do with it? Challenge the Shadowen to some sort of combat? Go charging around the countryside searching them out and destroying them one by one?

His face flushed. Shades! Why should he even *think* about doing such a thing?

He caught himself. Well, that was really the crux of things, wasn't it? Should he even consider doing what Allanon had asked—not so much the hunting of the Shadowen with the Sword of Shannara, but the hunting of the Sword of Shannara in the first place?

That was what needed deciding.

He tried pushing the matter from his mind for a moment, losing himself in the cool of the shadows where the cliffs still warded the pathway; but, like a frightened child clinging to its mother, it refused to release its grip. He saw Steff ahead of him saying something to Teel, then to Morgan and shaking his head vehemently as he did so. He saw the stiff set of Walker Boh's back. He saw Wren striding after her uncle as if she might walk right over him. All of them were as angry and frustrated as he was; there was no mistaking the look. They felt cheated by what they had been told—or not told. They had expected something more substantial, something definitive, something that would give them answers to the questions they had brought with them.

Anything besides the impossible charges they had been given!

Yet Allanon had said the charges were not impossible, that they could be accomplished, and that the three charged had the skills, the heart, and the right to accomplish them.

Par sighed. Should he believe that?

And again he was back to wondering whether or not he should even consider doing what he had been asked.

But he was already considering exactly that, wasn't he? What else was he doing by debating the matter, if not that?

He passed out of the cliff shadows onto the pebble-strewn trail leading downward to the campsite. As he did so, he made a determined effort to put aside his anger and frustration and to think clearly. What did he know that he could rely upon? The dreams had indeed been a summons from Allanon—that much appeared certain now. The Druid had come to them as he had come to Ohmsfords in the past, asking their help against dark magic that threatened the Four Lands. The only difference, of course, was that this time he had been forced to come as a shade. Cogline, a former Druid, had been his messenger in the flesh to assure that the summons was heeded. Cogline had Allanon's trust.

Par took a moment to consider whether or not he really believed that last statement and decided he did.

The Shadowen were real, he went on. They were dangerous, they were evil, they were certainly a threat of some sort to the Races and the Four Lands. They were magic.

He paused again. If the Shadowen were indeed magic, it would probably take magic to defeat them. And if he accepted that, it made much of what Allanon and Cogline had told them more convincing. It made possible the tale of the origin and growth of the Shadowen. It made probable the claim that the balance of things was out of whack. Whether you accepted the premise that the Shadowen were to blame or not, there was clearly much wrong in the Four Lands. Most of the blame for what was bad had been attributed by the Federation to the magic of the Elves and Druids—magic that the old stories claimed was good. But Par thought the truth lay somewhere in between. Magic in and of itself—if you believed in it as Par did—was never bad or good; it was simply power. That was the lesson of the wishsong. It was all in how the magic was used.

Par frowned. That being so, what if the Shadowen were using magic to cause problems among the Races in ways that none of them could see? What if the only way to combat such magic was to turn it against the user, to cause it to revert to the uses for which it was intended? What if Druids and Elves and talismans like the Sword of Shannara were indeed needed to accomplish that end?

There was sense in the idea, he admitted reluctantly.

But was there enough sense?

The campsite appeared ahead, undisturbed since their leave-taking the previous night, streaked by early sunlight and fading shadows. The horses nickered at their approach, still tied to the picket line. Par saw that Cogline's horse was among them. Apparently the old man had not returned here.

He found himself thinking of the way Cogline had come to them before, appearing unexpectedly to each, to Walker, Wren, and himself, saying what he had to say, then departing as abruptly as he had come. It had been that way each time. He had warned each of them what was required, then let them decide what they would do. Perhaps, he thought suddenly, that was what he had done this time as well—simply left them to decide on their own.

They reached the camp, still without having spoken more than a few brief words to one another, and came to an uneasy halt. There was some suggestion of eating or sleeping first, but everyone quickly decided against it. No one really wanted to eat or sleep; they were neither hungry nor tired. They were ready now to talk about what had happened. They wanted to put the matter to discussion and give voice to the thoughts and emotions that had been building and churning inside them during the walk back.

"Very well," Walker Boh said curtly, after a moment's strained silence. "Since no one else cares to say it, I will. This whole business is madness. Paranor is gone. The Druids are gone. There haven't been any Elves in the Four Lands in over a hundred years. The Sword of Shannara hasn't been seen for at least that long. We haven't, any of us, the vaguest idea of how to go about recovering any of them—if, indeed, recovery is possible. I suspect it isn't. I think this is just one more instance of the Druids playing games with the Ohmsfords. And I resent it very much!"

He was flushed, his face sharply drawn. Par remembered again how angry he had been back in the valley, almost uncontrolled. This was not the Walker Boh he remembered.

"I am not sure we can dismiss what happened back there as simple game-playing," Par began, but then Walker was all over him.

"No, of course not, Par—you see all this as a chance to satisfy your misguided curiosity about the uses of magic! I warned you before that magic was not the gift you envisioned, but a curse! Why is it that you persist in seeing it as something else?"

"Suppose the shade spoke the truth?" Coll's voice was quiet and firm, and it turned Walker's attention immediately from Par.

"The truth isn't in those cowled tricksters! When has the truth ever been in them? They tell us bits and pieces, but never the whole! They use us! They have always used us!"

"But not unwisely, not without consideration for what must be done—that's not what the stories tell us." Coll held his ground. "I am not necessarily advocating that we do as the shade suggested, Walker. I am only saying that it is unreasonable to dismiss the matter out of hand because of one possibility in a rather broad range."

"The bits and pieces you speak of—those were always true in and of themselves," Par added to Coll's surprisingly eloquent defense. "What you mean is that Allanon never told the whole truth in the beginning. He always held something back."

Walker looked at them as if they were children, shaking his head. "A half-truth can be as devastating as a lie," he said quietly. The anger was fading now, replaced by a tone of resignation. "You ought to know that much."

"I know that there is danger in either."

"Then why persist in this? Let it go!"

"Uncle," Par said, the reprimand in his voice astonishing even to himself, "I haven't taken it up yet."

Walker looked at him for a long time, a tall, pale-skinned figure against the dawn, his face unreadable in its mix of emotions. "Haven't you?" he replied softly.

Then he turned, gathered up his blankets and gear and rolled them up. "I will put it to you another way, then. Were everything the shade told us true, it would make no difference. I have decided on my course of action. I will do nothing to restore Paranor and the Druids to the Four Lands. I can think of nothing I wish less. The time of the Druids and Paranor saw more madness than this age could ever hope to witness. Bring back those old men with their magics and their conjuring, their playing with the lives of men as if they were toys?"

He rose and faced them, his pale face as hard as granite. "I would sooner cut off my hand than see the Druids come again!"

The others glanced at one another in consternation as he turned away to finish putting together his pack.

"Will you simply hide out in your valley?" Par shot back, angry now himself.

Walker didn't look at him. "If you will."

"What happens if the shade spoke the truth, Walker? What happens if all it has foreseen comes to pass, and the Shadowen reach extends even into Hearthstone? Then what will you do?"

"What I must."

"With your own magic?" Par spat. "With magic taught to you by Cogline?"

His uncle's pale face lifted sharply. "How did you learn of that?"

Par shook his head stubbornly. "What difference is there between your magic and that of the Druids, Walker? Isn't it all the same?"

The other's smile was hard and unfriendly. "Sometimes, Par, you are a fool," he said and dismissed him.

When he rose a moment later, he was calm. "I have done my part in this. I came as I was bidden and I listened to what I was supposed to hear. I have no further obligation. The rest of you must decide for yourselves what you will do. As for me, I am finished with this business."

He strode through them without pausing, moving down to where the horses were tethered. He strapped his pack in place, mounted, and rode out. He never once looked back.

The remaining members of the little company watched in silence. That was a quick decision, Par thought—one that Walker Boh seemed altogether too anxious to make. He wondered why.

When his uncle was gone, he looked at Wren. "What of you?"

The Rover girl shook her head slowly. "I haven't Walker's prejudices and predispositions to contend with, but I do have his doubts." She walked over to a gathering of rocks and seated herself.

Par followed. "Do you think the shade spoke the truth?"

Wren shrugged. "I am still trying to decide if the shade was even who it claimed, Par. I sensed it was, felt it in my heart, and yet . . ." She trailed off. "I know nothing of Allanon beyond the stories, and I know the stories but poorly. You know them better than I. What do you think?"

Par did not hesitate. "It was Allanon."

"And do you think he spoke the truth?"

Par was conscious of the others moving over to join them, silent, watchful. "I think there is reason to believe that he did, yes." He outlined his thoughts as far as he had developed them during the walk back from the valley. He was surprised at how convincing he sounded. He was no longer floundering; he was beginning to gain a measure of conviction in his arguments. "I haven't thought it through as much as I would like," he finished. "But what reason would the shade have for bringing us here and for telling us what it did if not to reveal the truth? Why would it tell us a lie? Walker seems convinced there is a deception at work in this, but I cannot find what form it takes or what purpose it could possibly serve.

"Besides," he added, "Walker is frightened of this business— of the Druids, of the magic, of whatever. He keeps something from us. I can sense it. He plays the same game he accuses Allanon of playing."

Wren nodded. "But he also understands the Druids." When Par looked confused, she smiled sadly. "They do hide things, Par. They hide whatever they do not wish revealed. That is their way. There are things being hidden here as well. What we were told was too incomplete, too circumscribed. However you choose to view it, we are being treated no differently from our ancestors before us."

There was a long silence. "Maybe we should go back into the valley tonight and see if the shade won't come to us again," Morgan suggested in a tone of voice that whispered of doubt.

"Perhaps we should give Cogline a chance to reappear," Coll added.

Par shook his head. "I don't think we will be seeing any more of either for now. I expect whatever decisions we make will have to be made without their help."

"I agree." Wren stood up again. "I am supposed to find the Elves and—how did he put it?—return them to the world of men. A very deliberate choice of words, but I don't understand them. I haven't any idea where the Elves are or even where to begin to look for them. I have lived in the Westland for almost ten years now, Garth for many more than that, and between us we have been everywhere there is to go. I can tell you for a fact that there are no Elves to be found there. Where else am I to look?"

She came over to Par and faced him. "I am going home. There is nothing more for me to do here. I will have to think on this, but even thinking may be of no use. If the dreams come again and tell me something of where to begin this search, then perhaps I will give it a try. But for now . . ."

She shrugged. "Well. Goodbye, Par."

She hugged and kissed him, then did the same for Coll and even Morgan this time. She nodded to the Dwarves and began gathering up her things. Garth joined her silently.

"I wish you would stay a bit longer, Wren," Par tried, quiet desperation welling up like a knot in his stomach at the thought of being left alone to wrestle with this matter.

"Why not come with me instead?" she answered. "You would probably be better off in the Westland."

Par looked at Coll, who frowned. Morgan looked away. Par sighed and shook his head reluctantly. "No, I have to make my own decision first. I have to do that before I can know where I should be."

She nodded, seeming to understand. She had her things together, and she walked up to him. "I might think differently if I had the magic for protection like you and Walker. But I don't. I don't have the wishsong or Cogline's teachings to rely on. I have only a bag of painted stones." She kissed him again. "If you need me, you can find me in the Tirfing. Be careful, Par."

She rode out of the camp with Garth trailing. The others watched them go, the curly haired Rover girl and her giant companion in his bright patchwork clothes. Minutes later, they were specks against the western horizon, their horses almost out of sight.

Par kept looking after them even when they had disappeared. The he glanced east again after Walker Boh. He felt as if parts of himself were being stolen away.

COLL INSISTED they have something to eat then, all of them, because it had been better than twelve hours since their last meal and there was no point in trying to think something through on an empty stomach. Par was grateful for the respite, unwilling to confront his own decision-making in the face of the disappointment he felt at the departure of Walker and Wren. He ate the broth that Steff prepared along with some hard bread and fruit, drank several cupfuls of ale, and walked down to the spring to wash. When he returned, he agreed to his brother's suggestion that he lie down for a few minutes and after doing so promptly fell asleep.

It was midday when he woke, his head throbbing, his body aching, his throat hot and dry. He had dreamed snatches of things he would have been just as happy not dreaming at all— of Rimmer Dall and his Federation Seekers hunting him through empty, burned-out city buildings; of Dwarves that watched, starving and helpless in the face of an occupation they could do nothing to ease; of Shadowen lying in wait behind every dark corner he passed in his flight; of Allanon's shade calling out in warning with each new hazard, but laughing as well at his plight. His stomach felt unsettled, but he forced the feeling aside. He washed again, drank some more ale, seated himself in the shade of an old poplar tree, and waited for the sickness to pass. It did, rather more quickly than he would have expected, and soon he was working on a second bowl of the broth.

Coll joined him as he ate. "Feeling better? You didn't look well when you first woke up."

Par finished eating and put the bowl aside. "I wasn't. But I'm all right now." He smiled to prove it.

Coll eased down next to him against the roughened tree trunk, settling his solid frame in place, staring out from the comfort of the shade into the midday heat. "I've been thinking," he said, the blocky features crinkling thoughtfully. He seemed reluctant to continue. "I've been thinking about what I would do if you decided to go looking for the Sword."

Par turned to him at once. "Coll, I haven't even . . ."

"No, Par. Let me finish." Coll was insistent. "If there's one thing I've learned about being your brother, it's to try to get the jump on you when it comes to making decisions. Otherwise, you make them first and once they're made, they might as well be cast in stone!"

He glanced over. "You may recall that we've had this discussion before? I keep telling you I know you better than you know yourself. Remember that time a few years back when you fell into the Rappahalladran and almost drowned while we were off in the Duln hunting that silver fox? There wasn't supposed to be one like it left in the Southland, but that old trapper said he'd seen one and that was enough for you. The Rappahalladran was cresting, it was late spring, and Dad told us not to try a crossing—made us promise not to try. I knew the minute you made that promise that you would break it if you had to. The very minute you made it!"

Par frowned. "Well, I wouldn't say . . ."

Coll cut him short. "The point is, I can usually tell when you've made up your mind about something. And I think Walker was right. I think you've made up your mind about going after the Sword of Shannara. You have, haven't you?"

Par stared at him, surprised.

"Your eyes say you're going after it, Par," Coll continued calmly, actually smiling. "Whether it's out there or not, you're going after it. I know you. You're going because you still think you can learn something about your own magic by doing so, because you want to do something fine and noble with it, because you have this little voice inside you whispering that the magic is meant for something. No, no, hold on, now—hear me out." He held up his hands at Par's attempt to dispute him. "I don't think there is anything wrong with that. I understand it. But I don't know if you do or whether you can admit to it. And you have to be able to admit to it because otherwise you won't ever be at peace with yourself about why you are going. I know

I don't have any magic of my own, but the fact is that in some ways I do understand the problem better than you."

He paused, somber. "You always look for the challenges no one else wants. That's part of what's happening here. You see Walker and Wren walk away from this and right away you want to do just the opposite. That's the way you are. You couldn't give it up now if you had to."

He cocked his head reflectively. "Believe it or not, I have always admired that in you."

Then he sighed. "I know there are other considerations as well. There's the matter of the folks, still under confinement back in the Vale, and us with no home, no real place to go, outlaws of a sort. If we abandon this search, this quest Allanon's shade has given us, where do we go? What possible thing can we do that will change matters more thoroughly than finding the Sword of Shannara? I know there's that. And I know . . ."

Par interrupted. "You said 'we.' "

Coll stopped. "What?"

Par was studying him critically. "Just then. You said 'we.' Several times. You said, what if 'we' abandon this search and where do 'we' go?"

Coll shook his head ruefully. "So I did. I start talking about you and almost before I know it I'm talking about me as well. But that's exactly the problem, I guess. We're so close that I sometimes think of us as if we were the same—and we're not. We're very different and no more so than in this instance. You have the magic and the chance to learn about it and I don't. You have the quest and I haven't. So what should I do if you go, Par?"

Par waited a moment, then said, "Well?"

"Well. After all is said and done, after all the arguments for and against have been laid on the table, I keep coming back to a couple of things." He shifted so he was facing Par. "First, I'm your brother and I love you. That means I don't abandon you, even when I'm not sure if I agree with what you're doing. I've told you that before. Second, if you go . . ." He paused. "You are going, aren't you?"

There was a long moment of silence. Par did not reply.

"Very well. If you go, it will be a dangerous journey, and you will need someone to watch your back. And that's what brothers are supposed to do for each other. That's second."

He cleared his throat. "Last, I've thought it all out from the point of view of what I would do if I were you, go or not go, measuring what I perceive to be the right and wrong of the matter." He paused. "If it were up to me, if I were you, I think I'd go."

He leaned back against the poplar trunk and waited. Par took a deep breath. "To be honest, Coll, I think that's just about the last thing I ever expected to hear from you."

Coll smiled. "That's probably why I said it. I don't like to be predictable."

"So you would go, would you? If you were me?" Par studied his brother silently for a moment, letting the possibility play itself out in his mind. "I don't know if I believe you."

Coll let the smile broaden. "Of course you do."

They were still staring at each other as Morgan wandered up and sat down across from them, faintly puzzled as he saw the same look registered on both faces. Steff and Teel came over as well. All three glanced at one another. "What's going on?" Morgan asked finally.

Par stared at him momentarily without seeing him. He saw instead the land beyond, the hills dotted with sparse groves, running south out of the barren stretches of the Dragon's Teeth, fading into a heat that made the earth shimmer. Dust blew in small eddies where sudden breezes scooped at the roadway leading down. It was still beneath the tree, and Par was thinking about the past, remembering the times that Coll and he had shared. The memories were an intimacy that comforted him; they were sharp and clear, most of them, and they made him ache in a sweet, welcome way.

"Well?" Morgan persisted.

Par blinked. "Coll tells me he thinks I ought to do what the shade said. He thinks I ought to try to find the Sword of Shannara." He paused. "What do you think, Morgan?"

Morgan didn't hesitate. "I think I'm going with you. It gets tiresome spending all of my time tweaking the noses of those Federation dunderheads who try to govern Leah. There's better uses for a man like me." He lunged to his feet. "Besides, I have a blade that needs testing against things of dark magic!" He reached back in a mock feint for his sword. "And as all here can bear witness, there's no better way to do so than to keep company with Par Ohmsford!"

Par shook his head despairingly. "Morgan, you shouldn't joke . . ."

"Joke! But that's just the point! All I've been doing for months now is playing jokes! And what good has it done?" Morgan's lean features were hard. "Here is a chance for me to do something that has real purpose, something far more important than causing Leah's enemies to suffer meaningless irritations and indignities. Come, now! You have to see it as I do, Par. You cannot dispute what I say." His eyes shifted abruptly. "Steff, how about you? What do you intend? And Teel?"

Steff laughed, his rough features wrinkling. "Well now, Teel and I share pretty much the same point of view on the matter. We have already reached our decision. We came with you in the first place because we were hoping to get our hands on something, magic or whatever, that could help our people break free of the Federation. We haven't found that something yet, but we might be getting closer. What the shade said about the Shadowen spreading the dark magic, living inside men and women and children to do so, might explain a good part of the madness that consumes the Lands. It might even have something to do with why the Federation seems so bent on breaking the backs of the Dwarves! You've seen it for yourself—that's surely what the Federation is about. There's dark magic at work there. Dwarves can sense it better than most because the deeper stretches of the Eastland have always provided a hiding place for it. The only difference in this instance is that, instead of hiding, it's out in the open like a crazed animal, threatening us all. So maybe finding the Sword of Shannara as the shade says will be a step toward penning that animal up again!"

"There, now!" Morgan cried triumphantly. "What better company for you, Par Ohmsford, than that?"

Par shook his head in bewilderment. "None, Morgan, but . . ."

"Then say you'll do it! Forget Walker and Wren and their

excuses! This has meaning! Think of what we might be able to accomplish!" He gave his friend a plaintive look. "Confound it, Par, how can we lose by trying when by trying we have everything to gain?"

Steff reached over and poked him. "Don't push so hard, Highlander. Give the Valeman room to breathe!"

Par stared at them each in turn, at the bluff-faced Steff, the enigmatic Teel, the fervently eager Morgan Leah, and finally Coll. He remembered suddenly that his brother had never finished revealing his own decision. He had only said that if he were Par, he would go.

"Coll . . ." he began.

But Coll seemed to read his thoughts. "If you're going, I'm going." His brother's features might have been carved from stone. "From here to wherever this all ends."

There was a long moment of silence as they faced each other, and the anticipation mirrored in their eyes was a whisper that rustled the leaves of their thoughts as if it were the wind.

Par Ohmsford took a deep breath. "Then I guess the matter's settled," he said. "Now where do we start?"

CHAPTER

17

S USUAL, Morgan Leah had a plan.

"If we expect to have any luck at all locating the Sword, we're going to need help. The five of us are simply too few. After all these years, finding the Sword of Shannara is likely to be like finding the proverbial needle in the haystack—and we don't begin to know enough about the haystack. Steff, you and Teel may be familiar with the Eastland, but Callahorn and the Borderlands are foreign ground. It's the same with the Valemen and myself—we simply don't know enough about the country. And let's not forget that the Federation will be prowling about every place we're likely to go. Dwarves and fugitives from the law aren't welcome in the South-land, the last I heard. We'll have to be on the lookout for Sha-dowen as well. Truth is, they seem drawn to the magic like wolves to the scent of blood, and we can't assume we've seen the last of them. It will be all we can to do watch our backs, let alone figure out what's happened to the Sword. We can't do it alone. We need someone to help us, someone who has a work-ing knowledge of the Four Lands, someone who can supply us with men and weapons."

He shifted his gaze from the others to Par and smiled that familiar smile that was filled with secretive amusement. "We need your friend from the Movement."

Par groaned. He was none too keen to reassociate with the outlaws; it seemed an open invitation to trouble. But Steff and Teel and even Coll liked the idea, and after arguing about it for

209

a time he was forced to admit that the Highlander's proposal made sense. The outlaws possessed the resources they lacked and were familiar with the Borderlands and the free territories surrounding them. They would know where to look and what pitfalls to avoid while doing so. Moreover, Par's rescuer seemed a man you could depend upon.

"He told you that if you ever needed help, you could come to him," Morgan pointed out. "It seems to me that you could use a little now."

There was no denying that, so the matter was decided. They spent what remained of the day at the campsite below the foothills leading to the Valley of Shale and the Hadeshorn, sleeping restlessly through the second night of the new moon at the base of the Dragon's Teeth. When morning came, they packed up their gear, mounted their horses and set out. The plan was simple. They would travel to Varfleet, search out Kiltan Forge at Reaver's End in the north city and ask for the Archer—all as Par's mysterious rescuer had instructed. Then they would see what was what.

They rode south through the scrub country that bordered the Rabb Plains until they crossed the east branch of the Mermidon, then turned west. They followed the river through midday and into early afternoon, the sun baking the land out of a cloudless sky, the air dry and filled with dust. No one said much of anything as they traveled, locked away in the silence of their own thoughts. There had been no further talk of Allanon since setting out. There had been no mention of Walker or Wren. Par fingered the ring with the hawk insigne from time to time and wondered anew about the identity of the man who had given it to him.

It was late afternoon when they passed down through the river valley of the Runne Mountains north of Varfleet and approached the outskirts of the city. It sprawled below them across a series of hills, dusty and sweltering against the glare of the westward fading sun. Shacks and hovels ringed the city's perimeter, squalid shelters for men and women who lacked even the barest of means. They called out to the travelers as they passed, pressing up against them for money and food, and Par and Coll handed down what little they had. Morgan glanced back reprovingly, somewhat as a parent might at a naive child, but made no comment.

A little farther on, Par found himself wishing belatedly that he had thought to disguise his Elven features. It had been weeks since he had done so, and he had simply gotten out of the habit. He could take some consolation from the fact that his hair had grown long and covered his ears. But he would have to be careful nevertheless. He glanced over at the Dwarves. They had their travel cloaks pulled close, the hoods wrapping their faces in shadow. They were in more danger than he of discovery. Everyone knew that Dwarves were not permitted to travel in the Southland. Even in Varfleet, It was risky.

When they reached the city proper and the beginnings of streets that bore names and shops with signs, the traffic increased markedly. Soon, it was all but impossible to move ahead. They dismounted and led their horses afoot until they found a stable where they could board them. Morgan made the transaction while the others stood back unobtrusively against the walls of the buildings across the way and watched the people of the city press against one another in a sluggish flow. Beggars came up to them and asked for coins. Par watched a fire-eater display his art to a wondering crowd of boys and men at a fruit mart. The low mutter of voices filled the air with a ragged sound.

"Sometimes you get lucky," Morgan informed them quietly as he returned. "We're standing in Reaver's End. This whole section of the city is Reaver's End. Kiltan Forge is just a few streets over."

He beckoned them on, and they slipped past the steady throng of bodies, working their way into a side street that was less crowded, if more ill-smelling, and soon they were hurrying along a shadowed alley that twisted and turned past a rutted sewage way. Par wrinkled his nose in distaste. This was the city as Coll saw it. He risked a quick glance back at his brother, but his brother was busy watching where he was stepping.

They crossed several more streets before emerging onto one that seemed to satisfy Morgan, who promptly turned right and led them through the crowds to a broad, two-storey barn with a sign that bore the name Kiltan Forge seared on a plaque of wood. The sign and the building were old and splintering, but the furnaces within burned red-hot, spitting and flaming as metals were fed in and removed by tenders. Machines ground, and hammers pounded and shaped. The din rose above the noise of the street and echoed off the walls of the surrounding buildings, to disappear finally into the suffocating embrace of the lingering afternoon heat.

Morgan edged his way along the fringes of the crowd, the others trailing silently after, and finally managed to work his way up to the Forge entrance. A handful of men worked the furnaces under the direction of a large fellow with drooping mustaches and a balding pate colored soot-black. The fellow ignored them until they had come all the way inside, then turned and asked, "Something I can help you with?"

Morgan said, "We're looking for the Archer."

The fellow with the mustaches ambled over. "Who did you say, now?"

"The Archer," Morgan repeated.

"And who's that supposed to be?" The other man was broad-shouldered and caked with sweat.

"I don't know," Morgan admitted. "We were just told to ask for him."

"Who by?"

"Look . . ."

"Who by? Don't you know, man?"

It was hot in the shadow of Kiltan Forge, and it was clear that Morgan was going to have trouble with this man if things kept going the way they were. Heads were already starting to turn. Par pushed forward impulsively, anxious to keep from drawing attention to themselves and said, "By a man who wears a ring that bears the insigne of a hawk."

The fellow's sharp eyes narrowed, studying the Valeman's face with its Elven features.

"This ring," Par finished and held it out.

The other flinched as if he had been stung. "Don't be showing that about, you young fool!" he snapped and shoved it away from him as if it were poison.

"Then tell us where we can find the Archer!" Morgan interjected, his irritation beginning to show through.

There was sudden activity in the street that caused them all to turn hurriedly. A squad of Federation soldiers was approaching, pushing through the crowd, making directly for the Forge. "Get out of sight!" the fellow with the mustaches snapped urgently and stepped away.

The soldiers came into the Forge, glancing about the fire-lit darkness. The man with the mustaches came forward to greet them. Morgan and the Valemen gathered up the Dwarves, but the soldiers were between them and the doorway leading to the street. Morgan edged them all toward the deep shadows.

"Weapons order, Hirehone," the squad leader announced to the man with the mustaches, thrusting out a paper. "Need it by week's end. And don't argue the matter."

Hirehone muttered something unintelligible, but nodded. The squad leader talked to him some more, sounding weary and hot. The soldiers were casting about restlessly. One moved toward the little company. Morgan tried to stand in front of his companions, tried to make the soldier speak with him. The soldier hesitated, a big fellow with a reddish beard. Then he noticed something and pushed past the Highlander. "You there!" he snapped at Teel. "What's wrong with you?" One hand reached out, pulling aside the hood. "Dwarves! Captain, there's . . . !"

He never finished. Teel killed him with a single thrust of her long knife, jamming the blade through his throat. He was still trying to talk as he died. The other soldiers reached for their weapons, but Morgan was already among them, his own sword thrusting, forcing them back. He cried out to the others, and the Dwarves and Valemen broke for the doorway. They reached the street, Morgan on their heels, the Federation soldiers a step behind. The crowd screamed and split apart as the battle careened into them. There were a dozen soldiers in pursuit, but two were wounded and the rest were tripping over one another in their haste to reach the Highlander. Morgan cut down the foremost, howling like a madman. Ahead, Steff reached a barred door to a warehouse, brought up the suddenly revealed mace, and hammered the troublesome barrier into splinters with a single blow. They rushed through the darkened interior and out a back door, turned left down an alley and came up against a fence. Desperately, they wheeled about and started back.

The pursuing Federation soldiers burst through the warehouse door and came at them.

Par used the wishsong and filled the disappearing gap between them with a swarm of buzzing hornets. The soldiers howled and dove for cover. In the confusion, Steff smashed enough boards of the fence to allow them all to slip through. They ran down a second alley, through a maze of storage sheds, turned right and pushed past a hinged metal gate.

They found themselves in a yard of scrap metal behind the Forge. Ahead, a door to the back of the Forge swung open. "In here!" someone called.

They ran without questioning, hearing the sound of shouting and blare of horns all about. They shoved through the opening into a small storage room and heard the door slam shut behind them.

Hirehone faced them, hands on hips. "I hope you turn out to be worth all the trouble you've caused!" he told them.

HE HID THEM in a crawlspace beneath the floor of the storage room, leaving them there for what seemed like hours. It was hot and close, there was no light, and the sounds of booted feet tramped overhead twice in the course of their stay, each time leaving them taut and breathless. When Hirehone finally let them out again, it was night, the skies overcast and inky, the lights of the city fragmented pinpricks through the gaps in the boards of the Forge walls. He took them out of the storage room to a small kitchen that was adjacent, sat them down about a spindly table, and fed them.

"Had to wait until the soldiers finished their search, satisfied themselves you weren't coming back or hiding in the metal," he explained. "They were angry, I'll tell you—especially about the killing."

Teel showed nothing of what she was thinking, and no one else spoke. Hirehone shrugged. "Means nothing to me either."

They chewed in silence for a time, then Morgan asked, "What about the Archer? Can we see him now?"

Hirehone grinned. "Don't think that'll be possible. There isn't any such person."

Morgan's jaw dropped. "Then why . . . ?"

"It's a code," Hirehone interrupted. "It's just a way of letting me know what's expected of me. I was testing you. Sometimes the code gets broken. I had to make sure you weren't spying for the Federation."

"You're an outlaw," Par said.

"And you're Par Ohmsford," the other replied. "Now finish up eating, and I'll take you to the man you came to see."

They did as they were told, cleaned off their plates in an old sink, and followed Hirehone back into the bowels of Kiltan Forge. The Forge was empty now, save for a single tender on night watch who minded the fire-breathing furnaces that were never allowed to go cold. He paid them no attention. They passed through the cavernous stillness on cat's feet, smelling ash and metal in a sulfurous mix, watching the shadows dance to the fire's cadence.

When they slipped through a side door into the darkness, Morgan whispered to Hirehone, "We left our horses stabled several streets over."

"Don't worry about it," the other whispered back. "You won't need horses where you're going."

They passed quietly and unobtrusively down the byways of Varfleet, through its bordering cluster of shacks and hovels and finally out of the city altogether. They traveled north then along the Mermidon, following the river upstream where it wound below the foothills fronting the Dragon's Teeth. They walked for the remainder of the night, crossing the river just above its north-south juncture where it passed through a series of rapids that scattered its flow into smaller streams. The river was down at this time of the year or the crossing would never have been possible without a boat. As it was, the water reached nearly to the chins of the Dwarves at several points, and all of them were forced to walk with their backpacks and weapons hoisted over their heads.

Once across the river, they came up against a heavily for-ested series of defiles and ravines that stretched on for miles into the rock of the Dragon's Teeth.

"This is the Parma Key," Hirehone volunteered at one point. "Pretty tricky country if you don't know your way."

That was a gross understatement, Par quickly discovered. The Parma Key was a mass of ridges and ravines that rose and fell without warning amid a suffocating blanket of trees and scrub. The new moon gave no light, the stars were masked by the canopy of trees and the shadow of the mountains, and the company found itself in almost complete blackness. After a brief penetration of the woods, Hirehone sat them down to wait for daybreak.

Even in daylight, any passage seemed impossible. It was perpetually shadowed and misted within the mountain forests of the Parma Key, and the ravines and ridges crisscrossed the whole of the land. There was a trail, invisible to anyone who hadn't known it before, a twisting path that Hirehone followed without effort but that left the members of the little company uncertain of the direction in which they were moving. Morning slipped toward midday, and the sun filtered down through the densely packed trees in narrow streamers of brightness that did little to chase the lingering fog and seemed to have strayed somehow from the outer world into the midst of the heavy shadows.

When they stopped for a quick lunch, Par asked their guide if he would tell them how much farther it was to where they were going.

"Not far," Hirehone answered. "There." He pointed to a massive outcropping of rock that rose above the Parma Key where the forest flattened against the wall of the Dragon's Teeth. "That, Ohmsford, is called the Jut. The Jut is the stronghold of the Movement."

Par looked, considering. "Does the Federation know it's there?" he asked.

"They know it's in here somewhere," Hirehone replied. "What they don't know is exactly where and, more to the point, how to reach it."

"And Par's mysterious rescuer, your still-nameless outlaw chief—isn't he worried about having visitors like us carrying back word of how to do just that?" Steff asked skeptically.

Hirehone smiled. "Dwarf, in order for you to find your way in again, you first have to find your way out. Think you could manage that without me?"

Steff smirked grudgingly, seeing the truth of the matter. A

man could wander forever in this maze without finding his way clear.

It was late afternoon when they reached the outcropping they had been pointing toward all day, the shadows falling in thick layers across the wilderness, casting the whole of the forest in twilight. Hirehone had whistled ahead several times during the last hour, each time waiting for an answering whistle before proceeding farther. At the base of the cliffs, a gated lift waited, settled in a clearing, its ropes disappearing skyward into the rocks overhead. The lift was large enough to hold all of them, and they stepped into it, grasping the railing for support as it hoisted them up, slowly, steadily, until at last they were above the trees. They drew even with a narrow ledge and were pulled in by a handful of men working a massive winch. A second lift waited and they climbed aboard. Again they were hoisted up along the face of the rock wall, dangling out precariously over the earth. Par looked down once and quickly regretted it. He caught a glimpse of Steff's face, bloodless beneath its sun-browned exterior. Hirehone seemed unconcerned and whistled idly as they rose.

There was a third lift as well, this one much shorter, and when they finally stepped off they found themselves on a broad, grassy bluff about midway up the cliff that ran back several hundred yards into a series of caves. Fortifications lined the edge of the bluff and ringed the caves, and there were pockets of defense built into the cliff wall overhead where it was riddled with craggy splits. There was a narrow waterfall spilling down off the mountain into a pool, and several clusters of broad-leaf trees and fir scattered about the bluff. Men scurried everywhere, hauling tools and weapons and crates of stores, crying out instructions, or answering back.

Out of the midst of this organized confusion strode Par's rescuer, his tall form clothed in startling scarlet and black. He was clean-shaven now, his tanned face weather-seamed and sharp-boned in the sunlight, a collection of planes and angles. It was a face that defied age. His brown hair was swept back and slightly receding. He was lean and fit and moved like a cat. He swept toward them with a deep-voiced shout of welcome, one arm extending first to hug Hirehone, then to gather in Par.

"So, lad, you've had a change of heart, have you? Welcome, then, and your companions as well. Your brother, a Highlander, and a brace of Dwarves, is it? Strange company, now. Have you come to join up?"

He was as guileless as Morgan had ever thought to be, and Par felt himself blush. "Not exactly. We have a problem."

"Another problem?" The outlaw chief seemed amused. "Trouble just follows after you, doesn't it? I'll have my ring back now."

Par removed the ring from his pocket and handed it over. The other man slipped it back on his finger, admiring it. "The hawk. Good symbol for a free-born, don't you think?"

"Who are you?" Par asked him bluntly.

"Who am I?" The other laughed merrily. "Haven't you figured that out yet, my friend? No? Then I'll tell you." The outlaw chief leaned forward. "Look at my hand." He held up the closed fist with the finger pointed at Par's nose. "A missing hand with a pike. Who am I?"

His eyes were sea-green and awash with mischief. There was a moment of calculated silence as the Valeman stared at him in confusion.

"My name, Par Ohmsford, is Padishar Creel," the outlaw chief said finally. "But you would know me better as the great, great, great, and then some, grandson of Panamon Creel."

And finally Par understood.

THAT EVENING, over dinner, seated at a table that had been moved purposefully away from those of the other occupants of the Jut, Par and his companions listened in rapt astonishment while Padishar Creel related his story.

"We have a rule up here that everyone's past life is his own business," he advised them conspiratorially. "It might make the others feel awkward hearing me talk about mine."

He cleared his throat. "I was a landowner," he began, "a grower of crops and livestock, the overseer of a dozen small farms and countless acres of forestland reserved for hunting. I inherited the better part of it from my father and he from his father and so on back some years further than I care to consider.

But it apparently all began with Panamon Creel. I am told, though I cannot confirm it of course, that after helping Shea Ohmsford recover the Sword of Shannara, he returned north to the Borderlands where he became quite successful at his chosen profession and accumulated a rather considerable fortune. This, upon retiring, he wisely invested in what would eventually become the lands of the Creel family."

Par almost smiled. Padishar Creel was relating his tale with a straight face, but he knew as well as the Valemen and Morgan that Panamon Creel had been a thief when Shea Ohmsford and he had stumbled on each other.

"Baron Creel, he called himself," the other went on, oblivious. "All of the heads of family since have been called the same way. Baron Creel." He paused, savoring the sound of it. Then he sighed. "But the Federation seized the lands from my father when I was a boy, stole them without a thought of recompense, and in the end dispossessed us. My father died when he tried to get them back. My mother as well. Rather mysteriously."

He smiled. "So I joined the Movement."

"Just like that?" Morgan asked, looking skeptical.

The outlaw chief skewered a piece of beef on his knife. "My parents went to the governor of the province, a Federation underling who had moved into our home, and my father demanded the return of what was rightfully his, suggesting that if something wasn't done to resolve the matter, the governor would regret it. My father never was given to caution. He was denied his request, and he and my mother were summarily dismissed. On their way back from whence they had come, they disappeared. They were found later hanging from a tree in the forests nearby, gutted and flayed."

He said it without rancor, matter-of-factly, all with a calm that was frightening. "I grew up fast after that, you might say," he finished.

There was a long silence. Padishar Creel shrugged. "It was a long time ago. I learned how to fight, how to stay alive. I drifted into the Movement, and after seeing how poorly it was managed, formed my own company." He chewed. "A few of the other leaders didn't like the idea. They tried to give me over to the Federation. That was their mistake. After I disposed of them, most of the remaining bands came over to join me. Eventually, they all will."

No one said anything. Padishar Creel glanced up. "Isn't anyone hungry? There's a good measure of food left. Let's not waste it."

They finished the meal quickly, the outlaw chief continuing to provide further details of his violent life in the same disinterested tone. Par wondered what sort of man he had gotten himself mixed up with. He had thought before that his rescuer might prove to be the champion the Four Lands had lacked since the time of Allanon, his standard the rallying point for all of the oppressed Races. Rumor had it that this man was the charismatic leader for which the freedom Movement had been waiting. But he seemed as much a cutthroat as anything. However dangerous Panamon Creel might have been in his time, Par found himself convinced that Padishar Creel was more dangerous still.

"So, that is my story and the whole of it," Padishar Creel announced, shoving back his plate. His eyes glittered. "Any part of it that you'd care to question me about?"

Silence. Then Steff growled suddenly, shockingly, "How much of it is the truth?"

Everyone froze. But Padisher Creel laughed, genuinely amused. There was a measure of respect in his eyes for the Dwarf that was unmistakable as he said, "Some of it, my Eastland friend, some of it." He winked. "The story improves with every telling."

He picked up his ale glass and poured a full measure from a pitcher. Par stared at Steff with newfound admiration. No one else would have dared ask that question.

"Come, now," the outlaw chief interjected, leaning forward. "Enough of history past. Time to hear what brought you to me. Speak, Par Ohmsford." His eyes were fixed on Par. "It has something to do with the magic, hasn't it? There wouldn't be anything else that would bring you here. Tell me."

Par hesitated. "Does your offer to help still stand?" he asked instead.

The other looked offended. "My word is my bond, lad! I said I would help and I will!"

He waited. Par glanced at the others, then said, "I need to find the Sword of Shannara."

He told Padishar Creel of his meeting with the ghost of Allanon and the task that had been given him by the Druid. He told of the journey that had brought the five of them gathered to this meeting, of the encounters with Federation soldiers and Seekers and the monsters called Shadowen. He held nothing back, despite his reservations about the man. He decided it was better neither to lie nor to attempt half-truths, better that it was all laid out for him to judge, to accept or dismiss as he chose. After all, they would be no worse off than they were now, whether he decided to help them or not.

When he had finished, the outlaw chief sat back slowly and drained the remainder of the ale from the glass he had been nursing and smiled conspiratorially at Steff. "It would seem appropriate for me to now ask how much of *this* tale is true!"

Par started to protest, but the other raised his hand quickly to cut him off. "No, lad, save your breath. I do not question what you've told me. You tell it the way you believe it, that's clear enough. It's only my way."

"You have the men, the weapons, the supplies and the network of spies to help us find what we seek," Morgan interjected quietly. "That's why we're here."

"You have the spirit for this kind of madness as well, I'd guess," Steff added with a chuckle.

Padishar Creel rubbed his chin roughly. "I have more than these, my friends," he said, smiling like a wolf. "I have a sense of fate!"

He rose wordlessly and took them from the table to the edge of the bluff, there to stand looking out across the Parma Key, a mass of treetops and ridgelines bathed in the last of the day's sunlight as it faded west across the horizon.

His arm swept the whole of it. "These are my lands now, the lands of Baron Creel, if you will. But I'll hold them no longer than the ones before them if I do not find a way to unsettle the Federation!" He paused. "Fate, I told you. That's what I believe in. Fate made me what I am and it will unmake me as easily, if I do not take a hand in its game. The hand I must take, I think, is the one you offer. It is not chance, Par Ohmsford, that you have come to me. It is what was meant to be. I know that to be true, now especially—now, after hearing what you seek. Do you see the way of it? My ancestor and yours, Panamon Creel and Shea Ohmsford, went in search of the Sword of Shannara more than three hundred years ago. Now it is our turn, yours and mine. A Creel and an Ohmsford once again, the start of change in the land, a new beginning. I can feel it!"

He studied them, his sharp face intense. "Friendship brought you all together; a need for change in your lives brought you to me. Young Par, there are indeed ties that bind us, just as I said when first we met. There is a history that needs repeating. There are adventures to be shared and battles to be won. That is what fate has decreed for you and me!"

Par was a bit confused in the face of all this rhetoric as he asked, "Then you'll help us?"

"Indeed, I will." The outlaw chief arched one eyebrow. "I hold the Parma Key, but the Southland is lost to me—my home, my lands, my heritage. I want them back. Magic is the answer now as it was those many years past, the catalyst for change, the prod that will turn back the Federation beast and send it scurrying for its cave!"

"You've said that several times," Par interjected. "Said it several different ways—that the magic can in some way undermine the Federation. But it's the Shadowen that Allanon fears, the Shadowen that the Sword is meant to confront. So why . . . ?"

"Ah, ah, lad," the other interrupted hurriedly. "You strike to the heart of the matter once again. The answer to your question is this—I perceive threads of cause and effect in everything. Evils such as the Federation and the Shadowen do not stand apart in the scheme of things. They are connected in some way, joined perhaps as Ohmsfords and Creels are joined, and if we can find a way to destroy one, we will find a way to destroy the other!"

The look he gave them was one of such fierce determination that for a long moment no one said anything further. The last of the sunlight was fading away below the horizon, and the gray of twilight cloaked the Parma Key and the lands south and west in a mantle of gauze. The men behind them were stirring from their eating tables and beginning to retire to sleeping areas that lay scattered about the bluff. Even at this high elevation, the summer night was warm and windless. Stars and the beginnings of the first quarter's moon were slipping into view.

"All right," Par said quietly. "True or not, what can you do to help us?"

Padishar Creel smoothed back the wrinkles in the scarlet sleeves of his tunic and breathed deeply the smells of the mountain air. "I can do, lad, what you asked me to do. I can help you find the Sword of Shannara."

He glanced over with a quick grin and matter-of-factly added, "You see, I think I know where it is."

CHAPTER

18

FOR THE NEXT TWO DAYS, Padishar Creel had nothing more to say about the Sword of Shannara. Whenever Par or one of the others of the little company tried to engage him in conversation on the matter, he would simply say that time would tell or that patience was a virtue or offer up some similar platitude that just served to irritate them. He was unfailingly cheerful about it, though, so they kept their feelings to themselves.

Besides, for all the show the outlaw chief made of treating them as his guests, they were prisoners of a sort, nevertheless. They were permitted the run of the Jut, but forbidden to leave it. Not that they necessarily could have left in any event. The winches that raised and lowered the baskets from the heights into the Parma Key were always heavily guarded and no one was allowed near them without reason. Without the lifts to carry them down, there was no way off the bluff from its front. The cliffs were sheer and had been carefully stripped of handholds, and what small ledges and clefts had once existed in the rock had been meticulously chipped away or filled. The cliffs behind were sheer as well for some distance up and warded by the pocket battlements that dotted the high rock.

That left the caves. Par and his friends ventured into the central cavern on the first day, curious to discover what was housed there. They found that the mammoth, cathedral-like central chamber opened off into dozens of smaller chambers where the outlaws stored supplies and weapons of all sorts, made their living quarters when the weather outside grew forbidding, and established training and meeting rooms. There were tunnels leading back into the mountain, but they were cordoned off and watched. When Par asked Hirehone, who had stayed on a few extra days, where the tunnels led, the master of Kiltan Forge smiled sardonically and told him that, like the trails in the Parma Key, the tunnels of the Jut led into oblivion.

The two days passed quickly despite the frustration of being put off on the subject of the Sword. All five visitors spent their time exploring the outlaw fortress. As long as they stayed away from the lifts and the tunnels they were permitted to go just about anywhere they wished. Not once did Padishar Creel question Par about his companions. He seemed unconcerned about who they were and whether they could be trusted, almost as if it didn't matter. Perhaps it didn't, Par decided after thinking it over. After all, the outlaw lair seemed impregnable.

Par, Coll, and Morgan stayed together most of the time. Steff went with them on occasion, but Teel kept away completely, as aloof and uncommunicative as ever. The Valemen and the Highlander became a familiar sight to the outlaws as they wandered the bluff, the fortifications, and the caverns, studying what man and nature had combined to form, talking with the men who lived and worked there when they could do so without bothering them, fascinated by everything they encountered.

But there was nothing and no one more fascinating than Padishar Creel. The outlaw chief was a paradox. Dressed in flaming scarlet, he was immediately recognizable from anywhere on the bluff. He talked constantly, telling stories, shouting orders, commenting on whatever came to mind. He was unremittingly cheerful, as if smiling was the only expression he had ever bothered to put on. Yet beneath that bright and ingratiating exterior was a core as hard as granite. When he ordered that something be done, it was done. No one ever questioned him. His face could be wreathed in a smile as warm as the summer sun while his voice could take on a frosty edge that chilled to the bone.

He ran the outlaw camp with organization and discipline. This was no ragtag band of misfits at work here. Everything was precise and thorough. The camp was neat and clean and kept that way scrupulously. Stores were separated and cataloged and anything could be found at a moment's notice. There were tasks assigned to everyone, and everyone made certain those tasks were carried out. There were a little more than three hundred men living on the Jut, and not one of them seemed to have the slightest doubt about what he was doing or whom he would answer to, if he were to let down.

On the second day of their stay, two of the outlaws were brought before Padishar Creel on a charge of stealing. The outlaw chief listened to the evidence against them, his face mild, then offered to let them speak in their own defense. One admitted his guilt outright, the other denied it—rather unconvincingly. Padishar Creel had the first flogged and sent back to work and the second thrown over the cliff. No one seemed to give the matter another thought afterward.

Later that same day, Padishar came over to Par when the Valeman was alone and asked if he was disturbed by what had happened. Barely waiting for Par's response, he went on to explain how discipline in a camp such as his was essential, and justice in the event of a breakdown must be swift and sure.

"Appearances often count for more then equities, you see," he offered rather enigmatically. "We are a close band here, and we must be able to rely on one another. If a man proves unreliable in camp, he most likely will prove unreliable in the field. And there's more than just his own life at stake there!"

He switched subjects abruptly then, admitting rather apologetically that he hadn't been entirely forthcoming about his background that first night and the truth of the matter was that his parents, rather than being landowners who had been strung up in the woods, had been silk merchants and had died in a Federation prison after they had refused to pay their taxes. He said the other simply made a better story.

When Par encountered Hirehone a short time later, he asked him—Padishar Creel's tale being still fresh in his mind at that point—whether he had known the outlaw chief's parents, and Hirehone said, "No, the fever took them before I came on board."

"In prison, you mean?" Par followed up, confused.

"Prison? Hardly. They died while on a caravan south out of Wayford. They were traders in precious metals. Padishar told me so himself."

Par related both conversations to Coll that night after dinner. They had secluded themselves at the edge of the bluff in a redoubt, where the sounds of the camp were comfortably distant and they could watch the twilight slowly unveil the nighttime sky's increasingly intricate pattern of stars. Coll laughed when Par was finished and shook his head. "The truth isn't in that fellow when it comes to telling anything about himself. He's more like Panamon Creel than Panamon probably ever thought of being!"

Par grimaced. "True enough."

"Dresses the same, talks the same—just as outrageous and quixotic." Coll sighed. "So why am I laughing? What are we doing here with this madman?"

Par ignored him. "What do you suppose he's hiding, Coll?"

"Everything."

"No, not everything. He's not that sort." Coll started to protest, but Par put out his hands quickly to calm him. "Think about it a moment. This whole business of who and what he is has been carefully staged. He spins out these wild tales deliberately, not out of whimsy. Padishar Creel has something else in common with Panamon, if we can believe the stories. He has re-created himself in the minds of everyone around him—drawn a picture of himself that doesn't square from one telling to the next, but is nevertheless bigger than life." He bent close. "And you can bet that he's done it for a reason."

Further speculation about the matter of Padishar Creel's background ended a few minutes later when they were summoned to a meeting. Hirehone collected them with a gruff command to follow and led them across the bluff and into the caves to a meeting chamber where the outlaw chief was waiting. Oil lamps on black chains hung from the chamber ceiling like spiders, their glimmer barely reaching into the shadows that darkened the corners and crevices. Morgan and the Dwarves were there, seated at a table along with several outlaws Par had seen before in the camp. Chandos was a truly ferocious-looking giant with a great black beard, one eye and one ear on the same side of his face missing, and scars everywhere. Ciba Blue was a young, smooth-faced fellow with lank blond hair and an odd cobalt birthmark on his left cheek that resembled a half-moon. Stasas and Drutt were lean, hard, older men with close-cropped dark beards, faces that were seamed and brown, and eyes that shifted watchfully. Hirehone ushered in the Valemen, closed the chamber door, and stood purposefully in front of it.

For just a moment Par felt the hair on the back of his neck prickle in warning.

Then Padishar Creel was greeting them, cheerful and reassuring. "Ah, young Par and his brother." He beckoned them onto benches with the others, made quick introductions, and said, "We are going after the Sword tomorrow at dawn."

"Where is it?" Par wanted to know at once.

The outlaw chief's smile broadened. "Where it won't get away from us."

Par glanced at Coll.

"The less said about where we're going, the better the chance of keeping it a secret." The big man winked.

"Is there some reason we need to keep it a secret?" Morgan Leah asked quietly.

The outlaw chief shrugged. "No reason out of the ordinary. But I am always cautious when I make plans to leave the Jut." His eyes were hard. "Humor me, Highlander."

Morgan held his gaze and said nothing. "Seven of us will go," the other continued smoothly. "Stasas, Drutt, Blue, and myself from the camp, the Valemen and the Highlander from without." Protests were already starting from the mouths of the others and he moved quickly to squelch them. "Chandos, you'll be in charge of the Jut in my absence. I want to leave someone behind I can depend upon. Hirehone, your place is back in Varfleet, keeping an eye on things there. Besides, you'd have trouble explaining yourself if you were spotted where we're going.

"As for you, my Eastland friends," he spoke now to Steff and Teel, "I would take you if I could. But Dwarves outside the Eastland are bound to draw attention, and we can't be having that. It's risky enough allowing the Valemen to come along with the Seekers still looking for them, but it's their quest."

"Ours as well now, Padishar," Steff pointed out darkly. "We have come a long way to be part of this. We don't relish being left behind. Perhaps a disguise?"

"A disguise would be seen through, particularly where we are going," the outlaw chief answered, shaking his head. "You are a resourceful fellow, Steff—but we can take no chances on this outing."

"There's a city and people involved, I take it?"

"There is."

The Dwarf studied him hard. "I would be most upset if there were games being played here at our expense."

There was a growl of warning from the outlaws, but Padishar Creel silenced it instantly. "So would I," he replied, and his gaze locked on the Dwarf.

Steff held that gaze for a long moment. Then he glanced briefly at Teel and nodded. "Very well. We'll wait.'

The outlaw chief's eyes swept the table. "We'll leave at first light and be gone about a week. If we're gone longer than that, chances are we won't be coming back. Are there any questions?"

No one spoke. Padishar Creel gave them a dazzling smile. "A drink, then? Outside with the others, so they can give us a toast and a wish for success! Up, lads, and strength to us who go to brave the lion in his den!"

He went out into the night, the others following. Morgan and the Valemen trailed, shuffling along thoughtfully.

"The lion in his den, eh?" Morgan muttered half to himself. "I wonder what he means by that?"

Par and Coll glanced at each other. Neither was certain that they wanted to know.

PAR SPENT A restless night, plagued by dreams and anxieties that fragmented his sleep and left him bleary-eyed with the coming of dawn. He rose with Coll and Morgan to find Padishar Creel and his companions already awake and in the midst of their breakfast. The outlaw chief had shed his scarlet clothing in favor of the less conspicuous green and brown woodsmen's garb worn by his men. The Valemen and the Highlander hurried to dress and eat, shivering a bit from the night's lingering chill. Steff and

Teel joined them, wordless shadows hunkered down next to the cooking fire. When the meal was consumed, the seven strapped on their backpacks and walked to the edge of the bluff. The sun was creeping into view above the eastern horizon, its early light a mix of gold and silver against the fading dark. Steff muttered for them to take care and, with Teel in tow, disappeared back into the dark. Morgan was rubbing his hands briskly and breathing the air as if he might never have another chance. They boarded the first lift and began their descent, passing wordlessly to the second and third, the winches creaking eerily in the silence as they were lowered. When they reached the floor of the Parma Key, they struck out into the misty forests, Padishar Creel leading with Blue, the Valemen and the Highlander in the middle, and the remaining two outlaws, Stasas and Drutt, trailing. Within seconds, the rock wall of the Jut had disappeared from view.

They traveled south for the better part of the day, turning west around midafternoon when they encountered the Mermidon. They followed the river until sunset, staying on its north shore, and camped that night just below the south end of the Kennon Pass in the shadow of the Dragon's Teeth. They found a cove sheltered by cypress where a stream fed down out of the rocks and provided them with drinking water. They built a fire, ate their dinner, and sat back to watch the stars come out.

After a time, Stasas and Drutt went off to take the first watch, one upstream, one down. Ciba Blue rolled into his blankets and was asleep in moments, his youthful face looking even younger in sleep. Padishar Creel sat with the Valemen and the Highlander, poking at the fire with a stick while he sipped at a flask of ale.

Par had been puzzling over their eventual destination all day, and now he said abruptly to the outlaw chief, "We're going to Tyrsis, aren't we?"

Padishar glanced over in surprise, then nodded. "No reason you shouldn't know now."

"But why look for the Sword of Shannara in Tyrsis? It disappeared from there over a hundred years ago when the Federation annexed Callahorn. Why would it be back there now?"

The other smiled secretively. "Perhaps because it never left."

Par and his companions stared at the outlaw chief in astonishment.

"You see, the fact that the Sword of Shannara disappeared doesn't necessarily mean that it went anywhere. Sometimes a thing can disappear and still be in plain sight. It can disappear simply because it doesn't look like what it used to. We see it, but we don't recognize it."

"What are you saying?" Par asked slowly.

Padishar Creel's smile broadened perceptibly. "I am saying that the Sword of Shannara may very well be exactly where it was three hundred years ago."

"Locked away in a vault in the middle of the People's Park in Tyrsis all these years and no one's figured it out?" Morgan Leah was aghast. "How can that possibly be?"

Padishar sipped speculatively at his flask and said, "We'll be there by tomorrow. Why don't we wait and see?"

Par Ohmsford was tired from the day's march and last night's lack of sleep, but he was awake a long time, nevertheless, after the others were already snoring. He couldn't stop thinking about what Padishar Creel had said. More than three hundred years ago, after Shea Ohmsford had used it to destroy the Warlock Lord, the Sword of Shannara had been embedded in a block of red marble and entombed in a vault in the People's Park in the Southland city of Tyrsis. There it had remained until the coming of the Federation into Callahorn. It was common knowledge that it had disappeared after that. If it hadn't, why did so many people believe it had? If it was right where it had been three hundred years ago, how come no one recognized it now?

He considered. It was true that much of what had happened during the time of Allanon had lost credibility; many of the tales had taken on the trappings of legend and folklore. By the time the Sword of Shannara disappeared, perhaps no one believed in it anymore. Perhaps no one even understood what it could do. But they at least knew it was *there*! It was a national monument, for goodness sake! So how could they say it was gone if it wasn't? It didn't make sense!

Yet Padishar Creel seemed so positive.

Par fell asleep with the matter still unresolved.

They rose again at sunrise, crossed the Mermidon at a shallows less than a mile upstream and turned south for Tyrsis. The day was hot and still, and the dust of the grasslands filled their nostrils and throats. They kept to the shade when they could, but the country south grew more open as the forests gave way to grasslands. They used their water sparingly and paced themselves as they walked, but the sun climbed steadily in the cloudless summer sky and the travelers soon were sweating freely. By midday, as they approached the walls of the city, their clothing lay damp against their skin.

Tyrsis was the home city of Callahorn, its oldest city, and the most impregnable fortress in the entire Southland. Situated on a broad plateau, it was warded by towering cliffs to the south, and a pair of monstrous battle walls to the north. The Outer Wall rose nearly a hundred feet above the summit of the plateau, a massive armament that had been breached only once in the city's history when the armies of the Warlock Lord had attacked in the time of Shea Ohmsford. A second wall sat back and within the first, a redoubt for the city's defenders. Once the Border Legion, the Southland's most formidable army, had defended the city. But the Legion was gone now, disbanded when the Federation moved in, and now only Federation soldiers patrolled the walls and byways, occupiers of lands that, until a hundred years ago, had never been occupied. The Federation soldiers were quartered in the Legion barracks within the first wall, and the citizens of the city still lived and worked within the second, housed in the city proper from where it ran back along the plateau to the base of the cliffs south.

Par, Coll, and Morgan had never been to Tyrsis. What they knew of the city, they knew from the stories they had heard of the days of their ancestors. As they approached it now, they realized how impossible it was for words alone to describe what they were seeing. The city rose up against the skyline like a great, hulking giant, a construction of stone blocks and mortar that dwarfed anything they had ever encountered. Even in the bright sunlight of midday, it had a black cast to it—as if the sunlight were being absorbed somehow in the rock. The city shimmered slightly, a side effect of the heat, and assumed a miragelike quality. A massive rampway led up from the plains to the base of the plateau, twisting like a snake through gates and causeways. Traffic was heavy, wagons and animals traveling in both directions in a steady stream, crawling through the heat and the dust.

The company of seven worked their way steadily closer. As they reached the lower end of the rampway, Padishar Creel turned back to the others and said, "Careful now, lads. Nothing to call attention to ourselves. Remember that it is as hard to get out of this city as it is to get in."

They blended into the stream of traffic that climbed toward the plateau's summit. Wheels thudded, traces jingled and creaked, animals brayed, and men whistled and shouted. Federation soldiers manned the checkpoints leading up, but made no effort to interfere with the flow. It was the same at the gates—massive portals that loomed so high overhead that Par was aghast to think that any army had managed to breach them—the soldiers seeming to take no notice of who went in or out. It was an occupied city, Par decided, that was working hard at pretending to be free.

They passed beneath the gates, the shadow of the gatehouse overhead falling over them like a pall. The second wall rose ahead, smaller, but no less imposing. They moved toward it, keeping in the thick of the traffic. The grounds between the walls were clear of everyone but soldiers and their animals and equipment. There were plenty of each, a fair-sized army housed and waiting. Par studied the rows of drilling men out of the corner of one eye, keeping his head lowered in the shadow of his hooded cloak.

Once through the second set of gates, Padishar pulled them from the Tyrsian Way, the main thoroughfare of homes and businesses that wound through the center of the city to the cliff walls and what was once the palace of its rulers, and steered them into a maze of side streets. There were shops and residences here as well, but fewer soldiers and more beggars. The buildings grew dilapidated as they walked and eventually they entered a district of ale houses and brothels. Padishar did not seem to notice. He kept them moving, ignoring the pleas of the beggars and street vendors, working his way deeper into the city.

At last they emerged into a bright, open district containing markets and small parks. A sprinkling of residences with yards separated the markets, and there were carriages with silks and ribbons on the horses. Vendors sold banners and sweets to laughing children and their mothers. Street shows were being performed on every corner—actors, clowns, magicians, musicians, and animal trainers. Broad, colorful canopies shaded the markets and the park pavilions where families spread their picnic lunches, and the air was filled with shouts, laughter, and applause.

Padishar Creel slowed, casting about for something. He took them through several of the stalls, along tree-shaded blocks where small gatherings were drawn by a multitude of delights, then stopped finally at a cart selling apples. He bought a small sackful for them all to share, took one for himself, and leaned back idly against a lamp pole to eat it. It took Par several moments to realize that he was waiting for something. The Valeman ate his apple with the others and looked about watchfully. Fruits of all sorts were on display in the stalls of a market behind him, there were ices being sold across the way, a juggler, a mime, a girl doing sleight of hand, a pair of dancing monkeys with their trainer, and a scattering of children and adults watching it all. He found his eyes returning to the girl. She had flaming red hair that seemed redder still against the black silk of her clothing and cape. She was drawing coins out of astonished children's ears, then making them disappear again. Once she brought fire out of the air and sent it spinning away. He had never seen that done before. The girl was very good.

He was so intent on watching her, in fact, that he almost missed seeing Padishar Creel hand something to a dark-skinned boy who had come up to him. The boy took what he was given without a word and disappeared. Par looked to see where he had gone, but it was as if the earth had swallowed him up.

They stayed where they were a few minutes longer, and then the outlaw chief said, "Time to go," and led them away. Par took a final look at the red-haired girl and saw that she was causing a ring to float in midair before her audience, while a tiny, blond-headed boy leaped and squealed after it.

The Valeman smiled at the child's delight.

ON THEIR WAY BACK through the gathering of market stalls, Morgan Leah caught sight of Hirehone. The master of Kiltan Forge was at the edge of a crowd applauding a juggler, his large frame wrapped in a great cloak. There was only a momentary glimpse of the bald pate and drooping mustaches, then he was gone. Morgan blinked, deciding almost immediately that he had been mistaken. What would Hirehone be doing in Tyrsis?

By the time they reached the next block, he had dismissed the matter from his mind.

THEY SPENT THE next several hours in the basement of a storage house annexed to the shop of a weapons-maker, a man clearly in the service of the outlaws, since Padishar Creel knew exactly where in a crevice by the frame to find a key that would open the door. He took them inside without hesitating. They found food and drink waiting, along with pallets and blankets for sleeping and water to wash up with. It was cool and dry in the basement, and the heat of the day quickly left them. They rested for a time, eating and talking idly among themselves, waiting for whatever was to come next. Only the outlaw chief seemed to know and, as usual, he wasn't saying. Instead, he went to sleep.

It was several hours before he awoke. He stood up, stretched, took time to wash his face, and walked over to Par. "We're going out," he said. He turned to the others. "Everyone else stay put until we get back. We won't be long and we won't be doing anything dangerous."

Both Coll and Morgan started to protest, then thought better of it. Par followed Padishar up the basement stairs, and the trapdoor closed behind them. Padishar took a moment at the outer door, then beckoned Par after him, and they stepped out into the street.

The street was still crowded, filled with tradesmen and artisans, buyers, and beggars. The outlaw chief took Par south toward the cliffs, striding rapidly as the shadows of late afternoon began to spread across the city. They did not return along any of the avenues that had brought them in, but followed a different series of small, rutted backstreets. The faces they passed were masks of studied disinterest, but the eyes were feral. Padishar ignored them, and Par kept himself close to the big man. Bodies pressed up against him, but he carried nothing of value, so he worried less than he might have otherwise.

As they approached the cliffs, they turned onto the Tyrsian Way. Ahead, the Bridge of Sendic lifted over the People's Park, a carefully trimmed stretch of lawn with broad-leaf trees that spread away toward a low wall and a cluster of buildings where the bridge ended. Beyond, a forest grew out of a wide ravine, and beyond that the spires and walls of what had once been the palace of the rulers of Tyrsis rose up against the fading light.

Par studied the park, the bridge, and the palace as they approached. Something about their configuration did not seem quite right. Wasn't the Bridge of Sendic supposed to have ended at the gates of the palace?

Padishar dropped back momentarily. "So, lad. Hard to believe that the Sword of Shannara could be hidden anywhere so open, eh?"

Par nodded, frowning. "Where is it?"

"Patience now. You'll have your answer soon enough." He put one arm about the Valeman and bent close. "Whatever happens next, do not act surprised."

Par nodded. The outlaw chief slowed, moved over to a flower cart and stopped. He studied the flowers, apparently trying to select a batch. He had done so when Par felt an arm go about his waist and turned to find the red-haired girl who practiced sleight of hand pressing up against him.

"Hello, Elf-boy," she whispered, her cool fingers brushing at his ear as she kissed him on the cheek.

Then two small children were beside them, a girl and a boy, the first reaching up to grasp Padishar's rough hand, the second reaching up to grasp Par's. Padishar smiled, lifted the little girl so that she squealed, kissed her, and gave half of the flowers to her and half to the boy. Whistling, he started the five of them moving into the park. Par had recovered sufficiently to notice that the red-haired girl was carrying a basket covered with a bright cloth. When they were close to the wall that separated the park from the ravine, Padishar chose a maple tree for them to sit under, the red-haired girl spread the cloth, and all of them began unpacking the basket which contained cold chicken, eggs, hard bread and jam, cakes, and tea.

Padishar glanced over at Par as they worked. "Par Ohmsford, meet Damson Rhee, your betrothed for purposes of this little outing."

Damson Rhee's green eyes laughed. "Love is fleeting, Par Ohmsford. Let's make the most of it." She fed him an egg.

"You are my son," Padishar added. "These other two children are your siblings, though their names escape me at the moment. Damson, remind me later. We're just a typical family, out for a late-afternoon picnic, should anyone ask."

No one did. The men ate their meal in silence, listening to the children as they chattered on and acted as if what was happening was perfectly normal. Damson Rhee looked after them, laughing right along with them, her smile warm and infectious. She was pretty to begin with, but when she smiled, Par found her beautiful. When they were finished eating, she did the coin trick with each child, then sent them off to play.

"Let's take a walk," Padishar suggested, rising.

The three of them strolled through the shade trees, moving without seeming purpose toward the wall that blocked away the ravine. Damson clung lovingly to Par's waist. He found he didn't mind. "Things have changed somewhat in Tyrsis since the old days," the outlaw chief said to Par as they walked. "When the Buckhannah line died out, the monarchy came to an end. Tyrsis, Varfleet, and Kern ruled Callahorn by forming the Council of the Cities. When the Federation made Callahorn a protectorate, the Council was disbanded. The palace had served as an assembly for the Council. Now the Federation uses it—except that no one knows exactly what they use it for."

They reached the wall and stopped. The wall was built of stone block to a height of about three feet. Spikes were embedded in its top. "Have a look," the outlaw chief invited.

Par did. The ravine beyond dropped away sharply into a mass of trees and scrub that had grown so thick it seemed to be choking on itself. Mist curled through the wilderness with an insistence that was unsettling, clinging to even the uppermost reaches of the trees. The ravine stretched away for perhaps a mile to either side and a quarter of that distance to where the palace stood, its doors and windows shuttered and dark, its gates barred. The stone of the palace was scarred and dirty, and the whole of it had the look of something that had not seen use for decades. A narrow catwalk ran from the buildings in the fore-ground to its sagging gates.

He looked back at Padishar. The outlaw chief was facing toward the city. "This wall forms the dividing line between past and present," he said quietly. "The ground we stand upon is called the People's Park. But the true People's Park, the one from the time of our ancestors—" He paused and turned back to the ravine. "—is down there." He took a moment to let that sink in. "Look. Below the Federation Gatehouse that wards the catwalk." Par followed his gaze and caught sight of a scattering of huge stone blocks barely poking up out of the forest. "That," the outlaw chief continued somberly, "is what remains of the real Bridge of Sendic. It was badly cracked, I am told, during the assault on Tyrsis by the Warlock Lord during the time of Pan-amon Creel. Some years later, it collapsed altogether. This other bridge," he waved indifferently, "is merely for show."

He glanced sideways at Par. "Now do you see?"

Par did. His mind was working rapidly now, fitting the pieces into place. "And the Sword of Shannara?" He caught a glimpse of Damson Rhee's startled look out of the corner of his eye.

"Down there somewhere, unless I miss my guess," Padishar replied smoothly. "Right where it's always been. You have some-thing to say, Damson?"

The red-haired girl took Par's arm and steered him away from the wall. "This is what you have come for, Padishar?" She sounded angry.

"Forbear, lovely Damson. Don't let's be judgmental."

The girl's grip tightened on Par's arm. "This is dangerous business, Padishar. I have sent men into the Pit before, as you well know, and not one of them has returned."

Padishar smiled indulgently. "The Pit—that's what Tyrsians call the ravine these days. Fitting, I suppose."

"You take too many risks!" the girl pressed.

"Damson is my eyes and ears and strong right arm inside Tyrsis," the other continued smoothly. He smiled at her. "Tell the Valeman what you know of the Sword, Damson."

She gave him a dangerous look, then swung her face away. "The collapse of the Bridge of Sendic occurred at the same time the Federation annexed Callahorn and began occupation of Tyrsis. The forest that now blankets the old People's Park, where the Sword of Shannara was housed, grew up virtually overnight. The new park and bridge came about just as quickly. I asked the old ones of the city some years ago what they remembered, and this is what I learned. The Sword didn't actually disappear from its vault; it was the vault that disappeared into the forest. People forget, especially when they're being told something else. Almost everyone believes there was only one People's Park and one Bridge of Sendic—the ones they see. The Sword of Shannara, if it ever existed, simply disappeared."

Par was looking at her in disbelief. "The forest, the bridge, and the park changed overnight?"

She nodded. "Just so."

"But . . . ?"

"Magic, lad," Padishar Creel whispered in answer to his unfinished question.

They walked on a bit, nearing the brightly colored cloth that contained the remains of their picnic. The children were back, nibbling contentedly at the cakes.

"The Federation doesn't use magic," Par argued, still confused. "They have outlawed it."

"Outlawed its use by others, yes," the big man acknowledged. "Perhaps the better to use it themselves? Or to allow someone else to use it? Or some*thing*?" He emphasized the last syllable.

Par looked over sharply. "Shadowen, you mean?"

Neither Padishar nor Damson said anything. Par's mind spun. The Federation and the Shadowen in league somehow, joined for purposes none of them understood—was that possible?

"I have wondered about the fate of the Sword of Shannara for a long time," Padishar mused, stopping just out of earshot of the waiting children. "It is a part of the history of my family as well. It always seemed strange to me that it should have vanished so completely. It was embedded in marble and locked in a vault for two hundred years. How could it simply disappear? What happened to the vault that contained it? Was it all somehow spirited away?" He glanced at Par. "Damson spent a long time finding out the answer. Only a few remembered the truth of how the disappearance came about. They're all dead now—but they left their story to me."

His smile was wolfish. "Now I have an excuse to discover whether that story is true. Is the Sword of Shannara down there in that ravine? You and I shall discover the answer. Resurrection of the magic of the Elven house of Shannara, young Ohmsford—the key, perhaps, to the freedom of the Four Lands. We must know."

Damson Rhee shook her titian head. "You are far too eager, Padishar, to throw your life away. And the lives of others like this boy. I will never understand."

She moved away from them to gather up the children. Par didn't care much for being called a boy by a girl who looked younger still.

"Watch out for that one, Par Ohmsford," the outlaw chief murmured.

"She doesn't have much faith in our chances," Par observed.

"Ah, she worries without cause! We have the strength of seven of us to withstand whatever might guard the Pit. And if there's magic as well, we have your wishsong and the Highlander's blade. Enough said."

He studied the sky. "It will be dark soon, lad." He put his arm about the Valeman companionably and moved them forward to join Damson Rhee and the children. "When it is," he whispered, "we'll have a look for ourselves at what's become of the Sword of Shannara."

CHAPTER

19

AS PADISHAR CREEL'S MAKESHIFT FAMILY reached the edge of the park and prepared to step out onto the Tyrsian Way, Damson Rhee turned to the outlaw chief and said, "The sentries who patrol the wall make a change at midnight in front of the Federation Gatehouse. I can arrange for a small disturbance that will distract them long enough for you to slip into the Pit—if you are determined on this. Be certain you go in at the west end."

Then she reached up and plucked a silver coin from behind Par's ear and gave it to him. The coin bore her likeness. "For luck, Par Ohmsford," she said. "You will be needing it if you continue to follow *him*."

She gave Padishar a hard look, took the children by the hand, and strode off into the crowds without looking back, her red hair shining. The outlaw chief and the Valeman watched her go.

"Who is she, Padishar?" Par asked when she was no longer in view.

Padishar shrugged. "Whoever she chooses to be. There are as many stories about her origins as there are about my own. Come now. Time for us to be going as well."

He took Par back through the city, keeping to the lesser streets and byways. The crowds were still heavy, everyone pushing and shoving, their faces dust-streaked and their tempers short. Twilight had chased the sunlight west, lengthening the shadows into evening, but the heat of midday remained trapped by the city's walls, rising out of the stone of the streets and buildings to hang in the still summer air. It was like being in a furnace. Par glanced skyward. Already the quarter-moon was visible northward, a sprinkling of stars east. He tried to think about what he had learned of the disappearance of the Sword of Shannara, but found himself thinking instead of Damson Rhee.

Padishar had him safely back down in the basement of the storage house behind the weapons shop before dark, where Coll and Morgan waited impatiently to receive them. Cutting short a flurry of questions, the outlaw chief smiled cheerfully and announced that everything was arranged. At midnight the Valemen, the Highlander, Ciba Blue, and he would make a brief foray into the ravine that fronted what had once been the palace of the city's rulers. They would descend using a rope ladder. Stasas and Drutt would remain behind. They would haul the ladder up when their companions were safely down and hide until summoned. Any sentries would be dispatched, the ladder would be lowered again, and they would all disappear back the way they had come.

He was succinct and matter-of-fact. He made no mention of why they were doing all this and none of his own men bothered to ask. They simply let him finish, then turned immediately back to whatever they had been doing before. Coll and Morgan, on the other hand, could barely contain themselves, and Par was forced to take them aside and tell them in detail everything that had happened. The three of them huddled in one corner of the basement, seated on sacks of scrubbing powder. Oil lamps lit the darkness, and the city above them began to go still.

When Par concluded, Morgan shook his head doubtfully.

"It is hard to believe that an entire city has forgotten there was more than one People's Park and Bridge of Sendic," he declared softly.

"Not hard at all when you remember that they have had more than a hundred years to work on it," Coll disagreed quickly. "Think about it, Morgan. How much more than a park and a bridge has been forgotten in that time? The Federation has saddled the Four Lands with three hundred years of revisionist history."

"Coll's right," Par said. "We lost our only true historian when

Allanon passed from the Lands. The Druid Histories were the only written compilations the Races had, and we don't know what's become of those. All we have left are the storytellers, with their word-of-mouth recitations, most of them imperfect."

"Everything about the old world has been called a lie," Coll said, his dark eyes hard. "We know it to be the truth, but we are virtually alone in that belief. The Federation has changed everything to suit its own purposes. After a hundred years, it is little wonder that no one in Tyrsis remembers that the People's Park and the Bridge of Sendic are not the same as they once were. The fact of the matter is, who even cares anymore?"

Morgan frowned. "Perhaps so. But something's still not right about this." His frown deepened. "It bothers me that the Sword of Shannara, vault and all, has been down in this ravine all these years and no one's seen it. It bothers me that no one who's gone down to have a look has come back out again."

"That troubles me, too," Coll agreed.

Par glanced briefly at the outlaws, who were paying no attention to them. "None of us thought for a minute that it wouldn't be dangerous trying to recover the Sword," he whispered, a hint of exasperation in his voice. "Surely you didn't expect to just walk up and take it? Of course no one's seen it! It wouldn't be missing if they had, would it? And you can bet that the Federation has made certain no one who got down into the Pit got back out again! That's the reason for the guards and the Gatehouse! Besides, the fact that the Federation has gone to so much trouble to hide the old bridge and park suggests to me that the Sword is down there!"

Coll looked at his brother steadily. "It also suggests that that's where it's meant to stay."

The conversation broke off and the three of them drifted away to separate corners of the basement. Evening passed quickly into nightfall and the heat of the day finally faded. The little company ate an uneventful dinner amid long stretches of silence. Only Padishar had much of anything to say, ebullient as always, tossing off stories and jokes as if this night were the same as any other, seemingly heedless of the fact that his audience remained unresponsive. Par was too excited to eat or talk and spent the time wondering if Padishar were as unaffected as he appeared. Nothing seemed to alter the mood of the outlaw chief. Padishar Creel was either very brave or very foolish, and it bothered the Valeman that he wasn't sure which it was

Dinner ended and they sat around talking in hushed voices and staring at the walls. Padishar came over to Par at one point and crouched down beside him. "Are you anxious to be about our business, lad?" he asked softly.

No one else was close enough to hear. Par nodded.

"Ah, well, it won't be long now." The outlaw patted his knee. The hard eyes held his own. "Just remember what we're about. A quick look and out again. If the Sword is there for the taking, fine. If not, no delays." His smile was wolfish. "Caution in all things." He slipped away, leaving Par to stare after him.

The minutes lengthened with the wearing slowness of shadows at midday. Par and Coll sat side by side without speaking. Par could almost hear his brother's thoughts in the silence. The oil lamps flickered and spat. A giant swamp fly buzzed about the ceiling until Ciba Blue killed it. The basement room began to smell close.

Then finally Padishar stood up and said it was time. They came to their feet eagerly, anticipation flickering in their eyes. Weapons were strapped down and cloaks pulled close. They went up the basement stairs through the trapdoor and out into the night.

The city streets were empty and still. Voices drifted out of ale houses and sleeping rooms, punctuated by raucous laughter and occasional shouts. The lamps were mostly broken or unlit on the back streets that Padishar took them down, and there was only moonlight to guide them through the shadows. They did not move furtively, only cautiously, not wishing to draw attention to themselves. They ducked back into alleyways several times to avoid knots of swaying, singing revellers who were making their way homeward. Drunks and beggars who saw them pass barely glanced up from the doorways and alcoves in which they lay. They saw no Federation soldiers. The Federation left the back streets and the poor of Tyrsis to manage for themselves.

When they reached the People's Park and the Bridge of Sendic, Padishar sent them across the broad expanse of the Tyrsian Way in twos and threes into the shadows of the park, dispatching them in different directions to regroup later, carefully watching the well-lighted Way for any approach of the Federation patrols he knew would be found there. Only one patrol passed, and it saw nothing of the company. A watch was posted before the Gatehouse at the center of the wall that warded the Pit, but the soldiers had lamplight reflecting all about them and could not see outside its glow to the figures lost in the dark beyond. Padishar took the company swiftly through the deserted park, west to where the ravine approached its juncture with the cliffs. There, he settled them in to wait.

Par crouched motionlessly in the dark and listened to the sound of his heart pumping in his ears. The silence about him was filled with the hum of insects. Locusts buzzed in raucous cadence in the black. The seven men were concealed in a mass of thicket, invisible to anyone without. But anyone beyond their concealment was invisible to them as well. Par was uneasy with their placement and wondered at its choice. He glanced at Padishar Creel, but the outlaw chief was busy overseeing the untangling of the rope ladder that would lower them into the ravine . . .

Par hesitated. The Pit. Lower them into the Pit. He forced himself to say the word.

He took a deep breath, trying to steady himself. He wondered if Damson Rhee was anywhere close.

A patrol of four Federation soldiers materialized out of the dark almost directly in front of them, walking the perimeter of the wall. Though the sound of their boots warned of their coming, it was chilling when they appeared, nevertheless. Par and the others flattened themselves in the scratchy tangle of their concealment. The soldiers paused, spoke quietly among themselves for a moment, then turned back the way they had come, and were gone.

Par exhaled slowly. He risked a quick glance over at the dark bowl of the ravine. It was a soundless, depthless well of ink.

Padishar and the other outlaws were fixing the rope ladder in place, preparing for the descent. Par came to his feet, eager to relieve the muscles that were beginning to cramp, anxious to be done with this whole business. He should have felt confident. He did not. He was growing steadily more uneasy and he couldn't say why. Something was tugging at him frantically, warning him, some sixth sense that he couldn't identify.

He thought he heard something—not ahead in the ravine, but behind in the park. He started to turn, his sharp Elf eyes searching.

Then abruptly there was a flurry of shouts from the direction of the Gatehouse, and cries of alarm pierced the night.

"Now!" Padishar Creel urged, and they bolted their cover for the wall.

The ladder was already knotted in place, tied down to a pair of the wall spikes. Quickly, they lowered it into the black. Ciba Blue went over first, the cobalt birthmark on his cheek a dark, hollow place in the moonlight. He tested the ladder first with his weight, then disappeared from view.

"Remember, listen for my signal," Padishar was saying hurriedly to Stasas and Drutt, his voice a rough whisper above the distant shouts.

He was turning to start Par down the ladder after Ciba Blue when a swarm of Federation soldiers appeared out of the dark behind them, armed with spears and crossbows, silent figures that seemed to come from nowhere. Everyone froze. Par felt his stomach lurch with shock. He found himself thinking, "I should have known, I should have sensed them," and thinking in the next breath that indeed he had.

"Lay down your weapons," a voice commanded.

For just an instant, Par was afraid that Padishar Creel would choose to fight rather than surrender. The outlaw chief's eyes darted left and right, his tall form rigid. But the odds were overwhelming. His face relaxed, he gave a barely perceptible smile, and dropped his sword and long knife in front of him wordlessly. The others of the little company did the same, and the Federation soldiers closed about. Weapons were scooped up and arms bound behind backs.

"There's another of them down in the Pit," a soldier advised the leader of their captors, a smallish man with short-cropped hair and commander's bars on his dark tunic.

The commander glanced over. "Cut the ropes, let him drop."

The rope ladder was cut through in a moment. It fell soundlessly into the black. Par waited for a cry, but there was none. Perhaps Ciba Blue had already completed his descent. He glanced at Coll, who just shook his head helplessly.

The Federation commander stepped up to Padishar. "You should know, Padishar Creel," he said quietly, his tone measured, "that you were betrayed by one of your own."

He waited momentarily for a response, but there was none. Padishar's face was expressionless. Only his eyes revealed the rage that he was somehow managing to contain.

Then the silence was shattered by a terrifying scream that rose out of the depths of the Pit. It lifted into the night like a stricken bird, hovering against the cliff rock until at last, mercifully, it dropped away.

The scream had been Ciba Blue's, Par thought in horror.

The Federation commander gave the ravine a perfunctory glance and ordered his prisoners led away.

THEY WERE TAKEN through the park along the ravine wall toward the Gatehouse, kept in single file and apart from each other by the soldiers guarding them. Par trudged along with the others in stunned silence, the sound of Ciba Blue's scream still echoing in his mind. What had happened to the outlaw down there alone in the Pit? He swallowed against the sick feeling in his stomach and forced himself to think of something else. Betrayed, the Federation commander had said. But by whom? None of them there, obviously—so someone who wasn't. One of Padishar's own . . .

He tripped over a tree root, righted himself and stumbled on. His mind whirled with a scattering of thoughts. They were being taken to the Federation prisons, he concluded. Once there, the grand adventure was over. There would be no more searching for the missing Sword of Shannara. There would be no further consideration of the charge given him by Allanon. No one ever came out of the Federation prisons.

He had to escape.

The thought came instinctively, clearing his mind as nothing else could. He had to escape. If he didn't, they would all be locked away and forgotten. Only Damson Rhee knew where they were, and it occurred suddenly to Par that Damson Rhee had been in the best position to betray them.

It was an unpleasant possibility. It was also unavoidable.

His breathing slowed. This was the best opportunity to break free that he would get. Once within the prisons, it would be much more difficult to manage. Perhaps Padishar would come up with a plan by then, but Par didn't care to chance it. Uncharitably, perhaps, he was thinking that Padishar was the one who had gotten them into this mess.

He watched the lights of the Gatehouse flicker ahead through the trees of the park. He only had a few minutes more. He thought he could manage it, but he would have to go alone. He would have to leave Coll and Morgan. There wasn't any choice.

Voices sounded from ahead, other soldiers waiting for their return. The line began to string out and some of the guards were straying a bit. Par took a deep breath. He waited until they were passing along a cluster of scrub birch, then used the wishsong. He sang softly, his voice blending into the sounds of the night, a whisper of breeze, a bird's gentle call, a cricket's brief chirp. He let the wishsong's magic reach out and fill the minds of the guards immediately next to him, distracting them, turning their eyes away from him, letting them forget that he was there . . .

And then he simply stepped into the birch and shadows and disappeared.

The line of prisoners passed on without him. No one had noticed that he was gone. If Coll or Morgan or any of the others had seen anything, they were keeping still about it. The Federation soldiers and their prisoners continued moving toward the lights ahead, leaving him alone.

When they were gone, he moved soundlessly off into the night.

HE MANAGED TO free himself almost immediately of the ropes that held his hands. He found a spike with a jagged edge on the ravine wall a hundred yards from where he had slipped away and, boosting himself up on the wall, sawed through the ropes in only minutes. No alarm had gone up yet from the watch; apparently he hadn't been missed. Maybe they hadn't bothered to count the original number of their prisoners, he reasoned. After all, it had been dark, and the capture had taken place in a matter of seconds.

At any rate, he was free. So what was he going to do now?

He worked his way back through the park toward the Tyrsian Way, keeping to the shadows, stopping every few seconds to listen for the sounds of the pursuit that never came. He was sweating freely, his tunic sticking to his back, his face streaked with dust. He was exhilarated by his escape and devastated by the realization that he didn't know how to take advantage of it. There was no help for him in Tyrsis and no help for him without. He didn't know who to contact within the city; there was no one he could afford to trust. And he had no idea how to get back into the Parma Key. Steff would help if he knew his companions were in trouble. But how would the Dwarf find out before it was too late to matter?

The lights of the Way came into view through the trees. Par stumbled to the edge of the park, close to its western boundaries, and collapsed in despair against the trunk of an old maple. He had to do something; he couldn't just wander about. He brushed at his face with his sleeve and let his head sink back against the rough bark. He was suddenly sick and it took every ounce of willpower he could muster to prevent himself from retching.

He had to get back to Coll and Morgan. He had to find a way to free them.

Use the wishsong, he thought.

But how?

A Federation patrol came down the Way, boots clumping in the stillness. Par shrank back into the shadows and waited until they were out of sight. Then he moved from his cover along the edge of the park toward a fountain bordering the walk. Once there, he leaned over and hurriedly splashed water on his hands and face. The water ran along his skin like liquid silver.

He paused, letting his head sink against his chest. He was suddenly very tired.

The arm that yanked him around was strong and unyielding, snapping his head back violently. He found himself face-to-face with Damson Rhee.

"What happened?" she demanded, her voice low.

Frantically, Par reached for his long knife. But his weapons were gone, taken by the Federation. He shoved at the girl, trying to rip free of her grip, but she sidestepped the blow without effort and kicked him so hard in the stomach that he doubled over.

"What are you doing, you idiot?" she whispered angrily.

Without waiting for an answer, she hauled him back into the concealing shadows of the park and threw him to the ground. "If you try something like that again with me, I will break both your arms!" she snapped.

Par pulled himself up to a sitting position, still looking for a way to escape. But she shoved him back against the ground and crouched close. "Why don't we try again, my beloved Elf-boy? Where are the others? What has happened to them?"

Par swallowed against his rage. "The Federation has them! They were waiting for us, Damson! As if you didn't know!"

The anger in her eyes was replaced by surprise. "What do you mean, 'as if I didn't know'?"

"They were waiting for us. We never got past the wall. We were betrayed! The Federation commander told us so! He said it was one of our own—an outlaw, Damson!" Par was shaking.

Damson Rhee's gaze was steady. "And you have decided that it was me, have you, Par Ohmsford?"

Par forced himself up on his elbows. "Who better than you? You were the only one who knew what we were about—the only one not taken! No one else knew! If not you, then who could it possibly have been?"

There was a long silence as they stared at each other in the dark. The sound of voices nearby grew slowly distinct. Someone was approaching.

Damson Rhee suddenly bent close. "I don't know. But it wasn't me! Now lie still until they pass!"

She pushed him into a gathering of bushes, then backed in herself and lay down beside him. Par could feel the warmth of her body. He could smell the sweet scent of her. He closed his eyes and waited. A pair of Federation soldiers worked their way out of the park, paused momentarily, then started back again and were gone.

Damson Rhee put her lips close against Par's ear. "Do they know you are missing yet?"

Par hesitated. "I can't be certain," he whispered back.

She took his chin with her smooth hand and turned his face until it was level with her own. "I didn't betray you. It may seem as if I must have, but I didn't. If I intended to betray you to the Federation, Par, I would have simply turned you over to that pair of soldiers and been done with it."

The green eyes glittered faintly with moonlight that had penetrated the branches of their concealment. Par stared at those eyes and found no hint of deception mirrored there. Still, he hesitated.

"You have to decide here and now whether you believe me," she said quietly.

He shook his head warily. "It isn't that easy!"

"It has to be! Look at me, Par. I have betrayed no one—not you or Padishar or the others, not now, not ever! Why would I do something like that? I hate the Federation as much as anyone!" She paused, exasperated. "I told you that this was a dangerous undertaking. I warned you that the Pit was a black hole that swallowed men whole. Padishar was the one who insisted you go!"

"That doesn't make him responsible for what happened."

"Nor me! What about the distraction I promised? Did it come about as I said it would?"

Par nodded.

"You see! I fulfilled my part of the bargain! Why would I bother if I intended your betrayal?"

Par said nothing.

Damson's nostrils flared. "You will admit to nothing, will you?" She shook back her auburn hair in a flash of color. "Will you at least tell me what happened?"

Par took a deep breath. Briefly, he related the events that surrounded their capture, including the frightening disappearance of the outlaw Ciba Blue. He kept deliberately vague the circumstances of his own escape. The magic was his business. Its secret belonged to him.

But Damson was not about to be put off. "So the fact of the matter is, you might as easily be the betrayer as I," she said. "How else is it that you managed to escape when the others could not?"

Par flushed, resentful of the accusation, irritated by her persistence. "Why would I do such a thing to my friends?"

"My own argument exactly," she replied.

They studied each other wordlessly, each measuring the strength of the other. Damson was right, Par knew. There was as much reason to believe that he had been the betrayer as she. But that didn't change the fact that he knew he wasn't while he didn't know the same of her.

"Decide, Par," she urged quietly. "Do you believe me or not?"

Her features were smooth and guileless in the scattering of light, her skin dappled with shadows from the tiny leaves of the bushes. He found himself drawn to her in a way he had not believed possible. There was something special about this girl, something that made him push aside his misgivings and cast out his doubts. The green eyes held him, insinuating and persuasive. He saw only truth in them.

"Okay, I believe you," he said finally.

"Then tell me how it is that you escaped when the others did not," she demanded. "No, don't argue the matter. I must have proof of your own innocence if we are to be of any use to each other or to our friends."

Par's resolve to keep to himself the secret of the wishsong slipped slowly away. Again, she was right. She was asking only what he would have asked in her place. "I used magic," he told her.

She inched closer, as if to judge better the truth of what he was saying. "Magic? What sort?"

He hesitated yet.

"Sleight of hand? Cloud spells?" she pressed. "Some sort of vanishing act?"

"Yes," he replied. She was waiting. "I have the ability to make myself invisible when I wish."

There was a long silence. He read the curiosity in her eyes. "You command real magic, don't you?" she said finally. "Not the pretend kind that I use, where coins appear and disappear and fire dances on the air. You have the sort that is forbidden. That is why Padishar is so interested in you." She paused. "Who are you, Par Ohmsford? Tell me."

It was still within the park now, the voices of the watch passed from hearing, the night gone deep and silent once more. There might have been no one else in all the world but the two of them. Par weighed the advisability of his reply. He was stepping on stones that floated in quicksand.

"You can see who I am for yourself," he said finally, hedging. "I am part Elf and that part of me carries the magic of my forebears. I have their magic to command—or some small part of it, at least."

She looked at him for a long time then, thinking. At last she seemed to have made up her mind. She crawled from the concealment of the bushes, pulling him out with her. They stood together in the shadows, brushing themselves off, breathing deeply the cool night air. The park was deserted.

She came up to him and stood close. "I was born in Tyrsis, the child of a forger of weapons and his wife. I had one brother and one sister, both older. When I was eight, the Federation discovered my father was supplying arms to the Movement. Someone—a friend, an acquaintance, I never knew who—betrayed him. Seekers came to our house in the middle of the night, fired it and burned it to the ground. My family was locked inside and burned with it. I escaped only because I was visiting my aunt. Within a year she was dead as well, and I was forced to live in the streets. That is where I grew up. My family was all gone. I had no friends. A street magician took me as his apprentice and taught me my trade. That has been my life." She paused. "You deserve to know why it is that I would never betray anyone to the Federation."

She reached up with her hand and her fingers brushed his cheek for just a moment. Then her hand trailed down to his arm and fastened there.

"Par, we must do whatever it is we are going to do tonight or it will be too late. The Federation knows who they have. Padishar Creel. They will send for Rimmer Dall and his Seekers to question Padishar. Once that happens, rescue will be pointless." She paused, making certain that he took her meaning. "We have to help them now."

Par went cold at the thought of Coll and Morgan in the hands of Rimmer Dall—let alone Padishar. What would the First Seeker do to the leader of the Movement?

"Tonight," she continued, her voice soft, but insistent. "While they are not expecting it. They will still have Padishar and the others in the cells at the Gatehouse. They won't have moved them yet. They will be tired, sleepy with the coming of morning. We won't get a better chance."

He stared at her incredulously. "You and I?"

"If you agree to come with me."

"But what can the two of us do?"

She pulled him close. Her red hair shimmered darkly in the moonlight. "Tell me about your magic. What can you do with it, Par Ohmsford?"

There was no hesitation now. "Make myself invisible," he said. "Make myself to appear to be different than I am. Make others think they are seeing things that aren't there." He was growing excited. "Just about anything that I want if it's not for too long and not too extended. It's just illusion, you understand."

She walked away from him, paced into the trees close by and stopped. She stood there in the shadows, lost in thought. Par waited where he was, feeling the cool night air brush his skin in a sudden breath of wind, listening to the silence that spread across the city like the waters of an ocean across its floor. He could almost swim through that silence, drifting away to better times and places. There was fear in him that he could not suppress—fear at the thought of returning for his friends, fear at the thought of failing in the attempt. But to attempt nothing at all was unthinkable.

Still, what could they do—just this slip of a girl and himself?

As if reading his mind she came back to him then, green eyes intense, seized his arms tightly, and whispered, "I think I know a way, Par."

He smiled in spite of himself.

"Tell me about it," he said.

CHAPTER

20

ALKER BOH JOURNEYED directly back to Hearthstone after taking leave of the company at the Hadeshorn. He rode his horse east across the Rabb, bypassed Storlock and its Healers, climbed the Wolfsktaag through the Pass of Jade, and worked his way upriver along the Chard Rush until he entered Darklin Reach. Three days later he was home again. He talked with no one on the way, keeping entirely to himself as he traveled, pausing only long enough to eat and sleep. He was not fit company for other men and he knew it. He was obsessed with thoughts of his encounter with the shade of Allanon. He was haunted by them.

The Anar was enveloped by a particularly violent midsummer storm within twenty-four hours of his return, and Walker secluded himself truculently in his cottage home while winds lashed its shaved-board walls and rains beat down upon its shingled roof. The forested valley was deluged, wracked by the crack and flash of lightning, shaken by the long, ominous peals of thunder, pelted and washed. The cadence of the rains obliterated every other sound, and Walker sat amid their constant thrum in brooding silence, wrapped in blankets and a blackness of spirit he would not have thought possible.

He found himself despairing.

It was the inevitability of things that he feared. Walker Boh, whatever name he chose to bear, was nevertheless an Ohmsford by blood, and he knew that Ohmsfords, despite their misgivings, had always been made to take up the Druid cause. It had been so with Shea and Flick, with Wil, and with Brin and Jair before him. Now it was to be his turn. His and Wren's and Par's. Par embraced the cause willingly, of course. Par was an incurable romantic, a self-appointed champion of the downtrodden and the abused. Par was a fool.

Or a realist, depending on how you viewed the matter. Because, if history proved an accurate indicator, Par was merely accepting without argument what Walker, too, would be forced to embrace—Allanon's will, the cause of a dead man. The shade had come to them like some scolding patriarch out of death's embrace—chiding them for their lack of diligence, scolding them for their misgivings, charging them with missions of madness and self-destruction. Bring back the Druids! Bring back Paranor! Do these things because I say they must be done, because I say they are necessary, because I—a thing of no flesh and dead mind—demand it!

Walker's mood darkened further as the weight of the matter continued to settle steadily over him, a pall mirroring the oppressiveness of the storms without. Change the whole of the face of the world—that was what the shade was asking of them, of Par, Wren, and himself. Take three hundred years of evolution in the Four Lands and dispense with it in an instant's time. What else was the shade asking, if not that? A return of the magic, a return of the wielders of that magic, of its shapers, of all the things ended by this same shade those three hundred years past. Madness! They would be playing with lives in the manner of creators—and they were not entitled!

Through the gray haze of his anger and his fear, he could conjure in his mind the features of the shade. Allanon. The last of the Druids, the keeper of the Histories of the Four Lands, the protector of the Races, the dispenser of magic and secrets. His dark form rose up against the years like a cloud against the sun, blocking away the warmth and the light. Everything that had taken place while he lived bore his touch. And before that, it was Bremen, and before that the Druids of the First Council of the Races. Wars of magic, struggles for survival, the battles between light and dark—or grays perhaps—had all been the result of the Druids.

And now he was being asked to bring all that back.

It could be argued that it was necessary. It had always been argued so. It could be said that the Druids merely worked to preserve and protect, never to shape. But had there ever been one without the other? And necessity was always in the eye of the beholder. Warlock Lords, Demons, and Mord Wraiths past—they had been exchanged for Shadowen. But what were these Shadowen that men should require the aid of Druids and magic? Could not men take it upon themselves to deal with the ills of the world rather than defer to power they scarcely understood? Magic carried grief as well as joy, its dark side as apt to influence and change as its light. Bring it back again, should he, only to give it to men who had repeatedly demonstrated that they were incapable of mastering its truths?

How could he?

Yet without it, the world might become the vision Allanon's shade had shown them—a nightmare of fire and darkness in which only creatures such as the Shadowen belonged. Perhaps it was true after all that magic was the only means of keeping the Races safe against such beings.

Perhaps.

The truth of the matter was that he simply didn't want to be part of what was to happen. He was not a child of the Races of the Four Lands, not in body or in spirit, and never had been. He had no empathy with their men and women. He had no place among them. He had been cursed with magic of his own, and it had stripped him of his humanity and his place among humans and isolated him from every other living thing. Ironic, because he alone had no fear of the Shadowen. Perhaps he could even protect against them, were he asked to do so. But he would not be asked. He was as much feared as they. He was the Dark Uncle, the descendent of Brin Ohmsford, the bearer of her seed and her trust, keeper of some nameless charge from Allanon . . .

Except, of course, that the charge was nameless no more. The charge was revealed. He was to bring back Paranor and the Druids, out of the void of yesteryear, out of the nothingness.

That was what the shade had demanded of him, and the demand tracked relentlessly through the landscape of his mind, hurdling arguments, circumventing reason, whispering that it was and therefore must be.

So he worried the matter as a dog would its bone, and the days dragged by. The storms passed and the sun returned to bake the plains dry but leave the forestlands weltering in the heat and damp. He went out after a time, walking the valley floor with only Rumor for company, the giant moor cat having wandered down out of the rain forests east with the changing of the weather, luminous eyes as depthless as the despair the Dark Uncle felt. The cat gave him companionship, but offered no solution to his dilemma and no relief from his brooding. They walked and sat together as the days and nights passed, and time hung suspended against a backdrop of events taking place beyond their refuge that neither could know nor see.

Until, on the same night that Par Ohmsford and his companions were betrayed in their attempt to lay hands upon the Sword of Shannara, Cogline returned to the valley of Hearthstone and the illusion of separateness that Walker had worked so hard to maintain was shattered. It was late evening, the sun had gone west, the skies were washed with moonlight and filled with stars, and the summer air was sweet and clean with the smell of new growth. Walker was coming back from a visit to the pinnacle, a refuge he found particularly soothing, the massive stone a source from which it seemed he could draw strength. The cottage door was open and the rooms within lighted as always, but Walker sensed the difference, even before Rumor's purr stilled and his neck ruff bristled.

Cautiously, he moved onto the porch and into the doorway.

Cogline sat at the old wooden dining table, skeletal face bent against the glare of the oil lamps, his gray robes a weathered covering for goods long since past repair. A large, squarish package bound in oilcloth and tied with cord rested close beside him. He was eating cold food, a glass of ale almost untouched at his elbow.

"I have been waiting for you, Walker," he told the other while he was still in the darkness beyond the entry.

Walker moved into the light. "You might have saved yourself the trouble."

"Trouble?" The old man extended a sticklike hand, and Rumor padded forward to nuzzle it familiarly. "It was time I saw my home again."

"Is this your home?" Walker asked. "I would have thought you more comfortable amid the relics of the Druid past." He waited for a response, but there was none. "If you have come to persuade me to take up the charge given me by the shade, then you should know at once that I will never do so."

"Oh, my, Walker. Never is such an impossible amount of time. Besides, I have no intention of trying to persuade you to do anything. A sufficient amount of persuading has already been done, I suspect."

Walker was still standing in the doorway. He felt awkward and exposed and moved over to the table to sit across from Cogline. The old man took a long sip of the ale.

"Perhaps you thought me gone for good after my disappearance at the Hadeshorn," he said softly. His voice was distant and filled with emotions that the other could not begin to sort out. "Perhaps you even wished it."

Walker said nothing.

"I have been out into the world, Walker. I have traveled into the Four Lands, walked among the Races, passed through cities and countrysides; I have felt the pulse of life and found that it ebbs. A farmer speaks to me on the grasslands below the Streleheim, a man worn and broken by the futility of what he has encountered. 'Nothing grows,' he whispers. 'The earth sickens as if stricken by some disease.' The disease infects him as well. A merchant of wooden carvings and toys journeys from a small village beyond Varfleet, directionless. 'I leave,' he says, 'because there is no need for me. The people cease to have interest in my work. They do nothing but brood and waste away.' Bits and pieces of life in the Four Lands, Walker—they wither and fade like a spotting that spreads across the flesh. Pockets here and pockets there—as if the will to go on were missing. Trees and shrubs and growing things fail; animals and men alike sicken and die. All become dust, and a haze of that dust rises up and fills the air and leaves the whole of the ravaged land a still life in miniature of the vision shown us by Allanon."

The sharp, old eyes squinted up at the other. "It begins, Walker. It begins."

Walker Boh shook his head. "The land and her people have

always suffered failings, Cogline. You see the shade's vision because you want to see it."

"No, not I, Walker." The old man shook his head firmly. "I want no part of Druid visions, neither in their being nor in their fulfillment. I am as much a pawn of what has happened as yourself. Believe what you will, I do not wish involvement. I have chosen my life in the same manner that you have chosen yours. You don't accept that, do you?"

Walker smiled unkindly. "You took up the magic because you wished to. Once-Druid, you had a choice in your life. You dabbled in a mixture of old sciences and magics because they interested you. Not so myself. I was born with a legacy I would have been better born without. The magic was forced upon me without my consent. I use it because I have no choice. It is a millstone that would drag me down. I do not deceive myself. It has made my life a ruin." The dark eyes were bitter. "Do not attempt to compare us, Cogline."

The other's thin frame shifted. "Harsh words, Walker Boh. You were eager enough to accept my teaching in the use of that magic once upon a time. You felt comfortable enough with it then to learn its secrets."

"A matter of survival and nothing more. I was a child trapped in a Druid's monstrous casting. I used you to keep myself alive. You were all I had." The white skin of his lean face was taut with bitterness. "Do not look to me for thanks, Cogline. I haven't the grace for it."

Cogline stood up suddenly, a whiplash movement that belied his fragile appearance. He towered above the dark-robed figure seated across from him, and there was a forbidding look to his weathered face. "Poor Walker," he whispered. "You still deny who you are. You deny your very existence. How long can you keep up this pretense?"

There was a strained silence between them that seemed endless. Rumor, curled on a rug before the fire at the far end of the room, looked up expectantly. An ember from the hearth spat and snapped, filling the air with a shower of sparks.

"Why have you come, old man?" Walker Boh said finally, the words a barely contained thrust of rage. There was a coppery taste in his mouth that he knew came not from anger, but from fear.

"To try to help you," Cogline said. There was no irony in his voice. "To give you direction in your brooding."

"I am content without your interference."

"Content?" The other shook his head. "No, Walker. You will never be content until you learn to quit fighting yourself. You work so hard at it. I thought that the lessons you received from me on the uses of the magic might have weaned you away from such childishness—but it appears I was wrong. You face hard lessons, Walker. Maybe you won't survive them."

He shoved the heavy parcel across the table at the other man. "Open it."

Walker hesitated, his eyes locked on the offering. Then he reached out, snapped apart the binding with a flick of his fingers and pulled back the oilcloth.

He found himself looking at a massive, leatherbound book elaborately engraved in gold. He reached out and touched it experimentally, lifted the cover, peered momentarily inside, then flinched away from it as if his fingers had been burned.

"Yes, Walker. It is one of the missing Druid Histories, a single volume only." The wrinkled old face was intense.

"Where did you get it?" Walker demanded harshly.

Cogline bent close. The air seemed filled with the sound of his breathing. "Out of lost Paranor."

Walker Boh came slowly to his feet. "You lie."

"Do I? Look into my eyes and tell me what you see."

Walker flinched away. He was shaking. "I don't care where you got it—or what fantasies you have concocted to make me believe what I know in my heart cannot possibly be so! Take it back to where you got it or let it sink into the bogs! I'll have no part of it!"

Cogline shook his wispy head. "No, Walker, I'll not take it back. I carried it out of a realm of yesterdays filled with gray haze and death to give to you. I am not your tormentor—never that! I am the closest thing to a friend you will ever know, even if you cannot yet accept it!" The weathered face softened. "I said before that I came to help you. It is so. Read the book, Walker. There are truths in there that need learning."

"I will not!" the other cried furiously.

Cogline stared at the younger man for long minutes, then sighed. "As you will. But the book remains. Read it or not, the choice is yours. Destroy it even, if you wish." He drained off the remainder of his ale, set the glass carefully on the table, and looked down at his gnarled hands. "I am finished here."

He came around the table and stood before the other. "Goodbye, Walker. I would stay if it would help. I would give you whatever it is within my power to give you if you would take it. But you are not yet ready. Another day, perhaps."

He turned then and disappeared into the night. He did not look back as he went. He did not deviate from his course. Walker Boh watched him fade away, a shadow gone back into the darkness that had made him.

The cottage, as if by his going, turned empty and still.

"IT WILL BE DANGEROUS, Par," Damson Rhee whispered. "If there were a safer way, I should snatch it up in an instant."

Par Ohmsford said nothing. They were deep within the People's Park once more, crouched in the shadows of a grove of cedar just beyond the broad splash of light cast by the lamps of the Gatehouse. It was midway toward dawn, the deepest, fullest hours of sleep, when everything slowed to a crawl amid dreams and rememberings. The Gatehouse rose up against the moonlit darkness like massive blocks stacked one upon the other by a careless child. Barred windows and bolted doors were shallow indentations in a skin made rough and coarse by weather and time. The walls warding the ravine ran off to either side and the crossing bridge stretched away behind, a spider web connecting to the tumbledown ruin of the old palace. A watch had been stationed before the main entry where a pair of matched iron portals stood closed behind a hinged grate of bars. The watch dozed on its feet, barely awake in the enveloping stillness. No sound or movement from the Gatehouse disturbed their rest.

"Can you remember enough of him to conjure up a likeness?" Damson asked, her words a brush of softness against his ear. Par nodded. It was not likely he would ever forget the face of Rimmer Dall.

She was quiet a moment. "If we are stopped, keep their attention focused on yourself. I will deal with any threats."

He nodded once more. They waited, motionless within their concealment, listening to the stillness, thinking their separate thoughts. Par was frightened and filled with doubts, but he was mostly determined. Damson and he were the only real chance Coll and the others had. They would succeed in this risky business because they must.

The Gate watch came awake as those patrolling the west wall of the park appeared out of the night. The guards greeted each other casually, spoke for a time, and then the watch from the east wall appeared as well. A flask was passed around, pipes were smoked, and then the guards dispersed. The patrols disappeared east and west. The Gate watch resumed their station.

"Not yet," Damson whispered as Par shifted expectantly.

The minutes dragged by. The solitude that had shrouded the Gatehouse earlier returned anew. The guards yawned and shifted. One leaned wearily on the haft of his poleaxe.

"Now," Damson Rhee said. She caught the Valeman by the shoulder and leaned into him. Her lips brushed his cheek. "Luck to us, Par Ohmsford."

Then they were up and moving. They crossed into the circle of light boldly, striding out of the shadows as if they were at home in them, coming toward the Gatehouse from the direction of the city. Par was already singing, weaving the wishsong's spell through the night's stillness, filling the minds of the watch with the images he wished them to see.

What they saw were two Seekers cloaked in forbidding black, the taller of the two First Seeker Rimmer Dall.

They snapped to attention immediately, eyes forward, barely looking at the two who approached. Par kept his voice even, the magic weaving a constant spell of disguise in the minds of the willing men.

"Open!" Damson Rhee snapped perfunctorily as they reached the Gatehouse entry.

The guards could not comply quickly enough. They pulled back the hinged grate, released the outer locks, and hammered anxiously on the doors to alert the guards within. A tiny door opened and Par shifted the focus of his concentration slightly. Bleary eyes peered out in grouchy curiosity, widened, and the locks released. The doors swung back, and Par and Damson pushed inside.

They stood in a wardroom filled with weapons stacked in wall racks and stunned Federation soldiers. The soldiers had been playing cards and drinking, clearly convinced the night's excitement was over. They were caught off guard by the appearance of the Seekers and it showed. Par filled the room with the faint hum of the wishsong, blanketing it momentarily with his magic. It took everything he had.

Damson understood how tenuous was his hold. "Everyone out!" she ordered, her voice flinty with anger.

The room emptied instantly. The entire squad dispersed through adjoining doors and disappeared as if formed of smoke. One guard remained, apparently the senior watch officer. He stood uncertainly, stiffly, eyes averted, wishing he were anywhere else but where he was, yet unable to go.

"Take us to the prisoners," Damson said softly, standing at the man's left shoulder.

The soldier cleared his throat after trying futilely to speak. "I'll need my commander's permission," he ventured. Some small sense of responsibility for his assigned duty yet remained to him.

Damson kept her eyes fixed on the man's ear, forcing him thereby to look elsewhere. "Where is your commander?" she asked.

"Sleeping below," the man answered. "I'll wake him."

"No." Damson stayed his effort to depart. "We'll wake him together."

They went through a heavily bolted door directly across the room and started down a stairwell dimly lit by oil lamps. Par kept the wishsong's music lingering in the frightened guard's ears, teasing him with it, letting him see them as much bigger than life and much more threatening. It was all going as planned, the charade working exactly as Damson and he had hoped. Down the empty stairs they went, circling from landing to landing, the thudding of their boots the only sound in the hollow silence. At the bottom of the well there were two doors. The one on the left was open and led into a lighted corridor. The guard took them through that door to another, stopped and knocked. When there was no response, he knocked again, sharply.

"What is it, drat you?" a voice snapped.

"Open up at once, Commander!" Damson replied in a voice so cold it made even Par shiver.

There was a fumbling about and the door opened. The Federation commander with the short-cropped hair and the unpleasant eyes stood there, his tunic half buttoned. Shock registered on his face instantly as the wishsong's magic took hold. He saw the Seekers. Worse, he saw Rimmer Dall.

He gave up trying to button his clothing and came quickly into the hall. "I didn't expect anyone this soon. I'm sorry. Is there a problem?"

"We'll discuss it later, Commander," Damson said severely. "For now, take us to the prisoners."

For just an instant there was a flicker of doubt in the other man's eyes, a shading of worry that perhaps everything was not quite right. Par tightened the hold of the magic on the man's mind, giving him a glimpse of the terror that awaited him should he question the order. That glimpse was enough. The commander hastened back down the corridor to the stairwell, produced a key from a ring at his waist, and opened the second door.

They stepped into a passageway lit by a single lamp hung next to the door. The commander took the lamp in hand and led the way forward. Damson followed. Par motioned the watch officer ahead of him and brought up the rear. His voice was beginning to grow weary from the effort of maintaining the charade. It was more difficult to project to several different points. He should have sent the second man away.

The passageway was constructed of stone block and smelled of mold and decay. Par realized that they were underground, apparently beneath the ravine. Things of considerable size darted from the light, and there were streaks of phosphorescence and dampness in the stone.

They had only gone a short distance when they came to the cells, a collection of low-ceilinged cages, not high enough for a man to stand in, dusty and cobwebbed, the doors constructed of rusted iron bars. The entire company was crammed into the first of these, crouched or sitting on a stone slab floor. Eyes blinked in disbelief, widened as the lie of the magic played hide-and-seek with the truth. Coll knew what was going on. He was already on his feet, pushing to the door, motioning the others up with him. Even Padishar obeyed the gesture, realizing what was about to happen.

"Open the door," Damson ordered.

Again, the eyes of the Federation commander registered his misgivings.

"Open the door, Commander," Damson repeated impatiently. "Now!"

The commander fumbled for a second key within the cluster at his belt, inserted it into the lock and turned. The cell door swung open. Instantly, Padishar Creel had the astonished man's neck in his hands, tightening his grip until the other could scarcely breathe. The watch officer stumbled back, turned, tried unsuccessfully to run over Par, was caught from behind by Morgan, and hammered into unconsciousness.

The prisoners crowded into the narrow passageway, greeting Par and Damson with handclasps and smiles. Padishar paid them no heed. His attention was focused entirely on the hapless Federation commander.

"Who betrayed us?" he said with an impatient hiss.

The commander struggled to free himself, his face turning bright red from the pressure on his throat.

"It was one of us, you said! Who?"

The commander choked. "Don't . . . know. Never saw . . ."

Padishar shook him. "Don't lie to me!"

"Never . . . Just a . . . message."

"Who was it?" Padishar insisted, the cords on the back of his hands gone white and hard.

The terrified man kicked out violently, and Padishar slammed his head sharply against the stone wall. The commander went limp, sagging like a rag doll.

Damson pulled Padishar about. "Enough of this," she said evenly, ignoring the fury that still burned in the other's eyes. "We're wasting time. He clearly doesn't know. Let's get out of here. There's been enough risk-taking for one day."

The outlaw chief studied her wordlessly for a moment, then let the unconscious man drop. "I'll find out anyway, I promise you," he swore.

Par had never seen anyone so angry. But Damson ignored it. She turned and motioned for Par to get moving. The Valeman led the way back up the stairwell, the others trailing behind him in a staggered line. They had devised no plan for getting out again when they had made the decision to come after their friends. They had decided that it would be best simply to take what opportunity offered and make do.

Opportunity gave them everything they needed this night. The wardroom was empty when they reached it, and they moved swiftly to pass through. Only Morgan paused, rummaging through the weapons racks until he had located the confiscated Sword of Leah. Smiling grimly, he strapped it across his back and went after the others.

Their luck held. The guards outside were overpowered before they knew what was happening. All about, the night was silent, the park empty, the patrols still completing their rounds, the city asleep. The members of the little band melted into the shadows and vanished.

As they hurried away, Damson swung Par around and gave him a brilliant smile and a kiss full on the mouth. The kiss was hungry and filled with promise.

Later, when there was time to reflect, Par Ohmsford savored that moment. Yet it was not Damson's kiss that he remembered most from the events of that night. It was the fact that the magic of the wishsong had proved useful at last.

CHAPTER

21

THE DRUID HISTORY BECAME for Walker Boh a challenge that he was determined to win.

For three days after Cogline's departure, Walker ignored the book. He left it on the dining table, still settled amid its oilcloth wrappings and broken binding cord, its burnished leather cover collecting motes of dust and gleaming faintly in sunshine and lamplight. He disdained it, going about his business as if it weren't there, pretending it was a part of his surroundings that he could not remove, testing himself against its temptation. He had thought at first to rid himself of it immediately, then decided against it. That would be too easy and too quickly second-guessed later on. If he could withstand its lure for a time, if he could live in its presence without giving in to his understandable desire to uncover its secrets, then he could dispose of it with a clean conscience. Cogline expected him either to open it or dispose of it at once. He would do neither. The old man would get no satisfaction in his efforts to manipulate Walker Boh.

The only one who paid any attention to the parcel was Rumor, who sniffed at it from time to time but otherwise ignored it. The three days passed and the book sat unopened.

But then something odd happened. On the fourth day of this strange contest, Walker began to question his reasoning. Did it really make any better sense to dispose of the book after a week or even a month than it did to dispose of it immediately? Would it matter either way? What did it demonstrate other than a sort of perverse hardheadedness on his part? What sort of game was he playing and for whose benefit was he playing it?

Walker mulled the matter over as the daylight hours waned and darkness closed about, then sat staring at the book from across the room while the fire in the hearth burned slowly to ash and the midnight hour neared.

"I am not being strong," he whispered to himself. "I am being frightened."

He considered the possibility in the silence of his thoughts. Finally he stood up, crossed the room to the dining table and stopped. For a moment, he hesitated. Then he reached down and picked up the Druid History. He hefted it experimentally.

Better to know the Demon that pursues you than to continue to imagine him.

He crossed back to his reading chair and seated himself once more, the book settled on his lap. Rumor lifted his massive head from where he slept in front of the fire, and his luminous eyes fixed on Walker. Walker stared back. The cat blinked and went back to sleep.

Walker Boh opened the book.

He read it slowly, working his way through its thick parchment pages with deliberate pacing, letting his eyes linger on the gold edges and ornate calligraphy, determined that now that the book was opened nothing should be missed. The silence after midnight deepened, broken only by an occasional throaty sound from the sleeping moor cat and the snapping of embers in the fire. Only once he thought to wonder how Cogline had really come by the book—surely not out of Paranor!—and then the matter was forgotten as the recorded history caught him up and swept him away as surely as if he were a leaf upon a windswept ocean.

The time chronicled was that of Bremen when he was among the last of the Druids, when the Warlock Lord and his minions had destroyed nearly all of the members of the Council. There were stories of the dark magic that had changed the rebel Druids into the horrors they had become. There were accounts of its varied uses, conjurings, and incantations that Bremen had uncovered but had been smart enough to fear. All of the frightening secrets of what the magic could do were touched upon, interspersed with the cautions that so many who tried to master the power would ignore. It was a time of upheaval and frightening change in the Four Lands, and Bremen alone had understood what was at stake.

Walker paged ahead, growing anxious now. Cogline had meant for him to read something particular within this history. Whatever it was, he had not yet come upon it.

The Skull Bearers had seized Paranor for themselves, the chronicles related. Paranor, they had thought, would now be their home. But the Warlock Lord had felt threatened there, wary of latent magic within the stones of the Keep, within the depths of the earth where the furnaces beneath the castle fortress burned. So he had called the Skull Bearers to him and gone north . . .

Walker frowned. He had forgotten that part. For a time Paranor had been abandoned completely when it could have belonged to the rebels. After all, the Second War of the Races had dragged on for years.

He paged ahead once more, skimming the words, searching without knowing exactly what it was he was searching for. He had forgotten his resolve of earlier, his promise to himself that he was not to be caught up in Cogline's snare. His curiosity and intellect were too demanding to be stayed by caution. There were secrets here that no man had set eyes upon for hundreds of years, knowledge that only the Druids had enjoyed, dispensing it to the Races as they perceived necessary and never otherwise. Such power! How long had it been hidden from everyone but Allanon, and before him Bremen, and before him Galaphile and the first Druids, and before them . . . ?

He stopped reading, aware suddenly that the flow of the narrative had changed. The script had turned smaller, more precise. There were odd markings amid the words, runes that symbolized gestures.

Walker Boh went cold to his bones. The silence that enveloped the room became enormous, an unending, suffocating ocean.

Shades! he whispered in the darkest corner of his mind. *It is the invocation for the magic that sealed away Paranor!*

His breathing sounded harsh in his own ears as he forced

his eyes away from the book. His pale face was taut. This was what Cogline had meant for him to find—why, he didn't know—but this was it. Now that he had found it, he wondered if he might not be better off closing the book at once.

But that was the fear whispering in his ear again, he knew.

He lowered his eyes once more and began to read. The spell was there, the invocation of magic that Allanon had used three hundred years ago to close away Paranor from the world of men. He found to his surprise that he understood it. His training with Cogline was more complete than he would have imagined. He finished the narrative of the spell and turned the page.

There was a single paragraph. It read:

Once removed, Paranor shall remain lost to the world of men for the whole of time, sealed away and invisible within its casting. One magic alone has the power to return it— that singular Elfstone that is colored Black and was conceived by the faerie people of the old world in the manner and form of all Elfstones, combining nevertheless in one stone alone the necessary properties of heart, mind, and body. Whosoever shall have cause and right shall wield it to its proper end.

That was all it said. Walker read on, found that the subject matter abruptly changed and skipped back. He read the paragraph again, slowly, searching for anything he might have missed. There was no question in his mind that this was what Cogline had meant for him to find. A Black Elfstone. A magic that could retrieve lost Paranor. The means to the end of the charge that the shade of Allanon had given him.

Bring back Paranor and restore the Druids. He could hear again the words of the charge in his mind.

Of course, there were no longer any Druids. But maybe Allanon intended that Cogline should take up the cause, once Paranor was restored. It seemed logical despite the old man's protestations that his time was past—but Walker was astute enough to recognize that where Druids and their magics were concerned logic often traveled a tortuous path.

He was two-thirds of the way through the history. He spent

another hour finishing it, found nothing further that he believed was intended for him, and turned back again to the paragraph on the Black Elfstone. Dawn was creeping out of the east, a faint golden light in the dark horizon. Walker rubbed his eyes and tried to think. Why was there so little digression on the purpose and properties of this magic? What did it look like and what could it do? It was a single stone instead of three—why? How was it that no one had ever heard of it before?

The questions buzzed around inside his head like trapped flies, annoying and at the same time intriguing him. He read the paragraph several times more—read it, in fact, until he could recite it from memory—and closed the book. Rumor stretched and yawned on the floor in front of him, lifted his head and blinked.

Talk to me, cat, Walker thought. *There are always secrets that only a cat knows. Maybe this is one of them.*

But Rumor only got up and went outside, disappearing into the fading shadows.

Walker fell asleep then and did not come awake again until midday. He rose, bathed and dressed anew, ate a slow meal with the closed book in front of him, and went out for a long walk. He passed south through the valley to a favorite glade where a stream rippled noisily over a meandering rock bed and emptied into a pool that contained tiny fish colored brilliant red and blue. He lingered there for a time, thinking, then returned again to the cottage. He sat on the porch and watched the sun creep westward in a haze of purple and scarlet.

"I should never have opened the book," he chided himself softly, for its mystery had proven irresistible after all. "I should have bound it back up and dropped it into the deepest hole I could find."

But it was too late for that. He had read it and knowledge acquired could not be readily forgotten. A sense of futility mingled with anger. He had thought it impossible that Paranor could be restored. Now he knew that there was a magic that could do exactly that. Once again, there was that sense of the inevitability of things prophesied by the Druids.

Still, his life was his own, wasn't it? He needn't accept the charge of Allanon's shade, whatever its viability.

But his curiosity was relentless. He found himself thinking of the Black Elfstone, even when he tried not to. The Black Elfstone was out there, somewhere, a forgotten magic. Where? Where was it?

That and all the other questions pressed in about him as the evening passed. He ate his dinner, walked again for a time, read from the few precious books of his own library, wrote a bit in his journal, and mostly thought of that single, beguiling paragraph on the magic that would bring back Paranor.

He thought about it as he prepared for bed.

He was still thinking about it as midnight approached.

Teasingly, insinuatingly, it wormed about restlessly inside his mind, suggesting this possibility and that, opening doors just a crack into unlighted rooms, hinting at understandings and insights that would bring him the knowledge he could not help but crave.

And with it, perhaps, peace of mind.

His sleep was troubled and restless. The mystery of the Black Elfstone was an irritation that would not be dispelled.

By morning, he had decided that he must do something about it.

PAR OHMSFORD CAME AWAKE that morning with a decision of his own to make. It had been five days since Damson and he had rescued Coll, Morgan, Padishar Creel, and the other two outlaws from the cells of the Federation Gatehouse, and the bunch of them had been on the run ever since. They had not attempted to leave the city, certain that the gates would be closely watched and the risk of discovery too great. They had not returned to the basement of the weapons-maker's shop either, feeling that it might have been compromised by their mysterious betrayer. Instead, they had skipped from one shelter to the next, never remaining more than one night, posting guards throughout their brief stay at each, jumping at every sound they heard and every shadow they saw.

Well, enough was enough. Par had decided that he was through running.

He rose from the makeshift bed he occupied in the attic of

the grain house and glanced over at Coll next to him, who was still asleep. The others were already up and presumably downstairs in the main warehouse, which was closed until the beginning of the work week. Gingerly he crossed to the tiny, shuttered window that let in what small amount of light the room enjoyed and peered out. The street below was empty except for a stray dog sniffing at a refuse bin and a beggar sleeping in the door of the tin factory across the way. Clouds hung low and gray across the skies, threatening rain before the close of the day.

When he crossed back to pull on his boots, he found Coll awake and looking at him. His brother's coarse hair was ruffled and his eyes were clouded with sleep and disgruntlement.

"Ho-hum, another day," Coll muttered and then yawned hugely. "What fascinating storage room will we be visiting today, do you suppose?"

"None, as far as I'm concerned." Par dropped down beside him.

Coll's eyebrows arched. "That so? Have you told Padishar?"

"I'm on my way."

"I suppose you have an alternative in mind—to hiding out, that is." Coll pushed himself up on one elbow. "Because I don't think Padishar Creel is going to give you the time of day if you don't. He hasn't been in the best of moods since he found out he might not be as well-loved among his men as he thought he was."

Par doubted that Padishar Creel ever had allowed himself to become deluded enough to believe that he was well-loved by his men, but Coll was certainly right enough about the outlaw chief's present temperament. His betrayal at the hands of one of his own men had left him taciturn and bitter. He had retreated somewhere deep inside himself these several days past, still clearly in command as he led them through the network of Federation patrols and checkpoints that had been thrown out across the city, still able to find them refuge when it seemed there could be none, but at the same time had become uncharacteristically withdrawn from everyone about him. Damson Rhee had come with them, whether by choice or not Par still wasn't sure, but even she could not penetrate the defenses the outlaw chief had thrown up around himself. Except for exercising his authority as leader, Padishar had removed himself from them as surely as if he were no longer physically present.

Par shook his head. "Well, we have to do something besides simply hop about from place to place for the rest of our lives." He was feeling rather sullen about matters himself. "If there's a need for a plan, Padishar should come up with one. Nothing's being accomplished the way things stand now."

Coll sat up and began dressing. "You probably don't want to hear this, Par, but it may be time to rethink this whole business of allying ourselves with the Movement. We might be better off on our own again."

Par said nothing. They finished dressing and went downstairs to find the others. There was cold bread, jam, and fruit for breakfast, and they ate it hungrily. Par could not understand how he could be so famished after doing so little. He listened as he ate to Stasas and Drutt compare notes on hunting in the forests of their respective homes somewhere below Varfleet. Morgan was keeping watch by the doors leading into the warehouse and Coll went to join him. Damson Rhee sat on an empty packing crate nearby, carving something. He had seen little of her during the past several days; she was often out with Padishar, scouting the city while the rest of them hid.

Padishar was nowhere to be seen.

After eating, Par went back upstairs to gather his things together, anticipating that, whatever the result of his confrontation with Padishar, it would likely involve a move.

Damson followed him up. "You grow restless," she observed when they were alone. She seated herself on the edge of his pallet, shaking back her reddish mane. "An outlaw's life is not what you had in mind, is it?"

He smiled faintly. "Sitting about in warehouses and basements isn't what I had in mind. What is Padishar waiting around for?"

She shrugged. "What we all wait around for from time to time—that little voice buried somewhere deep inside that tells us what to do next. It might be intuition or it might be common sense or then again it might be the advent of circumstances beyond our control." She gave him a wicked smile. "Is it speaking now to you?"

"Something certainly is." He sat down next to her. "Why are you still here, Damson? Does Padishar keep you?"

She laughed. "Hardly. I come and go as I please. He knows I was not the one who betrayed him. Or you, I think."

"Then why stay?"

She considered him thoughtfully for a moment. "Maybe I stay because you interest me," she said at last. She paused as if she wanted to say more, but thought better of it. She smiled. "I have never met anyone who uses real magic. Just the pretend kind, like me."

She reached up and deftly plucked a coin from behind his ear. It was carved from cherry wood. She handed it to him. It bore her likeness on one side and his on the other. He looked up at her in surprise. "That's very good."

"Thank you." He thought she colored slightly. "You may keep it with the other for good luck."

He tucked the coin into his pocket. They sat silent for a time, exchanging uncertain glances. "There isn't much difference, you know, between your kind of magic and mine," he said finally. "They both rely on illusion."

She shook her head. "No, Par. You are wrong. One is an acquired skill, the other innate. Mine is learned and, once learned, has become all it can. Yours is constantly growing, and its lessons are limitless. Don't you see? My magic is a trade, a way to make a living. Your magic is much more; it is a gift around which you must build your life."

She smiled, but there was a hint of sadness in it. She stood up. "I have work to do. Finish your packing." She moved past him and disappeared down the ladder.

The morning hours crawled past and still Padishar did not return. Par busied himself doing nothing, growing anxious for something—anything—to happen. Coll and Morgan drifted over from time to time, and he spoke to them of his intention to confront the outlaw chief. Neither seemed very optimistic about his chances.

The skies grew more threatening, the wind picking up until

it made a rather mournful howl about the loose-fitting jambs and shutters of the old building they were housed in, but still it didn't rain. Card games were played to pass the time and topics of conversation exhausted.

It was nearing midafternoon when Padishar returned. He slipped in through the front doors without a word, crossed the room to Par and motioned him to follow. He took the Valeman into a small office situated at the back of the main floor and shut the door behind them.

When they were alone, he seemed at a loss for words.

"I have been thinking rather carefully about what we should do," he said finally. "Or, if you prefer, what we should not do. Any mistake we make now could be our last."

He pulled Par over to a bench that had been shoved back against the wall and sat them both down. "There's the problem of this traitor," he said quietly. His eyes were bright and hard with something Par couldn't read. "I was certain at first that it must be one of us. But it isn't me or Damson. Damson is above suspicion. It isn't you. It might be your brother; but it isn't him either, is it?"

He made it a statement of fact rather than a question. Par shook his head in agreement.

"Or the Highlander."

Par shook his head a second time.

"That leaves Ciba Blue, Stasas, and Drutt. Blue is likely dead; that means that if he's the one, he was stupid enough to let himself get killed in the bargain. Doesn't sound like Blue. And the other two have been with me almost from the first. It is inconceivable that either of them would betray me—whatever the price offered or the reason supplied. Their hatred of the Federation is nearly a match for my own."

The muscles in his jaw tightened. "So perhaps it isn't any of us after all. But who else could have discovered our plan? Do you see what I mean? Your friend the Highlander mentioned this morning something he had almost forgotten. When we first came into the city and went down to the market stalls, he thought he saw Hirehone. He thought then he was mistaken; now he wonders. Forgetting momentarily the fact that Hirehone held my life in his hands any number of times before this and did not betray me, how would he have gone about doing so now? No one, outside of Damson and those I brought with me, knew the where, when, how, or why of what we were about. Yet those Federation soldiers were waiting for us. They knew."

Par had forgotten momentarily his plan to tell Padishar he was fed up with matters. "Then who was it?" he asked eagerly. "Who could it have been?"

Padishar's smile was forced. "The question plagues me like flies a sweating horse. I don't know yet. You may rest assured that sooner or later I will. For the moment, it doesn't matter. We have bigger fish to fry."

He leaned forward. "I spent the morning with a man I know, a man who has access to what happens within the higher circles of Federation authority in Tyrsis. He is a man I am certain of, one I can trust. Even Damson doesn't know of him. He told me some interesting things. It seems that you and Damson came to my rescue just in time. Rimmer Dall arrived early the next morning to see personally to my questioning and ultimate disposal." The outlaw chief's voice emitted a sigh of satisfaction. "He was very disappointed to find I had left early."

Padishar shifted his weight and brought his head close to Par's. "I know you are impatient for something to happen, Par. I can read the signs of it in you as if you were a notice posted on the wall by my bed. But haste results in an early demise in this line of work, so caution is always necessary." He smiled again. "But you and I, lad—we're a force to be reckoned with in this business of the Federation and their game-playing. Fate brought you to me, and she has something definite in mind for the two of us, something that will shake the Federation and their Coalition Council and their Seekers and all the rest right to the foundation of their being!"

One hand clenched before Par's face, and the Valeman flinched back in spite of himself. "So much effort has been put into hiding all traces of the old People's Park—the Bridge of Sendic destroyed and rebuilt, the old park walled away, guards running all about it like ants at a picnic dinner! Why? Because there's something down there that they don't want anyone to know about! I can feel it, lad! I am as convinced of it now as I was when we went in five nights ago!"

"The Sword of Shannara?" Par whispered.

Padishar's smile was genuine this time. "I'd stake ten years of my life on it! But there's still only one way to find out, isn't there?"

He brought his hands up to grip Par's shoulders. The weathered, sharp-boned face was a mask of cunning and ruthless determination. The man who had led them for the past five days had disappeared; this was the old Padishar Creel speaking.

"The man I spoke to, the one who has ears in the Federation chambers, tells me that Rimmer Dall believes we've fled. He thinks us back within the Parma Key. Whatever we came here for we've given up on, he's decided. He lingers in the city only because he has not decided what needs doing next. I suggest we give him some direction, young Par."

Par's eyes widened. "What . . . ?"

"What he least expects, of course!" Padishar anticipated his question and pounced on it. "The last thing he and his black-cloaked wolves will look for—that's what!" His eyes narrowed. "We'll go back down into the Pit!"

Par quit breathing.

"We'll go back down before they have a chance to figure out where we are or what we intend, back down into that most carefully guarded hidey-hole, and if the Sword of Shannara is there, why, we'll snatch it away from under their very noses!"

He brought an astonished Par to his feet with a jerk. "And we'll do it tonight!"

CHAPTER

22

IT WAS NEARING TWILIGHT by the time Walker Boh reached his destination. He had been journeying northward from Hearthstone since midmorning, traveling at a comfortable pace, not hurrying, allowing himself adequate time to think through what he was about to do. The skies had been clear and filled with sunshine when he had set out, but as the day lengthened toward evening clouds began to drift in from the west and the air turned dense and gray. The land through which he traveled was rugged, a series of twisting ridges and drops that broke apart the symmetry of the forests and left the trees leaning and bent like spikes driven randomly into the earth. Deadwood and outcroppings of rock blocked the trail repeatedly and mist hung shroudlike in the trees, trapped there it seemed, unmoving.

Walker stopped. He stared downward between two massive, jagged ridgelines into a narrow valley that cradled a tiny lake. The lake was barely visible, screened away by pine trees and a thick concentration of mist that clung tenaciously above its surface, swirling sluggishly, listlessly, haphazardly in the nearly windless expanse.

The lake was the home of the Grimpond.

Walker did not pause long, starting down into the valley almost immediately. The mist closed quickly about him as he went, filling his mouth with its metallic taste, clouding his vision of what lay ahead. He ignored the sensations that attacked him—the pressing closeness, the imagined whispers, the discomfiting deadness—and kept his concentration focused on putting one foot in front of the other. The air grew quickly cool, a damp layer against his skin that smelled of things decayed. The pines rose up about him, their numbers increasing until there was nowhere they did not stand watch. Silence cloaked the valley and there was only the soft scrape of his boots against the stone.

He could feel the eyes of the Grimpond watching.

It had been a long time.

Cogline had warned him early about the Grimpond. The Grimpond was the shade that lived in the lake below, a shade older than the world of the Four Lands itself. It claimed to pre-date the Great Wars. It boasted that it had been alive in the age of faerie. As with all shades, it had the ability to divine secrets hidden from the living. There was magic at its command. But it was a bitter and spiteful creature, trapped in this world for all eternity for reasons no one knew. It could not die and it hated the substanceless, empty existence it was forced to endure. It vented itself on the humans who came to speak with it, teasing them with riddles of the truths they sought to uncover, taunting them with their mortality, showing them more of what they would keep hidden than what they would reveal.

Brin Ohmsford had come to the Grimpond three hundred years earlier to find a way into the Maelmord so that she might confront the Ildatch. The shade toyed with her until she used the wishsong to ensnare it by trickery, forcing it to reveal what she wished to discover. The shade had never forgotten that; it was the only time a human had bested it. Walker had heard the story any number of times while growing up. It was only after he came north to Hearthstone to live, forsaking the Ohmsford name and legacy, that he discovered that the Grimpond was waiting for him. Brin Ohmsford might be dead and gone, but the Grimpond was alive forever and it had determined that someone must be made to pay for its humiliation. If not the one directly responsible, why, then another of that one's bloodline would do nicely.

Cogline advised him to stay clear. The Grimpond would see him destroyed if it was given the opportunity. His parents had been given the same advice and had heeded it. But Walker Boh had reached a point in his life when he was through making excuses for who and what he was. He had come to the Wilderun to escape his legacy; he did not intend to spend the rest of his life wondering if there was something out there that could undo him. Best to deal with the shade at once. He went looking for the Grimpond. Because the shade never appeared to more than one person at a time, Cogline was forced to remain behind. When the confrontation came, it was memorable. It lasted for almost six hours. During that time, the Grimpond assailed Walker Boh with every imaginable trick and ploy at its disposal, divulging real and imagined secrets of his present and his future, showering him with rhetoric designed to drive him into madness, revealing to him visions of himself and those he loved that were venomous and destructive. Walker Boh withstood it all. When the shade exhausted itself, it cursed Walker and disappeared back into the mist.

Walker returned to Hearthstone, feeling that the matter of the past was settled. He let the Grimpond alone and the Grimpond—though it could be argued that he had no choice since he was bound to the waters of the lake—did the same to him.

Until today, Walker Boh had not been back.

He sighed. It would be more difficult this time, since this time he wanted something from the shade. He could pretend otherwise. He could keep to himself the truth of why he had come—to learn from the Grimpond the whereabouts of the mysterious Black Elfstone. He could talk about this and that, or assume some role that would confuse the creature, since it loved games and the playing of them. But it was unlikely to make any difference. Somehow the Grimpond always divined the reason you were there.

Walker Boh felt the mist brush against him with the softness of tiny fingers, clinging insistently. This was not going to be pleasant.

He continued ahead as daylight failed and darkness closed about. Shadows, where they could find purchase in the graying haze, lengthened in shimmering parody of their makers. Walker wrapped his cloak closer to his body, thinking through the words he would say to the Grimpond, the arguments he would put forth, the games he would play if forced to do so. He recounted in his mind the events of his life that the shade was likely to play upon—most of them drawn from his youth when he was discomfited by his differences and beset by his insecurities.

"Dark Uncle" they had called him even then—the playmates of Par and Coll, their parents, and even people of the village of Shady Vale that didn't know him. Dark for the color of his life and being, this pale, withdrawn young man who could sometimes read minds, who could divine things that would happen and even cause them to be so, who could understand so much of what was hidden from others. Par and Coll's strange uncle, without parents of his own, without a family that was really his, without a history that he cared to share. Even the Ohmsford name didn't seem to fit him. He was always the "Dark Uncle," somehow older than everyone else, not in years but in knowledge. It wasn't knowledge he had learned; it was knowledge he had been born with. His father had tried to explain. It was the legacy of the wishsong's magic that caused it. It manifested itself this way. But it wouldn't last; it never did. It was just a stage he must pass through because of who he was. But Par and Coll did not have to pass through it, Walker would argue in reply. No, only you and I, only the children of Brin Ohmsford, because we hold the trust, his father would whisper. We are the chosen of Allanon . . .

He swept the memories from his mind angrily, the bitterness welling up anew. The "chosen of Allanon" had his father said? The "cursed of Allanon" was more like it.

The trees gave way before him abruptly, startling him with the suddenness of their disappearance. He stood at the edge of the lake, its rocky shores wending into the mist on either side, its waters lapping gently, endlessly in the silence. Walker Boh straightened. His mind tightened and closed down upon itself as if made of iron, his concentration focused, his thoughts cleared.

A solitary statue, he waited.

There was movement in the fog, but it emanated from more than one place. Walker tried to fix on it, but it was gone as quickly as it had come. From somewhere far away, above the haze that hung across the lake, beyond the rock walls of the ridgelines enfolding the narrow valley, a voice whispered in some empty heaven.

Dark Uncle.

Walker heard the words, tauntingly close and at the same time nowhere he would ever be, not from inside his head or from any other place discernible, but there nevertheless. He did not respond to them. He continued to wait.

Then the scattered movements that had disturbed the mist moments earlier focused themselves on a single point, coming together in a colorless outline that stood upon the water and began to advance. It took surer form as it came, growing in size, becoming larger than the human shape it purported to represent, rising up as if it might crush anything that stood in its way. Walker did not move. The ethereal shape became a shadow, and the shadow became a person . . .

Walker Boh watched expressionlessly as the Grimpond stood before him, suspended in the vapor, its face lifting out of shadow to reveal who it had chosen to become.

"Have you come to accept my charge, Walker Boh?" it asked.

Walker was startled in spite of his resolve. The dark, brooding countenance of Allanon stared down at him.

THE WAREHOUSE WAS HUSHED, its cavernous enclosure blanketed by stillness from floor to ceiling as six pairs of eyes fastened intently on Padishar Creel.

He had just announced that they were going back down into the Pit.

"We'll be doing it differently this time," he told them, his raw-boned face fierce with determination, as if that alone might persuade them to his cause. "No sneaking about through the park with rope ladders this go-around. There's an entry into the Pit from the lower levels of the Gatehouse. That's how we'll do it. We'll go right into the Gatehouse, down into the Pit and back out again—and no one the wiser."

Par risked a quick glance at the others. Coll, Morgan, Damson, the outlaws Stasas and Drutt—there was a mix of disbelief and awe etched on their faces. What the outlaw chief was proposing was outrageous; that he might succeed, even more so. No one tried to interrupt. They wanted to hear how he was going to do it.

"The Gatehouse watch changes shifts twice each day—once at sunrise, once at sunset. Two shifts, six men each. A relief comes in for each shift once a week, but on different days. Today is one of those days. A relief for the day shift comes in just after sunset. I know; I made it a point to find out."

His features creased with the familiar wolfish smile. "Today a special detail will arrive a couple of hours before the shift change because there's to be an inspection of the Gatehouse quarters this evening at the change, and the commander of the Gatehouse wants everything spotless. The day watch will be happy enough to let the detail past to do its work, figuring it's no skin off their noses." He paused. "That detail, of course, will be us."

He leaned forward, his eyes intense. "Once inside, we'll dispatch the night watch. If we're quiet enough about it, the day watch won't even know what's happening. They'll continue with their rounds, doing part of our job for us—keeping everyone outside. We'll bolt the door from within as a precaution in any case. Then we'll go down through the Gatehouse stairs to the lower levels and out into the Pit. It should still be light enough to find what we're looking for fairly quickly. Once we have it, we'll go back up the stairs and out the same way we came in."

For a moment, no one said anything. Then Drutt said, his voice gravelly, "We'll be recognized, Padishar. Bound to be some of the same soldiers there as when we were taken."

Padishar shook his head. "There was a shift change three days ago. That was the shift that was on duty when we were seized."

"What about that commander?"

"Gone until the beginning of the work week. Just a duty officer."

"We'd need Federation uniforms."

"We have them. I brought them in yesterday."

Drutt and Stasas exchanged glances. "Been thinking about this for a time, have you?" the latter asked.

The outlaw chief laughed softly. "Since the moment we walked out of those cells."

Morgan, who had been seated on a bench next to Par, stood

up. "If anything goes wrong and they discover what we're about, they'll be all over the Gatehouse. We'll be trapped, Padishar."

The big man shook his head. "No, we won't. We'll carry in grappling hooks and ropes with our cleaning equipment. If we can't go back the way we came, we'll climb out of the Pit using those. The Federation will be concentrating on getting at us through the Gatehouse entry. It won't even occur to them that we don't intend to come back that way."

The questions died away. There was a long silence as the six sifted through their doubts and fears and waited for something inside to reassure them that the plan would work. Par found himself thinking that there were an awful lot of things that could go wrong.

"Well, what's it to be?" Padishar's patience gave out. "Time's something we don't have to spare. We all know that there's risks involved, but that's the nature of the business. I want a decision. Do we try it or not? Who says we do? Who's with me?"

Par listened to the silence lengthen. Coll and Morgan were statues on the bench to either side of him. Stasas and Drutt, who it had seemed might speak first, now had their eyes fixed firmly on the floor. Damson was looking at Padishar, who in turn was looking at her. Par realized all at once that no one was going to say anything, that they were all waiting on him.

He surprised himself. He didn't even have to think about it. He simply said, "I'll go."

"Have you lost your mind?" Coll whispered urgently in his ear. Stasas and Drutt had Padishar's momentary attention, declaring that they, too, would go. "Par, this was our chance to get out!"

Par leaned close to him. "He's doing this for me, don't you see? I'm the one who wants to find the Sword! I can't let Padishar take all the risks! I have to go!"

Coll shook his head helplessly. Morgan, with a wink at Par over Coll's shoulder, cast his vote in favor of going as well. Coll just raised his hand wordlessly and nodded.

That left Damson. Padishar had his sharp gaze fixed on her, waiting. It suddenly occurred to Par that Padishar needn't have asked who wanted to go with him; he simply could have ordered it. Perhaps in asking he was also testing. There was still a traitor loose. Padishar had told him earlier that he didn't believe it was any of them—but he might have it in his mind to make sure.

"I will wait for you in the park," Damson Rhee said, and everyone stared at her. She did not seem to notice. "I would have to disguise myself as a man in order to go in with you. That is one more risk you would be taking—and to what end? There is nothing I can offer by being with you. If there is trouble, I will be of better use to you on the outside."

Padishar's smile was immediately disarming. "Your thinking is correct as usual, Damson. You will wait in the park."

It seemed to Par that he was a little too quick to agree.

GEYSERS EXPLODED and died from the flat, gray surface of the lake, and the spray felt like bits of ice where it landed on Walker Boh's skin.

"Tell me why you come here, Dark Uncle?" Allanon's shade whispered.

Walker felt the chill burn away as his determination caught fire. "I need tell you nothing," he replied. "You are not Allanon. You are only the Grimpond."

Allanon's visage shimmered and faded in the half-light, replaced by Walker's own. The Grimpond emitted a hollow laugh. "I am you, Walker Boh. Nothing more and nothing less. Do you recognize yourself?"

His face went through a flurry of transformations—Walker as a child, as a boy, as a youth, as a man. The images came and went so quickly that Walker could barely register them. It was somehow terrifying to watch the phases of his life pass by so quickly. He forced himself to remain calm.

"Will you speak with me, Grimpond?" he asked.

"Will you speak with yourself?" came the reply.

Walker took a deep breath. "I will. But for what purpose should I do so? There is nothing to talk about with myself. I already know all that I have to say."

"Ah, as do I, Walker. As do I."

The Grimpond shrank until it was the same size as Walker. It kept his face, taunting him with it, letting it reveal flashes of the age that would one day claim it, giving it a beaten cast as if to demonstrate the futility of his life.

"I know why you have come to me," the Grimpond said suddenly. "I know the private-most thoughts of your mind, the little secrets you would keep even from yourself. There need be no games between us, Walker Boh. You are surely my equal in the playing of them, and I have no wish to do battle with you again. You have come to ask where you must go to find the Black Elfstone. Fair enough. I will tell you."

Immediately, Walker mistrusted the shade. The Grimpond never volunteered anything without twisting it. He nodded in response, but said nothing.

"How sad you seem, Walker," soothed the shade. "No jubilation at my submission, no elation that you will have what you want? Is it so difficult then to admit that you have dispensed with pride and self-resolution, that you have forsaken your lofty principles, that you have been won over after all to the Druid cause?"

Walker stiffened in spite of himself. "You misread matters, Grimpond. Nothing has been decided."

"Oh, yes, Dark Uncle! Everything has been decided! Make no mistake. Your life weaves out before my eyes as a thread straight and undeviating, the years a finite number, their course determined. You are caught in the snare of the Druid's words. His legacy to Brin Ohmsford becomes your own, whether you would have it so or not. You have been shaped!"

"Tell me, then, of the Black Elfstone," Walker tried.

"All in good time. Patience, now."

The words died away into stillness, the Grimpond shifting within its covering of mist. Daylight had faded into darkness, the gray turned black, the moon and stars shut away by the valley's thick haze. Yet there was light where Walker stood, a phosphorescence given off by the waters beneath the air on which the Grimpond floated, a dull and shallow glow that played wickedly through the night.

"So much effort given over to escaping the Druids," the Grimpond said softly. "What foolishness." Walker's face dissipated and was replaced by his father's. His father spoke. "Remember, Walker, that we are the bearers of Allanon's trust. He gave it to Brin Ohmsford as he lay dying, to be passed from one generation to the next, to be handed down until it was needed, sometime far, far in the distant future . . ."

His father's visage leered at him. "Perhaps now?"

Images flared to life above him, borne on the air as if tapestries threaded on a frame, woven in the fabric of the mist. One after another they appeared, brilliant with color, filled with the texture and depth of real life.

Walker took a step back, startled. He saw himself in the images, anger and defiance in his face, his feet positioned on clouds above the cringing forms of Par and Wren and the others of the little company who had gathered at the Hadeshorn to meet with the shade of Allanon. Thunder rolled out of a darkness that welled away into the skies overhead, and lightning flared in jagged streaks. Walker's voice was a hiss amid the rumble and the flash, the words his own, spoken as if out of his memory. *I would sooner cut off my hand than see the Druids come again!* And then he lifted his arm to reveal that his hand, indeed, was gone.

The vision faded, then sharpened anew. He saw himself again, this time on a high, empty ridgeline that looked out across forever. The whole world spread away below him, the nations and their Races, the creatures of land and water, the lives of everyone and everything that were. Wind whipped at his black robes and whistled ferociously in his ears. There was a girl with him. She was woman and child both, a magical being, a creature of impossible beauty. She stunned him with the intensity of her gaze, depthless black eyes from which he could not turn away. Her long, silver hair flowed from her head in a shimmering mass. She reached for him, needing his balance to keep her footing on the treacherous rock—and he thrust her violently away. She fell, tumbling into the abyss below, soundless as she shrank from sight, silver hair fading into a ribbon of brightness and then into nothing at all.

Again, the vision faded, then returned. He saw himself a third time, now in a castle fortress that was empty of life and gray with disuse. Death stalked him relentlessly, creeping through walls and along corridors, cold fingers probing for signs of his life. He felt the need to run from it, knew that he must if he were to survive—and yet he couldn't. He stood immobile, letting Death approach him, reach for him, close about him. As his life ended, the cold filled him, and he saw that a dark, robed shape stood behind him, holding him fast, preventing him from fleeing. The shape bore the face of Allanon.

The visions disappeared, the colors faded, and the grayness returned, shifting sluggishly in the lake's phosphorescent glow. The Grimpond brought its robed arms downward slowly, and the lake hissed and spit with dissatisfaction. Walker Boh flinched from the spray that cascaded down upon him.

"What say you, Dark Uncle?" the Grimpond whispered. It bore Walker's pale face once more.

"That you play games still," Walker said quietly. "That you show lies and half-truths designed to taunt me. That you have shown me nothing of the Black Elfstone."

"Have I not?" The Grimpond shimmered darkly. "Is it all a game, do you think? Lies and half-truths only?" The laugh was mirthless. "You must think what you will, Walker Boh. But I see a future that is hidden from you, and it would be foolish to believe I would show you none of it. Remember, Walker. I am you, the telling of who and what you are—just as I am for all who come to speak with me."

Walker shook his head. "No, Grimpond, you can never be me. You can never be anyone but who you are—a shade without identity, without being, exiled to this patch of water for all eternity. Nothing you do, no game you play, can ever change that."

The Grimpond sent spray hissing skyward, anger in its voice. "Then go from me, Dark Uncle! Take with you what you came for and go!" The visage of Walker disappeared and was replaced by a death's head. "You think my fate has nothing to do with you? Beware! There is more of me in you than you would care to know!"

Robes flared wide, throwing shards of dull light into the mist. "Hear me, Walker! Hear me! You wish to know of the Black Elfstone? Then listen! Darkness hides it, a black that light can never penetrate, where eyes turn a man to stone and voices turn him mad! Beyond, where only the dead lie, is a pocket carved with runes, the signs of time's passing. Within that pocket lies the Stone!"

The death's head disappeared into nothingness, and only the robes remained, hanging empty against the fog. "I have given you what you wish, Dark Uncle," the shade whispered, its voice filled with loathing. "I have done so because the gift will destroy you. Die, and you will end your cursed line, the last of it! How I long to see that happen! Go, now! Leave me! I bid you swift journey to your doom!"

The Grimpond faded into the mist and was gone. The light it had brought with it dissipated as well. Darkness cloaked the whole of the lake and the shore surrounding it, and Walker was left momentarily sightless. He stood where he was, waiting for his vision to clear, feeling the chill touch of the mist as it brushed against his skin. The Grimpond's laughter echoed in the silence of his mind.

Dark Uncle came the harsh whisper.

He cast himself in stone against it. He sheathed himself in iron.

When his vision returned, and he could make out the vague shape of the trees behind him, he turned from the lake with his cloak wrapped close about him and walked away.

CHAPTER

23

AFTERNOON SLID TOWARD EVENING. A slow, easy rain fell on the city of Tyrsis, washing its dusty streets, leaving them slick and glistening in the fading light. Storm clouds brushed low against the trees of the People's Park, trailing downward in ragged streamers to curl about the roughened trunks. The park was empty, silent save for the steady patter of the rain.

Then footsteps broke the silence, a heavy thudding of boots, and a Federation squad of six materialized out of the gray, cloaked and hooded, equipment packs rattling. A pair of blackbirds perched on a peeling birch glanced over alertly. A dog rummaging amid the garbage slunk quickly away. From a still-dry doorway, a homeless child huddled against the chill and peered out, caution mirrored in its eyes. No other notice was taken. The streets were deserted, the city hunkered down and unseeing in the damp, unpleasant gloom.

Padishar Creel took his little band across the circle of the Tyrsian Way and into the park. Wrapped against the weather, they were indistinguishable one from the other, one from anyone else. They had come all the way from their warehouse lair without challenge. They had barely seen another living thing. Everything was going exactly as planned.

Par Ohmsford watched the faint, dark outline of the Gatehouse appear through the trees and felt his mind fold in upon itself. He hunched his shoulders against the chill of the rain and the heat of the sweat that ran beneath his clothing. He was trapped within himself and yet at the same time able to watch from without as if disembodied. The way forward was far darker than the day's light made it seem. He had stumbled into a tunnel, its walls round and twisting and so smooth he could not find a grip. He was falling, his momentum carrying him relentlessly toward the terror he sensed waiting ahead.

He was in danger of losing control of himself, he knew. He had been afraid before, yes—when Coll and he fled Varfleet, when the woodswoman appeared to confront them below the Runne, when Cogline told them what they must do, when they crossed the Rainbow Lake in night and fog with Morgan, when they fought the giant in the forests of the Anar, when they ran from the Gnawl in the Wolfsktaag, and when the Spider Gnomes and the girl-child who was a Shadowen seized him. He had been afraid when Allanon had come. But his fear then and since was nothing compared to what it was now. He was terrified.

He swallowed against the dryness he felt building in his throat and tried to tell himself he was all right. The feeling had come over him quite suddenly, as if it were a creature that had lain in wait along the rain-soaked streets of the city, its tentacles lashing out to snare him. Now he was caught up in a grip that bound him like iron and there was no way to break free. It was pointless to say anything to the others of what he was experiencing. After all, what could he say that would have any meaning—that he was frightened, even terrified? And what, did he suppose, were they?

A gust of wind shook the water-laden trees and showered him with droplets. He licked the water from his lips, the moisture cool and welcome. Coll was a bulky shape immediately ahead, Morgan another one behind. Shadows danced and played about him, nipping at his fading courage. This was a mistake, he heard himself whispering from somewhere deep inside. His skin prickled with the certainty of it.

He had a sense of his own mortality that had been missing before, locked away in some forgotten storeroom of his mind, kept there, he supposed, because it was so frightening to look upon. It seemed to him in retrospect as if he had treated everything that had gone before as some sort of game. That was ridiculous, he knew; yet some part of it was true. He had gone charging about the countryside, a self-declared hero in the mold of those in the stories he sang about, determined to confront the reality of his dreams, decided that he would know the truth of who and what he was. He had thought himself in control of his destiny; he realized now that he was not.

Visions of what had been swept through his mind in swift disarray, chasing one another with vicious purpose. He had caromed from one mishap to the next, he saw—always wrongly believing that his meddling was somehow useful. In truth, what had he accomplished? He was an outlaw running for his life. His parents were prisoners in their own home. Walker believed him a fool. Wren had abandoned him. Coll and Morgan stayed with him only because they felt he needed looking after. Padishar Creel believed him something he could never be. Worst of all, as a direct result of his misguided decision to accept the charge of a man three hundred years dead, five men were about to offer up their lives.

"Watch yourself," he had cautioned Coll in a vain attempt at humor as they departed their warehouse concealment. "Wouldn't want you tripping over those feet, duck's weather or no."

Coll had sniffed. "Just keep your ears pricked. Shouldn't be hard for someone like you."

Teasing, playing at being brave. Fooling no one.

Allanon! He breathed the Druid's name like a prayer in the silence of his mind. *Why don't you help me?*

But a shade, he knew, could help no one. Help could come only from the living.

There was no more time to think, to agonize over decisions past making, or to lament those already made. The trees broke apart, and the Gatehouse was before them. A pair of Federation guards standing watch stiffened as the patrol approached. Padishar never hesitated. He went directly to them, informed them of the patrol's purpose, joked about the weather, and had the doors open within moments. In a knot of lowered heads and tightened cloaks, the little band hastened inside.

The men of the night watch were gathered about a wooden table playing cards, six of them, heads barely lifting at the arrival of the newcomers. The watch commander was nowhere to be seen.

Padishar glanced over his shoulder, nodded faintly to Morgan, Stasas, and Drutt, and motioned them to spread out about the table. As they did so, one of the players glanced up suspiciously.

"Who're you?" he demanded.

"Clean-up detail," Padishar answered. He moved around behind the speaker and bent over to read his cards. "That's a losing hand, friend."

"Back off, you're dripping on me," the other complained.

Padishar hit him on the temple with his fist, and the man dropped like a stone. A second followed almost as fast. The guards surged to their feet, shouting, but the outlaws and Morgan felled them all in seconds. Par and Coll began pulling ropes and strips of cloth from their packs.

"Drag them into the sleeping quarters, tie and gag them," Padishar whispered. "Make sure they can't escape."

There was a quick knock at the door. Padishar waited until the guards were dispatched, then cracked the peep window. Everything was fine, he assured the guards without, who thought they might have heard something. The card game was breaking up; everyone thought it would be best to start getting things in order.

He closed the window with a reassuring smile.

After the men of the night watch were secured in the sleeping quarters, Padishar closed the door and bolted it. He hesitated, then ordered the locks to the entry doors thrown as well. No point in taking any chances, he declared. They couldn't afford to leave any of their company behind to make certain they were not disturbed.

With oil lamps to guide them, they descended through the gloom of the stairwell to the lower levels of the Gatehouse, the sound of the rain lost behind the heavy stone. The dampness penetrated, though, so chill that Par found himself shivering. He followed after the others in a daze, prepared to do whatever was necessary, his mind focused on putting one foot in front of the other until they were out of there. There was no reason to be frightened, he kept telling himself. It would all be over quick enough.

At the lower level, they found the watch commander sleeping—a new man, different from the one that had been waiting for them when they had tried to slip over the ravine wall. This one fared no better. They subdued him without effort, bound and gagged him, and locked him in his room.

"Leave the lamps," Padishar ordered.

They bypassed the watch commander's chambers and went down to the end of the hall. A single, ironbound door stood closed before them, twice as high as their tallest, the angular Drutt. A massive handle, emblazoned with the wolf's head insigne of the Seekers, jutted out. Padishar reached down with both hands and twisted. The latch gave, the door slid open. Murk and darkness filled the gap, and the stench of decay and mold slithered in.

"Stay close, now," Padishar whispered over his shoulder, his eyes dangerous, and stepped out into the gloom.

Coll turned long enough to reach back and squeeze Par's shoulder, then followed.

They stood in a forest of jumbled tree trunks, matted brush, vines, brambles, and impenetrable mist. The thick, sodden canopy of the treetops overhead all but shut out the little daylight that remained. Mud oozed and sucked in tiny bogs all about them. Creatures flew in ragged jumps through the jungle—birds or something less pleasant, they couldn't tell which. Smells assailed them—the decay and the mold, but something more as well, something even less tolerable. Sounds rose out of the murk, distant, indistinguishable, threatening. The Pit was a well of endless gloom.

Every nerve ending on Par Ohmsford's body screamed at him to get out of there.

Padishar motioned them ahead. Drutt followed, then Coll, Par, Morgan, and Stasas, a line of rain-soaked forms. They picked their way forward slowly, following the edge of the ravine, moving in the direction of the rubble from the old Bridge of Sendic. Par and Coll carried the grappling hooks and ropes, the others drawn weapons. Par glanced over his shoulder momentarily and

saw the light from the open door leading back into the Gatehouse disappear into the fog. He saw the Sword of Leah glint
dully in Morgan's hand, the rain trickling off its polished metal.

The earth they walked upon was soft and yielding, but it
held them as they pushed steadily into the gloom. The Pit had
the feel of a giant maw, open and waiting, smelling of things
already eaten, its breath the mist that closed them away. Things
wriggled and crawled through the pools of stagnant water, oozed
down decaying logs, and flashed through bits of scrub like
quicksilver. The silence was deafening; even the earlier sounds
had disappeared at their approach. There was only the rain,
slow and steady, seeping downward through the murk.

They walked for what seemed to Par a very long time. The
minutes stretched away in an endless parade until there was no
longer either beginning or end to them. How far could it be to
the fallen bridge, he wondered? Surely they should be there by
now. He felt trapped within the Pit, the wall of the ravine on
his left, the trees and mist to his right, gloom and rain overhead
and all about. The black cloaks of his companions gave them
the look of mourners at a funeral, buriers of the dead.

Then Padishar Creel stopped, listening. Par had heard it,
too—a sort of hissing sound from somewhere deep within the
murk, like steam escaping from a fissure. The others craned
their necks and peered unsuccessfully about. The hissing
stopped, the silence filling again with the sound of their breathing and the rain.

Padishar's broadsword glimmered as he motioned them ahead
once more. He took them more quickly now, as if sensing that
all was not right, that speed might have to take precedence over
caution. Scores of massive, glistening trunks came and went,
silent sentinels in the gloom. The light was fading rapidly, turned
from gray to cobalt.

Par sensed suddenly that something was watching them. The
hair on the back of his neck stiffened with the feel of its gaze,
and he glanced about hurriedly. Nothing moved in the mist;
nothing showed.

"What is it?" Morgan whispered in his ear, but he could only
shake his head.

Then the stone blocks of the shattered Bridge of Sendic came into view, bulky and misshapen as they jutted like massive teeth from the tangled forest. Padishar hurried forward, the others following. They moved away from the ravine wall and deeper into the trees. The Pit seemed to swallow them in its mist and dark. Bridge sections lay scattered amid the stone rubble beneath the covering of the forest, moss-grown and worn, spectral in the failing light.

Par took a deep breath. The Sword of Shannara had been embedded blade downward in a block of red marble and placed in a vault beneath the protective span of the Bridge of Sendic, the old legends told.

It had to be here, somewhere close.

He hesitated. The Sword was embedded in red marble; could he free it? Could he even enter the vault?

His eyes searched the mist. What if it was buried beneath the rubble of the bridge? How would they reach it then?

So many unanswered questions, he thought, feeling suddenly desperate. Why hadn't he asked them before? Why hadn't he considered the possibilities?

The cliffs loomed faintly through the murky haze. He could see the west corner of the crumbling palace of the Kings of Callahorn, a dark shadow through a break in the trees. He felt his throat tighten. They were almost to the far wall of the ravine. They were almost out of places to look.

I won't leave without the Sword, he swore wordlessly. *No matter what it takes, I won't!* The fire of his conviction burned through him as if to seal the covenant.

Then the hissing sounded again, much closer now. It seemed to be coming from more than one direction. Padishar slowed and stopped, turning guardedly. With Drutt and Stasas on either side, he stepped out a few paces to act as a screen for the Valemen and the Highlander, then began inching cautiously along the fringe of the broken stone.

The hissing grew louder, more distinct. It was no longer hissing. It was breathing.

Par's eyes searched the darkness frantically. Something was coming for them, the same something that had devoured Ciba Blue and all those before him who had gone down into the Pit and not come out again. His certainty of it was terrifying. Yet it wasn't for their stalker that he searched. It was for the vault that held the Sword of Shannara. He was desperate now to find it. He could see it suddenly in his mind, as clear as if it were a picture drawn and mounted for his private viewing. He groped for it uncertainly, within his mind, then without in the mist and the dark.

Something strange began to happen to him.

He felt a tightening within that seemed grounded in the magic of the wishsong. It was a pulling, a tugging that wrenched against shackles he could neither see nor understand. He felt a pressure building within himself that he had never experienced before.

Coll saw his face and went pale. "Par?" he whispered anxiously and shook him.

Red pinpricks of light appeared in the mist all about them, burning like tiny fires in the damp. They shifted and winked and drew closer. Faces materialized, no longer human, the flesh decaying and half-eaten, the features twisted and fouled. Bodies shambled out of the night, some massive, some gnarled, all misshapen beyond belief. It was as if they had been stretched and wrenched about to see what could be made of them. Most walked bent over; some crawled on all fours.

They closed about the little company in seconds. They were things out of some loathsome nightmare, the fragments and shards of sleep's horror come into the world of waking. Dark, substanceless wraiths flitted in and out of their bodies, through mouths and eyes, from the pores of skin and the bristles of hair.

Shadowen!

The pressure inside Par Ohmsford grew unbearable. He felt something drop away in the pit of his stomach. He was seeing the vision in his dreams come alive, the dark world of animal-like humans and Shadowen masters. It was seeing Allanon's promise come to pass.

The pressure broke free. He screamed, freezing his companions with the sharpness of his cry. The sound took form and became words. He sang, the wishsong ripping through the air as if a flame, the magic lighting up the darkness. The Shadowen jerked away, their faces horrible in the unexpected glare, the lesions and cuts on their bodies vivid streaks of scarlet. Par stiffened, flooded with a power he had never known the wish-song to possess. He was aware of a vision within his mind—a vision of the Sword of Shannara.

The light from the magic, only an illusion at first, was suddenly real. It brightened, lancing the darkness in a way Par found strangely familiar, flaring with intensity as it probed the gloom. It twisted and turned like a captured thing trying to escape, winding past the stone wreckage of the fallen Bridge of Sendic, leaping across the carcasses of fallen trees, burning through the ragged brush to where a singular stone chamber sat alone amid a tangle of vines and grasses not a hundred yards from where he stood.

He felt a surge of elation race through him.

There!

The word hissed in the white silence of his mind, cocooned away from the magic and the chaos. He saw weathered black stone, the light of his magic burning into its pocked surface, scouring its cracks and crevices, picking out the scrolled words carved into its facing:

> *Herein lies the heart and soul of the nations.*
> *Their right to be free men,*
> *Their desire to live in peace,*
> *Their courage . . .*

His strength gave out suddenly before he could complete his reading, and the magic flared sharply and died into blackness, gone as quickly as it had come. He staggered backward with a cry, and Coll caught him in his arms. Par couldn't hear him. He couldn't hear anything but the strange ringing that was the wishsong's residue, the leavings of a magic he now realized he had not yet begun to understand.

And in his mind the vision lingered, a shimmering image at the forefront of his thoughts—all that remained of what moments earlier the magic had uncovered in the mist and dark.

The weathered stone vault. The familiar words in scroll.

The Sword of Shannara.

Then the ringing stopped, the vision disappeared, and he was back in the Pit, drowning in weakness. The Shadowen were closing, shambling forward from all directions to trap them against the stone of the bridge. Padishar stepped forward, tall and forbidding, to confront the nearest, a huge bearish thing with talons for hands. It reached for him and he cut at it with the broadsword—once, twice, a third time—the strokes so rapid Par could barely register them. The creature sagged back, limbs drooping—but it did not fall. It barely seemed aware of what had been done to it, its eyes fixed, its features twisting with some inner torment.

Par watched the Shadowen through glazed eyes. Its limbs reconnected in the manner of the giant they had fought in the Anar.

"Padishar, the Sword . . ." he started to say, but the outlaw chief was already shouting, directing them back the way they had come, retreating along the wall of stone. "No!" Par shrieked in dismay. He could not put into words the certainty he felt. They had to reach the Sword. He lurched up, trying to break free of Coll, but his brother held him fast, dragging him along with the others.

The Shadowen attacked in a shambling rush. Stasas went down, dragged beyond the reach of his companions. His throat was ripped out and then something dark entered his body while he was still alive, gasping. It jerked him upright, brought him about to face them, and he became another attacker. The company retreated, swords slashing. Ciba Blue appeared—or what was left of him. Impossibly strong, he blocked Drutt's sword, caught hold of his arms, and wrapped himself about his former comrade like a leech. The outlaw shrieked in pain as first one arm and then the other was ripped from his body. His head went last. He was left behind, Ciba Blue's remains still fastened to him, feeding.

Padishar was alone then, besieged on all sides. He would have been dead if he were not so quick and so strong. He feinted and slashed, dodging the fingers that grappled for him, twisting to stay free. Hopelessly outnumbered, he began to give ground quickly.

It was Morgan Leah who saved him. Abandoning his role as defender of Par and Coll, the Highlander rushed to the aid of the outlaw chief. His red hair flying, he charged into the midst of the Shadowen. The Sword of Leah arced downward, catching fire as it struck. Magic surged through the blade and into the dark things, burning them to ash. Two fell, three, then more. Padishar fought relentlessly beside him, and together they began cutting a path through the gathering of eyes, calling wildly for Par and Coll to follow. The Valemen stumbled after them, avoiding the grasp of Shadowen who had slipped behind. Par abandoned all hope of reaching the Sword. Two of their number were already dead; the rest of them would be killed as well if they didn't get out of there at once.

Back toward the wall of the ravine they staggered, warding off the Shadowen as they went, the magic of the Sword of Leah keeping the creatures at bay. They seemed to be everywhere, as if the Pit were a nest in which they bred. Like the woods-woman and the giant, they seemed impervious to any damage done to them by conventional weapons. Only Morgan could hurt them; his was magic that they could not withstand.

The retreat was agonizingly slow. Morgan grew weary, and as his own strength drained away so did the power of the Sword of Leah. They ran when they could, but more and more fre-quently the Shadowen blocked their way. Par attempted in vain to invoke the magic of the wishsong; it simply would not come. He tried not to think of what that meant, still struggling to make sense of what had occurred, to understand how the magic had broken free. Even in flight, his mind wrestled with the memory. How could he have lost control like that? How could the magic have provided him with that strange light, a thing that was real and not illusion. Had he simply willed it to be? What was it that had happened to him?

Somehow they reached the wall of the ravine and sagged wearily against it. Shouts sounded from the park above and torches flared. Their battle with the Shadowen had alerted the Federation watch. In moments, the Gatehouse would be under siege.

"The grappling hooks!" Padishar gasped.

Par had lost his, but Coll's was still slung across his shoulder. The Valeman stepped back, uncoiled the rope, and heaved the heavy iron skyward. It flew out of sight and caught. Coll tested it with his weight and it held.

Padishar braced Par against the wall, and their eyes met. Behind him, the forests of the Pit were momentarily empty. "Climb," he ordered roughly. His breath came in short gasps. He pulled Coll to him as well. "Both of you. Climb until you are safely out, then flee into the park. Damson will find you and take you back to the Jut."

"Damson," Par repeated dumbly.

"Forget your suspicions and mine as well," the outlaw whispered harshly. There was a glint of something sad in his hard eyes. "Trust her, lad—she is the better part of me!"

The Shadowen materialized once more out of the murk, their breathing a slow hiss in the night air. Morgan had already pushed out from the wall to face them. "Get out of here, Par," he called back over his shoulder.

"Climb!" Padishar Creel snapped. "Now!"

"But you . . ." Par began.

"Shades!" the other exploded. "I remain with the Highlander to see that you escape! Don't waste the gesture!" He caught Par roughly by the shoulders. "Whatever happens to any of the rest of us, you must live! The Shannara magic is what will win this fight one day, and you are the one who must wield it! Now go!"

Coll took charge then, half-pushing and half-lifting Par onto the rope. It was knotted, and the Valeman found an easy grip. He began to climb, tears of frustration filling his eyes. Coll followed him up, urging him on, his blocky face taut beneath its sheen of sweat.

Par paused only once to glance downward. Shadowen ringed Padishar Creel and Morgan Leah as they stood protectively before the ravine wall.

Too many Shadowen.

The Valeman looked away again. Biting back against his rage, he continued to climb into black.

MORGAN LEAH DID NOT turn around as the scraping of boots on the ravine wall faded away; his eyes remained fixed on the encircling Shadowen. He was aware of Padishar standing at his left shoulder. The Shadowen were no longer advancing on them; they were hanging back guardedly at the edge of the mist's thick curtain, keeping their distance. They had learned what Morgan's weapon could do, and they had grown cautious.

Mindless things, the Highlander thought bitterly. *I could have come to a better end than this, you'd think!*

He feinted at the nearest of them, and they backed away.

Morgan's weariness dragged at him like chains. It was the work of the magic, he knew. Its power had gone all through him, a sort of inner fire drawn from the sword, an exhilarating rush at first, then after a time simply a wearing down. And there was something more. There was an insidious binding of the magic to his body that made him crave it in a way he could not explain, as if to give it up now, even to rest, would somehow take away from who and what he was.

He was suddenly afraid that he might not be able to relinquish it until he was too weak to do otherwise.

Or too dead.

He could no longer hear Par and Coll climbing. The Pit was again encased in silence save for the hissing of the Shadowen.

Padishar leaned close to him. "Move, Highlander!" he rasped softly.

They began to ease their way down the ravine wall, slowly at first, and then, when the Shadowen did not come at them right away, more quickly. Soon they were running, stumbling really, for they no longer had the strength to do anything more. Mist swirled about them, gray tendrils against the night. The trees shimmered in the haze of falling rain and seemed to move. Morgan felt himself ease into a world of unfeeling half-sleep that stole away time and place.

Twice more the Shadowen attacked as they fled, brief forays each time, and twice they were driven back by the magic of the Sword of Leah. Grotesque bodies launched themselves like slow rolling boulders down a mountainside and were turned to ash. Fire burned in the night, quick and certain, and Morgan felt a bit of himself fall away with each burst.

He began to wonder if in some strange way he was killing himself.

Above, where the park lay hidden behind the wall of the ravine, the shouts continued to grow, reaching out to them like a false lifeline of hope. There were no friends to be found there,

Morgan knew. He stumbled, and it required an incredible amount of effort to right himself.

And then, at last, the Gatehouse came into view, a shadowy, massive tower lifting out of the trees and mist.

Morgan was dimly aware that something was wrong.

"Get through the door!" Padishar Creel cried frantically, shoving at him so hard he almost fell.

Together they sprinted for the door—or where the door should have been, for it was unexplainably missing. No light seeped through the opening they had left; the stone wall was black and faceless. Morgan felt a surge of fear and disbelief well up in the pit of his stomach.

Someone—or something—had sealed off their escape!

With Padishar a step behind, he came up against the Gatehouse wall, against the massive portal that had admitted them into the Pit, now closed and barred against their re-entry. They heaved against it in desperation, but it was fastened securely. Morgan's fingers searched its edges, probing, finding to his horror small markings all about, markings they had somehow overlooked before, runes of magic that glowed faintly in the graying mist and prevented their escape more certainly than any lock and key ever could.

Behind him, he could hear the Shadowen massing. He wheeled away, rushed the night things in a frenzy and caused them to scatter. Padishar was hammering at the invisible lock, not yet aware that it was magic and not iron that kept them out.

Morgan turned back, his lean face a mask of fury. "Stand away, Padishar!" he shouted.

He went at the door as if it were one of the Shadowen, the Sword of Leah raised, its blade a brilliant silver streak against the dark. Down came the weapon like a hammer—once, twice, then again and again. The runes carved into the door's iron surface glowed a deep, wicked green. Sparks flew with each blow, shards of flame that screamed in protest. Morgan howled as if gone mad, and the power of the sword's magic drew the last of his strength from him in a rush.

Then everything exploded into white fire, and Morgan was consumed by darkness.

PAR LIFTED HIMSELF out of the Pit's murky blackness to the edge of the ravine wall and pulled himself over its spikes. Cuts and scrapes burned his arms and legs. Sweat stung his eyes, and his breath came in short gasps. For a moment, his vision blurred, the night about him an impenetrable mask dotted with weaving bits of light.

Torches, he realized, clustered about the entry to the Gatehouse. There were shouts as well and a hammering of heavy wood. The watch and whoever else had been summoned were trying to break down the bolted door.

Coll came over the wall behind him, grunting with the effort as he dropped wearily to the cool, sodden earth. Rain matted his dark hair where the hood of his cloak had fallen away, and his eyes glittered with something Par couldn't read.

"Can you walk?" his brother whispered anxiously.

Par nodded without knowing if he could or not. They came to their feet slowly, their muscles aching, their breathing labored. They stumbled from the wall into the shadow of the trees and paused in the blackness, waiting to discover if they had been seen, listening to the commotion that surrounded the Gatehouse.

Coll bent his head close. "We have to get out of here, Par." Par's eyes lifted accusingly. "I know! But we can't help them anymore. Not now, at least. We have to save ourselves." He shook his head helplessly. "Please!"

Par clasped him momentarily and nodded into his shoulder, and they stumbled ahead. They made their way slowly, keeping to the darkest shadows, staying clear of the paths leading toward the Gatehouse. The rain had stopped without their realizing it, and the great trees shed their surface water in sudden showers as the wind gusted in intermittent bursts. Par's mind spun with the memory of what had happened to them, whispering anew the warning it had given him earlier, teasing him with self-satisfied, purposeless glee. Why hadn't he listened, it whispered? Why had he been so stubborn?

The lights of the Tyrsian Way burned through the darkness ahead, and moments later they stumbled to the edge of the street. There were people clustered there, dim shapes in the night, faceless shadows that stood mute witness to the chaos beyond. Most were farther down near the park's entry and saw nothing of the two ragged figures who emerged. Those who did see quickly looked away when they recognized the Federation uniforms.

"Where do we go now?" Par whispered, leaning against Coll for support. He was barely able to stand.

Coll shook his head wordlessly and pulled his brother toward the street, away from the lights. They had barely reached its cobblestones when a lithe figure materialized out of the shadows some fifty feet away and moved to intercept them. *Damson*, Par thought. He whispered her name to Coll, and they slowed expectantly as she hurried up.

"Keep moving," she said quietly, boosting Par's free arm about her shoulders to help Coll support him. "Where are the others?"

Par's eyes lifted to meet hers. He shook his head slowly and saw the stricken look that crossed her face.

Behind them, deep within the park, there was a brilliant explosion of fire that rocketed skyward into the night. Gasps of dismay rose out of those gathered on the streets.

The silence that followed was deafening.

"Don't look back," Damson whispered, tight-lipped.

The Valemen didn't need to.

MORGAN LEAH LAY SPRAWLED upon the scorched earth of the Pit, steam rising from his clothing, the acrid stench of smoke in his mouth and nostrils. Somehow he was still alive, he sensed— barely. Something was terribly wrong with him. He felt broken, as if everything had been smashed to bits within his skin, leaving him an empty, scoured shell. There was pain, but it wasn't physical. It was worse somehow, a sort of emotional agony that wracked not only his body but his mind as well.

"Highlander!"

Padishar's rough voice cut through the layers of hurt and brought his eyes open. Flames licked the ground inches away.

"Get up—quickly!" Padishar was pulling at him, hauling him forcibly to his feet, and he heard himself scream. A muddled sea of trees and stone blocks swam in the mist and darkness, slowly steadied and at last took shape.

Then he saw. He was still gripping the hilt of the Sword of Leah, but its blade was shattered. No more than a foot remained, a jagged, blackened shard.

Morgan began to shake. He could not stop himself. "What have I done?" he whispered.

"You saved our lives, my friend!" Padishar snapped, dragging him forward. "That's what you did!" Light poured through a massive hole in the wall of the Gatehouse. The door that had been sealed against their return had disappeared. Padishar's voice was labored. "Your weapon did that. Your magic. Shattered that door into smoke! Gives us the chance we need, if we're quick enough. Hurry, now! Lean on me. Another minute or two. . ."

Padishar shoved him through the opening. He was dimly aware of the corridor they stumbled down, the stairs they climbed. The pain continued to rip through his body, leaving him incoherent when he tried to speak. He could not take his eyes from the broken sword. His sword—his magic—himself. He could not differentiate among them.

Shouts and a heavy thudding broke into his thoughts, causing him to flinch. "Easy, now," Padishar cautioned, the outlaw's voice a buzzing in his ears that seemed to come from very far away.

They reached the ward room with its weapons and debris. There was a frantic pounding on the entry doors. Their iron shielding was buckled and staved.

"Lie here," Padishar ordered, leaning him back against the wall to one side. "Say nothing when they enter, just keep still. With luck, they'll think us victims of what's happened here and nothing more. Here, give me that." He reached down and pried the broken Sword of Leah from Morgan's nerveless fingers. "Back in its case with this, lad. We'll see to its fixing later."

He shoved the weapon into its shoulder scabbard, patted Morgan's cheek, and moved to open the entry doors.

Black-garbed Federation soldiers poured into the room, shouting and yelling and filling the chamber with a din that was suffocating. A disguised Padishar Creel shouted and yelled back, directing them down the stairwell, into the sleeping quarters, over this way and out that. There was mass confusion. Morgan watched it all without really understanding or even caring. The sense of indifference he felt was outweighed only by his sense of loss. It was as if his life no longer had a purpose, as if any reason for it had evaporated as suddenly and thoroughly as the blade of the Sword of Leah.

No more magic, he thought over and over. I have lost it. I have lost everything.

Then Padishar was back, hauling him to his feet again, steering him through the chaos of the Gatehouse to the entry doors and from there into the park. Bodies surged past, but no one challenged them. "It's a fine madness we've let loose with this night's work," Padishar muttered darkly. "I just hope it doesn't come back to haunt us."

He took Morgan swiftly from the circle of the Gatehouse lights into the concealing shadows beyond.

Moments later, they were lost from sight.

CHAPTER

24

T WAS JUST AFTER DAWN when Par Ohmsford came awake the first time. He lay motionless on his pallet of woven mats, collecting his scattered thoughts in the silence of his mind. It took him awhile to remember where he was. He was in a storage shed behind a gardening shop somewhere in the center of Tyrsis. Damson had brought them there last night to hide after . . .

The memory returned to him in an unpleasant rush, images that swept through his mind with horrific clarity.

He forced his eyes open and the images disappeared. A faint wash of gray, hazy light seeped through cracks in the shuttered windows of the shed, lending vague definition to the scores of gardening tools stacked upright like soldiers at watch. The smell of dirt and sod filled the air, rich and pungent. It was silent beyond the walls of their concealment, the city still sleeping.

He lifted his head cautiously and glanced about. Coll was asleep beside him, his breathing deep and even. Damson was nowhere to be seen.

He lay back again for a time, listening to the silence, letting himself come fully awake. Then he rose, gingerly easing himself from beneath his blankets and onto his feet. He was stiff and cramped, and there was an aching in his joints that caused him to wince. But his strength was back; he could move about again unaided.

Coll stirred fitfully, turning over once before settling down again. Par watched his brother momentarily, studying the shadowed line of his blunt features, then stepped over to the nearest window. He was still wearing his clothing; only his boots had been removed. The chill of early morning seeped up from the plank flooring into his stockinged feet, but he ignored it. He put his eye to a crack in the shutters and looked out. It had stopped raining, but the skies were clouded and the world had a damp, empty look. Nothing moved within the range of his vision. A jumbled collection of walls, roofs, streets, and shadowed niches stared back at him from out of the mist.

The door behind him opened, and Damson stepped noiselessly into the shed. Her clothing was beaded with moisture and her red hair hung limp.

"Here, what are you doing?" she whispered, her forehead creasing with annoyance. She crossed the room quickly and took hold of him as if he were about to topple over. "You're not to be out of bed yet! You're far too weak! Back you go at once!"

She steered him to his pallet and forced him to lie down again. He made a brief attempt to resist and discovered that he had less strength than he first believed.

"Damson, listen . . ." he began, but she quickly put a hand over his mouth.

"No, you listen, Elf-boy." She paused, staring down at him as she might a curious discovery. "What is the matter with you, Par Ohmsford? Haven't you an ounce of common sense to call your own? You barely escaped with your life last night and already you are looking to risk it again. Haven't you the least regard for yourself?"

She took a deep breath, and he found himself thinking suddenly of how warm her hand felt against his face. She seemed to read his thoughts and lifted it away. Her fingers trailed across his cheek.

He caught her hand in his and held it. "I'm sorry. I couldn't sleep anymore. I was drifting in and out of nightmares about last night." Her hand felt small and light in his own. "I can't stop thinking about Morgan and Padishar . . ."

He trailed off, not wanting to say more. It was too frightening, even now. Next to him, Coll's eyes blinked open and fixed on him. "What's going on?" he asked sleepily.

Damson's fingers tightened on Par's. "Your brother cannot seem to sleep for worrying about everyone but himself."

Par stared up at her wordlessly for a moment, then said, "Is there any news, Damson?"

She smiled faintly. "I will make a bargain with you. If you promise me that you will try to go back to sleep for a time—or at least not leave this bed—I promise you that I will try to learn the answer to your question. Fair enough?"

The Valeman nodded. He found himself pondering anew Padishar's final admonition to him: *Trust her She is the better part of me!*

Damson glanced over at Coll. "I depend on you to make certain that he keeps his word." Her hand slipped from Par's and she stood up. "I will bring back something to eat as well. Stay quiet, now. No one will disturb you here."

She paused momentarily, as if reluctant even then to leave, then turned and disappeared out the door.

Silence filled the shadowed room. The brothers looked at each other without speaking for a moment, and then Coll said quietly, "She's in love with you."

Par flushed, then quickly shook his head. "No. She's just being protective, nothing more."

Coll lay back, sighed and closed his eyes. "Oh, is that it?" He let his breathing slow. Par thought he was sleeping again when he suddenly said, "What happened to you last night, Par?"

Par hesitated. "You mean the wishsong?"

Coll's eyes slipped open. "Of course I mean the wishsong." He glanced over sharply. "I know how the magic works better than anyone other than yourself, and I've never seen it do that. That wasn't an illusion you created; that was the real thing! I didn't think you could do that."

"I didn't either."

"Well?"

Par shook his head. What had happened indeed? He closed his eyes momentarily and then opened them again. "I have a theory," he admitted finally. "I came up with it between sleep and bad dreams, you might say. Remember how the magic of the wishsong came about in the first place? Wil Ohmsford used the Elfstones in his battle with the Reaper. He had to in order to save the Elf-girl Amberle. Shades, we've told that story often enough, haven't we? It was dangerous for him to do so because he hadn't enough true Elf blood to allow it. It changed him in a way he couldn't determine at first. It wasn't until after his children were born, until after Brin and Jair, that he discovered what had been done. Some part of the Elf magic of the Stones had gone into him. That part was passed to Brin and Jair in the form of the wishsong."

He raised himself up on one elbow; Coll did likewise. The light was sufficient now to let them see each other's faces clearly. "Cogline told us that first night that we didn't understand the magic. He said that it works in different ways—something like that—but that until we understood it, we could only use it in one. Then, later, at the Hadeshorn, he told us how the magic changes, leaving wakes in its passing like the water of a lake disturbed. He made specific reference to Wil Ohmsford's legacy of magic, the magic that became the wishsong."

He paused. The room was very still. When he spoke again, his voice sounded strange in his ears. "Now suppose for a moment that he was right, that the magic is changing all the time, evolving in some way. After all, that's what happened when the magic of the Elfstones passed from Wil Ohmsford to his children. So what if it has changed again, this time in me?"

Coll stared. "What do you mean?" he asked finally. "How do you think it could change?"

"Suppose that the magic has worked its way back to what it was in the beginning. The blue Elfstones that Allanon gave to Shea Ohmsford when they went in search of the Sword of Shannara all those years ago had the power to seek out that which was hidden from the holder."

"Par!" Coll breathed his name softly, the astonishment apparent in his voice.

"No, wait. Let me finish. Last night, the magic released itself in a way it has never done before. I could barely control it. You're right, Coll; there was no illusion in what it did. But it did respond in a recognizable way. It sought out what was hidden from me, and I think it did so because subconsciously I willed it." His voice was fierce. "Coll. Suppose that the power that once was inherent in the magic of the Elfstones is now inherent in the magic within me!"

There was a long silence between them. They were close now, their faces not two feet apart, their eyes locked. Coll's rough features were knotted in concentration, the enormity of what Par was suggesting weighing down on him like a massive stone block. Doubt mirrored in his eyes, then acceptance, and suddenly fear.

His face went taut. His rough voice was very soft. "The Elfstones possessed another property as well. They could defend the holder against danger. They could be a weapon of tremendous power."

Par waited, saying nothing, already knowing what was coming.

"Do you think that the magic of the wishsong can now do the same for you?"

Par's response was barely audible. "Yes, Coll. I think maybe it can."

By MIDDAY, the haze of early morning had burned away and the clouds had moved on. Sunshine shone down on Tyrsis, blanketing the city in heat. Puddles and streams evaporated as the temperature rose, the stone and clay of the streets dried, and the air grew humid and sticky.

Traffic at the gates of the Outer Wall was heavy and slow-moving. The Federation guards on duty, double the usual number as a result of the previous night's disturbance, were already sweating and irritable when the bearded gravedigger approached from out of the backstreets beyond the inner wall. Travelers and merchants alike moved aside at his approach. He was ragged and stooped, and he smelled to the watch as if he had been living in a sewer. He was wheeling a heavy cart in front of him, the wood rotted and splintered. There was a body in the cart, wrapped in sheets and bound with leather ties.

The guards glanced at one another as the gravedigger trudged up to them, his charge wheeled negligently before him, rolling and bouncing.

"Hot one for work, isn't it, sirs?" the gravedigger wheezed, and the guards flinched in spite of themselves from the stench of him.

"Papers," said one perfunctorily.

"Sure, sure." One ragged hand passed over a document that looked as if it had been used to wipe up mud. The gravedigger gestured at the body. "Got to get this one in the ground quick, don't you know. Won't last long on a day such as this."

One of the guards stepped close enough to prod the corpse with the point of his sword. "Easy now," the gravedigger advised. "Even the dead deserve some respect."

The soldier looked at him suspiciously, then shoved the sword deep into the body and pulled it out again. The gravedigger cackled. "You might want to be cleaning your sword there, sir—seeing as how this one died of the spotted fever."

The soldier stepped back quickly, pale now. The others retreated as well. The one holding the gravedigger's papers handed them hastily back and motioned him on.

The gravedigger shrugged, picked up the handles of the cart and wheeled his body down the long ramp toward the plain below, whistling tunelessly as he went.

What a collection of fools, Padishar Creel thought disdainfully to himself.

WHEN HE REACHED the first screening of trees north, the city of Tyrsis a distant grayish outline against the swelter, Padishar eased the handles of the cart down, shoved the body he had been hauling aside, took out an iron bar and began prying loose the boards of the cart's false bottom. Gingerly, he helped Morgan extricate himself from his place of hiding. Morgan's face was pale and drawn, as much from the heat and discomfort of his concealment as from the lingering effects of last night's battle.

"Take a little of this." The outlaw chief offered him an ale-skin, trying unsuccessfully not to look askance. Morgan accepted the offering wordlessly. He knew what the other was thinking—that the Highlander hadn't been right since their escape from the Pit.

Abandoning the cart and its body, they walked a mile further on to a river where they could wash. They bathed, dressed in clean clothes that Padishar had hidden with Morgan in the cart's false bottom, and sat down to have something to eat.

The meal was a silent one until Padishar, unable to stand it any longer, growled, "We can see about fixing the blade, Highlander. It may be the magic isn't lost after all."

Morgan just shook his head. "This isn't something anyone can fix," he said tonelessly.

"No? Tell me why. Tell me how the sword works, then. You explain it to me." Padishar wasn't about to let the matter alone.

Morgan did as the other asked, not because he particularly wanted to, but because it was the easiest way to get Padishar to stop talking about it. He told the story of how the Sword of Leah was made magic, how Allanon dipped its blade in the waters of the Hadeshorn so that Rone Leah would have a weapon with which to protect Brin Ohmsford. "The magic was in the blade, Padishar," he finished. He was having trouble being patient by now. "Once broken, it cannot be repaired. The magic is lost."

Padishar frowned doubtfully, then shrugged. "Well, it was lost for a good cause, Highlander. After all, it saved our lives. A good trade any day of the week."

Morgan looked up at him, his eyes haunted. "You don't understand. There was some sort of bond between us, the sword and me. When the sword broke, it was as if it was happening to me! It doesn't make any sense, I know—but it's there anyway. When the magic was lost, some part of me was lost as well."

"But that's just your sense of it now, lad. Who's to say that won't change?" Padishar gave him an encouraging smile. "Give yourself a little time. Let the wound heal, as they say."

Morgan put down his food, disinterested in eating, and hunched his knees close against his chest. He remained quiet, ignoring the fact that the outlaw chief was waiting for a response, contemplating instead the nagging recognition that nothing had gone right since their decision to go down into the Pit after the missing Sword of Shannara.

Padishar's brow furrowed irritably. "We have to go," he announced abruptly and stood up. When Morgan didn't move right away, he said, "Now, listen to me, Highlander. We're alive and that's the way we're going to stay, sword or no sword, and I'll not allow you to continue acting like some half-dead puppy . . ."

Morgan came to his feet with a bound. "Enough, Padishar! I don't need you worrying about me!" His voice sounded harsher than he had meant it to, but he could not disguise the anger he was feeling. That anger quickly found a focus. "Why don't you try worrying about the Valemen? Do you have any idea at all what's happened to them? Why have we left them behind like this?"

"Ah." The other spoke the word softly. "So that's what's really eating at you, is it? Well, Highlander, the Valemen are likely better off than we are. We were seen getting out of that Gatehouse, remember? The Federation isn't so stupid that it will overlook the report of what happened and the fact that two so-called guards are somehow missing. They'll have our description. If we hadn't gotten out of the city right away, we likely wouldn't have gotten out at all!"

He jabbed his finger at the Highlander. "Now the Valemen, on the other hand—no one saw them. No one will recognize their faces. Besides, Damson will have them in hand by now. She knows to bring them to the Jut. She'll get them out of Tyrsis easily enough when she has the chance."

Morgan shook his head stubbornly. "Maybe. Maybe not. You were confident as well about our chances of retrieving the Sword of Shannara and look what happened."

Padishar flushed angrily. "The risks involved in that were hardly a secret to any of us!"

"Tell that to Stasas and Drutt and Ciba Blue!"

The big man snatched hold of Morgan's tunic and yanked him forward violently. His eyes were hard with anger. "Those were my friends that died back there, Highlander—not yours. Don't be throwing it up in my face! What I did, I did for all of us. We need the Sword of Shannara! Sooner or later we're going to have to go back for it—Shadowen or not! You know that as well as I! As for the Valemen, I don't like leaving them any better than you do! But we had precious little choice in the matter!"

Morgan tried unsuccessfully to jerk free. "You might have gone looking for them, at least!"

"Where? Where would I look? Do you think they would be hidden in any place we could find? Damson's no fool! She has them tucked away in the deepest hole in Tyrsis! Shades, Highlander! Don't you realize what's happening back there? We uncovered a secret last night that the Federation has gone to great pains to conceal! I'm not sure either of us understands what it all means yet, but it's enough that the Federation thinks we might! They'll want us dead for that!"

His voice was a snarl. "I caught a glimpse of what's to come when I passed you through the gates. The Federation authorities no longer concern themselves merely with doubling guards and increasing watch patrols. They have mobilized the entire garrison! Unless I am badly mistaken, young Morgan Leah, they have decided to eliminate us once and for all—you and me and any other members of the Movement they can run to earth. We are a real threat to them now, because, for the first time, we begin to understand what they are about—and that's something they will not abide!"

His grip tightened, fingers of stone. "They'll come hunting us, and we had best not be anywhere we can be found!"

He released the Highlander with a shove. He took a deep breath and straightened. "In any case, I don't choose to argue the matter with you. I am leader here. You fought well back there in the Pit, and perhaps it cost you something. But that doesn't give you the right to question my orders. I understand the business of staying alive better than you, and you had best remember it."

Morgan was white with rage, but he kept himself in check. He knew there was nothing to be gained by arguing the matter further; the big man was not about to change his mind. He knew as well, deep down inside where he could admit it to himself, that what Padishar was saying about staying around in an effort to find Par and Coll was the truth.

He stepped away from Padishar and smoothed his rumpled clothing carefully. "I just want to be certain that we are agreed that the Valemen will not be forgotten."

Padishar Creel's smile was quick and hard. "Not for a moment. Not by me, at least. You are free to do as you choose in the matter."

He wheeled away, moving off into the trees. After a moment's hesitation, Morgan swallowed his anger and pride and followed.

PAR CAME AWAKE for the second time that day toward midafternoon. Coll was shaking him and the smell of hot soup filled the close confines of their shelter. He blinked and sat up slowly. Damson stood at a pruning bench, spooning broth into bowls, the steam rising thickly as she worked. She glanced over at the Valeman and smiled. Her flaming hair shimmered brightly in the shards of sunlight that filtered through the cracks in the shuttered windows, and Par experienced an almost irresistible need to reach out and stroke it.

Damson served the Valemen the soup together with fresh fruit, bread, and milk, and Par thought it was the most wonderful meal he had ever tasted. He ate everything he was given, Coll with him, both ravenous beyond what they would have thought possible. Par was surprised that he had been able to go back to sleep, but he was unquestionably the better for it, his body rested now and shed of most of its aches and pains. There was little talk during the meal, and that left him free to think. His mind had begun working almost immediately on waking, skipping quickly from the memory of last night's horrors to the prospect of what lay ahead—to sift through the information he had gathered, to consider carefully what he suspected, to make plans for what he now believed must be.

The process made him shudder inwardly with excitement and foreboding. Already, he discovered, he was beginning to relish the prospect of attempting the unthinkable.

When the Valemen had finished eating, they washed in a basin of fresh water. Then Damson sat them down again and told them what had become of Padishar and Morgan.

"They escaped," she began without preamble. Her green eyes reflected amusement and awe. "I don't know how they managed it, but they did. It took me awhile to verify that they had indeed gotten free, but I wanted to make certain of what I was being told."

Par grinned at his brother in relief. Coll stifled his own grin and instead simply shrugged. "Knowing those two, they probably talked their way out," he responded gruffly.

"Where are they now?" Par asked. He felt as if years had been added back onto his life. Padishar and Morgan had escaped—it was the best news he could have been given.

"That I don't know," Damson replied. "They seem to have disappeared. Either they have gone to ground in the city or—more likely—they have left it altogether and are on their way back to the Jut. The latter seems the better guess because the entire Federation garrison is mobilizing and there's only one reason they would do that. They mean to go after Padishar and his men in the Parma Key. Apparently, whatever he—and you—did last night made them very angry. There are all sorts of rumors afloat. Some say dozens of Federation soldiers were killed at the Gatehouse by monsters. Some say the monsters are loose in the city. Whatever the case, Padishar will have read the signs as easily as I. He'll have slipped out by now and gone north."

"You're certain the Federation hasn't found him instead?" Par was still anxious.

Damson shook her head. "I would have heard." She was propped against the leg of the pruning bench as they sat on the pallets that had served as their beds the night before. She let her head tilt back against the roughened wood so that the soft curve of her face caught the light. "It is your turn now. Tell me what happened, Par. What did you find in the Pit?"

With help from Coll, Par related what had befallen them, deciding as he did that he would do as Padishar had urged, that he would trust Damson in the same way that he had trusted the outlaw chief. Thus he told her not only of their encounter with the Shadowen, but of the strange behavior of the wishsong, of the unexpected way its magic had performed, even of his suspicions of the influence of the Elfstones.

When he had finished, the three of them sat staring wordlessly at one another for a moment, of different minds as they reflected on what the foray into the Pit had uncovered and what it all meant.

Coll spoke first. "It seems to me that we have more questions to answer now than we did when we went in."

"But we know some things, too, Coll," Par argued. He bent forward, eager to speak. "We know that there is some sort of connection between the Federation and the Shadowen. The Federation has to know what it has down there; it can't be ignorant of the truth. Maybe it even helped create those monsters. For all we know they might be Federation prisoners thrown into the Pit like Ciba Blue and changed into what we found. And why are they still down there if the Federation isn't keeping them so? Wouldn't they have escaped long ago if they could?"

"As I said, there are more questions than answers," Coll declared. He shifted his heavy frame to a more comfortable position.

Damson shook her head. "Something seems wrong here. Why would the Federation have any dealings with the Shadowen? The Shadowen represent everything the Federation is against—magic, the old ways, the subversion of the Southland and its people. How would the Federation even go about making such an arrangement? It has no defense against the Shadowen magic. How would it protect itself?"

"Maybe it doesn't have to," Coll said suddenly. They looked at him. "Maybe the Federation has given the Shadowen someone else to feed on besides itself, someone the Federation has no use for in any case. Perhaps that's what became of the Elves." He paused. "Perhaps that's what's happening now to the Dwarves."

They were silent as they considered the possibility. Par hadn't thought about the Dwarves for a time, the horrors of Culhaven and its people shoved to the back of his mind these past few weeks. He remembered what he had seen there—the poverty, the misery, the oppression. The Dwarves were being exterminated for reasons that had never been clear. Could Coll be right? Could the Federation be feeding the Dwarves to the Shadowen as a part of some unspeakable bargain between them?

His face tightened in dismay. "But what would the Federation get in return?"

"Power," Damson Rhee said immediately. Her face was still and white.

"Power over the Races, over the Four Lands," Coll agreed, nodding. "It makes sense, Par."

Par shook his head slowly. "But what happens when there is

no one left but the Federation? Surely someone must have thought of that. What keeps the Shadowen from feeding on them as well?"

No one answered. "We're still missing something," Par said softly. "Something important."

He rose, walked to the other side of the room, stood looking into space for a long moment, shook his head finally, turned, and came back. His lean face was stubborn with determination as he reseated himself.

"Let's get back to the matter of the Shadowen in the Pit," he declared quietly, "since that, at least, is a mystery that we might be able to solve." He folded his legs in front of him and eased forward. He looked at each of them in turn, then said, "I think that the reason they are down there is to keep anyone from getting to the Sword of Shannara."

"Par!" Coll tried to object, but his brother cut him off with a quick shake of his head.

"Think about it a moment, Coll. Padishar was right. Why would the Federation go to all the trouble of remaking the People's Park and the Bridge of Sendic? Why would they hide what remains of the old park and bridge in that ravine? Why, if not to conceal the Sword? And we've seen the vault, Coll! We've seen it!"

"The vault, yes—but not the Sword," Damson pointed out quietly, her green eyes intense as they met those of the Valemen.

"But if the Sword isn't down in the Pit as well, why are the Shadowen there?" Par asked at once. "Surely not to protect an empty vault! No, the Sword is still there, just as it has been for three hundred years. That's why Allanon sent me after it—he knew it was there, waiting to be found."

"He could have saved us a lot of time and trouble by telling us as much," said Coll pointedly.

Par shook his head. "No, Coll. That isn't the way he would do it. Think about the history of the Sword. Bremen gave it to Jerle Shannara some thousand years ago to destroy the Warlock Lord and the Elf King couldn't master it because he wasn't prepared to accept what it demanded of him. When Allanon chose Shea Ohmsford to finish the job five hundred years later, he decided that the Valeman must first prove himself. If he was not strong enough to wield it, if he did not want it badly enough, if he were not willing to give enough of himself to the task that finding it entailed, then the power of the Sword would prove too much for him as well. And he knew if that happened, the Warlock Lord would escape again."

"And he believes it will be the same now with you," Damson finished. She was looking at Par as if she were seeing him for the first time. "If you are not strong enough, if you are not willing to give enough, the Sword of Shannara will be useless to you. The Shadowen will prevail."

Par's answering nod was barely discernible.

"But why would the Shadowen—or the Federation, for that matter—leave the Sword in the Pit all these years?" Coll demanded, irritated that they were even talking about the matter after what had happened to them last night. "Why not simply remove it—or better yet, why not destroy it?"

Par's face was intense. "I don't think either the Federation or the Shadowen can destroy it—not a talisman of such power. I doubt that the Shadowen can even touch it. The Warlock Lord couldn't. What I can't figure out is why the Federation hasn't taken it out and hidden it."

He clasped his hands tightly before him. "In any case, it doesn't matter. The fact remains the Sword is still there, still in its vault." He paused, eyes level. "Waiting for us."

Coll gaped at him, realizing for the first time what he was suggesting. For a moment, he couldn't speak at all. "You can't be serious, Par," he managed finally, the disbelief in his voice undisguised. "After what happened last night? After seeing . . ." He forced himself to stop, then snapped, "You wouldn't last two minutes."

"Yes, I would," Par replied. His eyes were bright with determination. "I know I would. Allanon told me as much."

Coll was aghast. "Allanon! What are you talking about?"

"He said we had the skills needed to accomplish what was asked—Walker, Wren, and myself. Remember? In my case, I think he was talking about the wishsong. I think he meant that the magic of the wishsong would protect me."

"Well, it's done a rather poor job of it up to now!" Coll snapped, lashing out furiously.

"I didn't understand what it could do then. I think I do now."

"You think? You think? Shades, Par!"

Par remained calm. "What else are we to do? Run back to the Jut? Run home? Spend the rest of our days sneaking about?" Par's hands were shaking. "Coll, I haven't any choice. I have to try."

Coll's strong face closed in upon itself in dismay, his mouth tightening against whatever outburst threatened to break free. He wheeled on Damson, but the girl had her eyes locked on Par and would not look away.

The Valeman turned back, gritting his teeth. "So you would go back down into the Pit on the strength of an unproven and untested belief. You would risk your life on the chance that the wishsong—a magic that has failed to protect you three times already against the Shadowen—will somehow protect you now. And all because of what you perceive as your newfound insight into a dead man's words!" He drew his breath in slowly. "I cannot believe you would do anything so . . . stupid! If I could think of anything worse to call it, I would!"

"Coll . . ."

"No, don't say another word to me! I have gone with you everywhere, followed after you, supported you, done everything I could to keep you safe—and now you plan to throw yourself away! Just waste your life! Do you understand what you are doing, Par? You are sacrificing yourself! You still think you have some special ability to decide what's right! You are obsessed! You can't ever let go, even when common sense tells you you should!"

Coll clenched his fists before him. His face was rigid and furrowed, and it was all he could do to keep his voice level. Par had never seen him so angry. "Anyone else would back away, think it through, and decide to go for help. But you're not planning on any of that, are you? I can see it in your eyes. You haven't the time or the patience. You've made up your mind. Forget Padishar or Morgan or anyone else but yourself. You mean to have that Sword! You'd even give up your life to have it, wouldn't you?"

"I am not so blind . . ."

"Damson, you talk to him!" Coll interrupted, desperate now. "I know you care for him; tell him what a fool he is!"

But Damson Rhee shook her head. "No. I won't do that." Coll stared at her, stunned. "I haven't the right," she finished softly.

Coll went silent then, his rough features sagging in defeat. No one spoke immediately, letting the momentary stillness settle across the room. Daylight had shifted with the sun's movement west, gone now to the far side of the little storage shed, the shadows beginning to lengthen slightly in its wake. A scattering of voices sounded from somewhere in the streets beyond and faded away. Par felt an aching deep within himself at the look he saw on his brother's face, at the sense of betrayal he knew Coll was feeling. But there was no help for it. There was but one thing Par could say that would change matters, and he was not about to say it.

"I have a plan," he tried instead. He waited until Coll's eyes lifted. "I know what you think, but I don't propose to take any more chances than I have to." Coll gave him an incredulous look, but kept still. "The vault sits close to the base of the cliffs, just beneath the walls of the old palace. If I could get into the ravine from the other side, I would have only a short distance to cover. Once I had the Sword in my hands, I would be safe from the Shadowen."

There were several huge assumptions involved in that last statement, but neither Coll nor Damson chose to raise them. Par felt the sweat bead on his forehead. The difficulty of what he was about to suggest was terrifying.

He swallowed. "That catwalk from the Gatehouse to the old palace would give me a way across."

Coll threw up his hands. "You plan to go back into the Gatehouse yet a third time?" he exclaimed, exasperated beyond reason.

"All I need is a ruse, a way to distract . . ."

"Have you lost your mind completely? Another ruse won't do the trick! They'll be looking for you this go-around! They'll spy you out within two seconds of the time you . . ."

"Coll!" Par's own temper slipped.

"He is right," Damson Rhee said quietly.

Par wheeled on her, then caught himself. He jerked back toward his brother. Coll dared him to speak, red-faced, but silent. Par shook his head. "Then I'll have to come up with another way."

Coll looked suddenly weary. "The truth of the matter is, there isn't any other way."

"There might be one." It was Damson who spoke, her low voice compelling. "When the armies of the Warlock Lord besieged Tyrsis in the time of Balinor Buckhannah, the city was betrayed twice over from within—once by the front gates, the second time by passageways that ran beneath the city and the cliffs backing the old palace to the cellars beneath. Those passageways might still exist, giving us access to the ravine from the palace side."

Coll looked away wordlessly, disgust registering on his blocky features. Clearly, he had hoped for better than this from Damson.

Par hesitated, then said carefully, "That all happened more than four hundred years ago. I had forgotten about those passageways completely—even telling the stories as often as I do." He hesitated again. "Do you know anything about them—where they are, how to get into them, whether they can be traversed anymore?"

Damson shook her head slowly, ignoring the deliberate lift of Coll's eyebrows. She said, "But I know someone who might. If he will talk to us." Then she met Coll's gaze and held it. There was a sudden softness in her face that surprised Par. "We all have a right to make our own choices," she said quietly.

Coll's eyes seemed haunted. Par studied his brother momentarily, debating whether to say anything to him, then turned abruptly to Damson. "Will you take me to this person—tonight?"

She stood up then, and both Valemen rose with her. She looked small between them, almost delicate; but Par knew the perception was a false one. She seemed to deliberate before saying, "That depends. You must first promise me something. When you go back into the Pit, however you manage it, you will take Coll and me with you."

There was a stunned silence. It was hard to tell which of the Valemen was more astonished. Damson gave them a moment to recover, then said to Par, "I'm not giving you any choice in the matter, I'm afraid. I cannot. You would feel compelled to do the right thing and leave us both behind to keep us safe—which would be exactly the wrong thing. You need us with you."

The she turned to Coll. "And we need to be there, Coll. Don't you see? This won't end, any of it, not Federation oppression or Shadowen evil or the sickness that infects all the Lands, until someone makes it end. Par may have a chance to do that. But we cannot let him try it alone. We have to do whatever we can to help because this is our fight, too. We cannot just sit back and wait for someone else to come along and help us. No one will. If I've learned anything in this life, it's that."

She waited, looking from one to the other. Coll looked confused, as if he thought there ought to be an obvious alternative to his choices but couldn't for the life of him recognize what it was. He glanced briefly at Par and away again. Par had gone blank, his gaze focused on the floor, his face devoid of expression.

"It is bad enough that I must go," he said finally.

"Worse than bad," Coll muttered.

Par ignored him, looking instead at Damson. "What if it turns out that only I can go in?"

Damson came up to him, took his hands in her own and squeezed them. "That won't happen. You know it won't." She leaned up and kissed him softly. "Are we agreed?"

Par took a deep breath, and a frightening sense of inevitability welled up inside him. Coll and Damson Rhee—he was risking both their lives by going after the Sword. He was being stubborn beyond reason, intractable to the point of foolhardiness; he was letting himself be caught up in his own self-perceived needs and ambitions. There was every reason to believe that his insistence would kill them all.

Then give it up, he whispered fiercely to himself. *Just walk away*

But even as he thought it, he knew he wouldn't.

"Agreed," he said.

There was a brief silence. Coll looked up and shrugged. "Agreed," he echoed quietly.

Damson reached up to touch Par's face, then stepped over to Coll and hugged him. Par was more than a little surprised when his brother hugged her back.

CHAPTER

25

T WAS DUSK on the following day when Padishar Creel and Morgan Leah finally reached the Jut. Both were exhausted.

They had traveled hard since leaving Tyrsis, stopping only for meals. They had slept less than six hours the previous night. Nevertheless, they would have arrived even sooner and in better condition if not for Padishar's insistence on doing everything possible to disguise their trail. Once they entered the Parma Key, he backtracked continuously, taking them down ravines, through riverbeds, and over rocky outcroppings, all the while watching the land behind him like a hawk.

Morgan had thought the outlaw chief overcautious and, after growing impatient enough, had told him so. "Shades, Padishar— we're wasting time! What do you think is back there anyway?"

"Nothing we can see, lad," had been the other's enigmatic reply.

It was a sultry evening, the air heavy and still, and the skies hazy where the red ball of the sun settled into the horizon. As they rose in the basket lift toward the summit of the Jut, they could see night's shadows begin to fill the few wells of daylight that still remained in the forests below, turning them to pools of ink. Insects buzzed annoyingly about them, drawn by their body sweat. The swelter of the day lay across the land in a suffocating blanket. Padishar still had his gaze turned south toward Tyrsis, as if he might spy whatever it was he suspected had followed them. Morgan looked with him, but as before saw nothing. The big man shook his head. "I can't see it," he whispered. "But I can feel it coming."

He didn't explain what he meant by that and the Highlander didn't ask. Morgan was tired and hungry, and he knew that nothing either Padishar or he did was likely to change the plans of whatever might be out there. Their journey was completed, they had done everything humanly possible to disguise their passing, and there wasn't anything to be gained by worrying now. Morgan felt his stomach rumble and thought of the dinner that would be waiting. Lunch that day had been a sparse affair— a few roots, stale bread, hard cheese, and some water.

"I realize that outlaws are supposed to be able to subsist on next to nothing, but surely you could have done better than this!" he had complained. "This is pathetic!"

"Oh, surely, lad!" the outlaw chief had replied. "And next time you be the gravedigger and I'll be the body!"

Their differences had been put aside by then—not forgotten perhaps, but at least placed in proper perspective. Padishar had dismissed their confrontation five minutes after it ended, and Morgan had concluded by the end of the day that things were back to normal. He bore a grudging respect for the man—for his brash and decisive manner, because it reminded the Highlander of his own, for the confidence he so readily displayed in himself, and for the way he drew other men to him. Padishar Creel wore the trappings of leadership as if they were his birthright, and somehow that seemed fitting. There was undeniable strength in Padishar Creel; it made you want to follow him. But Padishar understood that a leader must give something back to his followers. Acutely aware of Morgan's role in bringing the Valemen north, he had made a point of acknowledging the legitimacy of the Highlander's concern for their safety. Several times after their argument he had gone out of his way to reassure Morgan that Par and Coll Ohmsford would never be abandoned, that he would make certain that they were safe. He was a complex, charismatic fellow, and Morgan liked him despite a nagging suspicion that Padishar Creel would never in the world be able to deliver everything he promised.

Outlaws clasped Padishar's hand in greeting at each station of their ascent. If they believe so strongly in him, Morgan asked himself, shouldn't I?

But he knew that belief was as ephemeral as magic. He thought momentarily of the broken sword he carried. Belief and magic forged as one, layered into iron, then shattered. He took a deep breath. The pain of his loss was still there, deep and insidious despite his resolve to put it behind him, to do as Padishar had suggested and to give himself time to heal. There was nothing he could do to change what had happened, he had told himself; he must get on with his life. He had lived for years without the use of the sword's magic—without even knowing it existed. He was no worse off now than he had been then. He was the same man.

And yet the pain lingered. It was an emptiness that scraped the bones of his body from within, leaving him fragmented and in search of the parts that would make him whole again. He could argue that he was unchanged, but what he had experienced through wielding of the magic had left its stamp upon him as surely as if he had been branded by a hot iron. The memories remained, the images of his battles, the impressions made by the power he had been able to call upon, the strength he had enjoyed. It was lost to him now. Like the loss of a parent or a sibling or a child, it could never be completely forgotten.

He looked out across the Parma Key and felt himself shrinking away to nothing.

When they reached the Jut, Chandos was waiting. Padishar's one-eyed second-in-command looked larger and blacker than Morgan remembered, his bearded, disfigured face furrowed and lined, his body wrapped in a great cloak that seemed to lend his massive body added size. He seized Padishar's hand and gripped it hard. "Good hunting?"

"Dangerous would be a better word for it," the big man replied shortly.

Chandos glanced at Morgan. "The others?"

"They've fought their last, save for the Valemen. Where's Hirehone? Somewhere about or gone back to Varfleet?"

Morgan glanced quickly at him. So Padishar was still looking to discover who had betrayed them, he thought. There had been no mention of the master of Kiltan Forge since Morgan had reported seeing him in Tyrsis.

"Hirehone?" Chandos looked puzzled. "He left after you did, same day. Went back to Varfleet like you told him, I expect. He's not here." He paused. "You have visitors, though."

Padishar yawned. "Visitors?"

"Trolls, Padishar."

The outlaw chief came awake at once. "You don't say? Trolls? Well, well. And how do they come to be here?"

They started across the bluff toward the fires, Padishar and Chandos shoulder to shoulder, Morgan trailing. "They won't say," Chandos said. "Came out of the woods three days back, easy as you please, as if finding us here wasn't any trouble at all for them. Came in without a guide, found us like we were camped in the middle of a field with our pennants flying." He grunted. "Twenty of them, big fellows, down out of the north country, the Charnals. Kelktic Rock, they call themselves. Just hung about until I went down to talk to them, then asked to speak with you. When I said you were gone, they said they'd wait."

"No, is that so? Determined, are they?"

"Like falling rock looking to reach level ground. I brought them up when they agreed to give over their arms. Didn't seem right leaving them sitting down in the Parma Key when they'd come all that way to find you—and done such a good job of it in the bargain." He smirked within his beard. "Besides, I figured three hundred of us ought to be able to stop a handful of Trolls."

Padishar laughed softly. "Doesn't hurt to be cautious, old friend. Takes more than a shove to bring down a Troll. Where are they?"

"Over there, the fire on the left."

Morgan and Padishar peered through the gloom. A cluster of faceless shadows were already on their feet, watching their approach. They looked huge. Unconsciously, Morgan reached back to finger the handle of his sword, remembering belatedly that a handle was just about all he had.

"The leader's name is Axhind," Chandos finished, his voice deliberately low now. "He's the Maturen."

Padishar strode up to the Trolls, his weariness shed somewhere back, his tall form commanding. One of the Trolls stepped forward to meet him.

Morgan Leah had never seen a Troll. He had heard stories about them, of course; everyone told stories about the Trolls. Once, long before Morgan was born, Trolls had come down out of the Northland, their traditional home, to trade with the members of the other Races. For a time, some of them had even lived among the men of Callahorn. But all that ended with the coming of the Federation and its crusade for Southland domination. Trolls were no longer welcome below the Streleheim, and the few who had come south quickly went north again. Reclusive by nature, it took very little to send them back to their mountain strongholds. Now, they never came out—or at least no one Morgan knew had ever heard of them coming out. To find a band this far south was very unusual.

Morgan tried not to stare at the visitors, but it was hard. The Trolls were heavily muscled, almost grotesque, their bodies tall and wide, their skin nut-brown and rough like bark. Their faces were flat and nearly featureless. Morgan couldn't find any ears at all. They wore leather and heavy armor, and great cloaks lay scattered about their fire like discarded shadows.

"I'm Baron Creel, Leader of the Movement." Padishar's voice boomed out.

The Troll facing him rumbled something incomprehensible. Morgan caught only the name Axhind. The two gripped hands briefly, then Axhind beckoned Padishar to sit with him at their fire. The Trolls stepped aside as the outlaw chief and his companions moved into the light to seat themselves. Morgan glanced about uneasily as the massive creatures closed about. He had never felt so unprotected. Chandos seemed unconcerned, positioning himself behind Padishar and a few feet back. Morgan eased down next to him.

The talk began in earnest then, but the Highlander didn't understand any of it. It was all done in the guttural language of the Trolls, a language of which Morgan knew nothing. Padishar seemed comfortable with it, however, pausing only infrequently to consider what he was saying. There was a great deal of what sounded like grunting, some heavy slurs, and much of what was said was emphasized by sharp gestures.

"How does Padishar speak their language?" Morgan whispered early on to Chandos.

The other never even glanced at him. "We see a bit more of life in Callahorn than you Highlanders," he said.

Morgan's hunger was threatening to consume him, but he forced it from his mind, holding himself erect against encroaching weariness, keeping himself deliberately still. The talk went on. Padishar seemed pleased with its direction.

"They want to join us," Chandos whispered after a time, apparently deciding that Morgan should be rewarded for his patience. He listened some more. "Not just these few—an entire twenty-one tribes!" He grew excited. "Five thousand men! They want to make an alliance!"

Morgan grew excited himself. "With us? Why?"

Chandos didn't answer right away, motioning for Morgan to wait. Then he said, "The Movement has approached them before, asked them to help. But they always believed it too divided, too undependable. They've changed their minds of late." He glanced over briefly. "They say Padishar has pulled the separate factions together sufficiently to reconsider. They're looking for a way to slow the Federation advance on their homelands." His rough voice was filled with satisfaction. "Shades, what a stroke of good fortune this might turn out to be!"

Axhind was passing out cups now and filling them with something from a great jar. Morgan took the cup he was offered and glanced down. The liquid it contained was as black as pitch. He waited until both the Troll leader and Padishar saluted, then drank. It was all he could do to keep from retching. Whatever he had been given tasted like bile.

Chandos caught the look on his face. "Troll milk," he said and smiled.

They drained the offering, even Morgan who found that it curbed his appetite instantly. Then they rose, Axhind and Padishar shook hands once more, and the Southlanders moved away.

"Did you hear?" Padishar asked quietly as they disappeared into the shadows. Stars were beginning to wink into view overhead, and the last of the daylight had faded away. "Did you hear it all, the whole of it?"

"Every last word," Chandos replied, and Morgan nodded wordlessly.

"Five thousand men! Shades! We could challenge the best that the Federation had to offer if we had a force like that!" Padishar was ecstatic. "There might be two thousand and some that the Movement could call upon, and more than that from the Dwarves! Shades!"

He slammed his fist into his open palm, then reached over and clapped both Chandos and Morgan heartily on the back. "It's about time something went our way, wouldn't you agree, lads?"

Morgan had dinner after that, sitting alone at a table near the cooking fire, his appetite restored by the smells that emanated from the stew kettles. Padishar and Chandos had gone off to confer on what had been happening during the former's absence, and Morgan saw no need to be part of that. He looked about for Steff and Teel, but there was no sign of either, and it wasn't until he was almost finished eating that Steff appeared out of the darkness and slumped down beside him.

"How did it go?" the Dwarf asked perfunctorily, forgoing any greeting, his gnarled hands clutched about a tankard of ale he had carried over. He looked surprisingly worn.

Briefly, Morgan related the events of the past week. When he was finished, Steff rubbed at his cinnamon beard and said, "You're lucky to be alive—any of you." His scarred face was haggard-looking; the mix of half-light and shadows seemed to etch more deeply its lines. "There's been some strange happenings taking place while you were away."

Morgan pushed back his plate and looked over, waiting.

The Dwarf cleared his throat, glancing about before he spoke. "Teel took sick the same day you left. They found her collapsed by the bluff about noon. She was breathing, but I couldn't bring her awake. I took her inside and wrapped her in blankets and sat with her for most of a week. I couldn't do anything for her. She just lay there, barely alive." He took a deep breath. "I thought she'd been poisoned."

His mouth twisted. "Could of been, it seemed to me. Lots

in the Movement have no use for the Dwarves. But then she woke finally, retching and so weak she could barely move. I fed her broth to give her back her strength, and she came around finally. She doesn't know what happened to her. She said the last thing she remembered was wondering something about Hirehone . . ."

Morgan's sharp intake of breath stopped him. "That mean something to you, Morgan?"

Morgan nodded faintly. "It might. I thought I saw Hirehone in Tyrsis after we arrived there. He shouldn't have been, and I decided then I must have been mistaken. I'm not so certain now. Someone gave us over to the Federation. It could have been Hirehone."

Steff shook his head. "Doesn't sound right. Why Hirehone, of all people? He could have turned us in that first time in Varfleet. Why wait until now?" The stocky form shifted. "Besides, Padishar trusts him completely."

"Maybe," Morgan muttered, sipping at his ale. "But Padishar was quick enough to ask about him when we got back here."

Steff considered that a moment, then dismissed the matter. "There's more. They found a handful of guards at the cliff edge two days back, night watch, the ones on the lifts, all dead, their throats torn out. No sign of who did it." He looked away momentarily, then back again. Shadows darkened his eyes. "The baskets were all up, Morgan."

They stared at each other. Morgan frowned. "So it was someone already here who did it?"

"Don't know. Seems like. But what was the reason for it, then? And if it was someone from the outside, how did they get up and then back down again with the baskets in place?"

Morgan looked off into the shadows and thought about it, but no answers would come. Steff rose. "I thought you should know. Padishar will hear on his own, I expect." He drained his tankard. "I've got to get back to Teel; I don't like leaving her alone after what's happened. She's still awfully weak." He rubbed his forehead and grimaced. "I don't feel so well myself."

"Off you go, then," Morgan said, rising with him. "I'll come see you both in the morning. Right now, though, I'm in desperate need of about two days' sleep." He paused. "You know about the Trolls?"

"Know about them?" Steff gave him a wry smile. "I've spoken with them already. Axhind and I go back a ways."

"Well, well. Another mystery. Tell me about it tomorrow, will you?"

Steff began moving away. "Tomorrow, it is." He was almost out of sight when he said, "Better watch your back, Highlander."

Morgan Leah had already decided as much.

HE SLEPT WELL that night and woke rested. The midmorning sun had crested the treeline and begun to heat up the day. There was activity in the outlaw camp, more so than usual, and Morgan was immediately anxious to find out what was happening. He thought momentarily that the Valemen might have returned, but then discarded the possibility, deciding that he would have been awakened if they had. He pulled on his clothing and boots, rolled up his blankets, washed, ate, and went down to the bluff edge. He caught sight of Padishar immediately, dressed once more in his crimson garb, shouting orders and directing men this way and that.

The outlaw chief glanced over as the Highlander approached and grunted. "I trust the noise didn't wake you." He turned to yell instructions to a group of men by the lifts before continuing in a normal tone of voice, "I would hate to think you were disturbed."

Morgan muttered something under his breath, but stopped when he caught a glimpse of the other's mocking grin. "Ah, ah. Just teasing you a bit, Highlander," the other soothed. "Let's not begin the day on the wrong foot—there's too much that needs doing. I've sent scouts to sweep the Parma Key to reassure myself that my neck hairs mislead me about what's out there, and I've sent south for Hirehone. We will see what we will see. Meanwhile, the Trolls await, Axhind and his brood. Close kin, the bunch of them, I'm told. Yesterday was merely an overture. Today we talk about the how and the wherefor of it all. You want to come along?"

Morgan did. Buckling on the scabbard that held the remains

of the Sword of Leah, which he was carrying now mostly out of habit, he followed Padishar along the bluff face and then back toward the campsite where the Trolls were already gathering. As they walked, he asked if there was any news of Par and Coll. There wasn't. He looked about expectantly for Steff and Teel, but there was no sign of either. He promised himself that he would seek them out later.

When they reached the Trolls, Axhind embraced the outlaw chief, then greeted the Highlander with a solemn nod and a handclasp like iron, and beckoned them both to take seats. Moments later, Chandos appeared with several companions, men Morgan didn't know, and the meeting got under way.

It lasted the remainder of the morning and the better part of the afternoon. Once again, Morgan was unable to follow what was being said, and this time Chandos was too preoccupied with his own participation to worry about him. Morgan listened attentively nevertheless, studying the gestures and movements of the bearish Trolls, trying to read something of what they were thinking behind their expressionless faces. He was mostly unsuccessful. They looked like great tree stumps brought to life and given the rudiments of human form to allow them to move about. Few did much of anything besides watch. The ones who spoke did so sparingly, even Axhind. There was an economy of effort behind everything they did. Morgan wondered briefly what they were like in a fight and decided that he probably already knew.

The sun moved across the sky, changing the light from dim to bright and back again, erasing and then lengthening shadows, filling the day with heat and then letting it linger in a suffocating swelter that left everyone shifting uncomfortably in a futile search for relief. There was a short break for lunch, an exchange of ales and wines, and even a brief allusion to the Highlander that had something to do with the extent of the support that the Movement enjoyed. Morgan stayed wisely silent during that exchange. He knew he had been brought there for support, not to contradict.

The afternoon was waning when the runner appeared, winded and frightened-looking. Padishar caught sight of him, frowned in annoyance at the interruption, and excused himself.

He listened intently to what the runner had to say, hesitated, then glanced at the Highlander and beckoned. Morgan came to his feet in a hurry. He did not care for what he saw in Padishar Creel's face.

Padishar dismissed the runner when Morgan reached them. "They found Hirehone," he said softly, evenly. "Out along the west edge of the Parma Key, close to the path we followed on our return. He's dead." His eyes shifted uncomfortably. "The patrol that found him said he looked as if he had been turned inside out."

Morgan felt his throat tighten at the image. "What's going on, Padishar?" he asked quietly.

"Be sure you let me know when you figure it out, Highlander. Meantime, there's worse news still. My neck hairs never lie. There's a Federation army not two miles off—the garrison at Tyrsis or I'm not my mother's favorite son." The hard face creased with lines of irony. "They're coming right for us, lad. Not a whit of deviation in their approach. Somehow they've discovered where we are—and I guess we both know how that might have happened, don't we?"

Morgan was stunned. "Who?" He barely breathed the word.

Padishar shrugged and laughed softly. "Does it really matter now?" He glanced over his shoulder. "Time to finish up here. I don't relish telling Axhind and his clan what's happened, but it wouldn't do to play games with them. If I were them, I'd disappear out of here faster than a hare gone to ground."

The Trolls were of a different mind, however. When the meeting broke up, Axhind and his companions showed no inclination to leave. Instead, they requested their weapons back— an impressive collection of axes, pikes, and broadswords—and on receiving them sat down and began in a leisurely fashion to sharpen the blades. It seemed as if they were looking for a fight.

Morgan went off to find the Dwarves. They were camped in a small, secluded grove of fir at the far end of the cliff base where an outcropping of rock formed a natural shelter from the weather. Steff greeted him without much enthusiasm. Teel was sitting up, her strange, masked face revealing nothing of her thoughts, though her eyes glittered watchfully. She looked stronger, her dusky hair brushed out, her hands steady as they accepted Morgan's own. He spoke with her briefly, but she said almost nothing in return. Morgan gave them the news of Hirehone and the approaching Federation army. Steff nodded soberly; Teel didn't even do that. He left them feeling vaguely dissatisfied with the entire visit.

The Federation army arrived with the coming of nightfall, spread out in the forestlands directly below the cliffs of the Jut, and began clearing the land for its use, working with the industrious determination of ants. They streamed out of the trees, several thousand strong, their pennants flying, their weapons gleaming. Standards were raised before each company—banners of solid black with one red and one white stripe where there were regular Federation soldiers and a grinning white wolf's head where there were Seekers. Tents went up, weapons racks were assembled, supplies were positioned to the rear, and fires sparked to life. Almost immediately teams of men began building siege weapons, and the sounds of saws felling trees and axes hewing limbs filled the air.

The outlaws watched from the heights, their own fortifications already in place. Morgan watched with them. They seemed relaxed and easy. There were only three hundred of them, but the Jut was a natural fortification that could resist an army five times the size of this one. The lifts had already been drawn to the bluff, and now there was no way up or down except by scaling the walls. That would require climbing by hand, ladder, or grappling hook. Even a handful of men could put a stop to that.

It was fully dark by the time Morgan was able to speak again with Padishar. They stood by the lifts, now under heavy guard, and looked out over the broad scattering of watch fires below. The men of the Federation continued to work, the sound of their building rising out of the darkened forests into the still night air.

"I don't mind telling you that all this effort bothers me," the outlaw chief muttered, his brow furrowing.

Morgan frowned with him. "Even with siege equipment, how can they possibly hope to reach us?"

Padishar shook his head. "They can't. That's what bothers me."

They watched a bit longer, then Padishar steered Morgan to a secluded part of the bluff, keeping him close as he whispered. "I needn't remind you that we've been betrayed twice now. Whoever's responsible is still out there—probably still among us. If the Jut's to be taken, that's my guess as to how it's to be done."

He turned to Morgan, his strong, weathered face close. "I'll do my part to see that the Jut's kept secure. But you keep your eyes open as well, Highlander. You might see things differently from me, being fresh here. Maybe you'll see something I'd otherwise miss. Watch us all, and it's a big favor I'll owe you if you turn up something."

Morgan nodded wordlessly. It gave him a purpose for being there, something he was beginning to suspect he lacked. He was consumed by the feeling of emptiness he had experienced on shattering his sword. He was distressed that he had been forced to leave Par and Coll Ohmsford behind. This charge, if nothing else, would give him something to concentrate on. He was grateful to Padishar for that.

When they finished, he went to the armorer and asked to be given a broadsword. He picked one that suited him, withdrew his own broken sword and replaced it with the new one. Then he hunted about for a discarded scabbard until he found one the Sword of Leah would fit, cut the scabbard to the sword's shortened length, bound the severed end, and strapped the makeshift sheath carefully to his belt.

He felt better about himself for the first time in days.

HE SLEPT WELL that night, too—even though the Federation continued to assemble its siege weapons until dawn. When the sun appeared, the building ceased. He woke then, the sudden stillness disconcerting, pulled on his clothes, strapped on his weapons, and hurried down to the bluff edge. The outlaws were settling into place, arms at the ready. Padishar was there, with Steff, Teel, and the contingent of Trolls. All watched silently what was taking place below.

The Federation army was forming up, squads into companies. They were well drilled, and there was no confusion as they marched into place. They encircled the base of the Jut, stretching from one end of the cliffs to the other, their lines just out of range of long bow and sling. Scaling ladders and ropes with grappling hooks were piled next to them. Siege towers stood ready, though the towers were crude and scarcely a third of the height of the cliffs leading up. Commanders barked orders crisply, and the gaps between companies slowly began to fill.

Morgan touched Steff briefly on the shoulder. The Dwarf glanced about uncertainly, nodded without saying anything, and looked away again.

Morgan frowned. Steff wasn't carrying any weapons.

Trumpets sounded, and the Federation lines straightened. Everything went still once more. Sunlight glinted off armor and weapons as the skies in the east brightened. Dew glistened off leaves and grasses, the birdsongs lifted cheerfully, the sound of water running came from somewhere distant, and it seemed to Morgan Leah that it might have been any of a thousand mornings he had greeted when he still roamed and hunted the hills of his homeland.

Then from back in the trees, behind the long lines of soldiers, something moved. There was a jerking of limbs and trunks and a rasping of scraped bark. The Federation ranks suddenly split in two, opening a hole that was better than a hundred feet across. The outlaws and their allies stiffened expectantly, frowns creasing their faces as the forest continued to shake with the approach of whatever was hidden there.

Shades, Morgan whispered to himself.

The thing emerged from out of the fading shadows. It was huge, a creature of impossible size, an apparition comprised of the worst bits and pieces of things scavengers might have left. It was formed of hair and sinew and bone, but at the same time of metal plates and bars. There were jagged ends and shiny surfaces, iron grafted onto flesh, flesh grown into iron. It had the look of a monstrous, misshapen crustacean or worm, but was neither. It shambled forward, its glittering eyes rolling upward to find the edge of the bluff. Pinchers clicked like knives and claws scraped heedlessly the roughened stone.

For an instant, Morgan thought it was a machine. Then, a heartbeat later, he realized it was alive.

"Demon's blood!" Steff cried in recognition, his gruff voice angry and frightened. "They've brought a Creeper!"

Hunching its way slowly through the ranks of the Federation army, the Creeper came for them.

26

ORGAN LEAH REMEMBERED the stories then.
It seemed as if there had always been stories of the
Creepers, tales that had been handed down from grand-
father to father, from father to son, from generation to
generation. They were told in the Highlands and in most parts
of the Southland he had visited. Men whispered of the Creepers
over glasses of ale around late night fires and sent shivers of
excitement and horror down the spines of boys like Morgan,
who listened at the circle's edge. No one put much stock in the
stories, though; after all, they were told in the same breath as
those wild imaginings of Skull Bearers and Mord Wraiths and
other monsters out of a time that was all but forgotten. Yet no
one was quite ready to dismiss them out-of-hand, either. Because
whatever the men of the Southland might believe, there were
Dwarves in the Eastland who swore by them.

Steff was one of those Dwarves. He had repeated the stories
to Morgan—long after Morgan had already heard them—not
as legend but as truth. They had happened, he insisted. They
were real.

It was the Federation, he told Morgan, who made the Creepers. A hundred years ago, when the war against the Dwarves
had bogged down deep in the wilderness of the Anar, when the
armies of the Southland were thwarted by the jungle and the
mountains and by the tangle of brush and the walls of rock that
prevented them from engaging and trapping their elusive quarry,
the Federation had called the Creepers to life. The Dwarves had

taken the offensive away from the Federation by then, a sizeable resistance force that was determined to avoid capture and to harass the invaders until they were driven from their homeland. From their fortress lairs within the maze of canyons and defiles of the Ravenshorn and the cavelike hollows of the surrounding forests, the Dwarves counterattacked the heavier and more cumbersome Federation armies almost at will and slipped away with the ease of night's shadows. The months dragged on as the Federation effort stalled, and it was then that the Creepers appeared.

No one knew for certain where they came from. There were some who claimed they were simply machines constructed by the Federation builders, juggernauts without capacity to think, whose only function was to bring down the Dwarf fortifications and the Dwarves with them. There were others who said that no machine could have done what the Creepers did, that such things possessed cunning and instinct. A few whispered that they were formed of magic. Whatever their origin, the Creepers materialized within the wilderness of the central Anar and began to hunt. They were unstoppable. They tracked the Dwarves relentlessly and, when they caught up to them, destroyed them all. The war ended in a little more than a month, the Dwarf armies annihilated, the backbone of the resistance shattered.

After that, the Creepers vanished as mysteriously as they had appeared, as if the earth had swallowed them whole. Only the stories remained, growing more lurid and at the same time less accurate with each telling, losing the force of truth as time passed, until only the Dwarves themselves remained certain of what had happened.

Morgan Leah stared downward for a moment longer as the stories of his childhood came to life, then wrenched his eyes away from the drop, away from the nightmare below, and looked frantically at Steff. The Dwarf was staring back at him, half-turned as if to bolt from the fortifications, his scarred face stricken.

"A Creeper, Morgan. A Creeper—after all these years. Do you know what that means?"

Morgan didn't have time to speculate. Padishar Creel was suddenly beside them, having heard the Dwarf speak. His hands gripped Steff's shoulders and he pulled the other about to face him. "Tell me now, quickly! What do you know of this thing?"

"It's a Creeper," Steff repeated, his voice stiff and unnatural, as if naming it said everything.

"Yes, yes, fine and well!" Padishar snapped impatiently. "I don't care what it is! I want to know how to stop it!"

Steff shook his head slowly, as if trying to clear it, as if dazed and unable to think. "You can't stop it. There isn't any way to stop it. No one has ever found a way."

There were mutterings from the men closest to them as they heard the Dwarf's words, and a sense of restless misgiving began to ripple through the lines of defenders. Morgan was stunned; he had never heard Steff sound so defeated. He glanced quickly at Teel. She had moved Steff away from Padishar protectively, her eyes bits of hard, glistening rock within her mask.

Padishar ignored them, turning instead to face his own men. "Stand where you are!" he roared angrily at those who had begun to whisper and move back. The whispers and the movement stopped immediately. "I'll skin the first rabbit who does otherwise!"

He gave Steff a withering glance. "No way, is there? Not for you, perhaps—though I would have thought it otherwise and you a better man, Steff." His voice was low, controlled. "No way? There's always a way!"

There was a scraping sound from below, and they all pushed back to the breastworks. The Creeper had reached the base of the cliff wall and was beginning to work its way up, securing a grip in cracks and crevices where human hands and feet could not hope to find purchase. Sunlight glinted off patches of armor-plating and bits of iron rod, and the muscles of its wormlike body rippled. The marching drums of the Federation had begun to sound, pounding a steady cadence to mark the monster's approach.

Padishar leaped recklessly atop the defenses. "Chandos! A dozen archers to me—now!"

The archers appeared immediately and as rapidly as they could manage sent a rain of arrows into the Creeper. It never slowed. The arrows bounced off its armor or buried themselves in its thick hide without effect. Even its eyes, those hideous black orbs that shifted and turned lazily with the movement of its body, seemed impervious.

Padishar withdrew the archers. A cheer went up from the ranks of the Federation army and a chanting began, matching the throb of the drums. The outlaw chief called for spearmen, but even the heavy wooden shafts and iron heads could not slow the monster's approach. They broke off or shattered on the rocks, and the Creeper came on.

Massive boulders were brought forward and sent rolling over the cliff edge. Several crashed into the Creeper. They grazed it or struck it full on, and the result was the same. It kept coming. The mutterings resumed, born of fear and frustration. Padishar shouted angrily to quiet them, but the task was growing harder. He called for brush to be brought forward, had it fired and sent tumbling into the Creeper—to no effect. Furious, he had a cask of cooking oil brought up, broken open and spilled down the cliff wall, then ignited. It burned ferociously against the barren rock, engulfing the approaching Creeper in a haze of black smoke and flames. Cries rose from the ranks of the Federation and the drums went still. Heat lifted into the morning air in waves so suffocating that the defenders were forced back. Morgan retreated with the rest, Steff and Teel next to him. Steff's face was drawn and pale, and he seemed strangely disoriented. Morgan helped him step away, unable to fathom what had happened to his friend.

"Are you sick?" he asked, whispering to the other as he eased him to a sitting position. "Steff, what's wrong?"

But the other didn't appear to have an answer. He simply shook his head. Then with an effort he said, "Fire won't stop it. It's been tried, Morgan. It doesn't work."

He was right. When the flames and the heat died away enough to permit the defenders to return to the walls, the Creeper was still there, working its way steadily upward, almost halfway up by now, as scorched and blackened as the rock to which it clung but otherwise unchanged. The drumming and the chanting from the Federation soldiers below resumed, an eager, confident swell of sound that engulfed the whole of the Jut.

The outlaws were dismayed. Arguments began to spring up,

and it was clear that by now no one believed that the Creeper could be stopped. What would they do when it reached them? Seemingly invulnerable to spears and arrows, could it be stopped by swords? The frantic outlaws could make a pretty good guess.

Only Axhind and his Rock Trolls seemed unperturbed by what was happening. They stood at the far end of the outlaw defenses, protecting a shelf that slanted down from the main bluff to the cliff wall, weapons held ready, a small island of calm amid the tumult. They were not talking. They did not appear nervous. They were watching Padishar Creel, apparently waiting to see what he would do next.

Padishar was quick to show them. He had noticed something that everyone else had missed, and it gave him a glimmer of hope for the besieged outlaws.

"Chandos!" he called out, shoving and pushing his men back into place as he walked down the breastworks. His burly, black-bearded lieutenant appeared. "Bring up whatever oil we've got—cooking, cleaning, anything! Don't waste time asking questions, just do it!"

Chandos closed his mouth and hurried off. Padishar wheeled and came back down the line toward Morgan and the Dwarves. "Ready one of the lifts!" he called past them. Then unexpectedly he stopped. "Steff. How are these things on slick surfaces, these Creepers? How do they grip?"

Steff looked at him blankly, as if the question were too perplexing for him to consider. "I don't know."

"But they have to grip to climb, don't they?" the other demanded. "What happens if they can't?"

He turned away without waiting for an answer. The morning had grown hot, and he was sweating heavily now. He stripped off his tunic, throwing it aside irritably. Snatching a set of cross belts from another outlaw, he buckled them on, picked up a short-handled axe, shoved it through one of the belt loops, and moved ahead to the lifts. Morgan followed, beginning to see now what the outlaw planned to do. Chandos hurried up from the caves, followed by a knot of men carrying casks of varying sizes and weights.

"Load them," Padishar ordered, motioning. When the loading was begun, he put his hands on his lieutenant's broad shoulders. "I'm going over in the lift, down where the beast climbs, and dump the oil on it."

"Padishar!" Chandos was horrified.

"No, listen now. The Creeper can't get up here if it can't climb, and it can't climb if it can't grip. The oil will make everything so slick the slug won't be able to move. It might even fall." He grinned fiercely. "Wouldn't that put a nice finish to things?"

Chandos shook his woolly head, a frantic look in his eyes. The Trolls had drifted over and were listening. "You think the Federation will let you get that far? Their bowmen will cut you to pieces!"

"Not if you keep them back, they won't." The grin vanished. "Besides, old friend—what other choice do we have?"

He sprang into the lift, crouching within the shelter of its railing to present the smallest target possible. "Just don't let me drop," he shouted and gripped the axe tightly.

The lift went over the side, Chandos letting it down quickly, bringing the boom close above where the Creeper worked its way upward, now high on the wall, a large black smudge that oozed across the rock. A howl went up from the Federation army as they saw what was happening, and lines of bowmen surged forward. The outlaws were waiting. Shooting unobstructed from their defenses far above, they broke the assault in moments. Immediately more lines rushed forward, and arrows began to shatter against the cliff face all about the dropping lift. The outlaws returned the Federation fire. Again, the assault broke apart and fell back.

But by now catapults had been brought forward, and massive rocks began to hurtle into the cliff face, smashing all about the fragile lift as Federation marksmen sought to find the range. One barrage of loose rock hammered into the lift and sent it careening into the wall. Wood splintered and cracked. From directly below, the Creeper looked up.

Morgan Leah stood at the edge of the bluff and watched in horror, Steff and Teel beside him. The lift with Padishar Creel twisted and spun as if caught in a fierce wind.

"Hold him!" Chandos screamed to the men on the ropes, turning back in dismay. "Hold him steady!"

But they were losing him. The rope slipped, and the effort to retrieve it dragged its handlers toward the cliff edge where they frantically struggled to brace themselves. Federation arrows raked the bluff, and two of the handlers dropped. No one took their place, uncertain what to do in the chaos of the attack. Chandos looked back over his shoulder, eyes wide. The rope slipped further.

They can't hold it, Morgan realized in horror.

He darted forward, shouting frantically. But Axhind was quicker. With a speed that belied his size, the Maturen of the Kelktic Rock bounded through the onlookers and seized the rope in his massive hands. The other holders fell back in confusion. Alone, the giant Troll held the lift and Padishar Creel. Then another Troll appeared and then two more. Bracing themselves, they hauled back on the rope as Chandos shouted instructions from the edge.

Morgan peered out over the bluff again. The Parma Key stretched away in a sea of deep green that disappeared into a midmorning sky that was cloudless and blue, filled with sweet smells and a sense of timelessness. The Jut was an island of chaos in its midst. At the base of the cliffs, Federation soldiers lay dying in heaps. The orderly lines were ragged now, their neat formations scattered in the rush to attack. Catapults launched their missiles and arrows flew from everywhere. The lift still dangled from its rope, a tiny bit of bait that was seemingly only inches above the black monstrosity that hunched its way steadily closer.

Then suddenly, almost unexpectedly, Padishar Creel was lifted into view, short-handled axe splintering the first of the oil casks and spilling its contents down the cliff side and over the Creeper. The head and upper body of the creature were saturated in the glistening liquid, and the Creeper stopped moving. The contents of a second cask followed the first, and then the contents of a third. The Creeper and the cliff wall were saturated. Arrows from the Federation bows pinged all about Padishar as he stood exposed. Then he was struck, once, twice, and he went down.

"Haul him up!" Chandos screamed.

The Trolls jerked on the line in response, the watching outlaws howling in fury and shooting down into the ranks of the Federation archers.

But then somehow Padishar was back on his feet, and the last two remaining casks were splintered and their contents dumped down the rock wall onto the Creeper. The beast hung there, no longer moving, letting the oil run down into it, under it, over it, streams of glistening oil and grease spreading down the cliff face in the harsh glare of the morning sun.

A catapult struck the lift squarely then and shattered it to pieces. The outlaws on the bluff cried out as the lift fell apart. But Padishar did not fall; he caught hold of the rope and dangled there, arrows and stones flying all about him, a perfect target. There was blood on his chest and arms, and the muscles of his body were corded with the effort it required for him to hang on.

Swiftly the rope came up, Padishar Creel was hauled to the edge of the bluff, and his men reached out to pull him to safety. For a moment the battle was forgotten. Chandos shouted in vain for everyone to get back, but the outlaws ignored him as they crowded around their fallen leader. Then Padishar was on his feet, blood streaming down his body from his wounds, arrows protruding from deep within his right shoulder and through the fleshy part of his left side, his face pale and drawn with pain. Reaching down, he snapped the arrow in his side in two and with a grimace pulled the shaft clear.

"Get back to the wall!" he roared. "Now!"

The outlaws scattered. Padishar pushed past Chandos and staggered to the breastworks, peering down at the Creeper.

The Creeper was still hanging there, still not moving, as if glued to the rock. The Federation archers and catapults were continuing their barrage on the outlaw defenses, but the effort had become a halfhearted one as they, too, waited to see what would happen.

"Fall, drat you!" Padishar cried furiously.

The Creeper stirred, shifting slightly, edging right, trying to maneuver away from the glistening sheet of oil. Claws rasped as it hunched and squirmed to keep its hold. But the oil had done its job. The creature's grip began to loosen, slowly at first, then more rapidly as one after another of its appendages slipped free.

A howl of dismay went up from the Federation ranks, a cheer from the outlaws. The Creeper was sliding down more quickly now, skidding on a track of oil that followed after it relentlessly, coating its tubular body. Its grip gave way altogether and down it went, tumbling, rolling, falling with a crunch of metal and bone. When it struck the earth at last, dust rose in a massive cloud, and the whole of the cliff face shook with the impact.

The Creeper lay motionless at the base of the cliffs, its oiled bulk shuddering.

"That's more like it!" Padishar Creel sighed and slid down the breastworks into a sitting position, his eyes closing wearily.

"You've finished him sure enough!" Chandos exclaimed, dropping into a crouch beside him. His smile was ferocious. Morgan, standing close at hand, found himself grinning as well.

But Padishar simply shook his head. "This doesn't finish anything. That was today's horror. Tomorrow will surely bring another. And what do we do for oil then, with the last of it spilled out today?" The dark eyes opened. "Cut this other arrow out of me so I can get some sleep."

THE FEDERATION DID NOT attack again that day. It withdrew its army to the edge of the forest, there to tend to the dead and wounded. Only the catapults were left in place, sending their loads skyward periodically, though most fell short and the assault proved more annoying than effective.

The Creeper, unfortunately, was not dead. After a time, it seemed to recover, and it rolled over sluggishly and crawled off into the shelter of the Parma Key. It was impossible to guess how badly it had been damaged, but no one was ready to predict that they had seen the last of it.

Padishar Creel was treated for his wounds, bound up, and put to bed. He was weak from loss of blood and in no small amount of pain, but his injuries would not leave him disabled. Even as Chandos was seeing to his care, Padishar was giving instructions for continuing the defense of the Jut. A special weapon was to be built. Morgan heard Chandos speak of it as he gathered a select group of men and sent them off into the largest of the caves to construct it. Work began almost immediately, but when Morgan asked what it was that was being assembled, Chandos was unwilling to talk about it.

"You'll see it when it's completed, Highlander," he responded gruffly. "Leave it at that."

Morgan did, but only because he hadn't any other choice. At something of a loss as to what to do with himself, he drifted over to where Steff had been taken by Teel and found his friend wrapped in blankets and feverish. Teel watched suspiciously as the Highlander felt Steff's forehead, a watchdog that no longer trusted anyone. Morgan could hardly blame her. He spoke quietly with Steff for a few moments, but the Dwarf was barely conscious. It seemed better to let him sleep. The Highlander stood up, glanced a final time at the unresponsive Teel, and walked away.

He spent the remainder of the day passing back and forth between the fortifications and the caves, checking on the Federation army and the secret weapon and on Padishar Creel and Steff. He didn't accomplish much, and the hours of the late morning and then the afternoon passed slowly. Morgan found himself wondering once again what good he was doing anyone, trapped at the Jut with these outlaws, resistance fighters or no, far from Par and Coll and what really mattered. How would he ever find the Valemen again, now that they had been separated? Certainly they would not attempt to come into the Parma Key, not while a Federation army had them under siege. Damson Rhee would never permit it.

Or would she? It suddenly occurred to Morgan that she might, if she thought there was a safe way to do so. That made him think. What if there was more than one way into the Jut? Didn't there have to be, he asked himself? Even with the defenses as strong as they were, Padishar Creel would never take the chance that they might somehow be breached, leaving the outlaws trapped against the rocks. He would have an escape route, another way out. Or in.

He decided to find out. It was almost dusk, however, before he got his chance. Padishar was awake again by then, and Morgan found him sitting on the edge of his bed, heavily bandaged, streaks of blood showing vividly against his weathered skin, studying a set of crudely sketched drawings with Chandos. Another man would still be sleeping, trying to regain his strength; Padishar looked ready to fight. The men glanced up as he approached, and Padishar tucked the drawings out of sight. Morgan hesitated.

"Highlander," the other greeted. "Come sit with me."

Surprised, Morgan came over, taking a seat on a packing crate filled with metal fittings. Chandos nodded, got up without a word, and walked out.

"And how is our friend the Dwarf?" Padishar asked, rather too casually. "Better, now?"

Morgan studied the other man. "No. Something is very wrong with him, but I don't know what it is." He paused. "You don't trust anyone, do you? Not even me."

"Especially not you." Padishar waited a moment, grinned disarmingly, and then made the smile disappear in the quickness of an eye's blink. "I can't afford to trust anyone anymore. Too much has happened to suggest that I shouldn't." He shifted his weight and grimaced with the pain it caused. "So tell me. What brings you to visit? Have you seen something you think I should know about?"

The truth was that with the excitement of the events of that morning, Morgan had forgotten about the charge that Padishar had given him to try to find out who it was that had betrayed them. He didn't say so, however; he simply shook his head.

"I have a question," he said. "About Par and Coll Ohmsford. Do you think that Damson Rhee might still try to bring them here? Is there another way into the Jut that she might use?"

The look that Padishar Creel gave him was at once indecipherable and filled with meaning. There was a long silence, and Morgan felt himself grow suddenly cold as he realized how it must look for him to be asking such a question.

He took a deep breath. "I'm not asking where it is, only if . . ."

"I understand what you're asking and why," the other said, cutting short his protestation. The hard face furrowed about the eyes and mouth. Padishar said nothing for a moment, studying the Highlander intently. "As a matter of fact, there is another way," he said finally. "You must have figured that out on your own, though. You understand enough of tactics to know that there must always be more than one way in or out of a refuge."

Morgan nodded wordlessly.

"Well, then, Highlander, I can only add that Damson would not put the Valemen at risk by trying to bring them here while the Jut was under siege. She would keep them safe in Tyrsis or elsewhere, whatever the situation might require."

He paused, eyes hard with hidden thoughts. Then he said, "No one but Damson, Chandos, and I know the other way—now that Hirehone is dead. Better that we keep it so until the identity of our traitor is discovered, don't you think? I wouldn't want the Federation walking in through the back door while we were busy holding shut the front."

Morgan hadn't considered the possibility of such a thing happening until now. It was a chilling thought. "Is the back way secure?" he asked hesitantly.

Padishar pursed his lips. "Very. Now take yourself off to dinner, Highlander. And remember to keep your eyes open."

He turned back to his drawings. Morgan hesitated a moment, thinking to say something more, then turned abruptly and left.

THAT NIGHT, as daylight faded into evening and stars began to appear, Morgan sat alone at the far end of the bluff where a grove of aspen trees sheltered a small grassy clearing, looked out across the valley of the Parma Key to where the moon, half-full again, lifted slowly out of the horizon into the darkening skies, and marshalled his powers of reason. The camp was quiet now except for the muffled sounds of work being done back in the caves on Padishar's secret weapon. The catapults and bows were stilled, the men of both the Federation army and the Movement sleeping or lost in their own private contemplations. Padishar was meeting with the Trolls and Chandos, a meeting to which Morgan had not been invited. Steff was resting, his fever seemingly no worse, but his strength sapped and his general health no better. There was nothing to be done, nothing to occupy the time but to sleep or think, and Morgan Leah had chosen the latter.

For as long as he could remember, he had been clever. It was a gift, admittedly, one that could be traced to his ancestors, to men such as Menion and Rone Leah—real Princes in those days, heroes—but an ability, too, that Morgan had worked long and hard to perfect. The Federation had supplied him with both a purpose and a direction for his skill. He had spent almost the whole of his youth concentrating on finding ways to outwit the Federation officials who occupied and governed his homeland, to irritate them at every opportunity so that they might never feel secure, to make them experience a futility and a frustration that would one day drive them from Leah forever. He was very good at it; perhaps he was the best there was. He knew all the tricks, had conceived most of them himself. He could outthink and outsmart almost anyone, if he were given time and opportunity to do so.

He smiled ruefully. At least, that was what he had always told himself. Now it was time to prove that it was so. It was time to figure out how the Federation had known so often what they were about, how it was that they had been betrayed—the outlaws, the Valemen, the little company from Culhaven, everyone connected with this misadventure—and most important of all, who was responsible.

It was something he could reason out.

He let his lean frame drape itself against the grassy base of a twisted, old trunk, drew his knees partway up to his chest, and considered what he knew.

The list of betrayals was a long one. Someone had informed the Federation when Padishar had taken them into Tyrsis to recover the Sword of Shannara. Someone had found out what they were going to do and gotten word to the Federation watch commander ahead of their arrival. One of your own, the watch commander had told Padishar. Then someone had revealed the location of the Jut to the army that now besieged it—again, someone who knew where it could be found and how to find it.

He frowned. The betrayals had actually begun before that,

though. If you accepted the premise—and he was now prepared to—that someone had sent the Gnawl to track them in the Wolfsktaag and had gotten word to the Shadowen on Toffer Ridge where the Spider Gnomes could snatch Par, why then, the betrayals went all the way back to Culhaven.

So had someone been tracking them all the way from Culhaven?

He discarded the possibility immediately. No one could have managed such a feat.

But there was more to the puzzle. There was the sighting of Hirehone in Tyrsis and his subsequent murder in the Parma Key. And there was the killing of the lift watch with the lifts still drawn up. What did those events have to do with anything?

He let all the pieces sift through his mind for a few minutes, waiting to see if he would discover something he had missed. Night birds called out from below in the darkness of the Parma Key, and the wind blew gently across his face, warm and fragrant. When nothing further occurred, he took each piece in turn and tried to fit it to the puzzle, working to see if a recognizable picture would emerge. The minutes paraded past him silently. The pieces refused to fit.

He was missing something.

He rubbed his hands together briskly. He would try it another way. He would eliminate what didn't work and see what was left. He took a steadying breath and relaxed.

No one could have followed them—not for all that time. So it must be someone among them. One of them. But if that someone were responsible for the Gnawl and the Shadowen as well as everything that had happened since their arrival at the outlaw camp, then didn't it have to be one of the members of the original company? Par, Coll, Steff, Teel, or himself? He went back to Teel momentarily, for he knew less of her than of any of them. He could not bring himself to believe it was either of the Valemen or Steff. But why was Teel any better as a candidate? Hadn't she suffered at least as much as Steff?

Besides, what did Hirehone have to do with any of this? Why were the men of the lift watch killed?

He caught himself. They were killed so that someone could either get in or get out of the outlaw camp undetected. It made sense. But the lifts were drawn up. They had to have been killed after bringing someone into the camp—killed perhaps to hide that someone's identity.

He wrestled with the possibilities. It all kept coming back to Hirehone. Hirehone was the key. What if it had been Hirehone he had seen in Tyrsis? What if Hirehone had indeed betrayed them to the Federation? But Hirehone had never returned to the Jut after leaving. So how could he have killed the watch? And why would he be killed after doing so in any case? And by whom? Could there be more than one traitor involved—Hirehone and someone else?

Something clicked into place.

Morgan Leah jerked forward in recognition. Who was the enemy here—the real enemy? Not the Federation. The real enemy was the Shadowen. Wasn't that what Allanon's shade had told them? Wasn't that what they had been warned against? And the Shadowen could take the form and body and speech of anyone. Some of them could, at least—the most dangerous. Cogline had said so.

Morgan felt his pulse quicken and his face flush with excitement. They weren't dealing with a human being in this matter. They were dealing with a Shadowen! The pieces of the puzzle suddenly began to fit together. A Shadowen could have hidden among them and they would not have known. A Shadowen could have summoned a Gnawl, sent word to Toffer Ridge to another of its kind, have gotten to Tyrsis ahead of Padishar's company, have spied out its purpose, and slipped away again before its return. A Shadowen could get close enough. And it could disguise itself as Hirehone. No, not disguise—it could *be* Hirehone! And it could have killed him when he had served his purpose, and killed the lift watch because they would have reported seeing it, no matter whose face it had worn. It had revealed the location of the Jut to the Federation army—even mapped a path for them to follow!

Who? All that remained was to determine . . .

Morgan sagged back slowly against the trunk of the aspen behind him, the puzzle suddenly complete. He knew who. Steff or Teel. It had to be one or the other. They were the only ones, besides himself, who had been with the company from the very beginning, from Culhaven to the Jut, to Tyrsis and back. Teel had been unconscious practically the entire time Padishar's band was in Tyrsis. That would have given either of the Dwarves, or more specifically the Shadowen within, the opportunity to slip away and then back again. They were alone much of the time in any case—just the two of them.

He stiffened against the weight of his suspicions as they bore down on him. For an instant, he thought he was crazy, that he should discard his reasoning entirely and start over again. But he couldn't do that. He knew he was right.

The wind brushed at him, and he pulled his cloak closer in spite of the evening's warmth. He sat without moving in the protective shadow of his haven and examined carefully the conclusions he had reached, the reasonings he had devised, the speculations that had slowly assumed the trappings of truth. It was silent now in the outlaw camp, and he could imagine himself to be the only human being living in all the vast, dark expanse of the Parma Key.

Shades.

Steff or Teel.

His instincts told him it was Teel.

CHAPTER

27

T WAS THREE DAYS after they had made their decision to go back down into the Pit to recover the Sword of Shannara that Damson at last took the Valemen from their garden shed hideaway into the streets of Tyrsis. By then Par was beside himself with impatience. He had wanted to go immediately; time was everything, he had argued. But Damson had flatly refused. It was too dangerous, she insisted. Too many Federation patrols were still combing the city. They had to wait. Par had been left with no choice but to do so.

Even now, when she finally judged the margin of risk small enough to permit them to venture forth, it was on a night when reasonable men would think twice about doing so, a night that was bone-cold, the city wrapped in a blanket of mist and rain that prevented even friends of long standing from recognizing each other from a distance of more than a few feet and sent the few citizens who had worked past their normal quitting time scurrying down the glistening, empty streets for the warmth and comfort of their homes.

Damson had provided the little company with foul-weather cloaks, hooded and caped, and they wore them now pulled close as they made their way through the damp and the silence. Their boots thudded softly on the stone roadway as they walked, echoing in the stillness, filling up the night with a strange, rushed cacophony. Water dripped from eaves and trickled down mortared grooves, and the mist settled on their skin with a chill, possessive adherence that was faintly distasteful. They followed the backstreets as always, avoiding the Tyrsian Way and the other main thoroughfares where Federation patrols still kept watch, steering into the narrow avenues that burrowed like tunnels through the colorless, semi-abandoned blocks of the city's poor and homeless.

They were on their way to find the Mole.

"That is how he is known," Damson told them just before they went out. "All of the street people call him that because that is what he chooses to call himself. If he ever had a real name, I doubt that he remembers it. His past is a closely kept secret. He lives in the sewers and catacombs beneath Tyrsis, a recluse. He almost never comes out into the light. His whole world is the underbelly of the city, and no one knows more about it than he does."

"And if there are still passageways that run beneath the palace of the Kings of Tyrsis, the Mole will know about them?" Par pressed.

"He will know."

"Can we trust him?"

"The problem is not whether we can trust him, but whether he will decide to trust us. As I said, he is very reclusive. He may not even choose to talk with us."

And Par said simply, "He must."

Coll said nothing. He had said little the entire day, barely a word since they had decided to go back into the Pit. He had swallowed the news of what they were going to do as if he had ingested a medicine that would either cure or kill him and he was waiting to see which it would be. He seemed to have decided that it was pointless to debate the matter further or to argue what he perceived as the folly of their course of action, so he had taken a fatalistic stance, bowing to the inevitability of Par's determination and the fortune or misfortune that would befall them because of it, and he had gone into a shell as hard and impenetrable as iron.

He trailed now as they made their way through the murk of the Tyrsian evening, tracking Par as closely as his own shadow, intruding with his mute presence in a way that distressed rather than comforted. Par didn't like feeling that way about his brother, but there was no help for it. Coll had determined his own role. He would neither accept what Par was doing nor cut himself free of it. He would simply stick it out, for better or worse, until a resolution was reached.

Damson steered them to the top of a narrow flight of stone steps that cut through a low wall connecting two vacant, unlighted buildings and wound its way downward into the dark. Par could hear water running, a low gurgle that splashed and chugged through some obstruction. They made a cautious descent of the slick stone, finding a loose, rusted railing that offered an uncertain handhold. When they reached the end of the stairs, they found themselves on a narrow walkway that ran parallel to a sewer trench. It was down the trench that the water ran, spilling from a debris-choked passageway that opened from underneath the streets above.

Damson took the Valemen into the tunnel.

It was black inside and filled with harsh, pungent smells. The rain disappeared behind them. Damson paused, fumbled about in the dark for a moment, then produced a torch coated with pitch on one end, which she managed to light with the aid of a piece of flint. The firelight brightened the gloom enough to permit them to see their way a few steps at a time, and so they proceeded. Unseen things scurried away in the darkness ahead, soundless but for the scratching of tiny claws. Water dripped from the ceiling, ran down the walls, and churned steadily through the trench. The air was chill and empty of life.

They reached a second set of stairs descending further into the earth and took them. They passed through several levels this time, and the sound of the water faded. The scratchings remained, however, and the chill clung to them with irritating persistence. The Valemen pulled their cloaks tighter. The stairs ended and a new passageway began, this one narrower than the other. They were forced to crouch in order to proceed, and the dampness gave way to dust. They moved ahead steadily, and the minutes slipped past. They were deep beneath the city by now, well within the core of rock and earth that formed the plateau on which Tyrsis rested. The Valemen had lost all sense of direction.

When they reached the bottom of a dry well with an iron ladder that led up, Damson paused. "It is not far now," she said quietly. "Just another several hundred yards when we reach the top of this ladder. We should find him then—or he us. He brought me here once long ago when I showed him a bit of kindness." She hesitated. "He is very gentle, but peculiar as well. Be careful how you treat him."

She took them up the ladder to a landing that opened into a series of passageways. It was warmer there, less dusty, the air stale but not malodorous. "These tunnels were bolt holes once for the city's defenders; at some points they lead all the way down to the plains." Her red hair shimmered as she brushed it back from her face. "Stay close to me."

They entered one of the corridors and started down. The pitch coating on the torch head sizzled and steamed. The tunnel twisted about, crisscrossed other tunnels, wound through rooms shored up with timbers and fastening bolts, and left the Valemen more confused than ever as to where they were. But Damson never hesitated, certain of her way, either reading signs that were hidden from them or calling to memory a map that she kept within her head.

At last they entered a room that was the first of several, all interconnected, large chambers with wooden beams, stone block floors, walls from which hangings and tapestries dangled, and a storehouse of bizarre treasures. Piled floor to ceiling, wall to wall, there were trunks of old clothing, piles of furniture crammed and laden with clasps, fittings, writings gone almost to dust, feathers, cheap jewelry, and toy animals of all sorts, shapes, and sizes. The animals were all carefully arranged, some seated in groups, some lined up on shelves and on divans, some placed at watch atop bureaus and at doorways. There were a few rusted weapons scattered about and an armful of baskets woven from cane and rush.

There were lights as well—oil lamps fastened to the beams overhead and the wall beneath, filling the rooms with a vague brightness, the residual smoke venting through airholes that disappeared at the corners of the room into the rock above.

The Valemen looked about expectantly. There was no one there.

Damson did not seem surprised. She led them into a room,

dominated by a trestle table and eight highback chairs of carved oak, and motioned for them to sit. There were animals occupying all the chairs, and the Valemen looked inquiringly at the girl.

"Choose your place, pick up the animal that's seated there, and hold it," she advised and proceeded to show them what she meant. She selected a chair with a worn, stuffed velvet rabbit resting on it, lifted the tattered creature, and placed it comfortably on her lap as she sat down.

Coll did the same, his face empty as he fixed his gaze on a spot on the far wall, as if convinced that what was happening was no stranger than what he had expected. Par hesitated, then sat down as well, his companion something that might have been either a cat or a dog—it was impossible to tell which. He felt slightly ridiculous.

They sat there then and waited, not speaking, barely looking at each other. Damson began stroking the worn fur backing on her rabbit. Coll was a statue. Par's patience began to slip as the minutes passed and nothing happened.

Then one after another, the lights went out. Par started to his feet, but Damson said quickly, "Sit still."

All of the lights but one disappeared. The one that remained was at the opening of the first room they had entered. Its glow was distant and barely reached to where they sat. Par waited for his eyes to adjust to the near darkness; when they did, he found himself staring at a roundish, bearded face that had popped up across from him two seats down from Damson. Blank, dilated ferret eyes peered at him, shifted to find Coll, blinked, and stared some more.

"Good evening to you, Mole," Damson Rhee said.

The Mole lifted his head a shade; his neck and shoulders came into view, and his hands and arms lifted onto the table. He was covered with hair, a dark, furry coat. It grew on every patch of skin showing, save for where his nose and cheeks and a swatch of forehead glimmered like ivory in the faint light. His rounded head swiveled slowly, and his child's fingers locked together in a pose of contentment.

"Good evening to you, lovely Damson," he said.

He spoke in a child's voice, but it sounded queer somehow,

as if he were speaking from out of a barrel or through a screen of water. His eyes moved from Par to Coll, from Coll to Par.

"I heard you coming and put on the lights for you," he said. "But I don't much like the lights, so now that you are here, I have put them out again. Is that all right?"

Damson nodded. "Perfectly."

"Whom have you brought with you on your visit?"

"Valemen."

"Valemen?"

"Brothers, from a village south of here, a long way away. Par Ohmsford. Coll Ohmsford."

She pointed to each and the eyes shifted. "Welcome to my home. Shall we have tea?"

He disappeared without waiting for an answer, moving so quietly that, try as he might, even in the almost utter silence, Par could not hear him. He could smell the tea as it was brought, yet failed to see it materialize until the cups were placed before him. There were two of them, one regular size and one quite tiny. They were old, and the paint that decorated them was faded and worn.

Par watched doubtfully while Damson offered a sip from the smaller cup to the toy rabbit she held. "Are all the children fine?" she asked conversationally.

"Quite well," the Mole replied, seated again now where he had first appeared. He was holding a large bear, to whom he offered his own cup. Coll and Par followed the ritual without speaking. "Chalt, you know, has been bad again, sneaking his tea and cookies when he wishes, disrupting things rather thoroughly. When I go up to hear the news through the street grates and wall passages, he seems to believe he has license to reorganize things to his own satisfaction. Very annoying." He gave the bear a cross look. "Lida had a very bad fever, but is recovered now. And Westra cut her paw."

Par glanced at Coll, and this time his brother glanced back.

"Anyone new to the family?" Damson asked.

"Everlind," the Mole said. He stared at her for a moment, then pointed to the rabbit she was holding. "She came to live with us just two nights ago. She likes it much better here than on the streets."

Par hardly knew what to think. The Mole apparently collected junk discarded by the people of the city above and brought it down into his lair like a pack rat. To him, the animals were real—or at least that was the game he played. Par wondered uneasily if he knew the difference.

The Mole was looking at him. "The city whispers of something that has upset the Federation—disruptions, intruders, a threat to its rule. The street patrols are increased and the gate watches challenge everyone. There is a tightening of the chains." He paused, then turned to Damson. He said, almost eagerly, "It is better to be here, lovely Damson—here, underground."

Damson put down her cup. "The disruption is part of the reason we have come, Mole."

The Mole didn't seem to hear. "Yes, better to be underground, safe within the earth, beneath the streets and the towers, where the Federation never comes."

Damson shook her head firmly. "We are not here for sanctuary."

The Mole blinked, disappointment registering in his eyes. He set his own cup aside and the animal he held with it, and he cocked his rounded head. "I found Everlind at the back of the home of a man who provides counting services for the Federation tax collectors. He is quick with numbers and tallies far more accurately than others of his skill. Once, he was an advisor to the people of the city, but the people couldn't pay him as well as the Federation, so he took his services there. All day long, he works in the building where the taxes are held, then goes home to his family, his wife and his daughter, to whom Everlind once belonged. Last week, the man bought his daughter a new toy kitten, silky white fur and green button eyes. He bought it with money the Federation gave him from what they had collected. So his daughter discarded Everlind. She found the new kitten far prettier to look upon."

He looked at them. "Neither the father nor the daughter understands what they have given up. Each sees only what is on the surface and nothing of what lies beneath. That is the danger of living above ground."

"It is," Damson agreed softly. "But that is something we must change, those of us who wish to continue to live there."

The Mole rubbed his hands again, looking down at them as he did so, lost in some contemplation of his own. The room was a still life in which the Mole and his visitors sat among the discards and rejects of other lives and listened to what might have been the whisper of their own.

The Mole looked up again, his eyes fixing on Damson. "Beautiful Damson, what is it that you wish?"

Damson's willowy form straightened, and she brushed back the stray locks of her fiery hair. "There were once tunnels beneath the palace of the Kings of Tyrsis. If they are still there, we need to go into them."

The Mole stiffened. "Beneath the palace?"

"Beneath the palace and into the Pit."

There was a long silence as the Mole stared at her unblinking. Almost unconsciously, his hands went out to retrieve the animal he had been holding. He patted it gently. "There are things out of darkest night and mind in the Pit," he said softly.

"Shadowen," Damson said.

"Shadowen? Yes, that name suits them. Shadowen."

"Have you seen them, Mole?"

"I have seen everything that lives in the city. I am the earth's own eyes."

"Are there tunnels that lead into the Pit? Can you take us through them?"

The Mole's face lost all expression, then pulled away from the table's edge and dropped back into shadow. For an instant, Par thought he was gone. But he was merely hiding, returned to the comfort of the dark to consider what he was being asked. The toy animal went with him, and the girl and the Valemen were left alone as surely as if the little fellow had truly disappeared. They waited patiently, not speaking.

"Tell them how we met," the Mole spoke suddenly from his concealment. "Tell them how it was."

Damson turned obediently to the Valemen. "I was walking in one of the parks at night, just as the dusk was ending, the stars brightening in the sky. It was summer, the air warm and filled with the smell of flowers and new grass. I rested on a bench for a moment, and Mole appeared beside me. He had seen me perform my magic on the streets, hidden somewhere beneath them as he watched, and he asked me if I would do a trick especially for him. I did several. He asked me to come back the next night, and I did. I came back each night for a week, and then he took me underground and showed me his home and his family. We became friends."

"Good friends, lovely Damson. The best of friends." The Mole's face slipped back into view, easing from the shadows. The eyes were solemn. "I cannot refuse anything you ask of me. But I wish you would not ask this."

"It is important, Mole."

"You are more important," the Mole replied shyly. "I am afraid for you."

She reached over slowly and touched the back of his hand. "It will be all right."

The Mole waited until she took her hand away, then quickly tucked his own under the table. He spoke reluctantly. "There are tunnels all through the rock beneath the palace of the Kings of Tyrsis. They connect with cellars and dungeons that lie forgotten. Some, one or two perhaps, open into the Pit."

Damson nodded. "We need you to take us there."

The Mole shivered. "Dark things—Shadowen—will be there. What if they find us? What will we do?"

Damson's eyes locked on Par. "This Valeman has use of magic as well, Mole. But it is not magic like mine that plays tricks and entertains, it is real magic. He is not afraid of the Shadowen. He will protect us."

Par felt his stomach tighten at the words—words that made promises he knew deep down inside he might not be able to keep.

The Mole was studying him once more. His dark eyes blinked. "Very well. Tomorrow I will go into the tunnels and make certain they can still be traversed. Come back when it is night again, and if the way is open I will take you."

"Thank you, Mole," Damson said.

"Finish your tea," the Mole said quietly, not looking at her.

They sat in silence in the company of the toy animals and did so.

IT WAS STILL raining when they left the maze of underground tunnels and sewer channels and slipped back through the empty streets of the city. Damson led the way, surefooted in the mist and damp, a cat that didn't mind the wet. She returned the Valemen to the storage shed behind the gardening shop and left them there to get some sleep. She said she would return for them after midday. There were things that she needed to do first.

But Par and Coll didn't sleep. They kept watch instead, sitting at the windows and looking out into a curtain of fog that was filled with the movement of things that weren't there and thick with the reflected light of the coming day. It was almost morning by then, and the sky was brightening in the east. It was cold in the shed, and the brothers huddled in blankets and tried to put aside their discomfort and the disquieting thought of what lay ahead.

For a long time neither of them spoke. Finally Par, his impatience used up, said to his brother, "What are you thinking about?"

Coll took a moment to consider, then simply shook his head.

"Are you thinking about the Mole?"

Coll sighed. "Some." He hunched himself within his blanket. "I should be worried about placing my life in the hands of a fellow who lives underground with the relics of other people's lives for possessions and toy animals for companions, but I'm not. I don't really know why that is. I guess it is because he doesn't seem any stranger than anyone else connected with what's happened since we left Varfleet. Certainly, he doesn't seem any crazier."

Par didn't respond to that. There wasn't anything he could say that hadn't already been said. He knew his brother's feelings. He pulled his own blanket tight and let his eyes close against the movement of the fog. He wished the waiting was over and that it was time to get started. He hated the waiting.

"Why don't you go to sleep?" he heard Coll say.

"I can't," he replied. His eyes slipped open again. "Why don't you?"

Coll shrugged. The movement seemed an effort. Coll was

lost within himself, struggling to maintain direction while mired in a steadily tightening morass of circumstances and events from which he knew he should extricate himself but could not.

"Coll, why don't you let me do this alone," Par said suddenly, impulsively. His brother looked over. "I know we've already had this discussion; don't bother reminding me. But why don't you? There isn't any reason for you to go. I know what you think about what I'm doing. Maybe you're right. So stay here and wait for me."

"No."

"But why not? I can look out for myself."

Coll stared. "As a matter of fact, you can't," he said quietly. His rough features crinkled with disbelief. "I think that might be the most ridiculous thing I've ever heard you say."

Par flushed angrily. "Just because . . ."

"There hasn't been a single moment during this entire expedition or trek or whatever you want to call it that you haven't needed help from someone." The dark eyes narrowed. "Don't misunderstand me. I'm not saying you were the only one. We've all needed help, needed each other—even Padishar Creel. That's the way life works." One strong hand lifted and a finger jabbed Par roughly. "The thing is, everyone but you realizes and accepts it. But you keep trying to do everything on your own, trying to be the one who knows best, who has all the answers, recognizes all the options, and has some special insight the rest of us lack that allows you to decide what's best. You blind yourself to the truth. Do you know what, Par? The Mole, with his family of toy animals and his underground hideout—you're just like him. You're exactly the same. You create your own reality—it doesn't matter what the truth is or what anyone else thinks."

He slipped his hand back into his blanket and pulled the covering tight again. "That's why I'm going. Because you need me to go. You need me to tell you the difference between the toy animals and the real ones."

He turned away again, directing his gaze back out the rain-streaked window to where the night's fading shadows continued to play games in the mist.

Par's mouth tightened. His brother's face was infuriatingly calm. "I know the difference, Coll!" he snapped.

Coll shook his head. "No you don't. It's all the same to you. You decide whatever you want to decide and that's the end of the matter. That's the way it was with Allanon's ghost. That's the way it was with the charge he gave you to find the Sword of Shannara. That's the way it is now. Toy animals or real ones, the fact of what they are doesn't matter. What matters is how you perceive it."

"That's not true!" Par was incensed.

"Isn't it? Then tell me this. What happens tomorrow if you're mistaken? About anything. What if the Sword of Shannara isn't there? What if the Shadowen are waiting for us? What if the wishsong doesn't work the way you think it will? Tell me, Par. What if you're just plain wrong?"

Par gripped the edges of his blanket until his knuckles were white.

"What happens if the toy animals turn out to be real ones? What do you plan to do then?" He waited a moment, then said, "That's why I'm going, too."

"If it turns out that I'm wrong, what difference will it make if you do go?" Par shouted furiously.

Coll didn't respond right away. Then slowly he looked over once again. He gave Par a small, ironic smile. "Don't you know?"

He turned away again. Par bit his lip in frustration. The rain picked up momentarily, the drops beating on the shed's wooden roof with fresh determination. Par felt suddenly small and frightened, knowing that his brother was right, that he was being foolish and impulsive, that his insistence in going back into the Pit was risking all their lives, but knowing too that it didn't make any difference; he must go. Coll was right about that as well; the decision had been made and he would not change it. He remained rigid and upright next to his brother, refusing to give way to his fears, but within he curled tight and tried to hide from the faces they showed him.

Then Coll said quietly, "I love you, Par. And I suppose when you get right down to it, that's why I'm going most of all."

Par let the words hang in the silence that followed, unwilling to disturb them. He felt himself uncurl and straighten, and a flush of warmth spread through him. When he tried to speak, he could not. He let his breath out in a long, slow, inaudible sigh.

"I need you with me, Coll," he managed finally. "I really do."

Coll nodded. Neither of them said anything after that.

CHAPTER

28

WALKER BOH RETURNED to Hearthstone following his confrontation with the Grimpond and for the better part of a week did nothing more than consider what he had been told. The weather was pleasant, the days warm and sunny, the air filled with fragrant smells from the woodland trees and flowers and streams. He felt sheltered by the valley; he was content to remain in seclusion there. Rumor provided all the company he required. The big moor cat trailed after him on the long walks he took to while away his days, padding silently down the solitary trails, along the moss-covered stream banks, through the ancient massive trees, a soundless and reassuring presence. At night, the two sat upon the cottage porch, the cat dozing, the man staring skyward at the canopy of moon and stars.

He was always thinking. He could not stop thinking. The memory of the Grimpond's words haunted him even at Hearthstone, at his home, where nothing should have been able to threaten him. The words played unpleasant games within his mind, forcing him to confront them, to try to reason through how much of what they whispered was truth and how much a lie. He had known it would be like this before he had gone to see the Grimpond—that the words would be vague and distressing and that they would speak riddles and half-truths and leave him with a tangled knot of threads leading to the answers he sought, a knot that only a clairvoyant could manage to sort out.

He had known and still he was not prepared for how taxing it would be.

He was able to determine the location of the Black Elfstone almost immediately. There was only one place where eyes could turn a man to stone and voices drive him mad, one place where the dead lay in utter blackness—the Hall of Kings, deep in the Dragon's Teeth. It was said that the Hall of Kings had been fashioned even before the time of the Druids, a vast and impenetrable cavern labyrinth in which the dead monarchs of the Four Lands were interred, a massive crypt in which the living were not permitted, protected by darkness, by statues called Sphinxes that were half-man, half-beast and could turn the living to stone, and by formless beings called Banshees who occupied a section of the caverns called the Corridor of Winds and whose wail could drive men mad instantly.

And the Tomb itself, where the pocket carved with runes hid the Black Elfstone, was watched over by the serpent Valg.

At least it was if the serpent was still alive. There had been a terrible battle fought between the serpent and the company under Allanon's leadership, who had gone in search of the Sword of Shannara in the time of Shea Ohmsford. The company had encountered the serpent unexpectedly and been forced to battle its way clear. But no one had ever determined if the serpent had survived that battle. As far as Walker knew, no one had ever gone back to see.

Allanon might have returned once upon a time, of course. But Allanon had never said.

The difficulty in any event was not in determining the mystery of the Elfstone's whereabouts, but in deciding whether or not to go after it. The Hall of Kings was a dangerous place, even for someone like Walker who had less to fear than ordinary men. Magic, even the magic of a Druid, might not be protection enough—and Walker's magic was far less than Allanon's had ever been. Walker was concerned as well with what the Grimpond hadn't told him. There was certain to be more to this than what had been revealed; the Grimpond never gave out everything it knew. It was holding something back, and that was probably something that could kill Walker.

There was also the matter of the visions. There had been three of them, each more disturbing than the one before. In the first, Walker had stood on clouds above the others in the little company who had come to the Hadeshorn and the shade of Allanon, one hand missing, mocked by his own claim that he would lose that hand before he would allow the Druids to come again. In the second, he had pushed to her death a woman with silver hair, a magical creature of extraordinary beauty. In the third, Allanon had held him fast while death reached to claim him.

There was some measure of truth in each of these visions, Walker knew—enough truth so that he must pay heed to them and not simply dismiss them as the Grimpond's tauntings. The visions meant something; the Grimpond had left it to him to try to figure out what.

So Walker Boh debated. But the days passed and still the answers he needed would not come. All that was certain was the location of the Black Elfstone—and its claim upon the Dark Uncle grew stronger, a lure that drew him like a moth to flame, though the moth understood the promise of death that waited and flew to it nevertheless.

And fly to it Walker did as well in the end. Despite his resolve to wait until he had puzzled out the Grimpond's riddles, his hunger to reclaim the missing Elfstone finally overcame him. He had thought the conversation through until he was sick of repeating it in his mind. He became convinced that he had learned all from it that he was going to learn. There was no other course of action left to him but to go in search of the Black Elfstone and to discover by doing what he could discover in no other way. It would be dangerous; but he had survived dangerous situations before. He resolved not to be afraid, only to be careful.

He left the valley at the close of the week, departing with the sunrise, traveling afoot, wearing a long forest cloak for protection against the weather and carrying only a rucksack full of provisions. Most of what he would need he would find on the way. He walked west into Darklin Reach and did not look back until Hearthstone was lost from view. Rumor remained behind. It was difficult to leave the big cat; Walker would have felt better having him along. Few things living would challenge a full-grown moor cat. But it would be dangerous for Rumor as well outside the protective confines of the Eastland, where he could not conceal himself as easily and where his natural protection would be stripped from him. Besides, this was Walker's quest and his alone.

The irony of his choosing to make the quest at all did not escape him. He was the one who had vowed never to have anything to do with the Druids and their machinations. He had gone grudgingly with Par on his journey to the Hadeshorn. He had left the meeting with the shade of Allanon convinced that the Druid was playing games with the Ohmsfords, using them to serve his own hidden purposes. He had practically thrown Cogline from his own home, insisting that the other's efforts to teach the secrets of the magic had retarded his growth rather than enhanced it. He had threatened to take the Druid History that the old man had brought him and throw it into the deepest bog.

But then he had read about the Black Elfstone, and somehow everything had changed. He still wasn't sure why. His curiosity was partly to blame, his insatiable need to know. Was there such a thing as the Black Elfstone? Could it bring back disappeared Paranor as the history promised? Questions to be answered—he could never resist the lure of their secrets. Such secrets had to be solved, their mysteries revealed. There was knowledge waiting to be discovered. It was the purpose to which he had dedicated his life.

He wanted to believe that his sense of fairness and compassion made him go as well. Despite what he believed about the Druids, there might be something in Paranor itself—if, indeed, the Druid's Keep could be brought back—that would help the Four Lands against the Shadowen. He was uneasy with the possibility that in not going he was condemning the Races to a future like that which the Druid shade had described.

He promised himself as he departed that he would do no more than he must and certainly no more than he believed reasonable. He would remain, first and always, his own master rather than the plaything that Allanon's shade would have him be.

The days were still and sultry, the summer's heat building as he traversed the forest wilderness. Clouds were massed in the west, somewhere below the Dragon's Teeth. There would be storms waiting in the mountains.

He passed along the Chard Rush, then climbed into the Wolfsktaag and out again. It took him three days of easy travel to reach Storlock. There he reprovisioned with the help of the Stors and on the morning of the fourth day set out to cross the Rabb Plains. The storms had reached him by then, and rain began to fall in a slow, steady drizzle that turned the landscape gray. Patrols of Federation soldiers on horseback and caravans of traders appeared and faded like wraiths without seeing him. Thunder rumbled in the distance, muted and sluggish in the oppressive heat, a growl of dissatisfaction echoing across the emptiness.

Walker camped that night on the Rabb Plains, taking shelter in a cottonwood grove. There was no dry wood for a fire and Walker was already drenched through, so he slept wrapped in his cloak, shivering with the damp and cold.

Morning brought a lessening of the rains, the clouds thinning and letting the sun's brightness shine through in a screen of gray light. Walker roused himself stoically, ate a cold meal of fruit and cheese, and struck out once more. The Dragon's Teeth rose up before him, sullen and dark. He reached the pass that led upward into the Valley of Shale and the Hadeshorn and, beyond, the Hall of Kings.

That was as far as he went that day. He made camp beneath an outcropping of rock where the earth was still dry. He found wood, built a fire, dried his clothes, and warmed himself. He would be ready now when tomorrow came and it was time to enter the caverns. He ate a hot meal and watched the darkness descend in a black pall of clouds, mist, and night across the empty reaches about him. He thought for a time about his boyhood and wondered what he might have done to make it different. It began to rain again, and the world beyond his small fire disappeared.

He slept well. There were no dreams, no nervous awakenings. When he woke, he felt rested and prepared to face whatever fate awaited him. He was confident, though not carelessly so. The rain had stopped again. He listened for a time to the sounds of the morning waking around him, searching for hidden warnings. There were none.

He wrapped himself in his forest cloak, shouldered his ruck-sack, and started up.

The morning slipped away as he climbed. He was more cautious now, his eyes searching across the barren rock, defiles, and crevices for movement that meant danger, his ears sorting through the small noises and scrapes for those that truly menaced. He moved quietly, deliberately, studying the landscape ahead before proceeding into it, choosing his path with care. The mountains about him were vast, empty, and still—sleeping giants rooted so utterly by time to the earth beneath that even if they somehow managed to wake they would find they could no longer move.

He passed into the Valley of Shale. Black rock glistened damply within its bowl, and the waters of the Hadeshorn stirred like a thick, greenish soup. He circled it warily and left it behind.

Beyond, the slope steepened and the climb grew more difficult. The wind began to pick up, blowing the mist away until the air was sharp and clear and there was only the gray ceiling of the clouds between Walker and the earth. The temperature dropped, slowly at first, then rapidly until it was below freezing. Ice began to appear on the rock, and snow flurries swirled past his face in small gusts. He wrapped his cloak about him more tightly and pressed on.

His progress slowed then, and for a very long time it seemed to Walker as if he were not moving at all. The pathway was uneven and littered with loose stone, twisting and winding its way through the larger rocks. The wind blew into him remorselessly, biting at his face and hands, buffeting him so that it threatened to knock him backward. The mountainside remained unchanging, and it was impossible to tell at any given point how far he had come. He quit trying to hear or see anything beyond what lay immediately in front of him and limited his concentration to putting one foot in front of the other, drawing into himself as far as he could to block away the cold.

He found himself thinking of the Black Elfstone, of how it would look and feel, of what form its magic might take. He played with the vision in the silence of his mind, shutting out the world he traveled through and the discomfort he was feeling. He held the image before him like a beacon and used it to brighten the way.

It was noon when he entered a canyon, a broad split between the massive peaks with their canopy of clouds that opened into a valley and beyond the valley into a narrow, twisting passageway that disappeared into the rock. Walker traversed the canyon floor to the defile and started in. The wind died away to a whisper, an echo that breathed softly in the suddenly enfolding stillness. Moisture trapped by the peaks collected in pools. Walker felt the chill lose its bite. He came out of himself again, newly alert, tense as he searched the dark rifts and corners of the corridor he followed.

Then the walls fell away and his journey was finished.

The entrance to the Hall of Kings stood before him, carved into the wall of the mountain, a towering black maw, bracketed by huge stone sentries fashioned in the shape of armor-clad warriors, the blades of their swords jammed downward into the earth. The sentries faced out from the cavern mouth, faces scarred by wind and time, eyes fastened on Walker as if they might somehow really see.

Walker slowed, then stopped. The way forward was wrapped in darkness and silence. The wind, its echo still ringing in his ears, had faded away completely. The mist was gone. Even the cold had mutated into a sort of numbing, empty chill.

What Walker felt at that moment was unmistakable. The feeling wrapped about him like a second skin, permeated his body, and reached down into his bones. It was the feeling of death.

He listened to the silence. He searched the blackness. He waited. He let his mind reach out into the world. He could discover nothing.

The minutes faded away.

Finally Walker Boh straightened purposefully, hitched up the rucksack, and started forward once again.

IT WAS MIDAFTERNOON in the Westland where the Tirfing stretched from the sun-baked banks of the Mermidon south along the broad, empty stretches of the Shroudslip. The summer had been a dry one, and the grasses were withered from the heat, even where there had been a measure of shade to protect them. Where there had been no shade at all, the land was burned bare.

Wren Ohmsford sat with her back against the trunk of a spreading oak, close to where the horses nosed into a muddy pool of water, and watched the sun's fire turn red against the west sky, edging toward the horizon and the day's close. The glare blinded her to anything approaching from that direction, and she shaded her eyes watchfully. It was one thing to be caught napping by Garth; it was something else again to let her guard down against whoever it was that was tracking them.

She pursed her lips thoughtfully. It had been more than two days now since they had first discovered they were being followed—sensed it, really, since their shadow had remained carefully hidden from them. He or she or it—they still didn't know. Garth had backtracked that morning to find out, stripping off his brightly colored clothing and donning mud-streaked plains garb, shading his face, hands, and hair, disappearing into the heat like a wraith.

Whoever was tracking them was in for an unpleasant surprise.

Still, it was nearing day's end and the giant Rover hadn't returned. Their shadow might be more clever than they imagined.

"What does it want?" she mused.

She had asked Garth the same question that morning, and he had drawn his finger slowly across his throat. She tried to argue against it, but she lacked the necessary conviction. It could be an assassin following them as easily as anyone else.

Her gaze wandered to the expanse of the plains east. It was disturbing enough to be tracked like this. It was even more disturbing to realize that it probably had something to do with her inquiries about the Elves.

She sighed fitfully, vaguely irritated with the way things were working out. She had come back from her meeting with the shade of Allanon in an unsettled state, dissatisfied with what she had heard, uncertain as to what she should do. Common sense

told her that what the shade had asked of her was impossible.
But something inside, that sixth sense she relied upon so heavily,
whispered that maybe it wasn't, that Druids had always known
more than humans, that their warnings and chargings to the
people of the Races had always had merit. Par believed. He was
probably already in search of the missing Sword of Shannara.
And while Walker had departed from them in a rage, vowing
never to have anything to do with the Druids, his anger had
been momentary. He was too rational, too controlled to dismiss
the matter so easily. Like her, he would be having second
thoughts.

She shook her head ruefully. She had believed her own decision irrevocable for a time. She had persuaded herself that
common sense must necessarily govern her course of action, and
she had returned with Garth to her people, putting the business
of Allanon and the missing Elves behind her. But the doubts had
persisted, a nagging sense of something being not quite right
about her determination to drop the matter. So, almost reluctantly, she had begun to ask questions about the Elves. It was
easy enough to do; the Rovers were a migrating people and
traveled the Westland from end to end during the course of a
year's time, trading for what they needed, bartering with what
they had. Villages and communities came and went, and there
were always new people to talk to. What harm could it do them
to inquire about the Elves?

Sometimes she had asked her questions directly, sometimes
almost jokingly. But the answers she had received were all the
same. The Elves were gone, had been since before anyone could
remember, since before the time of their grandfathers and grand-
mothers. No one had ever seen an Elf. Most weren't sure there
had ever really been any to see.

Wren had begun to feel foolish even asking, had begun to
consider giving up asking at all. She broke away from her people
to hunt with Garth, anxious to be alone to think, hoping to gain
some insight into the dilemma through solitary consideration of it.

And then their shadow had appeared, stalking them. Now
she was wondering if there wasn't something to be found out
after all.

She saw movement out of the corner of her eye, a vague blur in the swelter of the plains, and she came cautiously to her feet. She stood without moving in the shadow of the oak as the shape took form and became Garth. The giant Rover trotted up to her, sweat coating his heavily muscled frame. He seemed barely winded, a tireless machine that even the intense midsummer heat could not affect. He signed briefly, shaking his head. Whoever was out there had eluded him.

Wren held his gaze a moment, then reached down to hand him the waterskin. As he drank, she draped her lanky frame against the roughened bark of the oak and stared out into the empty plains. One hand came up in an unconscious movement to touch the small leather bag about her neck. She rolled the contents thoughtfully between her fingers. Make-believe Elf-stones. Her good luck charm. What sort of luck were they providing her now?

She brushed aside her uneasiness, her sun-browned face a mask of determination. It didn't matter. Enough was enough. She didn't like being followed, and she was going to put an end to it. They would change the direction of their travel, disguise their trail, backtrack once or twice, ride all night if need be, and lose their shadow once and for all.

She took her hand away from the bag and her eyes were fierce.

Sometimes you had to make your own luck.

WALKER BOH ENTERED the Hall of Kings on cat's feet, passing noiselessly between the massive stone sentinels, stepping through the cavern mouth into the blackness beyond. He paused there, letting his eyes adjust. There was light, a faint greenish phosphorescence given off by the rock. He would not need to light a torch to find the way.

A picture of the caverns flashed momentarily in his mind, a reconstruction of what he expected to find. Cogline had drawn it for him on paper once, long ago. The old man had never been into the caverns himself, but others of the Druids had, Allanon among them, and Cogline had studied the maps that they had devised and revealed their secrets to his pupil. Walker felt confident that he could find the way.

He started ahead.

The passageway was broad and level, its walls and floors free from sharp projections and crevices. The near-dark was wrapped in silence, deep and hushed, and there was only the faint echo of his boots as he walked. The air was bone-chilling, a cold that had settled into the mountain rock over the centuries and could not be dislodged. It seeped into Walker despite his clothing and made him shiver. A prickling of unpleasant feelings crept through him—loneliness, insignificance, futility. The caverns dwarfed him; they reduced him to nothing, a tiny creature whose very presence in such an ancient, forbidden place was an affront. He fought back against the feelings, recognizing what they would do to him, and after a brief struggle they faded back into the cold and the silence.

He reached the cave of the Sphinxes shortly after. He paused again, this time to steady his mind, to take himself deep down inside where the stone spirits couldn't reach him. When he was there, wrapped in whispers of caution and warning, blanketed in words of power, he went forward. He kept his eyes fixed on the dusty floor, watching the stone pass away, looking only at the next few feet he must cover.

In his mind, he saw the Sphinxes looming over him, massive stone monoliths fashioned by the same hands that had made the sentinels. The Sphinxes were said to have human faces carved on the bodies of beasts—creatures of another age that no living man had ever seen. They were old, so incredibly ancient that their lives could be measured by hundreds of generations of mortal men. So many monarchs had passed beneath their gaze, carried from life to endless rest within their mountain tombs. So many, never to return.

Look at us, they whispered! *See how wondrous we are!*

He could sense their eyes on him, hear the whisper of their voices in his mind, feel them tearing and ripping at the layers of protection he had fashioned for himself, begging him to look up. He moved more quickly now, fighting to banish the whispers, resisting the urge to obey them. The stone monsters seemed to howl at him, harsh and insistent.

Walker Boh! Look at us! You must!

He struggled forward, his mind swarming with their voices, his resolve crumbling. Sweat beaded on his face despite the cold, and his muscles knotted until they hurt. He gritted his teeth against his weakness, chiding himself, thinking suddenly of Allanon in a bitter, desperate reminder that the Druid had come this way before him with seven men under his protection and had not given in.

In the end, neither did he. Just as he thought he would, that he must, he reached the far end of the cavern and stepped into the passageway beyond. The whispers faded and were gone. The Sphinxes were left behind. He looked up again, carefully resisted the urge to glance back, then moved ahead once more.

The passageway narrowed and began to wind downward. Walker slowed, uncertain as to what might lurk around the darkened corners. The greenish light could be found only in small patches here, and the corridor was thick with shadows. He dropped into a crouch, certain that something waited to attack him, feeling its presence grow nearer with every step he took. He considered momentarily using his magic to light the passageway so that he might better see what hid from him, but he quickly discarded the idea. If he invoked the magic, he would alert whatever might be there that he possessed special powers. Better to keep the magic secret, he thought. It was a weapon that would serve him best if its use was unexpected.

Yet nothing appeared. He shrugged his uneasiness aside and pressed on until the passageway straightened and began to widen out again.

Then the sound began.

He knew it was coming, that it would strike all at once, and still he was not prepared when it came. It lashed out at him, wrapping about with the strength of iron chains, dragging him ahead. It was the scream of winds through a canyon, the howl and rip of storms across a plain, the pounding of seas against shoreline cliffs. And beneath, just under the skin of it, was the horrifying shriek of souls in unimaginable pain, scraping their bones against the rock of the cavern walls.

Frantically, Walker Boh brought his defenses to bear. He was in the Corridor of Winds, and the Banshees were upon him.

He blocked everything away in an instant, closing off the terrifying sound with a strength of will that rocked him, focusing
his thoughts on a single picture within his mind—an image of
himself. He constructed the image with lines and shadings, coloring in the gaps, giving himself life and strength and determination. He began to walk forward. He muffled the sound of the
Banshees until they were no more than a strange buzzing that
whipped and tore about him, trying to break through. He
watched the Corridor of Winds pass away about him, a bleak
and empty cavern in which everything was invisible but the
wailing, a whirl of color that flashed like maddened lightning
through the black.

Nothing Walker did would lessen it. The shrieks and howls
hammered into him, buffeting his body as if they were living
things. He could feel his strength ebbing as it had before the
onslaught of the Sphinxes, his defenses giving way. The fury of
the attack was frightening. He fought back against it, a hint of
desperation creeping through him as he watched the image he
had drawn of himself begin to shimmer and disappear. He was
losing control. In another minute, maybe two, his protection
would crumble completely.

And then, once again, he broke clear just when it seemed
he must give way. He stumbled from the Corridor of Winds
into a small cave that lay beyond. The screams of the Banshees
vanished. Walker collapsed against the closest wall, sliding down
the smooth rock into a sitting position, his entire body shaking.
He breathed in and out slowly, steadily, coming back to himself
in bits and pieces. Time slowed, and for a moment he allowed
his eyes to close.

When he opened them again, he was looking at a pair of
massive stone doors fastened to the rock by iron hinges. Runes
were carved into the doors, the ancient markings as red as fire.

He had reached the Assembly, the Tomb where the Kings
of the Four Lands were interred.

He climbed to his feet, hitched up the rucksack, and walked
to the doors. He studied the markings a moment, then placed
one hand carefully upon them and shoved. The door swung
open and Walker Boh stepped through.

He stood in a giant, circular cavern streaked by greenish

light and shadow. Sealed vaults lined the walls, the dead within closed away by mortar and stone. Statues stood guarding their entombed rulers, solemn and ageless. Before each was piled the wealth of the master in casks and trunks—jewels, furs, weapons, treasures of all sorts. They were so covered with dust that they were barely recognizable. The walls of the chamber loomed upward until they disappeared, the ceiling an impenetrable canopy of black.

The chamber appeared empty of life.

At its far end, a second pair of doors stood closed. It was beyond that the serpent Valg had lived. The Pyre of the Dead was there, an altar on which the deceased rulers of the Four Lands lay in state for a requisite number of days before their interment. A set of stone stairs led down from the altar to a pool of water in which Valg hid. Supposedly, the serpent kept watch over the dead. Walker wouldn't have been surprised to learn that he just fed on them.

He listened for long moments for the sound of anything moving, anything breathing. He heard nothing. He studied the Tomb. The Black Elfstone was hidden here—not in the cavern beyond. If he were quick and if he were careful, he might avoid having to discover whether or not the serpent Valg was still alive.

He began moving slowly, noiselessly past the crypts of the dead, their statues and their wealth. He ignored the treasures; he knew from Cogline that they were coated with a poison instantly fatal to anyone who touched them. He picked his way forward, skirting each bastion of death, studying the rock walls and the rune markings that decorated them. He circled the chamber and found himself back where he had started.

Nothing.

His brow furrowed in thought. Where was the pocket that contained the Black Elfstone?

He studied the cavern a second time, letting his eyes drift through the haze of greenish light, skipping from one pocket of shadows to the next. He must have missed something. What was it?

He closed his eyes momentarily and let his thoughts reach out, searching the blackness. He could feel something, a very small presence that seemed to whisper his name. His eyes snapped open again. His lean, ghostlike face went taut. The presence was not in the wall; it was in the floor!

He began moving again, this time directly across the chamber, letting himself be guided by what he sensed was waiting there. It was the Black Elfstone, he concluded. An Elfstone would have life of its own, a presence that it could summon if called upon. He strode away from the statues and their treasures, away from the vaults, no longer even seeing them, his eyes fastening on a point almost at the center of the cavern.

When he reached that point, he found a rectangular slab of rock resting evenly on the floor. Runes were carved in its surface, markings so faded that he could not make them out. He hesitated, uneasy that the writing was so obscured. But if the runes were Elven script, they might be thousands of years old; he could not expect to be able to read them now.

He knelt down, a solitary figure in the center of the cavern, isolated even from the dead. He brushed at the stone markings and tried a moment longer to decipher them. Then, his patience exhausted, he gave up. Using both hands, he pushed at the stone. It gave easily, moving aside without a sound.

He felt a momentary rush of excitement.

The hole beneath was dark, so cloaked in shadow that he could make nothing out. Yet there was something . . .

Casting aside momentarily the caution that had served him so well, Walker Boh reached down into the opening.

Instantly, something wrapped about his hand, seizing him. There was a moment of excruciating pain and then numbness. He tried to jerk free, but he could not move. Panic flooded through him. He still could not see what was down there.

Desperate now, he used the magic, his free hand summoning light and sending it swiftly down into the hole.

What he saw caused him to go cold. There was no Elfstone. Instead, a snake was fastened to his hand, coiled tightly about it. But this was no ordinary snake. This was something far more deadly, and he recognized it instantly. It was an Asphinx, a creature out of the old legends, conceived at the same time as its massive counterparts in the caves without, the Sphinxes. But the Asphinx was a creature of flesh and blood until it struck. Only then did it turn to stone.

And whatever it struck turned to stone as well.

Walker's teeth clenched against what he saw happening. His hand was already turning gray, the Asphinx still wrapped firmly about it, dead now and hardened, cemented against the floor of the compartment in a tight spiral from which it could not be broken loose.

Walker Boh pulled violently against the creature's grasp. But there was no escape. He was embedded in stone, fastened to the Asphinx and the cavern floor as surely as if by chains.

Fear ripped through him, tearing at him as a knife edge might his flesh. He was poisoned. Just as his hand was turning to stone, so would the rest of him. Slowly. Inexorably.

Until he was a statue.

CHAPTER

29

DAWN AT THE JUT brought a change in the weather as the leading edge of the storm that was passing through Tyrsis drifted north into the Parma Key. It was still dark when the first cloud banks began to blanket the skies, blotting out the moon and stars and turning the whole of the night an impenetrable black. Then the wind died, its whisper fading away almost before anyone still awake in the outlaw camp noticed it was gone, and the air became still and sullen. A few drops fell, splashing on the upturned faces of the watch, spattering onto the dry, dusty rock of the bluff in widening stains. Everything grew hushed as the drops came quicker. Steam rose off the floor of the forestland below, lifting above the treetops to mix with the clouds until there was nothing left to see, even with the sharpest eyes. When dawn finally broke, it came as a line of brightness along the eastern horizon so faint that it went almost unnoticed. By then, the rain was falling steadily, a heavy drizzle that sent everyone scurrying for shelter, including the watch.

Which was why no one saw the Creeper.

It must have come out of the forest under cover of darkness and begun working its way up the cliffside when the clouds took away the only light that would have revealed its presence. There were sounds of scraping as it climbed, the rasp of its claws and armor-plating as it dragged itself upward, but the sounds were lost in the rumble of distant thunder, the splatter of the rain, and the movement of men and animals in the camps. Besides, the outlaws on watch were tired and irritable and convinced that nothing was going to happen before dawn.

The Creeper was almost on top of them before they realized their mistake and began to scream.

The cries brought Morgan Leah awake with a start. He had fallen asleep in the grove of aspen at the far end of the bluff, still mulling over what to do about his suspicions as to the identity of the traitor. He was curled in a ball under the canopy of the largest tree, his hunting cloak wrapped about him for warmth. His muscles were so sore and cramped that at first he could not bring himself to stand. But the cries grew quickly more frantic, filled with terror. Ignoring his own discomfort, he forced himself to his feet, pulled free the broadsword he had strapped to his back, and stumbled out into the rain.

The bluff was in pandemonium. Men were charging back and forth everywhere, weapons drawn, dark shadows in a world of grayness and damp. A few torches appeared, bright beacons against the black, but their flames were extinguished almost immediately by the downpour. Morgan hurried ahead, following the tide, searching the gloom for the source of the madness.

And then the saw it. The Creeper was atop the bluff, rearing out of the chasm, looming over the outlaw fortifications and the men who threatened it, its claws digging into the rock to hold it fast. A dead man dangled from one of its massive pinchers, cut nearly in half—one of the watch who had realized what was happening.

The outlaws surged forward recklessly, seizing poles and spears, jamming them into the Creeper's massive body, trying desperately to force the monster back over the edge. But the Creeper was huge; it towered above them like a wall. Morgan slowed in dismay. They might as well have been trying to turn a river from its course. Nothing that large could be dislodged by human strength alone.

The Creeper lunged forward, throwing itself into its attackers. Poles and spears snapped and splintered as it hurtled down. The men caught beneath died instantly, and several more were quickly snatched up by the pinchers. An entire section of the Jut's fortifications collapsed under the creature's weight. The outlaws fell back as it hunched its way into them, smashing weapons, stores, and campsites, catching up anything that moved. Blows from swords and knives rained down on its body, but the Creeper seemed unaffected. It advanced relentlessly, stalking the men who retreated from it, destroying everything in its path.

"Free-born!" the cry rang out suddenly. "To me!"

Padishar Creel materialized from out of nowhere, a bright scarlet figure in the rain and mist, rallying his men. They cried out in answer and rushed to stand beside him. He formed them quickly into squads; half counterattacked the Creeper with massive posts to fend off the pinchers while the balance hacked at the monster's sides and back. The Creeper writhed and twisted, but came on.

"Free-born, free-born!" The cries sounded from everywhere, lifting into the dawn, filling the grayness with their fury.

Then Axhind and his Rock Trolls appeared, their massive bodies armored head to foot, wielding their huge battleaxes. They attacked the Creeper head-on, striking for the pinchers. Three died almost instantly, torn apart so fast that they disappeared in a blur of limbs and blood. But the others cut and hacked with such determination that they shattered the left pincher, leaving it broken and useless. Moments later, they cut it off entirely.

The Creeper slowed. A trail of bodies littered the ground behind it. Morgan still stood between the monster and the caves, undecided as to what he should do and unable to understand why. It was as if he had become mired in quicksand. He saw the beast lift itself clear of the earth. Its head and pincher came up, and it hung suspended like a snake about to strike, braced on the back half of its body, prepared to throw itself on its attackers and smash them. The Trolls and the outlaws fell back in a rush, shouting to one another in warning.

Morgan looked for Padishar, but the outlaw chief had disappeared. The Highlander could not find him anywhere. For an instant, he thought Padishar must have fallen. Rain trickled down his face into his eyes, and he blinked it away impatiently. His hand tightened on the handle of his broadsword, but still he hung back.

The Creeper was inching forward, casting right and left to

protect against flanking attacks. A twitch of its tail sent several men flying. Spears and arrows flew into it and bounced away. Steadily it came on, forcing the defenders ever closer to the caves. Soon, there would be nowhere left for them to go.

Morgan Leah was shaking. *Do something!* his mind screamed.

In that same instant Padishar reappeared at the mouth of the largest of the Jut's caves, calling out to his men to fall back. Something huge lumbered into view behind him, creaking and rumbling as it came. Morgan squinted through the gloom and mist. Lines of men appeared, hauling on ropes, and the thing began to take shape. Morgan could see it now as it cleared the cavern entrance and crawled into the light.

It was a great, wooden crossbow.

Padishar had its handlers wheel it into position facing the Creeper. Atop its base, Chandos used a heavy winch to crank back the bowstring. A massive, sharpened bolt was fitted in place.

The Creeper hesitated, as if to measure the potential danger of this new weapon. Then, lowering itself slightly, it advanced, its remaining pincher clicking in anticipation.

Padishar ordered the first bolt fired when the creature was still fifty feet away. The shot flew wide. The Creeper picked up speed as Chandos hurriedly rewound the bowstring. The crossbow fired again, but the bolt glanced off a section of armor-plating and caromed away. The Creeper was knocked sideways, slowed momentarily by the force of the blow, and then it straightened itself and came on.

Morgan saw at once that there would be no time for a third shot. The Creeper was too close. Yet Chandos stayed atop the crossbow, desperately cranking back the bowstring a third time. The Creeper was only yards away. Outlaws and Trolls harassed it from all sides, axes and swords hammering against it, but it refused to be deterred. It recognized the crossbow as the only thing it really had to fear and moved swiftly to destroy it.

Chandos shoved the third bolt into place and reached for the trigger.

He was too late. The Creeper lunged and came down atop the crossbow, smashing into its works. Wood splintered, and the wheels supporting the weapon gave way. Chandos was thrown into the night. Men scattered everywhere, crying out. The Creeper shifted atop the wreckage, then lifted free. It drew itself up deliberately, sensing its victory, knowing it needed only one further lunge to finish the job.

But Padishar Creel was quicker. While the other outlaws fled, Chandos lay unconscious in the darkness, and Morgan struggled with his indecision, Padishar attacked. Little more than a scarlet blur in the mist and half-light of the rain-soaked dawn, the outlaw chief seized one of the crossbow bolts that had been spilled from its rack, darted beneath the Creeper, and braced the bolt upright against the earth. The Creeper never saw him, so intent was it on destroying the crossbow. The monster hammered down, smashing through the already crippled weapon onto the iron-tipped bolt. The force of its lunge sent the bolt through iron and flesh, in one side of its body and out the other.

Padishar barely managed to roll clear as the Creeper struck the earth.

Back the monster reared, shuddering with pain and surprise, transfixed on the bolt. It lost its balance and toppled over, writhing madly in an effort to dislodge the killing shaft. It crashed to the ground, belly up, coiling into a ball. "Free-born!" Padishar Creel cried out, and the outlaws and Trolls were upon it. Bits and pieces of the creature flew apart as swords and axes hacked. The second pincher was sheared off. Padishar shouted encouragement to his men, attacking with them, swinging his broadsword with every ounce of strength he possessed.

The battle was ferocious. Though badly injured, the Creeper was still dangerous. Men were pinned beneath it and crushed, sent flying as it thrashed, and ripped by its claws. All efforts to put an end to it were stymied until finally another of the scattered crossbow bolts was brought forward and rammed through the monster's eye and into its brain. The Creeper convulsed one last time and went still.

Morgan Leah watched it all as if from a great distance, too far removed from what was happening to be of any use. He was still shaking when it ended. He was bathed in sweat. He had not lifted a finger to help.

THERE WAS A CHANGE in the outlaw camp after that, a shift in attitude that reflected the growing belief that the Jut was no longer invulnerable. It was apparent almost immediately. Padishar slipped into the blackest of moods, railing at everyone, furious at the Federation for using a Creeper, at the dead monster for the damage it had inflicted, at the watch for not being more alert, and at himself especially for not being better prepared. His men went about their tasks grudgingly, a dispirited bunch that slogged through the rain and murk and mumbled darkly to themselves. If the Federation had sent one Creeper, they said, what was to prevent it from sending another? If another was sent, what would they do to stop this one? And what would they do if the Federation sent something worse?

Eighteen men died in the attack and twice that number were injured, some of whom would be dead before the day was out. Padishar had the casualties buried at the far end of the bluff and the injured moved into the largest cave, which was converted into a temporary hospital. There were medicines and some few men with experience in treating battle wounds to administer them, but the outlaws did not have the services of a genuine Healer. The cries of the injured and dying lingered in the early morning stillness.

The Creeper was dragged to the edge of the bluff and thrown over. It was a difficult, exhausting task, but Padishar would not tolerate the creature's presence on the bluff a second longer than was necessary. Ropes and pulleys were used, one end of the lines fastened to the monster's dead bulk, the other end passed through the hands of dozens of men who pulled and strained as the Creeper was hauled inch by inch through the wreckage of the camp. It took the outlaws all morning. Morgan worked with them, not speaking to anyone, trying hard to remain inconspicuous, still struggling to understand what had happened to him.

He figured it out finally. He was still immersed in the effort to drag the Creeper to the bluff edge, his body aching and weary, but his mind grown unexpectedly sharp. It was the Sword of Leah that was responsible, he realized—or more accurately, the magic it contained, or had once contained. It was the loss of the magic that had crippled him and had caused him to be so indecisive, so frightened. When he had discovered the magic of the Sword, he had thought himself invincible. The feeling of power was like nothing he had ever experienced or would have believed possible. With that sort of power at his command, he could do anything. He could still remember what it had felt like to stand virtually alone against the Shadowen in the Pit. Wondrous. Exhilarating.

But draining, as well. Each time he invoked the power, it seemed to take something away from him.

When he had broken the Sword of Leah and lost all use of the magic, he had begun to understand just how much it was that had been taken from him. He sensed the change in himself almost immediately. Padishar had insisted he was mistaken, had told him he would forget his loss, that he would heal, and that time would see him back to the way he had been. He knew now that it wasn't so. He would never heal—not completely. Having once used the magic, he was changed irrevocably. He couldn't give it up; he wasn't the same man without it. Though he had possessed it only briefly, the effect of having had it for even that long was permanent. He hungered to have it back again. He needed to have it back. He was lost without it; he was confused and afraid. That was the reason he had failed to act during the battle with the Creeper. It was not that he lacked a sense of what he should do or how he should do it. It was that he no longer could invoke the magic to aid him.

Admitting this cost him something he couldn't begin to define. He continued to work, a machine without feelings, numbed by the idea that loss of the magic could paralyze him so. He hid himself in his thoughts, in the rain and the gray, hoping that no one—especially Padishar Creel—had noticed his failure, agonizing over what he would do if it happened again.

After a time, he found himself thinking about Par. He had never considered before what it must be like for the Valeman to have to continually struggle with his own magic. Forced to confront what the magic of the Sword of Leah meant to him, Morgan thought he understood how difficult it must be for Par. How had his friend learned to live with the uncertainty of the wishsong's power? What did he feel when it failed him, as it had so many times on their journey to find Allanon? How had he managed to accept his weakness? It gave Morgan a measure of renewed strength to know that the Valeman had somehow found a way.

By midday, the Creeper was gone and the damage it had caused to the camp was mostly repaired. The rain ceased finally as the storms drifted east, scraping along the rim of the Dragon's Teeth. The clouds broke apart, and sunlight appeared through the breaks in long, narrow streamers that played across the dark green spread of the Parma Key. The mist burned off, and all that remained was a sheen of dampness that blanketed everything with a lustrous silver coating.

The Federation immediately hauled forward its catapults and siege towers and renewed its assault on the Jut. The catapults flung their stones and the siege towers were lined with archers who kept a steady fire on the outlaw camp. No effort was made to scale the heights; the attack was limited to a constant barrage against the bluff and its occupants, a barrage that lasted through the afternoon and went on into the night, a steady, constant, ceaseless harassment. There was nothing that the outlaws could do to stop it; their attackers were too far away and too well-protected. There was nowhere outside of the caves where it was safe to walk. It seemed clear that the loss of the Creeper hadn't discouraged the Federation. The siege would not be lifted. It would go on until the defenders were sufficiently weakened to be overcome by a frontal assault. If it were to take days or weeks or months, the end would be the same. The Federation army was content to wait.

On the heights, the defenders dodged and darted through the rain of missiles, yelled defiantly down at their attackers, and went about their work as best they could. But in the privacy of their shelters they grumbled and muttered their suspicions with renewed conviction. No matter what they had once believed, the Jut could not be held.

Morgan Leah was faced with worries of his own. The Highlander had deliberately gone off by himself and was secluded once more within the shelter of the aspen grove at the far end of the bluff, away from the major defensive positions of the camp where most of the Federation attack was being concentrated. Having managed to put aside for the moment the matter of his inability to accept losing the magic of the Sword of Leah, he was now forced to confront the equally troubling dilemma of his suspicions as to the identity of the traitor.

It was difficult to know what to do. Surely he should tell someone. He *had* to tell someone. But who?

Padishar Creel? If he told Padishar, the outlaw chief might or might not believe him, but in either case he was unlikely to leave the matter to chance. Padishar didn't care a fig for either Steff or Teel at this point; he would simply do away with them—both of them. After all, there was no way of knowing which one it was—or even if it was either. And Padishar was in no mood to wait around for the answer.

Morgan shook his head. He couldn't tell Padishar.

Steff? If he chose to do that, he was deciding, in effect, that Teel was the traitor. That was what he wanted to believe, but was that the truth of the matter? Even if it was, he knew what Steff's reaction would be. His friend was in love with Teel. Teel had saved his life. He would hardly be willing to accept what Morgan was telling him without some sort of proof to back it up. And Morgan didn't have any proof—at least, nothing you could hold in your hand and point to. Speculation was all he had, well-reasoned or not.

He eliminated Steff.

Someone else? There wasn't anyone else. He would have told Par or Coll if they were there, or Wren, or even Walker Boh. But the members of the Ohmsford family were scattered to the four winds, and he was alone. There was no one he could trust.

He sat within the trees and listened to the distant shouts and cries of the defenders, to the sound of catapults and bows, the creaking of iron and wood, the hum of missiles sent flying, and the ping and crash and thud of their impact. He was isolated, an island within the heart of a battle that had somehow caught him up, lost in a sea of indecision and doubt. He had to do something—but the direction he should take refused to reveal itself. He had wanted so badly to be a part of the fight against the Federation, to come north to join the outlaws, to undertake the search for the Sword of Shannara, to see the Shadowen destroyed. Such aspirations he had harbored when he had set out—

such bold plans! He was to be shed of his claustrophobic existence in the Highlands, his meaningless tweaking of the noses
of the bureaucrats the Federation had sent to govern, finished
at last with conducting meaningless experiments in aggravation
against men who could change nothing, even if they wished to
do so. He was to do something grand, something wonderful . . .

Something that would make a difference.

Well, now he had his chance. He could make the difference
no one else could. And there he sat, paralyzed.

Afternoon drifted into evening, the siege continued unabated, and Morgan's dilemma remained unresolved. He left the
grove once to check on Steff and Teel—or more accurately,
perhaps, to spy on them, to see if they might give anything
away. But the Dwarves seemed no different from before. Steff
was still weak and able to converse for only a few minutes before
dropping off to sleep; Teel was taciturn, guarded. He studied
them both as surreptitiously as he could, working at seeing
something that would give him a clue as to whether his suspicions had any basis in fact—any possibility of truth at all—and
he left as empty-handed as he had come.

It was almost dark when Padishar Creel found him. He was
lost in thought, still trying to puzzle through what course of
action he should take, and he didn't hear the big man approach.
It wasn't until Padishar spoke that he realized anyone was there.

"Keeping to yourself quite a bit, aren't you?"

Morgan jumped. "What? Oh, Padishar. Sorry."

The big man sat down across from him. His face was tired
and streaked with dust and sweat. If he noticed Morgan's uneasiness, he didn't let on. He stretched his legs and leaned back,
supporting himself on his elbows, wincing from the pain of his
wounds. "This has been a foul day, Highlander," he said. It came
out in a long sigh of aggravation. "Twenty-two men dead now,
another two likely to be gone by morning, and here we cower
like foxes brought to bay."

Morgan nodded without responding. He was trying desperately to decide what he should say.

"Truth is, I don't much care for the way this is turning out."
The hard face was impossible to read. "The Federation will lay
siege to this place until we've all forgotten why it was that we

came here in the first place, and that doesn't do much to advance my plans or the hopes of the free-born. Bottled up like we are, we're not much use to anyone. There's other havens, and there'll be other times to square matters with those cowards who would send things conceived of dark magic to do their work rather than face us themselves." He paused. "So I've decided that it's time to think about getting out."

Morgan sat forward now. "Escape?"

"'Out that back door we talked about. I thought you should know. I'll be needing your help."

Morgan stared. "My help?"

Padishar straightened slowly to a sitting position. "I want someone to carry a message to Tyrsis—to Damson and the Valemen. They need to know what's happened. I'd go myself, but I have to stay to see the men safely out. So I thought you might be interested."

Morgan agreed at once. "I am. I'll do it."

The other's hand lifted in warning. "Not so fast. We won't be leaving the Jut right away, probably not for another three days or so. The injured shouldn't be moved just yet. But I'll want you to leave sooner. Tomorrow, in fact. Damson's a smart girl with a good head on her shoulders, but she's wilful. I've been thinking matters over a bit since you asked me whether she might attempt to bring the Valemen here. I could be wrong; she might try to do just that. You have to make certain she doesn't."

"I will."

"Out the back door, then—as I've said. And you go alone."

Morgan's brow furrowed.

"Alone, lad. Your friends stay with me. First, you can't be wandering about Callahorn with a pair of Dwarves in tow—even if they were up to it, which at least the one isn't. The Federation would have you in irons in two minutes. And second, we can't be taking any chances after all the treachery that's been done. No one is to know your plans."

The Highlander considered a moment. Padishar was right. There was no point in taking needless risks. He would be better off going by himself and telling no one what he was about—

especially Steff and Teel. He almost gave voice to what he was thinking, then thought better of it. Instead, he simply nodded.

"Good. The matter is settled. Except for one thing." Padishar climbed back to his feet. "Come with me."

He took Morgan through the camp and into the largest of the caves that opened on the cliffs backing the bluff, led him past the bay in which the wounded were being cared for and into the chambers beyond. The tunnels began there, a dozen or more, opening off each other, disappearing back into the darkness. Padishar had picked up a torch on their way in; now he touched it to one that burned from an iron bracket hammered into the cave wall, glanced about for a moment to reassure himself that no one was paying any special attention, then beckoned Morgan ahead. Ignoring the tunnels, he guided the Highlander through the piles of stores to the very deepest part of the caves, several hundred feet back into the cliff rock to a wall where crates were stacked twenty feet high. It was quiet there, the noise left behind. Again he glanced back, scanning the darkness.

Then, handing his torch to Morgan, he reached up with both hands, fitted his fingers into the seams of the crates and pulled. An entire section swung free, a false front on hidden hinges that opened into a tunnel beyond.

"Did you see how I did that, lad?" he asked softly. Morgan nodded.

Padishar took back his torch and poked it inside. Morgan leaned forward. The walls of the secret tunnel twisted and wound downward into the rock until they were lost from view.

"It goes all the way through the mountain," Padishar said. "Follow it to its end and you come out above the Parma Key just south of the Dragon's Teeth, east of the Kennon Pass." He looked at Morgan pointedly. "If you were to attempt to find your way through the other passageways—the ones I keep a guard on for show—we might never see you again. Understand?"

He shoved the secret door closed again and stepped back. "I'm showing you all this now because, when you're ready to go, I won't be with you. I'll be out there, keeping a close watch on your backside." He gave Morgan a small, hard smile. "Be certain you get clear quickly."

They went back through the storage chambers and out through the main cavern to the bluff. It was dark now, the last of the daylight faded into dusk. The outlaw chief stopped, stretched, and took a deep breath of evening air.

"Listen to me, lad," he said quietly. "There's one thing more. You have to stop brooding about what happened to that sword you carry. You can't haul that burden around with you and expect to stay clearheaded; it's much too heavy a load, even for a determined fellow like you. Lay it down. Leave it behind you. You've got enough heart in you to manage without it."

He knows about this morning, Morgan realized at once. He knows and he's telling me that it's all right.

Padishar sighed. "Every bone in my body aches, but none of them aches nearly so bad as my heart. I hate what's happened here. I hate what's been done to us." He looked squarely at Morgan. "That's what I mean about useless baggage. You think about it."

He turned and strode off into the dark. Morgan almost called him back. He even took a step after him, thinking that now he would tell him his suspicious about the traitor. It would have been easy to do so. It would have freed him of the frustration he felt at having to keep the matter to himself. It would have absolved him of the responsibility of being the only one who knew.

He wrestled with his indecision as he had wrestled with it all that day.

But once again he lost.

HE SLEPT AFTER THAT, wrapping himself in his cloak and curling up on the ground within the shadow of the aspen. The earth had dried after the morning rain; the night was warm, and the air was filled with the smells of the forest. His sleep was dreamless and complete. Worries and indecisions slipped away like water shed from his skin. Banished were the wraiths of his lost magic and of the traitor, driven from his mind by the weariness that wrapped protectively about him and gave him peace. He drifted, suspended in the passing of time.

And then he came awake.

A hand clutched his shoulder, tightening. It happened so abruptly, so shockingly, that for a moment he thought he was being attacked. He thrashed himself clear of his cloak and bounded to his feet, wheeling about frantically in the dark.

He found himself face-to-face with Steff.

The Dwarf was crouched before him, wrapped in his blankets, his hair stiff and spikey, his scarred face pale and drawn and sweating despite the night's comfortable feel. His dark eyes burned with fever, and there was something frightened and desperate in their look.

"Teel's gone," he whispered harshly.

Morgan took a deep, steadying breath. "Gone where?" he managed, one hand still fastened tightly about the handle of the dagger at his waist.

Steff shook his head, his breathing ragged in the night's silence. "I don't know. She left about an hour ago. I saw her. She thought I was sleeping, but . . ." He trailed off. "Something's wrong, Morgan. Something." He could barely speak. "Where is she? Where's Teel?"

And instantly, Morgan Leah knew.

CHAPTER

30

I T WAS ON THAT SAME NIGHT that Par Ohmsford went down into the Pit after the Sword of Shannara for the final time.

Darkness had descended on the city of Tyrsis, a cloak of impenetrable black. The rain and mist had turned into fog so thick that the roofs and walls of buildings, the carts and stalls of the markets, even the stones of the streets disappeared into it as if they had melted away. Neither moon nor stars could be seen, and the lights of the city flickered like candles that might be snuffed out at any instant.

Damson Rhee led the Valemen from the garden shed into the haze, cloaked and hooded once more. The fog was suffocating; it was damp and heavy and it clung to clothing and skin alike in a fine sheen. The day had ended early, shoved into nightfall by the appearance of the fog as it rose out of the grasslands below the bluff and built upon itself like a tidal wave until it simply rolled over Tyrsis' walls and buried her. The chill of the previous night had been replaced by an equally unpleasant warmth that smelled of must and rot. All day the people of the city muttered in ill-disguised concern over the strangeness of the weather; when the last of the day's thin, gray light began to fade, they barricaded themselves in their homes as if they were under siege.

Damson and the Valemen found themselves virtually alone in the silent, shrouded streets. When travelers passed by, once or twice only, their presence was but momentary, as if ghosts that had ventured forth from the netherworld only to be swallowed back up again. There were sounds, but they lacked both a source and a direction. Footsteps, the soft thudding of boots, rose into the silence from out of nowhere and disappeared the same way. Things moved about them, shapes and forms without definition that floated rather than walked and that came and went with the blink of an eye.

It was a night for imagining things that weren't there.

Par did his best to avoid that, but he was only partially successful. He harbored within him ghosts of his own making, and they seemed to find their identity in the shadows that played in the mist. There, left of the pinprick of light that was a street-lamp, rose the promise Par had made to keep Coll and Damson safe this night when they went down into the Pit—a small, frightened wisp of nothing. There, just behind it, was his belief that he possessed in the magic of the wishsong sufficient power to keep that promise, that he could somehow use the wishsong as the Elfstones had once been used—not as a maker of images and deceptions, but as a weapon of strength and power. His belief chased after his promise, smaller and frailer yet. Across the way, crawling along the barely visible wall of a shop front, hunching itself across the stone blocks as if mired in quicksand, was the guilt he felt at heeding no one but himself as he sought to vindicate both promise and belief—a guilt that threatened to rise up and choke him.

And hanging over all of them like a giant bird of prey—over promise, belief, and guilt, at home within the faceless night, blind and reckless and cast in stone—was his determination to heed the charge of the shade of Allanon and retrieve from the Pit and its Shadowen the missing Sword of Shannara.

It was down there in its vault, he reassured himself in the privacy of his thoughts. The Sword of Shannara. It was waiting for him.

But the ghosts would not be banished, and the whisper of their doubts swarmed about his paper-thin self-assurances like scavengers, insistent in their purpose, taunting him for his pride and his foolish certainty, teasing him with vivid images of the fate that awaited them all if he was wrong. He walled himself away from the ghosts, just as he had walled himself away all along. But he could not ignore their presence. He could not pretend they weren't there. He fled down inside himself as the three companions worked their way slowly, blindly through the empty city streets, the fog, and the damp and found refuge in the hard core of his resolve. He was risking everything on being right. But what if he wasn't? Who, besides Coll and Damson, would suffer for his mistake?

He thought for a time about those from whom he had become separated on his odyssey—those who had faded away into the events that had brought him to this night. His parents were Federation prisoners, under house arrest at their home in the village of Shady Vale—kind, gentle folk who had never hurt anyone and knew nothing of what this business was about. What, he wondered, would happen to them if he failed? What of Morgan Leah, the sturdy Dwarf Steff, and the enigmatic Teel? He supposed that even now they were hatching plans against the Federation, hidden away at the Jut, deep within the protective confines of the Parma Key. Would his failure exact a price from them as well? And what of the others who had come to the Hadeshorn? Walker Boh had returned to Hearthstone. Wren had gone back into the Westland. Cogline had disappeared.

And Allanon. What of the Druid shade? What of Allanon, who might never even have existed?

But this wasn't a mistake and he wasn't wrong. He knew it. He was certain of it.

Damson slowed. They had reached the narrow stone steps that wound downward to the sewers. She glanced back at Par and Coll momentarily, her green eyes hard. Then, beckoning them after, she began her descent. The Valemen followed. Par's ghosts went with him, closing tightly about, their breath as real as his own as it brushed against his face. Damson led the way; Coll brought up the rear. No one spoke. Par was not certain he could speak if he tried. His mouth and throat felt as if they were lined with cotton.

He was afraid.

Once again, Damson produced a torch to light the way, a flare of brightness in the dark, and they moved noiselessly ahead. Par glanced at Damson and Coll in turn. Their faces were pale and taut. Each met his gaze briefly and looked away.

It took them less than an hour to reach the Mole. He was

waiting for them when they climbed out of the dry well, hunched down in the shadows, a bristling cluster of hair from which two glittering eyes peeked out.

"Mole?" Damson called softly to him.

For a moment, there was no response. The Mole was crouched within a cleft in the rock wall of the chamber, almost invisible in the dark. If it hadn't been for the torch Damson bore, they would have missed him completely. He stared out at them without speaking, as if measuring the truth of who they appeared to be. Finally, he shuffled forward a foot or two and stopped.

"Good evening, lovely Damson," he whispered. He glanced briefly at the Valemen but said nothing to them.

"Good evening, Mole," Damson replied. She cocked her head. "Why were you hiding?"

The Mole blinked like an owl. "I was thinking."

Damson hesitated, her brow furrowing. She stuck the torch into a crack in the rock wall behind her where the light would not disturb her strange friend. Then she crouched down in front of him. The Valemen remained standing.

"What have you discovered, Mole?" Damson asked quietly.

The Mole shifted. He was wearing some sort of leather pants and tunic, but they were almost completely enveloped in the fur of his body. His feet were covered with hair as well. He wore no shoes.

"There is a way into the palace of the Kings of Tyrsis and from there into the Pit," the Mole said. He hunched lower. "There are also Shadowen."

Damson nodded. "Can we get past them?"

The Mole rubbed his nose with his hand. Then he studied her expectantly for a very long time, as if discovering something in her face that before this had somehow escaped his notice. "Perhaps," he said finally. "Shall we try?"

Damson smiled briefly and nodded again. The Mole stood up. He was tiny, a ball of hair with arms and legs that looked as if they might have been stuck on as an afterthought. What was he, Par wondered? A Dwarf? A Gnome? What?

"This way," the Mole said, and beckoned them after him into a darkened passageway. "Bring the torch if you wish. We may use it for a while." He glanced pointedly at the Valemen. "But there must be no talking."

So it began. He took them down into the bowels of the city, its deepest sewers, the catacombs that tunneled its basements and sublevels, passageways that no one had used for hundreds of years. Dust lay upon the rock and earthen floors in thick layers that showed no signs of having ever been disturbed. It was warmer here; the damp and fog did not penetrate. The corridors burrowed into the cliffs, rising and falling through rooms and chambers that had once been used as bolt holes for the defenders of the city, to store foodstuffs and weapons, and on occasion to hide the entire population—men, women, and children—of Tyrsis. There were doors now and then, all rusted and falling off their hinges, bolts broken and shattered, wooden timbers rotting. Rats stirred from time to time in the darkness, but fled at the approach of the humans and the light.

Time slipped away. Par lost all track of how long they navigated the underground channels, working their way steadily forward behind the squat form of the Mole. He let them rest now and again, though he himself did not appear to need to. The Valemen and the girl carried water and some small food to keep their strength up, but the Mole carried nothing. He didn't even appear to have a weapon. When they stopped, those few brief times, they sat about in a circle in the near-dark, four solitary beings buried under hundreds of feet of rock, three sipping water and nibbling food, the fourth watching like a cat, all of them silent participants in some strange ritual.

They walked until Par's legs began to ache. Dozens of corridors lay behind them, and the Valeman had no idea where they were or what direction they were going. The torch they had started out with had burned away and been replaced twice. Their clothing and boots were coated with dust, their faces streaked with it. Par's throat was so parched he could barely swallow.

Then the Mole stopped. They were in a dry well through which a scattering of tunnels ran. Against the far wall, a heavy iron ladder had been bolted into the rock. It rose into the dark and disappeared.

The Mole turned, pointed up and held one scruffy finger to his mouth. No one needed to be told what that meant.

They climbed the ladder in silence, one foot after the other, listening to the rungs creak and groan beneath their weight. The torchlight cast their shadows on the walls of the well in strange, barely recognizable shapes. The corridors beneath faded into the black.

At the top of the ladder there was a hatchway. The Mole braced himself on the ladder and lifted. The hatchway rose an inch or two, and the Mole peeked out. Satisfied, he pushed the hatchway open, and it fell over with a hollow thud. The Mole scrambled out, Damson and the Valemen on his heels.

They stood in a huge empty cellar, a stone-block dungeon with enormous casks banded by strips of iron, shackles and chains scattered about, cell doors fashioned of iron bars, and countless corridors that disappeared at every turn into black holes. A single broad stairway at the far end of the cellar lifted into shadow. The silence was immense, as if become so much a part of the stone that it echoed with a voice of its own. Darkness hung over everything, chased only marginally by the smoking light of the single torch the company bore.

The Mole edged close against Damson and whispered something. Damson nodded. She turned to the Valemen, pointed to where the stairs rose into the black and mouthed the word "Shadowen."

The Mole took them quickly through the cellar to a tiny door set into the wall on their right, unlatching it soundlessly, ushering them through, then closing it tightly behind them. They were in a short corridor that ended at another door. The Mole took them through this door as well and into the room beyond.

The room was empty, with nothing in it but some pieces of wood that might have come from packing crates, some loose pieces of metal shielding, and a rat that scurried hastily into a crack in the wall's stone blocks.

The Mole tugged at Damson's sleeve and she bent down to listen. When he had finished, she faced the Valemen.

"We have come under the city, through the cliffs at the west end of the People's Park and into the palace. We are in its lower levels, down where the prisons used to be. It was here that the armies of the Warlock Lord attempted a breakthrough in the time of Balinor Buckhannah, the last King of Tyrsis."

The Mole said something else. Damson frowned. "The Mole says that there may be Shadowen in the chambers above us— not Shadowen from the Pit, but others. He says he can sense them, even if he cannot see them."

"What does that mean?" Par asked at once.

"It means that sensing them is as close as he cares to get." Damson's face tilted away from the torchlight as she scanned the ceiling of the room. "It means that if he gets close enough to see them, they can undoubtedly see him as well."

Par followed her gaze uneasily. They had been talking in whispers, but was it safe to do even that? "Can they hear us?" he asked, lowering his voice further, pressing his mouth close to her ear.

She shook her head. "Not here, apparently. But we won't be able to talk much after this." She looked over at Coll. He was motionless in the dark. "Are you all right?" Coll nodded, white-faced nevertheless, and she looked back at Par. "We are some distance from the Pit still. We have to use the catacombs under the palace to reach the cliff hatch that will let us in. Mole knows the way. But we have to be very careful. There were no Shadowen in the tunnels yesterday when he explored, but that may have changed."

Par glanced at the Mole. He was squatting down against one wall, barely visible at the edge of the torchlight, eyes gleaming as he watched them. One hand stroked the fur of his arm steadily.

The Valeman felt a twinge of uneasiness. He shifted his feet until he had placed Damson between the Mole and himself. Then he said, so that he believed only she could hear, "Are you sure we can trust him?"

Damson's pale face did not change expression, but her eyes seemed to look somewhere far, far away. "As sure as I can be." She paused. "Do you think we have a choice?"

Par shook his head slowly.

Damson's smile was faint and ironic. "Then I guess there is no point worrying about it, is there?"

She was right, of course. There was no help for his suspicions unless he agreed to turn back, and Par Ohmsford had already decided that he would never do that. He wished that he could test the magic of the wishsong, that he had thought to do so earlier—just to see if it could do what he thought it could. That would provide some reassurance. Yet he knew, even as he completed the thought, that there was no way to test the magic, at least not in the way that he needed to—that it would not reveal itself. He could make images, yes. But he could not summon the wishsong's real power, not until there was something to use it against. And maybe not even then.

But the power was there, he insisted once again, a desperate reassurance against the whisperings of his ghosts. It had to be.

"We won't be needing this anymore," Damson said, gesturing with the torch. She handed it to Par, then fished through her pockets and produced a pair of strange white stones streaked with silver. She kept one and handed him the other. "Put out the torch," she instructed him. "Then place your hands tightly about the stone to warm it. When you feel its heat, open them."

Par doused the torch in the dust, smothering the flame. The room went completely black. He put the strange stone between his hands and held it there. After a few seconds, he could feel it grow warm. When he took one hand away, the stone gave off a meager silver light. As his eyes adjusted, he saw that the light was strong enough to reveal the faces of his companions and an area beyond of several feet.

"If the light begins to dim, warm the stone again with your hands."

She closed her hand over his, tight about the stone, held it there, then lifted it away. The silver light radiated even more brightly. Par smiled in spite of himself, the amazement in his eyes undisguised. "That's a nice trick, Damson," he breathed.

"A bit of my own magic, Valeman," she said softly, and her eyes fixed on him. "Street magic from a street girl. Not so wonderful as the real thing, but reliable. No smoke, no smell, easily tucked away. Better than torchlight, if we want to stay hidden."

"Better," he agreed.

The Mole took them from the room then, guiding them into the black without the benefit of any light at all, apparently needing none. Damson followed, carrying one stone, Par came after carrying the other, and Coll once again brought up the rear. They went out through a second door into a passageway that twisted about and ran past other doors and rooms. They moved soundlessly, their boots scraping softly on the stone, their breathing a shallow hiss, their voices stilled.

Par found himself wondering again about the Mole. Could the Mole be trusted? Was the little fellow what he claimed to be or something else? The Shadowen could appear as anyone. What if the Mole was a Shadowen? So many questions again, and no answers to be found. There was no one he could trust, he thought bleakly—no one but Coll. And Damson. He trusted Damson.

Didn't he?

He beat back the sudden cloud of doubt that threatened to envelop him. He could not afford to be asking such questions now. It was too late to make any difference, if the answers were the wrong ones. He was risking everything on his judgment of Damson, and he must believe that his judgment was correct.

Thinking again of the Shadowen enigma, the mystery of who and what they were and how they could be so many things, he was led to wonder suddenly if there were Shadowen in the outlaw camp, if the enemy they were so desperately seeking to remain hidden from was in fact already among them. The traitor that Padishar Creel sought could be a Shadowen, one that only looked human, that only seemed to be one of them. How were they to know? Was magic the only test that would reveal them? Was that to be the purpose of the Sword of Shannara, to reveal the true identity of the enemy they sought? It was what he had wondered from the moment Allanon had sent him in search of the Sword. But how impossible it seemed that the talisman could be meant for such endless, exhausting work. It would take forever to test it against everyone who might be a Shadowen.

He heard in his mind the whisper of Allanon's voice.

Only through the Sword can truth be revealed and only through truth shall the Shadowen be overcome.

Truth. The Sword of Shannara was a talisman that revealed truth, destroyed lies, and laid bare what was real against the pretense of what only seemed so. That was the use to which Shea Ohmsford had put it when the little Valeman had defeated the Warlock Lord. It must be the use for which the talisman was meant this time as well.

They climbed a long, spiral staircase to a landing. A door in the wall before them stood closed and bolted. The wall behind and the ceiling above were lost in shadow. The drop below seemed endless. They crowded together on the landing while the Mole worked the bolts, first one, then another, then a third. One by one, the metal grating softly, they slid free. The Mole twisted the handle slowly. Par could hear the sound of his own breathing, of his pulse, and of his heartbeat, all working in response to the fear that coursed through him. He could feel Shadowen watching, hidden in the dark. He could sense their presence. It was irrational, imagined—but there nevertheless.

Then the Mole had the door open, and they slipped quickly through.

They found themselves in a tiny, windowless room with a stairwell in the exact center that spiraled down into utter blackness and a door to the left that opened into an empty corridor. Light filtered through slits in the walls of the corridor, faint and wispy. At the corridor's far end, maybe a hundred feet away, a second door stood closed.

The Mole motioned them into the corridor and shut the first door behind them. Par edged over to one of the slits in the wall and peered out. They were somewhere in the palace, above-ground again. Cliffs rose up before him, their slopes a tangle of pine trees. Above the trees, clouds hung thick across the skyline, their underbellies flat and hard and sullen.

Par drew back. Darkness was beginning to give way to daylight. It was almost morning. They had been walking all night.

"Lovely Damson," the Mole was saying softly as Par joined them. "There is a catwalk ahead that crosses the palace court. Using it will save us considerable time. If you and your friends will keep watch, I will make certain the shadow things are nowhere about."

Damson nodded. "Where do you want us?"

Where he wanted them was at each end of the corridor, listening for the sound of anything that might approach. It was agreed that Coll would remain where he was. Par and Damson went on with the Mole to the corridor's far end. There, after a reassuring nod, the Mole slipped past them through the door and was gone.

The Valeman and the girl sat across from each other, close against the door. Par glanced back down the dimly lighted corridor to make certain that Coll was in sight. His brother's rough face lifted briefly, and Par gave a cursory wave. Coll waved back.

They sat in silence then, waiting. The minutes passed and the Mole did not return.

Par grew uneasy. He edged closer to Damson. "Do you think he is all right?" he asked in a whisper.

She nodded without speaking.

Par sat back again, took a deep breath, and let it out slowly. "I hate waiting like this."

She made no response. Her head tilted back against the wall and her eyes closed. She remained like that for a long time. Par thought she might be sleeping. He looked down the corridor again at Coll, found him exactly as he had left him, and turned back to Damson. Her eyes were open, and she was looking at him.

"Would you like me to tell you something about myself that no one else knows?" she asked quietly.

He studied her face wordlessly—her fine, even features, so intense now, her emerald eyes and pale skin shadowed under the sweep of her red hair. He found her beautiful and enigmatic, and he wanted to know everything about her.

"Yes," he replied.

She moved over until their shoulders were touching. She glanced at him briefly, then looked away. He waited.

"When you tell someone a secret about yourself, it is like giving a part of yourself away," she said. "It is a gift, but it is worth much more than something you buy. I don't tell many people things about myself. I think it is because I have never had much besides myself, and I don't want to give what little I have away."

She looked down and her hair spilled forward, veiling her face so that he couldn't see it clearly. "But I want to give something to you. I feel close to you. I have from the very beginning, from that first day in the park. Maybe it is because we have the magic in common—we share that. Maybe that is what makes me feel we're alike. Your magic is different from mine, but that doesn't matter. What matters is that using the magic is how we live. It is what we are. Magic gives us our identity."

She paused, and he thought she might be waiting for a response, so he nodded. He could not tell if she saw the nod or not.

She sighed. "Well, I like you, Elf-boy. You are stubborn and determined, and sometimes you don't take notice of anything or anyone around you—only of yourself. But I am like that, too. Maybe that is how we keep ourselves from becoming exactly like everyone else. Maybe it is how we survive."

She paused, then faced him. "I was thinking that if I were to die, I would want to leave something of myself with you, something that only you would have. Something special."

Par started to protest, but she put her fingers quickly against his mouth. "Just let me finish. I am not saying that I think I will die, but it is surely possible. So perhaps telling you this secret will protect me against it, like a talisman, and keep me safe from harm. Do you see?"

His mouth tightened and she took her fingers away. "Do you remember when I first told you about myself, that night you escaped from the Federation watch after the others were captured? I was trying to convince you that I was not your betrayer. We told ourselves some things about each other. You told me about the magic, about how it worked. Do you remember?"

He nodded. "You told me that you were orphaned when you were eight, that the Federation was responsible."

She drew her knees up like a child. "I told you that my family died in a fire set by Federation Seekers after it was discovered that my father was supplying weapons to the Movement. I told you a street magician took me in shortly after and that is how I learned my trade."

She took a deep breath and shook her head slowly. "What

I told you was not entirely true. My father didn't die in the fire. He escaped. With me. It was my father who raised me, not an aunt, not a street magician. I grew up with street magicians and that is how I learned my trade, but it was my father who looked after me. It is my father who looks after me still."

Her voice shook. "My father is Padishar Creel."

Par stared in wonderment. "Padishar Creel is your father?"

Her eyes never left him. "No one knows but you. It is safer that way. If the Federation found out who I was, they would use me to get to him. Par, what you needed to know that night when I told you about my childhood was that I could never betray anyone after the way my family was betrayed to the Federation. That much was true. That is why my father, Padishar Creel, is so furious that there might be a traitor among his own men. He can never forget what happened to my mother, brother, and sister. The possibility of losing anyone close to him again because of someone's treachery terrifies him."

She paused, studying him intently. "I promised never to tell anyone who I really was, but I am breaking that promise for you. I want you to know. It is something I can give you that will belong only to you."

She smiled then, and some of the tension drained out of him. "Damson," he said, and he found himself smiling back at her. "Nothing had better happen to you. If it does, it will be my fault for talking you into bringing me down here. How will I face Padishar, then?" His voice was a soft whisper of laughter. "I wouldn't be able to go within a hundred miles of him!"

She started laughing as well, shaking soundlessly at the thought, and she shoved him as if they were children at play. Then she reached over and hugged herself against him. He let her hold him without responding for a moment, his eyes straying to where Coll sat, a vague shadow at the other end of the hall. But his brother wasn't looking. There had been friends and traitors mixed up in this enterprise from the beginning, and it had been all but impossible to tell which was which. Except for Coll. And now Damson.

He put his arms around her and hugged her back.

Moments later, the Mole returned. He came upon them so quietly that they didn't even know he was there until the door began to open against them. Par released Damson and jumped to his feet, the blade of his long knife flashing free. The Mole peeked through the door and then ducked hurriedly out of sight again. Damson grabbed Par's arm. "Mole!" she whispered. "It's all right!"

The Mole's roundish face eased back into view. Upon seeing that the weapon had been put away, he came all the way through. Coll was already hastening down the corridor. When he joined them, the Mole said, calm again, "The catwalk is clear and will stay that way if we hurry. But be very quiet, now."

They slipped from the corridor and found themselves on a balcony that encircled a vast, empty rotunda. They moved quickly along it, passing scores of closed, latched doors and shadowed alcoves. Halfway around, the Mole led them into a hall and down its length to a set of iron-barred doors that opened out over the main courtyard of the palace. A catwalk ran across the drop to a massive wall. The courtyard had once been a maze of gardens and winding pathways; now there were only crumbling flagstones and bare earth. Beyond the wall lay the dark smudge of the Pit.

The Mole beckoned anxiously. They stepped onto the catwalk, feeling it sway slightly beneath their combined weight, hearing it creak in protest. The wind blew in quick gusts, and the sound it made as it rushed over the bare stone walls and across the empty courtyard was a low, sad moan. Weeds whipped and shuddered below them and debris scattered about the court, careening from wall to wall. There was no sign of life, no movement in the shadows and murk, no Shadowen in sight.

They crossed the catwalk quickly, once they were upon it, ignoring the creak and groan of its iron stays. They kept their feet moving, their hands on the railing, and their eyes focused carefully ahead, watching the palace wall draw closer. When the crossing was completed they stepped hurriedly onto the battlement, each reaching back to help the next person, grateful to be done.

The Mole took them into a stairwell where they found a fresh set of steps winding downward into blackness. Using the light of the stones Damson had supplied, they descended silently. They were close now; the stone of the wall was all that separated them from the Pit. Par's excitement sent the blood pumping through him, a pounding in his ears, and his nerve endings tightened.

Just a few more minutes . . .

At the bottom of the stairwell, there was a passageway that ended at a weathered, ironbound wooden door. The Mole walked to the door and stopped. When he turned back to face them, Par knew at once what lay beyond.

"Thank you, Mole," he said softly.

"Yes, thank you," echoed Damson.

The Mole blinked shyly. Then he said, "You can look through here."

He reached up and carefully pulled back a tiny shutter that revealed a slit in the wood. Par stepped forward and peered out.

The floor of the Pit stretched away before him, a vast, fog-bound wilderness of trees and rock, a bottomland that was strewn with decaying logs and tangled brush, a darkness in which shadows moved and shapes formed and faded again like wraiths. The wreckage of the Bridge of Sendic lay just to the right and disappeared into the gray haze.

Par squinted into the murk a moment longer. There was no sign of the vault that held the Sword of Shannara.

But he had seen it, right there, just beyond the wall of the palace. The magic of the wishsong revealed it. It was out there. He could feel its presence like a living thing.

He let Damson take a look, then Coll. When Coll stepped back, the three of them stood facing one another.

Par slipped out of his cloak. "Wait for me here. Keep watch for the Shadowen."

"Keep watch for them yourself," Coll said bluntly, shrugging off his own cloak. "I'm going with you."

"I'm going, too," said Damson.

But Coll blocked her way instantly. "No, you're not. Only one of us can go besides Par. Look about you, Damson. Look at where we are. We're in a box, a trap. There is no way out of the Pit except through this door and no way out of the palace except back up the stairs and across the catwalk. The Mole can watch the catwalk, but he can't watch this door at the same time. You have to do that."

Damson started to object, but Coll cut her short. "Don't argue, Damson. You know I'm right. I've listened to you when I should; this time you listen to me."

"It doesn't matter who listens to whom. I don't want either of you going," insisted Par sharply.

Coll ignored him, shifting his short sword in his belt until it was in front of him. "You don't have any choice."

"Why shouldn't I be the one to go?" Damson demanded angrily.

"Because he's my brother!" Coll's voice cracked like a whip, and his rough features were hard. But when he spoke next, his voice was strangely soft. "It has to be me; it's why I came in the first place. It's why I'm here at all."

Damson went still, frozen and voiceless. Her gaze shifted. "All right," she agreed, but her mouth was tight and angry as she said it. She turned away. "Mole, watch the catwalk."

The little fellow was glancing at each of them in turn, a mix of uncertainty and bewilderment in his bright eyes. "Yes, lovely Damson," he murmured and disappeared up the stairs.

Par started to say something more, but Coll took him by the shoulders and pushed him back up against the weathered door. Their eyes met and locked.

"Let's not waste any more time arguing about this, huh?" Coll said. "Let's just get it over with. You and me."

Par tried to twist free, but Coll's big hands were like iron clamps. He sagged back, frustrated. Coll released him. "Par," he said, and the words were almost a plea. "I spoke the truth. I have to go."

They faced each other in silence. Par found himself thinking of what they had come through to reach this point, of the hardships they had endured. He wanted to tell Coll that it all meant something, that he loved him, that he was frightened for him now. He wanted to remind his brother about his duck feet, to warn him that duck feet were too big to sneak around in. He thought he might scream.

But, instead, he said simply, "I know."

Then he moved to the heavy, weathered door, released its fastenings, and pulled on its worn handle. The door swung open, and the half-light and fog, the rancid smells and cloying chill, the hiss of swamp sounds, and the high, distant call of a solitary bird rushed in.

Par looked back at Damson Rhee. She nodded. That she would wait? That she understood? He didn't know.

With Coll beside him, he stepped out into the Pit.

CHAPTER

31

HERE WAS TEEL?

Morgan Leah knelt hurriedly beside Steff, touched his face, and felt the chill of his friend's skin through his fingers. Impulsively, he put his hands on Steff's shoulders and gripped him, but Steff did not seem to feel it. Morgan took his hands away and rocked back on his heels. His eyes scanned the darkness about him, and shivered with something more than the cold. The question repeated itself in his mind, racing from corner to corner as if trying to hide, a dark whisper.

Where was Teel?

The possibilities paraded before him in his mind. Gone to get Steff a drink of water, something hot to eat, another blanket perhaps? Gone to look around, spooked from her sleep by one of those instincts or sixth-senses that kept you alive when you were constantly being hunted? Close by, about to return?

The possibilities shattered into broken pieces and disappeared. No. He knew the answer. She had gone into the secret tunnel. She had gone there to lead the soldiers of the Federation into the Jut from the rear. She was about to betray them one final time.

No one but Damson, Chandos, and I know the other way—now that Hirehone is dead.

That was what Padishar Creel had told him, speaking of the hidden way out, the tunnel—something Morgan had all but forgotten until now. He shivered at the clarity of the memory. If his reasoning was correct and the traitor was a Shadowen who had taken Hirehone's identity to follow them to Tyrsis, then that meant the Shadowen had possession of Hirehone's memories and knew of the tunnel as well.

And if the Shadowen was now Teel . . .

Morgan felt the hairs on the back of his neck prickle. It would take the Federation months to take the Jut by siege. But what if the siege was nothing more than a decoy? What if the Creeper itself had been, even in failing, just a decoy? What if the Federation's intent from the beginning, was to take the Jut from within, by betrayal once again, through the tunnel that was to have been the outlaws' escape?

I have to so something!

Morgan Leah felt leaden. He must leave Steff and get to Padishar Creel at once. If his suspicions about Teel were correct, she had to be found and stopped.

If.

The horror of what he was thinking knotted in his throat—that Teel could be the very worst of the enemies that had hunted them all since Culhaven, that she could have deceived them so completely, especially Steff, who believed that he owed her his life and who was in love with her. The knot tightened. He knew that the horror he felt didn't come from the possibility of betrayal—it came from the certainty of it.

Steff saw something of that horror mirrored in his eyes and grappled angrily with him. "Where is she, Morgan? You know! I can see it!"

Morgan did not try to break away. Instead, he faced his friend and said, "I think I know. But you have to wait here, Steff. You have to let me go after her."

"No." Steff shook his head adamantly, his scarred face knotting. "I'm going with you."

"You can't. You're too sick . . ."

"I'm going, Morgan! Now where is she?"

The Dwarf was shaking with fever, but Morgan knew that he was not going to be able to free himself unless he did so by force. "All right," he agreed, taking a slow breath. "This way."

He put his arm under his friend to support him and started into the dark. He could not leave Steff behind, even knowing how difficult it would make things having his friend along. He would simply do what he must in spite of him. He stumbled suddenly and fought his way back to his feet, hauling Steff up with him, not having seen the coil of rope that lay on the ground in his path. He forced himself to slow, realizing as he did so that he hadn't even taken time yet to think through what he had surmised. Teel was the traitor. He must accept that. Steff could not, but he must. Teel was the one . . .

He stopped himself.

No. Not Teel. Don't call that thing Teel. Teel is dead. Or close enough to being dead that there is no distinction to be made. So, not Teel. The Shadowen that hid in Teel.

His breathing grew rapid as he hastened through the night, Steff clinging to him. The Shadowen must have left her body and taken Hirehone's in order to follow Padishar's little company to Tyrsis and betray it to the Federation. Then it had abandoned Hirehone's body, returned to the camp, killed the watch because it could not ascend the Jut unseen, and reinhabited Teel. Steff had never realized what was happening. He had believed Teel poisoned. The Shadowen had let him think as much. It had even managed to cast suspicion on Hirehone with that tale of following him to the bluff before falling into unconsciousness. He wondered how long Teel had been a Shadowen. A long time, he decided. He pictured her in his mind, nothing more than a shell, a hollow skin, and his teeth ground at the image. He remembered Par's description of what it had been like when the Shadowen on Toffer Ridge, the one who had taken the body of the little girl, had tried to come into him. He remembered the horror and revulsion the Valeman had expressed. That was what it must have been like for Teel.

There was no further time to consider the matter. They were approaching the main cave. The entrance was ablaze with torchlight. Padishar Creel stood there. The outlaw chief was awake, just as Morgan had hoped he would be, brilliant in his scarlet clothing, talking with the men who cared for the sick and injured, his broadsword and long knives strapped in place.

"What are you doing?" Steff cried angrily. "This is between you and me, Morgan! Not him!"

But Morgan ignored his protestations, dragging him into the

light. Padishar Creel turned as the two men staggered up to him and caught hold of them by the shoulders.

"Whoa, now, lads—slow down! What's the reason for charging about in the dark like this?" The other man's grip tightened as Steff tried to break free, and the rough voice lowered. "Careful, now. Your eyes say something's frightened you. Let's keep it to ourselves. What's happened?"

Steff was rigid with anger, and his eyes were hard. Morgan hesitated. The others in Padishar's company were looking at them curiously, and they were close enough to hear what he might say. He smiled disarmingly. "I think I've found the person you've been looking for," he said to the big man.

Padishar's face went taut momentarily, then quickly relaxed. "Ah, that's all, is it?" He spoke as much to his men as to them, his voice almost joking. "Well, well, come on outside a minute and tell me about it." He put his arm about their shoulders as if all was well, waved to those listening, and steered the Highlander and the Dwarf outside.

There he backed them into the shadows. "What is it you've found?" he demanded.

Morgan glanced at Steff, then shook his head. He was sweating now beneath his clothes, and his face was flushed. "Padishar," he said. "Teel's missing. Steff doesn't know what's happened to her. I think she might have gone down into the tunnel."

He waited, his gaze locked on the big man's, silently pleading with him not to demand more, not to make him explain. He still wasn't certain, not absolutely, and Steff would never believe him in any case.

Padishar understood. "Let's have a look. You and I, Highlander."

Steff seized him by the arm. "I'm coming too." His face was bathed in sweat, and his eyes were glazed, but there was no mistaking his determination in the matter.

"You haven't the strength for it, lad."

"That's my concern!"

Padishar's face turned sharply into the light. It was crisscrossed with welts and cuts from last night's battle, tiny lines that seemed to reflect the deeper scars the Dwarf bore. "And none of mine," he said quietly. "So long as you understand."

They went into the sick bay, where Padishar took one of the other outlaws aside and spoke softly to him. Morgan could just make out what was being said.

"Rouse Chandos," Padishar ordered. "Tell him I want the camp mobilized. Check the watch, be certain it's awake and alive. Make ready to move everyone out. Then he's to come after me into the hidden tunnel, the bolt hole. With help. Tell him I said that we're all done with secrecy, so it doesn't matter now who knows what he's about. Now get to it!"

The man scurried off, and Padishar beckoned wordlessly to Morgan and Steff. He led them through the main cavern into the deep recesses where the stores were kept. He lit three torches, kept one for himself and gave one each to the High-lander and the Dwarf. Then he took them into the very back of the farthest chamber where the cases were stacked against the rock wall, handed his torch to Morgan, grabbed the cases in both hands and pulled. The false front opened into the tunnel beyond. They slipped through the opening, and Padishar pulled the packing crates back into place.

"Stay close," he warned.

They hurried into the dark, the torches smoking above them, casting their weak yellow light against the shadows. The tunnel was wide, but it twisted and turned. Rock outcroppings made the passage hazardous; there were stalactites and stalagmites both, wicked stone icicles. Water dripped from the ceiling and pooled in the rock, the only sound in the silence other than their footsteps. It was cold in the caves, and the chill quickly worked its way through Morgan's clothes. He shivered as he trailed after Padishar. Steff trailed them both, walking haltingly on his own, his breathing ragged and quick.

Morgan wondered suddenly what they were going to do when they found Teel.

He made a mental check of his weapons. He had the newly acquired broadsword strapped across his back, a dagger in his belt, and another in his boot. At his waist, he wore the short-ened scabbard and the remains of the Sword of Leah.

Not much help against a Shadowen, he thought worriedly. And how much use would Steff be, even after he discovered the truth? What would he do?

If only I still had the magic

He forced that thought away from him, knowing what it would lead to, determined that he would not allow his indecision to bind him again.

The seconds ticked by, and the echo of their passing reverberated in the sound of the men's hurried footsteps. The walls of the tunnel narrowed down sharply, then broadened out again, a constant change of size and shape. They passed through a series of underground caverns where the torchlight could not even begin to penetrate the shadows that cloaked the hollow, vaulted roofs. A little farther on, a series of crevices opened before them, several almost twenty feet across. Bridges had been built to span them, wooden slats connected by heavy ropes, the ropes anchored in the rock by iron pins. The bridges swayed and shook as they crossed, but held firm.

All the while they walked, they kept watch for Teel. But there was no sign of her.

Steff was beginning to have trouble keeping up. He was enormously strong and fit when well, but whatever sickness had attacked him—if indeed it was a sickness and he had not been poisoned as Morgan was beginning to surmise—had left him badly worn. He fell repeatedly and had to drag himself up again each time. Padishar never slowed. The big man had meant what he said—Steff was on his own. The Dwarf had gotten this far on sheer determination, and Morgan did not see how he could maintain the pace the outlaw chief was setting much longer. The Highlander glanced back at his friend, but Steff didn't seem to see him, his haunted eyes searching the shadows, sweeping the curtain of black beyond the light.

They were more than a mile into the mountain when a glimmer of light appeared ahead, a pinprick that quickly became a glow. Padishar did not slow or bother to disguise his coming. The tunnel broadened, and the opening ahead brightened with the flicker of torches. Morgan felt his heartbeat quicken.

They entered a massive underground cavern ablaze with light. Torches were jammed into cracks in the walls and floors, filling the air with smoke and the smell of charred wood and burning pitch. At the center of the cavern a huge crevice split the chamber floor end to end, a twisted maw that widened and narrowed as it worked its way from wall to wall. Another bridge had been built to span the crevice at its narrowest juncture, this one a massive iron structure. Machinery had been installed on the near side of the crevice to raise and lower it. The bridge was down at the moment, linking the halves of the cavern floor. Beyond, the flat rock stretched away to where the tunnel disappeared once more into darkness.

Teel stood next to the bridge machinery, hammering.

Padishar Creel stopped, and Morgan and Steff quickly came up beside him. Teel hadn't heard or seen them yet, their torchlight enveloped by the cavern's own brightness.

Padishar laid down his torch. "She's jammed the machinery. The bridge can't be raised again." His eyes found Steff's. "If we let her, she will bring the Federation right to us."

Steff stared wildly. "No." he gasped in disbelief.

Padishar ignored him. He unsheathed his broadsword and started forward.

Steff lunged after him, tripping, falling, then crying out frantically, "Teel!"

Teel whirled about. She held an iron bar in her hands, the smooth surface bright with nicks from where she had been smashing the bridge works. Morgan could see the damage clearly now, winches split apart, pulleys forced loose, gears stripped. Teel's hair glittered in the light, flashing with traces of gold. She faced them, her mask revealing nothing of what she was thinking, an expressionless piece of leather strapped about her head, the eyeholes dark and shadowed.

Padishar closed both big hands about the broadsword, lifting its blade into the light. "End of the line for you, girl," he snapped

The echo filled the cavern, and Steff came to his feet, lurching ahead. "Padishar, wait!" he howled.

Morgan jumped to intercept him, caught hold of his arm, and jerked him about. "No, Steff, that isn't Teel! Not anymore!" Steff's eyes were bright with anger and fear. Morgan lowered his voice, speaking quickly, calmly. "Listen to me. That's a Shadowen, Steff. How long since you've seen the face beneath that mask? Have you looked at it? It isn't Teel under there anymore. Teel's been gone a long time."

The anger and fear turned to horror. "Morgan, no! I would know! I could tell if it wasn't her!"

"Steff, listen . . ."

"Morgan, he's going to kill her! Let me go!"

Steff jerked free and Morgan grabbed him again. "Steff, look at what she's done! She's betrayed us!"

"No!" the Dwarf screamed and struck him.

Morgan went down in a heap, the force of the blow leaving him stunned. His first reaction was surprise; he hadn't thought it possible that Steff could still possess such strength. He pushed himself to his knees, watching as the Dwarf raced after Padishar, screaming something the Highlander couldn't understand.

Steff caught up with the big man when they were just a few steps from Teel. The Dwarf threw himself on Padishar from behind, seizing his sword arm, forcing it down. Padishar shouted in fury, tried to break free and failed. Steff was all over him, wrapped about him like a second skin.

In the confusion, Teel struck. She was on them like a cat, the iron bar lifted. The blows hammered down, quick and unchallenged, and in a matter of seconds both Padishar and Steff lay bleeding on the cavern floor.

Morgan staggered to his feet alone to face her.

She came for him unhurriedly, and as she did so there was a moment in which all of his memories of her came together at once. He saw her as the small, waiflike girl that he had met at Culhaven in the darkened kitchen of Granny Elise and Auntie Jilt, her honey-colored hair just visible beneath the folds of her hooded cloak, her face concealed by the strange leather mask. He saw her listening at the edges of the campfire's light to the conversation shared by the members of the little company who had journeyed through the Wolfsktaag. He saw her crowded close to Steff at the base of the Dragon's Teeth before they went to meet with the shade of Allanon, suspicious, withdrawn, fiercely protective.

He forced the images away, seeing her only as she was now, striking down Padishar and Steff, too swift and strong to be what she pretended. Even so, it was hard to believe that she was a

Shadowen, harder still to accept that they had all been fooled so completely.

He pulled free the broadsword and waited. He would have to be quick. Maybe he would have to be more than quick. He remembered the creatures in the Pit. Iron alone hadn't been enough to kill them.

Teel went into a crouch as she reached him, her eyes dark pools within the mask, the look that was reflected there hard and certain. Morgan gave a quick feint, then cut viciously at the girl's legs. She sidestepped the blow easily. He cut again—once, twice. She parried, and the shock of the sword blade striking the iron bar washed through him. Back and forth they lunged, each waiting for the other to provide an opening.

Then a series of blows brought the flat of the broadsword against the iron bar and the blade shattered. Morgan ripped at the bar with what was left, the handle catching it and twisting it free. Both sword and bar skittered away into the dark.

Instantly Teel threw herself on Morgan, her hands closing about his throat. She was incredibly strong. He had only a moment to act as he fell backward. His hand closed on the dagger at his waist, and he shoved it into her stomach. She drew back, surprised. He kicked at her, thrusting her back, drew the dagger in his boot and jammed it into her side, ripping upward.

She backhanded him so hard that he was knocked off his feet. He landed with a grunt, jarred so that the breath was knocked from his body. Spots danced before his eyes, but he gasped air into his lungs and scrambled up.

Teel was standing where he had left her, the daggers still embedded in her body. She reached down and calmly pulled them free, tossing them away.

She knows I can't hurt her, he thought in despair. *She knows I haven't anything that can stop her.*

She seemed unhurt as she advanced on him. There was blood on her clothing, but not much. There was no expression to be seen behind the mask, nothing in her eyes or on her mouth, just an emptiness that was as chilling as ice. Morgan edged away from her, searching the cavern floor for any kind of weapon at all. He caught sight of the iron bar and desperately snatched it up.

Teel seemed unworried. There was a shimmer of movement all about her body, a darkness that seemed to lift slightly and settle back again—as if the thing that lived within her was readying itself.

Morgan backed away, maneuvering toward the crevice. Could he somehow manage to lure this thing close enough to the drop to shove it over? Would that kill it? He didn't know. He knew only that he was the only one left to stop it, to prevent it from betraying the entire Jut, all those men, to the Federation. If he failed, they would die.

But I'm not strong enough—not without the magic!

He was only a few feet from the crevice edge. Teel closed the gap that separated them, moving swiftly. He swung at her with the iron bar, but she caught the bar in her hand, broke his grip on it, and flung it away.

The she was on him, her hands at his throat, choking off his air, strangling him. He couldn't breathe. He fought to break free, but she was far too strong. His eyes squeezed shut against the pain, and there was a coppery taste in his mouth.

A huge weight dropped across him.

"Teel, don't!" he heard someone cry—a disembodied voice choked with pain and fatigue.

Steff!

The hands loosened marginally, and his eyes cleared enough so that he could see Steff atop Teel, arms locked about her, hauling back. There was blood streaking his face. A gaping wound had been opened at the top of his head.

Morgan's right hand groped at his belt and found the handle of the Sword of Leah.

Teel ripped free of Steff, turned and pulled him about. There was a fury in her eyes, in the way the cords of her throat went taut, that even the mask could not conceal. Yanking Steff's dagger from its sheath, she buried it deep in his chest. Steff toppled backward, gasping.

Teel turned back then to finish Morgan, half-raised over him, and he thrust the broken blade of his sword into her stomach.

Back she reared, screaming so that Morgan arched away from her in spite of himself. But he kept his hands fastened on the handle of the sword. Then something strange began to happen. The Sword of Leah grew warm and flared with light. He could feel it stir and come to life.

The magic! Oh, Shades—it was the magic!

Power surged through the blade, linking them together, flowing into Teel. Crimson fire exploded through her. Her hands tore at the blade, at her body, at her face, and the mask came free. Morgan Leah would never forget what lay beneath, a countenance born of the blackest pits of the netherworld, ravaged and twisted and alive with demons that he had only imagined might exist. Teel seemed to disappear entirely, and there was only the Shadowen behind the face, a thing of blackness and no substance, an emptiness that blocked and swallowed the light.

Invisible hands fought to thrust Morgan away, to strip him of his weapon and of his soul.

"Leah! Leah!" He sounded the battle cry of his ancestors, of the Kings and Princes of his land for a thousand years, and that single word became the talisman to which he clung.

The Shadowen's scream became a shriek. Then it collapsed, the darkness that sustained it crumbling and fading away. Teel returned, a frail, limp bundle, empty of life and being. She fell forward atop him, dead.

It TOOK SEVERAL MINUTES for Morgan to find the strength to push Teel away. He lay there in the wetness of his own sweat and blood, listening to the sudden silence, exhausted, pinned to the cavern floor by the dead girl's weight. His only thought was that he had survived.

Then slowly his pulse quickened. It was the magic that had saved him. It was the magic of the Sword of Leah. Shades, it wasn't gone after all! At least some part of it still lived, and if part of it lived then there was a chance that it could be completely restored, that the blade could be made whole again, the magic preserved, the power . . .

His ruminations scattered uncontrollably in their frantic passing and disappeared. He gulped air into his lungs, mustered his strength, and pushed Teel's body aside. She was surprisingly light. He looked down at her as he rolled onto his hands and knees. She was all shrunken in, as if something had dissolved her bones. Her face was still twisted and scarred, but the demons he had seen there were gone.

Then he heard Steff gasp. Unable to rise he crawled to his friend. Steff lay on his back, the dagger still protruding from his chest. Morgan started to remove it, then slowly drew back. He knew at a glance that it was too late to make any difference. Gently, he touched his friend's shoulder.

Steff's eyes blinked open and shifted to find him. "Teel?" he asked softly.

"She's dead," Morgan whispered back.

The Dwarf's scarred face tightened with pain, then relaxed. He coughed blood. "I'm sorry, Morgan. Sorry . . . I was blind, so this had to happen."

"It wasn't only you."

"I should have seen . . . the truth. Should have recognized it. I just . . . didn't want to, I guess."

"Steff, you saved our lives. If you hadn't awakened me . . ."

"Listen to me. Listen, Highlander. You are my closest friend. I want you . . . to do something." He coughed again, then tried to steady his voice. "I want you to go back to Culhaven and make certain . . . that Granny Elise and Auntie Jilt are all right." His eyes squeezed shut and opened again. "You understand me, Morgan? They will be in danger because Teel . . ."

"I understand," Morgan cut him short.

"They are all I have left," Steff whispered, reaching out to fasten his hand on Morgan's arm. "Promise me."

Morgan nodded wordlessly, then said, "I promise."

Steff sighed, and the words he spoke were little more than a whisper. "I loved her, Morgan."

Then his hand slid away, and he died.

EVERYTHING THAT HAPPENED after that was something of a blur to Morgan Leah. He stayed at Steff's side for a time, so dazed that he could think of doing nothing else. Then he remembered Padishar Creel. He forced himself to his feet and went over to check on the big man. Padishar was still alive, but unconscious, his left arm broken from warding off the blows struck by the iron bar, his head bleeding from a deep gash. Morgan wrapped the head injury to stop the blood loss, but left the arm alone. There was no time to set it now.

The machinery that operated the bridge was smashed and there was no way that he could repair it. If the Federation was sending an attack force into the tunnels tonight—and Morgan had to assume they were—then the bridge could not be raised to prevent their advance. It was only a few hours until dawn. That meant that Federation soldiers were probably already on their way. Even without Teel to guide them, they would have little trouble following the tunnel to the Jut.

He found himself wondering what had become of Chandos and the men he was supposed to bring with him. They should have arrived by now.

He decided he couldn't risk waiting for them. He had to get out of there. He would have to carry Padishar since his efforts to waken him had failed. Steff would have to be left behind.

It took several minutes to decide what was needed. First he salvaged the Sword of Leah, slipping it carefully back into its makeshift sheath. Then he carried Teel and afterward Steff to the edge of the crevice and dropped them over. He wasn't sure it was something he could do until after it was done. It left him feeling sick and empty inside.

He was incredibly tired by then, so weak that he did not think he could make it back through the tunnels by himself, let alone carrying Padishar. But somehow he managed to get the other across his shoulders and, with one of the torches to guide him, he started out.

He walked for what seemed like hours, seeing nothing, hearing only the sound of his own boots as they scraped across the stone. Where was Chandos, he asked himself over and over again. Why hadn't he come? He stumbled and fell so many times that he lost count, tripped up by the tunnel's rock and by his own weariness. His knees and hands were torn and bloodied, and his body began to grow numb. He found himself thinking of curious things, of his boyhood and his family, of the adventures he had shared growing up with Par and Coll, of the steady, reliable Steff and the Dwarves of Culhaven. He cried some of the time, thinking of what had become of them all, of how much of the past had been lost. He talked to Padishar when he felt himself on the verge of collapse, but Padishar slept on.

He walked, it seemed, forever.

Yet when Chandos finally did appear, accompanied by a swarm of outlaws and Axhind and his Trolls, Morgan was no longer walking at all. He had collapsed in the tunnel, exhausted.

He was carried with Padishar the rest of the way, and he tried to explain what had happened. He was never certain exactly what he said. He knew that he rambled, sometimes incoherently. He remembered Chandos saying something about a new Federation assault, that the assault had prevented him coming as quickly as he had wanted. He remembered the strength of the other's gnarled hand as it held his own.

It was still dark when they regained the bluff, and the Jut was indeed under attack. Another diversion, perhaps, to draw attention away from the soldiers sneaking through the tunnels, but one that required dealing with nevertheless. Arrows and spears flew from below, and the siege towers had been hauled forward. Numerous attempts at scaling the heights had already been repelled. Preparations for making an escape, however, were complete. The wounded were set to move out, those that could walk risen to their feet, those that couldn't placed on litters. Morgan went with the latter group as they were carried back into the caves to where the tunnels began. Chandos appeared, his fierce, black-bearded face hovering close to Morgan as he spoke.

"All is well, Highlander," Morgan would remember the other man saying, his voice a faint buzz. "There's Federation soldiers in the hidden tunnel already, but the rope bridges have been cut. That will slow them a bit—long enough for us to be safely away. We'll be going into these other tunnels. There's a way out through them as well, you see, one that only Padishar knows. It's rougher going, a good number of twists and turns and a few tricky choices to be made. But Padishar knows what to do. Never leaves anything to chance. He's awake again, bringing the rest of them down, making sure everyone's out. He's a tough one, old Padishar. But no tougher than you. You saved his life, you did. You got him out of there just in time. Rest now, while you can. You won't have long."

Morgan closed his eyes and drifted off to sleep. He slept poorly, brought awake time and again by the jostling of the litter on which he lay and by the sounds of the men who were crowded about him, whispering and crying out in pain. Darkness cloaked the tunnels, a hazy black that even torchlight could not cut through entirely. Faces and bodies passed in and out of view, but his lasting impression was of impenetrable night.

Once or twice, he thought he heard fighting, the clash of weapons, the grunts of men. But there was no sense of urgency in those about him, no indication that anything threatened, and he decided after a time that he must be dreaming.

He forced himself awake finally, not wishing to sleep any longer, afraid to sleep when he was not certain what was happening. Nothing around him appeared to have changed. It seemed that he could not have been asleep for more than a few moments.

He tried lifting his head, and pain stabbed down the back of his neck. He lay back again, thinking suddenly of Steff and Teel and of the thinness of the line that separated life and death.

Padishar Creel came up beside him. He was heavily bandaged about the head, and his arm was splinted and strapped to his side. "So, lad," he greeted quietly.

Morgan nodded, closed his eyes and opened them again.

"We're getting out now," the other said. "All of us, thanks to you. And to Steff. Chandos told me the story. He had great courage, that one." The rough face looked away. "Well, the Jut's lost but that's a small price to pay for our lives."

Morgan found that he didn't want to talk about the price of lives. "Help me up, Padishar," he said quietly. "I want to walk out of here."

The outlaw chief smiled. "Don't we all, lad," he whispered.

He reached out his good hand and pulled Morgan to his feet.

CHAPTER

32

T WAS A NIGHTMARISH WORLD where Par and Coll Ohmsford walked. The silence was intense and endless, a cloak of emptiness that stretched further than time itself. There were no sounds, no cries of birds or buzzings of insects, no small skitterings or scrapes, not even the rustle of the wind through the trees to give evidence of life. The trees rose skyward like statues of stone carved by some ancient civilization and left in mute testament to the futility of man's works. They had a gray and wintry look to them, and even the leaves that should have softened and colored their bones bore the look of a scarecrow's rags. Scrub brush and saw grass rubbed up against their trunks like stray children, and bramble bushes twisted together in a desperate effort to protect against life's sorrows.

The mist was there as well, of course. The mist was there first, last, and always, a deep and pervasive sea of gray that shut everything vibrant away. It hung limp in the air, unmoving as it smothered trees and brush, rocks and earth, and life of any kind or sort, a screen that blocked away the sun's light and warmth. There was an inconsistency to it, for in some places it was thin and watery and merely gave a fuzzy appearance to what it sought to cloak, while in others it was as impenetrable as ink. It brushed at the skin with a cold, damp insistence that whispered of dead things.

Par and Coll moved slowly, cautiously through their waking dream, fighting back against the feeling that they had become disembodied. Their eyes darted from shadow to shadow, searching for movement, finding only stillness. The world they had entered seemed lifeless, as if the Shadowen they knew to be hidden there were not in fact there at all but were simply a lie of the dream that their senses could not reveal.

They moved quickly to the rubble of the Bridge of Sendic so that they could follow its broken trail to the vault. Their footsteps were soundless in the tall grasses and the damp, yielding earth. At times their boots disappeared entirely in the carpet of mist. Par glanced back to the door they had come through. It was nowhere to be seen.

In seconds, the cliff face itself, the whole of what remained of the palace of the Kings of Tyrsis, had vanished as well.

As if it had never been, Par thought darkly.

He felt cold and empty inside, but hot where sweat made the skin beneath his clothing feel prickly and damp. The emotions that churned inside would not be sorted out or dispersed; they screamed with voices that were garbled and confused, each desperate to be heard, each mindless. He could feel his heart pounding within his chest, his pulse racing in response, and he sensed the imminency of his own death with every step he took. He wished again that he could summon for just a moment the magic, even in its most rudimentary form, so that he could be reassured that he possessed some measure of power to defend himself. But use of the magic would alert whatever lived within the Pit, and he wanted to believe that as yet that had not happened.

Coll brushed his arm, pointing to where the earth had opened before them in a wicked-looking crack that disappeared into blackness. They would have to go around. Par nodded, leading the way. Coll's presence was reassuring to him, as if the simple fact of his being there might somehow deter the evil that threatened. Coll—his large, blocky form like a rock at Par's back, his rough face so determined that it seemed his strength of will alone would see them through. Par was glad beyond anything words could express that his brother had come. It was a selfish reaction, he knew, but an honest one. Coll's courage in this business was to a large extent the source of his own.

They skirted the pitfall and worked their way back to the

tumbled remains of the bridge. Everything about them was un-changed, silent and unmoving, empty of life.

But then something shimmered darkly in the mists ahead, a squarish shape that lifted out of the rubble.

Par took a deep steadying breath. It was the vault.

They moved toward it hurriedly, Par in the lead, Coll just a step behind. Stone-block walls came sharply into focus, losing the surreal haziness in which the mists had cloaked them. Brush grew up against its sides, vines looped over its sloped roof, and moss colored its foundation in shadings of rust and dark green. The vault was larger than Par had imagined, a good fifty feet across and as much as twenty feet high at its peak. It had the look and feel of a crypt.

The Valemen reached its nearest wall and edged their way cautiously around the corner to the front. They found writing carved there in the pitted stone, an ancient scroll ravaged by time and weather, many of its words nearly erased. They stopped, breathless, and read:

Herein lies the heart and soul of the nations
Their right to be free men,
Their desire to live in peace,
Their courage to seek out truth.
Herein lies the Sword of Shannara

Just beyond, a massive stone door stood ajar. The brothers glanced at each other wordlessly, then started forward. When they reached the door, they peered inside. There was a wall that formed a corridor leading left; the corridor disappeared into darkness.

Par frowned. He hadn't expected the vault to be a complex structure; he had thought it would be nothing more than a single chamber with the Sword of Shannara at its center. This sug-gested something else.

He looked at Coll. His brother was clearly upset, peering about anxiously, studying first the entry, then the dark tangle of the forest surrounding them. Coll reached out and pulled on the door. It moved easily at his touch.

He bent close. "This looks like a trap," he whispered so softly that Par could barely hear him.

Par was thinking the same thing. A door to a vault that was three hundred years old and had been subjected to the climate of the Pit should not give way so readily. It would be a simple matter for someone to shut it again once he was inside.

And yet he knew he would go in anyway. He had already made up his mind to do so. He had come through too much to turn back now. He raised his eyebrows and gave Coll a questioning look. What was Coll suggesting, the look asked?

Coll's mouth tightened, knowing that Par was determined to continue, that the risks no longer made any difference. It took a supreme effort for him to speak the words. "All right. You go after the Sword; I'll stand guard out here." One big hand grasped Par's shoulder. "But hurry!"

Par nodded, smiled triumphantly, and clutched his brother back.

Then he was through the door, moving swiftly down the passageway into the dark. He went as far as he could with the faint light of the outside world to guide him, but it soon faded. He felt along the walls for the corridor's end, but couldn't find it. He remembered then that he still carried the stone Damson had given him. He reached into his pocket, took it out, clasped it momentarily between his hands to warm it, and held it out before him. Silver light flooded the darkness. His smile grew fierce. Again, he started forward, listening to the silence, watching the shadows.

He wound along the passageway, descended a set of stairs, and entered a second corridor. He traveled much further than he would have thought possible, and for the first time he began to grow uneasy. He was no longer in the vault, but somewhere deep underground. How could that be?

Then the passageway ended. He stepped into a room with a vaulted ceiling and walls carved with images and runes, and he caught his breath with a suddenness that hurt.

There, at the very center of the room, blade downward in a block of red marble, was the Sword of Shannara.

He blinked to make certain that he was not mistaking

what he saw, then moved forward until he stood before it. The blade was smooth and unmarked, a flawless piece of workmanship. The handle was carved with the image of a hand thrusting a torch skyward. The talisman glistened like new metal in the soft light, faintly blue in color.

Par felt his throat tighten. It was indeed the Sword.

A sharp rush of elation surged through him. He could hardly keep himself from calling out to Coll, from shouting aloud to him what he was feeling. A wave of relief swept over him. He had gambled everything on what had amounted to little more than a hunch—and his hunch had been right. Shades, it had been right all along! The Sword of Shannara had indeed been down in the Pit, concealed by its tangle of trees and brush, by the mist and night, by the Shadowen . . . !

He shoved aside his elation abruptly. Thinking of the Shadowen reminded him in no uncertain terms how precarious his position was. There would be time to congratulate himself later, when Coll and he were safely out of this rat hole.

There were stairs cut in a stone base on which rested the block of marble and the Sword embedded in it, and he started for them. But he had taken only a single step when something detached itself from the darkness of the wall beyond. Instantly, he froze, terror welling up in his throat.

A single word screamed out in his mind.

Shadowen!

But he saw at once that he was mistaken. It wasn't a Shadowen. It was a man dressed all in black, cloaked and hooded, the insigne of a wolf's head sew on his chest.

Par's fear did not lessen when he realized who the other was. The man approaching him was Rimmer Dall.

At the entrance to the vault, Coll waited impatiently. He stood with his back against the stone, just to one side of the opening, his eyes searching the mist. Nothing moved. No sound reached him. He was alone, it seemed; yet he did not feel that way. The dawn's light filtered down through the canopy of the trees, washing him in its cold, gray haze.

Par had been gone too long already, he thought. It shouldn't be taking him this much time.

He glanced quickly over his shoulder at the vault's black opening. He would wait another five minutes; then he was going in himself.

RIMMER DALL CAME to a stop a dozen feet away from Par, reached up casually and pulled back the hood of his cloak. His craggy face was unmasked, yet in the half-light of the vault it was so streaked with shadows as to be practically unrecognizable. It made no difference. Par would have known him anywhere. Their one and only meeting that night so many weeks ago at the Blue Whisker was not something he would ever forget. He had hoped it would never be repeated; yet here they were, face to face once more. Rimmer Dall, First Seeker of the Federation, the man who had tracked him across the length and breadth of Callahorn and nearly had him so many times, had caught up with him at last.

The door through which Par had entered remained open behind him, a haven that beckoned. The Valeman poised to flee.

"Wait, Par Ohmsford," the other said, almost as if reading his thoughts. "Are you so quick to run? Do you frighten so easily?"

Par hesitated. Rimmer Dall was a huge, rangy man; his red-bearded face might have been chiseled out of stone, so hard and menacing did it appear. Yet his voice—and Par had not forgotten it either—was soft and compelling.

"Shouldn't you hear what I have to say to you first?" the big man continued. "What harm can it do? I have been waiting here to talk to you for a very long time."

Par stared. "Waiting?"

"Certainly. This is where you had to come sooner or later once you made up your mind about the Sword of Shannara. You have come for the Sword, haven't you? Of course you have. Well, then, I was right to wait, wasn't I? We have much to discuss."

"I wouldn't think so." Par's mind raced. "You tried to arrest Coll and me in Varfleet. You imprisoned my parents in Shady Vale and occupied the village. You have been chasing after me and those with me for weeks."

Rimmer Dall folded his arms. Par noticed again how the left was gloved to the elbow. "Suppose I stand here and you stand there," the big man offered. "That way you can leave any time you choose. I won't do anything to prevent it."

Par took a deep breath and stepped back. "I don't trust you."

The big man shrugged. "Why should you? However, do you want the Sword of Shannara or don't you? If you want it, you must first listen to me. After you've done so, you can take it with you if you wish. Fair enough?"

Par felt the hairs on the back of his neck prickle in warning. "Why should you make a bargain like that after all you've done to keep me from getting the Sword?"

"Keep you from getting the Sword?" The other laughed, a low, pleasant chuckle. "Par Ohmsford. Did you once think to ask for the Sword? Did you ever consider the possibility that I might simply give it to you? Wouldn't that have been easier than sneaking about the city and trying to steal it like a common thief?" Rimmer Dall shook his head slowly. "There is so much that you don't know. Why not let me tell it to you?"

Par glanced about uncertainly, not willing to believe that this wasn't some sort of trick to put him off his guard. The vault was a maze of shadows that whispered of other things lurking there, hidden and waiting. Par rubbed briskly the stone that Damson had given him to brighten its light.

"Ah, you think I have others concealed in the darkness with me, is that it?" Rimmer Dall whispered, the words coming from somewhere deep down inside his chest to rumble through the silence. "Well, here then!"

He raised his gloved hand, made a quick motion with it, and the room was flooded with light. Par gasped in surprise and took another step back.

"Do you think, Par Ohmsford, that you are the only one who has use of magic?" Rimmer Dall asked quietly. "Well, you aren't. As a matter of fact, I have magic at my command that is much greater than yours, greater perhaps than that of the Druids of old. There are others like me, too. There are many in the Four Lands who possess the magic of the old world, of the world before the Four Lands and the Great Wars and man himself."

Par stared at him wordlessly.

"Would you listen to me now, Valeman? While you still can?"

Par shook his head, not in response to the question he had been asked, but in disbelief. "You are a Seeker," he said finally. "You hunt those who use magic. Any use—even by you—is forbidden!"

Rimmer Dall smiled. "So the Federation has decreed. But has that stopped you from using your magic, Par? Or your uncle Walker Boh? Or anyone who possesses it? It is, in fact, a foolish decree, one that could never be enforced except against those who don't care about it in the first place. The Federation dreams of conquest and empire-building, of uniting the lands and the Races under its rule. The Coalition Council schemes and plans, a remnant of a world that has already destroyed itself once in the wars of power. It thinks itself chosen to govern because the Councils of the Races are no more and the Druids gone. It sees the disappearance of the Elves as a blessing. It seizes the provinces of the Southland, threatens Callahorn until it submits, and destroys the wilful Dwarves simply because it can. It sees all this as evidence of its mandate to rule. It believes itself omniscient! In a final gesture of arrogance it outlaws magic! It doesn't once bother asking what purpose magic serves in the scheme of things—it simply denies it!"

The dark figure hunched forward, the arms unfolding. "The fact of the matter is that the Federation is a collection of fools that understands nothing of what the magic means, Valeman. It was magic that brought our world to pass, the world in which we live, in which the Federation believes itself supreme. Magic creates everything, makes everything possible. And the Federation would dismiss such power as if it were meaningless?"

Rimmer Dall straightened, looming up against the strange light he had created, a dark form that seemed only vaguely human.

"Look at me, Par Ohmsford," he whispered.

His body began to shimmer, then to separate. Par watched

in horror as a dark shape rose up against the shadows and half-light, its eyes flaring with crimson fire.

"Do you see, Valeman?" Rimmer Dall's disembodied voice whispered with a hiss of satisfaction. "I am the very thing the Federation would destroy, and they haven't the faintest idea of it!"

The irony of the idea was wasted on Par, who saw nothing beyond the fact that he had placed himself in the worst possible danger. He shrank from the man who called himself Rimmer Dall, the creature who wasn't in fact a man at all, but was a Shadowen. He edged backward, determined to flee. Then he remembered the Sword of Shannara, and abruptly, recklessly, changed his mind. If he could get to the Sword, he thought fiercely, he would have a weapon with which to destroy Rimmer Dall.

But the Shadowen seemed unconcerned. Slowly the dark shape settled back into Rimmer Dall's body and the big man's voice returned. "You have been lied to, Valeman. Repeatedly. You have been told that the Shadowen are evil things, that they are parasites who invade the bodies of men to subvert them to their cause. No, don't bother to deny it or to ask how I know," he said quickly, cutting short Par's exclamation of surprise. "I know everything about you, about your journey to Culhaven, the Wilderun, the Hadeshorn, and beyond. I know of your meeting with the shade of Allanon. I know of the lies he told you. Lies, Par Ohmsford—and they begin with the Druids! They tell you what you must do if the Shadowen are to be destroyed, if the world is to be made safe again! You are to seek the Sword, Wren the Elves, and Walker Boh vanished Paranor—I know!"

The craggy face twisted in anger. "But listen now to what you were not told! The Shadowen are not an aberration that has come to pass in the absence of the Druids! We are their successors! We are what evolved out of the magic with their passing! And we are not monsters invading men, Valeman—we are men ourselves!"

Par shook his head to deny what he was hearing, but Rimmer Dall brought up his gloved hand quickly, pointing to the Valeman. "There is magic in men now as there was once magic in the creatures of faerie. In the Elves, before they took themselves away. In the Druids later." His voice had gone soft and insistent. "I am a man like any other except that I possess the magic. Like you, Par. Somehow I inherited it over the generations of my family that lived before me in a world in which use of magic was commonplace. The magic scattered and seeded itself—not within the ground, but within the bodies of the men and women of the Races. It took hold and grew in some of us, and now we have the power that was once the province of the Druids alone."

He nodded slowly, his eyes fixed on Par. "You have such power. You cannot deny it. Now you must understand the truth of what having that power means."

He paused, waiting for Par to respond. But Par had gone cold to the bone as he sensed what was coming, and he could only howl silently in denial.

"I can see in your eyes that you understand," Rimmer Dall said, his voice softer still. "It means, Par Ohmsford, that you are a Shadowen, too."

COLL COUNTED THE SECONDS in his mind, stretching the process out for as long as he could, thinking as he numbered each that Par must surely appear. But there was no sign of his brother.

The Valeman shook his head in despair. He paced away from the craggy wall of the vault and back again. Five minutes was up. He couldn't wait any longer. He had to go in. It frightened him that in doing so he would be leaving their backs unprotected, but he had no choice. He had to discover what had happened to Par.

He took a deep breath to steady himself as he prepared to enter.

That was when the hands seized him from behind and dragged him down.

"YOU'RE LYING!" Par shouted at Rimmer Dall, forgetting his fear, taking a step forward threateningly.

"There is nothing wrong with being a Shadowen," the other answered sharply. "It is only a word that others have used to label something they don't fully understand. If you can forget the lies you have been told and think of the possibilities, you will be better able to understand what I am telling you. Suppose for a moment that I am right. If the Shadowen are simply men who are meant to be successors to the Druids, then wielding the magic is not only their right, it is their responsibility. The magic is a trust—wasn't that what Allanon told Brin Ohmsford when he died and marked her with his blood? The magic is a tool that must be used for the betterment of the Races and the Four Lands. What is so difficult to accept about that? The problem is not with myself or with you or with the others like us. The problem is with fools like those who govern the Federation and think that anything they cannot control must be suppressed! They see anyone different than themselves as an enemy!"

The strong face tightened. "But who is it that seeks domination over the Four Lands and its people? Who drives the Elves from the Westland, enslaves the Dwarves in the East, besieges the Trolls in the North, and claims all of the Four Lands as its own? Why is it, do you think, that the Four Lands begin to wither and die? Who causes that? You have seen the poor creatures who live in the Pit. Shadowen, you think them, don't you? Well, they are—but their condition is brought about by their keepers. They are men like you and me. The Federation locks them away because they show evidence of possessing magic and are thought dangerous. They become what they are thought to be. They are starved of the life the magic could feed them and they grow mad! That child on Toffer Ridge—what happened to her that caused her to become what she is? She was starved of the magic she needed, of the use of it, and of everything that would have kept her sane. She was driven into exile. Valeman, it is the Federation that causes disruption in the Four Lands with its foolish, blind decrees and its crushing rule! It is the Shadowen who have a chance to set things right!

"As for Allanon, he is first and always a Druid with a Druid's mind and ways. What he seeks is known only to him and likely to remain that way. But you are well advised to be cautious of accepting too readily what he tells you."

He spoke with such conviction that for the first time Par Ohmsford began to doubt. What if indeed the shade of Allanon had lied? Wasn't it true that the Druids had always played games with those from whom they wanted something? Walker had warned him that this was so, that it was a mistake to accept what Allanon was telling them. Something in what Rimmer Dall was saying seemed to whisper that it was true in this instance as well. It was possible, he thought in despair, that he had been misled completely.

The tall, cloaked form before him straightened. "You belong with us, Par Ohmsford," he said quietly.

Par shook his head quickly. "No."

"You are one of us, Valeman. You can deny it as long and as loudly as you like, but the fact remains. We are the same, you and I—possessors of the magic, successors to the Druids, keepers of the trust." He paused, considering. "You still fear me, don't you? A Shadowen. Even the name frightens you. It is the unavoidable result of having accepted as truth the lies you have been told. You think of me as an enemy rather than as kindred."

Par said nothing.

"Let us see who lies and who tells the truth. There." He pointed suddenly to the Sword. "Remove it from its stone, Valeman. It belongs to you; it is your bloodright as heir to the Elven house of Shannara. Pick it up. Touch me with it. If I am the black creature you have been warned against, then the Sword will destroy me. If I am an evil that hides within a lie, the Sword will reveal it. Take it in your hands, then. Use it."

Par remained motionless for a long moment, then bounded up the steps to the block of red marble, seized the Sword of Shannara in both hands, and pulled it forth. It slid free unhindered, gleaming and smooth. He turned quickly and faced Rimmer Dall.

"Come close, Par," the other whispered. "Touch me."

Memories whirled madly in Par's mind, bits and pieces of the songs he had sung, of the stories he had told. What he held now was the Sword of Shannara, the Elven talisman of truth against which no lie could stand.

He came down off the steps, the carved hilt with its burning torch pressed into his palm, the blade held cautiously before him. Rimmer Dall stood waiting. When Par was within striking distance, he stretched out the blade of the talisman and laid it firmly against the other's body.

Nothing happened.

Keeping his eyes riveted on the other, he held the blade steady and willed that the truth be revealed. Still nothing happened. Par waited for as long as he could stand it, then lowered the blade in despair and stepped away.

"Now you know. There is no lie about me," Rimmer Dall said. "The lie is in what you have been told."

Par found that he was shaking. "But why would Allanon lie? What purpose could that possibly serve?"

"Think for a moment on what you have been asked to do." The big man was relaxed, his voice calm and reassuring. "You have been asked to bring back the Druids, to restore to them their talismans, to seek our destruction. The Druids want to regain what was lost to them, the power of life and magic. Is that any different, Par, than what the Warlock Lord sought to do ten centuries ago?"

"But you hunted us!"

"To talk to you, to explain."

"You imprisoned my parents!"

"I kept them safe from harm. The Federation knew of you and would have used them to find you, if I hadn't gone to them first."

Par caught his breath, his arguments momentarily exhausted. Was what he was being told true? Shades, was everything the lie that Rimmer Dall claimed it to be? He could not believe it, yet he could not bring himself to disbelieve it either. His confusion wrapped him like a blanket and left him feeling small and vulnerable.

"I have to think," he said wearily.

"Then come with me and do so," Rimmer Dall responded at once. "Come with me and we shall talk more of this. You have many questions that require answers, and I can give them to you. There is much you need to know about how the magic can be used. Come, Valeman. Put aside your fears and misgivings. No harm shall come to you—never to one whose magic is so promising."

He spoke reassuringly, compellingly, and for an instant Par was almost persuaded. It would have been so easy to agree. He was tired, and he wanted this odyssey to end. It would be comforting to have someone to talk to about the frustrations of possessing the magic. Rimmer Dall would surely know, having experienced them himself. As much as he hated to admit it, he no longer felt threatened by the man. There seemed to be no reason to deny what he was asking.

But he did nevertheless. He did without really understanding why. "No," he said quietly.

"Think of what we can share if you come with me," the other persisted. "We have so much in common! Surely you have longed to talk of your magic, the magic you have been forced to conceal. There has never been anyone for you to do that with before me. I can feel the need in you; I can sense it! Come with me! Valeman, you have . . ."

"No."

Par stepped away. Something ugly whispered suddenly in his mind, some memory that did not yet have a face, but whose voice he clearly recognized.

Rimmer Dall watched him, his craggy features gone suddenly hard. "This is foolish, Valeman."

"I am leaving," Par said quietly, tense now, back on his guard. What was it that bothered him so? "And I am taking the Sword."

The black-cloaked form became another shadow in the halflight. "Stay, Valeman. There are dark secrets kept from you, things that would be better learned from me. Stay and hear them."

Par edged toward the passageway that had brought him in.

"The door is directly behind you," Rimmer Dall said suddenly, his voice sharp. "There are no passageways, no stairs. That was all illusion, my magic invoked to closet you long enough so that we might talk. But if you leave now, something precious will be destroyed. Truth waits for you, Valeman—and there is horror in its face. You cannot withstand it. Stay, and listen to me! You need me!"

Par shook his head. "You sounded for a moment, Rimmer

Dall, like those others, those Shadowen who look nothing like you outwardly, yet speak with your need. Like them, you would possess me."

Rimmer Dall stood silently before him, not moving, simply watching as he backed away. The light the First Seeker had produced faded, and the chamber slid rapidly into darkness.

Par Ohmsford grasped the Sword of Shannara in both hands and bolted for freedom.

RIMMER DALL HAD BEEN right about the passageways and stairs. There were none. It was all illusion, a magic Par should have recognized at once. He burst from the blackness of the vault directly into the gray half-light of the Pit. The damp and mist closed about him instantly. He blinked and whirled about, searching.

Coll

Where was Coll?

He stripped the cloak from his back and wrapped it hurriedly about the Sword of Shannara. Allanon had said he would need it—if Allanon was still to be believed. At the moment, he didn't know. But the Sword should be cared for; it must have purpose. Unless it had lost its magic. Could it have lost its magic?

"Par."

The Valeman jumped, startled by the voice. It was right behind him, so close that it might have been a whisper in his ear if not for the harshness of its sound. He turned.

And there was Coll.

Or what had once been Coll.

His brother's face was barely recognizable, ravaged by some inner torment that he could only begin to imagine, a twisting that had distorted the familiar features and left them slack and lifeless. His body was misshapen as well, all pulled out of joint and hunched over, as if the bones had been rearranged. There were marks on his skin, tears and lesions, and the eyes burned with a fever he recognized immediately.

"They took me," Coll whispered despairingly. "They made me. Please, Par, I need you. Hug me? Please?"

Par cried out, howling as if he would never stop, willing the thing before him to go away, to disappear from his sight and mind. Chills shook him, and the emptiness that opened inside threatened to collapse him completely.

"Coll!" he sobbed.

His brother stumbled and jerked toward him, arms outstretched. Rimmer Dall's warning whispered in Par's ear—the truth, the truth, the horror of it! Coll was a Shadowen, had somehow become one, a creature like the others in the Pit that Rimmer Dall claimed the Federation had destroyed! How? Par had been gone only minutes, it seemed. What had been done to his brother?

He stood there, stunned and shaking, as the thing before him caught hold of him with its fingers, then with its arms, enfolding him, whispering all the time, "hug me, hug me," as if it were a litany that would set it free. Par wished he were dead, that he had never been born, that he could somehow disappear from the earth and leave all that was happening behind. He wished a million impossible things—anything that could save him. The Sword of Shannara dropped from his nerveless fingers, and he felt as if everything he had known and believed in had in a single instant been betrayed.

Coll's hands began to rip at him.

"Coll, no!" he screamed.

Then something happened deep inside, something that he struggled against for only an instant's time before it overpowered him. A burning surged within his chest and spread outward through his body like a fire out of control. It was the magic—not the magic of the wishsong, the magic of harmless images and pretended things, but the other. It was the magic that had belonged once to the Elfstones, the magic that Allanon had given to Shea Ohmsford all those years ago, that had seeded itself in Wil Ohmsford and passed through generations of his family to him, changing, evolving, a constant mystery. It was alive in him, a magic greater than the wishsong, hard and unyielding.

It rushed through him and exploded forth. He screamed to Coll to let go of him, to get away, but his brother did not seem to hear. Coll, a ruined creature, a caricature of the blood and flesh human Par had loved, was consumed with his own inner madness, the Shadowen that he had become needing only to feed. The magic took him, enveloped him, and in an instant turned him to ash.

Par watched in horror as his brother disintegrated before his eyes. Stunned, speechless, he collapsed to his knees, feeling his own life disappear with Coll's.

Then other hands were reaching for him, grappling with him, pulling him down. A whirl of twisted, ravaged faces and bodies pressed into him. The Shadowen of the Pit had come for him as well. There were scores of them, their hands grasping for him, their fingers ripping and tearing as if to shred him. He felt himself coming apart, breaking beneath the weight of their bodies.

And then the magic returned, exploding forth once more, and they were flung away like deadwood.

The magic took form this time, an unbidden thought brought to life. It coalesced in his hands, a jagged shard of blue fire, the flames as cool and hard as iron. He did not understand it yet, did not comprehend its source or being—yet he understood instinctively its purpose. Power radiated through him. Crying out in fury he swung his newfound weapon in a deadly arc, cutting through the creatures about him as if they were made of paper. They collapsed instantly, their voices unintelligible and remote as they died. He lost himself in the haze of his killing, striking out like a madman, giving sweet release to the fury and despair that had been born with the death of his brother.

The death he had caused!

The Shadowen fell back from him, those he did not destroy, staggering and shambling like stringed puppets. Bellowing at them still, gripping the shard of magic fire in one hand, Par reached down and snatched up the fallen Sword of Shannara.

He felt it burn him, searing his hand, the pain harsh and shocking.

Instantly his own magic flared and died. He jerked back in surprise, tried to invoke it anew and found he could not. The Shadowen started for him at once. He hesitated, then ran. Down the line of bridge rubble he raced, tripping and sliding on the dampened earth, gasping in rage and frustration. He could not tell how close the creatures of the Pit were to him. He ran without looking back, desperate to escape, fleeing as much from the horror of what had befallen him as the Shadowen in pursuit.

He was almost to the wall of the cliff when he heard Damson call. He ran for her, his mind shriveled so that he could think of nothing but the need to get free. The Sword of Shannara was clutched tightly to his chest, the burning gone now, just a simple blade wrapped within his muddied cloak. He went down, sprawling on his face, sobbing. He heard Damson again, calling out, and he shouted back in answer.

Then she had him in her arms, hauling him back to his feet, pulling him away, asking, "Par, Par, what's wrong with you? Par, what's happened?"

And he, replying in gasps and sobs, "He's dead, Damson! Coll's dead! I've killed him!"

The door into the cliff wall stood open ahead, a black aperture with a small, furry, wide-eyed creature framed in the opening. With Damson supporting him, he stumbled through and heard the door slam shut behind him.

Then everything and everyone disappeared in the white sound of his scream.

CHAPTER

33

IT WAS RAINING in the Dragon's Teeth, a cold, gray, insistent drizzle that masked the skyline from horizon to horizon. Morgan Leah stood at the edge of a trailside precipice and stared out from beneath the hood of his cloak. South, the foothills appeared as low, rolling shadows against the haze. The Mermidon could not be seen at all. The world beyond where he stood was a vague and distant place, and he had an unpleasant sense of not being able to fit back into it again.

He blinked away the flurry of drops that blew into his eyes, shielding himself with his hands. His reddish hair was plastered against his forehead, and his face was cold. Beneath his sodden clothing, his body was scraped and sore. He shivered, listening to the sounds around him. The wind whipped across the cliffs and down through the trees, its howl rising momentarily above the thunder that rumbled far to the north. Flood streams cascaded through the rocks behind him, rushing and splashing, the water building on itself as it tumbled downward into mist.

It was a day for rethinking one's life, Morgan decided grimly. It was a day for beginning anew.

Padishar Creel came up behind him, a cloaked, bulky form. Rain streaked his hard face, and his clothing, like Morgan's, was soaked through.

"Time to be going?" he asked quietly.

Morgan nodded.

"Are you ready, lad?"

"Yes."

Padishar looked away into the rain and sighed. "It's not turned out as we expected, has it?" he said quietly. "Not a bit of it."

Morgan thought a minute, then replied, "I don't know, Padishar. Maybe it has."

Under Padishar's guidance, the outlaws had emerged from the tunnels below the Jut early that morning and made their way east and north into the mountains. The trails they followed were narrow and steep and made dangerously slick by the rain, but Padishar felt it was safer to travel them than to try to slip through the Kennon Pass, which would surely be watched. The weather, bad as it was, was more help than hindrance. The rain washed away their footprints, erasing any trace of where they had been or where they were going. They had seen nothing of the Federation army since their flight began. Any pursuit was either bogged down or confused. The Jut might be lost, but the outlaws had escaped to fight another day.

It was now midafternoon, and the ragtag band had worked its way to a point somewhere above the juncture of the Mermidon where it branched south to the Rainbow Lake and east to the Rabb Plains. On a bluff where the mountain trails diverged in all directions, they had paused to rest before parting company. The Trolls would turn north for the Charnals and home. The outlaws would regroup at Firerim Reach, another of their redoubts. Padishar would return to Tyrsis in search of Damson and the missing Valemen. Morgan would go east to Culhaven and keep his promise to Steff. In four weeks' time, they would all meet again at Jannisson Pass. Hopefully by then the Troll army would be fully mobilized and the Movement would have consolidated its splintered groups. It would be time to begin mapping out a specific strategy for use in the continuing struggle against the Federation.

If any of them were still alive to do the mapping, Morgan thought dismally. He wasn't convinced any longer that they would be. What had happened with Teel had left him angry and doubting. He knew now how easy it was for the Shadowen—and therefore their Federation allies—to infiltrate those who stood against them. Anyone could be the enemy; there was no way to tell. Betrayal could come from any quarter and likely would. What were they to do to protect themselves when they could never be certain whom to trust?

It was bothering Padishar as well, Morgan knew—though the outlaw chief would be the last to admit it. Morgan had been watching him closely since their escape, and the big man was seeing ghosts at every turn.

But, then, so was he.

He felt a dark resignation chill him as if seeking to turn him to ice. It might be best for both of them to be alone for a while.

"Will it be safe for you to try going back to Tyrsis so soon?" he asked abruptly, wanting to make some sort of conversation, to hear the other's voice, but unable to think of anything better to say.

Padishar shrugged. "As safe as it ever is for me. I'll be disguised in any case." He looked over, dipping his head briefly against a gust of wind and rain. "Don't be worrying, Highlander. The Valemen will be all right. I'll make certain of it."

"It bothers me that I'm not going with you." Morgan could not keep the bitterness from his voice. "I was the one who talked Par and Coll into coming here in the first place—or at least I had a lot to do with it. I abandoned them once already in Tyrsis, and here I am abandoning them again." He shook his head wearily. "But I don't know what else I can do. I have to do what Steff asked of me. I can't just ignore . . ."

What he was going to say caught sharply in his throat as the memory of his dying friend flashed through his mind and the pain of his loss returned, sharp and poignant. He thought momentarily that there might be tears, but there weren't. Perhaps he had cried them all out.

Padishar reached out and put a hand on his shoulder. "Highlander, you must keep your promise. You owe him that. When it's finished, come back. The Valemen and I will be waiting, and we'll all begin again."

Morgan nodded, still unable to speak. He tasted the rain on his lips and licked it away.

Padishar's strong face bent close, blocking out everything else for just an instant. "We do what we must in this struggle, Morgan Leah. All of us. We are free-born as the rally cry says—

Men, Dwarves, Trolls, all of us. There is no separate war to fight; it's a war that we all share. So you go to Culhaven and help those who need it there, and I'll go to Tyrsis and do the same. But we won't forget about each other, will we?"

Morgan shook his head. "No, we won't, Padishar."

The big man stepped back. "Well, then. Take this." He handed Morgan his ring with the hawk emblem. "When you need to find me again, show this to Matty Roh at the Whistledown in Varfleet. I'll see to it that she knows the way to where I'll be. Don't worry. It served the purpose once; it will serve it twice. Now, be on your way. And good luck to you."

He extended his hand and Morgan took it with a firm grasp. "Luck to you as well, Padishar."

Padishar Creel laughed. "Always, lad. Always."

He walked back across the bluff to a grove of towering fir where the outlaws and Trolls waited. Everyone who could came to their feet. Words of parting were spoken, distant and faint through the rain. Chandos was hugging Padishar, others were clapping him on the back, a few from their stretchers lifted their hands for him to take.

Even after all that's happened, he's still the only leader they want, Morgan thought in admiration.

He watched the Trolls begin to move north into the rocks, the huge, lumbering figures quickly becoming indistinguishable from the landscape through which they passed.

Padishar was looking at him now. He lifted his arm and waved in farewell.

He turned east into the foothills. The rain lashed at him, and he kept his head bent low to protect his face. His eyes focused on the path before him. When he thought to look back again, to see those he had fought beside and traveled with one final time, they had disappeared.

It occurred to him then that he said nothing to Padishar about the magic that still lingered in the broken Sword of Leah, the magic that had saved both their lives. He had never told the other how he had defeated Teel, how it was that he had managed to overcome the Shadowen. There had been no time to talk of it. He supposed that there had been no real reason. It was something he didn't yet fully understand. Why there was still magic in the blade, he didn't know. Why he had been able to summon it, he wasn't certain. He had thought it all used up before. Was it all used up now? Or was there enough left to save him one more time if the need should arise?

He found himself wondering how long it would be before he had to find out.

Moving cautiously down the mountainside, he faded away into the rain.

P AR OHMSFORD DRIFTED

He did not sleep, for in sleeping he would dream and his dreams haunted him. Nor did he wake, for in waking he would find the reality that he was so desperate to escape.

He simply drifted, half in and half out of any recognizable existence, tucked somewhere back in the gray in-between of what is and what isn't, where his mind could not focus and his memories remained scattered, where he was warm and secure from the past and future both, curled up deep inside. There was a madness upon him, he knew. But the madness was welcome, and he let it claim him without a struggle. It made him disoriented and distorted his perceptions and his thoughts. It gave him shelter. It cloaked him in a shroud of nonbeing that kept everything walled away—and that was what he needed.

Yet even walls have chinks and cracks that let through the light, and so it was with his madness. He sensed things—whispers of life from the world he was trying so hard to hide from. He felt the blankets that wrapped him and the bed on which he lay. He saw candles burning softly through a liquid haze, pin-pricks of yellow brightness like islands on a dark sea. Strange beasts looked down at him from cabinets, shelves, boxes, and dressers, and their faces were formed of cloth and fur with button eyes and sewn noses, with ears that drooped and tipped, and with studied, watchful poses that never changed. He listened as words were spoken, floating through the air as motes of dust on streamers from the sun.

"He's very sick, lovely Damson," he heard one voice say.

And the other replied, "He's protecting himself, Mole."

Damson and Mole. He knew who they were, although he

couldn't quite place them. He knew as well that they were talking about him. He didn't mind. What they were saying didn't make any difference.

Sometimes he saw their faces through the chinks and cracks.

The Mole was a creature with round, furry features and large, questioning eyes who stood above him, looking thoughtful. Sometimes he brought the strange beasts to sit close by. He looked very much the same as the beasts, Par thought. He called them by name. He spoke with them. But the beasts never answered back.

The girl fed him sometimes. Damson. She spooned soup into his mouth and made him drink, and he did so without argument. There was something perplexing about her, something that fascinated him, and he tried talking to her once or twice before giving up. Whatever it was he wished to say refused to show itself. The words ran away and hid. His thoughts faded. He watched her face fade with them.

She kept coming back, though. She sat beside him and held his hand. He could feel it from where he hid inside himself. She spoke softly, touched his face with her fingers, let him feel her presence even when she was doing nothing. It was her presence more than anything that kept him from drifting away altogether. He would have liked it better if she had let him go. He thought that it would happen that way eventually, that he would drift far enough that everything would disappear. But she prevented that, and, while it frustrated and even angered him at times, it also interested him. Why was she doing this? Was she anxious to keep him with her, or did she simply want to be taken along?

He began to listen more intently when she spoke. Her words seemed to grow clearer.

"It wasn't your fault," was what she told him most often. She told him that over and over, and for the longest time he didn't know why.

"That creature was no longer Coll." She told him that, too. "You had to destroy it."

She said these things, and once in a while he thought he almost understood. But fierce, dark shadows cloaked his understanding, and he was quick to hide from them.

But one day she spoke the words and he understood imme-

diately. The drifting stopped, the walls broke apart, and everything rushed in with the cold fury of a winter ice storm. He
began screaming, and he could not seem to stop. The memories
returned, sweeping aside everything he had so carefully constructed to keep them out, and his rage and anguish were boundless. He screamed, and the Mole shrank from him, the strange
beasts tumbled from his bedside, he could see the candles flickering through the tears he cried, and the shadows danced
with glee.

It was the girl who saved him. She fought past the rage and
anguish, ignored the screams, and held him to her. She held him
as if the drifting might begin anew, as if he were in danger of
being swept away completely, and she refused to let go. When
his screams finally stopped, he found that he was holding
her back.

He slept then, a deep and dreamless sleep that submerged
him completely and let him rest. The madness was gone when
he awoke, the drifting ended, and the gray half-sleep washed
away. He knew himself again; he knew his surroundings and the
faces of Damson Rhee and the Mole as they passed beside him.
They bathed him and gave him fresh clothes, fed him and let
him sleep some more. They did not speak to him. Perhaps they
understood that he could not yet respond.

When he woke this time, the memories from which he had
hidden surfaced in the forefront of his mind like creatures seeking air. They were no longer so loathsome to look upon, though
they made him sad and confused and left him feeling empty. He
faced them one by one, and allowed them to speak. When they
had done so, he took their words and framed them in windows
of light that revealed them clearly.

What they meant, he decided, was that the world had been
turned upside down.

The Sword of Shannara lay on the bed beside him. He wasn't
sure if it had been there all along or if Damson had placed it
there after he had come back to himself. What he did know was
that it was useless. It was supposed to provide a means to destroy
the Shadowen, and it had been totally ineffective against Rimmer Dall. He had risked everything to gain the Sword, and it

appeared that the risk had been pointless. He still did not possess the talisman he had been promised.

Of lies and truth there were more than enough and no way to separate one from the other. Rimmer Dall was lying surely—he could sense that much. But he had also spoken the truth. Allanon had spoken the truth—but he had been lying as well. Neither of them was entirely what he pretended to be. Nothing was completely as either portrayed it. Even he might be something other than what he believed, his magic the two-edged sword about which his uncle Walker had always warned him.

But the harshest and most bitter of the memories he faced was of poor, dead Coll. His brother had been changed into a Shadowen while trying to protect him, made a creature of the Pit, and Par had killed him for it. He hadn't meant to, certainly hadn't wanted to, but the magic had come forth unbidden and destroyed him. Probably there hadn't been anything he could have done to stop it, but such rationalization offered little in the way of solace or forgiveness. Coll's death was his fault. His brother had come on this journey because of him. He had gone down into the Pit because of him. Everything he had done had been because of Par.

Because Coll loved him.

He thought suddenly of their meeting with the shade of Allanon where so much had been entrusted to all of the Ohmsfords but Coll. Had Allanon known then that Coll was going to die? Was that why no mention had been made of him, why no charge had been given to him?

The possibility enraged Par.

His brother's face hovered in the air before him, changing, running through the gamut of moods he remembered so well. He could hear Coll's voice, the nuances of its rough intensity, the mix of its tones. He replayed in his mind all the adventures they had shared while growing up, the times they had gone against their parents' wishes, the places they had traveled to and seen, the people they had met and of whom they had talked. He retraced the events of the past few weeks, beginning with their flight from Varfleet. Much of it was tinged with his own sense of guilt, his need to assign himself blame. But most of it was free of everything but the wish to remember what his brother Coll had been like.

Coll, who was dead.

He lay for hours thinking of it, holding up the fact of it to the light of his understanding, in the silence of his thoughts, trying to find a way to make it real. It wasn't real, though—not yet. It was too awful to be real, and the pain and despair were too intense to be given release. Some part of him refused to admit that Coll was gone. He knew it was so, and yet he could not banish entirely that small, hopelessly absurd denial. In the end, he gave up trying.

His world compressed. He ate and he rested. He spoke sparingly with Damson. He lay in the Mole's dark underground lair amid the refuse of the upper world, himself a discard, only a little more alive than the toy animals that kept watch over him.

Yet all the while his mind was at work. Eventually he would grow strong again, he promised himself. When he did, someone would answer for what had been done to Coll.

CHAPTER

34

THE PRISONER CAME AWAKE, easing out of the drug-induced sleep that had kept him paralyzed almost from the moment he was taken. He lay on a sleeping mat in a darkened room. The ropes that had bound his hands and feet had been removed, and the cloths with which he had been gagged and blindfolded were gone. He was free to move about.

He sat up slowly, fighting to overcome a sudden rush of dizziness. His eyes adjusted to the dark, and he was able to make out the shape and dimensions of his jail. The room was large, more than twenty feet square. There was the mat, a wooden bench, a small table, and two chairs pushed into it. There was a window with metal shutters and a metal door. Both were closed.

He reached out experimentally and touched the wall. It was constructed of stone blocks and mortar. It would take a lot of digging to get through.

The dizziness passed finally, and he rose to his feet. There was a tray with bread and water on the table, and he sat down and ate the bread and drank the water. There was no reason not to; if they had wanted him dead, he would be so by now. He retained faint impressions of the journey that had brought him there—the sounds of the wagon in which he rode and the horses that pulled it, the low voices of the men, the rough grasp of the hands that held him when he was being fed and bedded, and the ache that he felt whenever he was awake long enough to feel anything.

He could still taste the bitterness of the drugs they had forced down his throat, the mix of crushed herbs and medicines that had burned through him and left him unconscious, drifting in a world of dreams that lacked any semblance to reality.

He finished his meal and came back to his feet. Where had they brought him, he wondered?

Taking his time, for he was still very weak, he made his way over to the shuttered window. The shutters did not fit tightly, and there were cracks in the fittings. Cautiously, he peered out.

He was a long way up. The summer sunlight brightened a countryside of forests and grassy knolls that stretched away to the edge of a huge lake that shimmered like liquid silver. Birds flew across the lake, soaring and diving, their calls ringing out in the stillness. High overhead, the faint traces of a vast, brightly colored rainbow canopied the lake from shoreline to shoreline.

The prisoner caught his breath in surprise. It was the Rainbow Lake.

He shifted his gaze hurriedly to the outer walls of his prison. He could just catch a glimpse of them as the window well opened up and dropped away.

They were formed of black granite.

This time his revelation stunned him. For a moment, he could not believe it. He was inside Southwatch.

Inside.

But who were his jailors—the Federation, the Shadowen, or someone else altogether? And why Southwatch? Why was he here? Why was he even still alive for that matter?

His frustration overcame him for a moment, and he lowered his head against the window ledge and closed his eyes. So many questions once again. It seemed that the questions would never end.

What had become of Par?

Coll Ohmsford straightened, and his eyes slipped open. He pressed his face back against the shutters, peered into the distant countryside, and wondered what fate his captors had planned for him.

THAT NIGHT COGLINE DREAMED. He lay in the shelter of the forest trees that ringed the barren heights on which ancient Paranor had once stood, tossing beneath the thin covering of his robes, beset by visions that chilled him more surely than any night wind. When he came awake, it was with a start. He was shaking with fear.

He had dreamed that the Shannara children were all dead.

For a moment he was convinced that it must be so. Then fear gave way to nervous irritation and that in turn to anger. He realized that what he had experienced was more probably a premonition of what might be than a vision of what was.

Steadying himself, he built a small fire, let it burn awhile to warm him, then took a pinch of silver powder from a pouch at his waist and dropped it into the flames. Smoke rose, filling the air before him with images that shimmered with iridescent light. He waited, letting them play themselves out, watching them closely until they had faded away.

Then he grunted in satisfaction, kicked out the fire, rolled himself back into his robes, and lay down again. The images told him only a little, but a little was all he needed to know. He was reassured. The dream was only a dream. The Shannara children lived. There were dangers that threatened them, of course—just as there had been from the beginning. He had sensed them in the images, monstrous and frightening, dark wraiths of possibility.

But that was as it must be.

The old man closed his eyes and his breathing slowed. There was nothing to be done about it this night.

Everything, he repeated, was as it must be.

Then he slept.

HERE ENDS BOOK ONE of *The Heritage of Shannara*. Book Two, *The Druid of Shannara*, will reveal more of Cogline, who calls himself a failed Druid, and of the troubles of the children of Shannara.

THE DRUID OF SHANNARA

TO LAURIE AND PETER,
FOR THEIR LOVE, SUPPORT, AND ENCOURAGEMENT
IN ALL THINGS

THE DRUID OF SHANNARA

CHAPTER

1

HE KING OF THE SILVER RIVER stood at the edge of the
Gardens that had been his domain since the dawn of
the age of faerie and looked out over the world of mortal men. What he saw left him sad and discouraged.
Everywhere the land sickened and died, rich black earth turning
to dust, grassy plains withering, forests becoming huge stands of
deadwood, and lakes and rivers either stagnating or drying away.
Everywhere the creatures who lived upon the land sickened and
died as well, unable to sustain themselves as the nourishment
they relied upon grew poisoned. Even the air had begun to turn
foul.

And all the while, the King of the Silver River thought, *the
Shadowen grow stronger.*

His fingers reached out to brush the crimson petals of the
cyclamen that grew thick about his feet. Forsythia clustered just
beyond, dogwood and cherry farther back, fuchsia and hibiscus,
rhododendrons and dahlias, beds of iris, azaleas, daffodils, roses,
and a hundred other varieties of flowers and flowering plants
that were always in bloom, a profusion of colors that stretched
away into the distance until lost from sight. There were animals
to be seen as well, both large and small, creatures whose evolution could be traced back to that distant time when all things
lived in harmony and peace.

In the present world, the world of the Four Lands and the
races that had evolved out of the chaos and destruction of the
Great Wars, that time was all but forgotten. The King of

the Silver River was its sole remnant. He had been alive when the world was new and its first creatures were just being born. He had been young then, and there had been many like him. Now he was old and he was the last of his kind. Everything that had been, save for the Gardens in which he lived, had passed away. The Gardens alone survived, changeless, sustained by the magic of faerie. The Word had given the Gardens to the King of the Silver River and told him to tend them, to keep them as a reminder of what had once been and what might one day be again. The world without would evolve as it must, but the Gardens would remain forever the same.

Even so, they were shrinking. It was not so much physical as spiritual. The boundaries of the Gardens were fixed and unalterable, for the Gardens existed in a plane of being unaffected by changes in the world of mortal men. The Gardens were a presence rather than a place. Yet that presence was diminished by the sickening of the world to which it was tied, for the work of the Gardens and their tender was to keep that world strong. As the Four Lands grew poisoned, the work became harder, the effects of that work grew shorter, and the boundaries of human belief and trust in its existence—always somewhat marginal— began to fail altogether.

The King of the Silver River grieved that this should be. He did not grieve for himself; he was beyond that. He grieved for the people of the Four Lands, the mortal men and women for whom the magic of faerie was in danger of being lost forever. The Gardens had been their haven in the land of the Silver River for centuries, and he had been the spirit friend who protected its people. He had watched over them, had given them a sense of peace and well-being that transcended physical boundaries, and gave promise that benevolence and goodwill were still accessible in some corners of the world to all. Now that was ended. Now he could protect no one. The evil of the Shadowen, the poison they had inflicted upon the Four Lands, had eroded his own strength until he was virtually sealed within his Gardens, powerless to go to the aid of those he had worked so long to protect.

He stared out into the ruin of the world for a time as his

despair worked its relentless will on him. Memories played hide-and-seek in his mind. The Druids had protected the Four Lands once. But the Druids were gone. A handful of descendents of the Elven house of Shannara had been champions of the races for generations, wielding the remnants of the magic of faerie. But they were all dead.

He forced his despair away, replacing it with hope. The Druids could come again. And there were new generations of the old house of Shannara. The King of the Silver River knew most of what was happening in the Four Lands even if he could not go out into them. Allanon's shade had summoned a scattering of Shannara children to recover the lost magic, and perhaps they yet would if they could survive long enough to find a means to do so. But all of them had been placed in extreme peril. All were in danger of dying, threatened in the east, south, and west by the Shadowen and in the north by Uhl Belk, the Stone King.

The old eyes closed momentarily. He knew what was needed to save the Shannara children—an act of magic, one so powerful and intricate that nothing could prevent it from succeeding, one that would transcend the barriers that their enemies had created, that would break past the screen of deceit and lies that hid everything from the four on whom so much depended.

Yes, *four*, not three. Even Allanon did not understand the whole of what was meant to be.

He turned and made his way back toward the center of his refuge. He let the songs of the birds, the fragrances of the flowers, and the warmth of the air soothe him as he walked and he drew in through his senses the color and taste and feel of all that lay about him. There was virtually nothing that he could not do within his Gardens. Yet his magic was needed without. He knew what was required. In preparation he took the form of the old man that showed himself occasionally to the world beyond. His gait became an unsteady shamble, his breathing wheezed, his eyes dimmed, and his body ached with the feelings of life fading. The birdsong stopped, and the small animals that had crowded close edged quickly away. He forced himself to separate from everything he had evolved into, receding into what he might have been, needing momentarily to feel human mortality in order to know better how to give that part of himself that was needed.

When he reached the heart of his domain, he stopped. There was a pond of clearest water fed by a small stream. A unicorn drank from it. The earth that cradled the pond was dark and rich. Tiny, delicate flowers that had no name grew at the water's edge; they were the color of new snow. A small, intricately formed tree lifted out of a scattering of violet grasses at the pond's far end, its delicate green leaves laced with red. From a pair of massive rocks, streaks of colored ore shimmered brightly in the sunshine.

The King of the Silver River stood without moving in the presence of the life that surrounded him and willed himself to become one with it. When he had done so, when everything had threaded itself through the human form he had taken as if joined by bits and pieces of invisible lacing, he reached out to gather it all in. His hands, wrinkled human skin and brittle bones, lifted and summoned his magic, and the feelings of age and time that were the reminders of mortal existence disappeared.

The little tree came to him first, uprooted, transported, and set down before him, the framework of bones on which he would build. Slowly it bent to take the shape he desired, leaves folding close against the branches, wrapping and sealing away. The earth came next, handfuls lifted by invisible scoops to place against the tree, padding and defining. Then came the ores for muscle, the waters for fluids, and the petals of the tiny flowers for skin. He gathered silk from the unicorn's mane for hair and black pearls for eyes. The magic twisted and wove, and slowly his creation took form.

When he was finished, the girl who stood before him was perfect in every way but one. She was not yet alive.

He cast about momentarily, then selected the dove. He took it out of the air and placed it still living inside the girl's breast where it became her heart. Quickly he moved forward to embrace her and breathed his own life into her. Then he stepped back to wait.

The girl's breast rose and fell, and her limbs twitched. Her eyes fluttered open, coal black as they peered out from her delicate white features. She was small boned and finely wrought like a piece of paper art smoothed and shaped so that the edges and corners were replaced by curves. Her hair was so white it seemed silver; there was a glitter to it that suggested the presence of that precious metal.

"Who am I?" she asked in a soft, lilting voice that whispered of tiny streams and small night sounds.

"You are my daughter," the King of the Silver River answered, discovering within himself the stirring of feelings he had thought long since lost.

He did not bother telling her that she was an elemental, an earth child created of his magic. She could sense what she was from the instincts with which he had endowed her. No other explanation was needed.

She took a tentative step forward, then another. Finding that she could walk, she began to move more quickly, testing her abilities in various ways as she circled her father, glancing cautiously, shyly at the old man as she went. She looked around curiously, taking in the sights, smells, sounds, and tastes of the Gardens, discovering in them a kinship that she could not immediately explain.

"Are these Gardens my mother?" she asked suddenly, and he told her they were. "Am I a part of you both?" she asked, and he told her yes.

"Come with me," he said gently.

Together, they walked through the Gardens, exploring in the manner of a parent and child, looking into flowers, watching for the quick movement of birds and animals, studying the vast, intricate designs of the tangled undergrowth, the complex layers of rock and earth, and the patterns woven by the threads of the Gardens' existence. She was bright and quick, interested in everything, respectful of life, caring. He was pleased with what he saw; he found that he had made her well.

After a time, he began to show her something of the magic. He demonstrated his own first, only the smallest bits and pieces of it so as not to overwhelm her. Then he let her test her own against it. She was surprised to learn that she possessed it, even more surprised to discover what it could do. But she was not hesitant about using it. She was eager.

"You have a name," he told her. "Would you like to know what it is?"

"Yes," she answered, and stood looking at him alertly.

"Your name is Quickening." He paused. "Do you understand why?"

She thought a moment. "Yes," she answered again.

He led her to an ancient hickory whose bark peeled back in great, shaggy strips from its trunk. The breezes cooled there, smelling of jasmine and begonia, and the grass was soft as they sat together. A griffin wandered over through the tall grasses and nuzzled the girl's hand.

"Quickening," the King of the Silver River said. "There is something you must do."

Slowly, carefully he explained to her that she must leave the Gardens and go out into the world of men. He told her where it was that she must go and what it was that she must do. He talked of the Dark Uncle, the Highlander, and the nameless other, of the Shadowen, of Uhl Belk and Eldwist, and of the Black Elfstone. As he spoke to her, revealing the truth behind who and what she was, he experienced an aching within his breast that was decidedly human, part of himself that had been submerged for many centuries. The ache brought a sadness that threatened to cause his voice to break and his eyes to tear. He stopped once in surprise to fight back against it. It required some effort to resume speaking. The girl watched him without comment—intense, introspective, expectant. She did not argue with what he told her and she did not question it. She simply listened and accepted.

When he was done, she stood up. "I understand what is expected of me. I am ready."

But the King of the Silver River shook his head. "No, child, you are not. You will discover that when you leave here. Despite who you are and what you can do, you are vulnerable nevertheless to things against which I cannot protect you. Be careful then to protect yourself. Be on guard against what you do not understand."

"I will," she replied.

He walked with her to the edge of the Gardens, to where the world of men began, and together they stared out at the encroaching ruin. They stood without speaking for a very long time before she said, "I can tell that I am needed there."

He nodded bleakly, feeling the loss of her already though she had not yet departed. *She is only an elemental,* he thought and knew immediately that he was wrong. She was a great deal more. As much as if he had given birth to her, she was a part of him.

"Goodbye, Father," she said suddenly and left his side.

She walked out of the Gardens and disappeared into the world beyond. She did not kiss him or touch him in parting. She simply left, because that was all she knew to do.

The King of the Silver River turned away. His efforts had wearied him, had drained him of his magic. He needed time to rest. Quickly he shed his human image, stripping away the false covering of skin and bones, washing himself clean of its memories and sensations, and reverting to the faerie creature he was.

Even so, what he felt for Quickening, his daughter, the child of his making, stayed with him.

CHAPTER

2

ALKER BOH CAME awake with a shudder.

Dark Uncle.

The whisper of a voice in his mind jerked him back from the edge of the black pool into which he was sliding, pulled him from the inky dark into the gray fringes of the light, and he started so violently that the muscles of his legs cramped. His head snapped up from the pillow of his arm, his eyes slipped open, and he stared blankly ahead. There was pain all through his body, endless waves of it. The pain wracked him as if he had been touched by a hot iron, and he curled tightly into himself in a futile effort to ease it. Only his right arm remained outstretched, a heavy and cumbersome thing that no longer belonged to him, fastened forever to the floor of the cavern on which he lay, turned to stone to the elbow.

The source of the pain was there.

He closed his eyes against it, willing it to disperse, to disappear. But he lacked the strength to command it, his magic almost gone, dissipated by his struggle to resist the advancing poison of the Asphinx. It was seven days now since he had come into the Hall of Kings in search of the Black Elfstone, seven days since he had found instead the deadly creature that had been placed there to snare him.

Oh, yes, he thought feverishly. Definitely to snare him.

But by whom? By the Shadowen or by someone else? Who now had possession of the Black Elfstone?

He recalled in despair the events that had brought him to

this end. There had been the summons from the shade of Allanon, dead three hundred years, to the heirs of the Shannara magic: his nephew Par Ohmsford, his cousin Wren Ohmsford, and himself. They had received the summons and a visit from the once-Druid Cogline urging them to heed it. They had done so, assembling at the Hadeshorn, ancient resting place of the Druids, where Allanon had appeared to them and charged them with separate undertakings that were meant to combat the dark work of the Shadowen who were using magic of their own to steal away the life of the Four Lands. Walker had been charged with recovering Paranor, the disappeared home of the Druids, and with bringing back the Druids themselves. He had resisted this charge until Cogline had come to him again, this time bearing a volume of the Druid Histories which told of a Black Elfstone which had the power to retrieve Paranor. That in turn had led him to the Grimpond, seer of the earth's and mortal men's secrets.

He searched the gloom of the cavern about him, the doors to the tombs of the Kings of the Four Lands dead all these centuries, the wealth piled before the crypts in which they lay, and the stone sentinels that kept watch over their remains. Stone eyes stared out of blank faces, unseeing, unheeding. He was alone with their ghosts.

He was dying.

Tears filled his eyes, blinding him as he fought to hold them back. He was such a fool!

Dark Uncle. The words echoed soundlessly, a memory that taunted and teased. The voice was the Grimpond's, that wretched, insidious spirit responsible for what had befallen him. It was the Grimpond's riddles that had led him to the Hall of Kings in search of the Black Elfstone. The Grimpond must have known what awaited him, that there would be no Elfstone but the Asphinx instead, a deadly trap that would destroy him.

And why had he thought it would be otherwise? Walker asked himself bleakly. Didn't the Grimpond hate him above all others? Hadn't it boasted to Walker that it was sending him to his doom by giving him what he asked for? Walker had simply gone out of his way to accommodate the spirit, anxiously rushing off to greet the death that he had been promised, blithely believing that he could protect himself against whatever evil he might encounter. Remember? he chided himself. Remember how confident you were?

He convulsed as the poison burned into him. Well and good. But where was his confidence now?

He forced himself to his knees and bent down over the opening in the cavern floor where his hand was pinned to the stone. He could just make out the remains of the Asphinx, the snake's stone body coiled about his own stone arm, the two of them forever joined, fastened to the rock of the mountain. He tightened his mouth and pulled up the sleeve of his cloak. His arm was hard and unyielding, gray to the elbow, and streaks of gray worked their way upward toward his shoulder. The process was slow, but steady. His entire body was turning to stone.

Not that it mattered if it did, he thought, because he would starve to death long before that happened. Or die of thirst. Or of the poison.

He let the sleeve fall back into place, covering the horror of what he had become. Seven days gone. What little food he'd brought with him had been consumed almost immediately, and he'd drunk the last of his water two days ago. His strength was failing rapidly now. He was feverish most of the time, his lucid periods growing shorter. He had struggled against what was happening at first, trying to use his magic to banish the poison from his body, to restore his hand and arm to flesh and blood. But his magic had failed him completely. He had worked at freeing his arm from the stone flooring, thinking that it might be pried loose in some way. But he was held fast, a condemned man with no hope of release. Eventually his exhaustion had forced him to sleep, and as the days passed he had slept more often, slipping further and further away from wanting to come awake.

Now, as he knelt in a huddle of darkness and pain, salvaged momentarily from the wreckage of his dying by the voice of the Grimpond, he realized with terrifying certainty that if he went to sleep again it would be for good. He breathed in and out rapidly, choking back his fear. He must not let that happen. He must not give up.

He forced himself to think. As long as he could think, he reasoned, he would not fall asleep. He retraced in his mind his conversation with the Grimpond, hearing again the spirit's words, trying anew to decipher their meaning. The Grimpond had not named the Hall of Kings in describing where the Black Elfstone could be found. Had Walker simply jumped to the wrong conclusion? Had he been deliberately misled? Was there any truth in what he had been told?

Walker's thoughts scattered in confusion, and his mind refused to respond to the demands he placed on it. He closed his eyes in despair, and it was with great difficulty that he forced them open again. His clothes were chill and damp with his own sweat, and his body shivered within them. His breathing was ragged, his vision blurred, and it was growing increasingly difficult to swallow. So many distractions—how could he think? He wanted simply to lie down and . . .

He panicked, feeling the urgency of his need threaten to swallow him up. He shifted his body, forcing his knees to scrape against the stone until they bled. A little more pain might help keep me awake, he thought. Yet he could barely feel it.

He forced his thoughts back to the Grimpond. He envisioned the wraith laughing at his plight, taking pleasure at it. He heard the taunting voice calling out to him. Anger gave him a measure of strength. There was something that he needed to recall, he thought desperately. There was something that the Grimpond had told him that he must remember.

Please, don't let me fall asleep!

The Hall of Kings did not respond to the urgency of his plea; the statues remained silent, disinterested, and oblivious. The mountain waited.

I have to break free! he howled wordlessly.

And then he remembered the visions, or more specifically the first of the three that the Grimpond had shown him, the one in which he had stood on a cloud above the others of the little company that had gathered at the Hadeshorn in answer to the summons of the shade of Allanon, the one in which he had said that he would sooner cut off his hand than bring back the Druids and then lifted his arm to show that he had done exactly that.

He remembered the vision and recognized its truth.

He banished the reaction it provoked in horrified disbelief

and let his head droop until it was resting on the cavern stone. He cried, feeling the tears run down his cheeks, the sides of his face, stinging his eyes as they mingled with his sweat. His body twisted with the agony of his choices.

No! No, he would not!

Yet he knew he must.

His crying turned to laughter, chilling in its madness as it rolled out of him into the emptiness of the tomb. He waited until it expended itself, the echoes fading into silence, then looked up again. His possibilities had exhausted themselves; his fate was sealed. If he did not break free now, he knew he never would.

And there was only one way to do so.

He hardened himself to the fact of it, walling himself away from his emotions, drawing from some final reserve the last of his strength. He cast about the cavern floor until he found what he needed. It was a rock that was approximately the size and shape of an axe-blade, jagged on one side, hard enough to have survived intact its fall from the chamber ceiling where it had been loosened by the battle four centuries earlier between Allanon and the serpent Valg. The rock lay twenty feet away, clearly beyond reach of any ordinary man. But not him. He summoned a fragment of the magic that remained to him, forcing himself to remain steady during its use. The rock inched forward, scraping as it moved, a slow scratching in the cavern's silence. Walker grew light-headed from the strain, the fever burning through him, leaving him nauseated. Yet he kept the rock moving closer.

At last it was within reach of his free hand. He let the magic slip away, taking long moments to gather himself. Then he stretched out his arm to the rock, and his fingers closed tightly about it. Slowly he gathered it in, finding it impossibly heavy, so heavy in fact that he was not certain he could manage to lift it let alone . . .

He could not finish the thought. He could not dwell on what he was about to do. He dragged the rock over until it was next to him, braced himself firmly with his knees, took a deep breath, raised the rock overhead, hesitated for just an instant, then in a rush of fear and anguish brought it down. It smashed into the stone of his arm between elbow and wrist, hammering it with such force that it jarred his entire body. The resulting pain was so agonizing that it threatened to render him unconscious. He screamed as waves of it washed through him; he felt as if he were being torn apart from the inside out. He fell forward, gasping for breath, and the axe-blade rock dropped from his nerveless fingers.

Then he realized that something had changed.

He pushed himself upright and looked down at his arm. The blow had shattered the stone limb at the point of impact. His wrist and hand remained fastened to the Asphinx in the gloom of the hidden compartment of the cavern floor. But the rest of him was free.

He knelt in stunned disbelief for a long time, staring down at the ruin of his arm, at the gray-streaked flesh above the elbow and the jagged stone capping below. His arm felt leaden and stiff. The poison already within it continued to work its damage. There were jolts of pain all through him.

But he was free! Shades, he was free!

Suddenly there was a stirring in the chamber beyond, a faint and distant rustling like something had come awake. Walker Boh went cold in the pit of his stomach as he realized what had happened. His scream had given him away. The chamber beyond was the Assembly, and it was in the Assembly that the serpent Valg, guardian of the dead, had once lived.

And might live still.

Walker came to his feet, sudden dizziness washing through him. He ignored it, ignored the pain and weariness as well, and stumbled toward the heavy, ironbound entry doors that had brought him in. He shut away the sounds of everything about him, everything within, concentrating the whole of his effort on making his way across the cavern floor to the passageway that lay beyond. If the serpent was alive and found him now, he knew he was finished.

Luck was with him. The serpent did not emerge. Nothing appeared. Walker reached the doors leading from the tomb and pushed his way through into the darkness beyond.

What happened then was never clear afterward in his mind. Somehow he managed to work his way back through the Hall of Kings, past the Banshees whose howl could drive men mad, and past the Sphinxes whose gaze could turn men to stone. He heard the Banshees wail, felt the gaze of the Sphinxes burning down, and experienced the terror of the mountain's ancient magic as it sought to trap him, to make him another of its victims. Yet he escaped, some final shield of determination preserving him as he made his way clear, an iron will combining with weariness and pain and near madness to encase and preserve him. Perhaps his magic came to aid him as well; he thought it possible. The magic, after all, was unpredictable, a constant mystery. He pushed and trudged through near darkness and phantasmagoric images, past walls of rock that threatened to close about him, down tunnels of sight and sound in which he could neither see nor hear, and finally he was free.

He emerged into the outside world at daybreak, the sun's light chill and faint as it shone out of a sky thick with clouds and rain that lingered from the previous night's storm. With his arm tucked beneath his cloak like a wounded child, he made his way down the mountain trail toward the plains south. He never looked back. He could just manage to look ahead. He was on his feet only because he refused to give in. He could barely feel himself anymore, even the pain of his poisoning. He walked as if jerked along by strings attached to his limbs. His black hair blew wildly in the wind, whipping about his pale face, lashing it until his eyes blurred with tears. He was a scarecrow figure of madness as he wandered out of the mist and gray.

Dark Uncle, the Grimpond's voice whispered in his mind and laughed in glee.

He lost track of time completely. The sun's weak light failed to disperse the stormclouds and the day remained washed of color and friendless. Trails came and went, an endless procession of rocks, defiles, canyons, and drops. Walker remained oblivious to all of it. He knew only that he was descending, working his way downward out of the rock, back toward the world he had so foolishly left behind. He knew that he was trying to save his life.

It was midday when he emerged at last from the high peaks into the Valley of Shale, a tattered and aimless bit of human wreckage so badly fevered and weakened that he stumbled halfway across the crushed, glistening black rock of the valley floor before realizing where he was. When he finally saw, his strength gave out. He collapsed in the tangle of his cloak, feeling the sharp edges of the rock cutting into the skin of his hands and face, heedless of its sting as he lay facedown in exhaustion. After a time, he began to crawl toward the placid waters of the lake, inching his way painfully ahead, dragging his stone-tipped arm beneath him. It seemed logical to him in his delirium that if he could reach the Hadeshorn's edge he might submerge his ruined arm and the lethal waters would counteract the poison that was killing him. It was nonsensical, but for Walker Boh madness had become the measure of his life.

He failed even in this small endeavor. Too weak to go more than a few yards, he lapsed into unconsciousness. The last thing he remembered was how dark it was in the middle of the day, the world a place of shadows.

He slept, and in his sleep he dreamed that the shade of Allanon came to him. The shade rose out of the churning, boiling waters of the Hadeshorn, dark and mystical as it materialized from the netherworld of afterlife to which it had been consigned. It reached out to Walker, lifted him to his feet, flooded him with new strength, and gave clarity once more to his thoughts and vision. Spectral, translucent, it hung above the dark, greenish waters—yet its touch felt curiously human.

—Dark Uncle—

When the shade spoke the words, they were not taunting and hateful as they had been when spoken by the Grimpond. They were simply a designation of who and what Walker was.

—Why will you not accept the charge I have given you—

Walker struggled angrily to reply but could not seem to find the words.

—The need for you is great, Walker. Not my need, but the need of the Lands and their people, the races of the new world. If you do not accept my charge, there is no hope for them—

Walker's rage was boundless. Bring back the Druids, who were no more, and disappeared Paranor? Surely, thought Walker in response. Surely, shade of Allanon. I shall take my ruined body in search of what you seek, my poisoned limb, though I be dying and cannot hope to help anyone, still I . . .

—Accept, Walker. You do not accept. Acknowledge the truth of yourself and your own destiny—

Walker didn't understand.

—Kinship with those who have gone before you, those who understood the meaning of acceptance. That is what you lack—

Walker shuddered, disrupting the vision of his dream. His strength left him. He collapsed at the Hadeshorn's edge, blanketed in confusion and fear, feeling so lost that it seemed to him impossible that he could ever again be found.

Help me, Allanon, he begged in despair.

The shade hung motionless in the air before him, ethereal against a backdrop of wintry skies and barren peaks, rising up like death's specter come to retrieve a fresh victim. It seemed suddenly to Walker that dying was all that was left to him.

Do you wish me to die? he asked in disbelief. *Is this what you demand of me?*

The shade said nothing.

Did you know that this would happen to me? He held forth his arm, jagged stone stump, poison-streaked flesh.

The shade remained silent.

Why won't you help me? Walker howled.

—Why won't you help me—

The words echoed sharply in his mind, urgent and filled with a sense of dark purpose. But he did not speak them. Allanon did.

Then abruptly the shade shimmered in the air before him and faded away. The waters of the Hadeshorn steamed and hissed, roiled in fury, and went still once more. All about the air was misted and dark, filled with ghosts and wild imaginings, a place where life and death met at a crossroads of unanswered questions and unresolved puzzles.

Walker Boh saw them for only a moment, aware that he was seeing them not in sleep but in waking, realizing suddenly that his vision might not have been a dream at all.

Then everything was gone, and he fell away into blackness.

W HEN HE CAME AWAKE AGAIN there was someone bending over him. Walker saw the other through a haze of fever and pain, a thin, sticklike figure in gray robes with a narrow face, a wispy beard and hair, and a hawk nose, crouched close like something that meant to suck away what life remained to him.

"Walker?" the figure whispered gently.

It was Cogline. Walker swallowed against the dryness in his throat and struggled to raise himself. The weight of his arm dragged against him, pulling him back, forcing him down. The old man's hands groped beneath the concealing cloak and found the leaden stump. Walker heard the sharp intake of his breath.

"How did you . . . find me?" he managed.

"Allanon," Cogline answered. His voice was rough and laced with anger.

Walker sighed. "How long have I . . . ?"

"Three days. I don't know why you're still alive. You haven't any right to be."

"None," Walker agreed and reached out impulsively to hug the other man close. The familiar feel and smell of the old man's body brought tears to his eyes. "I don't think . . . I'm meant to die . . . just yet."

Cogline hugged Walker back. He said, "No, Walker. Not yet."

Then the old man was lifting him to his feet, hauling him up with strength Walker hadn't known he possessed, holding him upright as he pointed them both toward the south end of the valley. It was dawn again, the sunrise unclouded and brilliant gold against the eastern horizon, the air still and expectant with the promise of its coming.

"Hold on to me," Cogline urged, walking him along the crushed black rock. "There are horses waiting and help to be had. Hold tight, Walker."

Walker Boh held on for dear life.

CHAPTER

3

OGLINE TOOK Walker Boh to Storlock. Even on horse-back with Walker lashed in place, it took until nightfall to complete the journey. They came down out of the Dragon's Teeth into a day filled with sunshine and warmth, turned east across the Rabb Plains, and made their way into the Eastland forests of the Central Anar to the legendary village of the Stors. Wracked with pain and consumed with thoughts of dying, Walker remained awake almost the entire time. Yet he was never certain where he was or what was happening about him, conscious only of the swaying of his horse and Cogline's constant reassurance that all would be well.

He did not believe that Cogline was telling him the truth.

Storlock was silent, cool and dry in the shadow of the trees, a haven from the swelter and dust of the plains. Hands reached up to take Walker from the saddle, from the smell of sweat and the rocking motion, and from the feeling that he must at any moment give in to the death that was waiting to claim him. He did not know why he was alive. He could give himself no reason. White-robed figures gathered all around, supporting him, easing him down—Stors, the Gnome Healers of the Village. Everyone knew of the Stors. Theirs was the most advanced source of healing in the Four Lands. Wil Ohmsford had studied with them once and become a healer, the only Southlander ever to do so. Shea Ohmsford had been healed after an attack in the Wolfsktaag. Earlier, Par had been brought to them as well, infected by the poison of the Werebeasts in Olden Moor. Walker

492

had brought him. Now it was Walker's turn to be saved. But Walker did not think that would happen.

A cup was raised to his lips, and a strange liquid trickled down his throat. Almost immediately the pain eased, and he felt himself grow drowsy. Sleep would be good for him, he decided suddenly, surprisingly. Sleep would be welcome. He was carried into the Center House, the main care lodge, and placed in a bed in one of the back rooms where the forest could be seen through the weave of the curtains, a wall of dark trunks set at watch. He was stripped of his clothes, wrapped in blankets, given something further to drink, a bitter, hot liquid, and left to fall asleep.

He did so almost at once.

As he slept, the fever dissipated, and the weariness faded away. The pain lingered, but it was distant somehow and not a part of him. He sank down into the warmth and comfort of his bedding, and even dreams could not penetrate the shield of his rest. There were no visions to distress him, no dark thoughts to bring him awake. Allanon and Cogline were forgotten. His anguish at the loss of his limb, his struggle to escape the Asphinx and the Hall of Kings, and his terrifying sense of no longer being in command of his own destiny—all were forgotten. He was at peace.

He did not know how long he slept, for he was not conscious of time passing, of the sweep of the sun across the sky, or of the change from night to day and back again. When he began to come awake once more, floating out of the darkness of his rest through a world of half-sleep, memories of his boyhood stirred unexpectedly, small snatches of his life in the days when he was first learning to cope with the frustration and wonder of discovering who and what he was.

The memories were sharp and clear.

He was still a child when he first learned he had magic. He didn't call it magic then; he didn't call it anything. He believed such power common; he thought that he was like everyone else. He lived then with his father Kenner and mother Risse at Hearthstone in Darklin Reach, and there were no other children to whom he might compare himself. That came later. It was his mother who told him that what he could do was unusual, that it made him different from other children. He could still see her face as she tried to explain, her small features intense, her white skin striking against coal black hair that was always braided and laced with flowers. He could still hear her low and compelling voice. Risse. He had loved his mother deeply. She had not had magic of her own; she was a Boh and the magic came from his father's side, from the Ohmsfords. She told him that, sitting him down before her on a brilliant autumn day when the smell of dying leaves and burning wood filled the air, smiling and reassuring as she spoke, trying unsuccessfully to hide from him the uneasiness she felt.

That was one of the things the magic let him do. It let him see sometimes what others were feeling—not with everyone, but almost always with his mother.

"Walker, the magic makes you special," she said. "It is a gift that you must care for and cherish. I know that someday you are going to do something wonderful with it."

She died a year later after falling ill to a fever for which even her formidable healing skills could not find a cure.

He lived alone with his father then, and the "gift" with which she had believed him blessed developed rapidly. The magic was an enabler; it gave him insight. He discovered that frequently he could sense things in people without being told—changes in their mood and character, emotions they thought to keep secret, their opinions and ideas, their needs and hopes, even the reasons behind what they did. There were always visitors at Hearthstone—travelers passing through, peddlers, tradesmen, woodsmen, hunters, trappers, even Trackers—and Walker would know all about them without their having to say a word. He would tell them so. He would reveal what he knew. It was a game that he loved to play. It frightened some of them, and his father ordered him to stop. Walker did as he was asked. By then he had discovered a new and more interesting ability. He discovered that he could communicate with the animals of the forest, with birds and fish, even with plants. He could sense what they were thinking and feeling just as he could with humans, even though their thoughts and feelings were more rudimentary and limited. He would disappear for hours on excursions of learning, on make-believe adventures, on journeys of testing and seeking out. He designated himself early as an explorer of life.

As time passed, it became apparent that Walker's special insight was to help him with his schooling as well. He began reading from his father's library almost as soon as he learned how the letters of the alphabet formed words on the fraying pages of his father's books. He mastered mathematics effortlessly. He understood sciences intuitively. Barely anything had to be explained. Somehow he just seemed to understand how it all worked. History became his special passion; his memory of things, of places and events and people, was prodigious. He began to keep notes of his own, to write down everything he learned, to compile teachings that he would someday impart to others.

The older he grew, the more his father's attitude toward him seemed to change. He dismissed his suspicions at first, certain that he was mistaken. But the feeling persisted. Finally he asked his father about it, and Kenner—a tall, lean, quick-moving man with wide, intelligent eyes, a stammer he had worked hard to overcome, and a gift for crafting—admitted it was true. Kenner did not have magic of his own. He had evidenced traces of it when he was young, but it had disappeared shortly after he had passed out of boyhood. It had been like that with his father and his father's father before that and every Ohmsford he knew about all the way back to Brin. But it did not appear to be that way with Walker. Walker's magic just seemed to grow stronger. Kenner told him that he was afraid that his son's abilities would eventually overwhelm him, that they would develop to a point where he could no longer anticipate or control their effects. But he said as well, just as Risse had said, that they should not be suppressed, that magic was a gift that always had some special purpose in being.

Shortly after, he told Walker of the history behind the Ohmsford magic, of the Druid Allanon and the Valegirl Brin, and of the mysterious trust that the former in dying had bequeathed to the latter. Walker had been twelve when he heard the tale. He had wanted to know what the trust was supposed to be. His father hadn't been able to tell him. He had only been able to relate the history of its passage through the Ohmsford bloodline.

"It manifests itself in you, Walker," he said. "You in turn will pass it on to your children, and they to theirs, until one day there is need for it. That is the legacy you have inherited."

"But what good is a legacy that serves no purpose?" Walker had demanded.

And Kenner had repeated, "There is always purpose in magic—even when we don't understand what it is."

Barely a year later, as Walker was entering his youth and leaving his childhood behind, the magic revealed that it possessed another, darker side. Walker found out that it could be destructive. Sometimes, most often when he was angry, his emotions transformed themselves into energy. When that happened, he could move things away and break them apart without touching them. Sometimes he could summon a form of fire. It wasn't ordinary fire; it didn't burn like ordinary fire and it was different in color, a sort of cobalt. It wouldn't do much of what he tried to make it do; it did pretty much what it wished. It took him weeks to learn to control it. He tried to keep his discovery a secret from his father, but his father learned of it anyway, just as he eventually learned of everything about his son. Though he said little, Walker felt the distance between them widen.

Walker was nearing manhood when his father made the decision to take him out of Hearthstone. Kenner Ohmsford's health had been failing steadily for several years, his once strong body afflicted by a wasting sickness. Closing down the cottage that had been Walker's home since birth, he took the boy to Shady Vale to live with another family of Ohmsfords, Jaralan and Mirianna and their sons Par and Coll.

The move became for Walker Boh the worst thing that had ever happened to him. Shady Vale, though little more than a hamlet community, nevertheless seemed constricting after Hearthstone. Freedom there had been boundless; here, there were boundaries that he could not escape. Walker was not used to being around so many people and he could not seem to make himself fit in. He was required to attend school, but there was nothing for him to learn. His master and the other children disliked and mistrusted him; he was an outsider, he behaved differently than they, he knew entirely too much, and they quickly decided that they wanted nothing to do with him. His magic became a snare he could not escape. It manifested itself

in everything he did, and by the time he realized he should
have hidden it away it was too late to do so. He was beaten a
number of times because he wouldn't defend himself. He was
terrified of what would happen if he let the fire escape.

He was in the village less than a year when his father died.
Walker had wished that he could die, too.

He continued to live with Jaralan and Mirianna Ohmsford,
who were good to him and who sympathized with the difficul-
ties he was encountering because their own son Par was just
beginning to exhibit signs of having magic of his own. Par was
a descendent of Jair Ohmsford, Brin's brother. Both sides of the
family had passed the magic of their ancestors down through
the bloodline in the years since Allanon's death, so the appearance of Par's magic was not entirely unexpected. Par's was a less
unpredictable and complicated form of magic, manifesting itself
principally in the boy's ability to create lifelike images with his
voice. Par was still little then, just five or six, and he barely
understood what was happening to him. Coll was not yet strong
enough to protect his brother, so Walker ended up taking the
boy under his wing. It seemed natural enough to do so. After
all, only Walker understood what Par was experiencing.

His relationship with Par changed everything. It gave him
something to focus on, a purpose beyond worrying about his
own survival. He spent time with Par helping him adjust to the
presence of the magic in his body. He counseled him in its use,
advised him in the cautions that were necessary, the protective
devices he must learn to employ. He tried to teach him how to
deal with the fear and dislike of people who would choose not
to understand. He became Par's mentor.

The people of Shady Vale began calling him "Dark Uncle."
It began with the children. He wasn't Par's uncle, of course; he
wasn't anybody's uncle. But he hadn't a firm blood tie in the
eyes of the villagers; no one really understood the relationship
he bore to Jaralan and Mirianna, so there were no constrictions
on how they might refer to him. "Dark Uncle" became the ap-
pellation that stuck. Walker was tall by then, pale skinned and
black haired like his mother, apparently immune to the brown-
ing effect of the sun. He looked ghostly. It seemed to the Vale
children as if he were a night thing that never saw the light of

day, and his relationship toward the boy Par appeared mysterious to them. Thus he became "Dark Uncle," the counseler of magic, the strange, awkward, withdrawn young man whose insights and comprehensions set him apart from everyone.

Nevertheless, the name "Dark Uncle" notwithstanding, Walker's attitude improved. He began to learn how to deal with the suspicion and mistrust. He was no longer attacked. He found that he could turn aside these assaults with not much more than a glance or even the set of his body. He could use the magic to shield himself. He found he could project wariness and caution into others and prevent them from following through on their violent intentions. He even became rather good at stopping fights among others. Unfortunately, all this did was distance him further. The adults and older youths left him alone altogether; only the younger children turned cautiously friendly.

Walker was never happy in Shady Vale. The mistrust and the fear remained, concealed just beneath the forced smiles, the perfunctory nods, and the civilities of the villagers that allowed him to exist among them but never gain acceptance. Walker knew that the magic was the cause of his problem. His mother and father might have thought of it as a gift, but he didn't. And he never would again. It was a curse that he felt certain would haunt him to the grave.

By the time he reached manhood, Walker had resolved to return to Hearthstone, to the home he remembered so fondly, away from the people of the Vale, from their mistrust and suspicion, from the strangeness they caused him to feel. The boy Par had adjusted well enough that Walker no longer felt concerned about him. To begin with, Par was a native of the Vale and accepted in a way that Walker never could be. Moreover, his attitude toward using magic was far different than Walker's. Par was never hesitant; he wanted to know everything the magic could do. What others thought did not concern him. He could get away with that; Walker never could. The two had begun to grow apart as they grew older. Walker knew it was inevitable. It was time for him to go. Jaralan and Mirianna urged him to stay, but understood at the same time that he could not.

Seven years after his arrival, Walker Boh departed Shady Vale. He had taken his mother's name by then, disdaining further use of Ohmsford because it linked him so closely with the legacy of magic he now despised. He went back into Darklin Reach, back to Hearthstone, feeling as if he were a caged wild animal that had been set free. He severed his ties with the life he had left behind him. He resolved that he would never again use the magic. He promised himself that he would keep apart from the world of men for the rest of his life.

For almost a year he did exactly as he said he would do. And then Cogline appeared and everything changed . . .

Half-sleep turned abruptly to waking, and Walker's memories faded away. He stirred in the warmth of his bed, and his eyes blinked open. For a moment he could not decide where he was. The room in which he lay was bright with daylight despite the brooding presence of a cluster of forest trees directly outside his curtained window. The room was small, clean, almost bare of furniture. There were a sitting chair and a small table next to his bed, the bed, and nothing else. A vase of flowers, a basin of water, and some cloths sat on the table. The single door leading into the room stood closed.

Storlock. That was where he was, where Cogline had brought him.

He remembered then what had happened to bring him here.

Cautiously, he brought his ruined arm out from beneath the bedding. There was little pain now, but the heaviness of the stone persisted and there was no feeling. He bit his lip in anger and frustration as his arm worked free. Nothing had changed beyond the lessening of the pain. The stone tip where the lower arm had shattered was still there. The streaks of gray where the poison worked its way upward toward his shoulder were there as well.

He slipped his arm from view again. The Stors had been unable to cure him. Whatever the nature of the poison that the Asphinx had injected into him, the Stors could not treat it. And if the Stors could not treat it—the Stors, who were the best of the Four Lands' Healers . . .

He could not finish the thought. He shoved it away, closed his eyes, tried to go back to sleep, and failed. All he could see was his arm shattering under the impact of the stone wedge.

Despair washed over him and he wept.

AN HOUR HAD PASSED when the door opened and Cogline entered the room, an intrusive presence that made the silence seem even more uncomfortable.

"Walker," he greeted quietly.

"They cannot save me, can they?" Walker asked bluntly, the despair pushing everything else aside.

The old man became a statue at his bedside. "You're alive, aren't you?" he replied.

"Don't play word games with me. Whatever's been done, it hasn't driven out the poison. I can feel it. I may be alive, but only for the moment. Tell me if I'm wrong."

Cogline paused. "You're not wrong. The poison is still in you. Even the Stors haven't the means to remove it or to stop its spread. But they have slowed the process, lessened the pain, and given you time. That is more than I would have expected given the nature and extent of the injury. How do you feel?"

Walker's smile was slow and bitter. "Like I am dying, naturally. But in a comfortable fashion."

They regarded each other without speaking for a moment. Then Cogline moved over to the sitting chair and eased himself into it, a bundle of old bones and aching joints, of wrinkled brown skin. "Tell me what happened to you, Walker," he said.

Walker did. He told of reading the ancient, leatherbound Druid History that Cogline had brought to him and learning of the Black Elfstone, of deciding to seek the counsel of the Grimpond, of hearing its riddles and witnessing its visions, of determining that he must go to the Hall of Kings, of finding the secret compartment marked with runes in the floor of the Tomb, and finally of being bitten and poisoned by the Asphinx left there to snare him.

"To snare someone at least, perhaps anyone," Cogline observed.

Walker looked at him sharply, anger and mistrust flaring in his dark eyes. "What do you know of this, Cogline? Do you play the same games as the Druids now? And what of Allanon? Did Allanon know . . ."

"Allanon knew nothing," Cogline interrupted, brushing aside the accusation before it could be completed. The old eyes glittered beneath narrowed brows. "You undertook to solve the

Grimpond's riddles on your own—a foolish decision on your part. I warned you repeatedly that the wraith would find a way to undo you. How could Allanon know of your predicament? You attribute far too much to a man three-hundred-years dead. Even if he were still alive, his magic could never penetrate that which shrouds the Hall of Kings. Once you were within, you were lost to him. And to me. It wasn't until you emerged again and collapsed at the Hadeshorn that he was able to discover what happened and summon me to help you. I came as quickly as I could and even so it took me three days."

One hand lifted, a sticklike finger jabbing. "Have you bothered to question why it is that you aren't dead? It is because Allanon found a way to keep you alive, first until I arrived and second until the Stors could treat you! Think on that a bit before you start casting blame about so freely!"

He glared, and Walker glared back at him. It was Walker who looked away first, too sick at heart to continue the confrontation. "I have trouble believing anyone just at the moment," he offered lamely.

"You have trouble believing anyone at any time," Cogline snapped, unappeased. "You cast your heart in iron long ago, Walker. You stopped believing in anything. I remember when that wasn't so."

He trailed off, and the room went silent. Walker found himself thinking momentarily of the time the old man referred to, the time when he had first come to Walker and offered to show him the ways in which the magic could be used. Cogline was right. He hadn't been so bitter then; he'd been full of hope.

He almost laughed. That was such a long time ago.

"Perhaps I can use my own magic to dispel the poison from my body," he ventured quietly. "Once I return to Hearthstone, once I'm fully rested. Brin Ohmsford had such power once."

Cogline dropped his eyes and looked thoughtful. His gnarled hands clasped loosely in the folds of his robe. It appeared as if he were trying to decide something.

Walker waited a moment, then asked, "What has become of the others—of Par and Coll and Wren?"

Cogline kept his gaze lowered. "Par has gone in search of the Sword, young Coll with him. The Rover girl seeks the Elves.

They've accepted the charges Allanon gave to them." He looked up again. "Have you, Walker?"

Walker stared at him, finding the question both absurd and troubling, torn between conflicting feelings of disbelief and uncertainty. Once he would not have hesitated to give his answer. He thought again of what Allanon had asked him to do: Bring back disappeared Paranor and restore the Druids. A ridiculous, impossible undertaking, he had thought at the time. Game playing, he had decried. He would not be a part of such foolishness, he had announced to Par, Coll, Wren, and the others of the little company that had come with him to the Valley of Shale. He despised the Druids for their manipulation of the Ohmsfords. He would not be made their puppet. So bold he had been, so certain. He would sooner cut off his hand than see the Druids come again, he had declared.

And the loss of his hand was the price that had been exacted, it seemed.

Yet had that loss truly put an end to any possibility of the return of Paranor and the Druids? More to the point, was that what he now intended?

He was conscious of Cogline watching him, impatient as he waited for Walker Boh's answer to his question. Walker kept his eyes fixed on the old man without seeing him. He was thinking suddenly of the Druid History and its tale of the Black Elfstone. If he had not gone in search of the Elfstone, he would not have lost his arm. Why had he gone? Curiosity, he had thought. But that was a simplistic answer and he knew it was given too easily. In any case, didn't the very fact of his going indicate that despite any protestations to the contrary he indeed had accepted Allanon's charge?

If not, what was it that he was doing?

He focused again on the old man. "Tell me something, Cogline. Where did you get that book of the Druid Histories? How did you find it? You said when you brought it to me that you got it out of Paranor. Surely not."

Cogline's smile was faint and ironic. "Why 'surely not,' Walker?"

"Because Paranor was sent out of the world of men by Allanon three hundred years ago. It doesn't exist anymore."

Cogline's face crinkled like crushed parchment. "Doesn't exist? Oh, but it does, Walker. And you're wrong. Anyone can reach it if they have the right magic to help them. Even you."

Walker hesitated, suddenly uncertain.

"Allanon sent Paranor out of the world of the men, but it still exists," Cogline said softly. "It needs only the magic of the Black Elfstone to summon it back again. Until then, it remains lost to the Four Lands. But it can still be entered by those who have the means to do so and the courage to try. It does require courage, Walker. Shall I tell you why? Would you like to hear the story behind my journey into Paranor?"

Walker hesitated again, wondering if he wanted to hear anything ever again about the Druids and their magic. Then he nodded slowly. "Yes."

"But you are prepared to disbelieve what I am going to tell you, aren't you?"

"Yes."

The old man leaned forward. "Tell you what. I'll let you judge for yourself."

He paused, gathering his thoughts. Daylight framed him in brightness, exposing the flaws of old age that etched his thin frame in lines and hollows, that left his hair and beard wispy and thin, and that gave his hands a tremulous appearance as he clasped them tightly before him.

"It was after your meeting with Allanon. He sensed, and I as well, that you would not accept the charge you had been given, that you would resist any sort of involvement without further evidence of the possibility that you might succeed. And that there was reason to want to. You differ in your attitude from the others—you doubt everything that you are told. You came to Allanon already planning to reject what you would hear."

Walker started to protest, but Cogline held up his hands quickly and shook his head. "No, Walker. Don't argue. I know you better than you know yourself. Just listen to me for now. I went north on Allanon's summons, seeming to disappear, leaving you to debate among yourselves what course of action you would follow. Your decision in the matter was a foregone conclusion. You would not do as you had been asked. Since that was so, I resolved to try to change your mind. You see, Walker,

I believe in the dreams; I see the truth in them that you as yet do not. I would not be a messenger for Allanon if there were any way to avoid it. My time as a Druid passed away long ago, and I do not seek to return to what was. But I am all there is and since that is so I will do what I think necessary. Dissuading you from refusing to involve yourself in the matter at hand is something I deem vital."

He was shaking with the conviction of his words and the look he extended Walker was one that sought to convey truths that the old man could not speak.

"I went north, Walker, as I said. I traveled out of the Valley of Shale and across the Dragon's Teeth to the valley of the Druid's Keep. Nothing remains of Paranor but a few crumbling outbuildings on a barren height. The forests still surround the spot on which it once stood, but nothing will grow upon the earth, not even the smallest blade of grass. The wall of thorns that once protected the Keep is gone. Everything has disappeared—as if some giant reached down and snatched it all away.

"I stood there, near twilight, looking at the emptiness, envisioning what had once been. I could sense the presence of the Keep. I could almost see it looming out of the shadows, rising up against the darkening eastern skies. I could almost define the shape of its stone towers and parapets. I waited, for Allanon knew what was needed and would tell me when it was time."

The old eyes gazed off into space. "I slept when I grew tired, and Allanon came to me in my dreams as he now does with all of us. He told me that Paranor was indeed still there, cast away by magic into a different place and time, yet there nevertheless. He asked me if I would enter and bring out from it a certain volume of the Druid Histories which would describe the means by which Paranor could be restored to the Four Lands. He asked if I would take that book to you." He hesitated, poised to reveal something more, then simply said, "I agreed.

"He reached out to me then and took my hand. He lifted me away from myself, my spirit out of my body. He cloaked me in his magic. I became momentarily something other than the man I am—but I don't know even now what that something was. He told me what I must do. I walked alone then to where the walls of the Keep had once stood, closed my eyes so that they would not deceive me, and reached out into worlds that lie beyond our own for the shape of what had once been. I found that I could do that. Imagine my astonishment when Paranor's walls materialized suddenly beneath my fingers. I risked taking a quick look at them, but when I did so there was nothing to see. I was forced to begin again. Even as a spirit I could not penetrate the magic if I violated its rules. I kept my eyes closed tightly this time, searched out the walls anew, discovered the hidden trapdoor concealed in the base of the Keep, pushed the catch that would release the locks, and entered."

Cogline's mouth tightened. "I was allowed to open my eyes then and look around. Walker, it was the Paranor of old, a great sprawling castle with towers that rose into clouds of ancient brume and battlements that stretched away forever. It seemed endless to me as I climbed its stairs and wandered its halls; I was like a rat in a maze. The castle was filled with the smell and taste of death. The air had a strange greenish cast; everything was swathed in it. Had I attempted to enter in my flesh-and-blood body, I would have been destroyed instantly; I could sense the magic still at work, scouring the rock corridors for any signs of life. The furnaces that had once been fueled by the fire at the earth's core were still, and Paranor was cold and lifeless. When I gained the upper halls I found piles of bones, grotesque and misshapen, the remains of the Mord Wraiths and Gnomes that Allanon had trapped there when he had summoned the magic to destroy Paranor. Nothing was alive in the Druid's Keep save myself."

He was silent for a moment as if remembering. "I sought out the vault in which the Druid Histories were concealed. I had a sense of where it was, quickened in part by the days in which I studied at Paranor, in part by Allanon's magic. I searched out the library through which the vault could be entered, finding as I did so that I could touch things as if I were still a creature of substance and not of spirit. I felt along the dusty, worn edges of the bookshelves until I found the catches that released the doors leading in. They swung wide, and the magic gave way before me. I entered, discovered the Druid Histories revealed, and took from its resting place the one that was needed."

Cogline's eyes strayed off across the sunlit room, seeking

visions that were hidden from Walker. "I left then. I went back the same way as I had come, a ghost out of the past as much as those who had died there, feeling the chill of their deaths and the immediacy of my own. I passed down the stairwells and corridors in a half-sleep that let me feel as well as see the horror of what now held sway in the castle of the Druids. Such power, Walker! The magic that Allanon summoned was frightening even yet. I fled from it as I departed—not on foot, you understand, but in my mind. I was terrified!"

The eyes swung back. "So I escaped. And when I woke, I had in my possession the book that I had been sent to recover and I took it then to you."

He went silent, waiting patiently as Walker considered his story. Walker's eyes were distant. "It can be done then? Paranor can be entered even though it no longer exists in the Four Lands?"

Cogline shook his head slowly. "Not by ordinary men." His brow furrowed. "Perhaps by you, though. With the magic of the Black Elfstone to help you."

"Perhaps," Walker agreed dully. "What magic does the Elfstone possess?"

"I know nothing more of it than you," Cogline answered quietly.

"Not even where it can be found? Or who has it?"

Cogline shook his head. "Nothing."

"Nothing." Walker's voice was edged with bitterness. He let his eyes close momentarily against what he was feeling. When they opened, they were resigned. "This is my perception of things. You expect me to accept Allanon's charge to recover disappeared Paranor and restore the Druids. I can only do this by first recovering the Black Elfstone. But neither you nor I know where the Elfstone is or who has it. And I am infected with the poison of the Asphinx; I am being turned slowly to stone. I am dying! Even if I were persuaded to . . ." His voice caught, and he shook his head. "Don't you see? There isn't enough time!"

Cogline looked out the window, hunching down into his robes. "And if there were?"

Walker's laugh was hollow, his voice weary. "Cogline, I don't know."

The old man rose. He looked down at Walker for a long time without speaking. Then he said, "Yes, you do." His hands clasped tightly before him. "Walker, you persist in your refusal to accept the truth of what is meant to be. You recognize that truth deep in your heart, but you will not heed it. Why is that?"

Walker stared back at him wordlessly.

Cogline shrugged. "I have nothing more to say. Rest, Walker. You will be well enough in a day or two to leave. The Stors have done all they can; your healing, if it is to be, must come from another source. I will take you back to Hearthstone."

"I will heal myself," Walker whispered. His voice was suddenly urgent, rife with both desperation and anger.

Cogline did not respond. He simply gathered up his robes and walked from the room. The door closed quietly behind him.

"I will," Walker Boh swore.

CHAPTER

4

IT TOOK MORGAN LEAH the better part of three days after parting with Padishar Creel and the survivors of the Movement to travel south from the empty stretches of the Dragon's Teeth to the forest-sheltered Dwarf community of Culhaven. Storms swept the mountains during the first day, washing the ridgelines and slopes with torrents of rain, leaving the trailways sodden and slick with the damp, and wrapping the whole of the land in gray clouds and mist. By the second day the storms had passed away, and sunshine had begun to break through the clouds and the earth to dry out again. The third day brought a return of summer, the air warm and fragrant with the smell of flowers and grasses, the countryside bright with colors beneath a clear, windswept sky, the slow, lazy sounds of the wild things rising up from the pockets of shelter where they made their home.

Morgan's mood improved with the weather. He had been disheartened when he had set out. Steff was dead, killed in the catacombs of the Jut, and Morgan was burdened with a lingering sense of guilt rooted in his unfounded but persistent belief that he could have done something to prevent it. He didn't know what, of course. It was Teel who had killed Steff, who had almost killed him as well. Neither Steff nor he had known until the very last that Teel was something other than what she appeared, that she was not the girl the Dwarf had fallen in love with but a Shadowen whose sole purpose in coming with them into the mountains was to see them destroyed. Morgan had suspected what she was, yet lacked any real proof that his suspicions were correct until the moment she had revealed herself and by then it was too late. His friends the Valemen, Par and Coll Ohmsford, had disappeared after escaping the horrors of the Pit in Tyrsis and not been seen since. The Jut, the stronghold of the members of the Movement, had fallen to the armies of the Federation, and Padishar Creel and his outlaws had been chased north into the mountains. The Sword of Shannara, which was what all them had come looking for in the first place, was still missing. Weeks of seeking out the talisman, of scrambling to unlock the puzzle of its hiding place, of hair-raising confrontations with and escapes from the Federation and the Shadowen, and of repeated frustration and disappointment, had come to nothing.

But Morgan Leah was resilient and after a day or so of brooding about what was past and could not be changed his spirits began to lift once more. After all, he was something of a veteran now in the struggle against the oppressors of his homeland. Before, he had been little more than an irritant to that handful of Federation officials who governed the affairs of the Highlands, and in truth he had never done anything that affected the outcome of larger events in the Four Lands. His risk had been minimal and the results of his endeavors equally so. But that had all changed. In the past few weeks he had journeyed to the Hadeshorn to meet with the shade of Allanon, he had joined in the quest for the missing Sword of Shannara, he had battled both Shadowen and Federation, and he had saved the lives of Padishar Creel and his outlaws by warning them of Teel before she could betray them one final time. He knew he had done something at last that had value and meaning.

And he was about to do something more.

He had made Steff a promise. As his friend lay dying, Morgan had sworn that he would go to Culhaven to the orphanage where Steff had been raised and warn Granny Elise and Auntie Jilt that they were in danger. Granny Elise and Auntie Jilt—the only parents Steff had ever known, the only kindred he was leaving—were not to be abandoned. If Teel had betrayed Steff, she would have betrayed them as well. Morgan was to help them get safely away.

It gave the Highlander a renewed sense of purpose, and that as much as anything helped bring him out of his depression. He had begun his journey disenchanted. He had lagged in his travel, bogged down by the weather and his mood. By the third day he had shaken the effects of both. His resolution buoyed him. He would spirit Granny Elise and Auntie Jilt out of Culhaven to somewhere safe. He would return to Tyrsis and find the Valemen. He would continue to search for the missing Sword of Shannara. He would find a way to rid Leah and the whole of the Four Lands of both Shadowen and Federation. He was alive and everything was possible. He whistled and hummed as he walked, let the sun's rays warm his face, and banished self-doubt and discouragement. It was time to get on with things.

Now and again as he walked his thoughts strayed to the lost magic of the Sword of Leah. He still wore the remains of the shattered blade strapped to his waist, cradled in the makeshift sheath he had constructed for it. He thought of the power it had given him and the way the absence of that power made him feel—as if he could never be whole again without it. Yet some small part of the magic still lingered in the weapon; he had managed to call it to life in the catacombs of the Jut when he destroyed Teel. There had been just enough left to save his life.

Deep inside, where he could hide it and not be forced to admit the implausibility of it, he harbored a belief that one day the magic of the Sword of Leah would be his again.

It was late afternoon on that third day of travel when he emerged from the forests of the Anar into Culhaven. The Dwarf village was shabby and worn where he walked, the refuge of those now too old and as yet too young who had not been taken by the Federation authorities to the mines or sold as slaves in the market. Once among the most meticulously maintained of communities, Culhaven was now a dilapidated collection of buildings and people that evidenced little of care or love. The forest grew right up against the outermost buildings, weeds intruding into yards and gardens, roadways rutted and choked with scrub. Wooden walls warped under peeling paint, tiles and shingles cracked and splintered, and trim about doorways and windows drooped away. Eyes peered out through the shadows, following after the Highlander as he made his way in; he could sense the people staring from behind windows and doors. The few Dwarves he encountered would not meet his gaze, turning quickly away. He walked on without slowing, his anger rekindled anew at the thought of what had been done to these people. Everything had been taken from them but their lives, and their lives had been brought to nothing.

He pondered anew, as Par Ohmsford had done when last they were there, at the purpose of it.

He kept clear of the main roads, staying on the side paths, not anxious to draw attention to himself. He was a Southlander and therefore free to come and go in the Eastland as he pleased, but he did not identify in any way with its Federation occupiers and preferred to stay clear of them altogether. Even if none of what had happened to the Dwarves was his doing, what he saw of Culhaven made him ashamed all over again of who and what he was. A Federation patrol passed him and the soldiers nodded cordially. It was all he could do to make himself nod back.

As he drew nearer to the orphanage, his anticipation of what he would find heightened perceptibly. Anxiety warred with confidence. What if he were too late? He brushed the possibility away. There was no reason to think that he was. Teel would not have risked jeopardizing her disguise by acting precipitately. She would have waited until she was certain it would not have mattered.

Shadows began to lengthen as the sun disappeared into the trees west. The air cooled and the sweat on Morgan's back dried beneath his tunic. The day's sounds began to fade away into an expectant hush. Morgan looked down at his hands, fixing his gaze on the irregular patchwork of white scars that crisscrossed the brown skin. Battle wounds were all over his body since Tyrsis and the Jut. He tightened the muscles of his jaw. Small things, he thought. The ones inside him were deeper.

He caught sight of a Dwarf child looking at him from behind a low stone wall with intense black eyes. He couldn't tell if it was a girl or a boy. The child was very thin and ragged. The eyes followed him a moment, then disappeared.

Morgan moved ahead hurriedly, anxious once more. He caught sight of the roof of the orphanage, the first of its walls, a window high up, a gable. He rounded a bend in the roadway and slowed. He knew instantly that something was wrong. The yard of the orphanage was empty. The grass was untended. There were no toys, no children. He fought back against the panic that rose suddenly within him. The windows of the old building were dark. There was no sign of anyone.

He came up to the gate at the front of the yard and paused. Everything was still.

He had assumed wrong. He was too late after all.

He started forward, then stopped. His eyes swept the darkness of the old house, wondering if he might be walking into some sort of trap. He stood there a long time, watching. But there was no sign of anyone. And no reason for anyone to be waiting here for him, he decided.

He pushed through the gate, walked up on the porch, and pushed open the front door. It was dark inside, and he took a moment to let his eyes adjust. When they had done so, he entered. He passed slowly through the building, searched each of its rooms in turn, and came back out again. There was dust on everything. It had been some time since anyone had lived there. Certainly no one was living there now.

So what had become of the two old Dwarf ladies?

He sat down on the porch steps and let his tall form slump back against the railing. The Federation had them. There wasn't any other explanation. Granny Elise and Auntie Jilt would never leave their home unless they were forced to. And they would never abandon the children they cared for. Besides, all of their clothes were still in the chests and closets, the children's toys, the bedding, everything. He had seen it in his search. The house wasn't closed up properly. Too much was in disarray. Nothing was as it would have been if the old ladies had been given a choice.

Bitterness flooded through him. Steff had depended on him; he couldn't quit now. He had to find Granny and Auntie. But where? And who in Culhaven would tell him what he needed to know? No one who knew anything, he suspected. The Dwarves surely wouldn't trust him—not a Southlander. He could ask until the sun rose in the west and set in the east.

He sat there thinking a long time, the daylight fading into dusk. After a while, he became aware of a small child looking at him through the front gate—the same child who had been watching him up the road. A boy, he decided this time. He let the boy watch him until they were comfortable with each other, then said, "Can you tell me what happened to the ladies who lived here?"

The boy disappeared instantly. He was gone so fast that it seemed as if the earth must have swallowed him up. Morgan sighed. He should have expected as much. He straightened his legs. He would have to devise a way to extract the information he needed from the Federation authorities. That would be dangerous, especially if Teel had told them about him as well as Granny and Auntie—and there was no reason now to believe that she hadn't. She must have given the old ladies up even before the company began its journey north to Darklin Reach. The Federation must have come for Granny and Auntie the moment Teel was safely beyond the village. Teel hadn't worried that Steff or Morgan or the Valemen would find out; after all, they would all be dead before it mattered.

Morgan wanted to hit something or someone. Teel had betrayed them all. Par and Coll were lost. Steff was dead. And now these two old ladies who had never hurt anyone . . .

"Hey, mister," a voice called.

He looked up sharply. The boy was back at the gate. An older boy stood next to him. It was the second boy who spoke, a hefty fellow with a shock of spiked red hair. "Federation soldiers took the old ladies away to the workhouses several weeks ago. No one lives here now."

Then they were gone, disappeared as completely as before. Morgan stared after them. Was the boy telling him the truth? The Highlander decided he was. Well and good. Now he had a little something to work with. He had a place to start looking.

He came to his feet, went back down the pathway, and out the gate. He followed the rutted road as it wound through the twilight toward the center of the village. Houses began to give way to shops and markets, and the road broadened and split in several directions. Morgan skirted the hub of the business district, watching as the light faded from the sky and the stars appeared. Torchlight brightened the main thoroughfare but was absent from the roads and paths he followed. Voices whispered in the stillness, vague sounds that lacked meaning and definition, hushed as if the speakers feared being understood. The houses changed character, becoming well tended and neat, the yards trimmed and nourished. Federation houses, Morgan thought— stolen from Dwarves—tended by the victims. He kept his bitterness at bay, concentrating on the task ahead. He knew where the workhouses were and what they were intended to accomplish. The women sent there were too old to be sold as personal slaves, yet strong enough to do menial work such as washing and sewing and the like. The women were assigned to the Federation barracks at large and made to serve the needs of the garrison. If that boy had been telling the truth, that was what Granny Elise and Auntie Jilt would be doing.

Morgan reached the workhouses several minutes later. There were five of them, a series of long, low buildings that ran parallel to each other with windows on both sides and doors at both ends. The women who worked them lived in them as well. Pallets, blankets, washbasins, and chamber pots were provided and pulled out from under the workbenches at night. Steff had taken Morgan up to a window once to let him peer inside. Once had been quite enough.

Morgan stood in the shadows of a storage shed across the way for long moments, thinking through what he would do. Guards stood at all the entrances and patroled the roadways and lanes. The women in the workhouses were prisoners. They were not permitted to leave their buildings for any reason short of sickness or death or some more benevolent form of release— and the latter almost never occurred. They were permitted visitors infrequently and then closely watched. Morgan couldn't remember when it was that visits were permitted. Besides, it didn't matter. It infuriated him to think of Granny Elise and Auntie Jilt being kept in such a place. Steff would not have waited to free them, and neither would he.

But how was he going to get in? And how was he going to get Granny and Auntie out once he did?

The problem defeated him. There was no way to approach the workhouses without being seen and no way to know in which of the five workhouses the old ladies were being kept in any case. He needed to know a great deal more than he did now before he could even think of attempting any rescue. Not for the first time since he had left the Dragon's Teeth, he wished Steff were there to advise him.

At last he gave it up. He walked down into the center of the village, took a room at one of the inns that catered to Southland traders and businessmen, took a bath to wash off the grime, washed his clothes as well, and went off to bed. He lay awake thinking about Granny Elise and Auntie Jilt until sleep finally overcame him.

When he awoke the following morning he knew what he needed to do to rescue them.

He dressed, ate breakfast in the inn dining room, and set out. What he was planning was risky, but there was no help for it. After making a few inquiries, he discovered the names of the taverns most frequented by Federation soldiers. There were three of them, and all were situated on the same street close to the city markets. He walked until he found them, picked the most likely—a dimly lit hall called the High Boot—entered, found a table close to the serving bar, ordered a glass of ale, and waited. Although the day was still young there were soldiers drifting in already, men from the night shift not yet ready for bed. They were quick to talk about garrison life and not much concerned with who might be listening. Morgan listened closely. From time to time he looked up long enough to ask a friendly question. Occasionally he commented. Once in a while he bought a glass for someone. Mostly he waited.

Much of the talk revolved around a girl who was rumored to be the daughter of the King of the Silver River. She had appeared rather mysteriously out of the Silver River country south and west below the Rainbow Lake and was making her way east. Wherever she went, in whatever villages and towns she passed through, she performed miracles. There had never been such magic, it was said. She was on her way now to Culhaven.

The balance of the tavern's chatter revolved around complaints about the way the Federation army was run by its officers. Since it was the common soldiers who were doing the complaining, the nature of the talk was hardly surprising. This was the part that Morgan was interested in hearing. The day passed away in lazy fashion, sultry and still within the confines of the hall with only the cold glasses of ale and the talk to relieve the heat and boredom. Federation soldiers came and went, but Morgan remained where he was, an almost invisible presence as he sipped and watched. He had thought earlier to circulate from one tavern to the next, but it quickly became apparent that he would learn everything he needed to know by remaining at the first.

By midafternoon he had the information he needed. It was time to act on it. He roused himself from his seat and walked across the roadway to the second of the taverns, the Frog Pond, an aptly named establishment if ever there was one. Seating himself near the back at a green cloth table that sat amid the shadows like a lily pad in a dark pool, he began looking for his victim. He found him almost immediately, a man close to his own size, a common soldier of no significant rank, drinking alone, lost in some private musing that carried his head so far downward it was almost touching the serving bar. An hour passed, then two. Morgan waited patiently as the soldier finished his final glass, straightened, pushed away from the bar, lurched out through the entry doors. Then he followed.

The day was mostly gone, the sun already slipping into the trees of the surrounding forests, the daylight turning gray with the approach of evening. The soldier shuffled unsteadily down the road through knots of fellow soldiers and visiting tradesmen, making his way back to the barracks. Morgan knew where he was going and slipped ahead to cut him off. He intercepted him as he came around a corner by a blacksmith's shop, seeming to bump into him by accident but in fact striking him so hard that the man was unconscious before he touched the ground. Morgan let him fall, muttered in mock exasperation, then picked the fellow up, hoisting him over one shoulder. The blacksmith and his workers glanced over together with a few passersby, and Morgan announced rather irritably that he supposed he would have to carry the fellow back to his quarters. Then off he marched in mock disgust.

He carried the unconscious soldier to a feed barn a few doors down and slipped inside. No one saw them enter. There, in near darkness, he stripped the man of his uniform, tied and gagged him securely, and shoved him back behind a pile of oat sacks. He donned the discarded uniform, brushed it out and straightened its creases, stuffed his own clothes in a sack he had brought, strapped on his weapons, and emerged once more into the light.

He moved quickly after that. Timing was everything in his plan; he had to reach the administration center of the workhouses just after the shift change came on at dusk. His day at the taverns had told him everything he needed to know about people, places, and procedures; he need only put the information to use. Already the twilight shadows were spreading across the forestland, swallowing up the few remaining pools of sunlight. The streets were starting to empty as soldier, trader, and citizen alike made their way homeward for the evening meal. Morgan kept to himself, careful to acknowledge senior officers in passing, doing what he could to avoid drawing attention to himself. He assumed a deliberate look and stance designed to keep others at bay. He became a rather hard-looking Federation soldier about his business—no one to approach without a reason, certainly no one to anger. It seemed to work; he was left alone.

The workhouses were lighted when he reached them, the day's activities grinding to a close. Dinner in the form of soup and bread was being carried in by the guards. The food smells wafted through the air, somewhat less than appetizing. Morgan crossed the roadway to the storage sheds and pretended to be checking on something. The minutes slipped past, and darkness approached.

At precisely sunset the shift change occurred. New guards replaced the old on the streets and at the doors of the workhouses. Morgan kept his eyes fixed on the administration center. The officer of the day relinquished his duty to his nighttime counterpart. An aide took up a position at a reception desk. Two men on duty—that was all. Morgan gave everyone a few minutes to settle in, then took a deep breath and strode out from the shadows.

He went straight to the center, pushed through the doors, and confronted the aide at the reception desk. "I'm back," he announced.

The aide looked at him blankly.

"For the old ladies," Morgan added, allowing a hint of irritation to creep into his voice. He paused. "Weren't you told?"

The aide shook his head. "I just came on . . ."

"Yes, but there should be a requisition order still on your desk from no more than an hour ago," Morgan snapped. "Isn't it there?"

"Well, I don't . . ." The aide cast about the desktop in confusion, moving stacks of papers aside.

"Signed by Major Assomal."

The aide froze. He knew who Major Assomal was. There wasn't a Federation soldier garrisoned at Culhaven who didn't. Morgan had found out about the major in the tavern. Assomal was the most feared and disliked Federation officer in the occupying army. No one wanted anything to do with him if they could help it.

The aide rose quickly. "Let me get the watch captain," he muttered.

He disappeared into the back office and emerged moments later with his superior in tow. The captain was clearly agitated. Morgan saluted the senior officer with just the right touch of disdain.

"What's this all about?" the captain demanded, but the question came out sounding more like a plea than a demand.

Morgan clasped his hands behind his back and straightened. His heart was pounding. "Major Assomal requires the services of two of the Dwarf women presently confined to the workhouses. I selected them personally earlier in the day at his request. I left so that the paperwork could be completed and now I am back. It seems, however, that the paperwork was never done."

The watch captain was a sallow-skinned, round-faced man who appeared to have seen most of his service behind a desk. "I don't know anything about that," he snapped peevishly.

Morgan shrugged. "Very well. Shall I take that message back to Major Assomal, Captain?"

The other man went pale. "No, no, I didn't mean that. It's just that I don't . . ." He exhaled sharply. "This is very annoying."

"Especially since Major Assomal will be expecting me back momentarily." Morgan paused. "With the Dwarves."

The watch captain threw up his hands. "All right! What difference does it make! I'll sign them out to you myself! Let's have them brought up and be done with it!"

He opened the registry of names and with Morgan looking on determined that Granny Elise and Auntie Jilt were housed in building four. Hurriedly he scribbled out a release order for the workhouse guards. When he tried to dispatch the aide to collect the old ladies, Morgan insisted that he go as well.

"Just to make certain there are no further mix-ups, Captain," he explained. "After all, I have to answer to Major Assomal as well."

The watch captain didn't argue, obviously anxious to be shed of the matter as quickly as possible, and Morgan went out the door with the aide. The night was still and pleasantly warm. Morgan felt almost jaunty. His plan, risky or not, was going to work. They crossed the compound to building four, presented the release order to the guards stationed at the front doors, and waited while they perused it. Then the guards unfastened the locks and beckoned for them to proceed. Morgan and the aide pushed through the heavy wooden doors and stepped inside.

The workhouse was crammed with workbenches and bodies and smelled of stale air and sweat. Dust lay over everything, and the lamplight shone dully against walls that were dingy and unwashed. The Dwarf women were huddled on the floor with cups of soup and plates of bread in hand, finishing their dinner. Heads and eyes turned hurriedly as the two Federation soldiers entered, then turned just as quickly away again. Morgan caught the unmistakable look of fear and loathing.

"Call their names," he ordered the aide.

The aide did so, his voice echoing in the cavernous room and near the back two hunched forms came slowly to their feet.

"Now wait outside for me," Morgan said.

The aide hesitated, then disappeared back through the doors.

Morgan waited anxiously as Granny Elise and Auntie Jilt made their way gingerly through the clutter of bodies, benches, and pallets to where he stood. He barely recognized them. Their clothes were in tatters. Granny Elise's fine gray hair was unkempt, as if it were fraying all around the edges; Auntie Jilt's sharp, birdlike face was pinched and harsh. They were bent over with more than age, moving so slowly that it appeared it hurt them even to walk.

They came up to him with their eyes downcast and stopped.

"Granny," he said softly. "Auntie Jilt."

They looked up slowly and their eyes widened. Auntie Jilt caught her breath. "Morgan!" Granny Elise whispered in wonder. "Child, it's really you!"

He bent down quickly then and took them in his arms, hugging them close. They collapsed into him, rag dolls lacking strength of their own, and he could hear them both begin to cry. Behind them, the other Dwarf women were staring in confusion.

Morgan eased the two old ladies gently away. "Listen now," he said softly. "We haven't much time. I've tricked the watch captain into releasing you into my custody, but he's liable to catch on if we give him the chance so we have to hurry. Do you have somewhere that you can go to hide, someplace you won't be found?"

Auntie Jilt nodded, her narrow face a mask of determination. "The Resistance will hide us. We still have friends."

"Morgan, where's Steff?" Granny Elise interrupted.

The Highlander forced himself to meet her urgent gaze. "I'm sorry, Granny. Steff is dead. He was killed fighting against the Federation in the Dragon's Teeth." He saw the pain that filled her eyes. "Teel is dead, too. She was the one who killed Steff. She wasn't what any of us thought, I'm afraid. She was a creature called a Shadowen, a thing of dark magic linked to the Federation. She betrayed you as well."

"Oh, Steff," Granny Elise whispered absently. She was crying again.

"The soldiers came for us right after you left," Auntie Jilt said angrily. "They took the children away and put us in this cage. I knew something had gone wrong. I thought you might have been taken as well. Drat it, Morgan, that girl was like our own!"

"I know, Auntie," he answered, remembering how it had been. "It has become difficult to know who to trust. What about the Dwarves you plan to hide with? Can they be trusted? Are you sure you will be safe?"

"Safe enough," Auntie replied. "Stop your crying, Elise," she said and patted the other woman's hand gently. "We have to do as Morgan says and get out of here while we have the chance."

Granny Elise nodded, brushing away her tears. Morgan stood up again. He stroked each gray head in turn. "Remember, you don't know me, you're just my charges until we get clear of this place. And if something goes wrong, if we get separated, go where you'll be safe. I made a promise to Steff that I would see to it that you did. So you make certain I don't break that promise, all right?"

"All right, Morgan," Granny Elise said.

They went out the door then, Morgan leading, the two old ladies shuffling along behind with their heads bowed. The aide was standing rigidly to one side by himself; the guards looked bored. With the Dwarf ladies in tow, Morgan and the aide returned to the administration center. The watch captain was waiting impatiently, the promised release papers clutched in his hand. He passed them across the reception desk to Morgan for his signature, then shoved them at the aide and stalked back into his office. The aide looked at Morgan uncomfortably.

Inwardly congratulating himself on his success, Morgan said, "Major Assomal will be waiting."

He turned and was in the process of ushering Granny Elise and Auntie Jilt outside when the door opened in front of them and a new Federation officer appeared, this one bearing the crossed bars of a divisional commander.

"Commander Soldt!" The aide leaped to his feet and saluted smartly.

Morgan froze. Commander Soldt was the officer in charge of supervising the confinement of the Dwarves, the ranking officer off the field for the entire garrison. What he was doing at the center at this hour was anybody's guess, but it was certainly not going to do anything to help further Morgan's plans.

The Highlander saluted.

"What's this all about?" Soldt asked, glancing at Granny Elise and Auntie Jilt. "What are they doing out of their quarters?"

"Just a requisition, Commander," replied the aide. "From Major Assomal."

"Assomal?" Soldt frowned. "He's in the field. What would he want with Dwarves . . ." He glanced again at Morgan. "I don't know you, soldier. Let me see your papers."

Morgan hit him as hard as he could. Soldt fell to the floor and lay unmoving. Instantly Morgan went after the aide, who backed away shrieking in terror. Morgan caught him and slammed his head against the desk. The watch captain emerged just in time to catch several quick blows to the face. He staggered back into his office and went down.

"Out the door!" Morgan whispered to Granny Elise and Auntie Jilt.

They rushed from the administration center into the night. Morgan glanced about hurriedly and breathed out sharply in relief. The sentries were still at their posts. No one had heard the struggle. He guided the old ladies quickly along the street, away from the workhouses. A patrol appeared ahead. Morgan slowed, moving ahead of his charges, assuming a posture of command. The patrol turned off before it reached them, disappearing into the dark.

Then someone behind them was shouting, calling for help. Morgan pulled the old ladies into an alleyway and hastened them toward its far end. The shouts were multiplying now, and there was the sound of running feet. Whistles blew and an assembly horn blared.

"They'll be all over us now," Morgan muttered to himself.

They reached the next street over and turned onto it. The shouts were all around them. He pulled the ladies into a shadowed doorway and waited. Soldiers appeared at both ends of the street, searching. Morgan's rescue plans were collapsing about him. His hands tightened into fists. Whatever happened, he couldn't allow the Federation to recapture Granny and Auntie.

He bent to them. "I'll have to draw them away," he whispered urgently. "Stay here until they come after me, then run. Once you're hidden, stay that way—no matter what."

"Morgan, what about you?" Granny Elise seized his arm.

"Don't worry about me. Just do as I say. Don't come looking

for me. I'll find you when this whole business is over. Goodbye, Granny. Goodbye, Auntie Jilt."

Ignoring their pleas to remain, he kissed and hugged them hurriedly, and darted into the street. He ran until he caught sight of the first band of searchers and yelled to them, "They're over here!"

The soldiers came running as he turned down an alleyway, leading them away from Granny Elise and Auntie Jilt. He wrenched the broadsword he wore strapped to his back from its scabbard. Breaking free of the alleyway, he caught sight of another band and called them after him as well, gesturing vaguely ahead. To them he was just another soldier—for the moment, at least. If he could just maneuver them ahead of him, he might be able to escape as well.

"That barn, ahead of us," he shouted as the first bunch caught up with him. "They're in there!"

The soldiers charged past, one knot, then the second. Morgan turned and darted off in the opposite direction. As he came around the corner of a feed building, he ran right up against a third unit.

"They've gone into . . ."

He stopped short. The watch captain stood before him, howling in recognition.

Morgan tried to break free, but the soldiers were on him in an instant. He fought back valiantly, but there was no room to maneuver. His attackers closed and forced him to the ground. Blows rained down on him.

This isn't working out the way I expected, he thought bleakly and then everything went black.

CHAPTER

5

THREE DAYS LATER she who was said to be the daughter
of the King of the Silver River arrived in Culhaven.
The news of her coming preceded her by half a day and
by the time she reached the outskirts of the village the
roadway leading in was lined with people for more than a mile.
They had come from everywhere—from the village itself, from
the surrounding communities of both the Southland and the
Eastland, from the farms and cottages of the plains and deep
forests, even the mountains north. There were Dwarves and
Men and a handful of Gnomes of both sexes and all ages. They
were ragged and poor and until now without hope. They jammed
the roadside expectantly, some come simply out of a sense of
curiosity, most come out of their need to find something to
believe in again.

The stories of the girl were wondrous. She had appeared
in the heart of the Silver River country close by the Rainbow
Lake, a magical being sprung full-blown from the earth. She
stopped at each village and town, farm and cottage, and performed miracles. It was said that she healed the land. She turned
blackened, withered stalks to fresh, green shoots. She brought
flowers to bloom, fruit to bear, and crops to harvest with the
smallest of touches. She gave life back to the earth out of death.
Even where the sickness was most severe, she prevailed. She
bore some special affinity to the land, a kinship that sprang
directly from her father's hands, from the legendary stewardship
of the King of the Silver River. For years it had been believed

that the spirit lord had died with the passing of the age of magic. Now it was known he had not; as proof he had sent his daughter to them. The people of the Silver River country were to be given back their old life. So the stories proclaimed.

No one was more anxious to discover the truth of the matter than Pe Ell.

It was midday, and he had been waiting for the girl within the shade of the towering old shagbark hickory on a rise at the very edge of town since just after sunrise when word had reached him that today was the day she would appear. He was very good at waiting, very patient, and so the time had gone quickly for him as he stood with the others of the growing crowd and watched the sun lift slowly into the summer sky and felt the heat of the day settle in. Conversation around him had been plentiful and unguarded, and he listened attentively. There were stories of what the girl had done and what it was believed she would do. There were speculations and judgments. The Dwarves were the most vehement in their beliefs—or lack thereof. Some said she was the savior of their people; some said she was nothing more than a Southland puppet. Voices raised in shouts, quarreled, and died away. Arguments wafted through the still, humid air like small explosions of steam out of a fiery earth. Tempers flared and cooled. Pe Ell listened and said nothing.

"She comes to drive out the Federation soldiers and restore our land to us, land that the King of the Silver River treasures! She comes to set us free!"

"Bah, old woman, you speak nonsense! There is nothing to say she is who she claims to be. What do you know of what she can or cannot do?"

"I know what I know. I sense what will be."

"Ha! That's the ache of your joints you feel, nothing more! You believe what you want to believe, not what is. The truth is that we have no more sense of who this girl is than we do of what tomorrow will bring. It is pointless to get our hopes up!"

"It is more pointless to keep them down!"

And so on, back and forth, an endless succession of arguments and counterarguments that accomplished nothing except to help pass the time. Pe Ell had sighed inwardly. He seldom argued. He seldom had cause to.

When at last she was said to approach, the arguments and conversation faded to mutterings and whispers. When she actually appeared, even the mutterings and whispers died away. A strange hush settled over those who lined the roadway suggesting that either the girl was not at all what they had expected or, perhaps, that she was something more.

She came up the center of the roadway surrounded by the would-be followers who had flocked to her during her journey east, a mostly bedraggled lot with tattered clothes and exhilarated faces. Her own garb was rough and poorly sewn, yet she evinced a radiance that was palpable. She was small and slight, but so exquisitely shaped as to seem not quite real. Her hair was long and silver, shining as water would when it shimmered in the moonlight. Her features were perfectly formed. She walked alone in a rush of bodies that crowded and stumbled about her yet could not bear to approach. She seemed to float among them. Voices called out anxiously to her, but she seemed unaware that anyone was there.

And then she passed by Pe Ell and turned deliberately to look at him. Pe Ell shuddered in surprise. The weight of that look—or perhaps simply the experience of it—was enough to stagger him. Almost immediately her strange black eyes shifted away again, and she was moving on, a sliver of brilliant sunlight that had momentarily left him blind. Pe Ell stared after her, not knowing what she had done to him, what it was that had occurred in that brief moment when their eyes met. It was as if she had looked into his heart and mind and read them quite clearly. It was as if with that single glance she had discovered everything there was to know about him.

He found her to be the most beautiful creature he had ever seen in his life.

She turned down the roadway into the village proper, the crowd trailing after, and Pe Ell followed. He was a tall, lean man, so thin that he appeared gaunt. His bones were prominent, and the muscles and skin of his body were molded tightly against them so as to suggest he might easily break. Nothing could have been further from the truth. He was as hard as iron. He had a long, narrow face with a hawk nose and a wide forehead with eyebrows set high above hazel eyes that were disarmingly frank to look upon. When he smiled, which was often, his mouth had a slightly lopsided appearance to it. His hair was brown and cropped close, rather spiky and uncontrolled. He slouched a bit when he walked and might have been either a gangly boy or a stalking cat. His hands were slim and delicate. He wore common forest clothing made of rough cloth dyed various shades of green and taupe, boots of worn leather laced back and across, and a short cloak with pockets.

He carried no visible weapon. The Stiehl was strapped to his thigh just below his right hip. The knife rode beneath his loose-fitting pants where it could not be seen but where it could be reached easily through a slit cut into a deep forward pocket.

He could feel the blade's magic warm him.

As he moved to keep up with the girl, people stepped aside—whether from what they saw in his face or the way he moved or the intangible wall they sensed surrounded him. He did not like to be touched, and everyone seemed instinctively to know it. As always, they shied away. He passed through them as a shadow chasing after the light, keeping the girl in sight as he did so, wondering. She had looked at him for a reason, and that intrigued him. He hadn't been certain what she would be like, how she would make him feel when he saw her for the first time—but he hadn't thought it would be anything like this. It surprised him, pleased him, and at the same time left him vaguely worried. He didn't like things that he couldn't control and he suspected that it would be difficult for anyone to exercise control over her.

Of course, he wasn't just anyone.

The crowd was singing now, an old song that told of the earth being reborn with the harvesting of new crops, the bearing of food from the fields to the tables of the people who had worked to gather it. There was praise for the seasons, for rain and sun, for the giving of life. Chants rose for the King of the Silver River; the voices grew steadily louder and more insistent. The girl seemed not to hear. She walked through the singing and the cries without responding, making her way first past the houses that lay at the edge of the village, then the larger shops that formed the core of the business center. Federation soldiers began to appear and tried to police the traffic as it surged ahead.

They were too few and too ill-prepared, thought Pe Ell. Apparently they had misjudged badly the extent of the community's response to the coming of the girl.

The Dwarves were feverish in their adoration. It was as if they had been given back the lives that had been stolen from them. A broken, subjugated people for so many years, there had been little enough to happen to give them hope. But this girl seemed to be what they had been waiting for. It was more than the stories, more than the claims of who she was and what she could do. It was the look and feel of her. Pe Ell could sense it as readily as the people who rallied about her. He could feel something of it in himself. She was different from anyone he had ever seen. She had come here for a reason. She was going to *do* something.

Business ground to a halt in Culhaven as the whole of the village, oppressed and oppressors alike, turned out to discover what was happening and became a part of it. Pe Ell had the sense of a wave gathering force out in the ocean, growing in size until it dwarfed the vast body of water that had given life to it. It was so with this girl. There was a sense of all other events beyond this one ceasing to exist. Everything but what she was faded away and lost meaning. Pe Ell smiled. It was the most wonderful feeling.

The wave swept on through the village, past the shops and businesses, the slave markets, the workhouses, the compounds and soldiers' quarters, the shabby homes of the Dwarves and the well-kept houses of the Federation officials, down the main thoroughfare, and out again. No one seemed able to guess where it was going. No one but the girl, for she led even at the center of the maelstrom of bodies, guiding somehow the edges of the wave, directing it as she wished. The cries and singing and chants continued unabated, exhilarated, rapturous. Pe Ell marveled.

And then the girl stopped. The crowd slowed, swirled about her, and grew still. She stood at the foot of the blackened slopes that had once been the Meade Gardens. She lifted her face to the stark line of the hill's barren crest much as if she might have been looking beyond it to a place that no one else could see. Few in the crowd looked where she was looking; they simply stared at her. There were hundreds of them now, and all of them waited to see what she would do.

Then slowly, deliberately she moved onto the slope. The crowd did not follow, sensing perhaps that it was not meant to, divining from some small movement or look that it was meant to wait. It parted for her, a sea of faces rapt with expectation. A few hands stretched out in an attempt to touch her, but none succeeded.

Pe Ell eased his way through the crowd until he stood at its foremost edge less than ten yards from the girl. Although he was purposeful in his advance, he did not yet know what he meant to do.

A knot of soldiers intercepted the girl, led by an officer bearing the crossed shoulder bars of a Federation commander. The girl waited for them. An unpleasant murmur rose from the crowd.

"You are not allowed here," announced the commander, his voice steady and clear. "No one is. You must go back down."

The girl looked at him, waiting.

"This is forbidden ground, young lady," the other continued, an officer addressing an inferior in a manner intended to demonstrate authority. "No one is permitted to walk upon this earth. A proclamation of the Coalition Council of the Federation government, which I have the honor to serve, forbids it. Do you understand?"

The girl did not answer.

"If you do not turn around and leave willingly, I shall be forced to escort you."

A scattering of angry cries sounded.

The girl came forward a step.

"If you do not leave *at once*, I shall have to . . ."

The girl gestured and instantly the man's legs were entwined in ground roots an inch thick. The soldiers who had accompanied him fell back with gasps of dismay as the pikes they were holding turned to gnarled staffs of deadwood that crumbled in their hands. The girl walked past them, unseeing. The blustering voice of the commander turned to a whisper of fear and then disappeared in the shocked murmur of the crowd.

Pe Ell smiled fiercely. Magic! The girl possessed real magic! The stories were true. It was more than he could have hoped for. Was she really the daughter of the King of the Silver River, he wondered?

The soldiers kept away from her now, unwilling to challenge the kind of power she obviously wielded. There were a few attempts at issuing orders by lesser officers, but no one was sure what to do after what had happened to the commander. Pe Ell glanced swiftly about. Apparently there were no Seekers in the village. In the absence of Seekers, no one would act.

The girl proceeded up the empty, burned surface of the slope toward its summit, and her passing barely stirred the dry earth on which she walked. The sun beat down fiercely out of the midday sky, turning the empty stretch of ground into a furnace. The girl seemed not to notice, her face calm as she passed through the swelter.

As he stared at her, Pe Ell felt himself drawn to the rim of a vast chasm, knowing that beyond was something so impossible that he could not imagine it.

What will she do?

She came to the summit of the slope and stopped, a slim, ethereal form outlined against the sky. She paused for a moment, as if searching for something in the air around her, an invisible presence that would speak to her. Then she knelt. She dropped down to the charred earth of the hillside and buried her hands within it. Her head lowered and her hair fell about her in a veil of silver light.

The world about her went absolutely still.

Then the earth beneath began to tremble and shake, and a rumbling sound rose out of its depths. The crowd gasped and fell back. Men steadied themselves, women snatched up children, and cries and shouts began to sound. Pe Ell came forward a step, his hazel eyes intense. He was not frightened. This was what he had been waiting for, and nothing could have chased him away.

Light seemed to flare from the hillside then, a glow that dwarfed even the sunlight's brilliance. Geysers exploded from the earth, small eruptions that burst skyward, showering Pe Ell and the foremost members of the crowd with dirt and silt. There was a heaving as if some giant buried beneath was rising from his sleep, and huge boulders began to jut from the ground like the bones of the giant's hunched shoulders. The burned surface of the hillside began to turn itself over and disappear. Fresh earth rose up to cover it, rich and glistening, filling the air with a pungent smell. Massive roots lifted out like snakes, twisting and writhing in response to the rumblings. Green shoots began to unfold.

In the midst of it all, the girl knelt. Her body was rigid beneath the loose covering of her clothes, and her arms were buried in the earth up to her elbows. Her face was hidden.

Many in the crowd were kneeling now, some praying to the forces of magic once believed to have controlled the destiny of men, some simply steadying themselves against tremors which had grown so violent that even the most sturdy trees were being shaken. Excitement rushed through Pe Ell and left him flushed. He wanted to run to the girl, to embrace her, to feel what was happening within her, and to share in the power.

Boulders grated and boomed as they rearranged themselves, changing the shape of the hillside. Terraced walls formed out of the rock. Moss and ivy filled the gaps. Trails wound down from one level to the next in gentle descent. Trees appeared, roots become small saplings, the saplings in turn thickening and branching out, compressing dozens of seasons of growth into scant minutes. Leaves budded and spread as if desperate to reach the sunlight. Grasses and brush spread out across the empty earth, turning the blackened surface a vibrant green. And flowers! Pe Ell cried out in the silence of his mind. There were flowers everywhere, springing forth in a profusion of bright colors that threatened to blind him. Blues, reds, yellows, violets— the rainbow's vast spectrum of shades and tones blanketed the earth.

Then the rumbling ceased and the silence that followed was broken by the singing of birds. Pe Ell glanced at the crowd behind him. Most were on their knees still, their eyes wide, their faces rapt with wonder. Many were crying.

He turned back to the girl. In a span of no more than a few minutes she had transformed the entire hillside. She had erased a hundred years of devastation and neglect, of deliberate razing, of purposeful burning off and leveling out, and restored to the Dwarves of Culhaven the symbol of who and what they were. She had given them back the Meade Gardens.

She was still on her knees, her head lowered. When she came back to her feet she could barely stand. All of her strength had been expended in her effort to restore the Gardens; she seemed to have nothing left to give. She swayed weakly, her arms hanging limply at her sides, her beautiful, perfect face drawn and lined, her silver hair damp and tangled. Pe Ell felt her eyes fix upon him once more and this time he did not hesitate. He went up the hillside swiftly, bounding over rocks and brush, skipping past the trails as if they were hindrances. He felt the crowd surging after him, heard their voices crying out, but they were nothing to him and he did not look back. He reached the girl as she was falling and caught her in his arms. Gently he cradled her, holding her as he might a captured wild creature, protectively and possessively at once.

Her eyes stared into his, he saw the intensity and brilliance of them, the depth of feeling they held, and in that moment he was bound to her in a way that he could not describe. "Take me to where I can rest," she whispered to him.

The crowd was all about them now, their anxious voices a babble he could not lock out. A sea of faces pressed close. He said something to those closest to reassure them that she was only tired and heard his words pass from mouth to mouth. He caught a glimpse of Federation soldiers at the fringes of the crowd, but they were wisely choosing to keep their distance. He began moving away, carrying the girl, amazed at how little she weighed. There was nothing to her, he thought. And everything.

A handful of Dwarves intercepted him, asking him to follow them, to bring the daughter of the King of the Silver River to their home, to let her rest with them. Pe Ell let himself be guided by them. One home was as good as another for now. The eyes of the crowd followed after, but already it was dispersing at its fringes, straying off into the paradise of the Gardens, discovering for themselves the beauty that it held. There was singing again, softer now, songs of praise and thanksgiving for the girl, lyrical and sweet.

Pe Ell descended the hillside and passed out of the Meade Gardens and back into the village of Culhaven with the girl asleep in his arms. She had given herself into his keeping. She had placed herself under his protection. He found it ironic.

After all, he had been sent there to kill her.

CHAPTER

6

E ELL CARRIED the daughter of the King of the Silver River to the home of the Dwarves who had offered to keep her, a family that consisted of a man, his wife, their widowed daughter, and two small grandchildren. Their home was a stone cottage at the east end of the village sheltered by white oak and red elm and set back against the wall of the forest close by the channel of the river. It was quiet there, isolated from the village proper, and by the time they reached it most of the following crowd had turned back. A handful chose to stay and set up camp at the edge of the property, most of them those who had followed the girl up from the country south, zealots who were determined that she would be their savior.

But she wasn't for them, Pe Ell knew. She belonged now to him.

With the help of the family he placed the girl in a bed in a tiny back room where the man and woman slept. The husband and his wife and widowed daughter went out again to prepare something to eat for those who had chosen to keep vigil over the girl, but Pe Ell remained. He sat in a chair next to the bed and watched her sleep. For a time the children remained, curious to see what would happen, but eventually they lost interest, and he was left alone. The daylight faded into darkness and still he sat, waiting patiently for her to wake. He studied the line of her body as she lay sleeping, the curve of her hip and shoulder, the soft rounding of her back. She was such a tiny thing, just a little bit of flesh and bone beneath the coverings, the smallest

534

spark of life. He marveled at the texture of her skin, at the coloring, at the absence of flaws. She might have been molded by some great artist whose reflection and skill had created a once-and-only masterpiece.

Fires were lit without, and the sound of voices drifted in through the curtained window. The sounds of night filled the silence between exchanges, the songs of birds and the buzzing of insects rising up against the faint rush of the river's waters. Pe Ell was not tired and had no need to sleep.

Instead, he used the time to think.

A WEEK EARLIER he had been summoned to Southwatch and a meeting with Rimmer Dall. He had gone because it pleased him and not because it was necessary. He was bored and he was hopeful that the First Seeker would give him something interesting to do, that he would provide him with a challenge. To Pe Ell's way of thinking, that was all that mattered about Rimmer Dall. The rest of what the First Seeker did with his life and the lives of others was of no interest to him. He had no illusions, of course. He knew what Rimmer Dall was. He simply didn't care.

It took him two days to make the journey. He traveled north on horseback out of the rugged hill country below the Battlemound where he made his home and arrived at Southwatch at sunset on the second day. He dismounted while still out of sight of the sentries and made his approach by foot. He need not have bothered; he could have come all the way in and gained immediate admittance. But he liked the idea of being able to come and go as he chose. He liked demonstrating his talent.

Especially to the Shadowen.

Pe Ell was as they were as he came into the black monolith, seemingly through the creases in the stone, a wraith out of darkness. He went past the sentries unseen and unheard, as invisible to them as the air they breathed. Southwatch was silent and dark, its walls polished and smooth, its corridors empty. It had the feel and look of a well-preserved crypt. Only the dead belonged here, or those who trafficked in death. He worked his way through its catacombs, feeling the pulse of the magic imprisoned in the earth beneath, hearing the whisper of it as it sought to break free. A sleeping giant that Rimmer Dall and his Shadowen thought they would tame, Pe Ell knew. They kept their secret well, but there was no secret that could be kept from him.

When he was almost to the high tower where Rimmer Dall waited, he killed one of those who kept watch, a Shadowen, but it made no difference. He did so because he could and because he felt like it. He melted into the black stone wall and waited until the creature came past him, drawn by a faint noise that he had caused, then drew the Stiehl from its sheath within his pants and cut the life out of his victim with a single, soundless twist. The sentry died in his arms, its shade rising up before him like black smoke, the body crumbling into ash. Pe Ell watched the astonished eyes go flat. He left the empty uniform where it could be found.

He smiled as he floated through the shadows. He had been killing for a long time now and he was very good at it. He had discovered his talent early in life, his ability to seek out and destroy even the most guarded of victims, his sense of how their protection could be broken down. Death frightened most people, but not Pe Ell. Pe Ell was drawn to it. Death was the twin brother of life and the more interesting of the two. It was secretive, unknown, mysterious. It was inevitable and forever when it came. It was a dark, infinitely chambered fortress waiting to be explored. Most entered only once and then only because they had no choice. Pe Ell wanted to enter at every opportunity and the chance to do so was offered through those he killed. Each time he watched someone die he would discover another room, glimpse another part of the secret. He would be reborn.

High within the tower, he encountered a pair of sentries posted before a locked door. They failed to see him as he eased close. Pe Ell listened. He could hear nothing, but he could sense that someone was imprisoned within the room beyond. He debated momentarily whether he should discover who it was. But that would mean asking, which he would never do, or killing the sentries, which he did not care to do. He passed on.

Pe Ell ascended a darkened flight of stairs to the apex of Southwatch and entered a room of irregular chambers that connected together like corridors in a maze. There were no doors, only entryways. There were no sentries. Pe Ell slipped inside, a soundless bit of night. It was dark without now, the blackness complete as clouds blanketed the skies and turned the world beneath opaque. Pe Ell moved through several of the chambers, listening, waiting.

Then abruptly he stopped, straightened, and turned.

Rimmer Dall stepped out of the blackness of which he was a part. Pe Ell smiled. Rimmer Dall was good at making himself invisible, too.

"How many did you kill?" the First Seeker asked in his hushed, whispery voice.

"One," Pe Ell said. His smile tugged at the corners of his mouth. "Perhaps I will kill another on the way out."

Dall's eyes shone a peculiar red. "One day you will play this game too often. One day you will brush up against death by mistake and she will snatch *you* up instead of your victim."

Pe Ell shrugged. His own dying did not trouble him. He knew it would come. When it did, it would be a familiar face, one he had seen all his life. For most, there was the past, the present, and the future. Not for Pe Ell. The past was nothing more than memories, and memories were stale reminders of what had been lost. The future was a vague promise—dreams and puffs of smoke. He had no use for either. Only the present mattered, because the present was the here and now of what you were, the happening of life, the immediacy of death, and it could be controlled as neither past nor future could. Pe Ell believed in control. The present was an ever-evolving chain of moments that living and dying forged, and you were always there to see it come.

A window opened on the night across a table and two chairs, and Pe Ell moved to seat himself. Rimmer Dall joined him. They sat in silence for a time, each looking at the other, but seeing something more. They had known each other for more than twenty years. Their meeting had been an accident. Rimmer Dall was a junior member of a policing committee of the Coalition Council, already deeply enmeshed in the poisonous politics of the Federation. He was ruthless and determined, barely out of boyhood, and already someone to be feared. He was a Shadowen, of course, but few knew it. Pe Ell, almost the same age, was an assassin with more than twenty kills behind him. They had met in the sleeping quarters of a man Rimmer Dall had come to dispatch, a man whose position in the Southland government he coveted and whose interference he had tolerated long enough. Pe Ell had gotten there first, sent by another of the man's enemies. They had faced each other in silence across the man's lifeless body, the night's shadows cloaking them both in the same blackness that mirrored their lives, and they had sensed a kinship. Both had use of the magic. Neither was what he seemed. Both were relentlessly amoral. Neither was afraid of the other. Without, the Southland city of Wayford buzzed and clanked and hissed with the intrigues of men whose ambitions were as great as their own but whose abilities were far less. They looked into each other's eyes and saw the possibilities.

They formed an irrevocable partnership. Pe Ell became the weapon, Rimmer Dall the hand that wielded it. Each served the other at his own pleasure; there were no constraints, no bonds. Each took what was needed and gave back what was required— yet neither really identified with nor understood what the other was about. Rimmer Dall was the Shadowen leader whose plans were an inviolate secret. Pe Ell was the killer whose occupation remained his peculiar passion. Rimmer Dall invited Pe Ell to eliminate those he believed particularly dangerous. Pe Ell accepted the invitation when the challenge was sufficiently intriguing. They nourished themselves comfortably on the deaths of others.

"Who is it that you keep imprisoned in the room below?" Pe Ell asked suddenly, breaking the silence, ending the flow of recollections.

Rimmer Dall's head inclined slightly, a mask of bones that gave his face the look of a fleshless skull. "A Southlander, a Valeman. One of two brothers named Ohmsford. The other brother believes he has killed this one. I arranged for him to think so. I planned it that way." The big man seemed pleased with himself. "When it is time, I will let them find each other again."

"A game of your own, it seems."

"A game with very high stakes, stakes that involve magic of

unimaginable proportions—magic greater than either yours or mine or anyone else's. Unbounded power."

Pe Ell did not respond. He felt the weight of the Stiehl against his thigh, the warmth of its magic. It was difficult for him to imagine a magic more powerful—impossible to envision one more useful. The Stiehl was the perfect weapon, a blade that could cut through anything. Nothing could withstand it. Iron, stone, the most impenetrable of defenses—all were useless against it. No one was safe. Even the Shadowen were vulnerable; even they could be destroyed. He had discovered as much some years back when one had tried to kill him, sneaking into his bedchamber like a stalking cat. It had thought to catch him sleeping; but Pe Ell was always awake. He had killed the black thing easily.

Afterward it had occurred to him that the Shadowen might have been sent by Rimmer Dall to test him. He hadn't chosen to dwell on the possibility. It didn't matter. The Stiehl made him invincible.

Fate had given him the weapon, he believed. He did not know who had made the Stiehl, but it had been intended for him. He was twelve years old when he found it, traveling with a man who claimed to be his uncle—a harsh, embittered drunkard with a penchant for beating anything smaller and weaker than himself—on a journey north through the Battlemound to yet another in an endless succession of towns and villages they frequented so that the uncle might sell his stolen goods. They were camped in a ravine in a desolate, empty stretch of scrub country at the edge of the Black Oaks, fence-sitting between the Sirens and the forest wolves, and the uncle had beaten him again for some imagined wrong and fallen asleep with his bottle tucked close. Pe Ell didn't mind the beatings anymore; he had been receiving them since he was orphaned at four and his uncle had taken him in. He hardly remembered what it was like not to be abused. What he minded was the way his uncle went about it these days—as if each beating was being undertaken to discover the limits of what the boy could stand. Pe Ell was beginning to suspect he had reached those limits.

He went off into the failing light to be alone, winding down the empty ravines, trudging over the desolate rises, scuffing his booted feet, and waiting for the pain of his cuts and bruises to ease. The hollow was close, no more than several hundred yards away, and the cave at its bottom drew him as a magnet might iron. He sensed its presence in a way he could not explain, even afterward. Hidden by the scrub, half-buried in loose rock, it was a dark and ominous maw opening down into the earth. Pe Ell entered without hesitation. Few things frightened him even then. His eyesight had always been extraordinary, and even the faintest light was enough to let him find his way.

He followed the cave back to where the bones were gathered—human bones, centuries old, scattered about randomly as if kicked apart. The Stiehl lay among them, the blade gleaming silver in the dark, pulsing with life, its name carved on its handle. Pe Ell picked it up and felt its warmth. A talisman from another age, a weapon of great power—he knew at once that it was magic and that nothing could withstand it.

He did not hesitate. He departed the cave, returned to the camp, and cut his uncle's throat. He woke the man first to make certain that he knew who had done it. His uncle was the first man he killed.

It had all happened a long time ago.

"THERE IS A GIRL," Rimmer Dall said suddenly and paused.

Pe Ell's gaze shifted back to the other's raw-boned face, silhouetted against the night. He could see the crimson eyes glitter.

The First Seeker's breath hissed from between his lips. "They say that she possesses magic, that she can change the character of the land simply by touching it, and that she can dispatch blight and disease and cause flowers to spring full grown from the foulest soil. They say that she is the daughter of the King of the Silver River."

Pe Ell smiled. "Is she?"

Rimmer Dall nodded. "Yes. She is who and what the stories claim. I do not know what she has been sent to do. She travels east toward Culhaven and the Dwarves. It appears that she has something specific in mind. I want you to find out what it is and then kill her."

Pe Ell stretched comfortably, his response unhurried. "Kill her yourself, why don't you?"

Rimmer Dall shook his head. "No. The daughter of the King of the Silver River is anathema to us. Besides, she would recognize a Shadowen instantly. Faerie creatures share a kinship that prohibits disguise. It must be someone other than one of us, someone who can get close enough, someone she will not suspect."

"Someone." Pe Ell's crooked smile tightened. "There are lots of someones, Rimmer. Send another. You have entire armies of blindly loyal cutthroats who will be more than happy to dispatch a girl foolish enough to reveal that she possesses magic. This business doesn't interest me."

"Are you certain, Pe Ell?"

Pe Ell sighed wearily. Now the bargaining begins, he thought. He stood up, his lean frame whiplike as he bent across the table so that he could see clearly the other's face. "I have listened to you tell me often enough how like the Shadowen you perceive me to be. We are much the same, you tell me. We wield magic against which there is no defense. We possess insight into the purpose of life which others lack. We share common instincts and skills. We smell, taste, sound, and feel the same. We are two sides of one coin. You go on and on. Well then, Rimmer Dall, unless you are lying I would be discovered by this girl as quickly as you, wouldn't I? Therefore, there is no point in sending me."

"It must be you."

"Must it, now?"

"Your magic is not innate. It is separate and apart from who and what you are. Even if the girl senses it, she will still not know who you are. She will not be warned of the danger you pose to her. You will be able to do what is needed."

Pe Ell shrugged. "As I said, this business doesn't interest me."

"Because you think there is no challenge in it?"

Pe Ell paused, then slowly sat down again. "Yes. Because there is no challenge."

Rimmer Dall leaned back in his chair and his face disappeared into shadow. "This girl is no simple flesh-and-blood creature; she will not be easily overcome. She has great magic, and her magic will protect her. It will take stronger magic still to kill her. Ordinary men with ordinary weapons haven't a chance. My legions of cutthroats, as you so disdainfully describe them, are worthless. Federation soldiers can get close to her, but cannot harm her. Shadowen cannot even get close. Even if they could, I am not certain it would make any difference. Do you understand me, Pe Ell?"

Pe Ell did not respond. He closed his eyes. He could feel Rimmer Dall watching him.

"This girl is dangerous, Pe Ell, the more so because she has obviously been sent to accomplish something of importance and I do not know what that something is. I have to find out and I have to put a stop to it. It will not be easy to do either. It may be too much even for you."

Pe Ell cocked his head thoughtfully. "Is that what you think?"

"Possibly."

Pe Ell was out of his chair with the swiftness of thought, the Stiehl snatched from its sheath and in his hand. The tip of the blade swept upward and stopped not an inch from Rimmer Dall's nose. Pe Ell's smile was frightening. "Really?"

Rimmer Dall did not flinch, did not even blink. "Do as I ask, Pe Ell. Go to Culhaven. Meet this girl. Find out what she plans to do. Then kill her."

Pe Ell was wondering if he should kill Rimmer Dall. He had thought about it before, contemplated it quite seriously. Lately the idea had begun to take on a certain fascination for him. He felt no loyalty to the man, cared nothing for him one way or the other beyond a vague appreciation of the opportunities he offered and even those were no longer as rewarding as they had once been. He was tired of the other's constant attempts to manipulate him. He no longer felt comfortable with their arrangement. Why not put an end to him?

The Stiehl wavered. The trouble was, of course, that there was no real point to it. Killing Rimmer Dall accomplished nothing, unless, of course, he was ready to discover what secrets might reveal themselves at the moment of the First Seeker's dying. That could prove interesting. On the other hand, why rush things? It was better to savor the prospect for a time. It was better to wait.

He sheathed the Stiehl with a quicksilver movement and backed away from Rimmer Dall. For just an instant he had a sense of missed opportunity, as if such a chance might never come again. But that was foolish. Rimmer Dall could not keep him away. The First Seeker's life was his to take when he chose.

He looked at Rimmer Dall for a moment, then spread his hands agreeably. "I'll do it."

He wheeled and started away. Rimmer Dall called after him. "Be warned, Pe Ell. This girl is more than a match for you. Do not play games with her. Once you have discovered her purpose, kill her quickly."

Pe Ell did not respond. He slipped from the room and melted back into the shadows of the keep, uninterested in anything Rimmer Dall thought or wished. It was enough that he had agreed to do what the Shadowen had asked. How he accomplished it was his own business.

He departed Southwatch for Culhaven. He did not kill any of the sentries on his way out. He decided it wasn't worth the effort.

MIDNIGHT APPROACHED. He grew tired of thinking and dozed in his chair as the hours slipped away. It was only several hours from dawn when the girl awoke. The cottage was silent, the Dwarf family asleep. The fires of those camped without had burned to coals and ash, and the last whispers of conversation had died away. Pe Ell came awake instantly as the girl stirred. Her eyes blinked open and fixed on him. She stared at him without speaking for a very long time and then slowly sat up.

"I am called Quickening," she said.

"I am Pe Ell," he replied.

She reached for his hand and took it in her own. Her fingers were as light as feathers as they traced his skin. Then she shivered and drew back.

"I am the daughter of the King of the Silver River," she said. She swung her legs off the bed and faced him. She smoothed back her tangled silver hair. Pe Ell was transfixed by her beauty, but she seemed completely unaware of it. "I need your help," she said. "I have come out of the Gardens of my father and into the world of men in search of a talisman. Will you journey with me to find it?"

The plea was so unexpected that for a moment Pe Ell did not respond but simply continued staring at the girl. "Why do you choose me?" he asked finally, confused.

And she said at once, "Because you are special."

It was exactly the right answer, and Pe Ell was astonished that she should know enough to give it, that she could sense what he wanted to hear. Then he remembered Rimmer Dall's warning and hardened himself. "What sort of talisman is it that we search for?"

She kept her eyes fastened on him. "One of magic, one with power enough to withstand even that of the Shadowen."

Pe Ell blinked. Quickening was so beautiful, but her beauty was a mask that distracted and confused. He felt suddenly stripped of his defenses, bared to his deepest corners, the light thrown on all his secrets. She knew him for what he was, he sensed. She could see everything.

In that instant, he almost killed her. What stopped him was how truly vulnerable she was. Despite her magic, formidable indeed, magic that could transform a barren, empty stretch of hillside back into what was surely no more than a memory in the minds of even the most elderly of the Dwarves, she lacked any form of defense against a killing weapon like the Stiehl. He could sense that it was so. She was helpless should he choose to kill her.

Knowing that, he decided not to. Not yet.

"Shadowen," he echoed softly.

"Are you frightened of them?" she asked him.

"No."

"Of magic?"

Pe Ell breathed in slowly. His narrow features twisted in upon themselves as he bent toward her. "What do you know of me?" he asked, his eyes searching her own.

She did not look away. "I know that I need you. That you will not be afraid to do what is necessary."

It seemed to Pe Ell that her words held more than one meaning, but he was unable to decide.

"Will you come?" she asked again.

Kill her quickly, Rimmer Dall had said. Find out her purpose and kill her. Pe Ell looked away, staring out the cottage window into the night, listening to the rushing sound of the river and the wind, soft and distant. He had never much bothered with the advice of others. Most of it was self-serving, useless to a man whose life depended on his ability to exercise his own judgment. Besides, there was a great deal more to this business than what Rimmer Dall had revealed. There were secrets waiting to be discovered. It might be that the talisman the girl searched for was something that even the First Seeker feared. Pe Ell smiled. What if the talisman happened to fall into his hands? Wouldn't that be interesting?

He looked back at her again. He could kill her anytime.

"I will come with you," he said.

She stood suddenly, reaching out her hands to take his own, drawing him up with her. They might have been lovers. "There are two more that must come with us, two like yourself who are needed," she said. "One of them is here in Culhaven. I want you to bring him to me."

Pe Ell frowned. He had already resolved to separate her from those fools camped without, misguided believers in miracles and fate who would only get in his way. Quickening belonged to him alone. He shook his head. "No."

She stepped close, her coal black eyes strangely empty. "Without them, we cannot succeed. Without them, the talisman is beyond our reach. No others need come, but they must."

She spoke with such determination that he found it impossible to argue with her. She seemed convinced that what she was saying was true. Perhaps it was, he decided; she knew more of what she was about at this point than he.

"Just two?" he asked. "No others? None of those without?"

She nodded wordlessly.

"All right," he agreed. No two men would be enough to cause him problems, to interfere with his plans. The girl would still be his to kill when he chose. "One man is here in the village, you say. Where am I to find him?"

For the first time since she had come awake, she turned away so that he could not see her.

"In the Federation prisons," she said.

CHAPTER

7

ORGAN LEAH.
That was the name of the man that Pe Ell was supposed to find and bring to the daughter of the King of the Silver River.

The streets of Culhaven were deserted save for the homeless huddled in the crooks and crannies of the shops, shapeless bundles of rags waiting out the night. Pe Ell ignored them as he made his way toward the center of town and the Federation prisons. Dawn was the better part of two hours away; he had more than sufficient time to do what was needed. He might have postponed this rescue business another night, but he saw no reason to do so. The quicker this fellow was found, the quicker they would all be on their way. He hadn't asked the girl yet where it was that they were going. It didn't matter.

He kept to the shadows as he moved ahead, mulling over in his mind the ambivalent effect she had on him. He was both exhilarated and appalled. She made him feel as if he were a man in the process of rediscovering himself and at the same time as if he were a fool. Rimmer Dall would certainly claim he was the latter, that he was playing the most dangerous of games, that he was being led about by the nose and deluding himself into thinking he was in command. But Rimmer Dall had no heart, no soul, no sense of the poetry of life and death. He cared nothing for anything or anyone—only for the power he wielded or sought to secure. He was a Shadowen, and the Shadowen were empty things. However Rimmer Dall saw it, Pe Ell was less like him than the First Seeker thought. Pe Ell understood the harsh realities of existence, the practical necessities of staying alive, and of making oneself secure; but he also could feel the beauty of things, particularly in the prospect of death. Death possessed great beauty. Rimmer Dall saw it as extinction. But when Pe Ell killed, he did so to discover anew the grace and symmetry that made it the most wondrous of life's events.

He was certain that there would be incredible beauty in the death of Quickening. It would be unlike any other killing he had ever done.

So he would not rush it, not hurry the irrevocable fact of it; he would take time to anticipate it. The feelings she invoked in him would not alter or adversely effect the course of action he had set for himself. He would not disparage himself for experiencing them; they were part of his makeup, a reaffirmation of his humanity. Rimmer Dall and his Shadowen could know nothing of such feelings; they were as unfeeling as stone. But not Pe Ell. Not ever.

He slipped past the workhouses, avoiding the lights of the compound and the Federation soldiers on watch. The surrounding forest was hushed and sleeping, a black void in which sounds were disembodied and somehow frightening. Pe Ell became a part of that void, comfortable within its cloaking as he moved soundlessly ahead. He could see and hear what no one else could; it had always been that way. He could feel what lived within the dark even though it hid from him. The Shadowen were like that; but even they could not assimilate as he could.

He paused at a lighted crossway and waited to be certain it was clear. There were patrols everywhere.

He pictured Quickening's image in the aura cast by a solitary streetlamp. A child, a woman, a magical being—she was all of these and much more. She was the embodiment of the land's most beautiful things—a sunlit woodland glen, a towering falls, a blue sky at midday, a rainbow's kaleidoscope of color, an endless sweep of stars at night viewed from an empty plain. She was a creature of flesh and blood, of human life, and yet she was a part of the earth as well, of fresh-turned soil, of mountain streams, of great old rocks that would not yield to anything but time. It baffled him, but he could sense things in her that were at once incongruous and compatible. How could that be? What was she, beyond what she claimed?

He moved swiftly through the light and melted back into the shadows. He did not know, but he was determined to find out.

The squarish dark bulk of the prisons loomed ahead. Pe Ell took a moment to consider his options. He knew the design of the Federation prisons at Culhaven; he had even been in them once or twice, though no one knew about it but Rimmer Dall. Even in prison, there were men who needed to be killed. But that was not to be the case tonight. Admittedly, he had considered killing this man he had been sent to rescue, this Morgan Leah. That would be one way to prevent the girl from insisting that he accompany them in their search for the missing talisman. Kill this one now, the other one later, and that would be the end of the matter. He could lie about how it happened. But the girl might guess the truth, might even divine it. She trusted him; why take a chance on changing that? Besides, perhaps she was right about needing these men to reclaim the talisman. He did not know enough yet of what they were about. It was better to wait and see.

He let his lean frame disappear into the stone of the wall against which he rested, thinking. He could enter the prisons directly, confront the commanding officer with his Shadowen insignia, and secure the release of the man without further fuss. But that would mean revealing himself, and he preferred not to do that. No one knew about him now besides Rimmer Dall. He was the First Seeker's private assassin. None of the other Shadowen even suspected that he existed; none had ever seen him. Those who had encountered him, Shadowen or otherwise, were all dead. He was a secret to everyone and he preferred to keep it that way. It would be better to take the man out in the usual way, in silence and stealth, alone.

Pe Ell smiled his lopsided smile. Save the man now so that he could kill him later. It was a strange world.

He eased himself out from the wall and snaked his way through the darkness toward the prisons.

MORGAN LEAH WAS not asleep. He lay wrapped in a blanket in his cell on a pallet of straw, thinking. He had been awake for most of the night, too restless to sleep, plagued by worries and regrets and a nagging sense of futility that he could not seem to banish. The cell was claustrophobic, barely a dozen feet square while more than twenty feet from floor to ceiling with an iron door several inches thick and a single barred window so high up he could not manage to reach it to look out even by jumping. The cell had not been cleaned since he had been thrown into it, so consequently it stank. His food, such as it was, was brought to him twice a day and shoved through a slot at the base of the door. He was given water to drink in the same way, but none with which to wash. He had been imprisoned now for almost a week and no one had come to see him. He was beginning to think that no one would.

It was an odd prospect. When they had caught him he had been certain they would be quick to use whatever means they had at their disposal to find out why he had gone to so much trouble to free two old Dwarf ladies. He wondered even now if Granny Elise and Auntie Jilt had escaped, if they remained free; he had no way of knowing. He had struck a Federation commander, perhaps killed him. He had stolen a Federation uniform to impersonate a Federation soldier, used a Federation major's name to secure entry to the workhouses, deceived the Federation officer on duty, and made the Federation army in general appear like a bunch of incompetents. All for the purpose of freeing two old ladies. A maligned and misused Federation command had to want to know why. They had to be anxious to repay him for the humiliation and hurt he had caused them. Yet they had left him alone.

He played mind games with the possibilities. It seemed unlikely he was going to be ignored indefinitely, that he was to be left in that cell until he was simply forgotten. Major Assomal, as he had discovered, was in the field; perhaps they were waiting for him to return to begin the questioning. But would Commander Soldt be patient enough to wait after what had been done to him? Or was he dead; had Morgan killed him after all? Or were they all waiting for someone else?

Morgan sighed. Someone else. He always came back to the

same inescapable conclusion. They were waiting for Rimmer Dall.

He knew that had to be it. Teel had betrayed Granny and Auntie to the Federation, but more particularly to the Shadowen. Rimmer Dall had to know of their connection to Par and Coll Ohmsford and all those who had gone in search of the Sword of Shannara. If someone tried to rescue them, surely he would be notified—and would come to see who it was that had been caught.

Morgan eased himself gingerly over on one side facing out from the wall into the blackness. He didn't hurt as much as he had the first few days; the aches and pains of his beating were beginning to heal. He was lucky nothing had been broken— lucky, in fact, that he was still alive.

Or not so lucky, he amended his assessment, depending on how you looked at it. His luck, it appeared, had run out. He thought momentarily of Par and Coll and regretted that he would not be able to go to them, to look after them as he had promised he would. What would become of them without him? What had happened to them in his absence? He wondered if Damson Rhee had hidden them after their escape from the Pit of Tyrsis. He wondered if Padishar Creel had found out where they were.

He wondered a thousand things, and there were no answers to be found for any of them.

Mostly he wondered how much longer he would be kept alive.

He rolled onto his back again, thinking of how different things might have been for him. In another age he would have been a Prince of Leah and one day ruled his homeland. But the Federation had put an end to the monarchy more than two hundred years ago, and today his family ruled nothing. He closed his eyes, trying to dispel any thoughts of might-have-beens and would-have-beens, finding no comfort there. He remained hopeful, his spirit intact despite all that had happened, the resiliency that had seen him through so much still in evidence. He did not intend to give up. There was always a way.

He just wished he could discover what it was.

He dozed for a bit, lost in a flow of imaginings that jumbled together in a wash of faces and voices, teasing him with their disjointed, false connectings, lies of things that never were and could never be.

He drifted into sleep.

Then a hand came down over his mouth, cutting off his exclamation of surprise. A second hand pinned him to the floor. He struggled, but the grip that held him was unbreakable.

"Quiet, now," a voice whispered in his ear. "Hush."

Morgan went still. A hawk-faced man in a Federation uniform was bent over him, peering into his eyes intently. The hands released, and the man sat back. A smile tugged at the corners of his mouth, and laugh lines wreathed his narrow face.

"Who are you?" Morgan asked softly.

"Someone who can get you free of this place if you're smart enough to do as I say, Morgan Leah."

"You know my name?"

The laugh lines deepened. "A lucky guess. Actually, I stumbled in here by chance. Can you show me the way out again?"

Morgan stared at him, a tall, gaunt fellow who had the look of a man who knew what he was about. The smile he wore seemed wired in place and there was nothing friendly about it. Morgan shoved his blanket aside and came to his feet, noticing the way the other backed off as he did so, always keeping the same amount of space between them. Cautious, thought Morgan, like a cat.

"Are you with the Movement?" he asked the man.

"I'm with myself. Put this on."

He tossed Morgan some clothing. When the Highlander examined it, he found he was holding a Federation uniform. The stranger disappeared back into the dark for a moment, then reemerged carrying something bulky over one shoulder. He deposited his burden on the pallet with a grunt. Morgan started as he realized it was a body. The stranger picked up the discarded blanket and draped it over the dead man to make it look as if he were sleeping.

"It will take them longer this way to discover you're missing," he whispered with that unnerving smile.

Morgan turned away and dressed as quickly as he could. The other man beckoned impatiently when he was finished and together they slipped out through the open cell door.

The corridor without was narrow and empty. Lamplight brightened the darkness only marginally. Morgan had seen nothing of the prisons when they brought him in, still unconscious from his beating, and he was immediately lost. He trailed after the stranger watchfully, following the passageway as it burrowed through the stone block walls past rows of cell doors identical to his own, all locked and barred. They encountered no one.

When they reached the first watch station, it was deserted as well. There appeared to be no one on duty. The stranger moved quickly to the corridor beyond, but Morgan caught a glint of metal blades through a half-open door to one side. He slowed, peering in. Racks of weapons lined the walls of a small room. He suddenly remembered the Sword of Leah. He did not want to leave without it.

"Wait a minute!" he whispered to the man ahead.

The stranger turned. Quickly Morgan pushed at the door. It gave reluctantly, dragging against something. Morgan shoved until there was enough space to get through. Inside, wedged against the back of the door, was another dead man. Morgan swallowed against what he was feeling and forced himself to search the racks for the Sword of Leah.

He found it almost immediately, still in its makeshift sheath, hung on a nail behind a brace of pikes. He strapped the weapon on hurriedly, grabbed a broadsword as well, and went out again.

The stranger was waiting. "No more delays," he said pointedly. "The shift change comes just after sunrise. It's almost that now."

Morgan nodded. They went down a second corridor, a back set of stairs supported by timbers that creaked and groaned as they descended, and out through a courtyard. The stranger knew exactly where he was going. There were no guards until they reached a post just inside the walls and even then they were not challenged. They passed through the gates and out of the prison just as the first faint tinges of light began to appear on the horizon.

The stranger took Morgan down the roadway a short distance, then into a barn through a backdoor where the shadows were so thick the Highlander had to feel his way. Inside, the stranger lit a lamp. Digging under a pile of empty feed sacks, he produced a change of clothing for each of them, woods garb, indistinguishable from what most Eastland laborers wore. They changed wordlessly, then stuffed the discarded Federation uniforms back beneath the sacks.

The stranger motioned Morgan after him and they went out again into the first light of the new day.

"A Highlander, are you?" the stranger asked abruptly as they walked eastward through the waking village.

Morgan nodded.

"Morgan Leah. Last name the same as the country. Your family ruled the Highlands once, didn't they?"

"Yes," Morgan answered. His companion seemed more relaxed now, his long strides slow and easy, though his eyes never stopped moving. "But the monarchy hasn't existed for many years."

They took a narrow bridge across a sewage-fouled tributary of the Silver River. An old woman passed them carrying a small child. Both looked hungry. Morgan glanced over at them. The stranger did not.

"My name is Pe Ell," he said. He did not offer his hand.

"Where are we going?" Morgan asked him.

The corners of the other's mouth tugged upward slightly. "You'll see." Then he added, "To meet the lady who sent me to rescue you."

Morgan thought at once of Granny Elise and Auntie Jilt. But how would they know someone like Pe Ell? The man had already said he was not a part of the Free-born Movement; it seemed unlikely that he was allied with the Dwarf Resistance either. Pe Ell, Morgan thought, was with exactly who he had said he was with—himself.

But who then was the lady on whose behalf he had come?

They passed down lanes that wound through the Dwarf cottages and shacks at the edge of Culhaven, crumbling stone and wood slat structures falling down around the heads of those who lived within. Morgan could hear the sluggish flow of the Silver River grow nearer. The houses separated as the trees thickened and soon there were few to be seen. Dwarves at work in their yards and gardens looked up at them suspiciously. If Pe Ell noticed, he gave no sign.

Sunlight was breaking through the trees ahead in widening streamers by the time they reached their destination, a small, well-kept cottage surrounded by a ragged band of men who had settled in at the edge of the yard and were in the process of completing breakfast and rolling up their sleeping gear. The men whispered among themselves and looked long and hard at Pe Ell as he approached. Pe Ell went past them without speaking, Morgan in tow. They went up the steps to the front door of the cottage and inside. A Dwarf family seated at a small table greeted them with nods and brief words of welcome. Pe Ell barely acknowledged them. He took Morgan to the back of the cottage and into a small bedroom and shut the door carefully behind them.

A girl sat on the edge of the bed.

"Thank you, Pe Ell," she said quietly and rose.

Morgan Leah stared. The girl was stunningly beautiful with small, perfect features dominated by the blackest eyes the Highlander had ever seen. She had long, silver hair that shimmered like captured light, and a softness to her that invited protection. She wore simple clothes—a tunic, pants cinched at the waist with a wide leather belt, and boots—but the clothes could not begin to disguise the sensuality and grace of the body beneath.

"Morgan Leah," the girl whispered.

Morgan blinked, suddenly aware that he was staring. He flushed.

"I am called Quickening," the girl said. "My father is the King of the Silver River. He has sent me from his Gardens into the world of Men to find a talisman. I require your help to do so."

Morgan started to respond and stopped, not knowing what to say. He glanced at Pe Ell, but the other's eyes were on the girl. Pe Ell was as mesmerized as he.

Quickening came up to him, and the flush in his face and neck traveled down his body in a warm rush. She reached out her hands and placed her fingers gently on the sides of his face.

He had never felt a touch like hers. He thought he might give anything to experience it again.

"Close your eyes, Morgan Leah," she whispered.

He did not question her; he simply did as she asked. He was immediately at peace. He could hear voices conversing somewhere without, the flow of the waters of the nearby river, the whisper of the wind, the singing of birds, and the scrape of a garden hoe. Then Quickening's fingers tightened marginally against his skin and everything disappeared in a wash of color.

Morgan Leah floated as if swept away in a dream. Hazy brightness surrounded him, but there was no focus to it. Then the brightness cleared and the images began. He saw Quickening enter Culhaven along a roadway lined with men, women, and children who cheered and called out to her as she passed, then followed anxiously after. He watched as she walked through growing crowds of Dwarves, Southlanders, and Gnomes to the barren stretch of hillside where the Meade Gardens had once flourished. It seemed that he became a part of the crowd, standing with those who had come to see what this girl would do, experiencing himself their sense of expectancy and hope. Then she ascended the hillside, buried her hands in the charred earth, and worked her wondrous magic. The earth was transformed before his eyes; the Meade Gardens were restored. The colors, smells, and tastes of her miracle filled the air, and Morgan felt an aching in his chest that was impossibly sweet. He began to cry.

The images faded. He found himself back in the cottage. He felt her fingers drop away and he brushed roughly at his eyes with the back of his hand as he opened them. She was staring at him.

"Was that real?" he asked, his voice catching in spite of his resolve to keep it firm. "Did that actually happen? It did, didn't it?"

"Yes," she answered.

"You brought back the Gardens. Why?"

Her smile was faint and sweet. "Because the Dwarves need to have something to believe in again. Because they are dying."

Morgan took a deep breath. "Can you save them, Quickening?"

"No, Morgan Leah," she answered, disappointing him, "I cannot." She turned momentarily into the room's shadows. "You can, perhaps, one day. But for now you must come with me."

The Highlander hesitated, unsure. "Where?"

She lifted her exquisite face back into the light. "North, Morgan Leah. To Darklin Reach. To find Walker Boh."

PE ELL STOOD to one side in the little cottage bedroom, momentarily forgotten. He didn't like what he was seeing. He didn't like the way the girl touched the Highlander or the way the Highlander responded to it. She hadn't touched him like that. It bothered him, too, that she knew the Highlander's name. She knew the other man's name as well, this Walker Boh. She hadn't known his.

She turned to him then, drawing him back into the conversation with Morgan Leah, telling them both they must travel north to find the third man. After they found him they would leave in search of the talisman she had been sent to find. She did not tell them what that talisman was, and neither of them asked. It was a result of the peculiar effect she had on them, Pe Ell decided, that they did not question what she told them, that they simply accepted it. They believed. Pe Ell had never done that. But he knew instinctively that this girl, this child of the King of the Silver River, this creature of wondrous magic, did not lie. He did not believe she was capable of it.

"I need you to come with me," she said again to the Highlander.

He glanced at Pe Ell. "Are you coming?"

The way he asked the question pleased Pe Ell. There was a measure of wariness in the Highlander's tone of voice. Perhaps even fear. He smiled enigmatically and nodded. Of course, Highlander, but only to kill you both when it pleases me, he thought.

The Highlander turned back to the girl and began explaining something about two old Dwarf ladies he had rescued from the workhouses and how he needed to know that they were safe because of some promise he had made to a friend. He kept staring at the girl as if the sight of her gave him life. Pe Ell shook his head. This one was certainly no threat to him. He could not imagine why the girl thought he was necessary to their recovery of the mysterious talisman.

Quickening told the Highlander that among those who had come with her to the cottage was one who would be able to discover what had become of the Dwarf ladies. He would make certain that they were well. She would ask him to do so immediately.

"Then if you truly need me, I will come with you," Morgan Leah promised her.

Pe Ell turned away. The Highlander was coming because he had no choice, because the girl had captured him. He could see it in the youth's eyes; he would do anything for her. Pe Ell understood that feeling. He shared something of it as well. The only difference between them was what they intended to do about it.

Pe Ell wondered again what it would feel like when he finally killed the girl. He wondered what he would discover in her eyes.

Quickening guided Morgan toward her bed so that he could rest. Pe Ell departed the room in silence and walked out of the cottage into the light. He stood there with his eyes closed and let the sun's warmth bathe his face.

8

OLL OHMSFORD WAS a prisoner at Southwatch for eight days before he discovered who had locked him away. His cell was the whole of his world, a room twenty feet square, high within the black granite tower, a stone-and-mortar box with a single metal door that never opened, a window closed off by metal shutters, a sleeping mat, a wooden bench, and a small table with two chairs. Light filtered through the shutters in thin, gray shafts when it was daytime and disappeared when it was night. He could peer through the cracks in the shutters and see the blue waters of the Rainbow Lake and the green canopy of the trees. He could catch glimpses of birds flying, cranes and terns and gulls, and he could hear their solitary cries.

Sometimes he could hear the howl of the wind blowing down out of the Runne through the canyons that channeled the Mermidon. Once or twice he could hear the howling of wolves.

Cooking smells reached him now and then, but they never seemed to emanate from the food that he was fed. His food came on a tray shoved through a hinged flap at the bottom of the iron door, a furtive delivery that lacked any discernible source. The food was consumed, and the trays remained where he stacked them by the door. There was a constant humming sound from deep beneath the castle, a sort of vibration that at first suggested huge machinery, then later something more akin to an earth tremor. It carried through the stone of the tower, and when Coll placed his hands against the walls he could feel the stone shiver. Everything was warm, the walls and floor, the door and window, the stone and mortar and metal. He didn't know how that could be with the nights sometimes chill enough to cause the air to bite, but it was. Sometimes he thought he could hear footsteps beyond his door—not when the food was delivered, but at other times when everything was still and the only other sound was the buzz of insects in the distant trees. The footsteps did not approach, but passed on without slowing. Nor did they seem to have an identifiable source; they might as easily come from below or above as without.

He could feel himself being watched, not often, but enough so that he was aware. He could feel someone's eyes fixed on him, studying him, waiting perhaps. He could not determine from where the eyes watched; it felt as if they watched from everywhere. He could hear breathing sometimes, but when he tried to listen for it he could hear only his own.

He spent most of his time thinking, for there was little else to do. He could eat and sleep; he could pace his cell and look through the cracks in the shutters. He could listen; he could smell and taste the air. But thinking was best, he found, an exercise that kept his mind sharp and free. His thoughts, at least, were not prisoners. The isolation he experienced threatened to overwhelm him, for he was closed away from everything and everyone he knew, without reason or purpose that he could discern, and by captors that kept themselves carefully hidden. He worried for Par so greatly that at times he nearly wept. He felt as if the rest of the world had forgotten him, had passed him by. Events were happening without him; perhaps everything he once knew had changed. Time stretched away in a slow, endless succession of seconds and minutes and hours and, after a while, days as well. He was lost in shadows and half-light and near-silence, his existence empty of meaning.

Thinking kept him together.

He thought constantly of how he might escape. The door and window were solidly seated in the stone of the fortress tower, and the walls and floor were thick and impenetrable. He lacked even the smallest digging tool in any event. He tried listening for those who patroled without, but the effort proved futile. He tried catching sight of those who delivered his meals, but they never revealed themselves. Escape seemed impossible.

He thought as well about what he might do to let someone know he was there. He could force a bit of cloth or a scrap of paper with a message scrawled on it through the cracks in the shutters of the window, but to what end? The wind would likely carry it away to the lake or the mountains and no one would ever find it. Or at least not in time to make any difference. He thought he might yell, but he knew he was so far up and away from any travelers that they would never hear him. He peered at the countryside unfailingly when it was light and never saw a single person. He felt himself to be completely alone.

He turned his thoughts finally to envisioning what was taking place beyond his door. He tried using his senses and when that failed, his imagination. His captors assumed multiple identities and behavioral patterns. Plots and conspiracies sprang to life, fleshed out with the details of their involvement of him. Par and Morgan, Padishar Creel and Damson Rhee, Dwarves, Elves, and Southlanders alike came to the black tower to free him. Brave rescue parties sallied forth. But all efforts failed. No one could reach him. Eventually, everyone gave up trying. Beyond the walls of Southwatch, life went on, uncaring.

After a week of this solitary existence, Coll Ohmsford began to despair.

Then, on the eighth day of his captivity, Rimmer Dall appeared.

It was late afternoon, gray and rainy, storm clouds low and heavy across the skies, lightning a wicked spider's web flashing through the creases, thunder rolling out of the darkness in long, booming peals. The summer air was thick with smells brought alive by the damp, and it felt chill within Coll's cell. He stood close against the shuttered window, peering out though the cracks in the fittings, listening to the sound of the Mermidon as it churned through the canyon rocks below.

When he heard the lock on the door to his room release he did not turn at first, certain that he must be mistaken. Then he saw the door begin to open, caught sight of the movement out of the corner of his eye, and wheeled about instantly.

A cloaked form appeared, tall and dark and forbidding, lacking face or limbs, seemingly a wraith come out of the night. Coll's first thought was of the Shadowen, and he dropped into a protective crouch, frantically searching his suddenly diminished cell for a weapon with which to defend himself.

"Don't be frightened, Valeman," the wraith soothed in an oddly familiar, whispery voice. "You are in no danger here."

The wraith closed the door behind it and stepped into the room's faint light. Coll saw by turns the black clothing marked with a white wolf's head, the left hand gloved to the elbow, and the rawboned, narrow face with its distinctive reddish beard.

Rimmer Dall.

Instantly Coll thought of the circumstances of his capture. He had gone with Par, Damson, and the Mole through the tunnels beneath Tyrsis into the abandoned palace of the old city's kings, and from there the Ohmsford brothers had gone on alone into the Pit in search of the missing Sword of Shannara. He had stood guard outside the entry to the vault that was supposed to contain the Sword, keeping watch while his brother went inside. It was the last time he had seen Par. He had been seized from behind, rendered unconscious, and spirited away. Until now he had not known who was responsible. It made sense that it should be Rimmer Dall, the man who had come for them weeks ago in Varfleet and hunted them ever since across the length and breadth of the Four Lands.

The First Seeker moved to within a few feet of Coll and stopped. His craggy face was calm and reassuring. "Are you rested?"

"That's a stupid question," Coll answered before he could think better of it. "Where's my brother?"

Rimmer Dall shrugged. "I don't know. When I last saw him he was carrying the Sword of Shannara from its vault."

Coll stared. "You were there—inside?"

"I was."

"And you let Par take the Sword of Shannara? You just let him walk away with it?"

"Why not? It belongs to him."

"You want me to believe," Coll said carefully, "that you don't care if he has possession of the Sword, that it doesn't matter to you?"

"Not in the way you think."

Coll paused. "So you let Par go, but you took me prisoner. Is that right?"

"It is."

Coll shook his head. "Why?"

"To protect you."

Coll laughed. "From what? Freedom of choice?"

"From your brother."

"From Par? You must think me the biggest fool who ever lived!"

The big man folded his arms across his chest comfortably. "To be honest with you, there is more to it than just offering you protection. You are a prisoner for another reason as well. Sooner or later, your brother will come looking for you. When he does, I want another chance to talk with him. Keeping you here assures me that I will have that chance."

"What really happened," Coll snapped angrily, "is that you caught me, but Par escaped! He found the Sword of Shannara and slipped past you somehow and now you're using me as bait to trap him. Well, it won't work. Par's smarter than that."

Rimmer Dall shook his head. "If I was able to capture you at the entrance to the vault, how is it that your brother managed to escape? Answer me that?" He waited a moment, then moved over to the table with its wooden chairs and seated himself. "I'll tell you the truth of things, Coll Ohmsford, if you'll give me a chance. Will you?"

Coll studied the other's face wordlessly for a moment, then shrugged. What did he have to lose? He stayed where he was, standing, deliberately measuring the distance between them.

Rimmer Dall nodded. "Let's begin with the Shadowen. The Shadowen are not what you have been led to believe. They are not monsters, not wraiths whose only purpose is to destroy the races, whose very presence has sickened the Four Lands. They are victims, for the most part. They are men, women and children who possess some measure of the faerie magic. They are the result of man's evolution through generations in which the magic was used. The Federation hunts them like animals. You

saw the poor creatures trapped within the Pit. Do you know
what they are? They are Shadowen whom the Federation has
imprisoned and starved into madness, changing them so that
they have become worse than animals. You saw as well the
woodswoman and the giant on your journey to Culhaven. What
they are is not their fault."

The gloved hand lifted quickly as Coll started to speak.
"Valeman, hear me out. You wonder how it is that I know so
much about you. I will explain if you will just be patient."

The hand came down again. "I became First Seeker in order
to hunt the Shadowen—not to harm or imprison them, but to
warn them, to get them to safety. That was why I came to you
in Varfleet—to see that you and your brother were protected. I
did not have the chance to do so. I have been searching for you
ever since to explain what I know. I thought that you might
return to the Vale and so placed your parents under my protection. I believed that if I could reach you first, before the Federation found you in some other way, you would be safe."

"I don't believe any of this," Coll interjected coldly.

Rimmer Dall ignored him. "Valeman, you have been lied to
from the beginning. That old man, the one who calls himself
Cogline, told you the Shadowen were the enemy. The shade of
Allanon warned you at the Hadeshorn in the Valley of Shale
that the Shadowen must be destroyed. Retrieve the lost magics
of the old world, you were advised. Find the Sword of Shannara.
Find the missing Elfstones. Find lost Paranor and bring back the
Druids. But were you told what any of this would accomplish?
Of course not. Because the truth of the matter is that you are
not supposed to know. If you did, you would abandon this business at once. The Druids care nothing for you and your kin and
never have. They are interested only in regaining the power
they lost when Allanon died. Bring them back, restore their
magics, and they will again control the destiny of the Races.
This is what they work for, Coll Ohmsford. The Federation,
unwittingly, ignorantly, helps them. The Shadowen provide the
perfect victim for both to prey upon. Your uncle recognized
the truth of things. He saw that Allanon sought to manipulate
him, to induce him to undertake a quest that would benefit no
one. He warned you all; he refused to be part of the Druid

madness. He was right. The danger is far greater than you realize."

He leaned forward. "I told all of this to your brother when he came into the vault after the Sword of Shannara. I was waiting there for him—had been waiting in fact for several days. I knew he would come back for the Sword. He had to; he couldn't help himself. That's what having the magic does to you. I know. I have the magic, too."

He stood up suddenly, and Coll shrank back in alarm. The black-clad body began to shimmer in the gloom as if translucent. Then it seemed to come apart, and Coll heard himself gasp. The dark form of a Shadowen lifted slowly out of Rimmer Dall's body, red eyes glinting, hung suspended in the air for a moment, and settled back again.

The First Seeker smiled coldly. "I am a Shadowen, you see. All of the Seekers are Shadowen. Ironic, isn't it? The Federation doesn't know. They believe us ordinary men, nothing more, men who serve their twisted interests, who seek as they do to rid the land of magic. They are fools. Magic isn't the enemy of the people. They are. And the Druids. And any who would keep men and women from being who and what they must."

One finger pointed at Coll like a dagger. "I told this to your brother, and I told him one thing more. I told him that he, too, is a Shadowen. Ah, you still don't believe me, do you? But listen, now. Par Ohmsford is in truth a Shadowen, whether either of you cares to admit it or not. So is Walker Boh. So is anyone who possesses real magic. That's what we are, all of us—Shadowen. We are sane, rational, and for the most part ordinary men, women, and children until we become hunted and imprisoned and driven mad by fools like the Federation. Then the magic overwhelms us and we become animals, like the woodswoman and the giant, like the things in the Pit."

Coll was shaking his head steadily. "No. This is all a lie."

"How is it that I know so much about you, do you think?" Rimmer Dall persisted, his voice maddeningly calm, even now. "I know all about your flight south down the Mermidon, your encounters with the woodswoman and the old man, how you met with that Highlander and persuaded him to join you, how you journeyed to Culhaven, then to Hearthstone, and finally to the Hadeshorn. I know of the Dwarves and Walker Boh. I know of your cousin Wren Ohmsford. I know of the outlaws and Padishar Creel and the girl and all the rest. I knew when you were going down into the Pit and tried to have you stopped. I knew that you would return and waited there for you. How, Valeman? Tell me."

"A spy in the outlaw camp," Coll answered, suddenly unsure. "Who?"

Coll hesitated. "I don't know."

"Then I will tell you. The spy was your brother."

Coll stared.

"Your brother, though he didn't realize it. Par is a Shadowen, and I sometimes know what other Shadowen think. When they use their magic, my own responds. It reveals to me their thoughts. When your brother used the wishsong, it let me know what he was thinking. That was how I found you. But Par's use of his magic alerted others as well. Enemies. That was why the Gnawl tracked you in the Wolfsktaag and the Spider Gnomes at Hearthstone.

"Think, Valeman! All that has befallen you has been the result of your own doing. I did not seek to harm you in Tyrsis. It was Par's decision to go down into the Pit that brought you to grief. I did not withhold the Sword of Shannara. Yes, I kept it hidden—but only to force Par to come to me so that I might save him."

Coll stiffened. "What do you mean?"

Rimmer Dall's pale eyes were intense. "I told you that the reason I brought you here was to protect you from your brother. I spoke the truth. The magic of a Shadowen is as two-edged as any sword. You have surely thought the same thing many times. It can be either salvation or curse. It can work to help or to hurt. But it is more complicated than that. A Shadowen can be affected by the stresses that use of the magic demands, particularly when he is threatened or hunted. The magic can grow frayed; it can escape. Remember the creatures in the Pit? Remember those you encountered on your travels? What do you think happened to them? Your brother has the wishsong as his magic. But the wishsong is only a thin shell covering the magic that lies beneath—a magic more powerful than your brother imagines. It begins to grow stronger as he runs and hides and tries to keep himself safe. If I don't reach him in time, if he continues to ignore my warnings, that magic will consume him."

A long silence followed. Coll reflected silently. He remembered Par telling him that he believed the magic of the wishsong was capable of doing much more than creating images, that he could feel it seeking a release. He remembered the way it had responded during their first venture into the Pit, casting a light through the gloom, illuminating the scroll of the vault. He thought of the creatures trapped there, become monsters and demons.

He wondered, just for an instant, if Rimmer Dall might not be telling him the truth.

The First Seeker came forward a single step and stopped. "Think about it, Coll Ohmsford," he suggested softly. He was big and dark against the gloom and frightening to look at. But his voice was reassuring. "Reason it through. You will have time enough to do so. I intend that you remain here until your brother comes looking for you or he uses his magic. One way or the other, I have to find him and warn him. I have to protect you both and those with whom you will eventually come in contact. Help me. We must find a way to reach your brother. We must try. I know you don't believe me now, but that will change."

Coll shook his head. "I don't think so."

Outside, distant and low, thunder rumbled and faded into the hissing of the rain. "So many lies have been told to you by others," Rimmer Dall said. "In time, you will see."

He moved back toward the cell door and stopped. "You have been kept in this room long enough. You may leave during the day. Just knock on the door when you wish to go out. Go down to the exercise yard and practice with the weapons. Someone will be there to help you. You should have some training. You need to learn better how to protect yourself. Make no mistake, though. You cannot leave. At night you will be locked in again. I wish it could be otherwise, but it cannot. Too much is at stake."

He paused. "I have a short visit to make, a journey of several days. Another requires my attention. When I return, we will talk again."

He seemed to consider Coll for a long moment, as if measuring him for something, then turned, and went out the way he had come. Coll watched him go, then walked back to the shuttered window and stood looking out again into the rain.

HE SLEPT POORLY that night, plagued by dreams of dark things that bore his brother's face, haunted when he came awake by what he had been told. *Nonsense*, was his first thought. *Lies*. But his instincts told him that some part of it, at least, was true—and that, in turn, suggested the unpleasant possibility that it might all be. Par a Shadowen. The magic a weapon that could destroy him. Both of them threatened by dark forces beyond their understanding or control.

He no longer knew what to believe.

When he woke, he rapped on the door. A black-cloaked Seeker released him and walked him down to the exercise yard. Another, a gruff fellow with a shaven head and knots and scars all over him, offered to spar with him. Using padded cudgels, they trained through the morning. Coll sweated and strained. It felt good to make use of his body again.

Later, alone in his cell, the afternoon clearing as the clouds thinned and sunshine broke through to the distant south, he evaluated his new situation. He was a prisoner still, but not so much so. He was no longer confined to a single room. He had been offered the means to stay fit and strong. He did not feel as threatened.

Whether or not Rimmer Dall was playing mind games with him remained to be seen, of course. In any case, the First Seeker had made a mistake. He had given Coll Ohmsford the opportunity to explore Southwatch.

And the further opportunity to find a way to escape.

CHAPTER

9

ALKER BOH LANGUISHED at Hearthstone in a prison far more forbidding than the one that had secured Morgan Leah. He had returned from Storlock filled with a fiery determination to cure the sickness that attacked him, to drive from his body the poison that the Asphinx had injected into it, and to heal himself as even the Stors could not. Within a week he had changed completely, grown dispirited and bitter, frightened that his hopes had been in vain, that he could not save himself after all. His days were long, heat-filled stretches of time in which he wandered the valley lost in thought, desperately trying to reason out what form of magic it would take to stem the poison's flow. His nights were empty and brooding, the dark hours expended in a silent, futile effort to implement his ideas.

Nothing worked.

He tried a little of everything. He began with a series of mind sets, inward delvings of his own magic that were designed to dissolve, break apart, turn back, or at least slow the poison's advance. None of these occurred. He used channeling of the magic in the form of an assault, the equivalent of an inner summoning of the fire that he sometimes used to protect and defend. The channeling could not seem to find a ready source; it scattered and lost its potency. He attempted spells and conjurings from the lore he had accumulated over the years, both that which was innate and that he had been taught. All failed. He resorted finally to the chemicals and powders that Cogline relied upon, the sciences of the old world brought into the new. He attacked the stone ruin of his arm and tried to burn it to the flesh so that cauterization might take place. He tried healing potions that were absorbed through the skin and permeated the stone. He used magnetic and electric fields. He used antitoxins. These, too, failed. The poison was too strong. It could not be overcome. It continued to work its way through his system, slowly killing him.

Rumor stayed at his side almost constantly, trailing silently after him on his long daytime walks, stretching out next to him in the darkness of his room as he struggled in vain to employ the magic in a way that would allow him to survive. The giant moor cat seemed to sense what was happening to Walker; it watched him as if fearful he might disappear at any moment, as if by watching closely it might somehow protect against this unseen thing that threatened. The luminous yellow eyes were always there, regarding him with intelligence and concern, and Walker found himself staring into them hopefully, searching for the answers he could find nowhere else.

Cogline, too, did what he could to help Walker in his struggle. Like the moor cat, he kept watch, albeit at a somewhat greater distance, afraid that Walker would not tolerate it if he came too close or stayed too long. There was still an antagonism between the two that would not be dispelled. It was difficult for them to remain in each other's presence for more than a few minutes at a time. Cogline offered what advice he could, mixing powders and potions at Walker's request, administering salves and healing medicines, suggesting forms of magic he thought might help. Mostly he provided what little reassurance he could that an antidote would be found.

Walker, though he would not admit it to the other, was grateful for that reassurance. For the first time in many years, he did not want to be alone. He had never given much thought to his own death, always convinced it was still far away and he would be prepared for it in any case when it arrived. He discovered now that he had been wrong on both counts. He was angry and frightened and confused; his emotions careened about inside him like stones tossed in a wagon bed, the debris of some emptied load. He fought to maintain his sense of balance, a belief in himself, some small measure of hope, but without the steadying presence of Cogline he would have been lost. The old man's face and voice, his movements, his idiosyncrasies, all so familiar, were handholds on the cliff to which Walker Boh clung, and they kept him from dropping away completely. He had known Cogline a long time; in the absence of Par and Coll, and to a lesser extent Wren, Cogline was his only link with the past—a past that he had in turn scorned, reviled, and finally cast away entirely, a past he was now desperate to regain as it was his link to the use of the magic that could save him. Had he not been so quick to disparage it, so anxious to be rid of its influence, had he taken more time to understand it, to learn from it, to master it and make it serve his needs, he might not be struggling so hard now to stay alive.

But the past is always irretrievable, and so Walker Boh found it here. Yet there was some comfort to be taken from the continued presence of the old man who had given him what understanding of the magic he had. With his future become so shockingly uncertain, he discovered a strange and compelling need to reach out to those things that remained his from the past. The most immediate of those was Cogline.

Cogline had come to him during the second year of his solitary life at Hearthstone. Risse had been dead fifteen years, Kenner five. He had been on his own ever since despite the efforts of Jaralan and Mirianna Ohmsford to make him a part of their family, an outcast from everyone because his magic would not let him be otherwise. While it had disappeared with the coming of age of all the Ohmsfords since Brin, it did not do so in him. Rather, it grew stronger, more insistent, more uncontrollable. It was bad enough when he lived in Shady Vale; it became intolerable at Hearthstone. It began to manifest itself in new ways—unwanted perceptions, strange foresights, harsh sensory recognition, and frightening exhibitions of raw power that threatened to shatter him. He could not seem to master them. He didn't understand them to begin with and therefore could not find a way to decipher their workings. It was best that he was alone; no one would have been safe around him. He found his sanity slipping away.

Cogline changed everything. He came out of the trees one afternoon, materializing from the mist that spilled down off the Wolfsktaag at autumn's close, a little old man with robes that hung precariously on his stick frame, wild unkempt hair, and sharp knowing eyes. Rumor was with him, a massive, immutable black presence that seemed to foreshadow the change that was to come into the Dark Uncle's life. Cogline related to Walker the history of his life from the days of Bremen and the Druid Council to the present, a thousand years of time. It was a straightforward telling that did not beg for acceptance but demanded it. Strangely enough, Walker complied. He sensed that this wild and improbable tale was the truth. He knew the stories of Cogline from the time of Brin Ohmsford, and this old man was exactly who and what the stories had described.

"I was sleeping the Druid sleep," Cogline explained at one point, "or I would have come sooner. I had not thought it was time yet, but the magic that resides within you, brought to life with your arrival at manhood, tells me that it is. Allanon planned it so when he gave the blood trust to Brin; there would come a time when the magic would be needed again and one among the Ohmsfords would be required to wield it. I think that perhaps you are meant to be that one, Walker. If so, you will need my help in understanding how the magic works."

Walker was filled with misgivings, but recognized that the old man might be able to show him how to bring the magic under control. He needed that control desperately. He was willing to take a chance that Cogline could give it to him.

Cogline stayed with him for the better part of three years. He revealed to Walker as a teacher to a student the lore of the Druids, the keys that would unlock the doors of understanding. He taught the ways of Bremen and Allanon, of going within to harness the magic's raw power, of working mind sets so that the power could be channeled and not loosed haphazardly. Walker had some knowledge to begin with; he had lived with the magic for many years and learned something of the self-denial and restraint that was necessary to survive its demands. Cogline expanded on that knowledge, advancing it into areas that Walker had not thought to go, instructing on methods he had not believed possible. Slowly, gradually, Walker began to find that the magic no longer governed his life; unpredictability gave way to self-control. Walker began to master himself.

Cogline instructed on the sciences of the old world as well, the chemicals and potions that he had developed and utilized over the years, the powders that burned through metal and exploded like fire, and the solutions that changed the form of both liquids and solids. Another set of doors opened for Walker; he discovered an entirely different form of power. His curiosity was such that he began to explore a combining of the two—old world and new world, a blending of magic and science that no one had ever successfully tried. He proceeded slowly, cautiously, determined that he would not become another of the victims that the power had claimed over the years, from the men of the old world who had brought about the Great Wars to the rebel Druid Brona, his Skull Bearers, and the Mord Wraiths who had sparked the Wars of the Races.

Then for some reason his thinking changed. Perhaps it was the exhilaration he felt when wielding the magic. Perhaps it was the insatiable need to know more. Whatever it was, he came to believe that complete mastery over the magic was not possible, that no matter how diligently he went about protecting himself against its adverse effects, the power would eventually claim him. His attitude toward using it reversed itself overnight. He tried to back away from it, to thrust it from him. His dilemma was enormous; he sought to distance himself from the magic yet could not do so successfully because it was an integral part of him. Cogline saw what was happening and tried to reason with him. Walker refused to listen, wondering all of a sudden why it was that Cogline had come to him in the first place, no longer believing it was simply to help. An effort was being made to manipulate him, a Druidic conspiracy that could be traced all the way back to the time of Shea Ohmsford. He would not be a part of it. He quarreled with Cogline, then fought. In the end, Cogline went away.

He came back, of course, over the years. But Walker would no longer accept instruction on use of the magic, fearing that further knowledge would result in an erosion of the control he had worked so hard to gain, that enhancement would lead to usurpation. Better simply to rely on what understanding he had, limited but manageable, and keep apart from the Races as he had planned from the first. Cogline could come and go, they could maintain their uneasy alliance, but he would not give himself over to the ways of Druids or once-Druids or anyone else. He would be his own person until the end.

And now that end had come, and he was no longer so sure of the path he had chosen to take. Death had arrived to claim him, and had he not distanced himself so from the magic he might have delayed its arrival a bit longer. Admission of the possibility required swallowing a bitter dose of pride. It was harsh to second-guess himself so, but it could not be avoided. Walker Boh had never in his life shied away from the truth; he refused to begin doing so now.

On the second week of his return from Storlock, sitting before the fire in the early evening hours, the pain of his sickness a constant reminder of things left undone, he said to Cogline, who was somewhere in the shadows behind rummaging through the books he kept at the cottage for his own use, "Come sit with me, old man."

He said it kindly, wearily, and Cogline came without argument, seating himself at Walker's elbow. Together they stared into the fire's bright glow.

"I am dying," Walker said after a time. "I have tried everything to dispel the poison, and nothing has worked. Even my magic has failed. And your science. We have to accept what that means. I intend to keep working to prevent it, but it seems that I will not survive." He shifted his arm uncomfortably against his side, a stone weight that worked relentlessly to pull him down, to make an end of him. "There are things I need to say to you before I die."

Cogline turned toward him and started to speak, but Walker shook his head. "I have embittered myself against you without reasonable cause. I have been unkind to you when you have been more than kind to me. I am sorry for that."

He looked at the old man. "I was afraid of what the magic would do to me if I continued to give myself over to it; I am still afraid. I have not changed my thinking completely. I still believe that the Druids use the Ohmsfords for their own purposes, that they tell us what they wish and direct us as they choose. It is a hard thing for me to accept, that I should be made their cat's-paw. But I was wrong to judge you one of them. Your purpose has not been theirs. It has been your own."

"As much as any purpose is mine and not one of circumstance and fate," Cogline said, and his face was sad. "We use so many words to describe what happens to us, and it all amounts to the same thing. We live out our lives as we are meant to live them—with some choice, with some chance, but mostly as a result of the persons we are." He shook his head. "Who is to say that I am any freer of the Druids and their manipulations than you, Walker? Allanon came to me in the same way as he did to you, young Par and Wren, and made me his. I cannot claim otherwise."

Walker nodded. "Nevertheless, I have been harsh with you and I wish I had not been. I wanted you to be the enemy because you were a flesh-and-blood person, not a Druid dead and gone or an unseen magic, and I could strike out at you. I wanted you to be the source of the fear I felt. It made things easier for me if I thought of you that way."

Cogline shrugged. "Do not apologize. The magic is a difficult burden for any to bear, but more so for you." He paused. "I don't believe you will ever be free of it."

"Except in death," Walker said.

"If death comes as swiftly as you think it will." The old eyes blinked. "Would Allanon establish a trust that could be thwarted so easily? Would he risk a complete undoing of his work on the chance that you might die too soon?"

Walker hesitated. "Even Druids can be wrong in their judgments."

"In this judgment?"

"Perhaps the timing was wrong. Another besides myself was meant to possess the magic beyond youth. I am the mistaken recipient. Cogline, what can possibly save me now? What is there left to try?"

The old man shook his head. "I do not know, Walker. But I sense that there is something."

They were silent then. Rumor, stretched out comfortably before the fire, lifted his head to check on Walker, and then let it drop again. The wood in the fireplace snapped loudly, and a whiff of smoke tinged the air of the room.

"So you think the Druids are not finished with me yet?" Walker said finally. "You think they will not let me give up my life?"

Cogline did not reply at once. Then he said, "I think you will determine what is to become of you, Walker. I have always thought that. What you lack is the ability to recognize what you are meant to do. Or at least an acceptance of it."

Walker felt a chill run through him. The old man's words echoed Allanon's. He knew what they meant. That he was to acknowledge that Brin Ohmsford's trust was meant for him, that he was to don the magic's armor and go forth into battle—like some invincible warrior brought forth out of time. That he was to destroy the Shadowen.

A dying man?

How?

The silence returned, and this time he did not break it.

THREE DAYS LATER Walker's condition took a turn for the worse. The medicines of the Stors and the ministerings of Cogline suddenly gave way before the onslaught of the poison. Walker woke feverish and sick, barely able to rise. He ate breakfast, walked out onto the porch to enjoy the warmth of the sun, and collapsed.

He remembered only snatches of what happened for several days after that. Cogline put him back to bed and bathed him with cold cloths while the poison's fever raged within him, an unquenchable fire. He drank liquids but could not eat. He dreamed constantly. An endless mirage of vile, frightening creatures paraded themselves before him, threatening him as he stood helpless, stripping him of his sanity. He fought back against them as best he could, but he lacked the necessary weapons. Whatever he brought to bear the monsters withstood. In the end, he simply gave himself over to them and drifted in black sleep.

From time to time he came awake and when he did so Cogline was always there. It was the old man's reassuring presence that saved him once again, a lifeline to which he clung, pulling him back from the oblivion into which he might otherwise have been swept. The gnarled hands reached out to him, sometimes gripping as if to hold him fast, sometimes stroking as if he were a child in need of comfort. The familiar voice soothed him, speaking words without meaning but filled with warmth. He could feel the other beside him, always near, waiting for him to wake.

"You are not meant to die, Walker Boh," he thought he heard more than once, though he could not be certain.

Sometimes he saw the old man's face bending close, leathery skin wrinkled and seamed, wispy hair and beard gray and disheveled, eyes bright and filled with understanding. He could smell the other, a forest tree with ancient limbs and trunk, but leaves as fresh and new as spring. When the sickness threatened to overwhelm him, Cogline was there to lift him free. It was because of the old man that he did not give up, that he fought back against the effects of the poison and willed himself to recover.

On the fourth day he awoke at midday and took some soup. The poison had been arrested temporarily, the medicines and ministerings and Walker's own will to survive taking command once more. Walker forced himself to explore the devastation of his shattered arm. The poison had progressed. His arm was turned to stone almost to the shoulder.

He wept that night in rage and frustration. Before he fell asleep he was aware of Cogline standing over him, a fragile presence against the vast, inexorable dark, telling him quietly that all would be well.

HE AWOKE AGAIN in the slow, aimless hours between midnight and dawn when time seems to have lost its way. It was instinct that woke him, a sense that something was impossibly wrong. He struggled up on one elbow, weak and disoriented, unable to pinpoint the source of his trepidation. An odd, unidentifiable sound rose out of the night's stillness, a buzz of activity from somewhere without that sleep and sickness rendered indistinct. His breathing was ragged as he pushed himself into a sitting position, shivering beneath his bedclothes against the chill of the air.

Light flared sharply, suddenly visible through the breaks in his curtained window.

He heard voices. No, he thought anxiously. Not voices. Guttural, inhuman sounds.

It took what strength he had to crawl from the bedside to the window, working his way slowly and painfully through fatigue and fever. He kept still, aware of a need for caution, sensing that he should not reveal himself. Without, the sounds had risen, and an overpowering smell of decay had descended over everything.

Groping, he found the windowsill before him and pulled himself level with its edge.

What he saw through the part in the curtains turned his stomach to ice.

COGLINE AWOKE when Rumor nudged him with his face, a rough, urgent shove that brought the old man upright instantly. He had not gone to bed until well after midnight, buried in his books of old world science, fighting to discover some means by which Walker Boh's life could be saved. Eventually he had fallen asleep in his chair before the fire, the book he was perusing still open in his lap, and it was there that Rumor found him.

"Confound it, cat," he muttered.

His first thought was that something had happened to Walker. Then he heard the sounds, faint still, but growing louder. Growls and snarls and hisses. Animal sounds. And no effort being made to disguise their coming.

He pushed himself to his feet, taking a moment to wipe the sleep from his eyes. A single lamp burned at the dining table; the fire in the hearth had gone out. Cogline drew his robes close and shuffled toward the front door, uneasy, anxious to discover what was happening. Rumor went with him, moving ahead. The fur along the ridge of his back bristled, and his muzzle was drawn back to expose his teeth. Whatever was out there, the moor cat didn't like it.

Cogline opened the door and stepped out onto the covered porch that fronted the cottage. The sky was clear and depthless. Moonlight flooded down through the trees, bathing the valley in white luminescence. The air was cool and brought Cogline fully awake. He stopped at the edge of the porch and stared. Dozens of pairs of tiny red lights blinked at him from out of the shadows of the forest, a vast scattering of delicate scarlet blossoms that shone in the black. They were everywhere, it seemed, ringing the cottage and its clearing.

Cogline squinted to better make them out. Then he realized that they were eyes.

He jumped as something moved amid the eyes. It was a man dressed in a black uniform with the silver insignia of a wolf's head sewn on his breast. Cogline saw him clearly as he stepped into the moonlight, big and rawboned with a face that was hollowed and pitted and eyes that were empty of life.

Rimmer Dall, he thought at once and experienced a terrible sinking feeling.

"Old man," the other said, and his voice was a grating whisper.

Cogline did not respond, staring fixedly at the other, forcing himself to keep from looking to his right, to where the window to Walker's bedroom stood open, to where Walker slept. Fear and anger raced through him, and a voice within screamed at him to run, to flee for his life. Quickly, it warned. Wake Walker. Help him escape!

But he knew it was already too late for that.

He had known for some time now that it would be.

"We are here for you, old man," whispered Rimmer Dall, "my friends and I." He motioned, and the creatures with him began to edge into the light, one after another, horrors all, Shadowen. Some were misshapen creatures like the woodswoman he had chased from the camp of Par and Coll Ohmsford weeks ago; some had the look of dogs or wolves, bent down on all fours, covered with hair, their faces twisted into animal muzzles, teeth and claws showing. The sounds they made suggested that they were anxious to feed.

"Failures," their leader said. "Men who could not rise above their weaknesses. They serve a better purpose now." He came forward a step. "You are the last, old man—the last who stands against me. All the Shannara children are gone, swept from the earth. You are all that remains, a poor once-Druid with no one to save him."

The lines that etched Cogline's face deepened. "Is that so?" he said. "Killed them all, did you?" Rimmer Dall stared at him. Not half a chance of it, Cogline decided instantly. The truth is he hasn't killed a one, just wants me to think he has. "And you came all this way to tell me about it, did you?" he said.

"I came to put an end to you," Rimmer Dall replied.

Well, there you have it, the old man thought. Whatever the First Seeker had managed to do about the Shannara children, it wasn't enough; so now he had come after Cogline as well, easier prey, perhaps. The old man almost smiled. To think it had all come down to this. Well, it wasn't as if he hadn't known. Allanon had warned him weeks ago, warned him in fact when he'd summoned him to retrieve the Druid History from Paranor. Oh, he hadn't told Walker, of course. He had thought about it, but hadn't done it. There just didn't seem to be any point. *Know this, Cogline, the shade had intoned, deep-voiced, prophetic. I have read the netherworld signs; your time in this world is nearly finished. Death stalks you and she is an implacable huntress. When next you see the face of Rimmer Dall, she will have found you. Remember, then. When that time comes, take back the Druid History from Walker Boh and hold it to you as if it were your life. Do not release it. Do not give it up. Remember, Cogline.*

Remember.

Cogline collected his thoughts. The Druid History rested within a niche in the stone fireplace inside the cottage, right where Walker had hidden it.

Remember.

He sighed wearily, resignedly. He'd asked questions, of course, but the shade had given no answers. Very like Allanon. It was enough that Cogline knew what was coming, it seemed. It wasn't necessary that he know the particulars.

Rumor snarled, his fur standing on end all over. He was crouched protectively before the old man, and Cogline knew there was no way to save the big cat. Rumor would never leave him. He shook his head. Well. An odd sense of calm settled over him. His thoughts were quite clear. The Shadowen had come for him; they knew nothing at all about Walker Boh being there. That was the way he intended to keep it.

His brow furrowed. Would the Druid History, if he could reach it, aid him in this?

His eyes found Rimmer Dall's. This time he did smile. "I don't think there's enough of you to do the job," he said.

His arm swept up and silver dust flew at the First Seeker, bursting into flame as it struck him. Rimmer Dall screamed in fury and staggered away, and the creatures with him attacked. They came at Cogline from everywhere, but Rumor met them with a lunge, stopped them short of the porch and tore the foremost to pieces. Cogline flung handfuls of the silver dust at his would-be destroyers and whole lines of them were set ablaze. The Shadowen screeched and howled, blundering into one another as they sought first to attack, then to escape. Bodies lurched wildly through the moonlight, filling the clearing with burning limbs. They began attacking each other. They died by the dozens. *Easy prey, do they think!* Cogline experienced a wild, perverse elation as he flung back his robes and sent the night exploding into white brilliance.

For an impossible moment, he thought he might actually survive.

But then Rimmer Dall reappeared, too powerful to be overcome by Cogline's small magic, and lashed out with fire of his own at the creatures he commanded, at his dogs and wolves and half-humans, at his near-mindless brutes. The Shadowen-kind, terrified of him, attacked in a renewed frenzy of hate and anger. This time they would not be driven off. Rumor savaged the first wave, quick and huge amid their smaller forms, and then they were all over him, a maelstrom of teeth and claws. Cogline could do nothing to help the gallant cat; even with the silver dust exploding all through them, the Shadowen came on. Rumor slowly began to give ground.

Despairing, Cogline used the last of his powder, dashing handfuls to the earth, igniting a wall of flame that for just an instant brought a halt to the beasts' advance. Swiftly he darted inside and snatched the Druid History from its hiding place.

Now we'll see.

He barely made the front door again before the Shadowen-kind were through the wall of fire and on him. He heard Rimmer Dall screaming at them. He felt Rumor press back against him protectively. There was nowhere to run and no point in trying, so he simply stood his ground, clutching the book to his chest, a scarecrow in tattered robes before a whirlwind. His attackers came on. When they had their hands on him, as his body was about to be ripped apart, he felt the rune markings on the book flare to life. Brilliant white fire burst forth, and everything within fifty feet was consumed.

It remains now for you, Walker, was Cogline's last thought.

He disappeared in the flames.

THE FINAL EXPLOSION threw Walker clear of the curtained window an instant before it was engulfed in flame. Even so, his face and hair were singed and his clothes were left steaming. He lay in a heap as the fire licked its way across the ceiling of his room. He ignored it, no longer caring what happened. He had been helpless to aid Cogline and Rumor, too weak to summon the magic, too weak even to rise and stand with them against the Shadowen, too weak to do anything but hang there on that window ledge and watch.

Useless! He screamed the word silently in his mind, rage and grief washing through him.

He lurched to his knees in desperation and peered out through the flames. Cogline and Rumor were gone. Rimmer Dall and what remained of the Shadowen-kind were melting back into the forest. He stared after them momentarily, and then his strength left him and he collapsed again.

Useless!

The fire's heat intensified about him. Timbers crashed down, fiery brands splintering off and searing his skin. His body jerked in pain, his stone arm an anchor that dragged against the wooden floor. His fate was assured, he realized. Another minute or two and he would be consumed. No one would come for him. No one even knew he was here. The old man and the giant moor cat had concealed his presence from the Shadowen; they had given up their lives to do so. . . .

He shuddered as an image of Rimmer Dall's face appeared in his mind, the dead eyes looking at him appraisingly.

He decided he did not want to die.

Almost without realizing what he was doing, he began to crawl.

CHAPTER

10

UICKENING FOUND HIM two days later. Pe Ell and Morgan Leah were with her, drawn on by the mystery of who and what she was, by her promise that they were needed to recover the talisman that she insisted she had been sent to find, by curiosity, by passion, and by a dozen other things that neither could begin to define. They had made the journey north out of Culhaven in three days' time, traveling openly and on foot along the Rabb where it bordered on the Anar, safely west of the Wolfsktaag and the dark things that lived there. Secrecy seemed the least of Quickening's concerns. She had chosen to depart in daylight rather than under cover of darkness, having told her band of would-be followers that they must remain behind and continue her work to help restore the health of the land, and she had kept to the open plains the entire way up the forestline. While Morgan Leah had been relieved that he would not have to venture into the Wolfsktaag again, he had been certain that Federation patrols along the Rabb would attempt to detain them. Curiously, that did not happen. They were seen more than once and approached, but each time the patrols got close they suddenly veered away. It was almost as if they had decided they were mistaken—as if they had decided that they hadn't seen anything after all.

It was nearing dusk when the three finally arrived at Hearthstone, the men footsore, sweaty, and vaguely disgruntled by the quick pace the girl had set and the fact that she could maintain it seemingly without effort. They had bypassed Storlock, crossed through the Pass of Jade and come down the Chard Rush into Darklin Reach. The sun was behind them, dropping quickly toward the rim of the mountains, and the skies ahead were sharply etched by the light. A column of thick black smoke rose before them like a snake. They could see the smoke long before they were able to determine its source. They watched it lift into the darkening eastern skies and dissipate, and Morgan Leah began to worry. Quickening said nothing, but it seemed to the Highlander that her face grew more intense. By the time they reached the rim of the valley and there was no longer any doubt, the girl's face looked stricken.

They followed the smoke to the ruins of the cottage. Charred rubble was all that remained; the fire that had consumed it was so hot that it was still burning in spots, wood and ash glowing red, sending the black smoke curling skyward. The clearing about it was seared and lifeless, and huge knots of earth had been exploded away. It looked as if two great armies had fought a war in the space of a hundred yards. There was nothing left that was recognizable. Bits and pieces were scattered about of what once might have been something human, but it was impossible to tell. Even Pe Ell, who was usually so careful not to reveal anything of what he was thinking, stared.

"The Shadowen were here," Quickening said, and that brought both men about to search the shadows of the forest behind them, until she added, "But they are gone now and will not return."

At the girl's direction, they searched the clearing for Walker Boh. Morgan's heart sank. He had been hoping that Walker was not there, that the Shadowen attack had been for some other reason. Nothing could have survived this, he thought. He watched Pe Ell kick halfheartedly at piles of rubble, clearly of the same mind. Morgan did not like the man. He didn't trust him; he didn't understand him. Despite the fact that Pe Ell had saved him from the Federation prisons, Morgan couldn't bring himself to feel any friendship toward the other. Pe Ell had rescued him at Quickening's request; he wouldn't have lifted a finger if the girl hadn't asked. He had already told Morgan as much; he had made a point of telling him. Who he was remained a mystery, but the Highlander didn't think anything good would come of his being there. Even now, picking his way across the blackened clearing, he had the look of a cat in search of something to play with.

Quickening found Walker Boh moments later, calling out urgently to the other two when she did. How she determined where he was hiding was anyone's guess. He was unconscious and buried several feet beneath the earth. Pe Ell and Morgan dug him free, discovering when they did that he had apparently been trapped in an underground passageway that led from the cottage to the edge of the forest. Although the passageway had collapsed, probably during the Shadowen attack, sufficient air had been able to reach him to allow him to survive. They pulled him into the failing light, and Morgan saw the remains of his arm, the lower part gone entirely, a stone stub protruding from the shoulder. Walker's breathing was faint and shallow, his skin drawn and white. At first, the Highlander didn't think he was even alive.

They laid him carefully on the ground, brushed the dirt from his face, and Quickening knelt next to him. Her two hands reached out to take his one. She held it a moment, and his eyes flickered open. Morgan drew back. He had never seen Walker's eyes like this; they were terrifying to look into, filled with dark madness.

"Don't let me die," the Dark Uncle whispered harshly.

The girl touched his face and he was instantly asleep. Morgan took a deep breath and let it out again slowly. Walker Boh wasn't asking for help out of fear; he was asking out of rage.

They made camp beside the ruins of the cottage that night, backed into the shelter of the trees as the light gave way to darkness. Quickening had a fire built close to where Walker Boh lay sleeping and she took up a position at his side and did not move. Sometimes she held his hand; sometimes she stroked him. Morgan and Pe Ell were forgotten. She did not seem to have need of them or wish that they intrude, so the Highlander built a second fire some distance away and prepared dinner from the supplies they carried—bread, some dried meat, cheese, and fruit. He offered some to the girl, but she shook her head and he moved away. He ate alone. Pe Ell took his food off into the dark.

After a time Quickening lay down next to Walker Boh and went to sleep, her body pressed close against his. Morgan watched stone-faced, a surge of jealousy sweeping through him at the thought that the Dark Uncle should be so close to her. He studied her face in the firelight, the curve of her body, the softness of her. She was so beautiful. He could not explain the effect she had on him; he did not think he could refuse her anything. It wasn't that he had a reasonable hope that she felt for him as he did for her—or even that she felt anything for him. It was the need she roused in him. He should not have come with her once he had escaped the prisons and made certain that Granny Elise and Auntie Jilt were safe. He should have gone after the Valemen, after Par and Coll Ohmsford. He had promised himself more than once while lying in the darkness and filth of that Federation cell that if he ever got free, he would. Yet here he was, chasing off into the deep Anar after this girl, searching out a talisman she said existed but hadn't once described, caught up with the enigmatic Pe Ell and now Walker Boh. It baffled him, but he didn't question it. He was there because he wanted to be there. He was there because the moment he had met Quickening he had fallen hopelessly in love with her.

He watched her until it hurt, then forced himself to look away. He was surprised when he saw Pe Ell standing back in the shadows at the edge of the trees watching too.

He was surprised again moments later when the other man came over to sit next to him by the fire. Pe Ell made it seem the most natural thing in the world, as if there had been no distance kept between them before, as if they were companions and not strangers. Hatchet-faced, as lean as a wire's shadow, he was not much more than a gathering of lines and angles that threatened to disappear in the dark. He sat cross-legged, his thin frame relaxed, hunched down, his mouth breaking into a faint smile as he saw Morgan frown. "You don't trust me," he said. "You shouldn't."

Morgan said, "Why not?"

"Because you don't know me and you never trust anyone you don't know. You don't trust most of those you do either.

That's just the way it is. Tell me, Highlander. Why do you think I'm here?"

"I don't know."

"I don't know either. I would be willing to bet that it is the same with you. We're here, you and I, because the girl tells us she needs us, but we really don't know what she means. It's just that we can't bring ourselves to tell her no." Pe Ell seemed to be explaining things as much to himself as to Morgan. He glanced Quickening's way briefly, nodding. "She's beautiful, isn't she? How can you say no to someone who looks like that? But it's more, because she has something inside as well, something special even in this world. She has magic, the strongest kind of magic. She brings dead things back to life—like the Gardens, like that one over there."

He looked back at Morgan. "We all want to touch that magic, to feel it through her. That's what I think. Maybe we can, if we're lucky. But if the Shadowen are involved in this, if there are things as bad as that to be dealt with, why then we're going to have to look out for one another. So you don't have to trust me or me you—maybe we shouldn't—but we have to watch each other's backs. Do you agree?"

Morgan wasn't sure whether he did or not, but he nodded anyway. What he thought was that Pe Ell didn't seem the kind who relied on anyone to watch his back. Or who watched anyone else's back either, for that matter.

"Do you know what I am?" Pe Ell asked softly, looking down into the fire. "I am a craftsman. I get myself in and out of places without anyone knowing. I move things aside that don't want to be moved. I make people disappear." He looked up. "I have a little magic of my own. You do, too, don't you?"

Morgan shook his head, cautious. "There's the man with the magic," he offered, indicating Walker Boh.

Pe Ell smiled doubtfully. "Doesn't seem to have done him much good against the Shadowen."

"It might have kept him alive."

"Barely, it appears. And what use is he to us with that arm?" Pe Ell folded his hands carefully. "Tell me. What can he do with his magic?"

Morgan didn't like the question. "He can do a lot of what you do. Ask him yourself when he's better."

"If he gets better." Pe Ell stood up smoothly, an effortless motion that caught Morgan by surprise. Quick, the Highlander thought. Much quicker than me. The other was looking at him. "I sense the magic in you, Highlander. I want you to tell me about it sometime. Later, when we've traveled together a bit longer, when we know each other a little better. When you trust me."

He moved away into the shadows at the fire's edge, spread his blanket on the ground, and rolled into it. He was asleep almost at once.

Morgan sat staring at him for a moment, thinking it would be a long time before he trusted that one. Pe Ell smiled easily enough, but it seemed that only his mouth wanted to participate in the act. Morgan thought about what the man had said about himself, trying to make sense of it. Get in and out of places without being seen? Move things that don't want to be moved? Make people disappear? What sort of double-talk was that?

The fire burned low and everyone around him slept. Morgan thought about the past for a moment, about his friends who were dead or disappeared, about the inexorable flow of events that was dragging him along in its wake. Mostly he thought about the girl who said she was the daughter of the King of the Silver River. Quickening. He wondered about her.

What was she going to ask of him?

What was he going to be able to give?

WALKER BOH CAME AWAKE at sunrise, rising up from the black pit of his unconsciousness. His eyes blinked open to find the girl peering down at him. Her hands were on his face, her fingers cool and soft against his skin, and it seemed that she drew him up with no more effort than it would require to lift a feather.

"Walker Boh," she spoke his name gently.

She seemed strangely familiar to him although he was certain they had never met. He tried to speak and found he couldn't. Something forbade it, a sense of wonder at the exquisite beauty of her, at the feelings she invoked within him. He found her like the earth, filled with strange magic that was simple and complex at once, a vessel of elements, of soil, air, and water, a part of everything that gave life. He saw her differently than Morgan Leah and Pe Ell, though he couldn't know that yet. He was not drawn to her as a lover or a protector; he had no wish to possess her. Rather, there was an affinity between them that transcended passion and need. There were bonds of immediate understanding that united them as emotions never could. Walker recognized the existence of those bonds even without being able to define them. This girl was something of what he had struggled all his life to be. This girl was a reflection of his dreams.

"Look at me," she said.

His eyes locked on her. She took her fingers from his face and moved them to the shattered remnants of his arm, to the stone stump that hung inert and lifeless from his shoulder. Her fingers reached within his clothing, stroking his skin, working their way to where the skin hardened into stone. He flinched at her touch, not wanting her to feel the sickness in him, or to discover the corruption of his flesh. But her fingers persisted; her eyes did not look away.

Then he gasped as everything disappeared in a white hot flash of pain. For an instant he saw the Hall of Kings again, the crypts of the dead, the stone slab with its rune markings, the black hole beneath, and the flash of movement as the Asphinx struck. After that he was floating, and there were only her eyes, black and depthless, folding him in a wave of sweet relief. The pain disappeared, drawing out of him in a red mist that dissipated into the air. He felt a weight lift away from him and he was at peace.

He might have slept for a time then; he was not certain. When he opened his eyes again, the girl was there beside him, looking down at him, and the dawn's light was faint and distant through the tips of the trees. He swallowed against the dryness in his mouth and throat, and she gave him water to drink from a skin. He was aware of Morgan Leah staring openmouthed at him from one side, his lean brown face a mask of disbelief. There was another man next to him, one he didn't know, hard-faced and cunning. They had both been there when the girl found him, he remembered. What were they seeing now that so astonished them?

Then he realized that something was different. His arm felt lighter, freer. There was no pain. He used what little strength he had to raise his head and look down at himself. His clothes had been pulled away from his shoulder, revealing pink, healed flesh where the stone wreckage of his sickness had been removed.

His arm was gone.

So, too, was the poison of the Asphinx.

What did he feel? His emotions jumbled together within him. He stared at the girl and tried unsuccessfully to speak.

She looked down at him, serene and perfect. "I am Quickening," she said. "I am the daughter of the King of the Silver River. Look into my eyes and discover me."

He did as he was told, and she touched him. Instantly he saw what Morgan Leah had seen before him, what Pe Ell had witnessed—the coming of Quickening into Culhaven and the resurrection of the Meade Gardens out of ash and dust. He felt the wonder of the miracle and he knew instinctively that she was who she claimed. She possessed magic that defied belief, magic that could salvage the most pitiful of life's wreckage. When the images were gone, he was struck again by the unexplainable sense of kinship he felt for her.

"You are well again, Walker Boh," she told him. "The sickness will trouble you no more. Sleep now, for I have great need of you."

She touched him once and he drifted away.

HE AWOKE AGAIN at midday, ravenous with hunger, dry with thirst. Quickening was there to give him food and water and to help him sit up. He felt stronger now, more the man he had been before his encounter with the Asphinx, able to think clearly again for the first time in weeks. His relief at being free of the poison of the Asphinx, at simply being alive for that matter, warred with his rage at what Rimmer Dall and the Shadowen had done to Cogline and Rumor. Just an old man and a bothersome cat, he had called them. He looked out across the clearing at the devastation. The girl did not ask him what had happened; she merely touched him and knew. All the images of that night's tragic events returned in a flood of memories that left him shaking and close to tears. She touched him again, to comfort and reassure, but he did not cry. He would not let himself. He kept his grief inside, walled away behind his determination to find and destroy those responsible.

Quickening said to him, away from Morgan Leah and the one she named Pe Ell, "You cannot give way to what you feel, Walker Boh. If you pursue the Shadowen now, they will destroy you. You lack the wisdom and the strength to overcome them. You will find both only through me."

Then, before he could respond, she called the other two over, seated them before her, and said, "I will tell you now of the need I have of you." She looked at them in turn and then seemed to look beyond. "A long time ago, in an age before Mankind, before the faerie wars, before everything you know, there were many like my father. They were the first of the faerie creatures, given life by the Word, given dominion over the land. Theirs was a trust to preserve and protect, and while they could, they did. But the world changed with the fading of the faerie creatures and the rise of Man. The evolution of the world took away almost everything that had existed in the beginning including those like my father. One by one, they died away, lost in the passing of the years and the changes of the world. The Great Wars destroyed many of them. The Wars of the Races destroyed more. Finally, there was only my father, a legend by now, the faerie Lord they called the King of the Silver River."

Her face lifted. "Except that my father was not alone as he believed. There was another. Even my father did not know of him at first, believing that all his kindred had died out long ago, that he alone had survived. My father was wrong. Another like himself still lived, changed so markedly as to now be all but unrecognizable. All of the first faeries drew their magic from the elements of the land. My father's strength derived from the rivers and lakes, from the waters that fed the earth. He built his Gardens to nourish them, to give them life, and draw life back again. His brother, the one he did not know had survived along with him, took his magic from the earth's stone. Where my father found strength in fluidity and change, his brother found strength in constancy and immutability."

She paused. "His name is Uhl Belk. He is the Stone King. He had no name in the old days; none of my father's kindred did. There was no need for names. My father was given his name by the people of the land; he did not ask for it. Uhl Belk took his name out of fear. He took it because he felt that only in having a name could he be certain of surviving. A name implied permanency, he believed. Permanency became everything for him. All around him, the world was changing, the old dying out, giving way to the new. He could not accept that he must change, for like the stone from which he drew his strength, he was unyielding. To survive, he embedded himself deeper in the ways that had sustained him for so long, burrowing into the earth on which he relied. He hid while the Great Wars destroyed almost everything. He hid again when the wars of magic, the Wars of the Races, threatened to do the same. He took his name and wrapped himself in stone. Like my father, his world was reduced to almost nothing, to a tiny bit of existence that was all his magic could protect. He clung to it desperately while the wars of Mankind raged through the centuries and he waited for a measure of sanity to return.

"But, unlike my father, Uhl Belk put aside the trust that the Word had given him. He lost sight of his purpose in his struggle to survive; he became convinced that simply to exist at whatever cost was all that mattered. His pledge to preserve and protect the land was forgotten; his promise to care for the land's life lost meaning. He hoarded and built upon his magic with one thought in mind—that when he grew strong enough he would make certain that his existence would never be threatened by anything or anyone again."

Quickening's eyes glanced down and lifted again, filled with wonder. "Uhl Belk is master of Eldwist, a finger of land far north and east above the Charnal Mountains where the Eastland ends at the Tiderace. After centuries of hiding, he has come forth to claim the world of Men for his own. He does this through his magic, which grows in strength as he applies it. He applies it indiscriminately to the land—the soil, the waters, the trees, the creatures that take nourishment from them. He turns everything to stone and takes back such magic as will make him stronger still. The whole of Eldwist is stone and the land about begins to turn as well. The Tiderace holds him captive for now because it is huge, and even Uhl Belk's magic is not yet sufficient to overcome an ocean. But Eldwist connects to the Eastland at its tip, and nothing prevents the magic's poison from spreading south. Except my father."

"And the Shadowen," Morgan Leah added.

"No, Morgan," she said, and it did not escape any of them that she called him by his first name alone. "The Shadowen are not Uhl Belk's enemy. My father alone seeks to preserve the Four Lands. The Shadowen, like the Stone King, would see the Lands made over in a way that would leave them unrecognizable—barren and stripped of life. The Shadowen and Uhl Belk leave each other alone because neither has anything to fear from the other. One day that may change, but by then it will no longer matter to any of us."

She looked at Walker. "Think of your arm, Walker Boh. The poison that claimed it is Uhl Belk's. The Asphinx belonged to him. Whatever living thing the Stone King or his creatures touch becomes as your arm did—hard and lifeless. That is the source of Uhl Belk's power, that constancy, that changelessness."

"Why did he choose to poison me?" Walker asked.

Her silver hair caught a ray of sunlight and shimmered in momentary brilliance. She shook the light away. "He stole a Druid talisman from the Hall of Kings, and he wanted to be certain that whoever discovered the theft would die before he could do anything about it. You were simply unlucky enough to be that one. The Druids, when they lived, were strong enough to challenge Uhl Belk. He waited until they were all gone to come forth again. His only enemy now is my father."

Her dark eyes shifted to Pe Ell. "Uhl Belk seeks to consume the land and to do so he must destroy my father. My father sends me forth to prevent that. I cannot do so without your help. I need you to come north with me into Eldwist. Once there, we must find and recover from the Stone King the talisman he stole from the Hall of Kings, from the Druids. That talisman is called the Black Elfstone. As long as he possesses it, Uhl Belk is invincible. We must take it away from him."

Pe Ell's long, narrow face remained expressionless. "How are we supposed to do that?" he asked.

"You will find a way," the girl said, looking at each of them in turn. "My father said you would, that you possess the means. But it will take all three of you to succeed. Each of you has the magic that is required; we have not spoken of it, but it is so. All three magics are needed. All three of you must go."

"All three." Pe Ell glanced doubtfully at Walker and Morgan. "What is it that this Black Elfstone does? What sort of magic does it possess?"

Walker leaned forward to hear her answer, and Quickening's black eyes fixed on him. "It steals away the power of other magics. It swallows them up and makes them its own."

There was stunned silence. Walker had never heard of such magic. Even in the old Druid legends, there was no mention of it. He thought about the words contained in the Druid History that Cogline had brought to him, the words that described how Paranor could be restored:

Once removed, Paranor shall remain lost to the world of men for the whole of time, sealed away and invincible within its casting. One magic alone has the power to return it—that singular Elfstone which is colored Black and was conceived by the faerie people of the old world in the manner and form of all Elfstones, combining nevertheless in one stone alone the necessary properties of heart, mind, and body. Whosoever shall have cause and right shall wield it to its proper end.

He had memorized the words before hiding the book in a crevice in the fireplace of the cottage before departing for the Hall of Kings. The words explained something of how the Black Elfstone could be used to bring back Paranor. If Druid magic had sealed it away, the Black Elfstone would negate the magic and restore the Keep. Walker frowned. That seemed awfully easy. Worse, the power of such a magic suggested that once employed, nothing could defeat it. Why would the Druids take the chance that something so powerful would fall into the hands of an enemy like Uhl Belk?

On the other hand, they had done what they could to protect it, he supposed. Almost no one could have retrieved it from the Hall of Kings. Or even known it was there. How had the Stone King discovered it, he wondered?

"If the Black Elfstone can take away other magics," Pe Ell said suddenly, putting an end to Walker's musings, "how can anything overcome it? Our own magic, any magic, will be useless against it."

"Especially mine, since I don't have any," Morgan spoke up suddenly, causing all of them to glance sharply at him. "At least, not enough to bother about."

"Is there something you can do to help us against the Stone King?" Walker asked. "Can you make use of your own magic in some way?"

"No," the girl said, and they went silent, staring at her. "My magic is useless until you have regained possession of the Black Elfstone from Uhl Belk. Nor must he be allowed to discover who I am. If he should, he would make a quick end of me. I will go with you and advise you when I can. I will help if possible. But I cannot use my magic—not the smallest amount, not for even the shortest time."

"But you think that we can?" Pe Ell demanded incredulously.

"The Stone King will find your magic of no consequence; he will not feel threatened by you."

Pe Ell's face assumed such a black look that Walker was momentarily distracted from wondering what it was that Quickening was hiding from them. He was certain now that she was hiding something. Not lying to them, he didn't think that. But there was definitely something she wasn't telling them. The problem was, he hadn't the faintest idea what.

She said then, "There is another reason that you should help me." Her eyes held them. "All things are possible if you come with me. Walker Boh. I have driven the poison from your body and made you well. I have healed your arm, but I cannot make you whole again. Come with me in search of the Black Elfstone and you will find a way to do so. Morgan Leah. You would restore the magic of your shattered Sword. Come with me. Pe Ell. You would seek out magic greater than that of the Shadowen. Come with me. My father tells me that together you possess the keys that will unlock all of these secrets. My father knows what is possible. He would not lie."

Her face lifted toward them. "The Four Lands and her people are threatened by the Shadowen; but no more so than by Uhl Belk. The means of ending one threat shall be found through ending the other. The Black Elfstone is the talisman that shall enable the ending of both. I know you cannot yet understand that; I know I cannot explain it to you. I do not know how you shall fare in this quest. But I shall go with you, live or die with you, succeed or fail with you. We shall be bound forever by what happens."

As we are somehow bound already, Walker thought to himself and wondered anew why the feeling persisted.

Silence crystallized about them. No one wanted to break its shell. There were questions yet unasked and answers yet ungiven; there were doubts and misgivings and fears to be conquered. A future that had been settled for them all not a week gone now stretched ahead, a dark and uncertain pathway that would take them where it chose. Uhl Belk, the Stone King, waited at the end of that path, and they were going to seek him out. It was already decided. Without anyone having said so, it was resolved. Such was the strength of Quickening's magic, the magic she exercised over the lives of others, a magic that not only restored life to what was believed dead and gone but also liberated hopes and dreams in the living.

It was like that now.

Morgan Leah was thinking what it would be like to have the Sword of Leah restored to him. He was remembering how it felt when its magic was his to command. Pe Ell was thinking what it would be like to have possession of a weapon that no one could stand against. He was remembering how it felt when he used the Stiehl. He was wondering if this would be the same.

But Walker Boh was thinking not so much of himself as of the Black Elfstone. It remained the key to all the locked doors. Could Paranor be restored; could the Druids be brought back again? Allanon's charge to him, part of what must be done if the Shadowen were to be destroyed. And now, for the first time since the dreams had come to him, he wanted them destroyed. More, he wanted to be the one to do it.

He looked into Quickening's black eyes, and it seemed as if she could read his thoughts. A Druid trick. A faerie gift.

And suddenly, shockingly, he remembered where he had seen her before.

HE WENT TO HER later that night to tell her. It took him a long time to decide to do so. It would have been easier to say nothing because in speaking he risked jeopardizing both his newfound friendship with her and his participation in the journey to Eldwist. But keeping silent would have been the same as lying, and he could not bring himself to do that. So he waited until Morgan and Pe Ell were slumbering, until the night was cloaked in blackness and time's passage slowed to a crawl, and he rose soundlessly from beneath his blankets, still aching and stiff from his ordeal, and crossed the fire-lit clearing to where she waited.

As he passed the ruins of the cottage, he glanced over. Earlier, while it was still light, he had searched the smoldering ashes for the missing Druid History. He had found nothing.

Quickening was not asleep; he knew she wouldn't be. She was sitting in the shadow of a massive fir where the trees that ringed the clearing were farthest from the sleepers. He was still weak and could not go far, but he did not wish to speak to her where the other two might hear. She seemed to sense this; she rose as he approached and went with him wordlessly into the forest. When they were a safe distance away, she slowed and faced him.

"What would you tell me, Walker Boh?" she asked and pulled him down with her onto the cool matting of the woodland floor.

It took him a moment to speak. He felt that odd kinship to her without yet understanding why, and it almost changed his mind, making him frightened of the words he had come to say and of the reaction they would cause.

"Quickening," he said finally, and the sound of her name coming from his lips stopped him anew. He tightened his resolve. "I was given a book of the Druid Histories by Cogline before he died. The book was destroyed in the fire. There was a passage in the book that said that the Black Elfstone is a Druid magic and possesses the power to bring back disappeared Paranor. That is the charge I was given by the shade of Allanon when I went to speak with him at the Hadeshorn some weeks ago—to restore Paranor and the Druids to the Four Lands. It was a charge that Cogline urged me to accept. He brought the Druid History to me to convince me it could be done."

"I know this," she said softly.

Her black eyes threatened to swallow him up, and he forced himself to look away. "I doubted him," he continued, the words coming harder now. "I questioned his purpose in telling me, accused him of serving the interests of the Druids. I wanted nothing to do with any of them. But my curiosity about the Black Elfstone persuaded me to pursue the matter anyway, even after he was gone. I decided to try to find out where the Elfstone was hidden. I went to see the Grimpond."

He looked up at her again and kept his gaze steady. "I was shown three visions. All three were of me. In the first I stood before the others in the company that had journeyed to the Hadeshorn to meet with the shade of Allanon and declared that I would sooner cut off my hand than help bring back the Druids. The vision mocked what I had said and showed me with my hand already gone. And now it is gone indeed. My hand and my arm both."

His voice was shaking. "The third vision is of no importance here. But in the second vision I stood at the crest of a ridgeline that looked out over the world. A girl was with me. She lost her balance and reached for me. When she did, I thrust her away, and she fell. That girl, Quickening, was you."

He waited for her response, the silence filling the space between them until it seemed to Walker as if nothing separated them. Quickening did not speak. She kept her eyes fixed on him, her features swept clean of expression.

"Surely you know of the Grimpond!" he exclaimed to her finally in exasperation.

Then he saw her blink and realized that she had been thinking of something else entirely. "It is an exiled spirit," she said.

"One that riddles and lies, but speaks a measure of truth as well, hiding it in devious ways. It did so with the first vision. My arm is gone. I would not have the same thing happen with your life!"

She smiled faintly then, just a trace of movement at the corners of her mouth. "You will not hurt me, Walker Boh. Are you worried that you must?"

"The vision," he repeated.

"The vision is that and nothing more," she interrupted gently. "Visions are as much illusion as truth. Visions tell us of possibilities and do not speak in absolutes. We are not bound by them; they do not govern what is to be. Especially those of a creature like the Grimpond. It teases with falsehoods; it deceives. Do you fear it, Walker Boh? No, not you. Nor I. My father tells me what is to be and that is enough. You will bring no harm to me."

Walker's face felt pinched and tight. "He might be mistaken in what he says; he might not see everything that is to be."

Quickening shook her head, reached out her slim hand, and touched his own. "You will be my protector on this journey, Walker Boh—all three of you, for as long as is necessary. Do not worry. I will be safe with you."

Walker shook his head. "I could remain behind . . ."

Her hand lifted quickly to his mouth and touched it as if to wipe away some new poison. "No." The word was sheathed in iron. "I will be safe if you are with me; I will be in danger only if you are not. You must come."

He stared at her doubtfully. "Can you tell me anything of what I am expected to do?"

She shook her head.

"Or of the means by which I am to claim the Black Elfstone from Uhl Belk?"

Again, no, firmly.

"Or even how I am to protect you when I have but one arm and . . . ?"

"No."

He let his body sag; he was suddenly very weary. The darkness was a cloak of doubt and indecision that hung about him in suffocating folds. "I am half a man," he whispered. "I have lost faith in who and what I am, in the promises I made to myself, in the tasks I set myself. I have been dragged about by Druid dreams and charges in which I do not believe. I have been stripped of my two closest friends, my home, and my sense of worth. I was the strongest of those who went to meet with Allanon, the one the others relied upon; now I am the weakest, barely able to stand on my own two feet. I cannot be as quick as you to dismiss the Grimpond's visions. I have been wrongly confident too many times. Now I must question everything."

"Walker Boh," she said.

He stared at her wonderingly as she reached out for him and brought him to his feet. "You will be strong again—but only if you believe."

She was so close he could feel the heat of her reaching out to him through the cool night air. "You are like me," she said quietly. "You have sensed as much already, though you fail to understand why it is so. It is because we are, before all other things, creatures of the magic we wield. The magic defines us, shapes us, and makes us who we are. For both of us, it is a birthright we cannot escape. You would protect me by telling me of this vision, by taking away the danger that your presence poses if the vision should be true. But, Walker Boh, we are bound in such a way that despite any vision's telling we cannot separate ourselves and survive. Do you not feel it? We must pick up the thread of this trail that leads to Eldwist and Uhl Belk and the Black Elfstone and follow it to its end. Visions of what might be cannot be allowed to deter us. Fears of our future cannot be permitted to intrude."

She paused. "Magic, Walker Boh. Magic governs my life's purpose, the magic given to me by my father. Can you say that it is any different for you?"

It wasn't a question she put to him; it was a statement of fact, of indisputable truth. He took a deep breath. "No," he acknowledged. "I cannot."

"We can neither deny it nor run from it, can we?"

"No."

"We have this in common—this, and separate charges to find the Black Elfstone and preserve the Four Lands, yours from the shade of Allanon, mine from my father. Beyond that, nothing matters. All paths lead to the Druid talisman." She lifted her face into the faint trailers of light that seeped downward through the trees from the starlit skies. "We must go in search of it together, Walker Boh."

She was so positive in her statement, so certain of what she said. Walker met her gaze, still filled with the doubts and fears she had urged him to cast aside, but comforted now in her sense of purpose and her strength of will. Once he had possessed both in equal measure. It made him ashamed and angry that he no longer did. He remembered Par Ohmsford's determination to do what was right, to find a use for his gift of magic. He thought of his own unspoken promise to the ghosts of Cogline and Rumor. He was still wary of the Grimpond's vision, but Quickening was right. He could not let it dissuade him from his quest.

He looked at her and nodded. A measure of determination returned. "We will not speak of the Grimpond's vision again," he promised.

"Not until there is need," she replied.

She took him by the arm and led him back through the darkened forest to sleep.

11

PAR OHMSFORD'S STRENGTH returned to him slowly. Two weeks passed while he lay bedded in the Mole's underground lair, a gaunt and motionless skeleton draped in old linen, dappled by a mingling of shadows and candlelight, and surrounded by the strange, changeless faces of the Mole's adopted children. Time had no meaning at first, for he was lost to anything remotely connected with the real world. Then the madness faded, and he began to come back to himself. The days and nights took on definition. Damson Rhee and the Mole became recognizable. The blur of darkness and light sharpened to reveal the shapes and forms of the subterranean rooms in which he rested. The stuffed castoffs grew familiar once more, button noses and eyes, thread-sewn mouths, worn cloth limbs and bodies. He was able to give them names. Words assumed meaning out of idle talk. There was nourishment and there was sleep.

Mostly, though, there were the memories. They tracked him through sleep and waking alike, wraiths that hovered at the edge of his thoughts, anxious to sting and bite. There were memories of the Pit, the Shadowen, Rimmer Dall, and the Sword of Shannara, but mostly of Coll.

He could not forgive himself. Coll was dead because of him—not simply because he had struck the fatal blow, the killing stroke of his wishsong's magic, not because he had failed to adequately protect his brother from the packs of Shadowen that roamed the Pit while he was engaged with Rimmer Dall, not for any of this, but because he had from the first, from the moment they had fled Varfleet and the Seekers, thought only of himself. His need to know the truth about the wishsong, the Sword of Shannara, the charges of Allanon, the purpose of the magic—this was what had mattered. He had sacrificed everything to discover that truth, and in the end that sacrifice had included his brother.

Damson Rhee strove mightily to persuade him otherwise, seeing his torment and instinctively recognizing its cause.

"He wanted to be there with you, Par," she would tell him, over and over, her face bent close, her red hair tumbling down about her slender shoulders, her voice soft and gentle. "It was his choice. He loved you enough that it could not have been otherwise. You did your best to keep him from coming, to keep him safe. But there was that in Coll that would not be compromised. A sense of what's right, what's necessary. He was determined to protect you from the dangers you both knew waited. He gave his life to keep you safe, don't you see? Don't be so quick to steal away what that sacrifice meant by insisting it was your fault. There were choices and he made them. He was strong-willed, and you could not have changed his mind even had you tried harder than you did. He understood, Par. He recognized the purpose and need in what you do. You believed that was true before; you must believe it now. Coll did. Don't let his death have been for nothing."

But Coll's death might have been for exactly that, he feared, and the fear chased after him in his darkest thoughts. Exactly what had his brother's death accomplished? What did he have to show for it? The Sword of Shannara? Yes, he had gained possession of the legendary blade of his Elven-blooded ancestors, the talisman the shade of Allanon had sent him to find. And what use was it? It had failed utterly as a weapon against Rimmer Dall, even after the First Seeker had revealed himself as a Shadowen. If the Sword was a necessary magic as Allanon had claimed, why hadn't it destroyed his greatest enemy? Worse, if Dall were to be believed, the Sword of Shannara could have been his simply for the asking. There was no need for their agonizing, destructive descent into the Pit—no need, then, for the death of Coll.

And no purpose to it either if Rimmer Dall was right about one thing more—that Par Ohmsford, like himself, was a Shadowen. For if Par were the very thing they were fighting to protect the Four Lands against . . .

If Coll had died to save a Shadowen . . .

Unthinkable? He was no longer sure.

So the memories plagued him, bitter and terrible, and he was awash in a slew of anguish and disbelief and anger. He fought through that morass, struggled to keep himself afloat, to breathe, to survive. The fever disappeared, the starkness of his emotions softened, the edges dulled, and the aching of his heart and body scarred and healed.

He rose at the end of the two weeks' time, determined to lie about no longer, and began to walk short distances within the Mole's dark quarters. He washed at the basin, dressed, and took his meals at the table. He navigated the lair end to end, doorway to doorway, testing himself, feeling his way through his weakness. He pushed back the memories; he kept them carefully at bay. He did so mostly through simple motion. Doing something, anything, helped to keep him from dwelling so much on what was over and done. He made note of the smells and tastes that hung upon the trapped air. He studied the texture of the ruined furniture, of the various discards of the upper world, and of the walls and floors themselves. His resolution stiffened. He was alive and there was a reason for it. He shifted in and out of the candlelight and shadows, a ghost impelled by an inner vision.

Even when he was too tired to move about further he was reluctant to rest. He spent hours seated on the edge of his bed examining the Sword of Shannara, pondering its mystery.

Why had it failed to respond to him when he had touched its blade to Rimmer Dall?

"Is it possible," Damson asked him at one point, her voice cautious, "that you have been deceived in some way and that this is not the Sword of Shannara?"

He thought carefully before he answered. "When I saw it in the vault, Damson, and then when I touched it, I knew it was the Sword. I was certain of it. I have sung the story of it so many times, pictured it so often. There was no doubt in my mind." He shook his head slowly. "I still feel it to be so."

She nodded. She was seated next to him on the bed, legs folded beneath her, green eyes intense. "But your anticipation of finding it might have colored your judgment, Par. You might have wanted it so badly that you allowed yourself to be fooled."

"It might have happened like that, yes," he agreed. "Then. But now, as well? Look at the blade. See here. The handle is worn, aged—yet the blade shines like new. Like Morgan's sword—magic protects it. And see the carving of the torch with its flame . . ."

His enthusiasm trailed off with a sigh. He saw the doubt mirrored in her eyes. "Yet it doesn't work, it's true. It doesn't do a thing. I hold it, and it seems right, what it should be—and it doesn't do anything, give back anything, or let me feel even the slightest hint of its magic. So how can it be the Sword?"

"Counter-magic," the Mole said solemnly. He was crouched in a corner of the room close to them, almost invisible in the shadows. "A mask that hides." He stretched his face with his hands to change its shape.

Par looked at him and nodded. "A concealment of some kind. Yes, Mole. It might be. I have considered the possibility. But what magic exists that is strong enough to suppress that of the Sword of Shannara? How could the Shadowen produce such a magic? And if they could, why not simply use it to destroy the blade? And shouldn't I be able to break past any counter-magic if I am the rightful bearer of the Sword?"

The Mole regarded him solemnly, voiceless. Damson gave no reply.

"I don't understand," he whispered softly. "I don't understand what's wrong."

He wondered, too, at how willingly Rimmer Dall had let him depart with the Sword. If it were truly the weapon it was supposed to be, the weapon that could destroy the Shadowen, Dall would surely not have let Par Ohmsford have it. Yet he had given it to the Valeman without argument, almost with encouragement in fact, telling him instead that what he had been told of the Shadowen and the Sword was a lie.

And then virtually proved it by demonstrating that the touch of the Sword would not harm him.

Par wandered the Mole's quarters with the blade in hand,

hefting it, balancing it, working to invoke the magic that lay within. Yet the secret of the Sword of Shannara continued to elude him.

Periodically Damson left their underground concealment and went up into the streets of Tyrsis. It was odd to think of an entire city existing just overhead, just beyond sight and sound, with people and buildings, sunlight and fresh air. Par longed to go with her, but she wisely counseled against it. He lacked strength yet for such an undertaking, and the Federation was still searching.

A week after Par had left his sickbed and begun moving about on his own, Damson returned with disquieting news.

"Some weeks ago," she advised, "the Federation discovered the location of the Jut. A spy in the outlaw camp apparently betrayed it. An army was dispatched from Tyrsis to penetrate the Parma Key and lay siege. The siege was successful. The Jut fell. It was taken close to the time, Par, when you escaped the Pit." She paused. "Everyone found there was killed."

Par caught his breath. "Everyone?"

"So the Federation claims. The Movement, it says, is finished."

There was momentary silence. They sat at the Mole's long table surrounded by his voiceless, unseeing children, saucers and cups set before them. It had become a midafternoon ritual.

"More tea, lovely Damson?" the Mole asked softly, his furry face poking up from the table's edge. She nodded without taking her eyes from Par.

Par frowned. "You don't seem distressed by this," he responded finally.

"I think it odd that it took weeks for word of this victory to reach the city."

"So it isn't true, then?"

She bit into one of the crackers that the Mole had provided for them and chewed. "It may be true that the Jut was taken. But I know Padishar Creel. It doesn't seem likely that he would let himself be trapped in his own lair. He's much too clever for that. More to the point, friends of the Movement here in the city with whom I spoke tell me that line soldiers with the army claim they killed almost no one, several dozen at most, and those were already dead when the Jut's summit was breached. What happened, then, to the others? There were three hundred men in that camp. Besides, if the Federation really had Padishar Creel, they'd spike his head atop the city gates to prove it."

"But there's no message from Padishar?"

She shook her head.

"And no word of Morgan or Steff or any of the others?"

She shook her head again. "They've vanished."

"So." He let the word hang.

She smiled ruefully. They finished their tea without speaking.

The following day, his body stronger, his mind determined, Par again announced that he wanted to go up into Tyrsis. He had been shut away long enough; he needed to see something of his own world again. He needed to feel sunlight on his skin and breathe fresh air. Besides, as long as he remained hidden away, nothing was being accomplished. It was time for him to *do* something.

Damson objected strongly, pointing out that he was not yet fully recovered and that it was extremely dangerous for him to go anywhere. The Federation knew who he was now; his description was everywhere. After his escape from the Pit, Seekers had begun searching the lower levels of the old palace and discovered the tunnels leading in. Now they were searching the tunnels as well. There were miles of tunnel and sewer to search, but the risk of discovery remained. For now, it was best to lie low.

In the end, they compromised. Par would be allowed to go into the tunnels close at hand as long as he was in the company of Damson or the Mole. He would not go aboveground, even for a moment. He would go where he was told and do what he was advised. But at least he would be out of his sick rooms. Par agreed.

He began his exploration eagerly, studying the lay of the tunnels as he trailed after Damson and the Mole, mapping it all out carefully in his mind. He tired quickly the first day and had to return early. He was stronger the second and continued to improve. He began to grow comfortable with his understanding of how the tunnels and sewers wove together—enough so that he believed he could find his way to the surface on his own should the need arise. The Mole advised him cautiously, watched him with intense, glittery eyes, and nodded in satisfaction. Damson stayed close, her hands constantly touching him, as if to shield against danger. He smiled inwardly at their protectiveness.

A week passed away. He was much better now, almost completely recovered. More than a month had elapsed since he had been carried beneath the city of Tyrsis and placed in hiding. He thought constantly of leaving, of picking up again the threads of his life.

At the same time he found himself wondering where he would begin.

IN THE END the decision was made for him.

It was late afternoon ten days after he had begun his exploration of the tunnels surrounding the Mole's lair. He was seated on the edge of his bed, once again examining the Sword of Shannara. Damson had gone up to the city to see what news she could learn of Padishar and the Federation. The Mole was a furtive shadow as he passed from room to room, straightening, arranging, and fussing with his possessions. Teatime had come and gone without the girl, and the Mole was unsettled. Par might have been if he had allowed himself to dwell on the matter, but as it was he was consumed with something else. His memory of the events surrounding the discovery of the Sword of Shannara and the death of Coll was still incomplete, the fragments piecing themselves back in place only intermittently as he recovered to form a complete picture. Now and then a new piece would recall itself. One did so now.

It had to do with the wishsong, actually. He remembered all too clearly how his magic had gathered within him, summoned on its own almost, when Coll—the thing that had been Coll—threatened him. Then, after Coll was gone and the others of the Shadowen in the Pit came for him, the wishsong had given him a flaming sword, a weapon unlike anything the magic had ever produced. It had destroyed the Shadowen effortlessly. For a few moments he had been possessed, infused with fury and madness, driven beyond any semblance of reason. He remembered how that had felt. But there was something more, something he had forgotten completely until now. When the Shadowen were destroyed and he had reached down to retrieve the Sword of Shannara from where it had fallen, the Sword had burned him—had seared his hand like fire. And instantly his own magic had died, and he had been unable to summon it again.

Why had the Sword of Shannara done that? What had happened to produce such a reaction?

He was pondering this, trying to make it fit with what little he knew of the mystery of the Sword, when Damson burst through the entry to the Mole's subterranean refuge, long hair disheveled, her breathing quick and frightened.

"Federation soldiers!" she announced, rushing up to Par, pulling him to his feet. "Dozens of them, hunting through the sewers, making a thorough sweep! Not at the palace, but here. I barely slipped in ahead of them. I don't know if someone betrayed us or if I was simply seen. But they have found the entry down and they're coming!" She paused, steadying herself. "If we stay, they will find us. We have to get out right away."

Par slung the Sword of Shannara over his shoulder and began shoving his few possessions into a sling pack. His thoughts scattered. He had been anxious to leave, but not like this.

"Mole!" Damson called out, and the furry fellow skittered quickly up to her. "You have to come with us. They will find you as well."

But the Mole shook his head solemnly, and his voice was calm. "No, beautiful Damson. This is my home. I will stay."

Damson knelt hurriedly. "You can't do that, Mole. You will be in great danger. These men will hurt you."

Par hurried over. "Come with us, Mole. Please. It is our fault that you are threatened."

The Mole regarded him quizzically. "I chose to bring you here. I chose to care for you. I did it for Damson—but for myself as well. I like you. I like how you make . . . lovely Damson feel."

Par saw Damson flush out of the corner of his eye and kept

his gaze focused on the Mole. "None of that matters now. What matters is that we are your friends, and friends look out for one another. You have to come with us."

"I will not go back into the world above," the Mole insisted quietly. "This is my home. I must look out for it. What of my children? What of Chalt and little Lida and Westra and Everlind? Would you have me leave them?"

"Bring them, if you must!" Par was growing desperate.

"We will help you find a new home," Damson added quickly.

But the Mole shook his head stubbornly. "The world up there wants nothing to do with any of us. We do not belong there, lovely Damson. We belong down here. Do not worry for us. We know these tunnels. There are places to hide where we will never be found. We will go to them if we must." He paused. "You could come with us, both of you. You would be safe."

Damson rose, her brow furrowed. "It will be enough if you are safe, Mole. We have brought too much danger already into your life. Just promise me that you will go to one of these hiding places now. Take your children and stay there until this hunt is finished and the tunnels are safe again. Promise me."

The Mole nodded. "I promise, sweet Damson."

Damson flew to gather her own possessions, then joined Par at the entryway. The Mole stood looking at them from out of the shadows, little more than a pair of glittering eyes lost in the jumble of discarded goods and faint candlelight.

Damson shouldered her pack. "Goodbye, Mole," she called softly, then lowered her pack, walked to where he waited, and reached down to embrace him. When she returned to Par, she was crying.

"I owe you my life, Mole," Par told him. "Thank you for everything you have done for me."

One small hand lifted in a faint wave.

"Remember your promise!" Damson warned almost angrily. "Hide yourself!"

Then they were through the entry and into the tunnel beyond, slipping soundlessly ahead. Damson carried no torch, but instead produced one of the strange stones that glowed when warmed by her hand. She used its small, sure light to guide them, opening her fingers to provide direction, closing them again to protect against discovery. They moved swiftly away from the Mole's lair, down one tunnel and into another, then up a metal ladder and into a pit.

From somewhere distant, they heard the sound of boots scraping.

Damson led Par away from the sound, along a tunnel that was dank and slick with moisture. Already the temperature was rising and the air filling with sewer smells. Rats skittered about in the dark recesses, and water trickled along the crevices of the rock. They wound their way steadily through the maze. Voices reached them once, unfocused, indistinct. Damson ignored them.

They arrived at a joining of several sewer ways, a ringed pit with water collecting in a deep, shadowed well. A central convergence, Par thought. He was breathing heavily, his strength failing already in the face of this sudden activity. The muscles of his legs and back ached, and he stretched himself gingerly to relieve them.

Damson glanced back at him, concern mirrored in her eyes. She hesitated, then guided him forward.

The voices rose again, closer now, coming from more than one direction. Torchlight flared behind them. Damson took Par up another ladder and into a tunnel that was so narrow they were forced to crawl to get through. Dampness and filth soaked into Par's clothing and clung to his skin. He forced himself to breathe through his mouth and then only when he could hold his breath no longer.

They emerged at the beginning of a wider tunnel, this one trenched down its middle so that there were stone walkways to either side of where the sewer water flowed. A pair of smaller tunnels intersected. There was a flicker of torchlight in each. Damson hurried on. They rounded a bend and found torchlight waiting ahead as well. Damson stopped, shoving Par back against the rock wall.

When she faced him, there was a hint of desperation in her eyes. "The only way out," she whispered, her mouth close to his ear, "lies ahead. If we go back, we'll be trapped."

She stepped back so that she could see his response. He glanced past her to the lights, approaching rapidly now, and heard the thudding of boots and the first hint of voices. Fear welled within and threatened to drown him. It felt as if the Federation had been hunting him forever; it seemed that the hunting would never stop. So many times he had escaped capture. It could not go on. Sooner or later his luck was going to run out. He had barely survived the Pit and the Shadowen. He was worn and sick at heart and he just wanted to be left alone. But the Federation would never leave him alone; the cycle was endless.

For an instant despair claimed him completely. Then abruptly he thought of Coll. He remembered his vow that someone would pay for what had become of his brother. Anger replaced the despair instantly. No, he would not be taken prisoner, he swore silently. He would not be given over to Rimmer Dall.

He thought momentarily to summon the magic that had aided him in the Pit, to call forth that fiery sword that would cut his enemies to pieces. He brushed the impulse aside. It was too much power to face again so soon and still with so little understanding. Cunning, not brute force, was needed here. He remembered suddenly how he had escaped from the Federation that night in the People's Park. Pulling Damson after him, he hastened to a shadowed niche in the tunnel wall formed by the bracing. Crouched in the darkness with the girl, he put a finger to his lips and signaled for her to remain still.

The Federation soldiers approached, five strong, torches lifted to provide sufficient light for their search, the metal of their weapons glinting. Par took a deep breath and slipped down within himself. He would have only one chance. Just one.

He waited until they were almost upon them, then used the wishsong. He kept it tightly in check, taking no chances with what it might do, carefully controlling its release. He cast a net about the soldiers of whispered warnings, a hint of something that disturbed the waters of the sewer farther ahead, a shadowy movement. He infused them with a need to hurry if they were to catch it.

Almost as one, the soldiers broke into a run and hastened past without looking. The Valeman and the girl pressed back against the tunnel rock, breathless. In moments the soldiers were gone.

Slowly Damson and Par came back to their feet. Then Damson reached out impulsively and hugged the Valeman. "You are well again, Par Ohmsford," she whispered, and kissed him. "This way, now. We're almost free."

They hurried down the passageway, crossed a confluent, and entered a dry well. The torches and boots and voices had receded into silence. There was a ladder leading up. Damson went first, pausing at the top to push up against a trapdoor. Twilight seeped through the crack. She listened, peered about, then climbed through. Par followed.

They stood within a shed, slat-walled and closed away. A single door led out. Damson moved to it, opened it cautiously and with Par in tow stepped out.

The city of Tyrsis rose around them, fortress walls, spiraled towers, jumbled buildings of stone and wood. The air was thick with smells and sounds. It was early evening, the day gone west, the city's people turned homeward. Life was slow and weary in the stillness of the summer heat. Overhead the sky was turning to black velvet, and stars were beginning to spread like scattered bits of crystal. A wondrously bright full moon beamed cold white light across the world.

Par Ohmsford smiled, the aches forgotten, his fears momentarily behind him. He adjusted the weight of the Sword of Shannara across his shoulders. It felt good to be alive.

Damson reached over and took his hand, squeezing it gently.

Together they turned down the street and disappeared into the night.

CHAPTER

12

QUICKENING KEPT HER little company at Hearthstone for several days to allow Walker Boh to regain his strength. It returned quickly, the healing process augmented as much by the girl's small touches and sudden smiles, by the very fact of her presence, as by nature's hand. There was magic all about her, an invisible aura that surrounded her, that reached out to everything with which she came in contact, and that restored and renewed with a thoroughness and rapidity that was astounding. Walker grew strong again almost overnight, the effects of his poisoning gone into memory, to some small extent at least joined by the pain of losing Cogline and Rumor. The haunted look disappeared from his eyes, and he was able to put away his anger and his fear, to lock them in a small dark corner of his mind where they would not disturb him and yet not be forgotten when the time came to remember. His determination returned, his confidence, his sense of purpose and resolve, and he became more like the Dark Uncle of old. His magic aided him in his recovery, but it was Quickening who provided the impetus, moment by moment, a warmth that outshone the sun.

She did more. The clearing where the cottage had stood became cleansed of its scars and burns, and the signs of the battle with the Shadowen slowly disappeared. Grasses and flowers blossomed and filled the emptiness, swatches of color and patches of fragrance that soothed and comforted. Even the ruins of the cottage settled into dust and at last faded from view completely. It seemed that whenever she chose she could make the world over again.

Morgan Leah began to talk to Walker when Pe Ell was not around, the Highlander still uneasy, admitting to Walker that he was not certain yet who the other really was or why Quickening had brought him along. Morgan had grown since Walker had seen him last. Brash and full of himself when he had first come to Hearthstone, he seemed subdued now, more controlled, a cautious man without lacking courage, a well-reasoned man. Walker liked him better for it and thought that the events that had conspired to separate him from the Ohmsfords and bring him to Culhaven had done much to mature him. The Highlander told Walker what had befallen Par and Coll, of their joining Padishar Creel and the Movement, their journey to Tyrsis and attempts to recover the Sword of Shannara from the Pit, their battles with the Shadowen, and their separation and separate escapes. He told Walker of the Federation assault on the Jut, Teel's betrayal, her death and Steff's, and the outlaw's flight north.

"She gave us all away, Walker," Morgan declared when he had finished his narrative. "She gave up Granny and Auntie in Culhaven, the Dwarves working with the Resistance that she knew about, everyone. She must have given Cogline up as well."

But Walker did not believe so. The Shadowen had known of Cogline and Hearthstone since Par had been kidnapped from the valley by Spider Gnomes some months earlier. The Shadowen could have come for Cogline at any time, and they had not chosen to do so until now. Rimmer Dall had told Cogline before he killed him that the old man was the last who stood against the Shadowen, and that meant that he believed Cogline had become a threat. More worrisome to him than how Rimmer Dall had found them was the First Seeker's claim that the children of Shannara were all dead. Obviously he was mistaken about Walker, but what of Par and Wren, the others of the Shannara line dispatched by the shade of Allanon in search of those things lost and disappeared that would supposedly save the Four Lands? Was Rimmer Dall mistaken about them as well or had they, too, gone the way of Cogline? He hadn't the means to discover the truth and he kept what he was thinking to himself. There was no point in saying anything to Morgan Leah, who was already struggling with the imagined consequences of his decision to follow after Quickening.

"I know I should not be here," he told Walker in confidence one afternoon. They were sitting within the shade of an aged white oak, listening to and watching the songbirds that darted overhead. "I kept my word to Steff and saw to the safety of Granny Elise and Auntie Jilt. But this! What of my promise to Par and Coll that I would protect them? I shouldn't be here; I should be back in Tyrsis looking for them!"

But Walker said, "No, Highlander, you should not. What good could you do even if you found them? How much help would you be against the Shadowen? You have a chance here to do something far more important—indeed, a need, if Quickening is right in what she says. Perhaps, too, you may find a way to restore the magic to your sword, just as I may find a way to restore my arm. Slim hopes for those of us with pragmatic minds, yet hopes nevertheless. We feel her need, Highlander, and we respond to it; we are her children, aren't we? I think we cannot dismiss such stirrings so easily. For now at least, we belong with her."

He had come to believe that, swayed by his midnight talk with Quickening when he had told her of the Grimpond's vision and his fear that it would come to pass, won over by her insistence and determination that it would not. Morgan Leah was no less thoroughly bound, mesmerized by her beauty, chained by his longings, drawn to her in ways he could not begin to understand but could not deny. For each of the three, the attraction to Quickening was different. Morgan's was physical, a fascination with the look and movement of her, with the exquisite line and curve of her face and body, and with a loveliness that transcended anything he had ever known or even imagined. Walker's was more ethereal, a sense of kinship with her born of their common birthright of magic, an understanding of the ways in which she was compelled to think and act because of it, a binding together through a common chain of links where each link was a shared experience of reasoning grown out of the magic's lure.

Pe Ell's purpose in coming was the most difficult to discern. He called himself an artist, at various times of sleight-of-hand and escape, but he was clearly something more. That he was extremely dangerous was no mystery to anyone, yet he kept any truths about himself carefully concealed. He seldom spoke to any of them, even to Quickening, though he was as attracted to her as either Walker or Morgan and looked after her as carefully as they. But Pe Ell's attraction was more that of a man for his possessions than a man for his lover or a kindred spirit. He seemed drawn to Quickening in the way of a craftsman to something he has created and offers up as evidence of his skill. It was an attitude that Walker found difficult to understand, for Pe Ell had been brought along in the same way as the rest of them and had done nothing to make Quickening who or what she was. Yet the feeling persisted in him that Pe Ell viewed the girl as his own and when the time was right he would attempt to possess her.

The days of the week played themselves out until finally Quickening decided Walker was well enough to travel, and the company of four departed Hearthstone. Traveling afoot, for the country would permit nothing better, they journeyed north through Darklin Reach and the forests of the Anar along the western edge of Toffer Ridge to the Rabb, crossed where the waters narrowed, and proceeded on toward the Charnals. Progress was slow because the country was heavily wooded, choked with scrub and slashed by ravines and ridges, and they were forced constantly to alter their direction of travel away from their intended course to find passable terrain. The weather was good, however, warm days of sunshine and soft breezes, the summer's close, a slow, lazy winding down of hours that made every day seem welcome and endless. There was sickness even this far north, wilting and poisoning of the earth and its life, yet not as advanced as in the middle sections of the Four Lands, and the smells and tastes, the sights and sounds, were mostly fresh and new and unfouled. Streams were clear and forests green, and the life within both seemed unaffected by the gathering darkness with which the Shadowen threatened to blanket everything.

Nights were spent camped in wooded clearings by ponds or

streams that provided fresh water and often fish for a meal, and there was talk now and then between the men, even by Pe Ell. It was Quickening who remained reticent, who kept herself apart when the day's travel was completed, who secluded herself back in the shadows, away from the firelight and the presence of the other three. It wasn't that she disdained them or hid from them; it was more that she needed the solitude. The wall went up early in their travels, an invisible distancing that she established the first night out and did not relinquish after. The three she had brought with her did not question, but instead watched her and each other surreptitiously and waited to see what would transpire. When nothing did, thrown together by her forced separation from them, they began to loosen up in each other's presence and to speak. Morgan would have talked in any case, an open and relaxed youth who enjoyed stories and the company of others. It was different with Walker and Pe Ell, both of whom were by nature and practice guarded and cautious. Conversations frequently became small battlegrounds between the two with each attempting to discover what secrets the other hid and neither willing to reveal anything about himself. They used their talk as a screen, careful to keep the conversation away from anything that really mattered.

They all speculated now and again on where they were going and what they were going to do when they got there. Those conversations ended quickly every time. No one would discuss what sort of magic he possessed, though Walker and Morgan already had some idea of each other's strengths, and no one would advance any plan of action for retrieving the talisman. They fenced with each other like swordsmen, probing for strengths and weaknesses, feinting with their questions and their suggestions, and trying to discover what sort of iron fortified the others. Walker and Pe Ell made little progress with each other, and while it became clear enough that Morgan was there because of the magic contained in the Sword of Leah it was impossible to learn anything substantive with the weapon shattered. Pe Ell, particularly, asked questions over and over again about what it was the Sword of Leah could do, what sort of materials it could penetrate, and how much power it contained. Morgan used all of his considerable talents to be both charming and confusing with his answers and to give the impression that the magic could do either anything or nothing. Eventually, Pe Ell left him alone.

The close of the first week of travel brought them north above the Anar to the foothills leading into the Charnals where for days thereafter they journeyed, always in the shadow of the mountains as they wound their way northeast toward the Tiderace. By now, they were beyond the lands any of them knew. Neither Morgan nor Pe Ell had ever been north of the Upper Anar, and Walker had not gone farther than the lower regions of the Charnals. In any case, it was Quickening who led them, seemingly unperturbed by the fact that she knew less of the country than any of them, responding to some inner voice that none of them could hear, to instincts that none of them could feel. She admitted that she did not know exactly where she was going, that she could sense enough to lead them for now, but that eventually they would have to cross the Charnals, and then she would be lost as the mountains would prove unfathomable to her. Eldwist lay beyond the Charnals, and they would have to have help in finding it.

"Have you the magic for that, Walker?" Pe Ell teased when she finished, but Walker only smiled and wondered the same thing.

Rain caught up with them as the second week ended and followed them relentlessly into the third, dampening their trail, their packs and clothing, and their spirits. Clouds massed overhead along the line of the peaks and refused to budge, dark and persistent. Thunder boomed and lightning flashed against the wall of the mountains as if giants were playing shadow games with their hands. There were not many travelers this far north; most of those they encountered were Trolls. Few spoke and fewer still had anything useful to tell. There were several passes that led through the mountains a day or two ahead, all of them beginning at a town high in the foothills called Rampling Steep. Yes, some of the passes led all the way east to the Tiderace. No, they had never heard of Eldwist.

"Makes you wonder if it really exists," Pe Ell muttered, persisting in his role as agitator, a smile creasing his narrow face, cold and empty and devoid of humor. "Makes you think."

That night, two days short of the completion of their third week of travel, he broached the subject in a manner that left no one in doubt as to his feelings. The rains were still falling, a gray haze that chilled and numbed the senses, and tempers had grown short.

"This town, Rampling Steep," he began, an edge to his voice that brought them all around in the stillness of the twilight, "that's where we lose any idea of where we're going, isn't it?" He asked the question of Quickening, who made no response. "We're lost after that, and I don't like being lost. Maybe it's time we talked a bit more about this whole business."

"What would you know, Pe Ell?" the girl asked quietly, unperturbed.

"You haven't told us enough about what lies ahead," he said. "I think you should. Now."

She shook her head. "You ask for answers I do not have to give. I have to discover them as well."

"I don't believe that," he said, shaking his head for emphasis, his voice low and hard. Morgan Leah was looking at him with undisguised irritation and Walker Boh was on his feet. "I know something about people, even ones who have the magic like yourself and I know when they're telling me everything they know and when they're not. You're not. You better do so."

"Or you might turn around and go back?" Morgan challenged sharply.

Pe Ell looked at him expressionlessly.

"Why don't you do that, Pe Ell? Why don't you?"

Pe Ell rose, his eyes flat and seemingly disinterested. Morgan stood up with him. But Quickening stepped forward, coming swiftly between them, moving to separate them without seeming to mean to do so, but as if she sought only to face Pe Ell. She stood before him, small and vulnerable, silver hair swept back as she tilted her face to his. He frowned and for a moment looked as if he felt threatened and might lash out. Whip-thin and sinewy, he curled back like a snake. But she did not move, either toward him or away, and the tension slowly went out of him.

"You must trust me," she told him softly, speaking to him as if he were the only other person alive in all the world, holding him spellbound by the force of her voice, the intensity of her black eyes, and the closeness of her body. "What there is to know of Uhl Belk and Eldwist, I have told you. What there is to know of the Black Elfstone, I have told you. As much, at least, as I am given to know. Yes, there are things I keep from you just as you keep things from me. That is the way of all living creatures, Pe Ell. You cannot begrudge me my secrets when you have your own. I keep nothing back that will harm you. That is the best I can do."

The lean man stared down at her without speaking, everything closed away behind his eyes where his thoughts were at work.

"When we reach Rampling Steep, we will seek help in finding our way," she continued, her voice still barely above a whisper, yet bell-clear and certain. "Eldwist will be known and someone will point the way."

And to the surprise of both Walker and Morgan Leah, Pe Ell simply nodded and stepped away. He did not speak again that night to any of them. He seemed to have forgotten they existed.

The following day they reached a broad roadway leading west into the foothills and turned onto it. The roadway wound ahead snakelike into the light and then into shadow when the sun dropped behind the peaks of the Charnals. Night descended and they camped beneath the stars, the first clear sky in many days. They talked quietly as the evening meal was consumed, a sense of balance restored with the passing of the rains. No mention was made of the previous night's events. Pe Ell seemed satisfied with what Quickening had told him, although she had told him almost nothing. It was the way in which she had spoken to him, Walker thought on reflection. It was the way she employed her magic to turn aside his suspicion and anger.

They set out again early the following morning, traveling northeast once more, the sunrise bright and warming. By late afternoon they had climbed high into the foothills, close against the base of the mountains. By sunset they had arrived at the town of Rampling Steep.

The light was nearly gone by then, a dim glow from behind the mountains west that colored the skyline in shades of gold and silver. Rampling Steep was hunkered down in a deep pool of shadows, cupped in a shallow basin at the foot of the peaks where the forest trees began to thin and scatter into isolated clumps between the ridges of mountain rock. The buildings of the town were a sorry bunch, ramshackle structures built of stone foundations and wooden walls and roofs with windows and doors all shuttered and barred and closed away like the eyes of frightened children. There was a single street that wound between them as if looking for a way out. The buildings of the town crouched down on either side save for a handful of shacks and cottages that were settled back on the high ground like careless sentries. Everything was desperately in need of repair. Boards from walls were broken and hung loose, roofing shingles had slipped away, and porch fronts sagged and buckled. Slivers of light crept through cracks and crevices. There were teams of horses hitched to wagons pulled up close against the buildings, each looking a little more ruined than the one before, and shadowed figures on two legs moved between them like wraiths.

As the company drew nearer Walker saw that the figures were mostly Trolls, great, hulking figures in the twilight, their barklike faces impossible to read. A few glanced at the four as they passed down the roadway, but none bothered to speak or to give a second look. The sound of voices reached out to them now, disembodied grunts and mutterings and laughter that the dilapidated walls could not keep in. But despite the talk and the laughter and the movement of men, Rampling Steep had an empty feel to it, as if it had long ago been abandoned by the living.

Quickening took them up the roadway without pausing, glancing neither left nor right, as sure of herself now as she had been from the start. Morgan followed no more than a step behind, staying close, keeping watch, being protective although there was probably no need for him to do so. Pe Ell had drifted out to the right, distancing himself. Walker trailed.

There was a series of ale houses at the center of Rampling Steep, and it appeared that everyone had gathered there. Music came from some, and men lurched and swaggered through the doors, passing in and out of the light in faceless anonymity. A few women passed as well, worn and hard looking. Rampling Steep appeared to be a place of ending rather than beginning.

Quickening took them into the first of the ale houses and asked the keeper if he knew of someone who could guide them through the mountains to Eldwist. She asked the question as if there were nothing unusual about it. She was oblivious to the stir her presence caused, to the stares that were directed at her from every quarter, and to the dark hunger that lay behind a good many of the eyes that fixed upon her, or at least she seemed to be. Perhaps, Walker thought, as he watched her, it was all simply of no consequence to her. He saw that no one tried to approach and no one threatened. Morgan stood protectively at her back, facing that unfriendly, rapacious gathering—as if one man could make a difference if they should decide to do something—but it was not the Highlander that deterred them or Walker or even the forbidding Pe Ell. It was the girl, a creature so stunning that like a thing out of some wild imagining it could not be disturbed for fear it would prove false. The men gathered in the ale house watched, that crowd of wild-eyed men, not quite believing but not willing to prove themselves wrong.

There was nothing to be learned at the first ale house, so they moved on to the next. No one followed. The scenario of the first ale house was repeated at the second, this one smaller and closer inside, the smoke of pipes and the smell of bodies thicker and more pungent. There were Trolls, Gnomes, Dwarves, and Men in Rampling Steep, all drinking and talking together as if it were the natural order of things, as if what was happening in the rest of the Four Lands was of no importance here. Walker studied their faces dispassionately, their eyes when their faces told him nothing, and found them secretive and scared, the faces and eyes of men who lived with hardship and disappointment yet ignored both because to do otherwise would mean they could not survive. Some seemed dangerous, a few even desperate. But there was an order to life in Rampling Steep as there was in most places, and not much happened to disturb that order. Strangers came and went, even ones as striking as Quickening, and life went on nevertheless. Quickening was something like a falling star—it happened a few times and you

were lucky if you saw it but you didn't do anything to change
your life because of it.

They moved on to a third ale house and then a fourth. At
each ale house, the answers to Quickening's questions were the
same. No one knew anything of Eldwist and Uhl Belk and no
one wanted to. There were maybe eight drinking houses in all
along the roadway, most offering beds upstairs and supplies from
storerooms out back, a few doubling as trading stations or exchanges. Because Rampling Steep was the only town for days in
either direction that fronted the lower side of the Charnals and
because it was situated where the trails leading down out of the
mountains converged, a lot of traffic passed through, trappers
and traders mostly, but others as well. Every ale house was filled
and most gathered were temporary or sometime residents on
their way to or from somewhere else. There was talk of all sorts,
of business and politics, of roads traveled and wonders seen, of
the people and places that made up the Four Lands. Walker
listened without appearing to and thought that Pe Ell was doing
the same.

At the fifth ale house they visited—Walker never even noticed the name—they finally got the response they were looking
for. The keeper was a big, ruddy-complexioned fellow with a
scarred face and a ready smile. He sized up Quickening in a
way that made even Walker uncomfortable. Then he suggested
that the girl should take a room with him for a few days, just
to see if maybe she might like the town enough to stay. That
brought Morgan Leah about with fire in his eyes, but Quickening screened him away with a slight shifting of her body, met
the keeper's bold stare, and replied that she wasn't interested.
The keeper did not press the suggestion. Instead, to everyone's
amazement in the face of the rejection he had just been handed,
he told her that the man she was seeking was down the street
at the Skinned Cat. His name, he said, was Horner Dees.

They went back out into the night, leaving the keeper looking as if he wasn't at all sure what he had just done. The look
was telling. Quickening had that gift; it was the essence of her
magic. She could turn you around before you realized it. She
could make you reveal yourself in ways you had never intended.
She could make you want to please her. It was the kind of thing

a beautiful woman could make a man do, but with Quickening it was something far more than her beauty that disarmed you. It was the creature within, the elemental that seemed human but was far more, an embodiment of magic that Walker thought reflected the father who had made her. He knew the stories of the King of the Silver River. When you met him, you told him what he wished to know and you did not dissemble. His presence alone was enough to make you *want* to tell him. Walker had seen how Morgan and Pe Ell and the men in the ale houses responded to her. And he as well. She was most certainly her father's child.

They found the Skinned Cat at the far end of the town, tucked back within the shadow of several massive, ancient shagbarks. It was a large, rambling structure that creaked and groaned simply from the movement of the men and women inside and seemed to hang together mostly out of stubbornness. It was crowded as the others, but there was more space to fill and it had been divided along its walls into nooks and partitions to make it feel less barnlike. Lights were scattered about like distant friends reaching out through the gloom, and the patrons were gathered in knots at the serving bar and about long tables and benches. Heads turned at their entrance as they had turned at the other ale houses, and eyes watched. Quickening moved to find the keeper, who listened and pointed to the back of the room. There was a man sitting at a table there, alone in a shadowed nook, hunched over and faceless, pushed away from the light and the crowd.

The four walked over to stand before him.

"Horner Dees," Quickening said in that silken voice.

Massive hands brought an ale mug slowly away from a bearded mouth and back to the tabletop, and a large, shaggy head lifted. The man was huge, a great old bear of a fellow with the better part of his years behind him. There was hair all over him, on his forearms and the backs of his hands, at his throat and on his chest, and on his head and face, grown over him so completely that except for his eyes and nose his features were obscured almost entirely. It was impossible to guess how old he was, but the hair was silver gray, the skin beneath it wrinkled and browned and mottled, and the fingers gnarled like old roots.

"I might be," he rumbled truculently from out of some giant's cave. His eyes were riveted on the girl.

"My name is Quickening," she said. "These are my companions. We search for a place called Eldwist and a man named Uhl Belk. We are told you know of both."

"You were told wrong."

"Can you take us there?" she asked, ignoring his response.

"I just said . . ."

"Can you take us there?" she repeated.

The big man stared at her without speaking, without moving, with no hint of what he was thinking. He was like a huge, settled rock that had survived ages of weathering and erosion and found them to be little more than a passing breeze. "Who are you?" he asked finally. "Who, other than your name?"

Quickening did not hesitate. "I am the daughter of the King of the Silver River. Do you know of him, Horner Dees?"

The other nodded slowly. "Yes, I know him. And maybe you are who you say. And maybe I am who you think. Maybe I even know about Eldwist and Uhl Belk. Maybe I'm the only one who knows—the only one who's still alive to tell about it. Maybe I can even do what you ask and take you there. But I don't see the point. Sit."

He gestured at a scattering of empty chairs, and the four seated themselves across the table from him. He looked at the men in turn, then his eyes returned to the girl. "You don't look as if you're someone who doesn't know what they're doing. Why would you want to find Uhl Belk?"

Quickening's black eyes were fathomless, intense. "Uhl Belk stole something that doesn't belong to him. It must be returned."

Horner Dees snorted derisively. "You plan to steal it back, do you? Or just ask him to return it? Do you know anything about Belk? I do."

"He stole a talisman from the Druids."

Dees hesitated. His bearded face twitched as he chewed on something imaginary. "Girl, nobody who goes into Eldwist ever comes out again. Nobody except me, and I was just plain lucky. There's things there that nothing can stand against. Belk, he's an old thing, come out of some other age, full of dark magic and evil. You won't ever take anything away from him, and he won't ever give anything back."

"Those who are with me are stronger than Uhl Belk," Quickening said. "They have magic as well, and theirs will overcome his. My father says it will be so. These three," and she named them each in turn, "will prevail."

As she spoke their names, Horner Dees let his eyes shift to identify each, passing over their faces quickly, pausing only once—so briefly that Walker wasn't sure at first that there had been a pause at all—on Pe Ell.

Then he said, "These are men. Uhl Belk is something more. You can't kill him like an ordinary man. You probably can't even find him. He'll find you and by then it will be too late." He snapped his fingers and sat back.

Quickening eyed him momentarily across the table, then reached out impulsively and touched the table's wooden surface. Instantly a splinter curled up, a slender stem forming, leafing out and finally flowering with tiny bluebells. Quickening's smile was as magical as her touch. "Show us the way into Eldwist, Horner Dees," she said.

The old man wet his lips. "It will take more than flowers to do in Belk," he said.

"Perhaps not," she whispered, and Walker had the feeling that for a moment she had gone somewhere else entirely. "Wouldn't you like to come with us and see?"

Dees shook his head. "I didn't get old being stupid," he said. He thought a moment, then sat forward again. "It was ten years ago when I went into Eldwist. I'd found it some time before that, but I knew it was dangerous and I wasn't about to go in there alone. I kept thinking about it though, wondering what was in there, because finding out about things is what I do. I've been a Tracker, a soldier, a hunter, everything there is to be, and it all comes down to finding out what's what. So I kept wondering about Eldwist, about what was in there, all those old buildings, all that stone, everywhere you looked. I went back finally because I couldn't stand not knowing anymore. I took a dozen men with me, lucky thirteen of us. We thought we'd find something of value in there, a place as secret and old as that. We knew what it was called; there's been legends about it for years in the high country, over on the other side of the mountains where some of us had been. The Trolls know it. It's a peninsula—just a narrow strip of land, all rock, jutting out into the middle of the Tiderace. We went out there one morning, the thirteen of us. Full of life. By dawn of the next day, the other twelve were dead, and I was running like a scared deer!"

He hunched his shoulders. "You don't want to go there," he said. "You don't want anything to do with Eldwist and Uhl Belk."

He picked up his mug, drained it, and slammed it down purposefully. The sound brought the keeper immediately, a fresh drink in hand, and away again just as quickly. Dees never looked at him, his eyes still fixed on Quickening. The evening was wearing on toward midnight by now, but few among the alehouse customers had drifted away. They clustered as they had since sunset, since long before in some cases, their talk more liquid and disjointed than earlier and their posture more relaxed. Time had lost its hold on them momentarily, victims of all forms of strife and misadventure, refugees huddled within the shelter of their intoxication and their loose companionship. Dees was not one of them; Walker Boh doubted that he ever would be.

Quickening stirred. "Horner Dees," she said, saying his name as if she were examining it, a young girl trying on an old man's identity. "If you do nothing, Uhl Belk will come for you."

For the first time, Dees looked startled.

"In time, he will come," Quickening continued, her voice both gentle and sad. "He advances his kingdom beyond what it was and it grows more swiftly with the passing of time. If he is not stopped, if his power is not lessened, sooner or later he will reach you."

"I'll be long dead," the old man said, but he didn't sound sure.

Quickening smiled, magical once again, something perfect and wondrous. "There are mysteries that you will never solve because you will not have the chance," she said. "That is not the case with Uhl Belk. You are a man who has spent his life finding out about things. Would you stop doing so now? How will you know which of us is right about Uhl Belk if you do not come with us? Do so, Horner Dees. Show us the way into Eldwist. Make this journey."

Dees was silent for a long time, thinking it through. Then he said, "I would like to believe that monster could be undone by something . . ." He shook his head. "I don't know."

"Do you need to?" the girl asked softly.

Dees frowned, then smiled, a great, gap-toothed grin that wreathed his broad face in weathered lines. "Never have," he said and laughed. The grin disappeared. "This is a hard walk we're talking about, not some stroll across the street. The passes are tough going any time of the year and once we're over and beyond, we'll be on our own. No help over there. Nothing but Trolls, and they don't care spit about outsiders. Nothing to help us but us. Truth is, none of you look strong enough to make it."

"We might be stronger than you think," Morgan Leah said quietly.

Dees eyed him critically. "You'll have to be," he said. "A lot stronger." Then he sighed. "Well, well. Come to this, has it? Me, an old man, about to go out into the far reaches one more time." He chuckled softly and looked back at Quickening. "You have a way about you, I'll say that. Talk a nut right out of its shell. Even a hard old nut like me. Well, well."

He shoved his chair back from the table and came to his feet. He was even bigger standing than he had been sitting, like some pitted wall that refused to fall down even after years of enduring adverse weather. He stood before them, hunched over and hoary looking, his big arms hanging loose, and his eyes squinting as if he had just come into the light.

"All right, I'll take you," he announced, leaning forward to emphasize his decision, keeping his voice low and even. "I'll take you because it's true that I haven't seen everything or found all the answers and what's life for if not to keep trying—even when I don't believe that trying will be enough. You meet me back here at sunrise, and I'll give you a list of what you need and where to find it. You do the gathering, I'll do the organizing. We'll give it a try. Who knows? Maybe some of us will even make it back."

He paused and looked at them as if seeing them for the first time. There was a hint of laughter around the edges of his voice as he said, "Won't it be a good joke on Belk if you really do have the stronger magic?"

Then he eased his way out from behind the table, shambled across the room and out the door, and disappeared into the night.

13

ORNER DEES WAS as good as his word, meeting them early the next morning to direct preparations for the journey that would take them across the Charnals and into Eldwist. He met them at the door of the rooming house on which they had finally settled for their night's lodgings, a creaky two-storied rambler that in former times had been first a residence then later a store, and without bothering to explain how he had found them provided a list of supplies they would need and directions on where to obtain them. He was even more rumpled and bearish seeming than he had been the previous night, wider than the door he stood before and hunched over like some sodden jungle shrub. He muttered and grumbled, and his instructions were delivered as if he were suffering from too much drink. Pe Ell thought him a worthless sot, and Morgan Leah found him just plain unpleasant. Because they could see that Quickening expected it, they accepted their instructions wordlessly. A little of Horner Dees went a long way. But Walker Boh saw something different. To begin with, he had worried enough the previous night about Dees to take Quickening aside after the old man's departure and suggest to her that maybe this wasn't the man they were looking for. After all, what did they know about Dees beyond what he had told them? Even if he actually had gone into Eldwist, that was ten years ago. What if he had since forgotten the way? What if he remembered just enough to get them hopelessly lost? But Quickening had assured him in that way she had of dispelling all doubt that Horner Dees was the man they needed. Now, as he listened to the old Tracker, he was inclined to agree. Walker had made a good many journeys in his time and he understood the kinds of preparations that were required. It was clear that Dees understood as well. For all of his gruff talk and his grizzled look, Horner Dees knew what he was doing.

The preparation time passed quickly. Walker, Morgan, and Pe Ell gathered together the foodstuffs, bedding, canvases, ropes, climbing tools, cooking implements, clothing, and survival gear that Dees had sent them to find. Dees himself arranged for pack animals, shaggy mules that could carry the heavy loads they would need and weather the mountain storms. They brought everything to an old stable situated at the north end of Rampling Steep, a building that seemed to serve Dees as both workshop and home. He lived in the tack room and when he wasn't issuing orders or checking on their efforts to carry them out he kept himself there.

Quickening was even more reclusive. When she wasn't with them, which was most of the time, they had no idea where she was. She seemed to drift in the manner of an errant cloud, more shadow than substance. She might have walked the woodlands away from the town, for she would have been more comfortable there. She might have simply hidden away. Wherever she went, she disappeared with the completeness of the sun at day's end, and they missed her as much. Only when she returned did they feel warmed again. She spoke to them each day, always singly, never together. She gave them a measure of herself, some small reassurance that they could not quite define but not mistake either. Had she been someone else, they would have suspected her of game playing. But she was Quickening, the daughter of the King of the Silver River, and there was no time or wish or even need for games in her life. She transcended such behavior, and while they did not fully understand her and sensed that perhaps they never would, they were convinced that deception and betrayal were beyond her. Her presence alone kept them together, bound them to her so that they would not turn away. She was incandescent, a creature of overpowering brilliance, so magical that they were as captivated by her as they would have been by a rainbow's arc. She caused them to look for her everywhere. They watched for her to appear and when she did found themselves beguiled anew. They waited for her to speak to them, to touch them, for even the briefest look. She spun them in the vortex of her being, and even as they found themselves spellbound they yearned for it to go on. They watched each other like hawks, uncertain of their roles in her plans, of their uses, and of their needs. They fought to learn something of her that would belong only to them and they measured the time they spent with her as if it were gold dust.

Yet they were not entirely without doubts or misgivings. In the secrecy of their most private thoughts they still worried— about her wisdom in selecting them, about her foresight in the quest they had agreed to undertake, and about whether wanting to be near her was sufficient reason for them to go on.

Pe Ell's ruminations were the most intense. He had come on this journey in the first place because the girl intrigued him, because she was different from the others he had been sent to kill, because he wanted to learn as much about her as he could before he used the Stiehl, and because he wanted to discover, too, if this talisman of which she spoke, this Black Elfstone, was as powerful as she believed and if so whether he could make it his own. It had annoyed him when she had insisted on bringing along the brash Highlander and the tall, pale one-armed man. He would have preferred that they go alone, because in truth he believed that he was all she would need. Yet he had held his tongue and remained patient, convinced that the other two would cause him no problem.

But now there was Horner Dees to contend with as well, and there was something about this old man that bothered Pe Ell. It was odd that Dees should trouble him like this; he seemed a worthless old coot. The source of his discomfort, he supposed, was the fact that he was beginning to feel crowded. How many more did the girl intend to add to their little company? Soon, he would be stumbling over cripples and misfits at every turn, none of them worth even the small effort it would eventually require to eliminate them. Pe Ell was a loner; he did not like groups. Yet the girl persisted in swelling their number and all for a rather vague purpose. Her magic seemed almost limitless; she could do things no one else could, not even him. He was convinced that despite her protestations to the contrary her magic was sufficient to guide them into Eldwist. Once there, she had no need of anyone but him. What was the purpose then of including the others?

Two nights earlier, just before the rains had ended, Pe Ell had confronted her out of frustration and discontent, intending to force from her the truth of the matter. Quickening had turned him aside somehow, calmed him, stripping him of his determination to unmask her. The experience had left him perplexed at the ease with which she had manipulated him, and for a time afterward he had thought simply to kill her and be done with it. He had discovered her purpose, hadn't he? Why not do as Rimmer Dall had advised and be finished with this business, forget the Black Elfstone, and leave these fools to chase after it without him? He had decided to wait. Now he was glad he had. For as he considered the irritating presence of Dees and the others, he began to think that he understood their purpose. Quickening had brought them to serve as a diversion, nothing more. After all, what other service could they provide? One's strength was contained in a broken sword, the other's in a broken body. What were such paltry magics compared to that of the Stiehl? Wasn't he the assassin, the master killer, the one whose magic could bring down anything? That was most certainly why she had brought him. She had never said as much, but he knew it was so. Rimmer Dall had been wrong to think she would not recognize what he was. Quickening, with her formidable insight and intuition, would not have missed such an obvious truth. Which was why she had brought him, of course— why she had come to him before any of the others. She needed him to kill Belk; he was the only one who could. She needed the magic of the Stiehl. The others, Dees included, were so much kindling to be thrown into the fire. In the end, she would have to depend on him.

Morgan Leah, if Pe Ell had bothered to ask him, might have agreed. He was the youngest and despite his brash attitude the most insecure. He was still closer to being a boy than a grown man, a fact he was forced to admit to himself if to no one else. He had traveled fewer places and done fewer things. He knew less about practically everything. Almost the whole of his life had been spent in the Highlands of Leah, and although he had found ways to make occupation of his homeland unpleasant for the Federation officials who sought to govern, he had done little else of note. He was hopelessly in love with Quickening and he had nothing to offer her. The Sword of Leah was the weapon she needed in her quest for the Black Elfstone, the talisman whose magic could defeat Uhl Belk. Yet the sword had lost the better part of its magic when it had shattered against the rune-marked doors leading from the Pit, and what remained was insufficient and, worse, unpredictable. Without it, he did not see how he would be of much use in this business. Perhaps Quickening was right when she said he might regain the Sword's magic if he went with her. But what would happen if she were threatened before then? Who among them would protect her? He had only a shattered sword. Walker Boh, without his arm, seemed less formidable than he had before, a man in search of himself. Horner Dees was old and gray. Only Pe Ell, with his still secret magic and enigmatic ways, seemed capable of defending the daughter of the King of the Silver River.

Nevertheless Morgan was determined to continue the quest. He was not entirely certain why. Perhaps it was pride, perhaps a stubborn refusal to give up on himself. Whatever it was, it kept alive a dim hope that somehow he would prove useful to this strange and wondrous girl he had fallen in love with, that he would somehow be able to protect her against whatever threatened, and that with time and patience he would discover a way to restore the magic to the Sword of Leah. He worked diligently at the tasks Horner Dees gave him to aid in outfitting the little company for its journey north, trying a little harder most times than the others. He thought of Quickening constantly, playing with images of her in his mind. She was a gift, he knew. She was the possibility of everything he had always hoped might one day be. It was more than the fact that she was beautiful, or the look or feel or way of her, or that she had rescued him from the Federation prisons or restored the Meade Gardens to the Dwarves of Culhaven. It was what he sensed lay between them, an intangible bond different than that linking her to the others. It was there when she spoke to him, when she called him by his first name as she did not do with the others.

It was there in the way she looked at him. It was something incredibly precious.

He made up his mind that he would not let it go, whatever it was, whatever It might turn out to be. It became, to his surprise and even his joy, the most important thing in his life.

Walker Boh had hold of something as well, but it was not as easily identifiable. As with Morgan's determination to love and Pe Ell's to kill, there was a bond that linked him to Quickening. There was that strange kinship between them, that sharing of magics that gave them insights into each other no one else possessed. Like the Highlander and the assassin, he believed his relationship with her different than that of the others, more personal and important, more lasting. He did not feel love for her as Morgan did and he had no wish to possess her like Pe Ell. What he needed was to understand her magic because in doing so he was convinced he would come to understand his own.

The dilemma lay in determining whether or not this was a good idea. It was not enough that his need was compelling; the deaths of Cogline and Rumor had made it that. He knew that he needed to understand the magic if he were to destroy the Shadowen. But he was frightened still of the consequences of such knowledge. With the magic, there was always a price. He had been intrigued with it since he had discovered he possessed it—and frightened of it as well. Fear and curiosity had pulled him in two directions all his life. It had been so when his father had told him of his legacy, when he had struggled unsuccessfully to make his home with the people of Shady Vale, when Cogline had come to him and offered to teach him how the magic worked, and when he had learned of the existence of the Black Elfstone from the pages of the Druid History and known that the charge given him by the shade of Allanon might be fulfilled. It was always the same. It was so now.

He had worried for a time that he had lost the magic entirely, that it had been destroyed by the poison of the Asphinx. But with the healing of his arm, his sense of himself had returned and with it an awareness that the magic had survived. He had tested it on this journey in little ways. He knew it was there, for example, when something within him reacted to Quickening's presence, to the way she used her own magic to bind Morgan and Pe Ell and himself to her, and to the effect she had on others. It was there, too, in the way he sensed things. He had caught the hesitation in the look Horner Dees gave Pe Ell—just a hint of recognition. He could feel the interaction between the members of the company and Quickening, a sense of the feelings that lay just beneath the surface of the looks and words they exchanged. He had insight, intuition, and foreknowledge in some cases. There was no doubt. The magic was still there.

Yet it was weakened and no longer the formidable weapon it had once been. That gave Walker pause. Here was an opportunity to move away from its influence, from the shadow it cast upon his life, from the legacy of Brin Ohmsford and the Druids, and from everything that had made him the Dark Uncle. If he did not probe, there would be no hurt. The magic would lie dormant, he believed, if it were not stirred. If left alone, it might let him break free.

But without it the Shadowen would be left free as well. And what purpose would it serve to make this journey into Eldwist and confront Uhl Belk if he did not intend to employ the magic? What use would he ever make of the Black Elfstone?

So they prowled within cages of their own making, Walker Boh and Morgan Leah and Pe Ell, suspicious cats with sharp eyes and hungry looks, their minds made up as to what they would do in the days that lay ahead and at the same time still quizzing themselves to make certain. They kept each other's company without ever getting close. Supplies were gathered and packs assembled, and the time passed quickly. Horner Dees seemed satisfied, but he was the only one. The other three chafed against the constraints of their uncertainty, impatience, and doubt despite their resolve to do otherwise, and nothing they could do or think would relieve them. There was a darkness that lay ahead, building upon itself like a stormcloud, and they could not see what waited beyond. They could see it rising up before them like a wall, a coming together of event and circumstance, an explosion of magic and raw strength, a revelation of need and purpose. Black and impenetrable, it would seek to devour them.

When it did, they sensed, not everyone would survive.

THREE DAYS LATER they departed Rampling Steep. They went out at sunrise, the skies thick with clouds that scraped against the mountains and shut away the light. The smell of rain was in the air, and the wind was sharp and chill as it swept down off the peaks. The town slept as they climbed away from it, hunkered down against the dark like a frightened animal, closed and still. A few forgotten oil lamps burned on porches and through the cracks of windows, but the people did not stir. As Walker Boh passed into the rocks he looked back momentarily at the cluster of colorless buildings and was reminded of locust shells, hollow and abandoned and fascinatingly ugly.

The rain began at midday and continued for a week without stopping. At times it slowed to a drizzle but never quit completely. The clouds remained locked in place overhead, thunder rumbled all about, and lightning flashed in the distance. They were cold and wet, and there was nothing they could do to relieve their discomfort. The foothills were forested lower down, but bare at the higher elevations. The wind swept over them unhindered and without the sun's warmth remained frost-edged and chill. Horner Dees set a steady pace, but the company could not travel rapidly while afoot and with mules in tow, and progress was slow. At night they slept beneath canvas shelters that kept the rain off and were able to strip away their wet clothing and wrap themselves in blankets. But there was no wood for a fire and the dampness persisted. They woke cramped and cold each morning, ate because it was necessary, and pressed ahead.

The foothills gave way to mountains after several days, and the path became less certain. The trail they had been following, broad and clear before, disappeared completely. Dees took them into a maze of ridges and defiles, along the rims of broad slides, and around massive boulders that would have dwarfed the buildings of Rampling Steep. The slope steepened dangerously, and they were forced to watch their footing at every turn. The clouds swept downward, filling the air with clinging moisture that sought to envelop them, that twisted about the rocks like some huge, substanceless worm, its skin a damp ooze. Thunder crashed, and it seemed as if they were at its center. Rain descended in torrents. They lost sight of everything that lay behind, and they could not discern what waited ahead.

Without Dees to guide them, they would have been lost. The Charnals swallowed them as an ocean would a stone. Everything looked the same. Cliffs were impassable walls through the mist and rain, canyons dropped into vast chasms of black emptiness, and the mountains spread away in a seemingly endless huddle of snowcapped peaks. It was so cold their skin grew numb. At times the rain turned to sleet and even to snow. They wrapped themselves in great cloaks and heavy boots and trudged on. Through it all Horner Dees remained steady and certain, a great shaggy presence they quickly learned to rely upon. He was at home in the mountains, comfortable despite the forbidding climate and terrain, at peace with himself. He hummed as he went, lost in private reveries of other times and places. He paused now and then to point something out that they would not have otherwise seen, determined that nothing should be missed. That he understood the Charnals was clear from the beginning; that he loved them soon became apparent. He spoke freely of that love, of the mix of wildness and serenity he found there, and of their vastness and permanency. His deep voice rumbled and shook as if filled with the tremors of the storms and the wind. He told stories of what life was like in the Charnals and he gave them a part of himself in the telling.

He gained no converts, however—except, perhaps, for Quickening, who as usual gave no indication of what she was thinking. The other three simply grumbled now and again, kept a studied silence the rest of the time, and fought a hopeless battle to ignore their discomfort. The mountains would never be their home; the mountains were simply a barrier they needed to get past. They labored stoically and waited for the journey to come to an end.

It did not do so. Instead it went on rather as if it were a lost dog searching for its master, the scent firmly in mind, yet distracted by other smells. The rains diminished and finally passed, but the air stayed frosty, the wind continued to buffet them, and the mountains stretched on. The men, the girl, and the animals trudged forward, shoved and pushed by the weather and the land. Midway through the second week Dees said they were starting down, but there was no way of knowing if that were

true; nothing in the rocks and scrub about them indicated it was
so. Wherever they looked, the Charnals were still there.

Twelve days out they were caught in a snowstorm high in
a mountain pass and nearly died. The storm came on them so
quickly that even Dees was caught by surprise. He quickly roped
them together and because there was no shelter to be found in
the pass he was forced to take them through. The air became a
sheet of impenetrable white and everything about them disappeared. Their feet and hands began to freeze. The mules broke
away in terror when part of the slope slid away, braying and
stumbling past the frantic men until they tumbled over the
mountainside and were lost. Only one was saved, and it carried
no food.

They found shelter, survived the storm, and pushed on. Even
Dees, who had shown himself to be the most durable among
them, was beginning to tire. The remaining mule had to be
destroyed the next day when it stepped in a snow-covered crevice and broke its leg. The heavy weather gear had been lost,
and they were reduced to backpacks which contained a meager
portion of food and water, some rope, and not much else.

That night the temperature plummeted. They would have
frozen if Dees had not managed to find wood for a fire. They
sat huddled together all night, pushed close to the flames, rubbing their hands and feet, talking to stay awake, afraid if they
didn't they would die in their sleep. It was an odd tableau, the
five of them settled back within the rocks, crouched close together about the tiny blaze, still wary of one another, protective
of themselves, and forced to share space and time and circumstance. Yet the words they spoke revealed them, not so much
for what was said as for how and when and why. It drew them
together in a strange sort of way, bonding them as not much
else could, and while the closeness that developed was more
physical than emotional and decidedly limited in any case, it at
least left them with a sense of fellowship that had been missing
before.

The weather improved after that, the clouds breaking up
and drifting on, the sun returning to warm the air, and the snow
and rain disappearing at last. The Charnals began to thin ahead
of them, and there was no mistaking the fact that they had

begun their descent. Trees returned, a scattering at first, then whole groves, and finally forests for as far as the eye could see, spilling down into distant valleys. They were able to fish and hunt game for food, to sleep in warm arbors, and to wake dry and rested. Spirits improved.

Then, fifteen days out of Rampling Steep, they arrived at the Spikes.

THEY STOOD FOR a long time on a ridgeline and looked down into the valley. It was nearing midday, the sun bright, the air warm and sweet smelling. The valley was broad and deep and shadowed by mountains that rose about it on either side. It was shaped like a funnel, wide mouth at the south end and narrow at the north where it disappeared into a line of distant hills. Trees grew thick upon its floor, but down its middle a jagged ridgeline rose, and the trees there had suffered a blight that had left them stripped of their foliage, bare trunks and branches jutting upward like the hackles on the back of a cornered animal.

Like spikes, Morgan Leah thought.

He glanced at Horner Dees. "What's down there?" he asked. His attitude toward the old Tracker had changed during the past two weeks. He no longer thought of him as an unpleasant old man. It had taken him longer than Walker Boh, but he had come to recognize that Dees was a thorough professional, better at what he did than anyone the Highlander had ever encountered. Morgan would have liked to be just half as good. He had begun paying attention to what the old man said and did.

Dees shrugged. "I don't know. It's been ten years since I passed this way." Dees, for his part, liked Morgan's enthusiasm and willingness to work. He liked the fact that Morgan wasn't afraid to learn. He narrowed his brows thoughtfully as he returned the other's glance. "I'm just being careful, Highlander."

They studied the valley some more.

"Something is down there," Pe Ell said quietly.

No one disputed him. Pe Ell had remained the most secretive among them, yet they knew enough of him by now to trust his instincts.

"We have to pass this way," Dees said finally, "or skirt the mountains on one side or the other. If we do that, we'll lose a week's time."

They continued their vigil for long moments without speaking, thinking the matter through separately, until finally Horner Dees said, "Let's get on with it."

They worked their way downward, discovering a pathway that led directly toward the center of the valley and the barren ridge. They moved quietly, Dees leading, Quickening behind him, Morgan, Walker, and Pe Ell bringing up the rear. They passed out of sunlight into shadow, and the air turned cool. The valley rose up to meet them and for a time swallowed them up. Then the trail lifted onto the ridgeline, and they found themselves in the midst of the blighted trees. Morgan studied the lifeless skeletons for a time, the blackening of the bark, the wilting of leaves and buds where there were any to be seen at all, and turned instinctively to look at Walker. The Dark Uncle's pale, drawn face lifted, and the hard eyes stared back at him. They were both thinking the same thing. The Spikes had been sickened in the same way as the rest of the land. The Shadowen were at work here, too.

They crossed a band of sunlight that had slipped through a break in the peaks and then dipped downward into a hollow. It was abnormally still there, a pool of silence that magnified the sound of their footsteps as they worked their way ahead. Morgan had grown increasingly edgy, reminded of his encounter with the Shadowen on the journey to Culhaven with the Ohmsfords. His nose tested the air for the rank smell that would warn of the other's presence, and his ears strained to catch even the smallest sound. Dees moved ahead purposefully, Quickening's long hair a slender bit of silver trailing after. Neither exhibited any sign of hesitation. Yet there was tension in all of them; Morgan could feel it.

They passed out of the hollow and back onto the open ridge. For a time they were high enough above the trees that Morgan could see the valley from end to end. They were more than halfway through now, approaching the narrow end of the funnel where the mountains split apart and the trees thinned with the beginning of the hills beyond. Morgan's edginess began to dissipate and he found himself thinking of home, of the Highlands of Leah, and of the countryside he had grown up in. He missed the Highlands, he realized—much more than he would have expected. It was one thing to say that his home no longer belonged to him because the Federation occupied it; it was another to make himself believe it. Like Par Ohmsford, he lived with the hope that things might one day change.

The trail dipped downward again and another hollow appeared, this one shaggy with brush and scrub that had filled the gaps left with the passing of the trees. They moved into it, shoving their way past brambles and stickers, angling for the open spaces where the trail wound ahead. Shadows lay thick across the hollow as the light began to creep westward. The forests about them formed a wall of dark silence.

They had just entered a clearing at the center of the hollow when Quickening suddenly slowed. "Stand still," she said.

They did so instantly, looking first at her, then at the brush all about them. Something was moving. Figures began to detach themselves, breaking their concealment, moving into the light. There were hundreds of them—small, squat creatures with hairy, gnarled limbs and bony features. They looked as if they had grown out of the scrub, so like it were they, and it was only the short pants and weapons that seemed to separate the two. The weapons were formidable—short spears and strangely shaped throwing implements with razor edges. The creatures held them threateningly as they advanced.

"Urdas," Horner Dees said quietly. "Don't move."

No one did, not even Pe Ell who was crouched in much the same way as the creatures who menaced him.

"Who are they?" Morgan asked of Dees, at the same time backing protectively toward Quickening.

"Gnomes," the other said. "With a little Troll thrown in. No one has ever been sure of the exact mix. You don't find them anywhere south of the Charnals. They're Northlanders as much as the Trolls. Tribal like the Gnomes. Very dangerous."

The Urdas were all about them now, closing off any chance of escape. They had thickly muscled bodies with short, powerful legs and long arms, and their faces were blunt and expressionless. Morgan tried to read something of what they might be thinking in their yellow eyes, but failed.

Then he noticed that they were all looking at Quickening.

"What do we do?" he asked Dees in an anxious whisper, worried now.

Dees shook his head.

The Urdas moved to within a dozen feet of the company and stopped. They did not threaten; they did not speak. They simply stood there, watching Quickening for the most part, but waiting as well.

Waiting for what? Morgan asked himself silently.

And at almost the same moment the brush parted, and a golden-haired man stepped into view. Instantly the Urdas dropped to one knee, heads bowed in recognition. The golden-haired man looked at the five beleaguered members of the surrounded company and smiled.

"The King has come," he said brightly. "Long live the King."

CHAPTER

14

OULD YOU LAY down your weapons, please?" the man called out to them cheerfully. "Just put them on the ground in front of you. Don't worry. You can pick them up again in a moment."

He sang:

> *"Nothing given freely is ever given up.*
> *It will be given back to you*
> *Through others' love and trust."*

The five from Rampling Steep stared at him.

"Please?" he said. "It will make things so much easier if you do."

Dees glanced at the others, shrugged, and did as he was asked. Neither Walker nor Quickening carried any weapons. Morgan hesitated. Pe Ell didn't move at all.

"This is only for the purpose of demonstrating your friendship," the man went on encouragingly. "If you don't lay down your weapons, my subjects won't allow me to approach. I'll have to keep shouting at you from over here."

He sang:

> *"High, low, wherever we may go,*
> *I'll have to keep on shouting out to you."*

Morgan, after a sharp glance from Dees, complied. It was hard to tell what Pe Ell might have done if Quickening hadn't

turned to him and whispered, "Do as he says." Pe Ell hesitated
even then before unstrapping his broadsword. The look on his
hard face was unmistakable. The broadsword notwithstanding,
Morgan was willing to bet that Pe Ell still had a weapon concealed on him somewhere.

"Much better," the stranger announced. "Now step back a
pace. There!" He beckoned, and the Urdas came quickly to
their feet. He was a man of average height and build, his movements quick and energetic, and his clean-shaven face handsome
beneath his long blond hair. His blue eyes twinkled. He gestured
at the Urdas and then at the weapons on the ground. The odd-
looking creatures muttered agreeably and heads began to nod.
He sang again, a short piece that the Urdas seemed to recognize,
his voice full and rich, his handsome face beaming. When he
finished, the circle parted to let him pass. He came directly up
to Quickening, bowed low before her, took her hand in his own
and kissed it. "My lady," he said.

He sang:

> "Five travelers crossed field and stream
> And Eastland forests wide.
> They crossed the Charnal Mountain range
> To gain the Northland side.
> Tra-la-la-diddie-oh-day.
>
> Five travelers came from afar
> And entered Urda Land.
> They braved the dangers of the Spikes
> To meet King Carisman.
> Tra-la-la-diddie-oh-day."

He bowed to Quickening again. "That is my name, Lady.
Carisman. And yours?"

Quickening gave it to him and those of her companions as
well. She seemed unconcerned that he knew. "Are you indeed
a king?" she asked.

Carisman beamed. "Oh, yes, Lady. I am king of the Urdas,
lord of all those you now survey and many, many more. To be
honest, I did not seek out the job. It was thrust upon me, as

they say. But come now. Time enough to tell that tale later. Pick up your weapons—carefully, of course. We mustn't alarm my subjects; they are very protective of me. I shall take you to my palace and we shall talk and drink wine and eat exotic fruits and fishes. Come now, come. It shall be a royal feast!"

Dees tried to say something, but Carisman was gone as swiftly as a feather caught by the wind, dancing away, singing some new song, and beckoning them to follow. The Tracker, Morgan, and Pe Ell retrieved their weapons and with Walker and Quickening in tow, started after. Urdas surrounded them on all sides, not pressing in on them, but staying uncomfortably close nevertheless. The odd creatures did not speak, but merely gestured to one another, their eyes shifting from Carisman to the travelers, inquisitive and cautious. Morgan returned the gaze of those closest and tried a smile. They did not smile back.

The gathering went down off the Spikes into the forested valley below, west of the ridgeline where the shadows were deepest. There was a narrow trail that wound through the trees, and the procession followed it dutifully, Carisman in the lead, singing as he went. Morgan had encountered some odd characters in his time, but Carisman struck him as odder than most. He could not help wondering why anyone, even the Urdas, would make this fellow their king.

Dees had dropped back a pace to walk with him, and he asked the old Tracker. "As I said, a tribal folk. Superstitious, like most Gnomes. Believe in spirits and wraiths and other nonsense."

"But Carisman?" Morgan questioned.

Dees shook his head. "I admit I can't figure it. Urdas usually don't want anything to do with outlanders. This one seems goofy as a week-old loon, but he's obviously found some way of gaining their respect. I never heard of him before this. Don't think anyone has."

Morgan peered over the heads of the Urdas at the prancing Carisman. "He seems harmless enough."

Dees snorted. "He probably is. Anyway, it isn't him you have to worry about."

They worked their way west toward the wall of the mountains, daylight fading rapidly now, dusk spreading until the whole of the forestland was enveloped. Morgan and Dees continued to exchange comments, but the other three kept their thoughts to themselves. Walker and Pe Ell were gaunt shadows, Quickening a burst of sunlight. The Urdas filtered out about them, appearing and disappearing in the heavy brush, strung out ahead, behind, and to either side. Carisman's words had suggested that they were guests, but Morgan couldn't shake the feeling that they were really prisoners.

After a little more than a mile, the trail ended at a clearing in which the village of the Urdas was settled. A stockade had been built to protect the village from raiders, and its gates opened now to let the hunters and those they shepherded pass through. A sea of women, children, and old people waited within, bony faced and staring, their voices a low, inaudible buzz. The village consisted of a cluster of small huts and open-sided shelters surrounding a lodge constructed of notched logs and a shingled roof. Trees grew inside the stockade, shading the village and providing supports for treeways and lifts. There were wells scattered about and smokehouses for curing meat. The Urdas, it appeared, had at least rudimentary skills.

The five from Rampling Steep were taken to the main lodge and led to a platform on which a rough-hewn chair draped with a garland of fresh flowers was situated. Carisman seated himself ceremoniously and beckoned his guests to take their places next to him on mats. Morgan and the others did as they were asked, keeping a wary eye on the Urdas, a large number of whom entered as well and took seats on the floor below the platform. When everyone was settled, Carisman came to his feet and sang some more, this time in a tongue that Morgan found impossible to identify. When he was finished, a handful of Urda women began to bring out platters of food.

Carisman sat down. "I have to sing to get them to do anything," he confided. "It is so tedious sometimes."

"What are you doing here anyway?" Horner Dees asked bluntly. "Where did you come from?"

"Ah," Carisman said with a sigh.

He sang:

"There was a young tunesmith from Rampling,
Who felt it was time to take wing.
He decided to hike,
North into the Spikes,
To the Urdas, who made him their king!"

He grimaced. "Not very original, I'm afraid. Let me try again."

He sang:

"Come hither, my fellows, and lady, come nigh,
There are worlds to discover more'n what meets the eye.
Far reaches to travel and people to see,
Wonders to gaze on and lives for to lead,
A million adventures to try.

Come hither, my fellows, and lady, come nigh,
A tunesmith's a man who must sing for to fly.
He searches the byways for songs telling truth,
Seeks out hidden meanings and offers of proof,
Of the reasons for being alive.

Come hither, my fellows, and lady, come nigh,
For life's to be found in the rivers and skies.
In the forests and mountains that lie far away,
In the creatures that frolic and gambol and play,
And beg me my songs to apply"

"Considerably better, don't you think?" he asked them, blue eyes darting from one face to the next, anxiously seeking their approval.

"A tunesmith, are you?" Dees grunted. "From Rampling Steep?"

"Well, by way of Rampling Steep. I was there a day or so once several years back." Carisman looked sheepish. "The rhyme works, so I use it." He brightened. "But a tunesmith, yes. All my life. I have the gift of song and the wit to make use of it. I have talent."

"But why are you here, Carisman?" Quickening pressed.

Carisman seemed to melt. "Lady, chance has brought me to this place and time and even to you. I have traveled the better part of the Four Lands, searching out the songs that would give wings to my music. There is a restlessness in me that will not let me stay in any one place for very long. I have had my chances to do so, and even ladies who wished to keep me— though none was as beautiful as you. But I keep moving. I wandered first west, then east, and finally north. I passed through Rampling Steep and found myself wondering what lay beyond. Finally I set out across the mountains to see."

"And survived?" Horner Dees asked incredulously.

"Just barely. I have a sense of things; it comes from my music, I think. I was well provisioned, for I had traveled in rough country before. I found my way by listening to my heart. I had the good fortune of encountering favorable weather. When I was finally across—exhausted and close to starving, I admit—I was found by the Urdas. Not knowing what else to do, I sang for them. They were enchanted by my music and they made me their king."

"Enchanted by limericks and snippets of rhyme?" Dees refused to let go of his skepticism. "A bold claim, Carisman."

Carisman grinned boyishly. "Oh, I don't claim to be a better man than any other."

He sang:

> "No matter how high or lofty the throne,
> What sits on it is the same as your own."

He brushed the matter aside. "Eat now, you must be very hungry after your journey. There is as much food and drink as you want. And tell me what brings you here. No one from the Southland ever comes this far north—not even the trappers. I never see anyone except Trolls and Gnomes. What brings you?"

Quickening told him that they were on a quest, that they had come in search of a talisman. It was more than Morgan would have revealed, but it seemed to matter little to Carisman, who did not even bother asking what the talisman was or why they needed it but only wanted to know if Quickening could teach him any new songs. Carisman was quick and bright, yet his focus was quixotic and narrow. He was like a child, inquisitive and distracted and full of the wonder of things. He seemed to genuinely need approval. Quickening was the most responsive, so he concentrated his attention on her and included the others in his conversation mostly by implication. Morgan listened disinterestedly as he ate, then noticed that Walker wasn't listening at all, that he was studying the Urdas below the platform. Morgan began studying them as well. After a time he saw that they were seated in carefully defined groups, and that the foremost group consisted of a mixed gathering of old and young men to whom all the others deferred. Chiefs, thought Morgan at once. They were talking intently among themselves, glancing now and then at the six seated on the platform, but otherwise ignoring them. Something was being decided, without Carisman.

Morgan grew nervous.

The meal ended and the empty plates were carried away. There was a sustained clapping from the Urdas, and Carisman rose to his feet with a sigh. He sang once more, but this time the song was different. This time it was studied and intricate, a finely wrought piece of music filled with nuances and subtleties that transcended the tune. Carisman's voice filled the lodge, it soared and swept aside everything that separated it from the senses, reaching down through the body to embrace and cradle the heart. Morgan was astounded. He had never been so affected—not even by the music of the wishsong. Par Ohmsford could capture your feeling for and sense of history in his song, but Carisman could capture your soul.

When the tunesmith was finished, there was utter silence. Slowly he sat down again, momentarily lost in himself, still caught up in what he had sung. Then the Urdas began thumping their hands on their knees approvingly.

Quickening said, "That was beautiful, Carisman."

"Thank you, Lady," he replied, sheepish again. "I have a talent for more than limericks, you see."

The silver-haired girl looked suddenly at Walker. "Did you find it beautiful, Walker Boh?"

The pale face inclined in thought. "It makes me wonder why someone who possesses such abilities chooses to share them with so few." The dark eyes fixed Carisman.

The tunesmith squirmed uncomfortably. "Well." The words suddenly would not seem to come.

"Especially since you said yourself that there is a restlessness in you that will not allow you to stay in one place. Yet you stay here among the Urdas."

Carisman looked down at his hands.

"They will not let you leave, will they?" Walker said quietly.

Carisman looked as if he would sink into the earth. "No," he admitted reluctantly. "For all that I am, a king notwithstanding, I remain a captive. I am allowed to be king only so long as I sing my songs. The Urdas keep me because they believe my song is magic."

"And so it is," Quickening murmured so softly that only Morgan, seated next to her, heard.

"What about us?" Dees demanded sharply. He shifted his bulk menacingly. "Are we captives as well? Have you brought us here as guests or prisoners, King Carisman? Or do you even have a say in the matter?"

"Oh, no!" the tunesmith exclaimed, clearly distraught. "I mean, yes, I have a say in the matter. And, no, you are not prisoners. I need only speak with the council, those men gathered there below us." He pointed to the group that Walker and Morgan had been observing earlier. Then he hesitated as he caught the black look on Pe Ell's face and came hurriedly to his feet. "I shall speak to them at once. If need be, I shall sing. A special song. You shall not remain here any longer than you wish, I promise. Lady, believe me, please. Friends."

He rushed from the platform and knelt next to the members of the Urda council, addressing them earnestly. The five who waited to discover whether they were guests or prisoners looked at one another.

"I don't think he can do anything to help us," Horner Dees muttered.

Pe Ell edged forward. "If I put a knife to his throat they will release us quick enough."

"Or kill us on the spot," Dees replied with a hiss. The two glared at each other.

"Let him have his chance," Walker Boh said, looking calmly at the assemblage. His face was unreadable.

"Yes," Quickening agreed softly. "Patience."

They sat silently after that until Carisman returned, detaching himself from the council, stepping back onto the platform to face them. His face told them everything. "I . . . I have to ask you to stay the night," he said, struggling to get the words out, discomforted beyond measure. "The council wishes to . . . debate the matter a bit. Just a formality, you understand. I simply require a little time . . ."

He trailed off uncertainly. He had positioned himself as far as possible from Pe Ell. Morgan held his breath. He didn't think the distance separating the two offered the tunesmith much protection. He found himself wondering, almost in fascination, what Pe Ell would do, what he *could* in fact do against so many.

He would not find out on this occasion. Quickening smiled reassuringly at Carisman and said, "We will wait."

They were taken to one of the larger huts and given mats and blankets for sleeping. The door was closed behind them, but not locked. Morgan didn't think it mattered either way. The hut sat in the center of the village, and the village was enclosed by the stockade and filled with Urdas. He had taken the trouble of asking Dees about the strange creatures during dinner. Dees had told him that they were a tribe of hunters. The weapons they carried were designed to bring down even the swiftest game. Two-legged intruders, he said, would not prove much of a challenge.

Pe Ell stood looking out through chinks in the hut's mud walls. "They are not going to let us leave," he said. No one spoke. "It doesn't matter what that play-king says, they'll try to keep us. We had better get away tonight."

Dees sat back heavily against one wall. "You make it sound as if leaving were an option."

Pe Ell turned. "I can leave whenever I choose. No prison can hold me."

He said it so matter-of-factly that the others, save Quickening, just stared at him. Quickening was looking off into space. "There is magic in his song," she said.

Morgan remembered her saying something like that before. "Real magic?" he asked.

"Close enough to be called so. I do not understand its source; I am not even certain what it can do. But a form of magic nevertheless. He is more than an ordinary tunesmith."

"Yes," Pe Ell agreed. "He is a fool."

"We might think you one as well if you persist in suggesting we can get out of here without him," Horner Dees snapped.

Pe Ell wheeled on him. There was such rage in his face that Dees came to his feet much more quickly than Morgan would have thought possible. Walker Boh, a dark figure at the hut's far end, turned slowly. Pe Ell seemed to consider his options, then stalked to where Quickening stood looking at him from beside Morgan. It was all the Highlander could do to stand his ground. Pe Ell's black look dismissed him with barely a flicker of a glance and fell instead on the girl.

"What do we need any of them for?" he whispered, his voice a hiss of fury. "I came because you asked me to; I could easily have chosen otherwise."

"I know that," she said.

"You know what I am." He bent close, his gaunt face hawk-like above her, his lean body taut. "You know I have the magic you need. I have all the magic you need. Be done with them. Let us go on alone."

Around him, the room seemed to have turned to stone, the others frozen into statues that could only observe and never act. Morgan Leah's hand moved a fraction of an inch toward his sword, then stopped. He would never be quick enough, he knew. Pe Ell would kill him before he could pull the blade clear.

Quickening seemed completely unafraid. "It is not yet time for you and I, Pe Ell," she whispered back, her voice soothing, cool. Her eyes searched his. "You must wait until it is."

Morgan did not understand what she was saying and he was reasonably certain that Pe Ell didn't either. The narrow face pinched and the hard eyes flickered. He seemed to be deciding something.

"My father alone has the gift of foresight," Quickening said softly. "He has foreseen that I shall have need of all of you when we find Uhl Belk. So it shall be—even though you might wish it otherwise, Pe Ell. Even though."

Pe Ell shook his head slowly. "No, girl. You are wrong. It shall be as I choose. Just as it always is." He studied her momentarily, then shrugged. "Nevertheless, what difference does it make? Another day, another week, it shall all come out the same in the end. Keep these others with you if you wish. At least for now."

He turned and moved away by himself, settling into a darkened corner.

The others stared after him in silence.

NIGHT DESCENDED and the village of the Urdas grew quiet as its inhabitants drifted off to sleep. The five from Rampling Steep huddled within the darkened confines of their shelter, separated from each other by the privacy of their thoughts. Horner Dees slept. Walker Boh was a shapeless bundle in the shadows, unmoving. Morgan Leah sat next to Quickening, neither speaking, eyes closed against the faint light of moon and stars that penetrated from without.

Pe Ell watched them all and raged silently against circumstance and his own stupidity.

What was *wrong* with him, he wondered bleakly? Losing his temper like that, exposing himself, nearly ruining his chance of accomplishing what he had set out to do. He was always in control. *Always!* But not this time, not when he was giving way to frustration and impatience, threatening the girl and all of her precious charges as if he were some schoolboy bully.

He was calm now, able to analyze what he had done, to sift through his emotions and sort out his mistakes. There were many of both. And it was the girl who was responsible, who undid him each time, he knew. She was the bane of his existence, an irritation and an attraction pulling him in opposite directions, a creature of beauty and life and magic that he would never understand until the moment he killed her. His yearning to do so grew stronger all the time, and it was becoming increasingly difficult to restrain. Yet he knew he must if he expected to gain possession of the Black Elfstone. The difficulty was in knowing how to withstand his obsession for her in the meantime. She incensed him, enflamed him, and left him twisted inside like fine wire. Everything that seemed obvious and uncomplicated to him appeared to be just the opposite to her. She insisted on having these fools accompany them—the one-armed man, the Highlander, and the old Tracker. *Shades! Useless foils!* How much longer would he have to tolerate them?

He felt the anger begin again and moved quickly to quell it. *Patience.* Her word, not his—but he had better try it on for size.

He listened to the sounds of the Urdas without, the guards, more than a dozen of them, crouched down in the darkness about the hut. He couldn't see them, but he could feel their presence. His instincts told him they were there. There was no sign of the tunesmith yet—not that it made any difference. The Urdas weren't about to set them free.

So many intrusions on what really matters!

His sharp eyes fixed momentarily on Dees. That old man. He was the worst of the lot, the hardest to figure out. There was something about him . . .

He caught himself again. Be patient. Wait. Events would undoubtedly continue to conspire to force him to do otherwise, but he must overcome them. He must remain in control.

Except that it was so difficult here. This was not his country, these were not his people, and the familiarity of surroundings and behavior, of people and customs that he had always been able to rely upon before was missing here. He was scaling a cliff he had never seen before and the footing was treacherous.

Perhaps staying in control this time would prove impossible.

He shook his head uneasily. The thought stayed with him and would not be dispelled.

It was after midnight when Carisman reappeared. Quickening brought Morgan awake with a touch of her hand to his cheek. He came to his feet and found the others already standing. The door unlatched and opened, and the tunesmith slipped inside.

"Ah, you are awake. Good." He moved at once to stand next

to Quickening, hesitant to speak, uncertain in their presence, like a boy forced to confess something he would prefer to keep secret.

"What has the council decided, Carisman?" Quickening prodded him gently, taking his arm and bringing him about to face her.

The tunesmith shook his head. "Lady, the best and the worst, I am afraid." He glanced at the others. "All of you are free to go when you choose." He turned back to Quickening. "Except you."

Morgan remembered at once the way the Urdas had looked at Quickening, recalling their fascination with her. "Why?" he demanded heatedly. "Why isn't she released as well?"

Carisman swallowed. "My subjects find her beautiful. They think she may be magic, like myself. They . . . wish her to marry me."

"Well now, this is an inventive tale!" Horner Dees snapped, his bristled face screwing up in disbelief.

Morgan seized Carisman by the tunic front. "I have seen the way you look at her, tunesmith! This is your idea!"

"No, no, I swear it is not!" the other cried in dismay, his handsome face contorted in horror. "I would never do such a thing! The Urdas . . ."

"The Urdas couldn't care less about . . ."

"Let him go, Morgan," Quickening said, interrupting, her voice low and steady. Morgan released his grip and stepped back instantly. "He speaks the truth," she said. "This is not his doing."

Pe Ell had shoved forward like a knifeblade. "It doesn't matter whose doing it is." His eyes fixed Carisman. "She goes with us."

Carisman's face went pale, and his eyes shifted anxiously from one determined face to the next. "They won't let her," he whispered, his gaze dropping. "And if they don't, she will end up like me."

He sang:

> "Long ago, in times gone by, there was a fair, fair maiden.
> She wandered fields and forest glens,
> With all the world her haven.

A mighty Lord a fancy took, demanded that she wed him.
When she refused, he took her home,
And locked her in his dungeon.
She pined away for what she'd lost, a life beyond her prison.
She promised everything she owned,
If she could have her freedom.
A fairy imp her plea did hear and quickly broke the door in.
Yet freed her not as she had asked,
But claimed her his possession.

The moral is: If you offer to give up everything,
Be prepared to keep nothing."

Horner Dees threw up his hands in exasperation. "What is it you are trying to say, Carisman?" he snapped.

"That your choices often undo you. That seeking everything sometimes costs you everything." It was Walker Boh who answered. "Carisman thought that in becoming a king he would find freedom and has instead found only shackles."

"Yes," the tunesmith breathed, sadness flooding his finely chiseled features. "I don't belong here any more than Quickening. If you would take her when you go, then you must take me as well!"

"No!" Pe Ell cried instantly.

"Lady," the tunesmith begged. "Please. I have been here for almost five years now—not just several as I claimed. I am caged as surely as that maiden in my song. If you do not take me with you, I shall be kept captive until I die!"

Quickening shook her head. "It is dangerous where we go, Carisman. Far more dangerous than it is here. You would not be safe."

Carisman's voice shook. "It doesn't matter! I want to be free!"

"No!" Pe Ell repeated, circling away like a cat. "Think, girl! Yet another fool to burden us? Why not an army of them, then? Shades!"

Morgan Leah was tired of being called a fool and was about to say so when Walker Boh caught him firmly by the arm and shook his head. Morgan frowned angrily, but gave way.

"What do you know of the country north, Carisman?" Horner Dees asked suddenly, his bulk backing the tunesmith away. "Ever been there?"

Carisman shook his head. "No. It doesn't matter what's there. It is away from here." His eyes darted furtively. "Besides, you have to take me. You can't get away if I don't show you how."

That stopped them. Everyone turned. "What do you mean?" Dees asked cautiously.

"I mean that you will be dead a dozen times over without my help," the tunesmith said.

He sang:

> "Sticks and stones will break your bones,
> But only if the spears don't.
> There's traps and snares placed everywhere,
> And none to warn if I don't.
> Fiddle-de-diddle-de-de."

Pe Ell had him by the throat so quickly that no one else had time to intervene. "You'll tell everything you know before I'm done with you or wish you had!" he threatened furiously.

But Carisman held steady, even forced back as he was, the hard eyes inches from his own. "Never," he gasped. "Unless . . . you agree . . . to take me with you."

His face lost all its color as Pe Ell's hand tightened. Morgan and Horner Dees glanced uncertainly at each other and then at Quickening, hesitating in spite of themselves. It was Walker Boh who stepped in. He moved behind Pe Ell and touched him in a manner they could not see. The gaunt man jerked back, his face rigid with surprise. Walker was quickly by him, his arm coming about Carisman and lifting him away.

Pe Ell whirled, cold rage in his eyes. Morgan was certain he was going to attack Walker, and nothing good could come of that. But Pe Ell surprised him. Instead of striking out, he simply stared at Walker a moment and then turned away, his face suddenly an expressionless mask.

Quickening spoke, diverting them. "Carisman," she said. "Do you know a way out of here?"

Carisman nodded, swallowing to speak. "Yes, Lady."

"Will you show it to us?"

"If you agree to take me with you, yes." He was bargaining now, but he seemed confident.

"Perhaps it would be enough if we helped you escape the village?"

"No, Lady. I would lose my way and they would bring me back again. I must go to wherever it is that you are going—far away from here. Perhaps," he said brightly, "I may turn out to be of some use to you."

When pigs fly, Morgan thought uncharitably.

Quickening seemed undecided, strange for her. She looked questioningly at Horner Dees.

"He's right about the Urdas bringing him back," the old Tracker agreed. "Us, too, if we aren't quick enough. Or smart enough."

Morgan saw Pe Ell and Walker Boh glaring at each other from opposite corners of the hut—harsh, dark wraiths come from exacting worlds, their silent looks full of warning. Who would survive a confrontation between those two? And how could the company survive while they were at such odds?

Then suddenly an idea occurred to him. "Your magic, Quickening!" he burst out impulsively. "We can use your magic to escape! You can control all that grows within the earth. That is enough to make the Urdas give way. With or without Carisman, we have your magic!"

But Quickening shook her head and for an instant she seemed almost to dissolve. "No, Morgan. We have crossed the Charnals into the country of Uhl Belk, and I cannot use my magic again until after we find the talisman. The Stone King must not discover who I am. If I use the magic, he will know."

The hut went silent again. "Who is the Stone King?" Carisman asked, and they all looked at him.

"I say we take him," Horner Dees said finally, bluff and to the point as always. His bulky figure shifted. "If he really can get us out of here, that is."

"Take him," Morgan agreed. He grinned. "I like the idea of having a king on our side as well—even if all he can do is make up songs."

Quickening glanced at the silent antagonists behind her. Pe Ell shrugged his indifference. Walker Boh said nothing.

"We will take you, Carisman," Quickening said, "though I am afraid to guess what this choice might cost you."

Carisman shook his head emphatically. "No price is too great, Lady, I promise you." The tunesmith was elated.

Quickening moved toward the door. "The night flies. Let us hurry."

Carisman held up his hand. "Not that way, Lady."

She turned. "There is another?"

"Indeed." He was beaming mischievously. "As it happens, I am standing on it."

CHAPTER

15

THE SPIKES AND the lands surrounding were filled with tribes of Urdas and other species of Gnomes and Trolls. Since they were all constantly at war with one another, they kept their villages fortified. A lot of hard lessons had been learned over the years, and one of them was that a stockade needed more than one way out. Carisman's bunch had dug tunnels beneath the village that opened through hidden trapdoors into the forests beyond. If the village were threatened by a prolonged siege or by an army of overwhelming numbers, the inhabitants still had a means of escape.

One of the entrances to the tunnels that lay inside the village was under the floor of the hut in which the five from Rampling Steep had been placed. Carisman showed them where it lay, buried a good foot beneath the earthen floor, sealed so tightly by weather and time that it took Horner Dees and Morgan working together to pull it free. It had clearly never seen use and perhaps been all but forgotten. In any case, it was a way out and the company was quick to seize upon it.

"I would feel better about this if we had a light," Dees muttered as he stood looking down into the blackness.

"Here," Walker Boh whispered impatiently, moving forward to take his place. He slipped down into the blackness where the walls of the tunnel shielded his actions and made a snapping motion with his fingers. Light blazed up about his hand, an aura of brightness that had no visible source. The Dark Uncle has at least a little of his magic left, Morgan thought.

"Carisman, is there more than one passage down here?" Walker's voice sounded hollow. The tunesmith nodded. "Then stay close to me and tell me how we are to go."

They dropped into the hole one by one, Carisman following Walker, Quickening and Morgan after them, Dees and Pe Ell last. It was black in the tunnel, even with Walker's light, and the air was close and full of earth smells. The tunnel ran in a straight line, then branched in three directions. Carisman took them right. It branched again, and this time he took them left. They had gone far enough, Morgan thought, that they must be beyond the stockade walls. Still the tunnel continued. Tree roots penetrated its walls, tangling their arms and feet, slowing their progress. At times the roots grew so thick that they had to be severed to permit passage. Even when the passageway was completely clear, it was hard for Horner Dees to fit through. He grunted and huffed and pushed ahead determinedly. Other tunnels intersected and passed on. Dirt and silt from their movements began to choke the air, and it grew hard to breathe. Morgan buried his face in his tunic sleeve and would not allow himself to think about what would happen if the tunnel walls collapsed.

After what seemed an impossibly long time they slowed and then stopped altogether. "Yes, this is it," Morgan heard Carisman say to Walker. He listened as the two struggled to free the trapdoor that sealed them in. They labored in wordless silence, grunting, digging, and shifting about in the cramped space. Morgan and the others crouched down in the blackness and waited.

It took them almost as long to loosen the trapdoor as it had to navigate the tunnel. When it finally fell back, fresh air rushed in and the six scrambled up into the night. They found themselves in a heavily wooded glen, the limbs of the trees grown so thick overhead that the sky was masked almost completely.

They stood wordlessly for a moment, breathing in the clean air, and then Dees pushed forward. "Which way to the Spikes?" he whispered anxiously to Carisman.

Carisman pointed and Dees started away, but Pe Ell reached out hurriedly and yanked him back. "Wait!" he warned. "There will be a watch!"

He gave the old Tracker a withering look, motioned them

all down and melted into the trees. Morgan sank back against the trunk of a massive fir, and the others became vague shadows through the screen of its shaggy limbs. He closed his eyes wearily. It seemed days since he had rested properly. He thought about how good it would feel to sleep.

But a touch on his shoulder brought him awake again almost immediately. "Easy, Highlander," Walker Boh whispered. The tall man slid down next to Morgan, dark eyes searching his own. "You tread on dangerous ground these days, Morgan Leah. You had better watch where you step."

Morgan blinked. "What do you mean?"

Walker's face inclined slightly, and Morgan could see the lines of tension and strain that creased it. "Pe Ell. Stay away from him. Don't taunt him, don't challenge him. Have as little to do with him as you can. If he chooses, he can strike you down faster than a snake in hiding."

The words were spoken in a whisper that was harsh and chilling in its certainty, a brittle promise of death. Morgan swallowed what he was feeling and nodded. "Who is he, Walker? Do you know?"

The Dark Uncle glanced away and back again. "Sometimes I am able to sense things by touching. Sometimes I can learn another's secrets by doing nothing more than brushing up against him. It happened that way when I took Carisman away from Pe Ell. He has killed. Many times. He has done so intentionally rather than in self-defense. He enjoys it. I expect he is an assassin."

A pale hand reached up to hold a startled Morgan in place. "Listen, now. He conceals a weapon of immense power beneath his clothing. The weapon he carries is magic. It is what he uses to kill."

"Magic?" Morgan's voice quivered in surprise despite his effort to keep it steady. His mind raced. "Does Quickening know?"

"She chose him, Highlander. She chose us all. She told us we possessed magic. She told us our magic was needed. Of course, she knows."

Morgan was aghast. "She deliberately brought an assassin? Is this how she plans to regain the Black Elfstone?"

Walker stared fixedly at him. "I think not," he said finally. "But I can't be sure."

Morgan slumped back in disbelief. "Walker, what are we doing here? Why has she brought us?" Walker did not respond. "I don't know for the life of me why I agreed to come. Or maybe I do. I am drawn to her, I admit; I am enchanted by her. But what sort of reason is that? I shouldn't be here. I should be back in Tyrsis searching for Par and Coll."

"We have had this discussion," Walker reminded him gently.

"I know. But I keep questioning myself. Especially now. Pe Ell is an assassin; what do we have to do with such a man? Does Quickening think us all the same? Does she think we are all killers of other men? Is that the use to which we are to be put? I cannot believe it!"

"Morgan." Walker spoke his name to calm him, then eased back against the tree until their heads were almost touching. Something in the way the Dark Uncle's body was bent reminded Morgan for a moment of how broken he had been when they had found him amid the ruins of his cottage at Hearthstone. "There is more to this than what you know," Walker whispered. "Or I, for that matter. I can sense things but not see them clearly. Quickening has a purpose beyond what she reveals. She is the daughter of the King of the Silver River—do not forget that. She has forbidden insight. She has magic that transcends any that we have ever seen. But she is vulnerable as well. She must walk a careful path in her quest. I think that we are here in part, at least, to see that she is able to keep to that path."

Morgan thought it over a moment and nodded, listening to the stillness of the night about them, staring out through the boughs of the old fir at the shadowy figures beyond, picking out Quickening's slim, ethereal form, a slender bit of movement that the night might swallow with no more than a slight shifting of the light.

Walker's voice tightened. "I have been shown a vision of her—a vision as frightening as any I have ever experienced. The vision told me that she will die. I warned her of this before we left Hearthstone; I told her that perhaps I should not come. But she insisted. So I came." He glanced over. "It is the same with all of us. We came because we knew we must. Don't try to understand why that is, Morgan. Just accept it."

Morgan sighed, lost in the tangle of his feelings and his needs, wishing for things that could never be, for a past that was lost and a future he could not determine. He thought of how far things had gone since the Ohmsfords had come to him in Leah, of how different they all now were.

Walker Boh rose, a rustle of movement in the silence. "Remember what I said, Highlander. Stay away from Pe Ell."

He pushed through the curtain of branches without looking back. Morgan Leah stared after him.

PE ELL WAS gone a long time. When he returned, he spoke only to Horner Dees. "It is safe now, old man," he advised softly. "Lead on."

They departed the glen wordlessly, following Carisman as he led them back toward the ridgeline, a silent procession of wraiths in the forest night. No one challenged them, and Morgan was certain that no one would. Pe Ell had seen to that.

It was still dark when they again caught sight of the Spikes. They climbed to the crest of the ridgeline and turned north. Dees moved them forward at a rapid pace, the pathway clear, the spine of the land bare and open to the light of moon and stars, empty save where the skeletal trees threw the spindly shadow of their trunks and branches crosswise against the earth like spiders' webs. They followed the Spikes through the narrow end of the valley's funnel and turned upward into the hills beyond. Daybreak was beginning to approach, a faint lightening of the skies east. Dees moved them faster still. No one had to bother asking why.

By the time the sun crested the mountains they were far enough into the hills that they could no longer see the valley at all. They found a stream of clear water and stopped to drink. Sweat ran down their faces and their breathing was labored.

"Look ahead," Horner Dees said, pointing. A line of peaks jutted into the sky. "That's the north edge of the Charnals, the last we have to cross. There's a dozen passes that lead over and the Urdas can't know which one we will take. It's all rock up there, hard to track anything."

"Hard for you, you mean," Pe Ell suggested unkindly. "Not necessarily hard for them."

"They won't go out of their mountains." Dees ignored him. "Once we're across, we'll be safe."

They hauled themselves back to their feet and went on. The sun climbed into the cloudless sky, a brilliant ball of white fire that turned the earth beneath into a furnace. It was the hottest Morgan could remember it being since he had left Culhaven. The hills rose toward the mountains, and the trees began to give way to scrub and brush. Once Dees thought he saw something moving in the forestlands far behind them, and once they heard a wailing sound that Carisman claimed was Urda horns. But midday came and went, and there was no sign of pursuit.

Then clouds began to move in from the west, a large threatening bank of black thunderheads. Morgan slapped at the gnats that flew against his sweat-streaked face. There would be a storm soon.

They stopped again as midafternoon approached, exhausted from their flight and hungry now as well. There was little to eat, just some roots and wild vegetables and fresh water. Horner Dees went off to scout ahead, and Pe Ell decided to backtrack to a bluff that would let him study the land behind. Walker sat by himself. Carisman began speaking with Quickening again about his music, insistent upon her undivided attention. Morgan studied the tunesmith's handsome features, his shock of blond hair, and his uninhibited gestures and was annoyed. Rather than show what he was feeling, the Highlander moved into the shade of a spindly pine and faced away.

Thunder rumbled in the distance, and the clouds pushed up against the mountains. The sky was a peculiar mix of sunshine and darkness. The heat was still oppressive, a suffocating blanket as it pressed down against the earth. Morgan buried his face in his hands and closed his eyes.

Both Horner Dees and Pe Ell were back quickly. The former advised that the passage that would take them across the last of the Charnals lay less than an hour ahead. The latter reported that the Urdas were after them in force.

"More than a hundred," he announced, fixing them with those hard, unreadable eyes. "Right on our heels."

They resumed their march at once, pressing ahead more quickly, a sense of urgency driving them now that had not been present before. No one had expected the Urdas to catch up with them this fast, certainly not before they were across the mountains. If they were forced to stand and fight here, they knew, they were finished.

They worked their way upward into the rocks, scrambling through huge fields of boulders and down narrow defiles, struggling to keep their footing on slides that threatened to send them careening away into jagged, bottomless fissures. The clouds scraped over the mountain peaks and filled the skies from horizon to horizon. Heavy drops of rain began to fall, spattering against the earth and their heated skin. Darkness settled over everything, an ominous black that echoed with the sound of thunder as it rolled across the empty, barren rock. Dusk was approaching, and Morgan was certain they would be caught in the mountains at nightfall, a decidedly unpleasant prospect. His entire body ached, but he forced himself to keep going. He glanced ahead to Carisman and saw that the tunesmith was in worse shape, stumbling and falling regularly, gasping for breath. Fighting back against his own exhaustion, he caught up with the other man, put an arm about him, and helped him to go on.

They had just gained the head of the pass that Dees had been shepherding them toward when they caught sight of the Urdas. The rugged, shaggy creatures appeared out of the rocks behind them, still more than a mile off, but charging ahead as if maddened, screaming and crying out, shaking their weapons with an unmistakable promise of what they would do with those they were pursuing when they finally caught up with them. The company, after no more than a moment's hesitation, fled into the pass.

The pass was a knife cut that sliced upward through the cliffs, a narrow passageway filled with twists and turns. The company spread out, snaking its way forward. The rain began to fall in earnest now, turning from a slow spattering into a heavy downpour. The footing became slippery, and tiny streams began to flow down out of the rocks, cutting away at the earth beneath their feet. They passed from the shadow of the cliffs and found themselves on a barren slope that angled left into a high-walled defile that was as black as night. Wind blew across the slope in frenzied gusts that sent silt flying into their faces. Morgan let go of Carisman and brought his cloak across his head to protect himself.

It required a tremendous effort to gain the defile, the wind beating against them so hard that they could progress only a little at a time. As they reached the darkened opening, the Urdas reappeared, very close now, come that last mile all too quickly. Darts, lances, and the razor-sharp throwing implements whizzed through the air, falling uncomfortably close. Hurriedly the company charged into the passageway and the protection of its walls.

Here, the rain descended in torrents and the light was almost extinguished. Jagged rock edges jutted out from the floor and walls of the narrow corridor and cut and scraped them as they passed. Time slowed to a standstill in the howl of wind and the roll of the thunder, and it seemed as if they would never get free. Morgan moved ahead to be with Quickening, determined to see that she was protected.

When they finally worked their way clear of the defile, they found themselves standing on a ledge that ran along a seam midway down a towering cliff face that dropped away into a gorge through which the waters of the Rabb raged in a churning, white-foamed maelstrom. Dees took them onto the ledge without hesitation, shouting something back that was meant to be encouraging but was lost in the sound of the storm. The line spread out along the broken seam, Dees in the lead, Carisman, Quickening, Morgan, and Walker Boh following, and Pe Ell last. The rain fell in sheets, the wind tore at them, and the sound of the river's rush was an impenetrable wall of sound.

When the foremost of the Urdas appeared at the mouth of the defile, no one saw. It wasn't until their weapons began to shatter against the rocks about the fleeing company that anyone realized they were there. A dart nicked Pe Ell's shoulder and spun him about, but he kept his footing and struggled on. The others began to advance more quickly, trying desperately to distance themselves from their pursuers, hastening along the ledge, booted feet slipping and sliding dangerously. Morgan glanced back and saw Walker Boh turn and throw something into the storm. Instantly the air flared with silver light. Darts and lances that were hurled into the brightness fell harmlessly away. The Urdas, frightened by the Dark Uncle's magic, fell back into the defile.

Ahead, the ledge broadened slightly and sloped downward. The far side of the mountains came into view, a sweeping stretch of forested hills that ran into the distance until it disappeared into a wall of clouds and rain. The Rabb churned below, cutting back on itself, rushing eastward through the rocks. The trail followed its bend, some fifty feet above its banks, the barren rock giving way to the beginnings of earth and scrub.

Morgan looked around one final time and saw that the Urdas were not following. Either Walker had frightened them off, or Horner Dees had been right about them not leaving their mountains.

He turned back.

In the next instant the entire cliff face was rocked with tremors as parts of it gave way under the relentless pounding of the wind and rain. The trail in front of him, an entire section of earth and rock, disappeared completely and took Quickening with it. She fell back against the slope, grasping. But there was nothing to hold on to, and she began to slide in a cloud of silt and gravel toward the river. Carisman, directly in front of her, almost went, too, but managed to throw himself forward far enough to clutch a tangle of roots from some mountain scrub and was saved.

Morgan was directly behind. He saw that Quickening could not save herself and that there was no one who could reach her. He didn't hesitate. He jumped from the crumbling trail into the gap, hurtling down the mountainside after her, the trailing shouts of his companions disappearing almost instantly. He struck the waters of the Rabb with jarring force, went under, and came up again gasping in shock at the cold. He caught a flash of Quickening's silver hair bobbing in a shower of white foam a few feet away, swam to her, seized her clothing, and drew her to him.

Then the current had them both, and they were swept away.

CHAPTER

16

I T WAS ALL that Morgan Leah could do to keep himself and Quickening afloat in the churning river, and while he might have considered trying to swim for shore if he had been unencumbered he gave no thought of doing so here. Quickening was awake and able to lend some assistance to his effort, but it was mostly Morgan's strength that kept them away from the rocks and out of the deep eddies that might have pulled them down. As it was, the river took them pretty much where it chose. It was swollen by the rains and overflowing its banks, and its surface waters were white with foam and spray against the darkness of the skies and land. The storm continued to rage, thunder rumbling down the canyon depths, lightning flashing against the distant peaks, and the rains falling in heavy sheets. The cliff face they had tumbled down disappeared from view almost immediately and with it their companions. The Rabb twisted and turned through the mountain rocks, and soon they lost any sense of where they were.

After a time a tree that had been knocked into the river washed by and they caught hold of it and let it carry them along. They were able to rest a bit then, clutching the slippery trunk side by side, doing what they could to protect their bodies from the rocks and debris, searching the river and the shoreline for a means to extract themselves. They did not bother trying to speak; they were too exhausted to expend the effort and the river would likely have drowned out their words in any case.

They simply exchanged glances and concentrated on staying together.

Eventually the river broadened, tumbling down out of the peaks into the hill country north, emptying into a forested basin where it pooled before being swept into a second channel that carried it south again. There was an island in the center of the basin, and the tree they were riding ran aground against it, spinning and bumping along its banks. Morgan and Quickening shoved away from their make-do raft and stumbled wearily ashore. Exhausted, their clothing hanging in tatters, they crawled through weeds and grasses for the shelter of the trees that grew there, a cluster of hardwoods dominated by a pair of monstrous old elms. Streams of water eddied and pooled on the ground about them as they fought their way along the island's rain-soaked banks, and the wind howled around their ears. Lightning struck the mainland shore nearby with a thunderous crack, and they flattened themselves while the thunder rolled past.

At last they gained the trees, grateful to discover that it was comparatively dry beneath the canopy of limbs and sheltered against the wind. They stumbled to the base of the largest of the elms and collapsed, sprawling next to each other on the ground, gasping for breath. They lay without moving for a time, letting their strength return. Then, after exchanging a long look that conveyed their unspoken agreement to do so, they pulled themselves upright against the elm's rough trunk and sat shoulder to shoulder, staring out into the rain.

"Are you all right?" Morgan asked her.

It was the first thing either of them had said. She nodded wordlessly. Morgan checked himself carefully for injuries, and finding none, sighed and leaned back—relieved, weary, cold, and unexplainably hungry and thirsty, too, despite being drenched. But there was nothing to eat or drink, so there was no point in thinking about it.

He glanced over again. "I don't suppose you could do anything about a fire, could you?" She shook her head. "Can't use magic of any kind, huh? Ah, well. Where's Walker Boh when you need him?" He tried to sound flippant and failed. He sighed.

She reached over and let her hand rest on his, and it warmed him despite his discomfort. He lifted his arm and placed it about her shoulders, easing her close. It brought them both some small measure of warmth. Her silver hair was against his cheek, and her smell was in his nostrils, a mix of earth and forest and something else that was sweet and compelling.

"They won't find us until this storm ends," she said.

Morgan nodded. "If then. There won't be any trail to follow. Just the river." He frowned. "Where are we, anyway? North or south of where we went into the river?"

"North and east," she advised.

"You know that?"

She nodded. He could feel her breathing, the slight movement of her body against him. He was shivering, but having her close like this seemed to make up for it. He closed his eyes.

"You didn't have to come after me," she said suddenly. She sounded uncomfortable. "I would have been all right."

He tried unsuccessfully to stifle a yawn. "I was due for a bath."

"You could have been hurt, Morgan."

"Not me. I've already survived attacks by Shadowen, Federation soldiers, Creepers, and other things I'd just as soon forget about. A fall into a river isn't going to hurt me."

The wind gusted sharply, howling through the branches of the trees, and they glanced skyward to listen. When the sound died away, they could hear the rush of the river again as it pounded against the shoreline.

Morgan hunched down within his sodden clothing. "When this storm blows itself out, we can swim to the mainland, get off this island. The river is too rough to try it now. And we're too tired to make the attempt in any case. But that's all right. We're safe enough right here. Just a little damp."

He realized that he was talking just to be doing something and went still again. Quickening did not respond. He could almost feel her thinking, but he hadn't a clue as to what she was thinking about. He closed his eyes again and let his breathing slow. He wondered what had become of the others. Had they managed to make it safely down that trail or had the collapse of the ledge trapped Walker and Pe Ell on the upper slope? He tried to envision the Dark Uncle and the assassin trapped with each other and failed.

It was growing dark now, dusk chasing away what little light remained, and shadows began to spread across the island in widening black stains. The rains were slowing, the sounds of thunder and wind receding in the distance, and the storm was beginning to pass. The air was not cooling as Morgan had expected, but instead was growing warm again, thick with the smells of heat and humidity. Just as well, he thought. They were too cold as it was. He thought about what it would feel like to be warm and dry again, to be secluded in his hunting lodge in the Highlands with hot broth and a fire, seated on the floor with the Ohmsfords, swapping lies of what had never been.

Or seated perhaps with Quickening, saying nothing because speaking wasn't necessary and just being together was enough, just touching . . .

The ache of what he was feeling filled him with both longing and fear. He wanted it to continue, wanted it to be there always, and at the same time he did not understand it and was certain that it would betray him.

"Are you awake?" he asked her, anxious suddenly for the sound of her voice.

"Yes," she replied.

He took a deep breath and breathed out slowly. "I have been thinking about why I'm here," he said. "Wondering about it since Culhaven. I haven't any magic anymore—not really. All I ever had was contained in the Sword of Leah, and now it's broken and what magic remains is small and probably won't be of much help to you. So there's just me, and I . . ." He stopped. "I just don't know what it is that you expect of me, I guess."

"Nothing," she answered softly.

"Nothing?" He could not keep the incredulity from his voice.

"Only what you are able and wish to give," she answered vaguely.

"But I thought that the King of the Silver River said . . ." He stopped. "I thought that your father said I was needed. Isn't that what you said? That he told you we were needed, all of us?"

"He did not say what it was that you were to do, Morgan. He told me to bring you with me in my search for the talisman and that you would know what to do, that we all would." She lifted away slightly and turned to look at him. "If I could tell you more, I would."

He scowled at her, frustrated with the evasiveness of her answers, with the uncertainty he was feeling. "Would you?"

She almost smiled. Even rain-streaked and soiled by the river's waters, she was the most beautiful woman he had ever seen. He tried to speak and failed. He simply sat there, mute and staring.

"Morgan," she said softly. "My father sees things that are hidden from all others. He tells me what I must know of these things, and I trust him enough to believe that what he tells me is enough. You are here because I need you. It has something to do with the magic of your Sword. I was told by my father and told you in turn that you will have a chance to make the Sword whole again. Perhaps then it will serve us both in a way we cannot foresee."

"And Pe Ell?" he pressed, determined now to know everything.

"Pe Ell?"

"Walker says he is an assassin—that he, too, carries a weapon of magic, a weapon that kills."

She studied him for a long moment before she said, "That is true."

"And he is needed, too?"

"Morgan." His name was spoken as a caution.

"Tell me. Please."

Her perfect features lowered into shadow and lifted again, filled with sadness. "Pe Ell is needed. His purpose, as yours, must reveal itself."

Morgan hesitated, trying to decide what to ask next, desperate to learn the truth but unwilling to risk losing her by crossing into territory in which he was not welcome.

His face tightened. "I would not like to think that I had been brought along for the same reason as Pe Ell," he said finally. "I am not like him."

"I know that," she said. She hesitated, wrestling with some inner demon. "I believe that each of you—Walker Boh included—is here for a different reason, to serve a different purpose. That is my sense of things."

He nodded, anxious to believe her, finding it impossible not to do so. He said, "I just wish I understood more."

She reached up and touched his cheek with her fingers, letting them slide down his jaw to his neck and lift away again. "It will be all right," she said.

She lay back again, folding into him, and he felt his frustration and doubt begin to fade. He let them go without a fight, content just to hold the girl. It was dark now, daylight gone into the west, night settled comfortably over the land. The storm had moved east, and the rains had been reduced to mist. The clouds were still thick overhead but empty now of thunder, and a blanket of stillness lay across the land as if to cover a child preparing for sleep. In the invisible distance the Rabb continued to churn, a sullen, now sluggish flow that lulled and soothed with its wash. Morgan peered into the night without seeing, finding its opaque curtain lowered to enclose him, to wrap about him as if an invisible shroud. He breathed the clean air and let his thoughts drift free.

"I could eat something," he mused after a time. "If there were anything to eat."

Quickening rose without speaking, took his hands in hers, and pulled him up after her. Together, they walked into the darkness, picking their way through the damp grasses. She was able to see as he could not and led the way with a sureness that defied him. After a time she found roots and berries that they could eat and a plant that when properly cut yielded fresh water. They ate and drank what they found, crouched silently next to each other, saying nothing. When they were finished, she took him out to the riverbank where they sat in silence watching the Rabb flow past in the dim, mysterious half-light, a murky sheen of movement against the darker mainland.

A light breeze blew into Morgan's face, filled with the rich scent of flowers and grasses. His clothes were still damp, but he was no longer chilled. The air was warm, and he felt strangely light-headed.

"It is like this sometimes in the Highlands," he told her. "Warm and filled with earth smells after a summer storm, the nights so long you think they might never end and wish they wouldn't." He laughed. "I used to sit up with Par and Coll Ohmsford on nights like this. I'd tell them that if a man wished hard enough for it, he could just . . . melt into the darkness like a snowflake into skin, just disappear into it, and then stay as long as he liked."

He glanced over to judge her reaction. She was still beside him, lost in thought. He brought his knees up to his chest and wrapped his arms around them. A part of him wanted to melt into this night so that it would go on forever, wanted to take her with him, away from the world about them. It was a foolish wish.

"Morgan," she said finally, turning. "I envy you your past. I have none."

He smiled. "Of course you . . ."

"No," she interrupted him. "I am an elemental. Do you know what that means? I am not human. I was created by magic. I was made from the earth of the Gardens. My father's hand shaped me. I was born full-grown, a woman without ever having been a child. My purpose in being has been determined by my father, and I have no say in what that purpose is to be. I am not saddened by this because it is all I know. But my instincts, my human feelings, tell me there is more, and I wish that it were mine as it has been yours. I sense the pleasure you take in remembering. I sense the joy."

Morgan was speechless. He had known she was magic, that she possessed magic, but it had never occurred to him that she might not be . . . He caught himself. Might not be what? As real as he was? As human? But she was, wasn't she? Despite what she thought, she was. She felt and looked and talked and acted human. What else was there? Her father had fashioned her in the image of humans. Wasn't that enough? His eyes swept over her. It was enough for him, he decided. It was more than enough.

He reached out to stroke her hand. "I admit I don't know anything about how you were made, Quickening. Or even anything about elementals. But you are human. I believe that. I would know if you weren't. As for not having any past, a past is nothing more than the memories you acquire, and that's something you're doing right now, acquiring memories—even if they're not the most pleasant in the world."

She smiled at the idea. "The ones of you will always be pleasant, Morgan Leah," she said.

He held her gaze. Then he leaned forward and kissed her, just a brief touching of their lips, and lifted away. She looked at him through those black, penetrating eyes. There was fear mirrored there, and he saw it.

"What frightens you?" he asked.

She shook her head. "That you make me feel so much."

He felt himself treading on dangerous ground, but went forward nevertheless. "You asked me before why I came after you when you fell. The truth is, I had to. I am in love with you."

Her face lost all expression. "You cannot be in love with me," she whispered.

He smiled bleakly. "I'm afraid I have no choice in the matter. This isn't something I can help."

She looked at him for a long time and then shuddered. "Nor can I help what I feel for you. But while you are certain of your feelings, mine simply confuse me. I do not know what to do with them. I have my father's purpose to fulfill, and my feelings for you and yours for me cannot be allowed to interfere with that."

"They don't have to," he said, taking her hands firmly now. "They can just be there."

Her silver hair shimmered as she shook her head. "I think not. Not feelings such as these."

He kissed her again and this time she kissed him back. He breathed her in as if she were a flower. He had never felt so certain about anything in his life as how he felt about her.

She broke the kiss and drew away. "Morgan," she said, speaking his name as if it were a plea.

They rose and went back through the damp grasses to the sheltering trees, to the elm where they had waited out the storm earlier, and sank down again by its roughened trunk. They held each other as children might when frightened and alone, protecting against nameless terrors that waited just beyond the bounds of their consciousness, that stalked their dreams and threatened their sleep.

"My father told me as I left the Gardens of my birth that there were things he could not protect me against," she whispered. Her face was close against Morgan's, soft and smooth, her breath warm. "He was not speaking of the dangers that would threaten me—of Uhl Belk and the things that live in Eldwist or even of the Shadowen. He was speaking of this."

Morgan stroked her hair gently. "There isn't much of anything that you can do to protect against your feelings."

"I can close them away," she answered.

He nodded. "If you must. But I will tell you first that I am not capable of closing my feelings away. Even if my life depended on it, I could not do so. It doesn't make any difference who you are or even what you are. Elemental or something else. I don't care how you were made or why. I love you, Quickening. I think I did from the first moment I saw you, from the first words you spoke. I can't change that, no matter what else you ask of me. I don't even want to try."

She turned in his arms, and her face lifted to find his. Then she kissed him and kept on kissing him until everything around them disappeared.

WHEN THEY WOKE the next morning the sun was cresting the horizon of a cloudless blue sky. Birds sang and the air was warm and sweet. They rose and walked to the riverbank and found the Rabb slow-moving and placid once more.

Morgan Leah looked at Quickening, at the curve of her body, the wild flow of her silver hair, the softness of her face, and the smile that came to his face was fierce and unbidden. "I love you," he whispered.

She smiled back at him. "And I love you, Morgan Leah. I will never love anyone again in my life the way I love you."

They plunged into the river. Rested now, they swam easily the distance that separated the island from the mainland. On gaining the far shore, they stood together for a moment looking back, and Morgan fought to contain the sadness that welled up within him. The island and their solitude and last night were lost to him except as memories. They were going back into the world of Uhl Belk and the Black Elfstone.

They walked south along the river's edge for several hours before encountering the others. It was Carisman who spied them first as he wandered the edge of a bluff, and he cried out in delight, summoning the rest. Down the steep slope he raced, blond hair flying, handsome features flushed. He skidded the last several yards on his backside, bounded up, and raced to intercept them. Throwing himself at Quickening's feet, he burst into song.

He sang:

> "Found are the sheep who have strayed from the fold,
> Saved are the lambs from the wolves and the cold,
> Wandering far, they have yet found their way,
> Now, pray we all, they are here for to stay
> Tra-la-la, tra-la-la, tra-la-la!"

It was a ridiculous song, but it made Morgan smile nevertheless. In moments, the others had joined them as well, gaunt Pe Ell, his dark anger at having lost Quickening giving way to relief that she had been found again; bearish Horner Dees, gruffly trying to put the entire incident behind them; and the enigmatic Walker Boh, his face an inscrutable mask as he complimented Morgan on his rescue. All the while, an exuberant Carisman danced and sang, filling the air with his music.

When the reunion finally concluded the company resumed its journey, moving away from the Charnals and into the forestlands north. Somewhere far ahead, Eldwist waited. The sun climbed into the sky and hung there, brightening and warming the lands beneath as if determined to erase all traces of yesterday's storm.

Morgan walked next to Quickening, picking his way through the slowly evaporating puddles and streams. They didn't speak. They didn't even look at each other. After a time, he felt her hand take his.

At her touch, the memories flooded through him.

CHAPTER

17

THEY WALKED NORTH for five days through the country beyond the Charnals, a land that was green and gently rolling, carpeted by long grasses and fields of wildflowers, dotted by forests of fir, aspen, and spruce. Rivers and streams meandered in silver ribbons from the mountains and bluffs, pooling in lakes, shimmering in the sunlight like mirrors, and sending a flurry of cooling breezes from their shores. It was easier journeying here than it had been through the mountains; the terrain was far less steep, the footing sure, and the weather mild. The days were sun-filled, the nights warm and sweet smelling. The skies stretched away from horizon to horizon, broad and empty and blue. It rained only once, a slow and gentle dampening of trees and grasses that passed almost unnoticed. The spirits of the company were high; anticipation of what lay ahead was tempered by renewed confidence and a sense of well-being. Doubts lay half-forgotten in the dark grottos to which they had been consigned. There was strength and quickness in their steps. The passage of the hours chipped away at uncertain temperaments with slow, steady precision and like a stonecutter's chisel etched and shaped until the rough edges vanished and only the smooth surface of agreeable companionship remained.

Even Walker Boh and Pe Ell called an unspoken truce. It could never be argued reasonably that they showed even the remotest inclination toward establishing a friendship, but they kept apart amiably enough, each maintaining a studied indifference to the other's presence. As for the remainder of the company, constancy was the behavioral norm. Horner Dees continued reticent and gruff, Carisman kept them all entertained with stories and songs, and Morgan and Quickening feinted and boxed with glances and gestures in a lovers' dance that was a mystery to everyone but them. There was in all of them, save perhaps Carisman, an undercurrent of wariness and stealth. Carisman, it seemed, was incapable of showing more than one face. But the others were circumspect in their dark times, anxious to keep their doubts and fears at bay, hopeful that some mix of luck and determination would prove sufficient to carry them through to the journey's end.

The beginning of that end came the following day with a gradual change in the character of the land. The green that had brightened the forests and hills south began to fade to gray. Flowers disappeared. Grasses withered and dried. Trees that should have been fully leafed and vibrant were stunted and bare. The birds that had flown in dazzling bursts of color and song just a mile south were missing here along with small game and the larger hoofed and horned animals. It was as if a blight had fallen over everything, stripping the land of its life.

They stood at the crest of a rise at midmorning and looked out over the desolation that stretched away before them.

"Shadowen," Morgan Leah declared darkly.

But Quickening shook her silvery head and replied, "Uhl Belk."

It grew worse by midday and worse still by nightfall. It was bad enough when the land was sickened; now it turned completely dead. All trace of grasses and leaves disappeared. Even the smallest bit of scrub disdained to grow. Trunks lifted their skeletal limbs skyward as if searching for protection, as if beseeching for it. The country appeared to have been so thoroughly ravaged that nothing dared grow back, a vast wilderness gone empty and stark and friendless. Dust rose in dry puffs from their boots as they stalked the dead ground, the earth's poisoned breath. Nothing moved about them, above them, beneath them—not animals, not birds, not even insects. There was no water. The air had a flat, metallic taste and smell to it. Clouds began to gather again, small wisps at first, then a solid bank that hung above the earth like a shroud.

They camped that night in a forest of deadwood where the air was so still they could hear each other breathe. The wood would not burn, so they had no fire. Light from a mix of elements in the earth reflected off the ceiling of clouds and cast the shadows of the trees across their huddled forms in clinging webs.

"We'll be there by nightfall tomorrow," Horner Dees said as they sat facing each other in the stillness. "Eldwist."

Dark stares were his only reply.

Uhl Belk's presence became palpable after that. He huddled next to them there in the fading dusk, slept with them that night, and walked with them when they set out the following day. His breath was what they breathed, his silence their own. They could feel him beckoning, reaching out to gather them in. No one said so, but Uhl Belk was there.

By midday, the land had turned to stone. It was as if the whole of it, sickened and withered and gone lifeless, had been washed of every color but gray and in the process petrified. It was all preserved perfectly, like a giant piece of sculpture. Trunks and limbs, scrub and grasses, rocks and earth—everything as far as the eye could see had been turned to stone. It was a starkly chilling landscape that despite its coldness radiated an oddly compelling beauty. The company from Rampling Steep found itself entranced. Perhaps it was the solidity that drew them, the sense that here was something lasting and enduring and somehow perfectly wrought. The ravages of time, the changing of the seasons, the most determined efforts of man—it seemed as if none of these could affect what had been done here.

Horner Dees nodded and the members of the company went forward.

A haze hung about them as they walked across this tapestry of frozen time, and it was only with difficulty that they were able, after several hours, to distinguish something else shimmering in the distance. It was a vast body of water, as gray as the land they passed through, blending into its bleakness, a backdrop merging starkly into earth and sky as if the transition were meaningless.

They had reached the Tiderace.

Twin peaks came into view as well, jagged rock spirals that lifted starkly against the horizon. It was apparent that the peaks were their destination.

Now and again the earth beneath them rumbled ominously, tremors reverberating as if the land were a carpet that some giant had taken in his hands and shaken. There was nothing about the tremors to indicate their source. But Horner Dees knew something. Morgan saw it in the way his bearded face tightened down against his chest and fear slipped into his eyes.

After a time the land about them began to narrow on either side and the Tiderace to close about, and they were left with a shrinking corridor of rock upon which to walk. The corridor was taking them directly toward the peaks, a ramp that might at its end drop them into the sea. The temperature cooled, and there was moisture in the air that clung to their skin in faint droplets. Their booted feet were strangely noiseless as they trod the hard surface of the rock, climbing steadily into a haze. Soon they became a line of shadows in the approaching dusk. Dees led, ancient, massive, and steady. Morgan followed with Quickening, the tall Highlander's face lined with wariness, the girl's smooth and calm. Handsome Carisman hummed beneath his breath while his gaze shifted about him as rapidly as a bird's. Walker Boh floated behind, pale and introspective within his long cloak. Pe Ell brought up the rear, his stalker's eyes seeing everything.

The ramp began to break apart before them, an escarpment out of which strange rock formations rose against the light. They might have been carvings of some sort save for the fact that they lacked any recognizable form. Like pillars that had been hewn apart by weather's angry hand over thousands of years, they jutted and angled in bizarre shapes and images, the mindless visions of a madman. The company passed between them, anxious in their shadow, and hurried on.

They arrived finally at the peaks. There was a rift between them, a break so deep and narrow that it appeared to have been formed by some cataclysm that had split apart what had once been a single peak to form the two. They loomed to either side, spirals of rock that thrust into the clouds as if to pin them fast.

Beyond, the skies were murky and misted, and the waters of the Tiderace crashed and rumbled against the rocky shores.

Horner Dees moved ahead and the others followed until all had been enveloped in shadows. The air was chill and unmoving in the gap, and the distant shrieks of seabirds echoed shrilly. What sort of creatures besides those of the sea could possibly live here? Morgan Leah wondered uneasily. He drew his sword. His whole body was rigid with tension, and he strained to catch some sign of the danger he sensed threatening them. Dees was hunched forward like an animal at hunt, and the three behind the Highlander were ghosts without substance. Only Quickening seemed unaffected, her head held high, her eyes alert as she scanned the rock, the skies, the gray that shrouded everything.

Morgan swallowed against the dryness in his throat. *What is it that waits for us?*

The walls of the break seemed to join overhead, and they were left momentarily in utter blackness with only the thin line of the passageway ahead to give them reassurance that they had not been entombed. Then the walls receded again, and the light returned. The rift opened into a valley that lay cradled between the peaks. Shallow, rutted, choked with the husks of trees and brush and with boulders many times the size of any man, it was an ugly catchall for nature's refuse and time's discards. Skeletons lay everywhere, vast piles of them, all sizes and shapes, scattered without suggestion of what creatures they might once have been.

Horner Dees brought them to a halt. "This is Bone Hollow," he said quietly. "This is the gateway to Eldwist. Over there, across the Hollow, through the gap in the peaks, Eldwist begins."

The others crowded forward for a better look. Walker Boh stiffened. "There's something down there."

Dees nodded. "Found that out the hard way ten years ago," he said. "It's called a Koden. It's the Stone King's watchdog. You see it?"

They looked and saw nothing, even Pe Ell. Dees seated himself ponderously on a rock. "You won't either. Not until it has you. And it won't matter much by then, will it? You could ask any of those poor creatures down there if they still had tongues and the stuff of life to use them."

Morgan scuffed his boot on a piece of deadwood as he listened. The deadwood was heavy and unyielding. Stone. Morgan looked at it as if understanding for the first time. Stone. Everything underfoot, everything surrounding them, everything for as far as the eye could see—it was all stone.

"Kodens are a kind of bear," Dees was saying. "Big fellows, live up in the cold regions north of the mountains, keep pretty much to themselves. Very unpredictable under any conditions. But this one?" He made his nod an enigmatic gesture. "He's a monster."

"Huge?" Morgan asked.

"A *monster*," Dees emphasized. "Not just in size, Highlander. This thing isn't a Koden anymore. You can recognize it for what it's supposed to be, but just barely. Belk did something to it. Blinded it, for one thing. It can't see. But its ears are so sharp it can hear a pin drop."

"So it knows we are here," Walker mused, edging past Dees for a closer look at the Hollow. His eyes were dark and introspective.

"Has for quite a while, I'd guess. It's down there waiting for us to try to get past."

"If it's still there at all," Pe Ell said. "It's been a long time since you were here, old man. By now it might be dead and gone."

Dees looked at him mildly. "Why don't you go on down there and take a look?"

Pe Ell gave him that lopsided, chilling smile.

The old Tracker turned away, his gaze shifting to the Hollow. "Ten years since I saw it and I still can't forget it," he whispered. He shook his grizzled head. "Something like that you don't ever forget."

"Maybe Pe Ell is right; maybe it is dead by now," Morgan suggested hopefully. He glanced at Quickening and found her staring fixedly at Walker.

"Not this thing," Dees insisted.

"Well, why can't we see it if it's all that big and ugly?" Carisman asked, peering cautiously over Morgan's shoulder.

Dees chuckled. His eyes narrowed. "You can't see it because it looks like everything else down there—like stone, all gray and hard, just another chunk of rock. Look for yourself. One of those mounds, one of those boulders, something that's down there that doesn't look like anything—that's it. Just lying there, perfectly still. Waiting."

"Waiting," Carisman echoed.

He sang:

> "Down in the valley, the valley of stone.
> The Koden lies waiting amid shattered bone.
> Amid all its victims,
> Within its gray home,
> The Koden lies waiting to make you its own."

"Be still, tunesmith," Pe Ell said, a warning edge to his voice. He scowled at Dees. "You got past this thing before, if we're to believe what you tell us. How?"

Dees laughed aloud. "I was lucky, of course! I had twelve other men with me and we just walked right in, fools to the last. It couldn't get us all, not once we started running. No, it had to settle for three. That was going in. Coming out, it only got one. Of course, there were just two of us left by then. I was the one it missed."

Pe Ell stared at him expressionlessly. "Like you said, old man—lucky for you."

Dees rose, as bearish as any Koden Morgan might have imagined, sullen and forbidding when he set his face as he did now. He faced Pe Ell as if he meant to have at him. Then he said, "There's all sorts of luck. Some you've got and some you make. Some you carry with you and some you pick up along the way. You're going to need all kinds of it getting in and out of Eldwist. The Koden, he's a thing you wouldn't want to dream about on your worst night. But let me tell you something. After you see what else is down there, what lies beyond Bone Hollow, you won't have to worry about the Koden anymore. Because the dreams you'll have on your worst nights after that will be concerned with other things!"

Pe Ell's shrug was scornful and indifferent. "Dreams are for frightened old men, Horner Dees."

Dees glared at him. "Brave words now."

"I can see it," Walker Boh said suddenly.

His voice was soft, almost a whisper, but it silenced the others instantly and brought them about to face him. The Dark Uncle was staring out across the broken desolation of the Hollow, seemingly unaware that he had spoken.

"The Koden?" Dees asked sharply. He came forward a step.

"Where?" Pe Ell asked.

Walker's gesture was obscure. Morgan looked anyway and saw nothing. He glanced at the others. None of them appeared to be able to find it either. But Walker Boh was paying no attention to any of them. He seemed instead to be listening for something.

"If you really can see it, point it out to me," Pe Ell said finally, his voice carefully neutral.

Walker did not respond. He continued to stare. "It feels . . ." he began and stopped.

"Walker?" Quickening whispered and touched his arm.

The pale countenance shifted away from the Hollow at last and the dark eyes found her own. "I must find it," he said. He glanced at each of them in turn. "Wait here until I call for you."

Morgan started to object, but there was something in the other man's eyes that stopped him from doing so.

Instead, he watched silently with the others as the Dark Uncle walked alone into Bone Hollow.

THE DAY WAS STILL, the air windless, and nothing moved in the ragged expanse of the Hollow save Walker Boh. He crossed the broken stone in silence, a ghost who made no sound and left no mark. There were times in the past few weeks when he had thought himself little more. He had almost died from the poison of the Asphinx and again from the attack of the Shadowen at Hearthstone. A part of him had surely died with the loss of his arm, another part with the failure of his magic to cure his sickness. A part of him had died with Cogline. He had been empty and lost on this journey, compelled to come by his rage at the

Shadowen, his fear at being left alone, and his wish to discover the secrets of Uhl Belk and the Black Elfstone. Even Quickening, despite ministering to his needs, both physical and emotional, had not been strong enough to give him back to himself. He had been a hollow thing, bereft of any sense of who and what he was supposed to be, reduced to undertaking this quest in the faint hope that he would discover his purpose in the world.

And now, here within this vast, desolate stretch of land, where fears and doubts and weaknesses were felt most keenly, Walker Boh thought he had a chance to come alive again.

It was the presence of the Koden that triggered this hope. Until now the magic had been curiously silent within him, a worn and tired thing that had failed repeatedly and at last seemed to have given up. To be sure, it was there still to protect him when he was threatened, to frighten off the Urdas when they came too close, to deflect their hurled weapons. Yet this was a poor and sorry use when he remembered what it had once been able to do. What of the empathy it had given him with other living things? What of his sense of emotions and thoughts? What of the knowledge that had always just seemed to come to him? What of the glimpses of what was to be? All of these had deserted him, gone away as surely as his old world, his life with Cogline and Rumor at Hearthstone. Once he had wished it would be so, that the magic would disappear and he would be left in peace, a man like any other. But it had become increasingly clear to him on this journey, his sense of who and what he was heightened by the passing of Cogline and his own physical and emotional devastation, that his wish had been foolish. He would never be like other men, and he would never be at peace without the magic. He could not change who and what he was; Cogline had known that and told him so. On this journey he had discovered it was true.

He needed the magic.

He required it.

Now he would test whether or not he could still call it his own. He had sensed the presence of the Koden before Pe Ell had. He had sensed what it was before Horner Dees had described it. Amid the strewn rock, hunched down and silent, it had reached out to him as creatures once had when he approached. He could feel the Koden call to him. Walker Boh was not certain of its purpose in doing so, yet knew he must respond. It was more than the creature's need that he was answering; it was also his own.

He moved directly through the jumble of boulders and petrified wood to where the Koden waited. It had not moved, not even an inch, since the company had arrived. But Walker knew where it lay concealed nevertheless, for its presence had brought the magic awake again. It was an unexpected, exhilarating, and strangely comforting experience to have the power within him stir to life, to discover that it was not lost as he had believed, but merely misplaced.

Or suppressed, he chided harshly. Certainly he had worked hard at denying it even existed.

Mist curled through the rocks, tendrils of white that formed strange shapes and patterns against the gray of the land. Far distant, beyond and below the peaks and the valley they cradled, Walker could hear the crash of the ocean waters against the shoreline, a dull booming that resonated through the silence. He slowed, conscious now that the Koden was just ahead, unable to dispel entirely his apprehension that he was being lured to his doom, that the magic would not protect him, and he would be killed. Would it matter if he was? he wondered suddenly. He brushed the thought away. Within, he could feel the magic burning like a fire stoked to life.

He came down from between two boulders into a depression, and the Koden rose up before him, cat-quick. It seemed to materialize out of the earth, as if the dust that lay upon the rock had suddenly come together to give it form. It was huge and old and grizzled, three times his own size, with great shaggy limbs and ragged yellow claws that curled down to grip the rock. It lifted onto its hind legs to show itself to him, and its twisted snout huffed and opened to reveal a glistening row of teeth. Sightless white eyes peered down at him. Walker stood his ground, his life a slender thread that a single swipe of one huge paw could sever. He saw that the Koden's head and body had been distorted by some dark magic to make the creature appear more grotesque and that the symmetry of shape that had once given grace to its power had been stripped away.

Speak to me, thought Walker Boh.

The Koden blinked its eyes and dropped down so close that the huge muzzle was no more than inches from the Dark Uncle's face. Walker forced himself to meet the creature's empty gaze. He could feel the hot, fetid breath.

Tell me, he thought.

There was an instant's time when he was certain that he was going to die, that the magic had failed him entirely, that the Koden would reach out and strike him down. He waited for the claws to rend him, for the end to come. Then he heard the creature answer him, the guttural sounds of its own language captured and transformed by the magic.

Help me, the Koden said.

A flush of warmth filled Walker. Life returned to him in a way he found difficult to describe, as if he had been reborn and could believe in himself again. A flicker of a smile crossed his face. The magic was still his.

He reached out slowly with his good arm and touched the Koden on its muzzle, feeling beneath his fingertips more than the roughness of its hide and fur, finding as well the spirit of the creature that was trapped beneath. The Dark Uncle read its history in that touch and felt its pain. He stepped close to study its massive, scarred body, no longer frightened by its size or its ugliness or its ability to destroy. It was a prisoner, he saw—frightened, angered, bewildered, and despairing in the manner of all prisoners, wanting only to be free.

"I will make you so," Walker Boh whispered.

He looked to discover how the Koden was bound and found nothing. Where were the chains that shackled it? He circled the beast, testing the weight and texture of the air and earth. The great head swung about, seeking to follow him, the eyes fixed and staring. Walker completed his circuit and stopped, frowning. He had found the invisible lines of magic that the Stone King had fashioned and he knew what it would take to set the creature free. The Koden was a prisoner of its mutation. It would have to be changed back into a bear again, into the creature it had been, and the stigma of Uhl Belk's touch cleansed. But Walker hadn't the magic for that. Only Quickening possessed such power, magic strong enough to bring back the

Meade Gardens out of the ashes of the past, to restore what once was, and she had already said she could not use her magic again until the Black Elfstone was recovered. Walker stood looking at the Koden helplessly, trying to decide if there were anything he could do. The beast shifted to face him, its great, ragged bulk a shimmer of rock dust against the landscape.

Walker reached out once more, and his fingers rested on the Koden's muzzle. His thoughts became words. *Let us pass, and we will find a way to set you free.*

The Koden stared out at him from the prison of its ruined body, sightless eyes hard and empty. *Go,* it said.

Walker lifted his hand away long enough to beckon his companions forward, then placed it back again. The others of the company came hesitantly, Quickening in the lead, then Morgan Leah, Horner Dees, Carisman, and Pe Ell. He watched them pass without comment, his arm outstretched, his hand steady. He caught a glimpse of what was in their eyes, a strange mix of emotions, understanding in Quickening's alone, fear and awe and disbelief in the rest. Then they were past. They walked from the rubble of Bone Hollow to the break in the cliffs beyond which they turned to wait for him.

Walker took his hand away and saw the Koden tremble. Its mouth gaped wide, and it appeared to cry out soundlessly. Then it wheeled away from him and lumbered down into the rocks.

"I won't forget," the Dark Uncle called after it.

The emptiness he felt made him shiver. Pulling his cloak close, he walked from the Hollow.

Morgan and the others, all but Quickening, asked Walker Boh when he reached them what had happened. How had he managed to charm the Koden so that they could pass? But the Dark Uncle refused to answer their questions. He would say only that the creature was a prisoner of the Stone King's magic and must be freed, that he had given his promise.

"Since you made the promise, you can worry about keeping it," Pe Ell declared irritably, anxious to dismiss the matter of the Koden now that the danger was behind them.

"We'll have trouble enough keeping ourselves free of the Stone King's magic," Horner Dees agreed.

Carisman was already skipping ahead, and Morgan suddenly found himself facing Walker Boh with no reply to give. It was Quickening who spoke instead, saying, "If you gave your promise, Walker Boh, then it must be kept." She did not, however, say how.

They turned away from Bone Hollow and passed into the break that opened out through the peaks to the Tiderace. The passage was shadowed and dark in the fading afternoon light, and a chill, rough-edged wind blew down off the slopes of the cliffs above, thrusting into them like a giant hand, shoving them relentlessly ahead. The sun had dropped into the horizon west, caught in a web of clouds that turned its light scarlet and gold. The smell of salt water, fish, and kelp filled the air, sharp and pungent.

Morgan glanced back once or twice at Walker Boh, still amazed at how he had been able to keep the Koden from attacking them, to walk right up to it as he had and touch it without coming to harm. He recalled the stories of the Dark Uncle, of the man before he had suffered the bite of the Asphinx and the loss of Cogline and Rumor, the man who had taught Par Ohmsford not to be frightened of the power of the Elven magic. Until now, he had thought Walker Boh crippled by the Shadowen attack on Hearthstone. He pursed his lips thoughtfully. Perhaps he had been wrong. And if wrong about Walker, why not wrong about himself as well? Perhaps the Sword of Leah could be made whole again and his own magic restored. Perhaps there was a chance for all of them, just as Quickening had suggested.

The defile opened suddenly before them, the shadows which had caged them brightened into gray, misty light, and they peeked through a narrow window in the cliffs. The Tiderace spread away below in an endless expanse, its waters roiling and white-capped as they churned toward the shoreline. The company moved ahead, back into the shadows. The trail they followed began to descend, to twist and turn through the rocks, damp and treacherous from the mist and the ocean spray. The walls split apart once more, this time forming ragged columns of stone that permitted brief glimpses of sky and sea. Underfoot, the rock was loose, and it felt as if everything was on the verge of breaking up.

Then they turned onto a slide so steep that they were forced to descend sitting and found themselves in a narrow passageway that curled ahead into a tunnel. They stooped to pass through, for the tunnel was filled with jagged rock edges. At its far end, the walls fell away, and the tunnel opened onto a shelf that lifted toward the sky. The company moved onto the shelf, discovered a pathway, and climbed to where it ended at a rampart formed of stone blocks.

They stood at the edge of the rampart and looked down. Morgan felt his stomach lurch. From where they stood, the land dropped away to a narrow isthmus that jutted into the sea. Connected to the isthmus was a peninsula, broad and ragged about the edges, formed all of cliffs against which the waters of the Tiderace pounded relentlessly. Atop the cliffs sat a city of towering stone buildings. The buildings were not of this time, but of the old world, of the age before the Great Wars destroyed the order of things and the new races were born. They rose hundreds of feet into the air, smooth and symmetrical and lined with banks of windows that yawned blackly against the gray light. Everything was set close together, so that the city had the look of a gathering of monstrous stone obelisks grown out of the rock. Seabirds wheeled and circled about the buildings, crying out mournfully in the failing light.

"Eldwist," Horner Dees announced.

Far west, the sun was sinking into the waters of the sea, losing its brightness and its color with the coming of night, the scarlet and gold fading to silver. The wind howled down off the cliffs behind them in a steady crescendo, and it felt as if even the pinnacle of rock on which they stood was being shaken. They huddled together against its thrust and the fall of night and watched raptly as Eldwist turned black with shadow. The wind howled through the city as well, down the canyons of its streets, across the drops of its cliffs. Morgan was chilled by the sound of it. Eldwist was empty and dead. There was only its stone, hard and unyielding, unchanging and fixed.

Horner Dees called out to them over the sound of the wind

as he turned away. He led them back to where a set of steps had been carved into the cliff face to lead downward to the city. The steps ran back against the wall, angling through the crevices and nooks, twisting once more into shadow. Night closed about as they descended, the sun disappearing, the stars winking into view in a sky that was clear and bright. Moonlight reflected off the Tiderace, and Morgan could see the stark, jutting peaks of the city lifting off the rocks. Mist rose in gauzy trailers, and Eldwist took on a surrealistic look—as if come out of time and legend. The seabirds flew away, the sound of their cries fading into silence. Soon there was only the roll of the waves as they slapped against the rocky shores.

At the base of the stairs they found an alcove sheltered by the rocks. Horner Dees brought them to a halt. "No sense in trying to go farther," he advised, sounding weary. The wind did not reach them here, and he talked in a normal tone of voice. "Too dangerous to try to go in at night. There's a Creeper down there . . ."

"A Creeper?" Morgan, who had been examining bits of grass and shrub that were perfectly preserved in stone, looked up sharply.

"Yes, Highlander," the other continued. "A thing that sweeps the streets of the city after dark, gathering up any stray bits and pieces of living refuse . . ."

A rumbling within the earth cut short the rest of what he was about to say. The source of the rumbling was Eldwist, and the members of the company turned quickly to look. The city stood framed against the night sky, all black save for where the light reflected off the stone. It was larger and more forbidding when viewed from below, Morgan thought as he peered into its shadows. More impenetrable . . .

Something huge surged out of the dark recesses he searched, a thing of such monstrous size as to give the momentary illusion that it dwarfed even the buildings. It rose from between the monoliths as if kindred, all bulk and weight, but long and sinewy like a snake as well, stone blocks turned momentarily liquid to reshape and re-form. Then jaws gaped wide—Morgan could see the jagged edge of the teeth clearly against the backdrop of the moon—and they heard a horrifying cry, like a strangled cough.

The earth reverberated with that cry, and the members of the company from Rampling Steep dropped into a protective crouch—all but Quickening, who remained erect, as if she alone were strong enough to withstand this nightmare.

A second later it was gone, dropping away as quickly and smoothly as it had come, the rumble of its passing hanging faintly in the air.

"That was no Creeper," Morgan whispered.

"And it wasn't here ten years ago either," a white-faced Horner Dees whispered back. "I'd bet on it."

"No," Quickening said softly, turning to face them now. Her companions came slowly to their feet. "It is newly born," she said, "barely five years old. It is still a baby."

"A baby!" Morgan exclaimed incredulously.

Quickening nodded. "Yes, Morgan Leah. It is called the Maw Grint." She smiled sadly. "It is Uhl Belk's child."

CHAPTER

18

THE SIX THAT FORMED the company from Rampling Steep spent the remainder of the night huddled in the shelter of the cliffs, crouched silently in the darkness, hidden away from the Maw Grint and whatever other horrors lay in wait within Eldwist. They built no fire—indeed, there was no wood to be gathered for one—and they ate sparingly of their meager food. Food and water would be a problem in the days to come since there was little of either to be found in this country of stone. Fish would become the staple of their diet; a small stream of rainwater that tumbled down off the rocks behind would quench their thirst. If the fish proved elusive or the stream dried up, they would be in serious trouble.

No one slept much in the aftermath of the Maw Grint's appearance. For a long while no one even tried. Their uneasiness was palpable as they waited out the night. Quickening used that time to relate to the others what she knew of the Stone King's child.

"My father told me of the Maw Grint when he sent me forth from his Gardens," she began, her black eyes distant as she spoke, her silver hair gleaming brightly in the moonlight. They sat in a half-circle, their backs settled protectively against the rocks, their eyes shifting warily from time to time toward the forbidding shadow of the city. All was silent now, the Maw Grint disappeared as mysteriously as it had come, the seabirds gone to roost, and the wind faded away.

Quickening's voice was carefully hushed. "As I am the child

of the King of the Silver River, so the Maw Grint is the child of Uhl Belk. Both of us were made by the magic, each to serve a father's needs. We are elementals, beings of earth's life, born out of the soil and not of woman's flesh. We are much the same, the Maw Grint and I."

It was such a bizarre statement that it was all Morgan Leah could do to keep from attacking it. He refrained from doing so only because there was nothing to be gained by voicing an objection and diverting the narration from its intended course.

"The Maw Grint was created to serve a single purpose," Quickening went on. "Eldwist is a city of the old world, one which escaped the devastation of the Great Wars. The city and the land on which it is settled mark the kingdom of Uhl Belk, his haven, his fortress against all encroachment of the world beyond. For a while, they were enough. He was content to burrow in his stone, to remain secluded. But his appetite for power and his fear of losing it were constant obsessions. In the end, they consumed him. He became convinced that if he did not change the world without, it would eventually change him. He determined to extend his kingdom south. But to do so he would have to leave the safety of Eldwist, and that was unacceptable. Like my father, his magic grows weaker the farther he travels from its source. Uhl Belk refused to take such a risk. Instead, he created the Maw Grint and sent his child in his place.

"The Maw Grint," she whispered, "once looked like me. It was human in form and walked the land as I do. It possessed a part of its father's magic as I do. But whereas I was given power to heal the land, the Maw Grint was given power to turn it to stone. A simple touching was all it took. By touching it fed upon the earth and all that lived and grew upon it, and everything was changed to stone.

"But Uhl Belk grew impatient with his child, for the transformation of the lands surrounding was not proceeding quickly enough to suit him. Surrounded by the waters of the Tiderace, which his magic could not affect, he was trapped upon this finger of land with only the way south open to him and only the Maw Grint to widen the corridor. The Stone King infused his child with increasingly greater amounts of his own magic, anxious for quicker and more extensive results. The Maw Grint began to change form as a result of the infusions of power, to transform itself into something more adaptable to what its father demanded. It became molelike. It began to tunnel into the earth, finding that change came quicker from beneath than above. It grew in size as it fed and changed again. It became a massive slug, a burrowing worm of immense proportions."

She paused. "It also went mad. Too much power, too quickly fed, and it lost its sanity. It evolved from a thinking, reasoning creature to one so mindless that it knew only to feed. It swept into the land south, burrowing deeper and deeper. The land changed quickly then, but the Maw Grint changed more quickly yet. And then one day Uhl Belk lost control of his child completely."

She glanced at the dark silhouette of the city and back again. "The Maw Grint began to hunt its father when it was not feeding off the land, aware of the power that the Stone King possessed and eager to usurp it. Uhl Belk discovered that he had fashioned a two-edged sword. On the one hand, the Maw Grint was tunneling into the Four Lands and changing them to stone. On the other, it was tunneling beneath Eldwist as well, searching for a way to destroy him. So powerful had the Maw Grint grown that father and son were evenly matched. The Stone King was in danger of being dispatched by his own weapon."

"Couldn't he simply change his son back again?" Carisman asked, wide-eyed. "Couldn't he use the magic to restore him to what he was?"

Quickening shook her head. "Not by the time he thought to do anything. By then it was too late. The Maw Grint would not let itself be changed—even though, my father tells me, a part of it realized the horror of what it had become and longed for release. That part, it seems, was too weak to act."

"So now it burrows the earth and sorrows over its fate," the tunesmith murmured.

He sang:

> "Made in the shape of humankind,
> To serve the Stone King's dark design,
> The Maw Grint tunnels 'neath the land,

A horror wrought by father's hand,
Become a monster out of need,
With no true hope of being freed,
It hunts."

"Hunts, indeed," Morgan Leah echoed. "Hunts us, probably."

Quickening shook her head. "It isn't even aware that we exist, Morgan. We are too small, too insignificant to catch its attention. Until we choose to use magic, of course. Then it will know."

There was a studied silence. "What was it doing when we saw it tonight?" Horner Dees asked finally.

"Crying out what it feels—its rage, frustration, hatred, and madness." She paused. "Its pain."

"Like the Koden, it is a prisoner of the Stone King's magic," Walker Boh said. His sharp eyes fixed the girl. "And somehow Uhl Belk has managed to keep that magic his own, hasn't he?"

"He has gained possession of the Black Elfstone," she replied. "He went out from Eldwist long enough to steal it from the Hall of Kings and replace it with the Asphinx. He took it back into his keep and used it against his child. Possession of the Elven magic shifted the balance of power back to Uhl Belk. Even the Maw Grint was not powerful enough to defeat the Stone."

"A magic that can negate the power of other magics," Pe Ell recited thoughtfully. "A magic that can turn them to its own use."

"The Maw Grint still threatens its father, but it cannot overcome the Elfstone. It lives because Uhl Belk wishes it to continue feeding on the land, to continue transforming living matter to stone. The Maw Grint is a useful, if dangerous, slave. By night, it tunnels the earth. By day, it sleeps. Like the Koden, it is blind—made so by the magic and the nature of what it does, burrowing within darkness, seldom seeing light." She looked again toward the city. "It will probably never know we are here if we are careful."

"So all we have to do is to steal the Elfstone." Pe Ell smiled. "Steal the Elfstone and let father and son feed on each other.

Nothing complicated about it, is there?" He glanced sharply at Quickening. "Is there?"

She met his gaze without flinching, but did not answer. Pe Ell's smile turned cold as he leaned back into the shadows.

There was a moment of strained silence, and then Morgan said to Horner Dees, "What about this Creeper you mentioned?"

Dees was looking sullen as well. He leaned forward ponderously, his eyes narrowed suspiciously. "Maybe the girl can tell you more about it than me," he answered quietly. "I've a feeling there's a great deal she knows and isn't telling."

Quickening's face was devoid of expression, coldly perfect as she faced the old Tracker. "I know what my father told me, Horner Dees—nothing more."

"King of the Silver River, Lord of the Gardens of Life," Pe Ell growled from the shadows. "Keeper of dark secrets."

"As you say, there is a Creeper in the city of Eldwist," Quickening went on, ignoring Pe Ell, her eyes on Dees. "Uhl Belk calls it the Rake. The Rake has been there for many years, a scavenger of living things serving the needs of its master. It comes out after dark and sweeps the streets and walkways of the city clean. We will have to be careful to avoid it when we go in."

"I've seen it at work," Dees grunted. "It took half a dozen of us on the first pass ten years ago, another two shortly after. It's big and quick." He was remembering now, and his anger at Quickening seemed to dissipate. He shook his head doubtfully. "I don't know. It hunts you out, finds you, finishes you. Goes into the buildings if it needs to. Did then, anyway."

"So it would be wise for us to find the Black Elfstone quickly, wouldn't it?" Pe Ell whispered.

They fell silent then, and after a few moments drifted away from each other into the shadows. They spent the remainder of the night attempting to sleep. Morgan dozed, but never for long. Walker was seated at the edge of the rocks watching the city when the Highlander nodded off and was still there when he woke. They were all tired and disheveled—all but Quickening. She stood fresh and new in the weak light of the morning sunrise, as beautiful as in the moment of their first meeting. Morgan found himself disturbed by the fact. In that way, certainly, she was something more than ordinary. He watched her, then looked quickly away when she turned toward him, afraid she would see. It bothered him to think that there might be differences between them after all and, worse, that those differences might be substantial.

They ate breakfast with the same lack of interest with which they had eaten dinner the night before. The land was a stark and ominous presence that watched them through hidden eyes. Fog hung across the peninsula, rising from the cliffs on which the city rested to the peaks of the tallest towers, giving the impression that Eldwist sat within the clouds. The seabirds had returned, gulls, puffins, and terns, wheeling and calling out above the dark waters of the Tiderace. A dampness had settled into the air with dawn's coming, and the water beaded on the faces of the six.

Having been warned by Dees of what lay ahead, they gathered rainwater from pools high in the rocks, wrapped what little food they still possessed against the wet, and set out to cross the isthmus.

It took them longer than they expected. The distance was short, but the path was treacherous. The rock was crisscrossed with crevices, its surface broken apart by ancient upheavals, damp and slick beneath their feet from the ocean's constant pounding. The wind gusted sharply, blowing spray in their faces, chilling their skin. Progress was slow. The sun remained a hazy white ball behind the low-hanging clouds, and the land ahead was filled with shadows. Eldwist rose before them, a cluster of vague shapes, dark and forbidding and silent. They watched it grow larger as they neared, rising steadily into the bleak skies, the sound of the wind echoing mournfully through its canyons.

Sometimes, as they walked, they could feel a rumbling beneath their feet, far distant, but ominously familiar. Apparently the Maw Grint didn't always sleep during the daylight hours.

Midday neared. The isthmus, which had been so narrow at points that the rock dropped away to either side of where they walked into dark cauldrons and whirlpools, broadened finally onto the peninsula and the outskirts of the city. The cliffs on which Eldwist had been built lifted before them, and the company was forced to climb a broad escarpment. Winding through a jumble of monstrous boulders along a pathway littered with loose stone, with their feet constantly sliding out from under them, they struggled resolutely ahead.

It took them the better part of two hours to gain the heights. By then the sun was already arcing west.

They paused to catch their breath at the city's edge, standing together at the end of a stone street that ran between rows of towering, vacant-windowed buildings and narrowed steadily until it disappeared into mist and shadow. Morgan Leah had never seen a city such as this one, the buildings flat and smooth, all constructed of stone, all symmetrically arranged like squares on a checkerboard. Broken rock littered the street, but beneath the rubble he could see the hard, even surface. It seemed as if it ran on forever, as if it had no end, a long, narrow corridor that disappeared only when the mist grew too thick for the eye to penetrate.

They began to walk it, a slow and cautious passage, spreading out along its corridor, listening and watching like cats at hunt. Other streets bisected it from out of the maze of tall buildings, these in turn disappearing right and left into shadow. There were no protective walls about Eldwist, no watchtowers or battlements or gates, only the buildings and the streets that fronted them. There appeared to be nothing living there. The streets and buildings came and went as the company pressed deeper, and the only sounds were those of the ocean and the wind and the seabirds. The birds flew overhead, the only sign of movement, winging their way past the caps of the buildings, down into the streets, across intersections and catwalks. Some roosted on the windowledges high overhead. After a time, Morgan saw that some of those he had believed roosting had been turned to stone.

Much of the debris that lay strewn about had once been something other than stone although most of it was not unrecognizable. Odd-looking poles stood at every street corner, and it was possible to surmise that these might have once been some form of lamps. The carcass of a monstrous carriage lay on its side against one building, a machine whose bones had been

703

stripped of their flesh. Scattered pieces of engines had survived time and weather, gear wheels and cylinders, flywheels and tanks. All had turned to stone. There were no growing things, no trees or shrubs, or even the smallest blade of grass.

They looked inside a few of the buildings and found the rooms cavernous and empty. Stairways ran upward into the stone shells, and they climbed one set all the way to the top so that they could look out across Eldwist and orient themselves. It was impossible to tell much, even as little as where the city began and ended. Clouds and mist obscured everything, revealing only glimpses of facings and roofs in a sea of swirling gray.

They did sight an odd dome at Eldwist's center, a structure unlike the tall obelisks that formed the balance of the city, and they chose to explore it next.

But coming down again into the streets they lost their sense of direction and turned the wrong way. They walked for the better part of an hour before deciding they had made a mistake; then they were forced to climb the stairs of another building in order to regain their bearings.

While they were doing so, the sun set. None of them had been paying any attention to how quickly the daylight had been fading.

When they emerged from their climb they were stunned to find the city in darkness.

"We'd better find a place to hide right now," Horner Dees admonished, glancing around uneasily. "The Rake will be out soon if it isn't already. It if finds us unprotected . . ."

He didn't have to finish the thought. For a moment they stared wordlessly at one another. None of them had bothered looking for a nighttime shelter.

Then Walker Boh said, "There was a small building several streets back with no windows on the lower levels, a small entry, a maze of corridors and rooms inside—like a warren."

"Safe enough for the moment," Pe Ell muttered, already heading down the street.

They began to backtrack through the city. It was so dark by now that they could barely find their way. The buildings loomed to either side in a wall made more solid by the thickening of the mist. The seabirds had again gone to roost, and the sound of ocean and wind had faded into a distant lull. The city was uncomfortably still.

Beneath them, the stone shell of the earth rumbled and shook.

"Something's awake and hungry," Pe Ell murmured and smiled coldly at Carisman.

The tunesmith laughed nervously, his handsome face white and drawn.

He sang:

> "Slip away, slip away, slip away home,
> Run for your bedcovers, no more to roam,
> Steal away quick from the things of the night,
> Keep yourself hidden and well out of sight."

They crossed an intersection that was flooded with pale moonlight that had found a break in the clouds and was streaming down in a splash of white fire. Pe Ell stopped abruptly, bringing the rest of them up short as well, listened for a moment, shook his head, and moved on. The rumbling beneath them came and went, sometimes close, sometimes far, never in one spot at any given time, seemingly all around. Morgan Leah peered ahead through mist and shadows. Was this the same street they had been on before? It didn't look quite the same . . .

There was a loud click. Pe Ell, still in the lead, catapulted backward, careening into Horner Dees and Quickening, who were closest, the force of his thrust knocking them both from their feet. They tumbled down in a heap, inches from the edge of a gaping hole that had opened in the street.

"Get back against the buildings!" he snapped, leaping to his feet and sweeping Quickening up with him as he raced from the chasm's edge.

The others were only a step behind. Another section of the street gave way, this one behind them, falling with a crash into blackness. The rumbling beneath crescendoed into a roar that deafened them, and they could hear the passing of something massive below. Morgan crouched deep within a shadowed alcove, pressed up against the stone wall, fighting to keep from screaming against his fear. The Maw Grint! He saw Horner

Dees next to him, his bearded face all but invisible as it turned away into the shadows. The thunder of the monster moving below peaked and then began to fade. Seconds later, it was gone.

The members of the little company came out of hiding then, one after another, white-faced and staring. They moved cautiously into the street, then started violently as the holes in the streets closed up again, the fallen sections lifting smoothly back into place.

"Trapdoors!" Pe Ell spat. There was fear and loathing in his face. Morgan caught sight of something white in his hand, a knife of some sort, its metal bright and shining. Then it was gone.

Pe Ell released Quickening from his grasp and turned away from them, moving back along the street, this time staying well up on the walkways that fronted the buildings. Wordlessly, eyes darting from one pool of shadows to the next, the others followed. They hastened down the walkway in single file, crossed the next intersection the same way, and hurried on. The rumbling sounded again, but far away now. The streets about them were quiet and empty once more.

Morgan Leah was still shaking. Those trapdoors had been placed there either to snare intruders or to let the Maw Grint into the city. Probably both. He swallowed against the dryness in his throat. They had been careless back there. They had better not be so again.

A heavy wall of mist blocked the way forward. Pe Ell hesitated as they approached it, then stopped. He looked back at Walker Boh, his eyes hard and penetrating. Some unspoken communication passed between them, a shared look that Morgan found almost feral. Walker glanced right. Pe Ell, after a moment's hesitation, turned that way.

They walked ahead, slowly now, listening to the silence again. The mist was all about them, fallen out of the clouds, seeped up from the stone, and come out of nowhere to envelop them. They moved with their hands stretched out to brush against the walls of the buildings for reassurance. Pe Ell was studying the path ahead carefully, aware now that the city was probably one vast collection of traps, that any part of the stone could drop away beneath their feet without warning.

Ahead, the mist began to clear.

Morgan thought he heard something, then decided he hadn't heard it, that he had sensed it instead. What?

They emerged from the shadow of the building next to them and the answer was waiting. The Rake stood in the center of the street, a huge, splay-legged metal monster with dozens of tentacles and feelers, pincers that gaped from its maw, and a whiplike tail. It was a Creeper like the one the outlaws of the Movement had faced at the Jut, comprised of metal and flesh, a hybrid nightmare of machine and insect. Except that this one was much bigger.

And much quicker. It came for them so fast that it was almost upon them before they had begun to scatter. Its wide, bent legs skittered like a centipede's. Tentacles swept out in a flurry of movement, the sound of metal scraping against stone a horrid rasp. The tentacles caught Dees and Carisman almost instantly, wrapping about them as they tried to flee. Pe Ell shoved Quickening across the walkway toward an open doorway, feinted as if to rush the monster, then darted away. Morgan drew his sword and would have attacked, having lost all sense of what he was doing at the thought of Quickening in danger, when Walker Boh caught hold of him and threw him back against the wall.

"Get inside!" The Dark Uncle cried, motioning toward a set of massive stone doors that gaped open.

Then Walker Boh threw back his cloak and his single arm came up. The Rake was almost on top of him when the arm lowered and a sheet of white light ignited. Morgan shrank back against the wall, blinded. He heard a harsh shriek and realized it was the Creeper. His vision cleared enough to see the creature's metal arms windmilling violently and caught a glimpse of Carisman and Horner Dees running from it. Then he was seized in an iron grip and thrust back through the black opening of the doorway.

It was Pe Ell who had yanked him inside. Quickening was already there. The white light of Walker's magic still burned through the darkness without, and they could hear the Rake thrashing against the building, the force of its attack so violent that stone chips were scattered everywhere. Walker burst into

view, Carisman and Horner Dees running before him, stunned
but freed. They stumbled across the floor and fell, then regained
their feet instantly as the Rake tore the giant entry doors from
their hinges, ripped the stone facing apart and shoved inside.

There was a broad staircase leading upward behind them,
and they bolted for it. The Rake came after them, staggering
slightly. If Walker's magic had done nothing else, it had momentarily disoriented the beast. Its tentacles lashed out wildly
in an effort to snare its prey. The six dashed up the stairs. A
single whiplash movement from below brought one arm across
the steps before them, but Pe Ell's strange knife flashed into
view, slicing across the arm and all but severing it. The arm
withdrew. They raced upward, springing from one landing to
the next, fleeing without looking back.

Finally, at a landing ten floors up, Walker brought them to
a ragged halt. Behind them there was only silence. They stood
in a knot, their breathing ragged as they listened.

"Perhaps it's given up," Carisman whispered, sounding hopeful.

"Not that thing," Horner Dees replied, his voice a muffled
rasp as he fought to catch his breath. "That thing won't ever
quit. I've seen what it can do."

Pe Ell thrust forward. "Since you claim to know so much
about it, tell us what it might do here!" he snarled.

Dees shook his bearish head obstinately. "I don't know. We
never made it as far as the buildings last time." Then he shuddered. "Shades! I can still feel those arms coming tight about
me!" He glanced sideways at Quickening. "I should never have
let you talk me into coming back here!"

"Hsssst!" Walker Boh was standing at the top of the stairs,
head cocked. "There's something . . ." he started to say and
stopped.

Pe Ell was next to him in a moment, crouched next to the
stair railing. Suddenly he jerked upright. "It's outside!" he snarled
and whirled about.

The once-glassed floor-to-ceiling latticework shattered into
pieces across the landing as the Rake clawed its way in. Morgan
was aghast. While the company had looked for it to come up
the stairs, the Rake had climbed the wall!

For a second time, it almost had them. Tentacles whipped across the small space and knocked most of them from their feet. Pe Ell was too quick for it, however, and the strange knife materialized in his hand, shredding the nearest arm. The Creeper flinched away, then came for him. But the diversion had given Walker Boh time to act. A fistful of Cogline's black powder appeared in his hand. He threw it at the beast and fire exploded forth.

The company raced up the stairs once more—one floor, two, three. Behind them, the Creeper thrashed against the fire. Then everything went still. They could no longer hear it; but they all knew where it was. There were openings through the walls on each floor where the windows had fallen away over the years. The Creeper could attack through any of them. It would keep coming after them, and sooner or later it would have them.

"We'll have to stand and fight!" Morgan cried out to the others, snatching free his broadsword.

"Do that and we'll all die, Highlander!" Horner Dees shouted back.

Then Pe Ell brought them up short, lunging ahead and wheeling to face them. "Back down those stairs, the bunch of you! Now! Stay close and I'll see you out of this!"

No one stopped to argue, not even Walker. They retraced their steps in a rush, descending in leaps and bounds, eyes on the window openings at each floor. Two flights down they caught a glimpse of the Rake as it pulled itself level with the frame. Tentacles snaked out, falling short. As they darted away, they could hear the monstrous thing reverse itself against the stone and start after them.

Another three flights, still far from the ground, Pe Ell brought them to a halt once more. "Here! This is the spot!" He pushed them down a long, high-ceilinged corridor. Behind them, the Rake gained the landing and lumbered swiftly in pursuit. The creature seemed to elongate as it came, changing the shape of its body to allow it access. Morgan was terrified. This Creeper could adapt to any situation. Narrow passageways and long climbs were not nearly enough to stop it.

At the end of the corridor was an enclosed catwalk that

crossed over to another building. "Get across as fast as you can!"
Pe Ell snapped.

Morgan and the others did as they were told. But the Highlander despaired of escape this way. Narrow as the catwalk might
be, it would not stop the Rake.

He reached the other side and turned with the others.
Pe Ell was kneeling at the far end of the walk where it joined to
the other building and sawing at the stone bracing with his
strange knife. Morgan stared. Had Pe Ell lost his mind? Did he
actually think his knife—any knife—could cut through stone?
The Rake was almost on top of him before he was back on his
feet. Cat-quick, he darted across the walk. He reached them just
as the Rake eased into view, snakelike now as it entered the
narrow tunnel opening.

And then the impossible happened. The bracing that Pe Ell
had been sawing snapped and gave way. The catwalk lurched
downward, held momentarily, then collapsed completely beneath the weight of the Rake. Down it plunged to the street,
shattering into fragments, dust and debris rising to mix with the
mist and the night.

The six from Rampling Steep stared downward, waiting.
Then they heard something—a scraping movement, the sound
of metal on stone.

"It's not dead!" Dees whispered in horror.

They stepped back hurriedly from the opening and slipped
down to the ground floor, exiting from a door on the far
side of the building onto the street. With Pe Ell and Walker in
the lead, they made their way silently through the dark. Behind them, they could hear the Creeper beginning to search
again.

Less than five blocks away they came upon the building
Walker Boh had been seeking, a squat, virtually windowless
bunker. They entered with anxious backward glances and peered
about. It was indeed a warren, a maze of rooms and corridors
with several sets of stairs and half a dozen entries. They climbed
four stories, settled themselves in a central room away from any
windows, and crouched down to wait.

The minutes passed and the Rake did not appear. An hour

came and went. They ate a cold meal and settled back. No one slept.

In the silence, their breathing was the only sound.

TOWARD DAWN, Morgan Leah grew restless. He found himself thinking of Pe Ell's knife, a blade that could cut through stone. The knife intrigued him. Like Pe Ell's presence on this journey, it was an unsolved mystery. The Highlander took a deep breath. Despite Walker's warning to stay clear of the man, he decided to see what he could learn. Climbing to his feet he moved to the darkened corner where the other sat with his back to the wall. He could see Pe Ell's eyes track him as he approached.

"What do you want?" Pe Ell asked coldly.

Morgan crouched down in front of him, hesitating in spite of his resolve. "I was curious about your knife," he admitted after a moment.

Their voices were barely audible whispers in the stillness. In the darkened room, no one else could hear.

Pe Ell's smile was cold. "You are, are you?"

"We all saw what it did."

Pe Ell had the knife out instantly, the blade held inches from Morgan's nose. Morgan held his breath and did not move. "The only thing you need to know about this," Pe Ell swore, "is that it can kill you before you can blink. You. Your one-armed friend. Anyone."

Morgan swallowed hard. "Even the Stone King?" He forced the question out, angry with himself for being frightened.

The blade disappeared back into the shadows. "Let me tell you something. The girl says you have magic about you. I don't believe it. You have nothing. One-arm is the only one among you who has magic, and his magic doesn't do anything! It doesn't kill. *He* doesn't kill. I can see it in his eyes. None of you matters in this business, whether you know it or not. You're nothing but a pack of fools."

He jabbed at Morgan with his finger. "Don't get in my way, Highlander. Any of you. And don't expect me to save you the next time that Creeper comes hunting. I'm all done with the lot of you." He withdrew his hand scornfully. "Now get away from me."

Morgan retreated wordlessly. He glanced briefly at Walker as he went, ashamed he had ignored the other's warning about Pe Ell. It was impossible to tell if the Dark Uncle had been watching. Dees and Carisman were asleep. Quickening was a faceless, barely distinguishable shadow.

Morgan sat cross-legged in a corner by himself, seething. He had learned nothing. All he had done was humiliate himself. His mouth tightened. One day he would have the use of his sword again. One day he would find a way to make it whole and recapture its magic—just as Quickening had said he would.

Then he would deal with Pe Ell.

He made himself a promise of it.

CHAPTER

19

THE COMPANY EMERGED from its concealment at daybreak. Clouds masked the skies over Eldwist from horizon to horizon, morning's arrival bleak and gray. A faint brightening of the damp, misty air was the best that dawn could manage, and night's shadows merely retreated into the city's alcoves and nooks to await their mistress' return.

There was no sign of the Rake. The six from Rampling Steep scanned the gloom cautiously. The buildings rose about them, massive and silent. The streets stretched away, canyons of stone. The only sounds were the howl of the wind, the crashing of the ocean, and the cries of the high-flying seabirds. The only movements were their own.

"As if it were never here," Horner Dees muttered as he shouldered his way past Morgan. "As if it were all a dream."

They began the search again for Uhl Belk. Rain fell through a curtain of smoky mist that tasted and smelled of the sea, and they were soaked through in minutes. A damp sheen settled across the stone walkways and streets, the walls of the buildings, the rubble and debris, a coating that mirrored the gloom and the shadows and played tricks with the light. The wind blew in sharp gusts, darting out of hiding at corners and alleyways, racing down the city's corridors with shrieks of delight, chasing itself endlessly. The morning wore on, a slow grinding of gears in some vast machine that could only be heard in the mind and felt in the wearing of the spirit. Time stole from them, they sensed. Time was a thief.

They found no trace of the Stone King. The city was vast and filled with hiding places, and even if they were sixty instead of six a thorough search could take weeks. None of them had any idea where to look for Uhl Belk or, worse, any idea what he looked like. Even Quickening could offer no help. Her father had not told her how the Stone King might appear. Did he look as they did? Was he human in form? Was he large or small? Morgan asked these questions as they trudged through the gloom, keeping well back on the walkways, close to the building walls. No one knew. They were searching for a ghost.

Midday passed. The buildings and streets of the city came and went in an endless procession of obelisks and gleaming black ribbons. The rain lessened, then increased. Thunder rumbled overhead, slow and ominous. The six ate a cold meal and drank a little in the dank, shadowed entry of one of the buildings while the rain turned into a downpour that flooded the streets with several inches of churning water. They peered outside and watched as the water gathered and flowed in small rivers to stone drains that swallowed it up.

They resumed walking when the rainfall lessened again and shortly afterward came upon the strange dome they had seen from the top of the building they had climbed the previous day. It sat amid the stone spires, a monstrous shell, its surface pitted and worn and cracked. They walked its circumference, searched for an entry, and found none. There were no doors, no stairs, no windows, nor openings of any kind. There were alcoves and niches and insets of varying sizes and shapes that gave its armor a sculpted look, but no way in or out. There were no footholds or ladders that would allow them to climb to its top. It was impossible to determine what it might have been used for. It sat there in the gloom and damp and defied them.

Mindful of time's rapid passing after yesterday's debacle, they returned early to their shelter. No one had much to say. They sat in the growing darkness, mostly apart from each other, mostly silent, and kept their thoughts to themselves.

There had been no sign of either the Maw Grint or the Rake that day. Nightfall brought them both out. They heard the Rake first, a skittering of metal legs on the stone street below, passing by without stopping as they held their collective breath. The Maw Grint came later, the sound of its approach a low rumbling that quickly became a roar. The monster burst forth, howling as it rose into the night. It was uncomfortably close; the stone of the building in which they hid shook with its cry. Then, just as quickly as it had come, it was gone again. No one made any attempt to try to catch a glimpse of it. Everyone stayed carefully put.

They slept better that night, perhaps because they were growing used to the city's night sounds, perhaps because they were so exhausted. They posted a watch and took turns standing it. The watch proved uneventful.

For three days afterward they continued their search. Fog and mist and rain hunted with them, persistent and unwelcome, and the city haunted their dreams. Eldwist was a stone forest filled with shadows and secrets, its towering buildings the trees that hemmed them in and closed them about. But unlike the green, living forests of the lands south the city was empty and lifeless. The girl and the men could form no affinity with Eldwist; they were trespassers here, unwanted and alone. Everything about the world in which they hunted was hard and unyielding. There were no recognizable signs, no familiar markings, and no changes in color or shape or smell or taste that would reveal to them even the smallest clue. There was only the enigma of the stone.

It began to affect the little company despite its resolve. Conversation diminished, tempers grew short, and there was a growing uncertainty as to what they were about. Horner Dees became more sullen and taciturn, his skills as a Tracker rendered useless, his experience from ten years previous used up. Pe Ell continued to distance himself, his eyes suspicious, his movements furtive and tense, a prowling cat at the edges of a jungle determined not to be brought to bay. Carisman quit singing almost completely. Morgan Leah found himself jumping at the smallest sound and was preoccupied with thoughts of the magic he had lost when the Sword of Leah had shattered. Walker Boh was a voiceless ghost, pale and aloof, floating through the gloom as if at any moment he might simply fade away.

Even Quickening changed. It was barely perceptible, a faint blurring of her exquisite beauty, an odd shading of her voice and movements, and a vague weariness in her eyes. Morgan, ever aware of what the girl was about, thought that he alone could tell.

But once, as they paused in their search in the shadow of a carriage husk, Walker Boh eased down beside the Highlander and whispered, "This city consumes us, Morgan Leah. Can you feel it? It has a life beyond what we understand, an extension of the Stone King's will, and it feeds on us. The magic is all about. If we do not find Uhl Belk soon, we will be in danger of being swallowed up entirely. Do you see? Even Quickening is affected."

And she was, of course. Walker drifted away again, and Morgan was left to wonder to what end they had been brought here. So much effort expended to reach this place and it all seemed for nothing. They were being drained of life, sapped of energy and purpose and will. He thought to speak of it to Quickening, but changed his mind. She knew what was happening. She always did. When it was time to do something, she would do it.

But it was Walker Boh who acted first. The fourth day of their hunt for the Stone King had concluded in the same manner as the previous three, without any of them having found even the smallest trace of their quarry. They were huddled in the shadows of their latest shelter; Pe Ell had insisted they change buildings in an effort to avoid discovery by the Rake, who still hunted them each night. They had not eaten a hot meal or enjoyed a fire's warmth since their arrival in Eldwist, and their water supply was in need of replenishing. Footsore and discouraged, they sat mired in silence.

"We need to search the tunnels beneath the city," the Dark Uncle said suddenly, his soft voice distant and cold.

The others looked up. "What tunnels?" Carisman wearily asked. The tunesmith, less fit than the others, was losing strength.

"The ones that honeycomb the rock beneath the buildings," Walker answered. "There are many of them. I have seen the stairways leading down from the streets."

Bearish Horner Dees shook his shaggy head. "You forget. The Maw Grint is down there."

"Yes. Somewhere. But it is a huge, blind worm. It won't even know of us if we're careful. And if the Maw Grint hides within the earth, maybe the Stone King hides there as well."

Morgan nodded. "Why not? They might both be worms. Maybe both are blind. Maybe neither likes the light. Goodness knows, there will be little enough of it down there. I think it is a good idea."

"Yes," Quickening agreed without looking at any of them.

Pe Ell stirred in the shadows and said nothing. The others muttered their assent. The darkness of their refuge went quickly still again.

That night Quickening slept next to Morgan Leah, something she had not done since their arrival in Eldwist. She came to him unexpectedly and burrowed close, as if she feared something would attempt to steal her away. Morgan reached around and held her for a time, listening to the sound of her breathing, feeling the pulse of her body against his own. She did not speak. After a time, he fell asleep holding her. When he awoke, she was gone again.

At dawn they departed their shelter and entered the catacombs beneath the city. A stairwell leading down from the building next to the one in which they were housed placed them on the first level. Other stairs ran deeper into the rock, spiraling down black holes of stone into emptiness. The tunnels on the first level were shaped from stone blocks and rails sat on beds of stone and cross ties as they disappeared into the dark. All had been turned to stone. There was no light beneath the city, so Walker Boh used one of Cogline's powders to coat the head of a narrow wedge of stone and create a firebrand. They moved ahead into the tunnels, following the line of the rails as they wound through the darkness. The rails passed platforms and other stairs leading up and down, and the tunnels branched and diverged. The air smelled musty, and loose stone crunched beneath their feet. After a time they came upon a giant carriage that lay upon its side, its wheels grooved to fit the rails, but broken and splintered now and fused to the axle and body by the magic's transformation. Once this carriage had ridden the rails, propelled in some mysterious way, carrying people of the old world from building to building, and from street to street.

The members of the company paused momentarily to gaze upon the wreck, then hurried on.

There were other carriages along the way, once an entire chamber full of them, some still seated upon the rails, some fallen and smashed along the way. There were piles of debris fallen by the rails that could not be identified and bits and pieces of what had been iron benches on the platforms they passed. Once or twice they ascended the stairs back to the streets of the city to regain their bearings before going down again. Below, far from where they walked, they could hear the rumble of the Maw Grint. Farther down still there was the sound of the ocean.

After several hours of exploring the network of tunnels without encountering any sign of the Stone King, Pe Ell brought them up short. "This is a waste of time," he said. "There's nothing to be found at this level. We need to go farther down."

Walker Boh glanced at Quickening, then nodded. Morgan caught sight of the looks on the faces of Carisman and Horner Dees and decided the same look was probably on his own.

They descended to the next level, winding down the stairwell into a maze of sewers. The sewers were empty and dry, but there was no mistaking what they had once been. The pipes that formed them were more than twenty feet high. Like everything else, they had been turned to stone. The company began following them, the light of Walker's makeshift torch a silver flare against the black, and the sound of their boots thudding harshly in the stillness. Not more than a hundred yards from where they had entered the sewers, a giant hole had been torn in the side of the stone pipe, shattering it apart as if it were paper. Something massive had burrowed through the rock and out again, something so huge that the sewer pipe had been no more than a blade of grass in its path.

From down the black emptiness of the burrowed tunnel came the rumble of the Maw Grint. The company crossed quickly through the rubble-strewn opening and continued on.

For two hours they wandered the sewers beneath the city, searching in vain for the lair of the Stone King. They twisted and wound about, and soon any sense of direction was irretrievably lost. There were fewer stairs leading up from this level, and many of them were nothing more than ladders hammered into the walls of drains. They came across the burrowings of the Maw Grint several times in the course of their hunt, the massive, jagged openings ripping upward through the earth and then disappearing down into it again, chasms of blackness large enough to swallow whole buildings. Morgan Leah stared into those chasms, realized they must honeycomb the peninsula rock, and wondered why the entire city didn't simply collapse into them.

Shortly after midday they stopped to rest and eat. They found a set of steps leading up to the first level and climbed to where an abandoned platform offered a set of battered stone benches. Seated there, Walker's odd torch planted in the rubble so that its light spilled over them like a halo, they stared wordlessly into the shadows.

Morgan finished before the others and moved over to where a thin shaft of daylight knifed down a stairwell leading to the streets of the city. He seated himself and stared upward, thinking of better times and places, wondering despondently if he would ever find them again.

Carisman came over to sit beside him. "It would be nice to see the sun again," the tunesmith mused and smiled faintly as Morgan glanced over. "Even for just a moment."

He sang:

> "Darkness is for bats and cats and frightened little mice,
> It's not for those of us who find the sunshine rather nice,
> So stay away from Eldwist's murk and take this good advice,
> Go someplace where your skin is warm instead of cold as ice."

He grinned rather sadly. "Isn't that a terrible piece of doggerel? It must be the worst song I've ever composed."

"Where did you come from, Carisman?" Morgan asked him. "I mean, before the Urdas and Rampling Steep. Where is your home?"

Carisman shook his head. "Anywhere. Everywhere. I call wherever I am my home, and I have been most places. I have been traveling since I was old enough to walk."

"Do you have a family?"

"No. Not that I know about." Carisman drew his knees up

to his chest and hugged them. "If I am to die here, there is no one who will wonder what has become of me."

Morgan snorted. "You're not going to die. None of us are. Not if we're careful." The intensity of Carisman's gaze made him uncomfortable. "I have a family. A father and mother back in the Highlands. Two younger brothers as well. I haven't seen them now in weeks."

Carisman's handsome face brightened. "I traveled the Highlands some years back. It was beautiful country, the hills all purple and silver in the early light, almost red when the sun set. It was quiet up there, so still you could hear the sound of the birds when they called out from far away." He rocked slightly. "I could have been happy there if I had stayed."

Morgan studied him a moment, watched him stare off into space, caught up in some inner vision. "I plan to go back when we're done with this business," he said. "Why don't you come home with me?"

Carisman stared at him. "Would that be all right? I would like that."

Morgan nodded. "Consider it done. But let's not have any more talk about dying."

They were silent for a moment before Carisman said, "Do you know that the closest thing I ever had to a family was the Urdas? Despite the fact that they kept me prisoner, they took care of me. Cared about me, too. And I cared about them. Like a family. Strange."

Morgan thought about his own family for a moment, his father and mother and brothers. He remembered their faces, the sound of their voices, the way they moved and acted. That led him to think of the Valemen, Par and Coll. Where were they? Then he thought of Steff, dead several weeks now, already becoming a memory, fading into the history of his past. He thought of the promise he had made to his friend—that if he found a magic that could aid the Dwarves in their struggle to be free again, he would use it—against the Federation—against the Shadowen. A rush of determination surged through him and dissipated again. Maybe the Black Elfstone would prove to be the weapon he needed. If it could negate other magics, if it were indeed powerful enough to bring back disappeared Paranor by counteracting the spell of magic that bound it . . .

"They liked the music, you know, but it was more than just that," Carisman was saying. "I think they liked me as well. They were a lot like children in need of a father. They wanted to hear all about the world beyond their valley, about the Four Lands and the peoples that lived there. Most of them had never been anywhere beyond the Spikes. I had been everywhere."

"Except here," Morgan said with a smile.

But Carisman only looked away. "I wish I had never come here," he said.

The company resumed its search of the sewers of Eldwist and continued to find them empty of life. They discovered nothing—not the smallest burrowing rodent, not a bat, not even the insects that normally thrived underground. There was no sign of Uhl Belk. There was only the stone that marked his passing. They wandered for several hours and then began to retrace their steps. Daylight would be gone shortly, and they had no intention of being caught outside when the Rake began its nocturnal scavenging.

"It may be, however, that it doesn't come down into the tunnels," Walker Boh mused.

But no one wanted to find out, so they kept moving. They followed the twisting catacombs, recrossed the burrowings of the Maw Grint, and pushed steadily ahead through the darkness. Grunting and huffing were the only sounds to be heard. Tension lined their faces. Their eyes reflected their discouragement and discontent. No one spoke. What they were thinking needed no words.

Then Walker brought them to a sudden halt and pointed off into the gloom. There was an opening in the tunnel, one that they had somehow missed earlier, smaller than the sewers and virtually invisible in the dimness. Walker crouched down to peer inside, then disappeared into the dark.

A moment later he returned. "There is a cavern and a stairwell leading down," he reported. "It appears there is yet another set of tunnels below.

They followed him through the opening to the chamber

beyond, a cave whose walls and floors were studded with jagged projections and rent with deep clefts. They found the stairwell and looked down into its gloom. It was impossible to see anything. They exchanged uneasy glances. Wordlessly, Walker moved to the head of the stairs. Holding the makeshift torch out in front of him, he started down. After a moment's hesitation, the others followed.

The stairs descended a long way, ragged and slick with moisture. The smell of the Tiderace was present here, and they could hear the trickle of seawater in the blackness. When they reached the end of the stairs, they found themselves standing in the middle of a broad, high tunnel in which the rock was crystallized and massive stone icicles hung from the ceiling in clusters, dripping water into black pools. Walker turned right, and the company moved ahead. The dampness chilled the air to ice, and the six pulled their cloaks tightly about them for warmth. Echoes of their footsteps reverberated through the stone corridor, chasing the silence.

Then suddenly there was something else, a sort of squealing that reminded Morgan Leah of a rusted iron lever being shifted after a long period of disuse. The members of the company stopped as one at its sound and stood in the faint silver glow of the torchlight, listening. The squealing continued; it was coming from somewhere behind them.

"Come," Walker Boh said sharply and began hurrying ahead. The others hastened after, spurred on by the unexpected urgency in his voice. Walker had recognized something in the sound that they had not. Morgan glanced over his shoulder as he went. What was back there?

They crossed a shallow stream of water that tumbled from a fissure in the rock wall, and Walker turned, motioning the rest of them past. The squealing sound was deafening now and coming closer. The Dark Uncle passed the torch to Morgan wordlessly, then lifted his arm and threw something into the black. A white fire flared to life, and the tunnel behind them was suddenly filled with light.

Morgan gasped. There were rats everywhere, a churning, scrambling mass of furred bodies. But these rats were giants, grown to three and four times their normal size, all claws and teeth. Their eyes were white and sightless, like everything else the company had encountered in Eldwist, and their bodies were sleek with the dampness of the sea. They looked ravenous. And maddened. They poured out of the rocks and came for the men and the girl.

"Run!" Walker cried, snatching the torch back from Morgan.

And run they did, charging frantically through the darkness with the sound of the squealing chasing after them in gathering waves, struggling to keep at the edges of the torchlight as they fought to escape the horror that pursued. The tunnel rose and fell in ragged slopes, and the rocks cut and scraped at them. They fell repeatedly, scrambled up again, and ran on.

A ladder! That was all that Morgan Leah could think. *We've got to find a ladder!*

But there was none. There were only the rock walls, the streams and pools of seawater, and the rats. And themselves, trapped.

Then from somewhere ahead came a new sound, the booming of waves against a shoreline, the pounding of the ocean against land.

They broke from the blackness of the tunnel into a faint, silvery brightness and staggered to a ragged halt. Before them a cliff dropped sharply into the Tiderace. The ocean churned and swirled below, crashing into the rocks, foaming white as it spilled over them. They were in an underground cavern so massive that its farthest reaches were lost in mist and shadow. Daylight spilled through clefts in the rock where the ocean had breached the wall. Other tunnels opened into the cavern as well, black holes far to the right and left. All were unreachable. The cliffs to either side were impassable. The drop below led to the rocks and the roiling sea. The only way left was back the way they had come.

Through the rats.

The rats were almost on top of the company now, their squeals rising up to overwhelm the thunder of the ocean's waters, their masses filling the lower half of the tunnel as they bit and clawed ahead. Morgan yanked out his broadsword, knowing even as he did so how futile the weapon would be. Pe Ell had moved to one side, clear of the others, and his strange silver knife was in his hand. Dees and Carisman were backed to the edge of the drop, crouched as if to jump.

Quickening stepped forward beside Morgan, her beautiful face strangely calm, her hands steady on his arm.

Then Walker Boh cast aside his torch and hurled a fistful of black powder into the horde of rats. Fire exploded everywhere, and the first rank was incinerated. But there were hundreds more behind that one, thousands of churning dark bodies. Claws scraped madly on the rocks, seeking to find a grip. Teeth and sightless eyes gleamed. The rats came on.

"Walker!" Morgan cried out desperately and shoved Quickening behind him.

But it wasn't the Dark Uncle who responded to Morgan's plea, or Pe Ell, or Horner Dees, or even Quickening. It was Carisman, the tunesmith.

He rushed forward, pushing past Morgan and Quickening, coming up beside Walker just as the rats burst through the tunnel opening onto the narrow ledge. Lifting his wondrous voice, he began to sing. It was a song that was different than any they had ever heard; it scraped like the rub of metal on stone, shrieked like the tearing of wood, and broke through the thunder of the ocean and the squeal of the rats to fill the cavern with its sound.

"Come to me!" Quickening cried out to the rest of them.

They bunched close at once, even Pe Ell, flattening themselves against one another as the tunesmith continued to sing. The rats poured out of the tunnel and swept toward them in a wave of struggling bodies. But then the wave split apart, flowing to either side of the tunesmith, passing by without touching any of them. Something in Carisman's song was turning them away. They twisted to either side, a churning mass. Onward they scrambled, heedless of everything, whether fleeing or being called it was impossible to tell, and tumbled into the sea.

Moments later, the last of them had been swallowed up or swept away. Carisman went still, then collapsed into Morgan's arms. The Highlander propped him up, and Quickening wiped cold seawater onto his face with the sleeve of her tunic. The others glanced about breathlessly, cautiously, scanning the dark tunnel opening, the empty rock, the waters of the sea.

"It worked," Carisman whispered in surprise as his eyes fluttered open again. "Did you see? It worked!" He struggled up and seized Quickening jubilantly by the arms. "I'd read something about it once, or heard about it maybe, but I had never thought I would . . . I mean, I had never tried such a thing before! Never! It was a cat song, Lady! A cat song! I didn't know what else to do, so I made those horrid rodents think we were giant cats!"

Everyone stared in disbelief. Only then did Morgan Leah appreciate how truly miraculous their escape had been.

20

ITH THE DESTRUCTION of the rats, they were able to retrace their steps through the tunnel that had brought them to the underground cavern, climb back into the sewers of Eldwist, climb from there to the level of tunnels above, and finally reach the streets of the city. It was already growing dark, and they hurried quickly through the descending gloom to gain the safety of their nighttime refuge. They only just succeeded. The Rake appeared almost at once, an invisible presence beyond the walls of the building, its armored legs scraping across the stone below, searching for them still. They sat huddled silently in the dark listening to it hunt until it had gone. Walker said he thought the creature could track by smell, only the rain and the number of trails they had left was confusing it. Sooner or later it would figure out where they were hiding.

Exhausted and aching and shaken by what had befallen them, they ate their dinner in silence and went quickly off to sleep.

The next morning Pe Ell, who following their escape from the tunnels had descended into a mood so black that no one dared approach him, announced that he was going out on his own.

"There are too many of us stumbling about to ever find anything," he declared, his voice calm and expressionless, his narrow face unreadable. He spoke to Quickening, as if only she mattered. "If there truly is a Stone King, he knows by now that we are here. This is his city; he can hide in it forever if he chooses. The only way to find him is to catch him off guard, sneak up on him, and surprise him. There will be none of that if we continue to hunt like a pack of dogs."

Morgan started to intervene, but Walker's fingers closed about his arm like iron bands.

Pe Ell glanced around. "The rest of you can keep bumbling about as long as you wish. But you'll do it without me. I've spent enough time shepherding you around. I should have gone off on my own from the first. If I had, this business would be finished by now." He turned back to Quickening. "When I have found Uhl Belk and the Black Elfstone, I will come back for you." He paused, meeting her gaze squarely. "If you are still alive."

He strode past them contemptuously and disappeared down the hall. His boots thudded softly on the stairs and faded into silence.

Horner Dees spit. "We're well rid of that one," he muttered.

"He is correct, though," Walker Boh said, and they all turned to look at him. "In one respect at least. We must divide ourselves up into groups if we are ever to complete this search. The city is too large, and we are too easy to avoid while we stay together."

"Two groups then," Dees agreed, nodding his shaggy head. "No one goes out alone."

"Pe Ell doesn't seem worried about hunting alone," Morgan noted.

"He's a predator, sure enough," Dees replied. He looked at Quickening speculatively. "How about it, girl? Does he have any chance of finding Belk and the Elfstone on his own?"

But Quickening only said, "He will return."

They seated themselves to work out a strategy, a method by which the city could be searched from end to end. The buildings ran mostly north of where they were concealed, so it was decided to divide Eldwist in two with one group taking the east half and the other the west. The search would concentrate on the buildings and streets, not the tunnels. If nothing were found aboveground, they would change their approach.

"Pe Ell may be wrong when he says that the Stone King must know we are here," Quickening said in closing. She brought her slender fingers up in a quick, birdlike movement. "We are insignificant in his eyes, and he may not yet have even noticed us. We are the reason he keeps the Rake in service. Besides, the Maw Grint occupies his time."

"How do we divide ourselves up?" Carisman asked.

"You will go with me," Quickening answered at once. "And Walker Boh."

Morgan was surprised. He had expected her to choose him. The disappointment he felt cut deeply. He started to dispute her choice, but her black eyes fixed him with such intensity that he went instantly still. Whatever her reasons for making this decision, she did not want it questioned.

"That leaves you and me, Highlander," Horner Dees grunted and clapped one heavy hand on Morgan's shoulder. "Think we can manage to disappoint Pe Ell and keep our skins whole?"

His sudden laugh was so infectious that Morgan found himself smiling in response. "I'd bet on it," he replied.

They gathered up their gear and went down into the street. Sheets of gloom draped the buildings, hung from skies thick with clouds and mist. The air was damp and chill, and their breath exhaled in a haze of white. They wished each other well and began moving off in separate directions, Morgan and Horner Dees going west, Quickening, Walker, and Carisman east.

"Take care of yourself, Morgan," Quickening whispered, her exquisite face a mix of shadow and light beneath the sweep of her silver hair. She touched him softly on the shoulder and hurried after Walker Boh.

"Tra-la-la-la, a-hunting we will go!" Carisman sang merrily as they disappeared.

Rain began to fall in a steady drizzle. Morgan and Horner Dees slogged ahead with their cloaks pulled tightly about their shoulders and their heads bent. They had agreed that they would follow the street to its end, until they were at the edge of the city, then turn north to track the peninsula's shoreline. There had been little enough found within the core of the city; perhaps there was something outside—particularly if the Stone King's magic was ineffective against water. They kept to the walkways and glanced cautiously down the darkened corridors of the side-streets they passed. Rainwater collected on the city's stone skin in puddles and streams, shimmering darkly in the gloom. Sea-birds huddled in nooks and crevices, waiting out the storm. In the shadows, nothing moved.

It was nearing midmorning when they reached the Tiderace, the land ending in cliffs which dropped hundreds of feet into the sea. Craggy outcroppings of rock rose out of the churning waters, worn and pitted. Waves crashed against the cliffs, the sound of their pounding mixing with the wind as it swept off the water in a rising howl. Morgan and Dees melted back into the shelter of the outer buildings, seeking to protect themselves. Rain and ocean spray soaked them quickly through, and they were soon shivering beneath their clothes. For two hours they skirted the city's western boundaries without finding anything. By midday, when they stopped to eat, they were disgruntled and worn.

"There's nothing to be found out here, Highlander," Dees observed, chewing on a bit of dried beef—his last. "Just the sea and the wind and those confounded birds, shrieking and calling like madwomen."

Morgan nodded without answering. He was trying to decide whether he could eat a seabird if he had to. Their food supplies were almost exhausted. Soon they would be forced to hunt. What else was there besides those birds? Fish, he decided firmly. The birds looked too rangy and tough.

"You miss the Highlands?" Dees asked him suddenly.

"Sometimes." He thought about his home and smiled faintly. "All the time."

"Me, too, and I haven't seen them in years. Thought they were the most beautiful piece of work nature ever made. I liked how they made me feel when I was in them."

"Carisman said he liked it there, too. He said he liked the quiet."

"The quiet. Yes, I remember how quiet it was in those hills." They had found shelter in a building's shadowed entry. The big man shifted himself away from a widening stain where the rain had trickled down the wall and collected on the steps where they were seated, backs to the wall, facing out into the weather.

He leaned forward. "Let me tell you something," he said softly. "I know this fellow, Pe Ell."

Morgan looked over, intrigued. "From where?"

"From before. Long before. Almost twenty years. He was just a kid then; I was already old." Dees chuckled darkly. "Some kid. A killer even then. An assassin right from the beginning— as if that was what he was born to be and he couldn't ever be anything else but." He shook his grizzled head. "I knew him. I knew it was bad luck if you crossed him."

"Did you?"

"Cross him? Me? No, not me. I know well enough who to stand up to and who to back away from. Always have. That's how I've stayed alive. Pe Ell is the kind who once he takes a dislike to you will keep coming till you're dead. Doesn't matter how long it takes him or how he gets the job done. He'll just keep at it." He pointed at Morgan. "You better understand something. I don't know what he's doing here. I don't know why the girl brought him. But he's no friend to any of you. You know what he is? He's a Federation assassin. Their best, in fact. He's Rimmer Dall's favorite boy."

Morgan froze, the blood draining from his face. "That can't be."

"Can and is," Dees said emphatically. "Unless things have changed from how they used to be, and I doubt they have."

Morgan shook his head in disbelief. "How do you know all this, Horner?"

Horner Dees smiled, a wide, hungry grin. "Funny thing about that. I remember him even though he doesn't remember me. I can see it in his eyes. He's trying to figure out what it is I know that he doesn't. Have you seen the way he looks at me? Trying to figure it out. Been too long, I guess. He's killed too many men, has too many faces in his past to remember many of them. Me, I been gone a long time. I don't have so many ghosts to worry about." He paused. "Truth is, Highlander, I was one of them myself."

"One of them?" Morgan asked quietly.

The other gave a sharp laugh, like a bark. "I was with the Federation! I tracked for them!"

As quick as that Morgan Leah's perception of Horner Dees changed. The big, bearish fellow was no longer just a gruff, old

Tracker whose best days were behind him; he was no longer even a friend. Morgan started to back away and then realized there was nowhere to back to. He reached for his broadsword.

"Highlander!" Dees snapped, freezing him. The big man clenched one massive fist, then relaxed it. "Like I said, that was long ago. I been gone from those people twenty years. Settle back. You haven't any reason to fear me."

He placed his hands in his lap, palms up. "Anyway, that's how I came to see the Highlands, believe it or not—in the service of the Federation. I was tracking Dwarf rebels for them, hunting the Rainbow Lake and Silver River country. Never found much. Dwarves are like foxes; they go to ground quick as a wink when they know they're being hunted." He smiled unexpectedly. "I didn't try very hard in any case. It was a worthless sort of job."

Morgan released his grip on the broadsword and sat back again.

"I was with them long enough to find out about Pe Ell," the other went on, and now his eyes were distant and troubled. "I knew most of what was happening back then. Rimmer Dall had me slated to be a Seeker. Can you imagine? Me? I thought that wolf's head stuff was nonsense. But I learned about Pe Ell while Dall was working on me. Saw him come and go once, when he didn't know it. Dall arranged for me to see because he liked putting one over on Pe Ell. It was a sort of game with the two of them, each trying to show up the other. Anyway, I saw him and heard what he did. A few others heard things, too. Everyone knew to stay away from him."

He sighed. "Just a little while after that, I quit the bunch of them. Left when no one was looking, came north through the Eastland, traveled about until I reached Rampling Steep, and decided that was where I'd live. Away from the madness south, the Federation, the Seekers, all of it."

"All of it?" Morgan repeated doubtfully, still trying to decide what to make of Horner Dees. "Even the Shadowen?"

Dees blinked. "What do you know of the Shadowen, Morgan Leah?"

Morgan leaned forward. Windblown mist had left Horner's

face damp and shining, and droplets of water clung to his hair and beard. "I want to know something from you first. Why are you telling me all this?"

The other's smile was strangely gentle. "Because I want you to know about Pe Ell, and you can't know about him without knowing about me. I like you, Highlander. You remind me a little of myself when I was your age—kind of reckless and headstrong, not afraid of anything. I don't want there to be secrets about me that might come out in a bad way. Like if Pe Ell should remember who I am. I want you for a friend and ally. I don't trust anyone else."

Morgan studied him wordlessly for a moment. "You might do better with someone else."

"I'll chance it. Now, how about it? I've answered your question. You tell me how you know about the Shadowen."

Morgan drew up his knees and hugged them to his chest, making up his mind. Finally, he said, "My best friend was a Dwarf named Steff. He was with the Resistance. The woman he loved was a Shadowen, and she killed him. I killed her."

Horner Dees arched his eyebrows quizzically. "I was given to understand that nothing but magic could kill those things."

Morgan reached down and drew out the shattered end of the Sword of Leah. "There was magic in this Sword once," he said. "Allanon put it there himself—three hundred years ago. I broke it during a battle with the Shadowen in Tyrsis before the start of all this. Even so, there was still enough magic left to avenge Steff and save myself." He studied the blade speculatively, hefted it, waited in vain to feel its warmth, then looked back at Dees. "Maybe there's still some. Anyway, that's why Quickening brought me along. This Sword. She said there was a chance it could be restored."

Horner Dees frowned. "Are you to use it against Belk then?"

"I don't know," Morgan admitted. "I haven't been told anything except that it could be made whole again." He slipped the broken blade back into its scabbard. "Promises," he said and sighed.

"She seems like the kind who keeps hers," the other observed after a moment's thought. "Magic to find magic. Magic to prevail over magic. Us against the Stone King." He shook his head. "It's too complicated for me. You just be sure you remember what I said about Pe Ell. You can't turn your back on him. And you mustn't go up against him either. You leave that to me."

"You?" Morgan declared in surprise.

"That's right. Me. Or Walker Boh. One-armed or not, he's a match for Pe Ell or I've misjudged him completely. You concentrate on keeping the girl safe." He paused. "Shouldn't be too hard, considering how you feel about each other."

Morgan flushed in spite of himself. "It's mostly me that's feeling anything," he muttered awkwardly.

"She's the prettiest thing I've ever seen," the old man said, smiling at the other's discomfort. "I don't know what she is, human or elemental or what, but she can charm the boots right off you. She looks at you, that face softens, she speaks the way she does, and you'll do anything for her. I should know. I wasn't ever going to come back to this place and here I am. She's done it to all of us."

Morgan nodded. "Even to Pe Ell. He's as much hers as the rest of us."

But Dees shook his head. "I don't know, Highlander. You look careful next chance you get. He's hers, but he isn't. She walks a fine line with that one. He could turn quick as a cat. That's why I tell you to look after her. You remember what he is. He's not here to do us any favors. He's here for himself. Sooner or later, he'll revert to form."

"I think so, too," Morgan agreed.

Dees gave a satisfied smirk. "But it won't be so easy for him now, will it? Because we'll be watching."

They packed up, tightened their cloaks against the weather, and stepped back out into the downpour. They continued to follow the shoreline as the afternoon lengthened, reaching the northernmost point of the peninsula without finding anything, and turned back again into the city. The rain finally ended, changing to a fine mist that hung like smoke against the gray sky and buildings. The air warmed. Shadows yawned and stretched in alleyways and nooks like waking spirits, and steam rose off the streets.

From somewhere underground the rumble of the Maw Grint sounded, a distant thunder that shook the earth.

"I'm beginning to think we're not ever going to find anything," Horner Dees muttered at one point.

They followed the dark corridors of the streets and searched the brume that lay all about, the doorways and windows that gaped open like mouths in search of food, and the flat, glistening walkways and passages. Everywhere the city lay abandoned and dead, stripped of life and filled with hollow, empty sounds. It walled them away with its stone and its silence; it wrapped about them with such persistence that despite memory and reason it seemed that the world beyond must have fallen away and that Eldwist was all that remained.

They grew weary with the approach of evening; the sameness of their surroundings dulled their senses and wore against their resistance. They began to stray a bit, to wander closer to the walkway's edge, to look upward more often at the stone heights that loomed all about, and to give themselves over to a dangerous and persistent wish that something—*anything*—would happen. Their boredom was acute, their sense of being unable to change or affect the things about them maddening. They had been in Eldwist almost a week. How much longer would they be forced to remain?

Ahead, the street deadended. They rounded the corner of the building they were following and discovered that the street widened into a square. At the square's center was an odd depression with steps leading down on all sides to a basin from which a statue rose, a winged figure with streamers and ribbons trailing from its body. Almost without thinking, they turned into the square, beguiled by its look, so different from anything else they had seen. *A park,* they thought to themselves without speaking. What was it doing here?

They were halfway across the street when they heard the catch that secured the trapdoor beneath them release.

They had no chance of saving themselves. They were standing in the center of the door when it dropped, and they plunged into the void beneath. They fell a long way, struck the side of a chute, and began to slide head-downward. The chute was rough, its surface littered with loose rock that cut and bit into their faces and hands. They clawed frantically in an attempt to slow their descent, heedless of the pain. Boots and knees dug in; hands and fingers grasped. The slide broadened and its slope decreased. They quit rolling, flattened themselves in a spread-eagle position, and came to a grinding halt.

Morgan lifted his head gingerly and peered about. He lay facedown on a slab of rock that stretched so far away into the shadows on either side that he could not see its end. Loose rock lay upon the slide like a carpet, bits and pieces of it still tumbling away. There was a faint glimmer of light from somewhere above, a narrow shaft that sought in vain to penetrate the gloom, so thin that it barely reached to where Morgan lay. He forced himself to look down. Horner Dees lay some twenty feet below him on his right, sprawled on his back with his arms and legs thrown wide, unmoving. Farther down, like a giant, hungry mouth, was a chasm of impenetrable blackness.

Morgan swallowed against the dust in his throat. "Horner?" he whispered hoarsely.

"Here," the other said, his voice a faint rasp.

"Are you all right?"

There was a grunt. "Nothing broken, I think."

Morgan took a moment to look about. All he could see was the slide, the shaft of light above, and the chasm below. "Can you move?" he called down softly.

There was silence for a moment, then the sound of rocks clattering away into the dark. "No," the reply came. "I'm too fat and old, Highlander. If I try to get up to you, I'll start sliding and won't be able to stop."

Morgan heard the strain in his voice. And the fear. Dees was helpless, laying on that loose rock like a leaf on glass; even the slightest movement would send him spinning away into the void.

Me, too, if I make any attempt to help, the Highlander thought darkly.

Yet he knew that he had to try.

He took a deep breath and brought his hand up slowly to his mouth. A shower of loose rock rattled away, but his body stayed in place on the slide. He brushed at the silt on his lips and closed his eyes, thinking. There was a rope in his backpack, a thin, strong coil, some fifty feet of it. His eyes opened again. Could he find a way to fasten it to something and haul himself up?

A familiar rumbling shook the earth, rising from below, shaking the carpet of rock about him so that small showers of it slid into the abyss. There was a thunderous huffing and a great, long sigh as if an enormous amount of air was being released.

Morgan Leah glanced down, cold to the bone. In the depths below, right beneath where they hung, the Maw Grint lay sleeping.

Morgan looked up again quickly. His breath came in short, frantic gasps, and he had to struggle to overcome an almost overpowering urge to claw his way out of there as fast as he could. The Maw Grint. That close. It was huge beyond belief; even his vague glimpse of it had been enough to tell him that. He couldn't begin to guess how much of it there was, where it began and ended, how far it stretched away.

He gripped at the rock until his hands hurt, fighting back against his fear and nausea. He had to get out of there! He had to find a way!

Almost without thinking about what he was doing, he reached beneath his stomach and began working free the broken remains of the Sword of Leah. It was a slow, agonizing process, for he was unable to lift up without fear of beginning his slide down again. And now, more than he had ever wanted anything, he did not want that.

"Don't try to move, Horner!" he called down softly, his voice dry and rough. "Stay where you are!"

There was no response. Morgan inched the Sword of Leah clear of its scabbard and out from under him, bringing it level with his face. The polished metal surface of the broken blade glittered brightly in the faint light. He pushed it above his head with one hand, then reached up with the other until he could grip it firmly with both. Turning the jagged end of the blade downward, he began to slide it into the rock. He felt it bite into the stone slab beneath.

Please! he begged.

Jamming the Sword of Leah into the stone, he hauled himself

up. The blade held, and he pulled his face level with its handle.
Bits of rock fell away beneath him, tumbling and sliding into the
void. The Maw Grint did not stir.

Morgan freed the Sword, reached upward to jam it into the
rock again, gripped it with every ounce of strength he possessed,
and pulled himself level once more. He closed his eyes and lay
next to it panting, then felt a rush of heat surge through his
body. *The magic?* He opened his eyes quickly to see, searching
the Sword's gleaming length. Nothing.

Holding himself in place with one hand, he used the other
to dive into his pack and secure the length of rope and a grappling hook. A handful of cooking implements and a blanket
worked free in the process and fell onto the chute. Ignoring
them, the Highlander slipped the rope about his waist and shoulders and tied it in a harness.

"Horner!" he whispered.

The old Tracker looked up, and Morgan threw the rope to
him. It fell across his body, and he seized it with both hands.
He started to slip almost immediately, swinging over until he
was beneath Morgan. Then the rope went taut, catching him.
The shock to Morgan's body was staggering, an immense,
wrenching weight that threatened to pull him down. But he had
both hands fastened once more on the Sword of Leah, and the
blade held firm.

"Climb to me!" he whispered down harshly.

Horner Dees began to do so, slowly, torturously, hand over
hand up the rope and the slide. As he passed the cooking implements and blanket that had fallen from Morgan's pack, he
kicked them free, and they tumbled farther down in a shower
of rock.

This time the Maw Grint coughed and came awake.

It grunted, a huffing sound that reverberated against the stone
walls. It lifted itself, its massive body thudding against the walls
of the tunnel in which it slept, shaking the earth violently. It
rolled and pitched and began to move. Morgan hung on to the
pommel of his sword, and Dees clung to the slender rope, both
gritting their teeth against the strain on muscle and bone. The
Maw Grint shook itself, and Tracker and Highlander could hear
a spraying sound and then a hiss of steam.

The Maw Grint slid away into the black and the sound of its passing faded. Morgan and Dees looked down cautiously.

An odd, greenish stain was working its way up the stone of the chute, just visible at the far edge of the shaft of light several dozen feet below Dees. It glistened darkly and steamed like a fire advancing through brush. They watched as it reached the blanket that had fallen from Morgan's pack. When it touched it, the rough wool turned instantly to stone.

Horner Dees began climbing again at once, a furious assault on the loose stone of the slide. When he was almost to Morgan, the Highlander stopped him, beckoned for slack on the rope, and began his own ascent, jamming the sword blade down into the rock, pulling himself up, jamming and pulling, over and over again.

They went on that way for what seemed an endless span of time. Daylight beckoned them, drawing them like a beacon toward the surface of the city and safety. Sweat ran down Morgan's face and body until he was drenched in it. His breathing grew labored, and his entire body was wracked with pain. It grew so bad at one point that he thought he must quit. But he could not. Below, the stain continued to advance, the poison given off by the Maw Grint's body solidifying everything in its path. The blanket went first, then the handful of cooking implements that hadn't fallen into the abyss. Soon there was nothing left save Morgan and Horner Dees.

And it was gaining steadily on them.

They struggled on, hauling themselves upward foot by foot. Morgan's mind closed down on his thoughts like an iron lid on a trunk of useless relics, and all of his efforts became concentrated on the climb. As he labored, he felt the heat spread through him once more, stronger this time, more insistent. He could feel it turning inside him like an auger, boring and twisting at the core of his being. It reached from head to heels and back again, from fingers to toes, through the muscles and bone and blood, until it was all he knew. At some point—he never knew exactly when—he looked at the Sword of Leah and saw it glowing as bright as day, the white fire of its magic burning through the shadows. *Still there,* he thought in furious determination. *Still mine!*

Then suddenly there was a ladder, rungs lining the walls of the chute above him, rising up from the darkness of their prison toward the fading daylight and the city. The light, he saw, came from a narrow airshaft. He scrambled toward it, jamming, hauling, releasing, starting all over again. He heard Horner Dees calling to him from below, his hoarse voice almost a sob, and looked down long enough to see the poison of the Maw Grint inches from the old Tracker's boots. He reached down impulsively with one hand and calling on a strength he didn't know he possessed, hauled upward on the rope, pulling Dees clear. The other kicked and scrambled toward him, bearded face a mask of dust and sweat. Morgan's hand released the rope and closed over the bottommost rung of the ladder. Dees continued to climb, digging his boots into the loose stone. The light was failing quickly now, gone gray already, slipping rapidly into darkness. Below, the Maw Grint's muffled roar shook the earth.

Then they were both on the ladder, scrambling upward, feet and hands gripping, bodies pressing against the stone. Morgan jammed the Sword of Leah back into his belt, safely in place. *Still magic!*

They burst from the airshaft into the street and fell on the walkway in exhaustion. Together, they crawled to the doorway of the nearest building and collapsed in the cool of its shadows.

"I knew . . . I was right . . . in wanting you for a friend," Horner Dees gasped.

He reached over, this great bearish man, and pulled the Highlander close. Morgan Leah could feel him shake.

CHAPTER

21

PE ELL SPENT the day sleeping.

After he walked out on Quickening and the others of the little company from Rampling Steep he went directly to a building less than a block away that he had chosen for himself two days earlier. Rounding the corner of the building so that he was out of sight of anyone who might be watching, he entered through a side door, climbed the stairs one floor, followed the hallways to the front of the building, and turned into a large, well-lighted chamber with windows that ran almost floor to ceiling and opened on the street below and the buildings across, one of which was where his once-companions were presently hiding.

He permitted himself a brief smile. They were such a pack of fools.

Pe Ell had a plan. He believed, as Quickening did, that the Stone King was hidden somewhere in the city. He did not believe the others of the company would find him even if they searched from now until next summer. He alone could do so. Pe Ell was a hunter by instinct and experience; the others were something less—each to a varying degree, but all hopeless. He had not lied when he told them he would be better off on his own. He would. Horner Dees was a Tracker, but a Tracker's skills were useless in a city of stone. Carisman and Morgan Leah had no skills worth talking about. Quickening disdained the use of her magic—maybe with good reason, although he wasn't convinced of that yet. The only one who might have been useful to him was Walker Boh. But the man with one arm was his most dangerous enemy, and he did not want to have to worry about watching his back.

His plan was simple. The key to finding Uhl Belk was the Rake. The Creeper was the Stone King's house pet, a giant watchdog that kept his city free of intruders. He turned it loose at night, and it swept the streets and buildings clean. What it missed one night, it went after the next. But only at night, not during the day. Why was that? Pe Ell asked himself. And the answer was obvious. Because like everything else that served the Stone King, willingly or not, it could not see. It hunted by using its other senses. The night was its natural ally. Daylight might even hinder it.

Where did it go during the day? Pe Ell then asked. Again, the answer seemed obvious. Like any house pet, it went back to its master. That meant that if Pe Ell could manage to follow the Rake to its daytime lair he had a good chance of finding the Stone King.

Pe Ell thought he could do so. The night was his ally as well; he had done most of his own hunting in the dark. His own senses were as sharp as those of the Creeper. He could hunt the Rake as easily as the Rake could hunt him. The Rake was a monster; there was no point in thinking he stood a chance against such a beast in a face-to-face confrontation, even with the aid of the Stiehl. But Pe Ell could be a shadow when he chose, and nothing could bring him to bay. He would take his chances; he would play cat and mouse with the Rake. Pe Ell was feeling many things, but fear wasn't one of them. He had a healthy respect for the Creeper, but he was not frightened of it. After all, he was the smarter of the two.

Come nightfall, he would prove it.

So he slept the daylight hours away, stretched out of sight just beneath the windows where he could feel the faint, hazy sunlight on his face and hear the sounds of anyone or anything passing in the street below.

When it grew dark, the shadows cooling the air to a damp chill, the light fading away, he rose and slipped down the stairs and out the door. He stood listening in the gloom for a long time. He had not heard the others of the company return from their daytime hunt; that was odd. Perhaps they had come into their shelter through another door, but he thought he would have heard them nevertheless. For a moment he considered stealing in for a quick look, but abandoned the idea almost immediately. What happened to them had nothing to do with him. Even Quickening no longer mattered as much. Now that he was away from her, he discovered, she had lost something of her hold over him. She was just a girl he had been sent to kill, and kill her he would if she was still alive when he returned from his night's hunt.

He would kill them all.

The cries of the seabirds were distant and mournful in the evening stillness, faint whimpers carried on the ocean wind. He could hear the dull pounding of the waters of the Tiderace against Eldwist's shores and the low rumble of the Maw Grint somewhere deep beneath the city.

He could not hear the Creeper.

He waited until it was as black as it would get, the skies obscured by clouds and mist, the gloom settled down about the buildings, spinning shadow webs. He had listened to and identified all of the dark's sounds by then; they were as familiar as the beating of his pulse. He began to move, just another shadow in the night. He slipped down the streets in quick, cautious dartings that carried him from one pool of darkness to the next. He did not carry any weapon but the Stiehl, and the Stiehl was safely sheathed within the covering of his pants. The only weapons he needed right now were instinct and stealth.

He found a juncture of streets where he could crouch in wait within a deeply shadowed entry that opened out of a tunnel stairwell and gave him a clear view of everything for almost two blocks. He settled himself back against the stone centerpost and waited.

Almost immediately, he began thinking of the girl.

Quickening, the daughter of the King of the Silver River—she was a maddening puzzle who stirred such conflicting feelings within him that he could barely begin to sort them out. It would have been better simply to brush them all aside and do as Rimmer Dall had said he must—kill her. Yet he could not quite bring himself to do so. It was more than defiance of Dall and his continued attempts to subvert him to the Shadowen cause, more than his determination that he would handle matters in his own way; it was the doubt and hesitation she roused in him, the feeling that somehow he wasn't as much in control of matters as he believed, that *she* knew things about him he did not. Secrets—she was a harborer of so many. If he killed her, those secrets would be lost forever.

He pictured her in his mind as he had done for so many nights during their journey north. He could visualize the perfection of her features, the way the light's movement across her face and body made every aspect seem more stunning than the one before. He could hear the music in her voice. He could feel her touch. She was real and impossible at once: an elemental by her own admission, a thing made of magic, yet human as well. Pe Ell was a man whose respect for life had long since been deadened by his killings. He was a professional assassin who had never failed. He did not understand losing. He was a wall that could not be breached; he was unapproachable by others save for those brief moments he chose to tolerate their presence.

But Quickening—this strange, ephemeral girl—threatened all of that. She had it in her, he believed, to ruin everything he was and in the end to destroy him. He didn't know how, but he believed it was so. She had the power to undo him. He should have been anxious to kill her then, to do as Rimmer Dall had asked. Instead, he was intrigued. He had never encountered anyone until now who he felt might threaten him. He wanted to rid himself of that threat; yet he wanted to get close to it first.

He stared out into the streets of Eldwist, down the corridors between the silent, towering buildings, and into the tunnels of endless gloom, unbothered by the seeming contradiction in his wants. The shadows reached out to him and drew him close. He was as much at home here as he had been at Southwatch, a part of the night, the emptiness, the solitude, the presence of death and absence of life. How little difference there was, he marveled, between the kingdoms of Uhl Belk and the Shadowen.

He relaxed. He belonged in the anonymity of darkness.

It was *she* and those who stayed with her that required the light.

He thought of them momentarily. It was a way to pass the time. He pictured each as he had pictured Quickening and considered the potential of each as a threat to him.

Carisman. He dismissed the tunesmith almost immediately.

Horner Dees. What was it about that old man that bothered him so? He hated the way the bearish Tracker looked at him, as if seeing right through skin and bone. He reflected on it momentarily, then shrugged it away. Dees was used up. He wielded no magic.

Morgan Leah. He disliked the Highlander because he was so obviously Quickening's favorite. She might even love him in her own way, although he doubted she was capable of real feeling—not her—not the elemental daughter of the King of the Silver River. She was simply using him as she was using them all, her reasons her own, carefully concealed. The Highlander was young and rash and probably would find a way to kill himself before he became a real problem.

That left Walker Boh.

As always, Pe Ell took an extra measure of time to ponder him. Walker Boh was an enigma. He had magic, but he didn't seem comfortable using it. Quickening had practically raised him from the dead, yet he seemed almost uninterested in living. He was preoccupied with matters of his own, things that he kept hidden deep down inside, secrets as puzzling as those of the girl. Walker Boh had a sense of things that surprised Pe Ell; he might even be prescient. Once, some years ago, Pe Ell had heard of a man who lived in the Eastland and could commune with animals and read the changes in the Lands before they came to pass. This man, perhaps? He was said to be a formidable opponent; the Gnomes were terrified of him.

Pe Ell rocked forward slowly and clasped his hands together. He would have to be especially careful of One-arm, he knew. Pe Ell wasn't frightened of Walker Boh, but neither was Walker Boh frightened of him.

Yet.

The minutes drifted away, the night deepened, and the streets remained empty and still. Pe Ell waited patiently, knowing the Rake would eventually come as it had come each night,

searching for their hiding place, seeking them out, and determined to exterminate them as it had been trained to do. Tonight
would be no exception.

He let himself consider for a time the implications of having
possession of a magic like the Black Elfstone—a magic that could
negate all other magics. Once he had it in his grasp—as he
eventually would—what would he do with it? His narrow, sharp
features crinkled with amusement. He would use it against Rimmer Dall for starters. He would use it to negate Dall's own
magic. He would slip into Southwatch, find the First Seeker,
and put an end to him. Rimmer Dall had grown more annoying
than useful; Pe Ell no longer cared to tolerate him. It was time
to sever their partnership once and for all. After that, he might
use the talisman against the rest of the Shadowen, perhaps make
himself their leader. Except that he really didn't want anything
to do with them. Better, perhaps, simply to eliminate them all—
or as many as he could reach. He smiled expectantly. That
would be an interesting challenge.

He leaned back contentedly in the shadows of his shelter.
He would have to learn how to use the magic of the Elfstone
first, of course. Would that prove difficult? Would he have to
rely on Quickening to instruct him? Would he have to find a
way to keep her alive awhile longer? He shivered with anticipation. The solution would present itself when it was time. For
now, he must concentrate on gaining possession of the Elfstone.

Almost an hour passed before he finally heard the approach
of the Rake. The Creeper came from the east, its metal legs
scraping softly on the stone as it slipped through the gloom. It
came right toward Pe Ell, and the assassin melted back into the
darkness of the stairwell until his eyes were level with the street.
The creature looked enormous from this angle, its immense body
balanced on iron-encased legs, its whiplike tail curled and ready,
and its tentacles outstretched and sweeping the damp air like
feelers. Steam rose from its iron shell, the heat of its body re-
acting to the cool air, condensation forming and dripping onto
the street. It sent its tentacles snaking into doorways and windows, along the gutters below the walkways, down the sewers,
and into the wrecks of the ancient skeletons of the toppled stone

carriages. For an instant Pe Ell thought the beast would spy him out, but then something caught the Creeper's attention and it scuttled past and disappeared into the night.

Pe Ell waited until he could just barely hear it, then slipped from his hiding place in pursuit.

He tracked the Rake for the remainder of the night, down streets and alleyways, through the foyers and halls of massive old buildings, and along the edges of the cliffs that bounded the city west and north. The Creeper went everywhere, a beast at hunt, constantly on the move. Pe Ell stalked it relentlessly. Most of the time he could only hear it, not see it. He had to be very sure he did not get too close. If he did, the creature would sense his presence and come after him. Pe Ell made himself a part of the shadows, just another piece of an endless stone landscape, a thing of vapor and nonbeing that not even the Rake could detect. He kept on the walkways and close to the building walls, avoided the streets and their maze of trapdoors, and stayed clear of any open spaces. He did not hurry; he kept his pace steady. Playing cat and mouse required a careful exercise of patience.

And then suddenly, near dawn, the Rake disappeared. He had glimpsed it only minutes earlier as it skittered away down a street in the central section of the city, rather close to where the others of the company were hiding. He could hear its legs and tentacles scrape, its body turn, and then there was nothing. Silence. Pe Ell slowed, stopped, and listened. Still there was nothing. He moved ahead cautiously, following a narrow alleyway until it emerged into a street. Still concealed within the shadows of the alleyway, he peered out. Left, the street tunneled into the gloom past rows of buildings that stretched skyward, flat faced and unrevealing. Right, the street was bisected by a cross street and bracketed by twin towers with huge, shadowed foyers that disappeared into complete blackness.

Pe Ell searched the street both ways, listened again, and began to fume. How could he have lost it so suddenly? How could it have just disappeared?

He was aware again of a brightening of the air, a hint of the sun's pending emergence into the world beyond the clouds and mist and gloom of Eldwist. It was daybreak. The Rake would go into hiding now. Perhaps it already had. Pe Ell frowned, then scanned the impenetrable shadows of the buildings across the way. Was that its hiding place, he wondered?

He started from his own concealment for a look when that sixth sense he relied upon so heavily warned him what was happening. The Rake was in hiding all right, but not for the reason he had first imagined. It was in hiding because it was setting a trap. It knew the intruders were still loose in the city, somewhere close. It knew they would have to kill it or it would kill them. So on the chance that they had followed, it had set a trap. It was waiting now to see if anything fell into it.

Pe Ell felt a rush of cold determination surge through him as he shrank back into the gloom of the alleyway. Cat and mouse, that's all it was. He smiled and waited.

Long minutes passed and there was only silence. Pe Ell continued to wait.

Then abruptly the Rake emerged from the shadows of the building across the street to the left, dancing almost gracefully into view, body poised. Pe Ell held his breath as the monster tested the air, turning slowly about. Satisfied, it moved on. Pe Ell exhaled slowly and followed.

It was growing brighter now, and the night air evolved into a sort of gray haze that reflected the dampness so that it became even more difficult to see what lay ahead. Yet Pe Ell did not slow, relying on his hearing to warn him of any danger, always conscious of the sound of the Rake moving ahead. It was no longer worrying about pursuit. Its night's work was finished; it was headed home.

To the lair of the Stone King, Pe Ell thought, impatient for the first time since his hunt had begun.

He caught up with the Rake as it slowed before a flat-sided building with a shadowed alcove thirty feet high and twice that across. The Rake's feelers probed the stone at the top of the alcove, and a section of the wall within swung silently away, lifting into the gloom. Without a backward glance, the Rake slipped through the opening. When it was inside, the wall swung back into place.

Got you! Pe Ell thought fiercely.

Nevertheless, he stood where he was for almost an hour afterward, waiting to see if anything else would happen, making certain that this was not another trap. When he was sure that it was safe, he emerged and darted along the edge of the buildings, following the walkways until he stood before the hidden entry.

He took a long time to study it. The stone facing was flat and smooth. He could trace the seams of the opening from within the frame of the alcove, but he would never have noticed the door without first knowing it was there. Far above him, just visible against the gray of the stone, he could detect a kind of lever. A release, he thought triumphantly. A way in.

He stood there for a while longer, thinking. Then he moved away, searching the buildings across the street for a hiding place. Once safely concealed, he would sit down and figure out a way to trip that lever. Then he would sleep again until it was dark. When night came, he would wake and wait for the Rake to go out.

When it did, he would go in.

CHAPTER

22

NIGHT LAY ACROSS the Westland in a humid, airless pall, the heat of the day lingering with sullen determination long after the sun's fiery ball had disappeared into the horizon. Darkness disdained to offer even the smallest measure of relief, empty of cool breezes, devoid of any suggestion of a drop in the temperature. The day's swelter was rooted in the earth, a stubborn presence that would not be dispelled, breathing fire out of its concealment like an underground dragon. Insects buzzed and hummed and flew in erratic, random bursts. Trees were heat-ravaged giants, drooping and exhausted. A full moon crawled across the southern horizon, gibbous and shimmering against the haze. The only sounds that broke the stillness were those dredged from the throats of hunted creatures an instant before their hunters silenced them forever.

Even on the hottest of nights, the game of life and death played on.

Wren Ohmsford and the big Rover Garth turned their horses down the rutted trail that led into the town of Grimpen Ward. It had taken them a week to journey there from the Tirfing, navigating hidden passes of the Irrybis that only the Rovers knew, following the trails of the Wilderun north and west, shying well clear of the treacherous Shroudslip, winding at last over Whistle Ridge and down into the dank mire of the Westland's most infamous lair.

When there was nowhere else to run or hide, it was said, there was always Grimpen Ward. Thieves, cutthroats, and misfits of all sorts came to the outlaw town to find refuge. Walled away by the Irrybis and the Rock Spur, swallowed up by the teeming jungle of the Wilderun, Grimpen Ward was a haven for renegades of every ilk.

It was also a deathtrap from which few escaped, a pit of vipers preying on one another because there was no one else, devouring their own kind with callous indifference and misguided amusement, feeding in a frenzy of need and boredom. Of those who came to Grimpen Ward seeking to stay alive, most ended up disappointed.

The town grew visible through the trees, and Wren and Garth slowed. Lights burned through the window glass of buildings black with grime, their shutters sagging and broken, their walls and roofs and porches so battered and ravaged by time and neglect that they seemed in immediate danger of collapse. Doors stood ajar in a futile effort to dispel the heat trapped within. Laughter broke sharply against the forest silence, rough, forced, desperate. Glasses clinked and sometimes shattered. Now and again, a scream sounded, solitary and disembodied.

Wren glanced at Garth and then signed, *We'll leave the horses hidden here.* Garth nodded. They turned their mounts into the trees, rode them some distance from the road until a suitable clearing was found, and tethered them in a stand of birch.

"Softly," Wren whispered, fingers moving.

They worked their way back to the roadway and continued down. Dust rose from beneath their boots and settled in a dark sheen on their faces. They had been riding all day, a slow journey through impossible heat, unable to force the pace without risking the health of their horses. The Wilderun was a morass of midsummer dampness and decay, the wood of the forests rotting into mulch, the ground soft and yielding and treacherous, the streams and drinking pools dried or poisoned, and the air a furnace that parched and withered. No matter how terrible the heat might be in other parts of the Four Lands, it was always twice as bad here. A stagnant, inhospitable cesspool, the Wilderun had long been regarded as a place to which the discards of the population of the Four Lands were welcome.

Bands of Rovers frequently came to Grimpen Ward to barter and trade. Accustomed to the vagaries and treacheries of Men,

outsiders themselves from society, branded outlaws and troub-
lemakers everywhere, the Rovers were right at home. Even so,
they traveled in tight-knit families and relied on strength of numbers to keep themselves safe. Seldom did they venture into
Grimpen Ward alone as Wren and Garth were doing.

A chance encounter with a small family of coin traders had
persuaded the girl and her giant protector to accept the risk.
Just a day after Garth's unsuccessful attempt to backtrack and
trap their shadow, they had come upon an old man and his sons
and their wives traveling north out of the passes, returning from
a journey through the pit. Eating with them, sharing tales, Wren
had asked simply out of habit if any among them knew of the
fate of the Westland Elves, and the old man had smiled, broken
toothed and wintry, and nodded.

"Not me, girl, you understand," he had rasped softly, chewing at the end of the pipe he smoked, his gray eyes squinting
against the light. "But at the Iron Feather in Grimpen Ward they
be an old woman that does. The Addershag, she's called. Haven't
spoke to her myself, for I don't frequent the ale houses of the
Ward, but word has it the old woman knows the tale. A seer,
they say. Queer as sin, maybe mad." He'd leaned into the fire's
glow. "They's making use of her someway, I hear. A pack of
them snakes. Making her give them secrets to take others'
money." He shook his head. "We stayed clear."

Later, they had talked it over, Wren and Garth, when the
family was asleep and they were left alone. The reasons to stay
out of the Wilderun were clear enough; but there were reasons
to go in as well. For one, there was the matter of their shadow. It
was back there still, just out of view and reach, carefully hidden
away like the threat of winter's coming. They could not catch
it and despite all their efforts and skill they could not shake it.
It clung to them, a trailing spider's web floating invisibly in their
wake. The Wilderun, they reflected, might be less to its taste
and might, with a bit of luck, bring it to grief.

For another, of course, there was the indisputable fact that
this was the first instance since Wren had started asking about
the Elves that she had received a positive response. It seemed
unreasonable not to test its merit.

So they had come, just the two of them, defying the odds,

determined to see what sort of resolution a visit to Grimpen Ward would bring. Now, a week's journey later, they were about to find out.

They passed down through the center of the town, eyes quick but thorough in their hunt. Ale houses came and went, and there was no Iron Feather. Men lurched past them, and a handful of women, tough and hard all, reeking of ale and the stale smell of sweat. The shouts and laughter grew louder, and even Garth seemed to sense how frantic they were, his rough face grim-set and fierce. Several of the men approached Wren, drunken, unseeing, anxious for money or pleasure, blind to the danger that mirrored in Garth's eyes. The big Rover shoved them away.

At a juncture of cross-streets, Wren caught sight of a cluster of Rovers working their way back toward their wagons at the end of an unlit road. She hailed them down and asked if they knew of the Iron Feather. One made a face and pointed. The band hurried off without comment. Wren and Garth continued on.

They found the ale house in the center of Grimpen Ward, a sprawling ramshackle structure framed of splitting boards and rusting nails, the veranda fronting painted a garish red and blue. Wide double doors were tied open with short lengths of rope; within, a crush of men sang and drank against a long bar and about trestle benches. Wren and Garth stepped inside, peering through the haze of heat and smoke. A few heads turned; eyes stared momentarily and looked away again. No one wanted to meet Garth's gaze. Wren moved up to the bar, caught the attention of the server, and signaled for ale. The server, a narrow-faced man with sure, steady hands brought the mugs over and waited for his money.

"Do you know a woman called the Addershag?" Wren asked him.

Expressionless, the man shook his head, accepted his money, and walked away. Wren watched him stop and whisper something to another man. The man slipped away. Wren sipped at her mug, found the ale unpleasantly warm, and moved down the serving bar, repeating her question as she went. No one knew of the Addershag. One grinned, leered, and made an unimaginative suggestion. Then he saw Garth and hurried off. Wren continued on. A second man reached out at her, and she flicked his arm away. When he reached again, she brought the heel of her hand into his face so hard he was knocked unconscious. She stepped around him, anxious to be done with this business. It was dangerous to continue on, even with Garth to protect her.

She reached the end of the serving bar and slowed. At the very back of the room a group of men occupied a table in the shadows. One of them beckoned, waited until he was certain she had seen, then beckoned again. She hesitated, then moved forward, pushing through the crowd, Garth at her back. She came up to the table and stopped when she was just out of reach of the men seated there. They were a rough bunch—dirty, unshaven, their skin the color of paste, their eyes ferretlike and dangerous. Ale mugs sat before them, sweating.

The man who had beckoned said, "Who is it you're looking for, girl?"

"A seer called the Addershag," she answered and then waited, certain that he already knew who she was looking for and probably where she would look.

"What do you want with her?"

"I want to ask her about the Elves."

The man snorted. "There aren't any Elves."

Wren waited.

The man eased forward in his chair. He was thick-featured, and his eyes were empty of feeling. "Suppose I decided to help you. Just suppose. Would you do something for me in turn?" The man studied her face a moment and grinned insolently. "Not that. I just want you to talk to her for me, ask her something. I can tell what you are by your clothes. You're a Rover. See, the Addershag is a Rover, too." He paused. "Didn't know that, did you? Well, she doesn't feel like talking to us, but she might feel different about you, one of her own." His gaze on her was hard and sullen. All pretense was gone now, the game under way. "So if I take you to her, then you have to ask a question or two for me. That a deal?"

Wren knew already that the man was planning to kill her. It was simply a question of how and when he and his friends would try. But she also knew he might really be able to take her to the Addershag. She weighed the risks and rewards momentarily, then said, "Agreed. But my friend goes with me."

"Whatever you say." The man smirked. "Course, my friends go, too. So I'll feel safe. Everyone goes."

Wren looked at the man appraisingly. Heavyset, muscular, an experienced cutthroat. The others the same. If they got her in a tight place . . .

"Garth," she said, looking back at him. She signed quickly, screening her movements from the men at the table. Garth nodded. She turned back to the table. "I'm ready."

The speaker rose, the others with him, an anxious, hungry-looking bunch. There was no mistaking what they were about. The speaker began ambling along the rear wall toward a door leading out. Wren followed, cautious, alert. Garth was a step behind; the remainder of the table trailed. They passed through the door into an empty hall and continued toward a back entrance. The sounds of the ale house disappeared abruptly as the door closed.

The man spoke over his shoulder. "I want to know how she reads the gaming cards like she does. How she reads the dice roll. I want to know how she can see what the players are thinking." He grinned. "Something for you, girl; something for me. I have to make a living, too."

He stopped unexpectedly before a side door, and Wren tensed. But the man ignored her, reaching into his pocket to extract a key. He inserted it in the lock and twisted. The lock released with a click and the door swung open. There were stairs beyond leading down. The man groped inside and brought forth an oil lamp, lit it, and handed it to Wren.

"She's in the cellar," he said, motioning through the door. "That's where we're keeping her for the moment. You talk to her. Take your friend if you want. We'll wait here." His smile was hard and unpleasant. "Just don't come back up without something to trade for my helping you out. Understand?"

The men with him had crowded up behind them, and the reek of them filled the narrow hall. Wren could hear the ragged sound of their breathing.

She moved close to the speaker and put her face inches from

his own. "What I understand is that Garth will remain here with you." She held his gaze. "Just in case."

He shrugged uncomfortably. Wren nodded to Garth, indicating the door and the gathering of men. Then holding the lamp before her, she started down the steps.

It was a shadowy descent. The stairway wound along a dirt wall shored up with timbers, the earth smell thick and pungent. It was cooler here, if only marginally. Insects skittered from underfoot. Strands of webbing brushed her face. The steps angled left along a second wall and ended. The cellar opened up before her in the lamplight.

An old woman sat slumped against the far wall, almost lost in the gloom. Her body was a dried husk, and her face had withered into a maze of lines and furrows. Ragged white hair tumbled down about her frail shoulders, and her gnarled hands were clasped before her. She wore a cloth shift and old boots. Wren approached and knelt before her. The ancient head lifted, revealing eyes that were milky and fixed. The old woman was blind.

Wren placed the oil lamp on the floor beside her. "Are you the seer they call the Addershag, old mother?" she asked softly.

The staring eyes blinked and a thin voice rasped, "Who wishes to know? Tell me your name."

"My name is Wren Ohmsford."

The white head tilted, shifting toward the stairway and the door above. "Are you with them?"

Wren shook her head. "I'm with myself. And a companion. Both of us are Rovers."

Aged hands reached out to touch her face, exploring its lines and hollows, scraping along the girl's skin like dried leaves. Wren did not move. The hands withdrew.

"You are an Elf."

"I have Elven blood."

"An Elf!" The old woman's voice was rough and insistent, a hiss against the silence of the ale house cellar. The wrinkled face cocked to one side as if reflecting. "I am the Addershag. I am the seer of the future and what it holds, the teller of truths. What do you wish of me?"

Wren rocked back slightly on the heels of her boots. "I am

searching for the Westland Elves. I was told a week ago that you might know where to find them—if they still exist."

The Addershag cackled softly. "Oh, they exist, all right. They do indeed. But it's not to everyone they show themselves—to none at all in many years. Is it so important to you, Elf-girl, that you see them? Do you search them out because you have need of your own kind?" The milky eyes stared unseeing at Wren's face. "No, not you. Despite your blood, you're a Rover before everything, and a Rover has need of no one. Yours is the life of the wanderer, free to travel any path you choose, and you glory in it." She grinned, nearly toothless. "Why, then?"

"Because it is a charge I have been given—a charge I have chosen to accept," Wren answered carefully.

"A charge, is it?" The lines and furrows of the old woman's face deepened. "Bend close to me, Elf-girl."

Wren hesitated, then leaned forward tentatively. The Addershag's hands came up again, the fingers exploring. They passed once more across Wren's face, then down her neck to her body. When they touched the front of the girl's blouse, they jerked back as if burned and the old woman gasped. "Magic!" she howled.

Wren started, then seized the other's wrists impulsively. "What magic? What are you saying?"

But the Addershag shook her head violently, her lips clamped shut, and her head sunk into her shrunken breast. Wren held her a moment longer, then let her go.

"Elf-girl," the old woman whispered then, "who sends you in search of the Westland Elves?"

Wren took a deep breath against her fears and answered, "The shade of Allanon."

The aged head lifted with a snap. "Allanon!" She breathed the name like a curse. "So! A Druid's charge, is it? Very well. Listen to me, then. Go south through the Wilderun, cross the Irrybis and follow the coast of the Blue Divide. When you have reached the caves of the Rocs, build a fire and keep it burning three days and nights. One will come who can help you. Do you understand?"

"Yes," Wren replied, wondering at the same time if she really did. Rocs, did the old woman say? Weren't they supposed to have been a form of giant coastal bird?

"Beware, Elf-girl," the other warned, a stick-thin hand lifting. "I see danger ahead for you, hard times, and treachery and evil beyond imagining. My visions are in my head, truths that haunt me with their madness. Heed me, then. Keep your own counsel, girl. Trust no one!"

She gestured violently, then slumped back again, her blind gaze fixed and hard. Wren glanced down the length of her body and started. The Addershag's worn dress had slipped back from her boots to reveal an iron chain and clamp fastened to her leg.

Wren reached out and took the aged hands in her own. "Old mother," she said gently. "Let me get you free of this place. My friend and I can help you, if you'll let us. There is no reason for you to remain a prisoner."

"A prisoner? Ha!" The Addershag lurched forward, teeth bared like an animal at bay. "What I look and what I am are two very different things!"

"But the chain . . ."

"Holds me not an instant longer than I wish!" A wicked smile creased the wrinkled face until its features almost disappeared. "Those men, those fools—they take me by force and chain me in this cellar and wait for me to do their bidding!" Her voice lowered. "They are small, greedy men, and all that interests them is the wealth of others. I could give them what they want; I could do their bidding and be gone. But this is a game that interests me. I like the teasing of them. I like the sound of their whining. I let them keep me for a time because it amuses me. And when I am done being entertained, Elf-girl, when I tire of them and decide again to be free, why . . . this!"

Her stick hands freed themselves, then twisted sharply before Wren's eyes and were transformed into writhing snakes, tongues darting, fangs bared, hissing into the silence. Wren jerked away, shielding her face. When she looked again, the snakes had disappeared.

She swallowed against her fear. "Were . . . they real?" she asked thickly, her face flushed and hot.

The Addershag smiled with dark promise. "Go, now," she whispered, shrinking back into the shadows. "Take what I told you and use it as you will. And guard yourself closely, Elf-girl. Beware."

Wren hesitated, pondering whether she should ask answers to the rush of questions that flooded through her. She decided against it. She picked up the oil lamp and rose. "Goodbye, old mother," she said.

She went back through the darkness, squinting into the light of the oil lamp to find the stairs, feeling the sightless gaze of the Addershag follow after her. She climbed the steps swiftly and slipped back through the cellar doorway into the ale house hall.

Garth was waiting for her, facing the knot of men who had come with them from the front room. The sounds of the ale house filtered through the closed door beyond, muffled and raucous. The eyes of the men glittered. She could sense their hunger.

"What did the old woman tell you?" the leader snapped.

Wren lifted the oil lamp to shed a wider circle of light and shook her head. "Nothing. She doesn't know of the Elves or if she does, she keeps it to herself. As for gaming, she won't say a word about that either." She paused. "She doesn't seem any kind of a seer to me. I think she's mad."

Anger reflected in the other man's eyes. "What a poor liar you are, girl."

Wren's expression did not change. "I'll give you some good advice, cutthroat. Let her go. It might save your life."

A knife appeared in the other's hand, a glint of metal come out of nowhere. "But not yours . . ."

He didn't finish because Wren had already slammed the oil lamp onto the hallway floor before him, shattering the glass, spilling the oil across the wood, exploding the flames everywhere. Fire raced across the wooden planks and up the walls. The speaker caught fire, shrieked, and stumbled back into the unwilling arms of his fellows. Garth and Wren fled the other way, reaching the backdoor in seconds. Shoulder lowered, Garth hammered into the wooden barrier and it flew from its hinges as if made of paper. The girl and the big Rover burst through the opening into the night, howls of rage and fear chasing after them. Down between the buildings of the town they raced, swift and silent, and moments later emerged back onto the main street of Grimpen Ward.

They slowed to a walk, glanced back, and listened. Nothing. The shouts and laughter of the ale houses nearest them drowned out what lay behind. There was no sign of fire. There was no indication of pursuit.

Side by side, Wren and Garth walked back up the roadway in the direction they had come, moving through the revelers, the heat and the gloom, calm and unhurried.

"We're going south to the Blue Divide," Wren announced as they reached the edge of the town, signing the words.

Garth nodded and made no response.

Swiftly they disappeared into the night.

CHAPTER

23

HEN WALKER BOH, Quickening, and Carisman left Morgan and Horner Dees, they traveled only a short distance east through the darkened streets of Eldwist before slowing to a halt. Walker and the girl faced each other. Neither had said anything about stopping; it was as if they had read each other's mind. Carisman looked from one face to the other in confusion.

"You know where the Stone King is hiding," Quickening said. She made it a statement of fact.

"I think I do," Walker answered. He stared into the depthless black eyes and marveled at the assurance he found there. "Did you sense that when you chose to come with me?"

She nodded. "When he is found, I must be there."

She didn't explain her reasoning, and Walker didn't ask. He glanced into the distance, trying futilely to penetrate the gloom, to see beyond the mist and darkness, and to find something of what he was meant to do. But there was nothing to be found out there, of course. The answers to his questions lay somewhere within.

"I believe the Stone King hides within the dome," he said quietly. "I suspected as much when we were there several days ago. There appear to be no entrances, yet as I touched the stone and walked about the walls I sensed life. There was a presence that I could not explain. Then, yesterday, when we were beneath the earth, trapped in that underground cavern, I again sensed that presence—only it was above us this time. I took a quick calculation when we emerged from the tunnels. The dome is seated directly above the cavern."

He stopped momentarily and glanced about. "Eldwist is the creation of its master. Uhl Belk has made this city of the old world his own, changing to stone what wasn't already, expanding his domain outward symmetrically where the land allows it. The dome sits centermost, a hub in a wheel of streets and buildings, walls and wreckage."

His pale face turned to meet hers. "Uhl Belk is there."

He could almost see the life brighten in her eyes. "Then we must go to meet him," she said.

They started off again, following the walkway to the end of the block and then turning abruptly north. Walker led, keeping them carefully back from the streets, against the walls of the buildings, clear of the open spaces, and away from the danger of trapdoors. Neither he nor Quickening spoke; Carisman hummed softly. They watched the gloom like hawks, listened for strange sounds, and smelled and tasted the damp, stale air warily. A brief rain caught up with them and left them shedding water from their cloaks and hoods, their feet chilled within their boots.

Walker Boh thought of home. He had done so increasingly of late, driven by the constant, unrelenting pressure of being hemmed about by the city's stone and darkness to seek out something of what had once been pleasant and healing. For a time he had sought to banish all thoughts of Hearthstone; its memories cut at him like broken glass. The cottage that he had adopted as his home had been burned to the ground in the battle with the Shadowen. Cogline and Rumor had died there. He had barely escaped dying himself, and keeping his life had cost him his arm. He had once believed himself invulnerable to the intrusions of the outside world. He had been vain and foolish enough to boast that what lay beyond Hearthstone presented no danger to him. He had denied the dreams that Allanon had sent him from the spirit world, the pleas that Par Ohmsford had extended for his help, and in the end the charge he had been given to go in search of Paranor and the Druids. He had encased himself in imaginary walls and believed himself secure. When those walls began collapsing, he had found that they could not be replaced and those things he had thought secure were lost.

Yet there were older memories of Hearthstone that transcended the recent tragedies. There were all those years when he had lived in peace in the valley, the seasons when the world outside did not intrude and there was time enough for everything. There were the smells of flowers, trees, and fresh water springs; the sounds of birds in early spring and insects on warm summer nights; the taste of dawn on a clear autumn morning; the feeling of serenity that came with the setting sun and the fall of night. He could reach back beyond the past few weeks and find peace in those memories. He did so now because they were all he had left to draw on.

Yet even his strongest memories provided only a momentary haven. The harsh inevitabilities of the present pressed in about him and would not be banished. He might escape for brief moments into the past, into the world that had sheltered him for a time before he was swept away by the tide of events he had sought foolishly to ignore. Escape might soothe and strengthen the spirit, but it was transitory and unresolving. His mind darted away into his memories only to find the past forever beyond his reach and the present forever at hand. He was struggling with his life, he discovered. He was adrift, a castaway fighting to keep afloat amid the wreckage of his confusion and doubt. He could almost feel himself sinking.

They reached the dome at midmorning and began their search. Working together, not willing to separate if there was any chance at all that the Stone King waited within, they began to explore the dome's surface, walking its circumference, feeling along its walls, and searching even the ground it sat upon. It was perfectly formed, although its ageing shell was pitted and cracked, rising several hundred feet into the air at its peak, spreading from wall to wall several hundred feet more. Depressions that had the look of giant thumbprints decorated the dome's peak along its upper surface, laid open like the petals of a flower, separated by bands of stone that curved downward to the foundation. Niches and alcoves indented its walls at ground level, offering no way inside, leading nowhere. Sculpted designs marked its stone, most of them almost completely worn away by time's passage, no longer decipherable, the runes of a world that had long since passed away.

"I can feel a presence still," Walker Boh said, slowing, folding his cloak about him. He glanced skyward. It was raining again, a slow, persistent drizzle. "There's something here. Something."

Quickening stood close beside him. "Magic," she whispered.

He stared at her, surprised that she had been so quick to recognize a truth that had eluded him. "It is so," he murmured. His hand stretched forth, searching. "All about, in the stone itself."

"He is here," Quickening whispered.

Carisman stepped forward and stroked the wall tentatively. His handsome brow furrowed. "Why does he not respond? Shouldn't he come out long enough to see what we want?"

"He may not even know we are here. He may not care." Quickening's soft face lifted. "He may even be sleeping."

Carisman frowned. "Then perhaps a song is needed to wake him up!"

He sang:

> *"Awake, awake, oh aged King of Stone,*
> *Come forth from your enfolding lair,*
> *We wait without, a worn and tired band,*
> *So lacking in all hope and care.*
>
> *Awake, awake, oh aged King of Stone,*
> *Be not afraid of what we bring,*
> *'Tis nothing more than finite spirit,*
> *A measure of the song I sing.*
>
> *Awake, awake, oh aged King of Stone,*
> *You who have seen all passing time,*
> *Share with us weak and mortal creatures,*
> *The truths and secrets of Mankind."*

His song ended, and he stood looking expectantly at the broad expanse of the dome. There was no response. He glanced at Quickening and Walker and shrugged. "Not his choice of music, perhaps. I shall think of another."

They moved away from the dome and into the shelter of an entry in a building that sat adjacent. Seating themselves with their backs to the wall so that they could look out at the dome, they pooled from their backpacks a collection of old bread and dried fruit for their lunch. They ate silently, staring out from the shadows into the gray rain.

"We are almost out of food," Walker said after a time. "And water. We will have to forage soon."

Carisman brightened. "I shall fish for us. I was a very good fisherman once—although I only fished for pleasure. It was a pleasing way to pass the time and compose. Walker Boh, what did you do before you came north?"

Walker hesitated, surprised by the question, unprepared to give an answer. What did he do? he asked himself. "I was a caretaker," he decided finally.

"Of what?" Carisman pressed, interested.

"Of a cottage and the land about it," he said softly, remembering.

"Of an entire valley and all the creatures that lived within it," Quickening declared, her eyes drawing Carisman's. "Walker Boh preserved life in the manner of the Elves of old. He gave of himself to replenish the land."

Walker stared at her, surprised once again. "It was a poor effort," he suggested awkwardly.

"I will not permit you to be the judge of that," the girl replied. "It is for others to determine how successful you have been in your work. You are too harsh in your criticism and lack the necessary distancing to be fair and impartial." She paused, studying him, her black eyes calm and reasoning. "I believe it will be judged that you did all that you could."

They both knew what she was talking about. Walker was strangely warmed by her words, and once again he experienced that sense of kinship. He nodded without responding and continued to eat.

When they had finished their meal they stood facing the dome once more, debating what approach to take next.

"Perhaps there is something to be seen from above," Quickening suggested. "An opening through the top of the dome or an aberration in the stone that would suggest a way in."

Walker glanced about. There was an ornate building less than a block distant that opened at its top into a belltower and gave a clear view of the dome below. They crossed to it cautiously, forever wary of trapdoors, and gained its entrance. Sculptures of winged angels and robed figures decorated its walls and ceilings. They moved inside cautiously. The central chamber was vast, the glass of its windows long disintegrated, the furnishings turned to dust. They found the stairway leading to the belltower and began to climb. The stairs had fallen away in spots, and only the bracing remained. They maneuvered along its spans, working their way upward. Floors came and went, most ragged with holes and cluttered with debris, all turned to stone, their collapse preserved in perfect relief.

They gained the belltower without difficulty and walked to the windows facing out. The city of Eldwist spread away on all sides, misted and gray, filled with the shadows of daylight's passing and night's approach. The rain had diminished, and the buildings rose like stone sentries across the span of the peninsula. The clouds had lifted slightly, and the choppy slate surface of the Tiderace and the ragged cliffs of the mainland beyond the isthmus could be seen in snatches through gaps in the lines of stone walls.

The dome sat directly below them, as closed and unrevealing at its top as it had been at its bottom. There was nothing to see, no hint of an opening, no suggestion of a way in. Nonetheless, they studied it for some time, hoping to discover something they had missed.

In the midst of their study a horn sounded, startling them.

"Urdas!" Carisman cried.

Walker and Quickening looked at each other in surprise, but Carisman had already dashed to the south window of the tower and was peering in the direction of the isthmus and the cliffs leading down.

"It must be them; that is their call!" he shouted, excitement and concern reflecting in his voice. He shaded his eyes against the glare of the dampened stone. "There! Do you see them?"

Walker and Quickening hastened to join him. The tunesmith was pointing to where the stairway descending the cliffs from the overlook was barely visible through the mist. There were glimpses of movement to be seen on the stairs, small, hunched figures crouched low as if to hide even from the shadows. Urdas, Walker recognized, and they were coming down.

"What is it that they think they are doing!" Carisman exclaimed, obviously upset. "They cannot come here!"

The Urdas faded into a patch of fog and were lost from view. Carisman wheeled on his companions, stricken. "If they are not stopped, they will all be killed!"

"The Urdas are no longer your responsibility, Carisman," Walker Boh declared softly. "You are no longer their king."

Carisman looked unconvinced. "They are children, Walker! They have no understanding of what lives down here. The Rake or the Maw Grint, either one will destroy them. I can't imagine how they slipped past the Koden . . ."

"In the same way as Horner Dees did ten years ago," Walker cut him short. "With a sacrifice of lives. And still they come ahead. They are not as worried about themselves, it appears, as you are."

Carisman wheeled on Quickening. "Lady, you've seen the way they react to things. What do they know of the Stone King and his magic? If they are not stopped . . ."

Quickening seized his arms and held them. "No, Carisman. Walker Boh is right. The Urdas are dangerous to you now as well."

But Carisman shook his head vehemently. "No, Lady. Never to me. They were my family before I abandoned them."

"They were your captors!"

"They cared for me and protected me in the only way they knew how. Lady, what am I to do? They have come here to find me! Why else would they be taking such a risk? I think they have never come so far away from home. They are here because they think you stole me away. Can I abandon them a second time, this time to die for a mistake that I can prevent them from making?" Carisman pulled free, slowly, gently. "I have to go to them. I have to warn them."

"Carisman . . ."

The tunesmith was already backing toward the belltower stairs. "I have been an orphan of the storm all of my life, blown from one island to the next, never with family or home, always in search of somewhere to belong and someone to belong to. The Urdas gave me what I have of both, little as it may seem to you. I cannot let them die needlessly."

He turned and started quickly down the stairs. Quickening and Walker exchanged wordless glances and hurried after.

They caught up with him on the street below. "We'll come with you then," Walker said.

Carisman whirled about at once. "No, no, Walker! You cannot show yourselves to them! If you do, they might think I am threatened by you—perhaps even that I am a prisoner! They might attack, and you could be hurt! No. Let me deal with them. I know them; I can talk with them, explain what has happened, and turn them back before it is too late." His handsome features crinkled with worry. "Please, Walker? Lady?"

There was nothing more to be said. Carisman had made up his mind and would not allow them to change it. As a final concession they demanded that they be allowed to accompany him at least as far as was reasonable to assure that they would be close at hand in case of trouble. Carisman was reluctant to agree even to that much, concerned that he was taking them away from work that was more important, that he was delaying their search for the Stone King. Both Quickening and Walker refused to argue the point. They walked in silence, single file along the walkways, down the tunneled streets, traveling south through the city. He would meet the Urdas at the city's south edge, Carisman told them, sweeping back his blond hair, squaring himself for his encounter. Walker found him odd and heroic at once, a strange parody of a man aspiring to reality yet unable quite to grasp it. Give thought to what you are doing, he begged the tunesmith at one point. But Carisman's answering smile was cheerfully beguiling and filled with certainty. He had done all the thinking he cared to do.

When they neared the boundaries of the city, the rocky flats of the isthmus peeking through the gaps in the buildings, Carisman brought them to a halt.

"Wait for me here," he told them firmly. Then he made them promise not to follow after him. "Do not show yourselves;

it will only frighten the Urdas. Give me a little time. I am certain I can make them understand. As I said, my friends—they are like children."

He clasped their hands in farewell and walked on. He turned at one point to make certain they were doing as he had asked, then waved back to them. His handsome face was smiling and assured. They watched the mist curl about him, gather him up, and finally cause him to disappear.

Walker glanced at the buildings surrounding them, chose a suitable one, and steered Quickening toward it. They entered, climbed the stairs to the top floor, and found a room where a bank of windows gaped open to the south. From there they could watch the Urdas approach. The gnarled figures were strung out along the isthmus, making their way cautiously past the crevices and ruts. There were perhaps twenty of them, several obviously injured.

They watched until the Urdas reached the edge of the city and disappeared into the shadow of the buildings.

Walker shook his head. "I find myself wishing we had not agreed to this. Carisman is almost a child himself. I cannot help thinking he would have been better off not coming with us at all."

"He chose to come," Quickening reminded him. Her face tilted into the light, out of a striping of shadows. "He wanted to be free, Walker Boh. Coming with us, even here, was better than staying behind."

Walker glanced through the windows a final time. The stone of the isthmus flats and the streets below glistened with the damp, empty and still. He could hear the distant thunder of the ocean, the cries of the seabirds, and the rushing of the wind down the cliffs. He felt alone.

"I wonder sometimes how many like Carisman there are," he said finally. "Orphans, as he called himself. How many left to roam the land, made outcasts by Federation rule, their magic not the gift it was intended to be, but a curse they must disguise if they would keep their lives."

Quickening seated herself against the wall and studied him. "A great many, Walker Boh. Like Carisman. Like yourself."

He eased down beside her, folding his cloak about him, lifting his pale face toward the light. "I was not thinking of myself."

"Then you must do so," she said simply. "You must become aware."

He stared at her. "Aware of what?"

"Of the possibilities of your life. Of the reasons for being who you are. If you were an elemental, you would understand. I was given life for a specific purpose. It would be terrifying to exist without that purpose. Is it not so for you?"

Walker felt his face tighten. "I have purpose in my life."

Her smile was unexpected and dazzling. "No, Walker Boh, you do not. You have thrust from you any sense of purpose and made yourself an outcast twice over—first, for having been born with the legacy of Brin Ohmsford's magic, and second, for having fallen heir to her trust. You deny who and what you are. When I healed your arm, I read your life. Tell me this is not so."

He took a deep breath. "Why is it that I feel we are so much alike, Quickening? It is neither love nor friendship. It is something in between. Am I joined to you somehow?"

"It is our magic, Walker Boh."

"No," he said quickly. "It is something more."

Her beautiful face masked all traces of the emotion that flickered in her eyes. "It is what we have come here to do."

"To find the Stone King and take back from him the stolen Black Elfstone. Somehow." Walker nodded solemnly. "And for me, to regain the use of my arm. And for Morgan Leah, to regain the magic of the Sword of Leah. All somehow. I have listened to your explanations. Is it true that you have not been told how any of this is to be accomplished? Or are there secrets that you hide from us as Pe Ell charges?"

"Walker Boh," she said softly. "You turn my questions into your own and ask of me what I would ask of you. We both keep something of the truth at bay. It cannot be so for much longer. I will make a bargain with you. When you are ready to confront your truth, I shall confront mine."

Walker struggled to understand. "I no longer fear the magic I was born with," he said, studying the lines of her face, tracing

its curves and angles as if she were in danger of disappearing
before he could secure a memory of her. "I listened once to my
nephew Par Ohmsford admonish me that the magic was a gift
and not a curse. I scorned him. I was frightened of the implications of having the magic. I feared . . ."

He caught himself, an iron grip that tightened on his voice
and thoughts instantly. A shadow of something terrifying had
shown itself to him, a shadow that had grown familiar to him
over the years. It had no face, but it spoke with the voices of
Allanon and Cogline and his father and even himself. It whispered of history and need and the laws of Mankind. He thrust
it away violently.

Quickening leaned forward and with gentle fingers touched
his face. "I fear only that you will continue to deny yourself,"
she whispered. "Until it is too late."

"Quickening . . ."

Her fingers moved across his mouth, silencing him. "There
is a scheme to life, to all of its various happenings and events,
to everything we do within the time allotted to us. We can
understand that scheme if we let ourselves, if we do not become
frightened of knowing. Knowledge is not enough if there is not
also acceptance of that knowledge. Anyone can give you knowledge, Walker Boh, but only you can learn how to accept it.
That must come from within. So it is that my father has sent
me to summon you and Pe Ell and Morgan Leah to Eldwist; so
it is that the combination of your magics shall free the Black
Elfstone and begin the healing process of the Lands. I know that
this is to be. In time, I shall know how. But I must be ready to
accept its truths when that happens. It is so as well for you."

"I will . . ."

"No, you will not be ready, Walker," she anticipated him,
"if you continue to deny truths already known to you. That is
what you must realize. Now speak no more of it to me. Only
think on what I have said."

She turned away. It was not a rebuff; she did not intend it
that way. It was a simple breaking off, an ending of talk, done
not to chastise but to allow him space in which to explore himself. He sat staring at her for a time, then turned introspective.
He gave himself over to the images her words conjured. He

found himself thinking of other voices in other times, of the world he had come from with its false measure of worth, its fears of the unknown, its subjugation to a government and rules it did not wish to comprehend. *Bring back the Druids and Paranor,* Allanon had charged him. And would that begin a changing back of the world, of the Four Lands, into what they had been? And would that make things better? He doubted, but he found his doubts founded more in a lack of understanding than in his fears. What was he to do? He was to recover the Black Elfstone, carry it to disappeared Paranor, and somehow, in some way, bring back the Keep. Yet what would that accomplish? Cogline was gone. All of the Druids were gone. There was no one . . .

But himself.

No! He almost screamed the word aloud. It bore the face of the thing he feared, the thing he struggled so hard to keep from himself. It was the terrifying possibility that had scratched and clawed around the edges of his self-imposed shield for as long as he could remember.

He would not take up the Druid cause!

Yet he was Brin Ohmsford's last descendent. He was bearer of the trust that had been left to her by Allanon. *Not in your lifetime. Keep it safe for generations to come. One day it will be needed again.* Words from the distant past, spoken by the Druid's shade after death, haunting, unfulfilled.

I haven't the magic! he wailed in desperation, in denial. *Why should it be me? Why?*

But he already knew. Need. Because there was need. It was the answer that Allanon had given to all of the Ohmsfords, to each of them, year after year, generation after generation. Always.

He wrestled with the specter of his destiny in the silence of his thoughts. The moments lengthened. Finally he heard Quickening say, "It grows dark, Walker Boh."

He glanced up, saw the failing of the light as dusk approached. He climbed to his feet and peered south into the flats. The isthmus was empty. There was no sign of the Urdas.

"It's been too long," he muttered and started for the stairs.

They descended quickly, emerged from the building, and began following the walkway south toward the city's edge. Shadows were already spreading into dark pools, the light chased west to the fringes of the horizon. The seabirds had gone to roost, and the pounding of the ocean had faded to a distant moan. The stone beneath their feet echoed faintly with their footsteps as if whispering secrets to break the silence.

They reached the fringe of the city and slowed, proceeding more cautiously now, searching the gloom for any signs of danger. There was no movement to be found. The mist curled its damp tendrils through vacant windows and down sewer grates, and there was a sense of a hidden presence at work. Ahead, the isthmus flats stretched out into the darkness, broken and ragged and lifeless.

They stepped clear of the building walls and stopped.

Carisman's body was slumped against a pillar of rock at the end of the street, pinned fast by a dozen spears. He had been dead for some time, the blood from his wounds washed away by the rain.

It appeared that the Urdas had gone back the way they had come.

They had taken Carisman's head with them.

Even children can be dangerous, Walker Boh thought bleakly. He reached over for Quickening's hand and locked it in his own. He tried to imagine what Carisman's thoughts had been when he realized his family had disowned him. He tried to tell himself that there was nothing he could have done to prevent it.

Quickening moved close to him. They stood staring at the dead tunesmith wordlessly for a moment more, then turned and walked back into the city.

24

THEY DID NOT RETURN to their normal place of concealment that night; it was already dusk when they departed the flats and the distance back through the city
was too great to cover safely. Instead, they found a
building close at hand, a low, squat structure with winding, narrow halls and rooms with doors opening through at both ends
to provide a choice of escape routes if the Rake should appear.
Settled deep within the stone interior of the building, shut away
with barely enough light to see each other at arm's length, they
ate their dinner of dried fruits and vegetables, stale bread, and
a little water and tried to banish the ghost of Carisman from
their presence. The dead tunesmith surfaced in memories, in
unspoken words, and in the faint, soft roll of the ocean's distant
waters. His face blossomed in the shadows they cast, and his
voice whispered in the sound of their breathing. Walker Boh
regarded Quickening without seeing her; his thoughts were of
Carisman and of how he had let the tunesmith go when he could
have stopped him from doing so. When Quickening touched
him on the arm, he was barely aware of the pressure of her
fingers. When she read his thoughts in the touch, he was oblivious. He felt drained and empty and impossibly alone.

Later, while she slept, he grew aware of her again. His
self-reproach had exhausted itself, his sorrow had dried up; Carisman's shade was banished, consigned at last to the place and
time in which it belonged. He sat in a box of darkness, the stone
of the walls and ceiling and floor pressing in around him, the

silence a blanket that would suffocate him, time the instrument by which he measured the approach of his own death. Could it be far away now for any of them? He watched the girl sleeping next to him, watched the rise and fall of her breast as she breathed, turned on her side, her face cradled in the crook of her arm, her silver hair fanned back in a sweep of brightness. He watched the slow, steady beat of her pulse along the slim column of her throat, searched the hollows of her face where the shadows draped and pooled, and traced the line of her body within the covering of clothes that failed to hide its perfection. She was a fragile bit of life whatever her magic, and he could not escape the feeling that despite the confidence she evidenced in her father and the command with which she had brought them north she was in peril. The feeling was elusive and difficult to credit, but it took life in his instincts and his prescience, born of the magic that he had inherited from Brin Ohmsford, magic that still ebbed and flowed within him as the tide of his belief in himself rose and fell. He could not disregard it. Quickening was at risk, and he did not know how to save her.

The night deepened and still he did not sleep. They were all at risk, of course. What he sensed of danger to the daughter of the King of the Silver River was possibly no more than what he sensed of danger to them all. It had caught up with Carisman. It would eventually catch up with Quickening as well. Perhaps what he feared was not that Quickening would die, but that she would die before she revealed the secrets she knew. There were many, he suspected. That she hid them so completely infuriated him. He was surprised at the anger his realization provoked. Quickening had brought him face to face with the darkest of his fears and then left him to stand alone against it. His entire life had been shadowed by his apprehension that Allanon's mysterious trust to the Ohmsfords, given over three hundred years ago to Brin and passed unused from generation to generation, might somehow require fulfillment by him. He had lived with the specter of it since childhood, aware of its existence as all of his family had been, finding it a ghost that would not be banished, that instead grew more substantial with the passing of the years. The magic of the Ohmsfords was alive in him as it had not been in his ancestors. The dreams of Allanon had come only to him. Cogline had made him his student and taught him the history of his art and of the Druid cause. Allanon had told him to go in search of the Druids and lost Paranor.

He shivered. Each step took him closer to the inevitable. The trust had been held for him. The phantom that had haunted him all these years had revealed a terrifying face.

He was to take the Black Elfstone and bring back Paranor.

He was to become the next Druid.

He could have laughed at the ridiculousness of the idea if he had not been so frightened of it. He despised what the Druids had done to the Ohmsfords; he saw them as sinister and self-serving manipulators. He had spent his life trying to rid himself of their curse. But it was more than that. Allanon was gone— the last of the real Druids. Cogline was gone—the last of those who had studied the art. He was alone; who was to teach him what a Druid must know? Was he to divine the study of magic somehow? Was he to teach himself? And how many years would that take? How many centuries? If the magic of the Druids was required to combat the Shadowen, such magic could not be drawn leisurely from the Histories and the tomes that had taught all the Druids who had gone before. Time did not permit it.

He clenched his teeth. It was foolish to think that he could become a Druid, even if he were willing, even if he wished it, even if the specter he had feared so for all these years turned out to be himself.

Foolish!

Walker's eyes glittered as he searched the shadows of the room for an escape from his distress. Where were the answers that he needed? Did Quickening hide those answers? Were they a part of the truths she concealed? Did she know what was to become of him? He started to reach for her, intending to shake her awake. Then he caught himself and drew back. No, he reasoned. Her knowledge was as small and imperfect as his own. With Quickening, it was more a sensing of possibilities, a divining of what might be, a prescience like his own. It was a part of the reason he felt her to be kindred; there was that sharing of abilities and uses of the magics they wielded. He forced his thoughts to slow and his mind to open and he gazed upon her as if his eyes might swallow her up. He felt something warm and generous touch him, her sleep presence, unbidden and revealed. It reminded him of his mother's when he was small and still in need of her reassurance and comfort. She was in some way a rendering of his future self. She opened him up to the possibilities of what he might be. He saw the colors of his life, the textures and the patterns that might be woven, and the styles that might be tried. He was cloth to be cut and shaped, but he lacked the tools and understanding. Quickening was doing what she could to give him both.

He dozed then for a time, still upright against the chamber wall, his legs and arms folded tightly together against his body, his face tilted forward into his cloak. When he came awake again, Quickening was looking at him. They studied each other wordlessly for a moment, each searching the other's eyes, seeking out some reading of the other's needs.

"You are afraid, Walker Boh," the girl said finally.

Walker almost smiled. "Yes, Quickening. I have been afraid forever. Afraid of this—of what is happening now—all of my life. I have run from it, hidden from it, wished it away, begged that it would disappear. I have fought to contain it. Exercising a strict and unyielding control over my life was the technique that seemed to work best. If I could dictate my own fate, then it could have no power over me. The past would be left for others; the present would belong to me."

He let his legs unfold and straightened them gingerly before him. "The Druids have affected the lives of so many of the Ohmsfords, of the children of Shannara, for generations. We have been used by them; we have been made over to serve their causes. They have changed what we are. They have made us slaves of the magic rather than simply wielders. They have altered the composition of our minds and bodies and spirits; they have subverted us. And still they are not satisfied. Look at what they expect of us now! Look at what is expected of me! I am to transcend the role of slave and become master. I am to take up the Black Elfstone—a magic I do not begin to understand. I am to use it to bring back lost Paranor. And even that is not enough. I am to bring back the Druids as well. But there are no Druids. There is only me. And if there is only me, then . . ."

He choked on the words. His resolve faltered. His patience

failed him. His anger returned, a raw and bitter echo in the silence.

"Tell me!" he begged, trying to contain his urgency.

"But I do not know," she whispered.

"You must!"

"Walker . . ."

There were tears in his eyes. "I cannot be what Allanon wants me to be—what he demands that I be! I cannot!" He took a quick, harsh breath to steady himself. "Do you see, Quickening? If I am to bring back the Druids by becoming one, if I must because there is no other way that the Races can survive the Shadowen, must I then be as they once were? Must I take control of the lives of those I profess to help, those others who are Ohmsfords, Par and Coll and Wren? For how many generations yet to come? If I am to be a Druid, must I do this? Can I do anything else?"

"Walker Boh." When she spoke his name her voice was soft and compelling. "You will be what you must, but you will still be yourself. You are not trapped in some spider's web of Druid magic that has predetermined your life, that has fated you to be but one way and one way only. There is always a choice. Always."

He had the sudden sense that she was talking of something else completely. Her perfect face strained against some inner torment, and she paused to reshape it, chasing quickly the furrows and lines. "You are frightened of your fate without knowing what it is to be. You are paralyzed by doubts and misgivings that are of your own making. Much has happened to you, Dark Uncle, and it is enough to make any man doubt. You have lost loved ones, your home, a part of your body and spirit. You have seen the specter of a childhood fear take form and threaten to become real. You are far from everything you know. But you must not despair."

His eyes were haunted. "But I do. I am adrift, Quickening. I feel myself slipping away completely."

She reached out her hand and took his own. "Then cling to me, Walker Boh. And let me cling to you. If we keep hold of each other, the drifting will stop."

She moved against him, her silver hair spilling across his

dark cloak as her head lowered into his chest. She did not speak, but simply rested there, still holding his hand, her warmth mixing with his own. He lowered his chin to her hair and closed his eyes.

He slept then, and there were no dreams or sudden wakings, only a gentle cradling by soft, invisible threads that held him firm. His drifting ceased, just as she had promised it would. He was no longer plagued by troubling and uncertain visions; he was left at peace. Calm enfolded him, soothing and comforting. It had a woman's hands, and the hands belonged to Quickening.

He woke again at daybreak, easing from the chilly stone floor to his feet as his eyes adjusted to the thin gray light. From beyond the maze of rooms and corridors that buffered him from the outside world, he could hear the soft patter of rain. Quickening was gone. Vaguely worried, he searched until he found her standing at a bank of windows on the north wall, staring out into the haze. The stone buildings and streets shimmered wetly, reflecting their own images in grotesque parody, mirroring their deadness. Eldwist greeted the new day as a corpse, sightless and stiff. It stretched away into the distance, rows of buildings, ribbons of streets, a symmetry of design and construction that was flat and hard and empty of life. Walker stood next to Quickening and felt the oppressiveness of the city close about him.

Her black eyes shifted to find his own, her mane of silver hair the sole brightness in the gloom. "I held you as tightly as I could, Walker Boh," she told him. "Was it enough?"

He took a moment to answer. The stump of his missing arm ached and the joints of his body were stiff and slow to respond. He felt himself to be a large shell in which his spirit had shriveled to the size of a pebble. Yet he was strangely resolved.

"I am reminded of Carisman," he said finally, "determined to be free at any cost. I would be free as well. Of my fears and doubts. Of myself. Of what I might become. That cannot be until I have learned the secret of the Black Elfstone and the truth behind the dreams of the shade of Allanon."

Quickening's faint smile surprised him. "I would be free, too," she said softly. She seemed anxious to explain, then looked quickly away. "We must find Uhl Belk," she said instead.

They departed their shelter and went out into the rain. They walked the silent streets of Eldwist north through the shadows and gloom, hunched within the protection of their forest cloaks, lost in their private thoughts.

Quickening said, "Eldwist is a land in midwinter waiting for spring. She is layered in stone as other parts of the earth at times are layered in snow. Can you feel her patience? There are seeds planted, and when the snow melts those seeds can be brought to bloom."

Walker wasn't sure what she was talking about. "There is only stone in Eldwist, Quickening. It runs deep and long, from shore to shore, the length and breadth of the peninsula. There are no seeds here, nothing of the woodlands or the fields, no trees, no flowers, no grasses. Only Uhl Belk and the monsters that serve him. And us."

"Eldwist is a lie," she said.

"Whose lie?" he asked. But she wouldn't answer.

They followed the street for close to an hour, keeping carefully to the walkways, listening for the sound of anything moving. Except for the steady patter of the rain, there was only silence. Even the Maw Grint slept, it seemed. Water pooled and was channeled into streams, and it swept down the gutters in sluggish torrents that eddied and splashed and washed away the silt and dust the wind had blown in. The buildings watched in mute and indifferent testimony, unfeeling sentinels. Clouds and mist mixed and descended to wrap them about, easing steadily downward until they scraped the earth. Things began to disappear, towers first, then entire walls, then bits and pieces of the streets themselves. Walker and Quickening felt a changing in the world, as if a presence had been loosed. Phantasms came out to play, dark shadows risen from the earth to dance at the edges of their vision, never entirely real, never quite completely formed. Eyes watched, peering downward from the heights, staring upward through the stone. Fingers brushed at their skin, droplets of rain, trailers of mist, and something more. Walker let himself become one with what he was feeling, an old trick, a blending of self with external sensations, all to gain a small measure of insight into the origin of what was unseen. He could sense a presence after a time, dark, brooding, ancient, a thing of vast power. He could hear it breathing. He could almost see its eyes.

"Walker," Quickening whispered.

A figure appeared out of the haze before them, cloaked and hooded as they were and uncomfortably close. Walker stepped in front of Quickening and stopped. The figure stopped as well. Wordlessly, they faced each other. Then the clouds shifted, changing the slant of the light, the shadows re-formed, and a voice called out uncertainly. "Quickening?"

Walker Boh started forward again. It was Morgan Leah.

They clasped hands on meeting, and Quickening hugged the sodden and disheveled Highlander close, kissing his face passionately. Walker watched without speaking, already aware of the attraction shared by the two, surprised that Quickening would allow it to be. He watched the way her eyes closed when Morgan held her and thought he understood. She was letting herself feel because it was all still new. She was no older than the time of her creation, and even if her father had given her human feelings she would not have experienced them firsthand until now. He felt an odd twinge of sadness for her. She was trying so hard to live.

"Walker." Morgan moved over to him, one arm still wrapped about the girl. "I've been searching everywhere. I thought something had happened to you as well."

He told them what had befallen Horner Dees and himself, how they had been snared by the trapdoor and tumbled onto the slide, and how they had found themselves confronted by the horror of the Maw Grint slumbering directly below. His eyes were fierce and bright as he struggled to describe how he had somehow managed to release the magic of the Sword of Leah once again, magic he had feared lost. With its aid they had escaped. They had taken refuge for the night close by, then made their way at dawn to where they had left the others of the little company. But the building had been empty and there had been no sign of anyone's return. Worried for Quickening— for all of them, he hastened to add—he had left Dees to keep watch for them in case they returned and gone hunting alone.

"Horner Dees was prepared to come as well, but I refused

to allow it. The truth is, he would never move again if he could arrange it—at least not until it was time to leave this place." The Highlander smiled broadly. "He's had enough of Eldwist and its traps; he wants the ale house at Rampling Steep again!" He paused then, looking past them speculatively. "Where's Carisman?"

It was their turn to speak, and Quickening did so, her voice steady and strangely comforting as she related the events that had led to the death of the tunesmith. Even so, Morgan Leah's face was lined with despair and anger by the time she had finished.

"He never understood anything, did he?" the Highlander said, the emotions he was holding inside threatening to choke him. "He just never understood! He thought his music was a cure for everything. Shades!"

He looked away a moment, shielding his expression, hands clasped on his hips defiantly, as if stubbornness might somehow change what had happened. "Where do we go now?" he asked finally.

Walker glanced at Quickening. "We believe that Uhl Belk hides within the dome," the girl spoke for him. "We were looking for a way in when the Urdas appeared. We are returning to continue the search."

Morgan turned, his face set. "Then I am coming with you. Horner will be better off resting right where he is. We can rejoin him at nightfall." The look he gave them was almost defiant. "That's the way it should be anyway. Just the three of us."

"Come if you wish, Morgan," Quickening soothed, and Walker nodded without comment.

They resumed walking, three rain-soaked figures nearly lost in the mist and shadows. Walker led, a lean and white-faced ghost against the gloom, leader now because Quickening had moved a step back to be with Morgan, content to follow. He hunched his narrow shoulders against the weather, felt the bite of the wind as it gusted momentarily, and felt the emptiness inside threaten to engulf him. He reached into that emptiness and tried to secure some part of his magic, a strength he could rely upon. It eluded him, like a snake in flight. He peered ahead through the thin curtain of the rain and watched the shadows chase after the light. The specter of his fate leered at him, a faint shimmer in a pool of water, a wisp of fog in a doorway, a darkening of stone where the dampness reflected like a mirror. In each instance, it wore the face of Allanon.

The street ended, and the dark bulk of the dome lifted before them like the shell of some sleeping crustacean. The three stepped down off the walkway and crossed to stand before it, dwarfed by its size. Walker stared at the dome without speaking, aware that Morgan and Quickening were waiting on him, conscious that something else was waiting on him as well. *It.* The presence he had sensed before was back again, stronger here, readier, more assured. And watching. Silently watching. Walker did not move. He felt eyes all around him, as if there were nowhere he might run that he could not be seen. The stone of the city was a hand that cradled him yet might close without warning to crush out his life. The presence wanted him to know that. It wanted him to know how insignificant he was, how futile his quest, and how purposeless his life. It bore down on him, pressed about like the mist and rain. Go home, he heard it whisper. Leave while you can.

He did not leave. He did not even step away. He had faced enough threats in his time, enough dark things that roamed the land, to know when he was being tested. The effort was not a crushing one; it was teasing and fey, as if designed to insinuate an opposite effect than the one indicated. Don't really leave, it seemed to say. Just remember that you were asked.

Walker Boh stepped forward to where the wall was broadest between the bands of stone. Death brushed up against him, a soft sprinkle of rain caught in the wind. It was odd, but he sensed Cogline close beside him, the old man's ghost risen from the ashes of Hearthstone, come to watch his student practice the craft he had taught him, come perhaps to judge how well he performed. You will never be free of the magic, he could hear the other say. He stared momentarily at the pitted, worn surface of the wall, watching the rainwater snake downward along its irregular paths, silver streamers that glistened like strands of Quickening's hair. He reached down again within himself for the magic and this time fastened on it. He drew its strength about him like armor, banded himself with it as if to match the stone of the shell before him, then reached out with his one remaining hand and pressed his fingers to the wall.

He felt the magic rise within him, flowing hot like fire, extending from his chest to his arm to the tips of his fingers to . . .

There was a shudder, and the stone before him drew back, flinching away as if human flesh that had been burned. There was a long, deep groan that was the sound of stone grating on stone and a thin shriek as if a life had been pressed between. Quickening crouched like a startled bird, her silver hair flung back, her eyes bright and strangely alive. Morgan Leah drew out the broadsword strapped across his back in a single swift motion.

The wall before them opened—not as a door would swing wide or a panel lift, but as a cloth torn asunder. It opened, stretched wide from foundation to apex, a mouth that sought to feed. When it was twenty feet across, it stopped, immobile once more, the stone edges smooth and fixed, imbued with the look of a doorway that had always been there and clearly belonged.

A way in, thought Walker Boh. Exactly what they had come searching for.

Quickening and Morgan Leah stood beside him expectantly. He did not look at either of them. He kept his eyes focused on the opening before him, on the darkness within, on its sea of impenetrable shadows. He searched and listened, but nothing revealed itself.

Still, he knew what waited.

Carisman's voice sang softly in his mind. *Come right in, said the spider to the fly*

With the girl and the Highlander flanking him, Walker Boh complied.

CHAPTER

25

SHADOWS ENVELOPED THEM almost immediately, layers of darkness that began less than a dozen feet inside the opening to the dome and entirely concealed everything that lay beyond. They slowed on Walker's lead, waiting for their eyes to adjust, listening to the hollow echoes of their booted feet fade into the silence. Then there was only the sound of their breathing. Behind them, the faint gray daylight was a slender thread connecting them to the world without, and an instant later it was severed. Stone grated on stone once more, and the opening that had admitted them disappeared. No one moved to prevent it from happening; indeed, they had all expected as much. They stood together in the silence that followed, each conscious of the reassuring presence of the others, each straining to hear the sound of any foreign movement, each waiting for some small measure of sight to return. The sense of emptiness was complete. The interior of the dome had the feel of a monstrous tomb in which nothing living had walked in centuries. The air had a stale and musty smell, devoid of any recognizable scents, and it was cold, a bone-biting chill that entered through the mouth and nostrils and worked its way instantly to the pit of the stomach and lodged there. They began to shiver almost immediately. Even in the impenetrable darkness it seemed to Walker Boh that he could see the clouding of his breath.

The seconds dragged by, heartbeats in the unbroken stillness. The three waited patiently. Something would happen.

Someone would appear. Unless they had been brought into the dome to be killed, Walker speculated in the silence of his thoughts. But he didn't think that was the case. In fact, he no longer believed as he had in the beginning that there was any active effort being made to eliminate them. The character of their relationship with Eldwist suggested on close study that the city functioned in an impersonal way to rid itself of intruders, but that it did not exert any special effort if it immediately failed. Eldwist did not rely on speed; it relied on the law of averages. Sooner or later intruders would make a mistake. They would grow incautious and either the trapdoors or the Rake would claim them. Walker was willing to wager that Quickening had guessed right, that until very recently the Stone King hadn't even been aware of their presence—or if he had, hadn't bothered himself about it. It wasn't until Walker had used magic against the shell of his enclosure that he had roused himself. Not even using magic against the Rake had made any difference to him. But now, Walker believed, he was curious—and that was why they had been brought inside . . .

Walker caught himself. He had missed something. Nothing was going to happen if they just stood there in the darkness, not if they waited all that day and all the next. The Stone King had brought them inside for a reason. He had brought them inside to see what they would do.

Or, perhaps, *could* do.

He reached out with his good arm to grip first Morgan and then Quickening and bent their heads gently to press close against his own. "Whatever happens, Quickening," he whispered, speaking only to the girl, his voice so soft it was barely audible, "remember your vow to do nothing to reveal that you have any use of the magic."

Then he released them, stepped away, brought up his hand, snapped his fingers, and sparked a single silver flame to life.

They looked about. They were standing in a tunnel that ran forward a short distance to an opening. Holding the flame before him, Walker led them forward. When they reached the tunnel's end, he extinguished the flame, summoned his magic a second time, and sent a scattering of silver fire into the darkness.

Walker inhaled sharply. The shower of light flew into the

unknown, soaring through the shadows, chasing them as it went, and rising until everything about them lay revealed. They stood at the entrance to a vast rotunda, an arena ringed by row upon row of seats that lifted away into the gloom. The roof of the dome stretched high overhead, its rafters of stone arcing downward from peak to foundation. Lines of stairs ran upward to the rows of seats, and railings encircled the arena. The arena and stands, like the rafters, were stone, ancient and worn by time, hard and flat against the darkness that cloaked them. A string of shadowed tunnels similar to the one that had admitted them opened through the stands, black holes that burrowed and disappeared.

At the very center of the arena stood a massive stone statue, rough-hewn and barely recognizable, of a man hunched over in thought.

Walker let the fire settle in place, its light extending. The dome was vast and empty, silent save for the sound of their footfalls, seemingly bereft of any life but their own. Out of the corner of his eye he saw Morgan start forward and reached out quickly to hold him back. Quickening moved over to take the Highlander's arm protectively in her own. Walker's gaze swept the arena, the black tunnels that opened onto it, the stands that surrounded it, the rafters and ceiling, and then the arena again. He stopped when he reached the statue. Nothing moved. But there was something there. He could feel it, more strongly now than before, the same presence he had sensed when he had stood without.

He started forward, slowly, cautiously. Morgan and Quickening trailed. He was momentarily in command of matters now, Quickening's deference in some way become an acknowledgment of her need. She was not to use magic. She was to rely on him. He discovered an unexpected strength of resolution in the fact that he had made her dependent on him. There was no time now for drifting, for self-doubts and fears, or for the uncertainties of who and what he was meant to be. A fiery determination burned through him. It was better this way, he realized, better to be in command, to accept responsibility for what was to happen. It had always been that way. At that moment he understood for the first time in his life that it always would.

The statue loomed directly before them, a massive chunk of stone that seemed to defy the light Walker had evoked to defuse the darkness. The thinker faced away from them, a gnarled and lumpish form, kneeling half-seated and half-slumped, one arm folded across his stomach, the second closed to a fist and cocked to brace his chin. It might have been intended that there be a cloak thrown about him or he might simply have been covered with hair; it was impossible to discern. There was no writing on the base he rested upon; indeed, it was a rather awkward pedestal that seemed to join the legs of the statue to the dome's floor as if the rock had simply melted away once upon a distant time.

They reached the statue and began to circle it. The face came slowly into view. It was a monster's face, ravaged and pocked, a mass of protuberances and knots, all misshapen in the manner of a sculpture partially formed and then abandoned. Eyes of stone stared blankly from beneath a glowering brow. There was horror written in the statue's features; there were demons captured in the shaping that could never be dislodged. Walker glanced away uneasily to search again the dome's shadows. The silence winked back at him.

Suddenly Quickening stopped, freezing in place like a startled deer. "Walker," she whispered, her voice a low hiss.

She was looking at the statue. Walker wheeled catlike to follow her gaze.

The eyes of the statue had shifted to fix on him.

He heard Morgan's blade clear its sheath in a rasp of metal.

The statue's misshapen head began moving, the stone grating eerily as it shifted, not breaking off or cracking, but rearranging somehow, as if become both solid and liquid. The grating echoed through the hollow shell of the dome like the shifting of massive mountain boulders in a slide. Arms moved and shoulders followed. The torso swiveled, the stone rubbing and grinding until the short hairs on Walker's neck were rigid.

Then it spoke, mouth opening, stone rubbing on stone.

—Who are you—

Walker did not reply, so astonished at what he was seeing that he could not manage to answer. He simply stood there, dumbfounded. The statue was alive, a thing of stone, frighteningly shaped by a madman's hand, lacking blood and flesh, yet somehow alive.

In the next instant he realized what he was seeing and even then he could not speak the creature's name. It was Quickening who spoke for him.

"Uhl Belk," she whispered.

—Who are you—

Quickening stepped forward, looking tiny and insignificant in the shadow of the Stone King, her silver hair swept back.

"I am called Quickening," she replied. Her voice, surprisingly strong and steady, reverberated through the stillness. "These are my companions, Walker Boh and Morgan Leah. We have come to Eldwist to ask you to return the Black Elfstone."

The head shifted slightly, stone crackling and grinding.

—The Black Elfstone belongs to me—

"No, Uhl Belk. It belongs to the Druids. You stole it from them. You stole it from the Hall of Kings and brought it into Eldwist. Now you must give it back."

There was a long pause before the Stone King spoke again.

—Who are you—

"I am no one."

—Have you magic to use against me—

"No."

—What of these others, do they have magic—

"Only a little. Morgan Leah once had use of a sword given him by the Druids which possessed the magic of the Hadeshorn. But it is broken now, the blade shattered, and its magic failed. Walker Boh once had the use of magic he inherited from his ancestors, from the Elven house of Shannara. But he lost the use of most of that magic when he suffered damage to his arm and his spirit. He has yet to gain it back. No, they have no magic that can harm you."

Walker was so astonished he could barely credit what he was hearing. In a matter of seconds, Quickening had undone them completely. She had revealed not only what it was that they had come to find but also that they lacked any reasonable chance of gaining possession of it. She had admitted that they were virtually powerless against this spirit creature, that they were unable to force it to comply with their demands. She had removed even the possibility that they might run a bluff. What was she thinking?

Uhl Belk was apparently wondering the same thing.

—I am to give up the Black Elfstone simply because you ask me to do so, give it up to three mortals of finite lives, a girl with no magic, a one-armed man, and a swordsman with a broken blade—

"It is necessary, Uhl Belk."

—I determine what is necessary in the Kingdom of Eldwist; I am the law and the power that enforces that law; there is no right but mine and therefore no necessity but mine; who would dare say no to me; not any of you; you are as insignificant as the dust that blows across the surface of my skin and washes into the sea—

He paused.

—The Black Elfstone is mine—

Quickening did not respond this time, but simply continued to stare into the Stone King's scarred eyes. Uhl Belk's massive body shifted again, moving as if mired in quicksand, the stone grinding resolutely, a wheel of time and certainty given the skin of substance.

—You—

He pointed to Walker, a finger straightening.

—The Asphinx claimed a part of you; I can sense its stink upon your body; yet somehow you still live; are you a Druid—

"No," Quickening answered instantly. "He is a messenger of the Druids, sent by them to recover the Black Elfstone. His Elven magic saved him from the poison of the Asphinx. His claim to the Black Elfstone is the rightful one, granted him by the Druids."

—The Druids are all dead—

Quickening said nothing, waiting for the Stone King, standing fearlessly beneath him. A sudden movement of one massive arm and she would be crushed. She seemed unconcerned. Walker glanced quickly at Morgan, but the Highlander's eyes were on the face of Uhl Belk, transfixed by the ugliness of it, hypnotized by the power he saw there. He wondered what he was expected to do. Anything? He wondered suddenly what he was doing there at all.

Then the Stone King spoke again, a slow rasping in the silence.

—I have been alive forever and I will live on long after you are dust; I was created by the Word and I have survived all that were given life with me save one and that one will soon be gone as well; I care nothing for the world in which I exist save for the preservation of that over which I was given dominion— eternal stone; it is stone that weathers all things, that is unchanging and fixed and therefore as close to perfection as life can achieve; I am the giver of stone to the world and the architect of what is to become; I use all necessary means to see that my purpose is fulfilled; therefore I took the Black Elfstone and made it mine—

The dome echoed with his words, and then the echoes died away into silence. The shadows were lengthening already as Walker's light began slowly to fail, the magic fading. Walker felt the futility of what they were about. Morgan's sword arm had lowered uselessly to his side; what purpose was there in trying to employ a weapon of iron against something as ancient and immutable as this? Only Quickening seemed to believe there was any hope.

—The Druids were as nothing compared to me; their precautions to hide and protect their magic were futile; I left the Asphinx to show my disdain for what they had attempted to do; they were believers in the laws of nature and evolution, foolish purveyors of the creed of change; they died and left nothing; stone is the only element of the earth's body that endures, and I shall live in that stone forever—

"Constant," Quickening whispered.

—Yes—

"Eternal."

—Yes—

"But what of your trust, Uhl Belk? What of that? You have disdained to be that which you were created—a balancing force, a preservationist of the world as it was created to be." Her voice was low and compelling, a web weaving images that seemed to take form and shimmer in the dead air before her. "I was told your story. You were given life to preserve life; that was the trust given you by the Word. Stone preserves nothing of life.

You were not instructed to transform, yet you have taken it upon yourself to subvert everything, to alter forever the composition of life upon the land, to change living matter to stone— all this to create an extension of who and what you are. And look what it has done to you."

She braced herself against the anger already forming on the Stone King's brow. "Give back the Black Elfstone, Uhl Belk. Let us help you become free again."

The massive stone creature shifted on his bed of rock, joints grating, the sounds cracking through the arena as if some invisible audience sought to respond. Uhl Belk spoke, and his voice had a new and frightening edge to it.

—You are more than you pretend to be; I am not deceived; yet it does not matter; I care nothing for who you are or what you want; I admitted you to me so that I might examine you; the magic with which you touched me caught my attention and made me curious as to who you might be; but I need nothing from you; I need nothing from any living thing; I am complete; think of me as the land on which you walk and you as the tiniest of fleas that live upon me; if you should become a bother I will eliminate you in an instant; if you should survive this day you will probably not survive another—

The great brow knitted, and the gnarled face re-formed its ridges and lines.

—What am I if not the whole of your existence; look about you and I am everything you see; look where you stand within Eldwist and I am everything you touch; I have made myself so; I have made myself one with the land I create; I am free of all else and shall ever be—

Suddenly Walker Boh understood. Uhl Belk wasn't a living thing in the conventional sense of the words. He was a spirit in the same way as the King of the Silver River. He was more than the statue that crouched before them. He was everything they walked upon; he was the entire Kingdom of Eldwist. The stone was his skin, he had said—a part of his living self. He had found a way to infuse himself into everything he created, ensuring his permanency in a way that nothing else could.

But that meant he was a prisoner as well. That was why he didn't rise to greet them or come hunting for them or involve himself directly in any way in what they were about. That was why his legs were sunk down into the stone. Mobility was beyond him, an indulgence meant for lesser creatures. He had evolved into something greater; he had evolved into his own world. And it held him trapped.

"But you are not free, are you?" Quickening questioned boldly, as if reading Walker's thoughts. "If you were, you would give us the Black Elfstone, for you would have no real need of it." Her voice was hard and insistent. "But you cannot do that, can you, Uhl Belk? You need the Black Elfstone to stay alive. Without it, the Maw Grint would have you."

—No—

"Without it, the Maw Grint would destroy you."

—No—

"Without it . . ."

—No—

A stone fist crashed downward, barely missing the girl, shattering a portion of the ground next to her, sending jagged cracks along its surface for a hundred yards in every direction. The Stone King shuddered as if stricken.

"The Maw Grint is your child, Uhl Belk," Quickening continued, ramrod straight before him, as if it were she who had the size and the power and not the Stone King. "But your child does not obey you."

—You know nothing; the Maw Grint is an extension of me, as is everything in Eldwist an extension of me; it has no life except what I would give; it serves my purpose and no other, turning the lands adjoining and all that live within them to stone, the permanency of myself—

The girl's black eyes were bright and quick. "And the Black Elfstone?"

The Stone King's voice was resonant with some strange mix of emotions that refused to be identified.

—The Black Elfstone allows—

The jagged mouth ground closed and the Stone King hunched down into himself, limbs and body knotting together as though they might disappear into a single massive rock.

"Allows?" Quickening breathed softly.

The flat, empty eyes lifted.

—Watch—

The word reverberated like a splitting of the Stone King's soul. Rock grated and ground once more, and the wall of the dome behind them parted. Gray, hazy daylight spilled through as if to flee the steady curtain of rain that fell without. Clouds and mist drifted past, bending and twisting about the buildings that loomed beyond, cloaking them as if they were a gathering of frozen giants set patiently at watch. An eerie wail burst from the Stone King's mouth and it filled the emptiness of the city with a sound like a thin sheet of metal vibrating in the wind. It rose and died quickly, but its echo lingered as if it would last forever.

—Watch—

They heard the Maw Grint before they saw it, its approach signaled by a rumble deep beneath the city's streets that rose steadily as the creature neared, a low growl building to a roar that jolted everything and brought the three from Rampling Steep to their knees. The Maw Grint burst into view, shattering apart the stone that was Uhl Belk's skin, splitting it wide just beyond the wall of the dome, just without the opening through which they stared wide-eyed and helpless. They could see the Stone King flinch with pain. The Maw Grint rose and seemed to keep rising, a leviathan of impossible size that dwarfed even the buildings themselves, swaying like a snake, a loathsome cross between burrowing worm and serpent, as black as pitch with foul liquid oozing from a rock-encrusted body, eyeless, headless, its mouth a sucking hole that seemed intent on drinking first the rain and then the air itself. It shot into view with a suddenness that was terrifying and filled the void of the dome's opening like a wave of darkness that would collapse it completely.

Walker Boh went cold with disbelief and horror. The Maw Grint wasn't real; it was impossible even to imagine such a thing. For the first time in his life he wanted to run. He watched Morgan Leah stagger back and drop to his knees. He watched Quickening freeze in place. He felt himself lose strength and only barely managed to keep from falling. The Maw Grint writhed against the skyline, a great spineless mass of black ooze that nothing could withstand.

Yet the Stone King did not waver. A thick, gnarled hand lifted, the one that had cradled his chin when they had thought him a statue, and the fingers slowly began to open. Light burst forth—yet it was light the like of which none of them had ever seen. It sprayed in all directions at first and did not illuminate in the manner of ordinary light but instead turned everything it touched dark.

This is not light, Walker Boh realized as he fought to hold back a flood of sensations that threatened to overwhelm him. *This is the absence of light!*

Then the fingers of the Stone King spread wide, and they could see what he held. It was a perfectly formed gemstone, its center as black and impenetrable as night. The stone glittered as it reflected the thin streamers of gray daylight and let not even the smallest trace pass within. It looked tiny cradled in Uhl Belk's massive stone palm, but the darkness it cast stretched away into the farthest corners of the dome, into the deepest recesses, seeking out and enveloping the whole of Walker's scattered luminescence so that in a matter of seconds the only light remaining came from the rent in the dome's stone skin.

Walker Boh felt his own magic stir within him in recognition.

They had found the Black Elfstone.

Uhl Belk cried out then, a thundering howl that rose above even the sounds of the Maw Grint's coming, of the wind and the rain and the sea far beyond, and he thrust the Black Elfstone before him. The blackness gathered and tightened into a single band that shot forward to strike the Maw Grint. The Maw Grint did not resist. Instead, it simply hung there, transfixed. It shuddered—pained and pleasured both somehow, wracked with feelings that the humans crouched before it could only imagine. It twisted, and the blackness twisted in response. The blackness spread, widening, flowing out, then back again, until the Stone King was enveloped as well. They could hear him groan, then sob, again with feelings that were mixed in some veiled way, not clearly defined and not meant to be. The Elfstone's magic joined them, father and son, monsters each, a substanceless lock that bound them as surely as iron chains.

What is happening? Walker Boh wondered. *What is the magic doing to them?*

Then the nonlight disappeared, a line of shadow fading, steadily dissipating like ink soaking into and through white netting, the air brightening until the daylight returned and the link between the Stone King and the Maw Grint had vanished. The Maw Grint sank from sight, oozing back into the earth. The hole that it had made closed after it, the stone knitting into place, as smooth and hard as before, leaving the street whole again, creating the illusion that nothing at all had happened. The rain washed away all traces of the creature's coming, streams of water loosening the greenish film of poison secreted from its body and carrying it from sight.

Uhl Belk's fingers closed once more about the Black Elfstone, his eyes lidded, his face transformed in a way that Walker could not describe, as if he had been made over somehow, created anew. Yet he was more frightening looking than ever, his features harsher, less human, and more a part of the rock that encased him. He withdrew the Elfstone, his hand clasping it tightly to his body. His voice rumbled.

—Do you see—

They did not, not even Quickening. The puzzlement in her dark eyes was evident. They stood mute before the Stone King, all three, feeling tiny and uncertain.

"What has happened to you, Uhl Belk?" the girl asked finally.

Rain hammered down, and the wind ripped through the dome's rent.

—Go—

The massive pitted head began to turn away, the stone grating ominously.

"You must give us the Black Elfstone!" Quickening shouted.

—The Black Elfstone is mine—

"The Shadowen will take it from you—just as you took it from the Druids!"

Uhl Belk's voice was weary, disinterested.

—The Shadowen are children; you are all children; you do not concern me; nothing that you do can harm or affect me;

look at me; I am as old as the world and I shall last as long; you shall be gone in the blink of an eye; take yourselves out of my city; if you remain, if you come to me again, if I am disturbed by you in any way, I shall summon the Rake to dispose of you and you shall be swept away at once—

The floor rippled beneath them, a shudder that sent them tumbling backward toward the opening in the wall. The Stone King had flinched the way an animal would in an effort to shed itself of some bothersome insect. Walker Boh rose, pulling Quickening back with him, beckoning to Morgan. There was nothing to be gained by staying. They would not have the Black Elfstone this day—if indeed ever. Uhl Belk was a creature evolved far beyond any other. He was right; what could they do that would harm or affect him?

Yet Quickening seemed unconvinced. "It is you who shall be swept away!" she shouted as they backed through the opening into the street. She was shaking. "Listen to me, Uhl Belk!"

The craggy face was turned again into shadow, the massive shoulders hunched down, the thinker's pose resumed. There was no response.

Standing outside in the rain they watched the wall seal over, the skin knit, the rent fade away as if it had never been. In moments the dome was an impenetrable shell once more.

Morgan moved to place his hands on Quickening's shoulders. The girl seemed unaware of him, a thing of stone herself. The Highlander leaned close and began whispering.

Walker Boh moved away from them. When he was alone, he turned once again to face Uhl Belk's haven. A fire consumed him and at the same time he felt detached. He was there and he was not. He realized that he no longer knew himself. He had become an enigma he could not solve. His thoughts tightened like a cinched cord. The Stone King was an enemy that none of them could defeat. He was not simply ruler of a city; he was the city itself. Uhl Belk had become Eldwist. He was a whole world, and no one could change an entire world. Not Allanon or Cogline or all of the Druids put together.

Rain streamed down his face. No one.

Yet he already knew that he was going to try.

CHAPTER

26

PE ELL HAD CHANGED his mind twice before finally settling the matter. Now he slipped down the darkening
street and ducked into the doorway of the building in
which the others had concealed themselves with his
misgivings comfortably stowed. Rain dripped from his cloak,
staining the stone of the stairs he followed, tracking his progress
in a steady, meandering trail. He paused at the landing to listen,
heard nothing, and went on. The others were probably out
searching. There or not, it made no difference to him. Sooner
or later, they would return. He could wait.

He passed down the hallway without bothering to conceal
his approach and stalked through the doorway of their hiding
place. At first glance the room appeared empty, but his instincts
warned him instantly that he was being watched and he stopped
a dozen feet through. Shadows dappled the room in strange
patterns, clustered about haphazardly as if stray children chased
inside by the weather. The patter of the rain sounded steadily
in the silence as Pe Ell stood waiting.

Then Horner Dees appeared, slipping noiselessly from the
shadows of a doorway to one side, moving with a grace and ease
that belied his bulky frame. He was scratched and bruised and
his clothing was torn. He looked as if some animal had gotten
hold of him. He fixed Pe Ell with his grizzled look, as rough
and suspicious as ever, an ageing bear come face to face with a
familiar enemy.

"You constantly amaze me," Pe Ell said, meaning it, still curious about this troublesome old man.

Dees stopped, keeping his distance. "Thought we'd seen the last of you," he growled.

"Did you, now?" Pe Ell smiled disarmingly, then moved across the room to where a collection of withered fruits sat drying in a makeshift bowl. He picked one up and took a bite. It was bitter tasting, but edible. "Where are the others?"

"Out and about," Dees answered. "What difference does it make to you?"

Pe Ell shed his damp cloak and seated himself. "None. What happened to you?"

"I fell down a hole. Now what do you want?"

Pe Ell's smile stayed in place. "A little help."

It was difficult to tell if Horner Dees was surprised or not; he managed to keep his face from showing anything but seemed at a momentary loss for a response. He hunched down a few inches, as if settling himself against an attack, studied Pe Ell wordlessly, then shook his head.

"I know you, Pe Ell," he declared softly. "I remember you from the old days, from the time you were just beginning. I was with the Federation then, a Tracker, and I knew you. Rimmer Dall had plans for me as well; but I decided not to go along with them. I saw you once or twice, saw you come and go, heard the rumors about you." He paused. "I just want you to know."

Pe Ell finished the fruit and tossed the pit aside. He wasn't sure how he felt about this unexpected revelation. He guessed it really didn't matter. At least now he had an inkling of what it was that bothered him so about Dees.

"I don't remember you," he said finally. "Not that it matters." The hatchet face inclined away from the light. "Just so we understand each other, Rimmer Dall's plans for me didn't work out quite as he expected either. I do what I choose. I always have."

Dees rugged face nodded. "You kill people."

Pe Ell shrugged. "Sometimes. Are you frightened?"

The other man shook his head. "Not of you."

"Good. Then if we've finished with that topic of conversation, let's move back to the other. I need a little help. Care to lend me some?"

Horner Dees stood mute a moment, then moved over to seat himself. He settled down with a grunt and stared at Pe Ell without speaking, apparently assessing the offer. That was fine with Pe Ell. He had thought the matter through carefully before coming back, weighing the pros and cons of abandoning his plan of entering the Rake's shelter alone, of seeking assistance in determining whether or not the Stone King hid within. He had nothing to hide, no intention to deceive. It was always best to take a straightforward approach when you could.

Dees stirred. "I don't trust you."

Pe Ell laughed tonelessly. "I once told the Highlander he was a fool if he did. I don't care if you trust me; I'm not asking for your trust. I'm asking for your help."

Dees was intrigued despite himself. "What sort of help?"

Pe Ell hid his satisfaction. "Last night I tracked the Rake to its lair. I watched it enter, saw where it hides. I believe it likely that where the Rake hides, the Stone King hides as well. When the Rake goes out tonight to patrol the streets of the city, I intend to go in for a look."

He shifted forward, bringing Dees into the circle of his confidence. "There is a catch that releases a door through which the Rake passes. If I trip it, I should be able to go in. The trouble is, what if the door closes behind me? How will I get out?"

Dees rubbed his bearded chin, digging at the thick whiskers as though they itched. "So you want someone to watch your back for you."

"It seems like a good idea. I had planned to go in alone, to confront the Stone King, kill him if need be, and take the Stone. That's still my plan, but I don't want to have to worry about the Rake crawling up my back when I'm not watching."

"So you want me to watch for you."

"Afraid?"

"You keep asking that. Fact is, I should be asking you. Why should you trust me? I don't like you, Pe Ell. I'd be just as happy if the Rake would get you. That makes me a poor choice for this job, don't you think?"

Pe Ell unfolded his legs and stretched his lean body back against the wall. "Not necessarily. You don't have to like me. I don't have to like you. And I don't. But we both want the same thing—the Black Elfstone. We want to help the girl. Doesn't seem likely either of us can do much alone—although I have a better chance than you do. The point is, if you give your word that you will keep watch for me, I think that's what you'll do. Because your word means something to you, doesn't it?"

Dees laughed dryly. "Don't tell me you're about to make a plea to my sense of honor. I don't think I could stomach that."

Pe Ell quit smiling. "I have my own code of honor, old man, and it means every bit as much to me as yours does to you. If I give my word, I keep it. That's more than most can say. I'm telling you I'll watch out for you if you watch out for me—just until this business is finished. After that, we each go back to watching out for ourselves." He cocked his head. "Time is slipping away. We have to be in place by sunset. Are you coming or not?"

Horner Dees took a long time to answer. Pe Ell would have been surprised and suspicious if he had not. Whatever else Dees was, he was an honest man, and Pe Ell was certain he would not enter into an arrangement he did not think he could abide by. Pe Ell trusted Dees; he wouldn't have asked the old man to watch his back if he didn't. Moreover, he thought Dees capable, the best choice of all, in some ways, not inexperienced like the Highlander or flighty like Carisman. Nor was he unpredictable like Walker Boh. Dees was nothing more nor less than what he appeared to be.

"I told the Highlander about you," Dees announced, watching. "He's told the others by now."

Pe Ell shrugged once more. "I don't care about that." And he didn't.

Dees hunched his heavy frame forward, squinting into the faint gray light. "If we get possession of the Stone, either of us, we bring it back to the girl. Your word."

Pe Ell smiled in spite of himself. "You would accept my word, old man?"

Dees' features were hard and certain. "If you try to break it, I'll find a way to make you sorry you did."

Pe Ell believed him. Horner Dees, for all of being old and used up, for the weathered look of him and the wear of the years, would be a dangerous adversary. A Tracker, a woodsman, and a hunter, Dees had kept himself alive for a long time. He might not be Pe Ell's equal in a face-to-face confrontation, but there were other ways to kill a man. Pe Ell smiled inwardly. Who should know better than he?

Pe Ell reached out his hand and waited for the old man to take it. "We have a bargain," he said. Their hands tightened, held momentarily and broke. Pe Ell came to his feet like a cat. "Now let's be off."

They went out the door of the room and down the stairs again, Pe Ell leading. The gloom without had thickened, the darkness growing steadily as nightfall approached. They hunched their cloaked shoulders against the rain and started away. Pe Ell's thoughts drifted to his bargain. It had been an easy one to make. He would return the Elfstone to the girl because not to do so would be to risk losing her completely and to face an eternity of being tracked by all of them.

Never leave your enemies alive to follow after you, he thought.

Better to kill them when you had the chance.

DAYLIGHT WAS FADING rapidly by the time Walker, Morgan, and Quickening approached the building Pe Ell and Horner Dees had vacated less than an hour earlier. The rain was falling steadily, a dark curtain that shaded the tall, somber buildings of the city, that masked away the skies and the mountains and the sea. Morgan walked with his arm protectively encircling the girl's shoulders, his head lowered to hers, two shadowed and hooded figures against the mist. Walker stayed apart, leaving them to each other. He saw how Quickening leaned into the Highlander. She seemed to welcome his embrace, an uncharacteristic response. Something had happened to her during the confrontation with the Stone King that he had missed, and he was only now beginning to make sense of what it was.

A thick stream of rainwater clogged the gutter ahead, blocking the walkway's end like a moat, and he was forced to move outside and around it. He was leading still, choosing their path, his cloaked form darkened by rain and gloom. A wraith, perhaps, he thought. A Grimpond, he corrected. He had not thought of the Grimpond for a long time, the memory too painful to retrieve from the corner of his mind to which he had confined it. It was the Grimpond with its twisted riddles who had led him to the Hall of Kings and his encounter with the Asphinx. It was the Grimpond who had cost him his arm, his spirit, and something of what he had been. Wounded in body and spirit—that was how he saw himself. It would make the Grimpond glad if it knew.

He lifted his face momentarily and let the rain wash over it, cooling his skin. He hadn't thought it possible to be so hot in such dank weather.

It was the Grimpond's visions, of course, that haunted him— the three dark and enigmatic glimpses of the future, not accurate necessarily, lies twisted into half-truths, truths shaded by lies, but real. The first had already come to pass; he had sworn he would cut off his hand before he would take up the Druid cause and that was exactly what he had done. Then he had taken up the cause anyway. Ironic, poetic, terrifying.

The second vision was of Quickening. The third . . .

His good hand clenched. The truth was, he never got beyond thinking about the second. Quickening. In some way, he would fail her. She would reach out to him for help, he would have the chance to save her from falling, and he would let her die. He would stand there and watch her tumble away into some dark abyss. That was the Grimpond's vision. That was what would come to pass unless he could find a way to prevent it.

He had not, of course, been able to prevent the first.

Disgust filled him, and he banished his memory of the Grimpond back to the distant corner from which it had been set loose. The Grimpond, he reminded himself, was itself a lie. But, then, wasn't he a lie as well? Wasn't that what he had become, so determined to keep himself clear of Druid machinations, so ready to disdain all use of the magic except that which served to sustain his own narrow beliefs, and so certain that he could be master of his own destiny? He had lied to himself repeatedly, deceived himself knowingly, pretended all things, and made his life a travesty. He was mired in his misconceptions and pretenses. He was doing what he had sworn he would never do—the work of the Druids, the recovery of their magic, the undertaking of their will. Worse, he was committed to a course of action which could only result in his destruction—a confrontation with the Stone King to take back the Black Elfstone. Why? He was clinging to this course of action as if it were the only thing that would stop his drifting, as if it were all that was left that would keep him from drowning, the only choice that remained.

Surely it was not.

He peered through the damp at the city and realized again how much he missed the forestlands of Hearthstone. It was more than the city's stone, its harsh and oppressive feel, its constant mist and rain. There was no color in Eldwist, nothing to wash clean his sight, to brighten and warm his spirit. There were only shadings of gray, a blurring of shadows layered one upon another. He felt himself in some way a mirror of the city. Perhaps Uhl Belk was changing him just as he changed the land, draining off the colors of his life, reducing him to something as hard and lifeless as stone. How far could the Stone King reach? he wondered. How deep into your soul? Was there any limit? Could he stretch his arms out all the way to Darklin Reach and Hearthstone? Could he find a human heart? In time, probably. And time was nothing to a creature that had lived so long.

They crossed to the front entry of their after-dark refuge and began to climb the stairs. Because Walker led, he saw the stains of rainwater preceding him on the stone steps that his own trailing dampness masked to those following. Someone had entered and gone out again recently. Horner Dees? But Dees was supposedly already there and waiting for their return.

They moved down the maze of hallways to the room which served as their base of operations. The room was empty. Walker's eyes swept the trail of dampness to the shadows of the doors exiting through each wall; his ears probed the quiet. He crossed to where someone had seated himself and eaten.

His instincts triggered unexpectedly.

He could almost smell Pe Ell.

"Horner? Where are you?" Morgan was peering into other

rooms and corridors, calling for the old Tracker. Walker met Quickening's gaze and said nothing. The Highlander ducked out momentarily, then back in again. "He said he would wait right here. I don't understand."

"He must have changed his mind," Walker offered quietly.

Morgan looked unconvinced. "I think I'll take a look around."

He went out the door they had come through, leaving the Dark Uncle and the daughter of the King of the Silver River staring at each other in the gloom.

"Pe Ell was here," she said, her black eyes locked on his.

He let the fire of her gaze warm him; he felt that familiar sense of kinship, of shared magics. "I don't sense a struggle," he said. "There is no blood, no disruption."

Quickening nodded soberly and waited. When he didn't speak further, she crossed to stand before him. "What are you thinking, Walker Boh?" she asked, discomfort in her eyes. "What have you been thinking all the way back, so lost within yourself?"

Her hands reached out to take his arm, to hold it tight. Her face lifted and the silver hair tumbled back, bathed in the weak gray light. "Tell me."

He felt himself laid bare, a thin, rumpled, battered life with barely enough strength remaining to keep from crumbling entirely. The ache in him stretched from his severed limb to his heart, physical and emotional both, an all-encompassing wave that threatened to sweep him away.

"Quickening." He spoke her name softly, and the sound of it seemed to steady him. "I was thinking you are more human than you would admit."

Puzzlement flashed across her perfect features.

He smiled, sad, ironic. "I might be a poor judge of such things, less responsive than I should be, a refugee from years of growing up a boy with no friends and few companions, of living alone too much. But I see something of myself in you. You are frightened by the feelings you have discovered in yourself. You admit to possessing the human emotions your father endowed you with when he created you, but you disdain to accept what you perceive to be their consequences. You love the Highlander—yet you try to mask it. You shut it away. You despise

Pe Ell—yet you play with him as a lure would a fish. You grapple with your emotions, yet refuse to acknowledge them. You work so hard to hide from your feelings."

Her eyes searched his. "I am still learning."

"Reluctantly. When you confronted the Stone King, you were quick to state what had brought you. You told him everything; you hid nothing. There was no attempt at deception or ruse. Yet when Uhl Belk refused your demand—as you surely knew he would—you grew angry, almost . . ." He searched for the word. "Almost frantic," he finished. "It was the first time I can remember when you allowed your feelings to surface openly, without concern for who might witness them."

He saw a flicker of understanding in her eyes. "Your anger was real, Quickening. It was a measure of your pain. I think you wanted Uhl Belk to give you the Black Elfstone because of something you believe will happen if he does not. Is that so?"

She hesitated, torn, then let her breath escape slowly, wearily. "Yes."

"You believe that we will gain the Elfstone. I know that you do. You believe it because your father told you it would be so."

"Yes."

"But you also believe, as he told you, that it will require the magics of those you brought with you to secure it. No amount of talking, no manner of persuasion, will convince Uhl Belk to give it up. Yet you felt you had to try."

Her eyes were stricken. "I am frightened . . ." Her voice caught.

He bent close. "Of what? Tell me."

Morgan Leah appeared in the doorway. He slowed, watched Walker Boh draw back from Quickening, and completed his entrance. "Nothing," he said. "No sign of Horner. It's dark out now; the Rake will be about. I'll have to postpone any search until tomorrow." He came up to them and stopped. "Is something wrong?" he asked quietly.

"No," said Quickening.

"Yes," said Walker.

Morgan stared. "Which is it?"

Walker Boh felt the shadows of the room close about, as if darkness had descended all at once, intending to trap them there.

They stood facing one another across a void, the Highlander, the Dark Uncle, and the girl. There was a sense of having reached an expected crossroads, of now having to choose a path which offered no return, of having to make a decision from which there was no retreat.

"The Stone King . . ." Quickening began in a whisper.

"We're going back for the Black Elfstone," Walker Boh finished.

BARELY A MILE AWAY, at a window two floors up in a building fronting the lair of the Rake, Pe Ell and Horner Dees waited for the Creeper to emerge. They had been in position for some time, settled carefully back in the shadows with the patience of experienced hunters. The rain had stopped finally, turned to mist as the air cooled and stilled. A thin vapor rose off the stone of the streets in wisps that curled upward like snakes. From somewhere deep underground came the faint rumble of the Maw Grint awakening.

Pe Ell was thinking of the men he had killed. It was strange, but he could no longer remember who they were. For a time he had kept count, first out of curiosity, later out of habit, but eventually the number had grown so large and the passing of time so great that he simply lost track. Faces that had been clear in the beginning began to merge and then to fade altogether. Now it seemed he could remember only the first and the last clearly.

The fact that his victims had lost all sense of identity was disconcerting. It suggested that he was losing the sharpness of mind that his work required. It suggested that he was losing interest.

He stared into the blackness of the night and felt an unfamiliar weariness engulf him.

He forced the weariness away irritably. It would be different, he promised himself, when he killed the girl. He might forget the faces of these others from Rampling Steep, the one-armed man, the Highlander, the tunesmith, and the old Tracker; after all, killing them was nothing more than a matter of necessity. But he would never forget Quickening. Killing her was a matter of pride. Even now he could visualize her as clearly as if she was seated next to him, the soft curve and sweep of the skin over her bones, the tilting of her face when she spoke, the way her eyes drew you in, the weave and sway of her hands when they moved. Surely she was the most wondrous of creatures, spellbinding in a way that defied explanation. Hers was the magic of the King of the Silver River and therefore as old as the beginning of life. He wanted to drink in that magic when he killed her; he believed he could. Once he had done so, she would be a part of him, living inside, a presence stronger than even the most indelible memory, stirring within him as nothing else could.

Horner Dees shifted softly beside him, relieving cramped muscles. Still wrapped in his private thoughts, Pe Ell did not glance over. He kept his eyes fixed on the flat surface of the hidden entry across the street. The shadows that cloaked it remained still and unmoving.

What would happen when he slid the blade of the Stiehl into her body? he wondered. What would he see in those depthless black eyes? What would he feel? The anticipation of the moment burned through him like fire. He had not thought of killing her for some time, waiting because he had no other choice if he was to secure the Black Elfstone, letting events take matters where they would. But the moment was close now, he believed. Once he had gained entry into the lair of the Rake, once he had discovered the hiding place of the Stone King, once he had secured possession of the Black Elfstone and disposed of Horner Dees . . .

He jerked upright.

Despite his readiness he was startled when across the way the stone panel lifted and the Rake emerged. He quickly dispensed with all further thoughts of Quickening. The Creeper's dark body glimmered where thin streamers of starlight managed to penetrate the blanket of clouds and reflect off the plates of armor. The monster stepped through the entry, then paused momentarily as if something had alarmed it. Feelers lifted and probed the air tentatively; the whiplike tail curled and snapped. The two in hiding shrank lower into the shadows. The Creeper remained motionless a moment longer, then, apparently satisfied, reached back and triggered the release overhead. The stone panel slid silently into place. The Rake turned and scuttled away into the mist and gloom, its iron legs scraping the stone like trailing chains.

Pe Ell waited until he was certain it was gone, then motioned for Horner Dees to follow him. Together they slipped down to the street, crossed, and stood before the Rake's lair. Dees produced the rope and grappling hook he was carrying and flung them toward a stone outcropping that projected above the secret entry. The grappling hook caught with a dull clank and held. Dees tested the rope, nodded, and passed the end to Pe Ell. Pe Ell climbed effortlessly, hand over hand, until he was level with the release. He triggered it, and the entry panel began to lift. Pe Ell dropped down quickly and with Horner Dees beside him, watched the black cave of the building's interior open into view.

Cautiously, they edged forward.

The entry ran back into deep shadow. Faint gray light slipped through the building's upper windows, seeped downward through gaps in the ruined floors, and illuminated small patches of the blackness. There was no sound from within. There was no movement.

Pe Ell turned to Dees. "Watch the street," he whispered. "Whistle if there's trouble."

He moved into the blackness, fading into it as comfortably as if he were one of its shadows. He was immediately at home, confident within its cloaking, his eyes and ears adjusting to its sweep. The walls of the building were bare and worn with age, damp in places where the rain had seeped through the mortar and run down the stone, tall and rigid against the faint light. Pe Ell slipped ahead, picking his way slowly, cautiously, waiting for something to show itself. He sensed nothing; the building seemed empty.

Something crunched underfoot, startling him. He peered down into the blackness. Bones littered the floor, hundreds of them, the remains of creatures the Rake had gathered in its nightly sweeps and carried back to its lair to consume.

The entry turned down a vast corridor to a larger hall and ended. No doors opened in, no passageways led out. The hall had once been an inner court and rose hundreds of feet through the building to a domed ceiling speckled with strange light patterns and the slow movement of shadows thrown by the clouds. The hall was silent. Pe Ell stared about in distress. He knew at once that there was nothing to discover—not the Stone King, not the Black Elfstone. He had guessed wrong. Anger and disappointment welled up within him, forcing him to continue his search even after he knew it was pointless. He started toward the far wall, scanning the mortared seams, the lines of floor and ceiling, desperate to find something.

Then Horner Dees whistled.

At almost the same moment Pe Ell heard the soft scrape of metal on stone.

He wheeled instantly and darted back through the darkened hall. The Rake had returned. There was no reason for it to have done so unless it had detected them. How? His mind raced, clawing back the layers of confusion. The Rake was blind, it relied on its other senses. It could not have seen them. Could it have smelled them? He had his answer instantly. Their scent about the doorway had alerted it; that was why it had paused. It had pretended to go out, waited, then circled back.

Pe Ell raged at his own stupidity. If he didn't get out of there at once, he would be trapped.

He burst into the darkened entry just in time to discover that he was too late. Through the raised door he caught a glimpse of the Rake rounding the corner of the building across the way, moving as fast as its metal legs would carry it toward its lair. The rope and Horner Dees were gone. Pe Ell melted into the darkest section of one wall, sliding forward soundlessly. He had to reach the entrance and get past the Creeper before it triggered the release. If he failed, he would be caught in the creature's lair. Even the Stiehl would not be enough to save him then.

The Rake rumbled up to the opening, iron claws rasping, and tentacles lashing out against the stone walls, beginning its probe within. Pe Ell slipped the Stiehl free of its sheath and crouched down against the dark. He would have to be quick. He was oddly calm, the way he was before a kill. He watched the monster fill the opening and start to move through.

At once he was up and running. The Rake sensed him instantly, its instincts even keener than Pe Ell's. A tentacle lashed out and caught him, inches from the door. The Stiehl whipped up, severing the limb, freeing the assassin once more. The Rake wheeled about, huffing. Pe Ell tried to run, but there were snaking arms everywhere.

Then the grappling hook shot out of the darkness behind the advancing Creeper, wrapping about its back legs. The rope securing it went taut, and the monster was jerked backward. Its limbs flailed, and its claws dug in. For a moment its attention was diverted. That moment was enough. Pe Ell was past it in a split second, racing into the street, darting to safety. Almost immediately Horner Dees was running beside him, his bearish form laboring from the strain. Behind them, they heard the rope snap and the Rake start after in pursuit.

"Here!" Dees yelled, pulling Pe Ell left into a gaping doorway.

They ran through an entry, up several flights of stairs, down a hall, and out onto a back ramp that crossed to another building. The Creeper lumbered behind, smashing everything that blocked its way. The men hastened into the building at the end of the ramp and down a second set of stairs to the street again. The sounds of pursuit were beginning to fade. They slowed, rounded a corner, peered cautiously down the empty street, then followed the walkway south several blocks to where a cluster of smaller buildings offered an impassable warren into which they quickly crept. Safe within, they slid down wearily, backs to the wall, side by side, breathing heavily in the stillness.

"I thought you'd run," Pe Ell said, gasping.

Dees grunted, shook his head. "I would have, but I gave my word. What do we do now?"

Pe Ell's body steamed with sweat, but deep inside a cold fury was building. He could still feel the Rake's tentacle wrapped about his body. He could still feel it beginning to squeeze. He experienced such revulsion that he could barely keep from screaming aloud.

Nothing had ever come so close to killing him.

He turned to Horner Dees, watched the rough, bearded face furrow, the eyes glitter. Pe Ell's voice was chilly with rage. "You can do what you wish, old man," he whispered. "But I'm going back and kill that thing."

27

ORGAN LEAH WAS appalled. "What do you mean we're going back?" he demanded of Walker Boh. He was not just appalled; he was terrified. "Who gave you the right to decide anything, Walker? Quickening is leader of this company, not you!"

"Morgan," the girl said softly. She tried to take his hand, but he stepped quickly away.

"No. I want this settled. What's going on here? I leave the room for just a moment, just long enough to make sure Horner isn't . . . and when I come back I find you close enough to . . ." He choked on the words, his brown face flushing as the impact of what he was saying caught up with him. "I . . ."

"Morgan, listen to me," Quickening finished. "We have to recover the Black Elfstone. We have to."

The Highlander's fists clenched helplessly. He was aware of how foolish he looked, how young. He made a studied effort to control himself. "If we go back there, Quickening, we will be killed. We didn't know what we were up against before; now we do. Uhl Belk is too much for us. We all saw the same thing—a creature changed into something only vaguely human, armored in stone, and capable of brushing us aside like we were nothing. He's part of the land itself! How do we fight something like that? He'll swallow us whole before we have a chance even to get close!"

He forced his breathing to slow. "And that's only if he doesn't call the Maw Grint or the Rake first. We can't stand up to *them* let alone *him*. Think about it, will you? What if he chooses to use the Elfstone against us! Then what do we do—you without any magic at all that you can use, me with a broken sword that's lost most of its magic, and Walker with . . . I don't know, what? With what, Walker? What are you?"

The Dark Uncle was unfazed by the attack, his pale face expressionless, his eyes steady as they fixed on the Highlander. "I am what I always was, Morgan Leah."

"Less an arm!" Morgan snapped and regretted it immediately. "No, I'm sorry, I didn't mean that."

"But it is true," the other replied quietly.

Morgan looked away awkwardly for a moment, then back again. "Look at us," he whispered. "We're barely alive. We've trekked all the way to the end of the world and it's just about finished us. Carisman's already dead. Maybe Horner Dees as well. We're beaten up. We look like scarecrows. We haven't had a bath in weeks, unless you want to count getting rained on. We're dressed in rags. We've been running and hiding so long we don't know how to fight anymore. We're caught in this gray, dismal world where all we see is stone and rain and mist. I hate this place. I want to see trees and grass and living things again. I don't want to die here. I especially don't want to die when there is no reason for it! And that's exactly what will happen if we go looking for the Stone King. Tell me, Walker, what chance do we have?"

To his surprise, Walker Boh said, "A better chance than you think. Sit down a minute and listen."

Morgan hesitated, suspicion mirrored in his eyes. Then slowly he sat, his anger and frustration momentarily spent. He allowed Quickening to move next to him again, to wrap her arms about him. He let the heat of her body soak through him.

Walker Boh crossed his legs before him and pulled his dark cloak close. "It is true that we appear to be little more than beggars off some Southland city street, that we have nothing with which to threaten Uhl Belk, that we are as insignificant to him as the smallest insects that crawl upon the land. But that appearance may be an illusion we can use. It may give us the chance we need to defeat him. He sees us as nothing. He does not fear us. He disdains to worry about us at all. It is possible that he has already forgotten us. He believes himself invulnerable. Perhaps we can use that against him."

The dark eyes were intense. "He is not what he believes, Highlander. He has evolved beyond the spirit creature he was born, beyond anything he was intended to be. I believe he has evolved even beyond the King of the Silver River. But his evolution has not been a natural one. His evolution has been brought about by his usage of the Black Elfstone. It is ironic, but the Druids protected their magic better than Uhl Belk realizes. He thinks that he stole it easily and uses it without consequence. But he is wrong. Just by calling up the Elfstone's magic, he is destroying himself."

Morgan Leah stared. "What are you talking about?"

"Listen to him, Morgan," Quickening cautioned, her soft face bent close, her dark eyes expectant.

"I did not understand before today what it was that the Black Elfstone was intended to do," Walker Boh continued, hurrying now, anxious to complete his explanation. "I was given the Druid History by Cogline and told to read it. I learned that the Black Elfstone existed and that its purpose was to release Paranor from its spell and return it to the world of men. I learned from Quickening that the Black Elfstone's magic was conceived to negate the effects of other magics—thus the magic that sealed away Paranor could be dispelled. Such power, Highlander! How could such power exist? I kept wondering if it was possible, and if possible, why the Druids—who were so careful in such matters—took no better precautions to protect against its misuse. After all, the Black Elfstone was the only magic that could restore their Keep, that could initiate the process that would restore them to power. Would they let that magic slip away so easily? Would they allow it to be utilized by others, even a creature as powerful as Uhl Belk?

"I knew, of course, that they would not. But how could they prevent it? Today I discovered the answer to that question. I watched the Stone King summon the Maw Grint; I watched what passed between father and son. Did you see it? When Uhl Belk invoked the power of the Stone, there was a binding of the two, a bringing together. The magic was a catalyst. But what did it do? I wondered. It seemed to give life to them both. It was clearly addictive; they reveled in its use. The magic of the Black Elfstone was stronger than their own in the moment of its release. It was so strong that they could not resist what it was doing to them; in fact, they welcomed its coming."

He paused, and his voice lowered to a guarded whisper. The room's shadows cloaked them like conspirators. "This is what I believe must happen when the magic is invoked. Yes, it negates whatever magic it is directed against, just as the Druid History suggests, just as Quickening was told by her father. It confronts and steals away that magic's power. But it must do more. It cannot simply cause the magic to disappear. It cannot take a magic and change it into air. Something must happen to that magic. The laws of nature require it. What it does, I believe, is to absorb and transfer the effects of that other magic to the user of the Stone. When Uhl Belk turns the Black Elfstone on the Maw Grint he takes his child's magic and makes it his own; he takes the poison that transforms the land and its creatures to stone and alters himself as well. That is why he has evolved as he has. And perhaps even more important than that, each time he siphons off a part of the Maw Grint's magic, Uhl Belk is brought close again for a few moments to the son he created. Using the Black Elfstone to share the Maw Grint's magic has given them a bond they could not otherwise enjoy. They hate and fear each other, but they need each other as well. They feed on each other, a giving and taking that only the Black Elfstone can facilitate. It is as close as they can come to a father/son relationship. It is the only bond they can share."

He hunched forward. "But it is killing Uhl Belk. It is changing him to stone entirely. In time, he will disappear into the stone that encases him. He will become like any other statue— inanimate. He is doing it to himself without even realizing it. That is the way the Elfstone works; that is why he was able to steal it so easily. The Druids didn't care. They knew that anyone using it would suffer the consequences eventually. Magic cannot be absorbed without consequence. Uhl Belk is addicted to that magic. He needs the feeling of transformation, of adding to his stone body, to his land, to his kingdom of self. He could not stop now even if he tried."

"But how does this help us?" Morgan asked, impatient once

more. He hunched forward curiously, caught up in the possibilities that Walker's explanation offered. "Even if you're right, what difference does it make? You're not suggesting that we simply wait until Uhl Belk kills himself, are you?"

Walker Boh shook his head. "We haven't time enough for that. The process may take years. But Uhl Belk is not as invulnerable as he believes. He has become largely dependent on the Black Elfstone, cocooned within his stone keep, changed mostly to stone himself, interested not so much in what is happening about him as in the feeding he requires so that his mutation can continue. He is largely stationary. Did you watch him when he tried to move? He cannot change positions quickly; he is welded to the rock of the floor. His magic is old and unused; most of what he does relates to feeding himself through use of the Stone. Fear of losing the Black Elfstone, of being deprived of his source of feeding, and of being left to the questionable mercy of his maddened child dominates his thinking. He has crippled himself with his obsessions. That gives us a chance to defeat him."

Morgan studied the other's face wordlessly for several long moments, thinking the matter through in spite of his reluctance to believe there was any possibility of succeeding, conscious of Quickening's eyes on him as he did so. He had always believed in Walker Boh's ability to reason matters through when others could not. He was the one who had suggested Par and Coll Ohmsford go to their uncle when they needed advice in dealing with the dreams of Allanon. He was frightened by what the Dark Uncle was suggesting, but not so big a fool as to discount it entirely.

Finally he said, "Everything you say may be so, Walker, but you have forgotten something. We still have to get inside the dome to have any chance of overcoming Uhl Belk. And he's not going to invite us in a second time. He's already made that clear. Since we haven't been able to find a way in on our own, how are we supposed to get close enough to do anything?"

Walker folded his hands before him thoughtfully. "Uhl Belk made a mistake when he admitted us to the dome. I was able to sense things that were hidden from me before, when I was forced to stand without. I was able to divine the nature of his fortress keep. He has settled himself above that cavern where the rats cornered us while we were searching the tunnels beneath the city. He places the Tiderace between himself and the Maw Grint's underground lair. But he miscalculated in doing so. The constant changing of the tide has worn and eroded portions of the stone on which he rests."

The Dark Uncle's eyes narrowed. "There is an opening that leads into the dome from beneath."

ANOTHER PAIR OF EYES narrowed as well, these in disbelief as Horner Dees weighed the implications of Pe Ell's words in the dark silence of the building in which the two men were crouched. "Kill it?" he questioned finally, unable to keep himself from repeating the other's words. "Why would you want to do that?"

"Because it's out there!" Pe Ell snapped impatiently, as if that explained everything.

His stare challenged the Tracker, daring him to object. When Dees did not respond, Pe Ell bent forward like a hawk at hunt. "How long have we been in this city, old man—a week, two? I can't even remember anymore. It seems as if we've been here forever! One thing I do know. Ever since we arrived, that thing has been hunting us. Every night, everywhere we go! The Rake, sweeping up the streets, cleaning up the garbage. Well, I've had enough!"

He was stiff with rage, fighting back against the memory of that iron tentacle wrapped about him, struggling to control his revulsion. When he killed, it was quick and clean. Not a slow squeezing, not a death that choked and strangled. And nothing ever touched him. Nothing ever got close.

Not until now.

His failure to find the Stone King in the Rake's lair hadn't done anything to improve his disposition either. He had been certain that he would find Uhl Belk and the Black Elfstone. Instead, he had almost succeeded in getting himself killed.

His knife-blade face was set and raw with feeling. "I won't be hunted anymore. A Creeper can die like anything else." He paused. "Think about this. Once it's dead, maybe the Stone King will show himself. Maybe he'll come out to see what killed his watchdog. Then we'll have him!"

Horner Dees did not look convinced. "You're not thinking straight."

Pe Ell flushed. "Are you frightened once more, old man?"

"Of course. But that doesn't have anything to do with the matter. The fact is, you're supposed to be a professional killer, an assassin. You don't kill without a reason and never without being sure that the odds are in your favor. I don't see any evidence of that here."

"Then you're not looking hard enough!" Pe Ell was furious. "You already have the reason! Haven't you been listening? It doesn't have to be money and it doesn't have to be someone else's idea! Do you want to find Uhl Belk or not? As for the odds, I'll find a way to change them!"

Pe Ell rose and wheeled away momentarily to face the dark. He shouldn't care one way or the other what this old man thought; it shouldn't matter in the least. But somehow, for some reason, it did, and he refused to give Dees the satisfaction of thinking he was somehow misguided. He hated to admit that Horner Dees might have saved his life, even that he might have helped him escape. The old man was a thorn in his side that needed removing. Dees had come out of his past like a ghost, come out of a time he had thought safely buried. No one alive should know who he was or what he had done save Rimmer Dall. No one should be able to talk about him.

He found suddenly that he wanted Horner Dees dead almost as much as he wanted to dispose of the Rake.

Except that the Rake was the more immediate problem.

He turned back to the old Tracker. "I've wasted enough time on you," he snapped. "Go back to the others. I don't need your help."

Horner Dees shrugged. "I wasn't offering it."

Pe Ell started for the door.

"Just out of curiosity," Dees called after him, rising now as well, "how do you plan to kill it?"

"What difference does it make to you?" Pe Ell called over his shoulder.

"You don't have a plan, do you?"

Pe Ell stopped dead in the doorway, seized by an almost

overpowering urge to finish off the troublesome Dees here and now. After all, why wait any longer? The others would never know. His hand dropped through the crease in his pants to close about the Stiehl.

"Thing is," Horner Dees said suddenly, "you can't kill the Rake even if you manage to get close enough to use that blade of yours."

Pe Ell's fingers released. "What do you mean?"

"I mean that even if you lay in wait for the thing, say you drop on it from above or sneak up on it from underneath—not likely, but say that you do—you still can't kill it quick enough." The sharp eyes glittered. "Oh, you can cut off a tentacle or two, maybe sever a leg, or even put out an eye. But that won't kill it. Where do you stab it that will kill it, Pe Ell? Do you know? I don't. Before you've taken two cuts, the Rake will have you. Damage the thing? A Creeper builds itself right back again, finds spare pieces of metal and puts what it's lost back in place."

Pe Ell smiled—mean, sardonic, empty of warmth. "I'll find a way."

Dees nodded. "Sure you will." He paused deliberately, his bearish frame shifting, changing his weight from one foot to the other. In the near darkness, he seemed like a piece of the wall breaking loose. "But not without a plan."

Pe Ell looked away in disgust, shook his head, then looked back again. He'd spent too much time trudging about this dismal city, this tomb of stone and damp. He'd been fighting too long to keep from being swallowed up in its belly. That coupled with prolonged exposure to Quickening's magic had eroded his instincts, dulled the edge of his sharpness, and twisted the clearness of his thought. He was at a point where the only thing that mattered was getting back to where he had started from, to the world beyond Eldwist, and to the life that he had so fully controlled.

But not without the Black Elfstone. He would not give it up.

And not without Quickening's life. He would not give that up either.

Meanwhile, Horner Dees was trying to tell him something. It never hurt to listen. He made himself go very still inside—everything, right down to his thoughts. "You have a plan of your own, don't you?" he whispered.

"I might."

"I'm listening."

"Maybe there's something to what you say about killing the Rake. Maybe that will bring Belk out of hiding. Something has to be tried." The admission came grudgingly.

"I'm still listening."

"It'll take the two of us. Same agreement as before. We look out for each other until the matter's done. Then it's every man for himself. Your word."

"You have it."

Horner Dees shuffled forward until he was right in front of Pe Ell, much closer than Pe Ell wanted him, wheezing like he'd run a mile, grinning through his shaggy beard, big hands knotting into fists.

"What I think we ought to do," he said softly, "is drop the Rake down a deep hole."

MORGAN LEAH STARED at Walker Boh wordlessly for a moment, then shook his head. He was surprised at how calm his voice sounded. "It won't work. You said yourself that the Stone King isn't just a moving statue; he's made himself a part of the land. He's everything in Eldwist. You saw what he did when he finally decided to let us into the dome and then after, when he summoned the Maw Grint. He just split the rock wall apart. His own skin, Walker. Don't you think he'll know if we try to climb through that same skin from beneath? Don't you think he'll be able to feel it? What do you think will happen to us then? Squish!"

Morgan made a grinding motion with his palms. A dark flush crept into his face; he found that he was shaking.

Walker's expression never changed. "What you suggest is possible, but unlikely. Uhl Belk may be the heart and soul of the land he has created, but he is also, like it, a thing of stone. Stone feels nothing, senses nothing. Uhl Belk would not have even discovered we were here if he had been forced to rely on his external senses. It was our use of magic that alerted him. There may remain enough of him that is human to detect intruders, but he relies principally on the Rake. If we can avoid using magic we can enter the dome before he knows what we are about."

Morgan started to object, then cut himself short. Quickening was clutching his arm so hard it hurt. "Morgan," she whispered urgently. "We can do it. Walker Boh is right. This is our chance."

"Our chance?" Morgan looked down at her, fighting to keep his balance as the black eyes threatened to drown him, finding her impossibly beautiful all over again. "Our chance to do what, Quickening?" He forced his gaze away from her, fixing on Walker. "Suppose that you are right about all this, that we can get into the dome without Belk knowing it. What difference does it make? What are we supposed to do then? Use our broken magics, the three of us—a weaponless girl, a one-armed man, and a man with half a sword? Aren't we right back where we started with this conversation?"

He ignored Quickening's hands as they pulled at him. "I won't pretend with you, Walker. You can see what I'm thinking. You can with everyone. I'm terrified. I admit it. If I had the Sword of Leah whole again, I would stand a chance against something like Uhl Belk. But I don't. And I don't have any innate magic like you and Par. I just have myself. I've stayed alive this long by accepting my limitations. That's how I was able to fight the Federation officials who occupy my homeland; that's how I managed to survive against something far bigger and stronger. You have to pick and choose your battles. The Stone King is a monster with monsters to command, and I don't see how the three of us can do anything about him."

Quickening was shaking her head. "Morgan . . ."

"No," he interrupted quickly, unable to stop himself now. "Don't say anything. Just listen. I have done everything you asked. I have given up other responsibilities I should have fulfilled to come north with you in search of Eldwist and Uhl Belk. I have stayed with you to find the Black Elfstone. I want you to succeed in what your father has sent you to do. But I don't know how that can happen, Quickening. Do you? Can you tell me?"

She moved in front of him, her face lifting. "I can tell you that it will happen. My father has said it will be so."

"With my magic and Walker's and Pe Ell's. I know. Well, then, what of Pe Ell? Isn't he supposed to go with us? Don't we need him if we are to succeed?"

She hesitated before giving her answer. "No. Pe Ell's magic will be needed later."

"Later. And your own?"

"I have no magic until you recover the Elfstone."

"So it is left to Walker and me."

"Yes."

"Somehow."

"Yes."

Walker Boh stepped forward impatiently, his pale face hard. "Enough, Highlander. You make it sound as if this were some mystical process that required divine intervention or the wisdom of the dead. There is nothing difficult about what we are being asked to do. The Stone King holds the Black Elfstone; he must be made to give it up. We must sneak through the floor of the dome and surprise him. We must find a way to shock him, to stun him, to do something that will make him release his grip on the Stone, then snatch it from him. We don't have to stand against him in battle; we don't have to slay him. This isn't a contest of strength; it is a contest of will. And cleverness. We must be more clever than he."

The Dark Uncle's eyes burned. "We have not come all this way, Morgan Leah, just to turn around and go back again. We knew there were no answers to be given to our questions, that we would have to find a way to do everything that was required. We have done so. We need do so only one time more. If we don't, the Elfstone is lost to us. That means that the Four Lands are lost as well. The Shadowen have won. Cogline and Rumor died for nothing. Your friend Steff died for nothing. Is that what you wish? Is that your intent? Is it, Morgan Leah?"

Morgan pushed past Quickening and seized the front of the other's cloak. Walker seized his in turn. For an instant they braced each other without speaking, Morgan's face contorted with rage, Walker's smooth and intense.

"I am frightened, too, Highlander," Walker Boh said softly. "I have fears that go far beyond what we are being asked to do here. I have been charged by the shade of Allanon with using the Black Elfstone to bring back Paranor and the Druids. If using the Elfstone on the Maw Grint turns Uhl Belk to stone, what will using it on disappeared Paranor do to me?"

There was a long, empty silence in which the question hung skeletal and forbidding against the dark of the room. Then Walker whispered, "It doesn't matter, you see. I have to find out."

Morgan let the other's cloak slip from his fingers. He took a slow step back. "Why are we doing this?" he whispered in reply. "Why?"

Walker Boh almost smiled. "You know why, Morgan Leah. Because there is no one else."

Morgan laughed in spite of himself. "Brave soldiers? Or fools?"

"Maybe both. And maybe we are just stubborn."

"That sounds right." Morgan sighed wearily, pushing back the oppressiveness of the dark and damp, fighting through his sense of futility. "I just think there should be more answers than there are."

Walker nodded. "There should. Instead, there are only reasons and they will have to suffice."

Morgan's mind spun with memories of the past, of his friends missing and dead, of his struggle to stay alive, and of the myriad quests that had taken him from his home in the Highlands and brought him at last to this farthest corner of the world. So much had happened, most of it beyond his control. He felt small and helpless in the face of those events, a tiny bit of refuse afloat in the ocean, carried on tides and by whim. He was sick and worn; he wanted some form of resolution. Perhaps only death was resolution enough.

"Let me speak with him," he heard Quickening say.

Alone, they knelt at the center of the room in shadow, facing each other, their faces so close that Morgan could see his reflection in her dark eyes. Walker had disappeared. Quickening's hands reached out to him, and he let her fingers come to rest on his face, tracing the line of his bones.

"I am in love with you, Morgan Leah," she whispered. "I want you to know that. It sounds strange to me to say such a thing. I never thought I would be able to do so. I have fears of my own, different from yours and Walker Boh's. I am afraid of being too much alive."

She bent forward and kissed him. "Do you understand what I mean when I say that? An elemental gains life not out of the love of a man and a woman for each other but out of magic's need. I was created to serve a purpose, my father's purpose, and I was told to be wary of things that would distract me. What could distract me more, Morgan Leah, than the love I have for you? I cannot explain that love. I do not understand it. It comes from the part of me that is human and surfaces despite my efforts to deny it. What am I to do with this love? I tell myself I must disdain it. It is . . . dangerous. But I cannot give it up because the feeling of it gives me life. I become more than a thing of earth and water, more than a bit of clay made whole. I become real."

He kissed her back, hard and determined, frightened by what she was telling him, by the sound of the words, by the implications they carried. He did not want to hear more.

She broke away. "You must listen to me, Morgan. I had thought to keep to my father's path and not to stray. His advice seemed sound. But I find now that I cannot heed it. I must love you. It does not matter what is meant for either of us; we are not alive if we do not respond to our feelings. So it is that I will love you in every way that I am able; I will not be frightened any longer by what that means."

"Quickening . . ."

"But," she said hurriedly, "the path remains clear before us nevertheless and we must follow it, you and I. We have been shown where it leads, and we must continue to its end. The Stone King must be overcome. The Black Elfstone must be recovered. You and I and Walker Boh must see that these things are done. We must, Morgan. We must."

He was nodding as she spoke, helpless in the face of her persistence, his love for her so strong that he would have done anything she asked despite the gravest reservations. The tears started in his eyes, but he forced them back, burying his face in her shoulder, hugging her close. He combed her silver hair with his fingers; he stroked the curve of her back. He felt her slim arms go around him, and her body tremble.

"I know," he answered softly.

He thought then of Steff, dying at the hands of the girl he had loved, thinking her something she was not. Would it be so with him? he wondered suddenly. He thought, too, of the promise he had once made his friend, a promise they had all made, Par and Coll and he, that if any of them found a magic that would help free the Dwarves, they would do what they could to recover it and see that it was used. Surely the Black Elfstone was such a magic.

He felt a calm settle through him, dissipating the anger and foreboding, the doubt and uncertainty. The path was indeed laid out for him, and he had never had any choice but to follow it.

"We'll find a way," he whispered to her and felt her own tears dampen his cheek.

STANDING IN THE BLACKNESS of the room beyond, Walker Boh looked back at the lovers as they embraced and felt the warmth of their closeness reach out to him like a lost child's tiny hands. He turned away. There could be no such love for him. He felt an instant's remorse and brushed it hastily aside. His future was a shining bit of certainty in the darkness of his present. Sometimes his prescience revealed a cutting edge.

He moved soundlessly through the building until he reached an open window high above the street and looked down into the roil of mist and gloom. The world of Eldwist was a maze of stone obstructions and corridors that glared back at him through a hard, wet sheen. It was harsh and certain and pointless and it reminded him of the direction of his life.

Yet now, at last, his life might become something more.

One puzzle remained. The Highlander had touched on it, brushed by it in his effort to understand how it was that they could stand against a being with the power of Uhl Belk. The puzzle had been with them since the beginning of their journey, a constant presence, and an enigma that refused to be revealed.

The puzzle was Quickening. The daughter of the King of the Silver River, created out of the elements of the Garden, given life out of magic—she was a riddle of words in another tongue. She had been sent to bring them all into Eldwist. But wouldn't a summons have done the job as well? Or even a dream? Instead the King of the Silver River had sent a living, breathing bit of wonder, a creature so beautiful she defied belief. Why? She was here for a reason, and it was a reason beyond that which she had revealed.

Walker Boh felt a dark place inside shiver with the possibilities.

What was it that Quickening had really been sent to do?

CHAPTER

28

A T DAWN THE THREE LEFT their concealment and went down into the streets. The rain had ceased to fall, the clouds had lifted above the peaks of the buildings, and the light was gray and iron hard. Silence wrapped the bones of Eldwist like a shroud, the air windless, unmisted, and empty. Far distant, the ocean was a faint murmur. Their footfalls thudded dully and receded into echoes that seemed to hang like whispers against the skies. Unsuccessfully, they searched the city for life. There was no sign of either Horner Dees or Pe Ell. The Rake had retreated to its daylight lair. The Maw Grint slept within the earth. And in his domed fortress, Uhl Belk was a dark inevitability awaiting confrontation.

Yet Walker Boh was at peace.

He strode before Morgan and Quickening, surprised at the depth of his tranquility. He had given so much of himself to the struggle to understand and control the purpose of his life, battling with the twin specters of legacy and fate. Now all that was cast aside. Time and events had rushed him forward to this moment, an implacable whirlwind that would resolve the purpose of his life for him. His meeting with the Stone King would settle the matter of who and what he was. Either he merited the charge that the shade of Allanon had given him or he did not. Either he was meant to possess the Black Elfstone and bring back Paranor and the Druids or he was not. Either he would survive Uhl Belk or he would not. He no longer questioned that his doubt must give way to resolution; he did not choose to mire himself further in the "what ifs" that had plagued him for so long. Circumstance had placed him here, and that was enough. Whether he lived or died, he would finally be free of the past. Was the Shannara magic alive within him, strong beyond the loss of his arm to the poison of the Asphinx, powerful enough to withstand the fury of the Stone King? Was the trust Allanon had given to Brin Ohmsford meant for him? He would find out. Knowledge, he thought with an irony that he could not ignore, was always liberating.

Morgan Leah was less certain.

Half-a-dozen steps back, his hand clasped in Quickening's, the Highlander was a fragile shell through which fears and misgivings darted like trapped flies. In contrast to Walker Boh, he already knew far too much. He knew that Walker was not the Dark Uncle of old, that the myth of his invincibility had been shattered along with his arm, and that he was swept along on the same tide of prophecies and promises as the rest of them. He knew that he himself was even less able, a man without a whole weapon, bereft of the magic that had barely sustained him through previous encounters with far lesser beings. He knew that there were only the two of them, that Quickening could not intervene, that she might share their fate but could not affect it. He could say that he understood her need to gain possession of the Black Elfstone, her belief in her father's promises, and her confidence in them—he could speak the words. He could pray that they would find some way to survive what they were undertaking, that some miracle would save them. But the fears and the misgivings would not be captured by words and prayers; they would not be allayed by false hope. They darted within like startled deer, and he could feel the beating of his heart in response to their flight.

What would he do, he wondered desperately, when the Stone King turned those empty eyes on him? Where would he find his strength?

He glanced covertly at Quickening, at the lines and shadows of her face, and at the darkly reassuring glitter of her eyes.

But Quickening walked beside him without seeing.

They passed down the empty streets toward the heart of the

city, stalking like cats along the stone ribbon of the walkways, their backs to the building walls. They could almost feel the earth beneath them pulse with the Stone King's life; they could almost hear the sound of his breathing through the hush. An old god, a spirit, a thing of incomprehensible power—they could feel his eyes upon them. The minutes slipped away, and the streets and buildings came and went with a sameness that whispered of ages come and gone and lives before their own that had passed this way without effect. An oppressive certainty settled down about them, an unspoken voice, a barely remembered face, a feathered touch, all designed to persuade them of the futility of their effort. They felt its presence and reacted, each differently, each calling up what defenses could be found. No one turned back. No one gave way. Locked together by their determination to make an end of this nightmare, they continued on.

In the east, dawn's faint gray light brightened to a chilly silver mist that mingled with the clouds and left the city crystallized.

They caught their first glimpse of the dome shortly after and when Walker Boh, still leading, pressed them back into the shadows of the building they followed as if afraid the dome could see. He took them back along the walkway and down a secondary street, then over and down another, winding this way and that, twisting about through the maze. They slid along the dampness like a trail of water seeking its lowest level and never slowed. Their path meandered, but the dome drew closer beyond the walls that concealed them.

Finally Walker stopped, head lifting within the cowl of his dark cloak as if to sniff the air. He was lost within himself, casting about in the darkness of his mind, the magic working to lead him to where his eyes could not see. He started out again, taking them across a street, down an alleyway and out again, down another street to where a building entry opened onto a set of broad stairs. The stairs took them into the earth beneath the building, a dark and engulfing descent into a cavernous chamber where dozens of the ancient carriages of the old world sat resting on their stone tracks. Massive hulks, broken apart by time and age, the carriages gave the chamber the look of a boneyard. Light fell across the carcasses in narrow stripes, and dust motes decorated the air in a thin, choking haze.

The stairs went farther down, and the three continued their descent. They entered an anteroom with a circular portal set in the far wall, stepped through hesitantly, and found themselves back in the city's sewers. The sewers burrowed in three directions into the darkness, catacombs wrapped in silence and the smell of dead things. Walker's good hand lifted and silver light wrapped about it. He paused once more, as if testing the air. Then he took them left.

The tunnel swallowed them effortlessly, its stone walls massive and impenetrable, threatening to hold them fast forever. Silence was a stealthy, invisible watcher. They heard nothing of the Maw Grint—not a rumble, not even the tremor of its breathing. Eldwist had the feel of a tomb once more, deserted of life, a haven for the dead. They stretched ahead in a line, Walker leading, Quickening next, and Morgan last. No words were exchanged, no glances. They kept their eyes on the light that Walker held forth, on the rock of the tunnel floor they followed, and on the movement of the shadows they cast.

Walker slowed, then stopped. His lighted hand moved to one side, then the other. A faint glimmer caught the outline of a dark opening in the wall left and stairs beyond.

Once again they started down, following damp, slick, roughened steps through a wormhole in the earth. They began to smell the Tiderace, then to hear the faint roar of its waters against Eldwist's shore. They listened closely, guardedly for the squealing of the rats, but it did not come. When they reached the end of these stairs, Walker took them right into a narrow gap studded with stone projections honed razor-sharp by nature and time. They moved slowly, inching their way along, hunched up close to each other to keep within the circle of the light. The dampness spread up the walls before them, a dark stain. Things began moving in the light, skittering away. Morgan caught a glimpse of what they were. Sea life, he recognized in surprise. Tiny black crabs. Were they far enough down from Uhl Belk that such things could live? Were they close enough to the water?

Then they emerged once more into the subterranean cavern that lay beneath the city. Rock walls circled away from the ledge on which they stood and the ocean crashed wildly into the rocks below. Mist churned overhead, draping the cavern's farthest reaches with curtains of white. Daylight brightened the shadows where the rocks were cleft to form small, nearly colorless rainbows against the mist.

The ledge ran away to either side, dipping, climbing, jagged and uneven, disappearing into rock and shadow. Walker Boh cast both ways, feeling for the presence he knew he would find, sensing the pulse of its magic. His eyes lifted toward the unseen. Uhl Belk.

"This way," he said quietly, turning left.

Then the rumble of the Maw Grint's waking sounded, elevating from a stir to a roar, and the whole of Eldwist shook with fury.

THE PLAN WAS SIMPLE, but then simple plans were the ones that usually worked best. The only trouble with this one, thought Pe Ell as he stood in the shadows of the building across from the Rake's lair, was that he was the one taking all the chances while Horner Dees remained safe and sound.

The plan, of course, had been the old man's.

Like Quickening, Walker, and Morgan Leah, they had gone out at dawn, slipping from their refuge back to the streets, greeting the cheerless gray light with squinted eyes and suspicious frowns. A brief exchange of glances and they had been off, going first to the Rake's lair, then tracing the route that Pe Ell would lure the Creeper down. When Dees had satisfied himself that Pe Ell had memorized it, they hooked the old man's harness in place, checked the leverage on the makeshift pulley, and parted company.

Pe Ell had backtracked to the Rake's lair, and now there he stood, waiting.

Stealth and speed were what he would need, first the one, then the other, and not too much of either—an assassin's tools.

He listened to the silence for a long time, judging the distance he must cover and measuring the retreat he would make.

There would be no one to help him escape this time if things went wrong. His narrow face turned this way and that, lifted into the smell of the sea and the stone, knifed against the mist, sifted through the instincts that warned him the Creeper was still awake.

He smiled his cold, empty smile. The anger was gone. The anticipation of killing calmed him like Quickening's touch, soothed him, and gave him peace. He was still and settled within himself, everything ready, in place, as sharp as the edge of the Stiehl and as certain.

Noiselessly, he crossed the street to the door of the lair. He carried the grappling hook and rope firmly in hand. Standing before the door, he tossed the hook skyward to wrap about the same stone projection they had used the previous night. The grappling hook caught with a sharp clang and held. Pe Ell backed away, waiting. But the door remained closed. The Rake had either not heard or was preparing itself for whatever would happen next. Pe Ell had hoped that the noise of the hook would bring the beast out and save him the trouble of making the climb. But he knew that was asking too much.

He took a deep breath. This was where the plan became really dangerous.

He stepped forward, grasped the rope that dangled from the grappling hook, and began to climb. He went swiftly, hand over hand, strong enough that he did not require the use of his legs. Once up, he gripped the release that triggered the hidden entry to the lair, yanked violently on it, and immediately dropped away, skinning down the rope like a cat. The door was already coming up when he struck the ground. There was a whisper of sound from within, and he sprang back instantly. A tentacle barely missed catching him, whistling past his feet. The Rake was already moving, lumbering forward, a nest of tentacles outstretched and grasping.

In another instant the door to the lair was completely up. The Creeper rushed forth, skittering madly, wildly, heedless of the fact that it was no longer night. Enraged by Pe Ell's invasion, it gave immediate pursuit. The assassin raced away, darting just ahead of the maddened beast, racing into the shadows of the alleyway across the street. The Creeper followed, faster than

Pe Ell had expected. For an instant he wondered if he had misjudged his chances. But there was no time to ponder the matter now, and the doubts evaporated in a surge of determination that propelled him forward.

Down the alleyway he ran and out into the adjoining street. He skidded to a halt. Careful of the traps, he thought. Careful you don't get caught in one yourself. That was what they had planned for the Rake, the old man and he—a long drop down a deep hole, a drop into the bowels of Eldwist. If he could stay alive that long.

The Creeper crashed through the entry of the building next to him, choosing its own route now, almost catching him by surprise. He barely eluded the closest tentacles, knife thin as he twisted away, gone almost before the beast could track him. He darted along the building's edge, the Rake in pursuit. The iron that armored the creature clanked and grated, thudded and scraped. He could feel the size of the thing looming over him, an avalanche waiting to fall. He went through one building, through a second, and emerged another street over. Close now, just two blocks more. But the beast? He turned, searching. He could hear it coming, but the sound seemed to project from everywhere at once. Where . . . ?

Out from the shadows of a darkly recessed entry the Creeper tore, iron arms slamming into the earth inches from Pe Ell as the assassin leaped free. Pe Ell howled in fury and dismay.

So quick!

He wanted to turn and fight, to see the monster react to the cold iron of the Stiehl as he slashed its body to ribbons. He wanted to *feel* the Creeper die. Instead he ran once more, racing along the stone paths of the city, down the streets, along the building walls, through shadows and gray light, a wisp of something darker than night. Tentacles rustled and slithered after him, catching at doors and windowframes, tearing them apart, leaving showers of stone dust scattered in their wake. The massive body hammered and careened, and the legs tore at the walk. The Rake seemed to pick up speed, coming faster still. If daylight bothered it, if blindness inhibited it, it showed nothing of it here. Pe Ell could feel its rage as if it were palpable.

The chase took them down another street and around a final

corner. Pe Ell could sense that he was losing ground. Ahead, the street deadended at a stone park. A basin of steps led down to a statue of a winged figure with streamers and ribbons trailing from its body—and to a trap, the same trap that had snared the old man and the Highlander days before.

Horner Dees was waiting, secured in his harness, standing at the edge of the hidden door, bait for the trap. Pe Ell leaped sideways to a walkway and picked up speed as the Rake rounded the corner behind him, tentacles whipping. He went past Horner Dees on the fly, caught a glimpse of his rough face, pale beneath the heavy beard, and sprang onto the wall where the lines securing the harness were laid. He pulled them taut, hoisting Dees out over the hidden pit. He heard the Creeper rumble into the street, heard Horner Dees yell. The Rake became aware of the old man, deviated direction slightly, and charged. Dees tried to backpedal in spite of himself as the juggernaut bore down on him, metal parts shrieking.

Then the trapdoor dropped open, and the monster began to fall. It tumbled wildly down the stone ramp, its armored body rasping. It had been so eager to reach the Tracker that it had forgotten where it was. Now it was caught, sliding away, disappearing from view. Pe Ell howled with delight.

But suddenly the tentacles lashed out and began snaring stone projections—a corner of the basin stairs, a section of a crumbling wall, anything within reach. The sliding stopped. Dust rose into the air, obscuring everything. Pe Ell hesitated, forgetting momentarily to pull in on the harness that secured Dees. Then he heard the old man scream. Yanking frantically on the ropes, he found they would not move. Something was pulling from the other end, something far stronger than himself. He had waited too long. The Rake had Horner Dees.

Pe Ell never hesitated. He wasn't thinking of his promise; keeping his word had never much concerned him. He simply reacted. He dropped the ropes, leaped from the wall, and raced through the basin park into the street. He saw the old Tracker sliding across the stone toward the edge of the drop, hands grasping and feet kicking, a tentacle wrapped about his stout body. He caught up with Horner Dees just as the old man was about to be pulled from view. One slice of the Stiehl severed the tentacle that bound him; a second severed the ropes of the harness.

"Run!" he screamed, shoving the bulky form away.

A tentacle snaked about him, trying to pin his arms fast. He twisted, the Stiehl's blade glowing white with magic, and the tentacle dropped away. Pe Ell raced left, cutting at the tentacles that secured the Rake, severing its hold. There was dust everywhere, rising into the gray light, mingling with the mist until it was uncertain where anything lay. Pe Ell was moving on instinct. He darted and skipped through the tangle of arms, hacked at each, heard the scraping begin again, and the sliding resume.

Then there was a rush of metal and flailing arms and the Rake was gone. It dropped into the chute and fell, tumbling down into the chasm. Pe Ell smothered his elation, racing back the way he had come, searching for Dees. He found him crawling weakly along the basin stairs. "Get up!" he cried, hauling him to his feet in a frenzied lunge, propelling him ahead.

The earth behind them exploded, the street shattering apart, stone fragments flying everywhere. The two men stumbled and fell and turned to look.

The remaining pieces of Horner Dees' plan tumbled into place.

Out of the depths of Eldwist rose the Maw Grint, awakened by the impact of the Rake's fall, aroused and angered. The monster roared and shook itself as it lifted skyward, worm body glistening, all ridges and scales, so huge that it blocked even the faint gray daylight. The Rake dangled from its mouth, turning to stone as the poison coated it, its struggles beginning to lessen. The Maw Grint held it firm a moment, then tossed it as a dog might a rat. The Rake flew through the air and struck the side of a building. The wall collapsed with the impact, and the Rake shattered into pieces.

Back down into the tunnels slid the Maw Grint, its thunder already fading to silence. Clouds of dust settled in its wake, and the light brightened to slate.

Impulsively Pe Ell reached out and locked hands with Horner Dees. Their labored breathing was the only sound in the stillness that followed.

UNDERGROUND, IN THE CAVERN beneath the Stone King's fortress dome, the rumble of the Maw Grint's waking disappeared into the pounding of the Tiderace against Eldwist's rocky shores. Morgan Leah's sun-browned face lifted to peer through the mists.

"What happened?" he whispered.

Walker Boh shook his head, unable to answer. He could still feel the tremors in the earth, lingering echoes of the monster's fury. Something had caused it to breach—something beyond normal waking. The creature's response had been different than when the Stone King had summoned it, more impatient, more intense.

"Is it sleeping again?" the Highlander pressed, anxious now, concerned with being trapped.

"Yes."

"And him?" Morgan pointed into the mists. "Does *he* know?"

Uhl Belk. Walker probed, reaching through the layers of rock in an effort to discover what might be happening. But he was too far away, the stone too secure to be penetrated by his magic. Not unless he used his touch, and if he did that the Stone King would be warned.

"He rests still," Quickening answered unexpectedly. She came forward to stand next to him, her face smooth and calm, her eyes distant. The wind rushed into her silver hair and scattered it about her face. She braced against its thrust. "Be at ease, Morgan. He does not sense the change."

But Walker sensed it, whatever it was, just as the girl had. Barely perceptible yet, but the effects were beginning to reach and swell. It was something beyond the passing of time and the erosion of rock and earth. The wind whispered it, the ground echoed with it, and the air breathed it. Born of the magic, the daughter of the King of the Silver River and the Dark Uncle had both felt its ripple. Only the Highlander was left unaware.

Walker Boh felt a rough, unexpected urgency clutch at him. Time was slipping away.

"We have to hurry," he said at once, starting away again. "Quickly, now. Come."

He took them left down the rocky outcropping of the ledge, across its ragged, slippery surface. They inched along with their backs to the wall, the ledge no more than several feet wide in places, the ocean's spray redampening its surface with each newly broken wave. Beyond where they stood the cavern spread away like some vast hidden world, and it seemed as if they could feel the eyes of its invisible inhabitants peering out at them.

The ledge ended at a cave that burrowed into darkness. Walker Boh lifted the magic of his silver light to the black and a staircase appeared, winding away, circling upward into the rock.

With Quickening and Morgan following shadowlike, the Dark Uncle began to climb.

CHAPTER

29

WHEN MORGAN LEAH was a boy he often played in the crystal-studded caves that lay east of the city. The caves had been formed centuries earlier, explored and forgotten by countless generations, their stone floors worn smooth by the passing of time and feet. They had survived the Great Wars, the Wars of the Races, the intrusions of living creatures of all forms, and even the earth fires that simmered just beneath their surface. The caves were pockets of bright luminescence, their ceilings thick with stalactites, floors dotted with pools of clear water and darkly shadowed sinkholes, and their chambers connected by a maze of narrow, twisting tunnels. It was dangerous to go into the caves; there was a very high risk of becoming lost. But for an adventure-seeking Highland boy like Morgan Leah, any prospect of risk was simply an attraction.

He found the caves when he was still very small, barely old enough to venture out on his own. There were a handful of boys with him when he discovered an entrance, but he was the only one brave enough to venture in. He went only a short distance that day, intimidated more than a little; it seemed a very real possibility that the caves ran to the very center of the earth. But the lure of that possibility was what called him back in the end, and before long he was venturing ever farther. He kept his exploits secret from his parents, as did all the boys; there were restrictions enough on their lives in those days. He played at being an explorer, at discovering whole worlds unknown to those he had left behind. His imagination would soar when he was inside the caves; he could become anyone and anything. Often he went into them alone, preferring the freedom he felt when the other boys were not about to constrict the range of his playacting, for their presence imposed limits he was not always prepared to accept. Alone, he could have things just as he wished.

It was while he was alone one day, just after the anniversary of the first year of his marvelous discovery, that he became lost. He was playing as he always played, oblivious of his progress, confident in his ability to find his way back because he had done so every time before, and all of a sudden he didn't know where he was. The tunnel he followed did not appear familiar; the caves he encountered had a different, foreign look; the atmosphere became abruptly and chillingly unfriendly. It took him a while to accept that he was really lost and not simply confused, and then he simply stopped where he was and waited. He had no idea what it was that he was waiting for at first, but after a time it became clear. He was waiting to be swallowed. The caves had come alive, a sleeping beast that had finally roused itself long enough to put an end to the boy who thought to trifle with it. Morgan would remember how he felt at that moment for the rest of his life. He would remember his sense of despair as the caves transformed from inanimate rock into a living, breathing, seeing creature that wrapped all about him, snakelike, waiting to see which way he would try to run. Morgan did not run. He braced himself against the beast, against the way it hunched down about him. He drew the knife he carried and held it before him, determined to sell his life dearly. Slowly, without realizing what he was doing, he disappeared into the character he had played at being for so many hours. He became someone else. Somehow that saved him. The beast drew back. He walked ahead challengingly, and as he did so the strangeness slowly vanished. He began to recognize something of where he was, a bit of crystallization here, a tunnel's mouth there, something else, something more, and all of a sudden he knew where he was again.

When he emerged from the caves it was night. He had been lost for several hours—yet it seemed only moments. He went home thinking that the caves had many disguises to put on, but that if you looked hard enough you could always recognize the face beneath.

He had been a boy then. Now he was a man and the beliefs of boyhood had long since slipped away. He had seen too much of the real world. He knew too many hard truths.

Yet as he climbed the stairs that curled upward through the rock walls of the cavern beneath Eldwist he was struck by the similarity of what he felt now and what he had felt then, trapped both times in a stone maze from which escape was uncertain. There was that sense of life in the rock, Uhl Belk's presence, stirring like a pulse in the silence. There was that sense of being spied upon, of a beast awakened and set at watch to see which way he would try to run. The weight of the beast pressed down upon him, a thing of such size that it could not be measured in comprehensible terms. A peninsula, a city and beyond, an entire world—Eldwist was all of these and Uhl Belk was Eldwist. Morgan Leah searched in vain for the disguise that had fooled him as a boy, for the face that he had once believed hidden beneath. If he did not find it, he feared, he would never get free.

They ascended in silence, those who had come from Rampling Steep, the only ones left who could face the Stone King. Morgan was so cold he was shivering, and the cold he felt derived from far more than the chill of the cavern air. He could feel the sweat bead along his back, and his mind raced with thoughts of what he would do when the stairs finally came to an end and they were inside the dome. Draw his sword, the one of ordinary metal, yet whole? Attack a thing that was nearly immortal with only that? Draw his shattered talisman, a stunted blade? Attack with that? What? What was it that he was expected to do?

He watched Quickening move ahead of him, small and delicate against Walker Boh's silver light, a frail bit of flesh and blood that might in a single sweep of Uhl Belk's stone hand scatter back into the elements that had formed it. Quickening gone—he tried to picture it. Fears assailed him anew, darts that pierced and burned. Why were they doing this? Why should they even try?

Walker slipped on the mist-dampened steps and grunted in

pain as he struck his knee. They slowed while he righted himself, and Morgan waited for Uhl Belk to stir. Hunter and hunted—but which was which? He wished he had Steff to stand beside him. He wished for Par Ohmsford, for Padishar Creel. He wished for any and all of them, for even some tiny part of them to appear. But wishing was useless. None of them were there; none of them would come. He was alone.

With this girl he loved, who could not help.

And with Walker Boh.

An unexpected spark of hope flashed inside the Highlander. Walker Boh. He stared at the cloaked figure leading them, one-armed, escaped from the Hall of Kings, risen from the ashes of Hearthstone. A cat with many lives, he thought. The Dark Uncle of old, evolved perhaps from the invincible figure of the legends, but a miracle nevertheless, able to defy Druids, spirits, and the Shadowen and live on. Come here to Eldwist, to fulfill a destiny promised by the shade of Allanon or to die—that was what Walker Boh had elected to do. Walker, who had survived everything until now, Morgan reminded himself, was not a man who could be killed easily.

So perhaps it was not intended that the Dark Uncle be killed this time either. And perhaps—just perhaps—some of that immortality might rub off on him.

Ahead, Walker slowed. A flick of his fingers and the silver light vanished. They stood silently in the dark, waiting, listening. The blackness lost its impenetrability as their eyes adjusted, and their surroundings slowly took shape—stairs, ceiling, and walls, and beyond, an opening.

They had reached the summit of their climb.

Still Walker kept them where they were, motionless. When Morgan thought he could stand it no longer, they started ahead once more, slowly, cautiously, one step at a time, shadows against the gloom. The steps ended and a corridor began. They passed down its length, invisible and silent save for their thoughts which seemed to Morgan Leah to hang naked and screaming and bathed in light.

When the corridor ended they stopped again, still concealed within its protective shadow. Morgan stepped forward for an anxious look.

The Stone King's dome opened before them, vast and hazy and as silent as a tomb. The stands that circled the arena stretched away in symmetrical, stair-step lines, a still life of shadows and half-light that lifted to the ceiling, its highest levels little more than a vague suggestion against the aged stone. Below, the arena was flat and hard and empty of movement. The giant form of Uhl Belk crouched at its center, turned away so that only a shading of the rough-hewn face was visible.

Morgan Leah held his breath. The silence of the dome seemed to whisper the warnings that screamed inside his head.

Walker Boh moved back to stand beside him, and the pale, hollowed face bent close so that the other's mouth was at his ear. "Circle left. I'll go right. When I strike him, be ready. I shall try to cause him to drop the Stone. Seize hold of it if he does. Then run. Don't look back. Don't hesitate. Don't stop for anything." The other's hand seized his wrist and held it. "Be swift, Highlander. Be quick."

Morgan nodded voicelessly. For an instant Quickening's black eyes met his own. He could not read what he saw there.

Then Walker was gone, slipping from the mouth of the corridor into the arena, moving to his right along the front wall of the stands into the gloom. Morgan followed, turning left. He pushed aside his dread and gave himself over to the Dark Uncle's command. He passed across the stone like a wraith, quick and certain, finding a surprising reassurance simply from being in motion. But his fear persisted, a cornered beast within his skin. Shadows seemed to circle about him as he went, and the dome's silence hissed at him in his mind, a voiceless snake. His eyes fixed on the bulky form at the arena's center; he found himself searching for even the smallest movement. There was none. Uhl Belk was carved stone against the gray, still and fixed. Quick, now, thought Morgan as he went. Quick as light. He saw Walker at the far side of the arena, a lean and furtive figure, nearly invisible in the gloom. Another few moments, he thought. And then . . .

Quickening.

He suddenly realized that in his haste to obey Walker he had forgotten about the girl. Where was she? He stopped abruptly, casting about for her without success, scanning the risers, the tunnels, the shadows that issued from everywhere. He felt something drop in his chest. Quickening!

Then he saw her—not safely concealed or well back from where they crept, but fully revealed, striding out from the corridor into the arena directly toward the massive figure of Uhl Belk. His breath caught sharply in his throat. What was she doing?

Quickening!

His cry was silent, but the Stone King seemed to hear, responding with an almost inaudible grunt, stirring to life, lifting away from his crouch, beginning to turn . . .

Brilliant white light flared across the canopy of the dome, so blinding that for an instant even Morgan had to look away. It was as if the sun had exploded through the clouds, the gray haze, the stone itself, to set fire to the air imprisoned there. Morgan saw Walker Boh with his single arm raised, thrust out from his dark robes, the magic bursting from his fingers. Uhl Belk howled in surprise, his massive body shuddering, arms raising to shield his eyes, his stone parts grinding with the effort.

Walker Boh leaped forward then, a shadow against the light, charging at the Stone King as the latter flailed ponderously at the painful brightness. Again his good arm raised, thrusting forth. An entire bag of Cogline's volatile black powder flew at Uhl Belk and exploded, hammering into the Stone King. Bits and pieces of the ragged body shattered into fragments. Fire burned along his arm to where his fist clenched the Black Elfstone.

But still he held the talisman fast.

And suddenly Morgan Leah found that he could not move. He was frozen where he stood. Just as had happened at the Jut when the Creeper had gained the heights under cover of darkness and the outlaws of the Movement had gone to meet its attack, he found himself paralyzed. All his fears and doubts, all his misgivings and terrors descended on him. They seized him with their clawed fingers and bound him up as surely as if he had been wrapped in chains. What could he do? How could he help? His magic was lost, his Sword blade shattered. He watched helplessly as Uhl Belk began to turn, to fight past Walker Boh's assault, and to brush back his magic. The Dark Uncle renewed his attack, but this time he struck without the element of surprise to aid him and the Stone King barely flinched. Already the brightness of Walker's false sun was beginning to fade and the gray of the dome's true light to return.

Walker Boh's words echoed tauntingly in Morgan's ears.

Be swift, Highlander. Be quick.

Morgan fought through his immobility and wrenched free from its scabbard the broadsword he wore strapped to his back. But his fingers refused to hold it; his hands would not obey. The broadsword slipped away, tumbling to the arena floor with a hollow clang.

The Stone King's breath hissed as one monstrous hand swept out to seize Walker Boh and crush the life from him. The Dark Uncle had gotten too close; there was no chance for him to escape. Then suddenly he was gone, reappearing first as two images, then four, and then countless more—Jair Ohmsford's favorite trick, three centuries ago. The Stone King grabbed at the images, and the images evaporated at his touch. The true Walker Boh sprang at the monster, scattered new fire into his face, and slid nimbly away.

The Stone King howled in rage, clawed at his face, and shook himself like an animal seeking to rid itself of flies. The whole of the arena shuddered in response. Fissures opened in jagged lines across the floor, the stands buckled and snapped, and a shower of dust and debris descended from the ceiling. Morgan lost his footing and fell, the impact of the stone jarring him to his teeth.

He felt pain, and with the coming of that pain the paralyzing chains fell away.

The Stone King's fist came up, and the fingers of his hand began to open. The nonlight of the Elfstone seeped through, devouring what remained of Walker Boh's fading magic. The Dark Uncle threw up a screen of fire to slow the magic's advance, but the nonlight enveloped it in a wave of blackness. Walker stumbled backward toward the shadows, chased by the nonlight, harried by the fissures and the cracking of stone.

Another few seconds and he would be trapped.

Then Quickening caught fire.

There was no other way to explain it. Morgan watched it

happen and still couldn't believe what he was seeing. The daughter of the King of the Silver River, less than twenty feet away from Uhl Belk by now, standing exposed and unprotected beneath his shadow, elevated like a creature made of air, until she was level with the giant's head, then burst into flames. The fire was golden and pure, its blaze a cloaking of light, flaring all along her body and limbs, leaving her illuminated as if by the midday sun. She was, in that instant, more beautiful than Morgan had ever seen her, radiant and flawless and exquisite beyond belief. Her silver hair lifted away from her, feathering outward against the fire, and her eyes glistened black within the gold. She hung there revealed, all wondrous, impossible magic come to life.

She is trying to distract him, Morgan realized in disbelief. *She is giving herself away, revealing who she is, in an effort to distract him from us!*

The Stone King turned at the unexpected flaring of light, his already crumpled face twisting until his features virtually ceased to exist. The slash of his mouth gaped at the sight of her and his voice sounded in anguish.

—You—

Uhl Belk forgot about Walker Boh. He forgot about the Dark Uncle's magic. He forgot about everything but the burning girl. In a frenzy of grinding stone limbs and joints, he struggled to reach her, surging up against the stone floor that welded him fast, grappling futilely for her, then in desperation bringing the hand that cupped the Black Elfstone to bear against her. His voice was a terrifying moan become a frenzied roar. The earth shuddered with the urgency of his need.

Morgan acted then, finally, desperately, even hopelessly. Surging back to his feet, his eyes fastened on Quickening and on the monster who sought to destroy her, he attacked. He went without thought, without reason, driven by need and armored in determination he had not thought he could ever possess. He raced into the haze of dust and debris, leaping past the fissures and drops, speeding as if he were carried on the strong autumn winds of his homeland. One hand dropped to his waist, and he pulled forth the shattered blade of his ancestors, the jagged remnant of the Sword of Leah.

Though he was not aware of it, the sword shone white with magic.

He screamed the battle cry of his homeland. "Leah! Leah!"

He reached the Stone King just as the other became aware of his presence and the hard, empty eyes began to turn. He sprang onto a massive bent leg, vaulted forward, seized the arm that extended the Black Elfstone, and drove the shattered blade of the Sword of Leah deep into its stone.

Uhl Belk screamed, not in surprise or anger this time, but in terrifying pain. White fire burst from the shattered blade into the Stone King's body, lines of flame that penetrated and seared. Morgan stabbed Uhl Belk again and yet again. The stone hands trembled and clutched, and the stricken monster shuddered.

The Black Elfstone tumbled from his fingers.

Instantly Morgan yanked free his Sword and scrambled down in an effort to retrieve it. But the Stone King's damaged arm blocked his way, swinging toward him like a hammer. He dodged wildly, desperate to escape its sweep, but it clipped him anyway and sent him tumbling back, arms and legs flying. He barely managed to keep hold of his weapon. He caught a brief glimpse of Quickening, an oddly clear vision, her face bright even though the magic of her fire had faded. He caught a snatch of dark motion as Walker Boh appeared next to her out of the shadows. Then he struck the wall, the force of the blow knocking the breath from him, jamming the joints of his body so that he thought he had broken everything. Even so, he refused to stay down. He staggered back to his feet, dazed and battered, determined to continue.

But there was nothing more to do. As quickly as that, the battle was ended. Walker Boh had gained possession of the fallen Elfstone. He braced the Stone King, the Druid talisman clutched menacingly in his raised hand. Quickening stood beside him, returned to herself, the magic she had summoned gone again. As his vision slowly cleared, as his sense of balance restored itself, Morgan saw her again in his mind, all on fire. He was still astonished at what she had done. Despite her vow she had used the magic, revealed herself to Uhl Belk, and risked everything to give them a chance to survive.

The questions whispered at him then, insidious tricksters.

Had she known that he would come to save her?

Had she known what his Sword would do?

The gloom of the dome's interior returned again with the fading of the magic, cloaking Uhl Belk's massive form in shadow. The Stone King faced them from a cloud of swirling dust, his body sagging as if melted by the heat of his efforts to defend himself, still joined to the stone of Eldwist in the chaining that had undone him. Try as he might, he had not been able to rise and break free. By choosing to become the substance of his kingdom he had rendered himself virtually immobile. His face was twisted into something unrecognizable, and when he spoke there was horror and madness reflected in his voice.

—Give the Elfstone back to me—

They stared up at him, the three from Rampling Steep, and it seemed none of them could find words to speak.

"No, Uhl Belk," Walker Boh replied finally, his own voice strained from the effort of his battle. "The Elfstone was never yours in the first place. It shall not be given back to you now."

—I shall come for you then; I shall take it from you—

"You cannot move from where you stand. You have lost this battle and with it the Elfstone. Do not think to try and steal it back."

—It is mine—

The Dark Uncle did not waiver. "It belongs to the Druids."

Dust geysered from the ravaged face as the creature's breath exploded in a hiss of despair.

—There are no Druids—

The accusation died away in a grating echo. Walker Boh did not respond, his face chiseled with emotions that seemed to be tearing him apart from within. The Stone King's arms rose in a dramatic gesture.

—Give the Black Elfstone back to me, human, or I shall command Eldwist to crush the life from you; give the talisman back now or see yourself destroyed—

"Attack me or those with me," Walker Boh said, "and I shall turn the Elfstone's magic against this city! I shall summon power enough to shatter the stone casing that preserves it and turn it and you to dust! Do not threaten further, Uhl Belk! The power is no longer yours!"

The silence that followed was profound. The Stone King's hand closed into a fist and the sound of grinding rose out of it.

—You cannot command me, human; no one can—

Walker's response was immediate. "Release us, Uhl Belk. The Black Elfstone is lost to you."

The statue straightened with a groan, and the sound of its voice was thick with weeping.

—It will come for me; the Maw Grint will come; my son, the monster I have made will descend upon me, and I shall be forced to destroy it; only the Black Elfstone kept it at bay; it will see me old and wearied and believe me without strength to defend against its hunger; it shall try to devour me—

Depthless hard eyes fixed on Quickening.

—Child of the King of the Silver River, daughter of he who was my brother once, give thought to what you do; you threaten to weaken me forever if you steal away the Stone; the Maw Grint's life is no less dear to me than your own to your father; without him there can be no expansion of my land, no fulfillment of my trust; who are you that you should be so quick to take what is mine; are you completely blind to what I have made; there is in the stone of my land a changeless beauty that your father's Gardens will never have; worlds may come and go but Eldwist will remain; it would be better for all worlds to be so; your father believes himself right in what he does, but his vision of life is no clearer than my own; am I not entitled to do what I see is right as the Word has given me to see right—

"You subvert what you touch, Uhl Belk," the girl whispered.

—And you do not; your father does not; all who live within nature do not; can you pretend otherwise—

Quickening's frail form eased a step closer to the giant, and the light that had radiated from her before flared anew.

"There is a difference between nurturing life and making it over," she said. "It was to nurture that you were charged when given your trust. You have forgotten how to do so."

The Stone King's hand brushed at the particles of light that floated from her body, an unconscious effort to shield himself. But then he drew his hand back sharply, the intake of his breath harsh with pain.

—No—

The word was an anguished cry. He straightened, caught by some invisible net that wrapped him and held him fast.

—Oh, child; I see you now; I thought that in the Maw Grint I had created a monster beyond all belief; but your father has done worse in you—

The rough voice gasped, choked as if it could not make the words come further.

—Child of change and evolution, you are the ceaseless, quicksilver motion of water itself; I see in truth what you have been sent to do; I have indeed been stone too long to have missed it; I should have realized when you came to me that you were madness; I am mired in the permanency I sought and have been as blind as those who serve me; the end of my life is written out before me by the scripting of my own hand—

"Uhl Belk," Quickening whispered the name as if it were a prayer.

—How can you give what has been asked after tasting so much—

Morgan did not understand what the Stone King was talking about. He glanced at Quickening and started in surprise. Her face was stricken with guilt, a mirror of the hidden secrets that he had always suspected but never wanted to believe she kept.

The Stone King's voice was a low hiss.

—Take yourself from me, child; go into the world again and do what you must to seal all our fates; your victory over me must seem hollow and bitter when the price demanded for it is made so dear—

Walker Boh was staring as well, his mouth shaped with a frown, his brow furrowed. He did not seem to understood what Uhl Belk was saying either. Morgan started to ask Quickening what was happening and hesitated, unsure of himself.

Then Uhl Belk's head jerked up with a sharp crack.

—Listen—

The earth began to shudder, a low rumbling that emanated from deep within, rising to the surface in gathering waves of sound. Morgan Leah had heard that rumble before.

—It comes—

The Maw Grint.

Walker began backing away, yelling at Morgan and Quickening to follow. He shouted at the Stone King, "Release us, Uhl Belk, if you would save yourself! Do so now! Quickly!"

Walker's arm lifted, threatening with the fist that held the Black Elfstone. Uhl Belk barely seemed to notice. His face had become more haggard, more collapsed than ever, a parody of human features, a monster's face grown hideous beyond thought. The giant's voice hissed like a serpent's through the roar of the Maw Grint's approach.

—Flee, fools—

There was no anger in the voice—only frustration and emptiness. And something more, Morgan Leah thought in amazement. There was hope, just a glimmer of it, a recognition beyond the Highlander's understanding, a seeing of some possibility that transcended all else.

A section of the dome's massive wall split apart directly behind them, stone blocks grinding with the movement, gray daylight spilling through.

—Flee—

Morgan Leah broke for the opening instantly, chased by demons he did not care to see. He felt, rather than saw, the Stone King watch him go. Quickening and Walker followed. They gained the opening in a rush and were through, running from the fury of the Maw Grint's coming, racing away into the gloom.

CHAPTER

30

IT APPEARED THAT the Maw Grint had gone mad.
Twice before the three who fled had observed the
monster's coming, once when it had surfaced as they
stood on the overlook above the city and once when it
had been summoned by Uhl Belk. There hadn't been a day since
they had arrived in Eldwist that they hadn't heard the creature
moving through the tunnels below them, astir at the coming of
each sunset to prowl with the dark. Each time its approach had
been prefaced with the same unmistakable deep, low rumbling
of the earth. Each time the city had trembled in response.

But there had never been anything like this.

The city of Eldwist was like a beast shaking itself awake from
a bad dream. Towers and spires rocked and trembled, shedding
bits and pieces of loose stone amid a shower of choking dust.
The streets threatened to buckle, stone cracking in jagged fissures, trapdoors dropping away as their catches released, supports and trestles snapping apart. Whole stairways leading
downward to the tunnels crumbled and disappeared, and sky-
bridges connecting one building to another collapsed. Against a
screen of gray haze and clouds Eldwist shimmered like a vanishing mirage.

Racing to escape the Stone King's dome, Walker Boh barely
gained the closest walkway before the tremors drove him to his
knees. He pitched forward, his outstretched arm curling against
his body to protect his hold on the Black Elfstone. He took the
force of the fall on his shoulder, a sharp, jarring blow, and kept

skidding. He struck the wall of the building ahead of him, and the breath left his body. For a moment he was stunned, bright pinpricks of light dancing before his eyes. When his vision cleared he saw Quickening and Morgan sprawled in the street behind him, knocked from their feet as well.

He rose with an effort and started away again, yelling for them to follow. As he watched them struggle up, his mind raced. He had threatened Uhl Belk with the Black Elfstone by saying that he would invoke its magic against the city if they were not released. The threat had been an idle one. He could not use the Elfstone that way without destroying himself. It was fortunate for them all that Uhl Belk still did not understand how the Druid magic worked. Even so they were not free yet. What would they do if the Maw Grint came after them? There was every reason to believe that it would. The magic of the Black Elfstone had provided a link between father and son, spirit lord and monster, that Walker Boh had broken. The Maw Grint already sensed that break; it had awakened in response. Once it discovered that the Elfstone was gone, that the Stone King no longer had possession of it, what was to prevent the beast from giving chase?

Walker Boh grimaced. There wasn't any question as to how such a chase would end. He couldn't use the Black Elfstone on the Maw Grint either.

A stone block large enough to bury him crashed into the street a dozen feet ahead, sending the Dark Uncle sprawling for the second time. Quickening darted past, her beautiful face oddly stricken, and raced away into the gloom. Morgan appeared, reached down as he caught up with Walker, and hauled him back to his feet. Together they ran on, sidestepping through the gathering debris, dodging the cracks and fissures.

"Where are we going?" the Highlander cried out, ducking his head against the dust and silt.

Walker gestured vaguely. "Out of the city, off the peninsula, back up on the heights!"

"What about Horner Dees?"

Walker had forgotten the Tracker. He shook his head. "If we can find him, we'll take him with us! But we can't stop to look! There isn't time!" He shoved the Elfstone into his tunic and reached out to grasp the other as they ran. "Highlander, stay close to Quickening. This matter is not yet resolved! She is in some danger!"

Morgan's eyes were white against his dust-streaked face. "What danger, Walker? Do you know something? What was Uhl Belk talking about back there when he spoke about her victory being hollow, about the price she was paying? What did he mean?"

Walker shook his head wordlessly. He didn't know—yet sensed at the same time that he should, that he was overlooking something obvious, forgetting something important. The street yawned open before them, a trapdoor sprung. He yanked the Highlander aside just in time, pulling him clear, propelling him back onto the walkway. The roaring of the Maw Grint was fading slightly now, falling back as the Stone King's fortressed dome receded into the distance.

"Catch up to her, Highlander!" Walker yelled, shoving him ahead. "Keep an eye out for Dees! We'll meet back at the building where we hid ourselves from the Rake!" He glanced over his shoulder and back again, shouting, "Careful, now! Watch yourself!"

But Morgan Leah was already gone.

Pe Ell AND HORNER DEES HAD only just reached the building to which the others now fled when the tremors began. Their battle with the Rake completed, they had come in search of the remainder of the company from Rampling Steep, each for his own reasons, neither sharing much of anything with the other. The truce they had called had ended with the destruction of the Rake, and they watched each other now with careful, suspicious eyes.

They whirled in surprise as the rumbling began to build, deeper and more pronounced than at any time before. The city shuddered in response.

"Something's happened," Horner Dees whispered, his bearded face lifting. "Something more."

"It's come awake again," Pe Ell cried with loathing. When

they had left the Maw Grint it was sunk back down into the earth and gone still.

The street on which they faced shook with the impact of the creature's rising.

Pe Ell gestured. "Look upstairs. See if anyone is there."

Dees went without argument. Pe Ell stood rooted on the walk while the city's tremors washed over him. He was taut and hard within himself, the battle with the Rake still alive inside, driving through him like the rushing of his blood. Things were coming together now; he could sense the coalescing of events, the weaving of the threads of fate of the five from Rampling Steep. It would be over soon, he sensed. It would be finished.

Horner Dees reappeared at the building entry. "No one."

"Then wait here for their return," Pe Ell snapped, starting quickly away. "I'll look toward the center of the city."

"Pe Ell!"

The hatchet face turned. "Don't worry, old man. I'll be back." *Perhaps,* he added to himself.

He darted into the gloom, leaving the ageing Tracker to call uselessly after him. Enough of Horner Dees, he thought bitterly. He was still rankled by the fact that he had saved the bothersome Tracker from the Rake, that he had acted on instinct rather than using common sense, that he had risked his life to save a man he fully intended to kill anyway.

On the other hand his plans for Dees and the other fools who had come with Quickening were beginning to change. He could feel those plans settling comfortably into place even now. Everything always seemed much clearer when he was moving. It was all well and good to anticipate the event, but circumstances and needs evolved, and the event did not always turn out as expected, the coming about of it not always as foreseen. Pe Ell revised his earlier assessment of the necessity of killing his companions. Quickening, of course, would have to die. He had already promised Rimmer Dall that he would kill her. More important, he had promised himself. Quickening's fate was unalterable. But why bother with killing the others? Unless they got in his way by trying to interfere with his plans for the girl, why expend the effort? If he somehow managed to gain possession of the Black Elfstone there was no possible harm they could cause him. And even if he was forced to abandon that part of his plan—as it now appeared he would have to—the old Tracker, the one-armed man, the Highlander, and the tunesmith offered no threat to him. Even if they escaped Eldwist to follow him he had little to fear. How would they find him? And what would they do if they did?

No, he need not kill them—though he would, he added, almost as an afterthought, if the right opportunity presented itself.

The tremors continued, long and deep, the growl of the earth protesting the coming of the monster worm. Pe Ell darted this way and that along the empty walkways, down streets littered with debris and past buildings weakened by ragged, wicked cracks that scarred their smooth surface. His sharp eyes searched the shadows for movement, seeking those who had come with him or even perhaps some sign of the elusive Stone King. He hadn't given up completely on the Black Elfstone. There was still a chance, he told himself. Everything was coming together, caught in a whirlpool. He could feel it happening . . .

Out of the haze before him raced Quickening, silver hair flying as she ran, her reed-thin body a quicksilver shadow. Pe Ell moved to intercept her, catching her about the waist with one arm before she realized what was happening. She gasped in surprise, stiffened, and then clung to him.

"Pe Ell," she breathed.

There was something in the way she spoke his name that surprised him. It was a measure of fear mingled with relief, an odd combination of dismay and satisfaction. He tightened his grip instinctively, but she did not try to break away.

"Where are the others?" he asked.

"Coming after me, escaped from Uhl Belk and the Maw Grint." Her black eyes fixed on him. "It is time to leave Eldwist, Pe Ell. We found the Stone King and we took the Black Elfstone away from him—Morgan, Walker Boh, and I."

Pe Ell fought to stay calm. "Then we are indeed finished with this place." He glanced past her into the gloom. "Who has the Elfstone now?"

"Walker Boh," she replied.

Pe Ell's jaw tightened. It would have to be Walker Boh, of

course. It would have to be him. How much easier things would be if the girl had the Stone. He could kill her now, take it from her, and be gone before any of them knew what had happened. The one-armed man seemed to stand in his way at every turn, a shadowy presence he could not quite escape. What would it take to be rid of him?

He knew, of course, what it would take. He felt his plans begin to shift back again.

"Quickening!" a voice called out.

It was the Highlander. Pe Ell hesitated, then made up his mind. He clamped his hand about Quickening's mouth and hauled her into the shadows. Surprisingly, the girl did not struggle. She was light and yielding, almost weightless in his arms. It was the first time he had held her since he had carried her from the Meade Gardens. The feelings she stirred within him were distractingly soft and pleasant, and he forced them roughly aside. Later for that, he thought, when he used the Stiehl . . .

Morgan Leah burst into view, pounding along the walkway, shouting for the girl, searching. Pe Ell held Quickening close and watched the Highlander run past. A moment later, he was gone.

Pe Ell released his hand from the girl's mouth, and she turned to face him. There was neither surprise nor fear in her eyes now; there was only resignation. "It is almost time for us, Pe Ell," she whispered.

A flicker of doubt tugged at his confidence. She was looking at him in that strange way she had, as if he were transparent to her, as if everything about him were known. But if everything were known, she would not be standing there so calmly. She would be attempting to flee, to call after the Highlander, or to do something to save herself.

The rumbling beneath the city increased, then faded slightly, a warning of the slow, inevitable avalanche bearing down on them.

"Time for us to do what?" he managed hesitantly, unable to break away from her gaze.

She did not answer. Instead she glanced past him, her black eyes searching. He turned to stare with her and watched the dark form of Walker Boh materialize from out of the haze of dust and gray light.

Unlike the Highlander, the Dark Uncle had seen them.

Pe Ell swung the girl in front of him and unsheathed the Stiehl from its hiding place, the blade gleaming bright with the magic. The one-armed man slowed perceptibly, then came on.

"Pe Ell," he whispered softly, as if the name itself were venomous.

"Stand back from me, Walker Boh," Pe Ell ordered. The other stopped. "We've seen enough of each other to know what we are capable of doing. No need to test it. Better that we part now and go our separate ways. But first give me the Stone."

The tall man stood without moving, seemingly without life, eyes fixed on the assassin and his hostage. He appeared to be weighing something.

Pe Ell's smile was sardonic. "Don't be foolish enough to think you might be quicker than me."

"We might neither of us be quick enough to survive this day. The Maw Grint comes."

"It will find me gone when it does. Give me the Black Elfstone."

"If I do so, will that be enough to satisfy you?" the other asked quietly, his gaze intense, as if trying to read Pe Ell's thoughts.

Like the girl, Pe Ell thought. Two of a kind. "Pass it to me," he commanded, ignoring the question.

"Release Quickening."

Pe Ell shook his head. "When I am safely away. Then I promise that I will set her free." *Free, forever.*

They stood staring at each other wordlessly for a moment, hard looks filled with unspoken promises, with visions of possibilities that were dark and forbidding. Then Walker Boh reached down into his tunic and brought forth the Stone. He held it out in his palm, dark and glistening. Pe Ell smiled faintly. The Elfstone was as black as midnight, opaque and depthless, seamless and unflawed. He had never seen anything like it before. He could almost feel the magic pulsing within.

"Give it to me," he repeated.

Walker Boh reached down to his belt and worked free a leather pouch marked with brilliant blue runes. Carefully he used the fingers of his solitary hand to maneuver the Stone into the pouch and pull the drawstrings tight. He looked at Pe Ell and said, "You cannot use the Black Elfstone, Pe Ell. If you try, the magic will destroy you."

"Life is filled with risks," Pe Ell replied. Dust churned in the air about them, sifted by a faint sea breeze. The stone of the city shimmered, swept up in the earth's distant rumble, wrapped in a gauze of mist and clouds. "Toss it to me," he ordered. "Gently."

He used the hand with the Stiehl to keep tight hold of Quickening. The girl did not stir. She waited passively, her slender body pressed against him, so compliant she might have been sleeping. Walker held out the pouch with the Black Elfstone and carefully lobbed it. Pe Ell caught it and shoved it into his belt, securing the strings to his buckle.

"Magic belongs to those who are not afraid to use it," he offered, smiling, backing cautiously away. "And to those who can keep it."

Walker Boh stood rock-still against the roiling dust and tremors. "Beware, Pe Ell. You risk everything."

"Don't come after me, Walker Boh," Pe Ell warned darkly. "Better for you if you remain here and face the Maw Grint."

With Quickening securely in his grasp he continued to move away, following the line of the walkway until the other man vanished into the haze.

WALKER BOH REMAINED MOTIONLESS, staring after the disappearing Pe Ell and Quickening. He was wondering why he had given up the Black Elfstone so easily. He had not wanted to, had resolved not to in fact, and had been prepared instead to attack Pe Ell, to go to the girl's rescue—until he looked into her eyes and saw something there that stopped him. Even now he wasn't sure what it was that he had seen. Determination, resignation, some private insight that transcended his own—something. Whatever it was, it had changed his mind as surely as if she had used her magic.

His head lowered and his dark eyes narrowed.

Had she, he wondered, used her magic?

He stood lost in thought. A light dusting of water sprinkled his face. It was beginning to rain again. He looked up, remembering where he was, what he was about, and hearing again the thunder caused by the movement of the Maw Grint beneath the city, feeling the vibration of its coming.

Cogline's voice was a whisper in his ear, reminding him gently to understand who he was. He had always wondered before. Now he thought he knew.

He summoned his magic, feeling it rise easily within him, strong again since his battle with the Stone King, as if that confrontation had freed him of constraints he had placed upon himself. It gathered at the center of his being, whirling like a great wind. The rune markings on the pouch in which the Black Elfstone rested would be its guide. With barely a lifting of his head he sent it winging forth in search of Pe Ell.

Then he followed after.

PE ELL RAN, dragging Quickening behind him. She came without resisting, moving obediently to keep pace, saying nothing, asking nothing, her eyes distant and calm. He glanced back at her only once and quickly turned away again. What he saw in those dark eyes bothered him. She was seeing something that he could not, something old and immutable, a part of her past or her future—he wasn't sure which. She was an enigma still, the one secret he had not yet been able to solve. But soon now he would, he promised himself. The Stiehl would give him an answer to what she hid. When her life was fading from her she would stand revealed. There would be no secrets then. The magic would not permit it. Just as it had been with all the others he had killed, there would be only truth.

He felt the first drops of rain strike his heated face.

He darted left along a cross street, angling away from the direction Morgan Leah had gone and Walker Boh would follow. There was no reason to give them any chance of finding him. He would slip quickly from the city onto the isthmus, cross to the stairs, gain the heights of the overlook, and then with time and privacy enough to take full advantage of the moment he would kill her. Anticipation washed through him. Quickening, the daughter of the King of the Silver River, the most wondrous magical creature of all, would be his forever.

Yet the flicker of doubt continued to burn within him. What was it that bothered him so? He searched for the answer, pausing briefly as he remembered what she had said about needing their magics, the magics of all three—the Highlander, Walker Boh, and himself. All three were required, the King of the Silver River had proclaimed. That was why she had recruited them, persuaded them to come, and kept them together through all the anger and mistrust. But it had been Walker Boh and the Highlander alone who had discovered the hiding place of Uhl Belk and secured the Black Elfstone. He had done nothing—except to destroy the Rake. Was that the use for which his magic had been intended? Was that the reason for his coming? It didn't seem enough somehow. It seemed there should be something more.

Pe Ell slid through the murk of Eldwist's deepening morning, holding the girl close to him as he went, thinking to himself that this whole journey had been a puzzle with too many missing pieces. They had come in search of the Stone King—yet the others, not Pe Ell, had found him. They had come to retrieve the Black Elfstone—yet the others, not Pe Ell, had done so. The magic of the Stiehl was the most deadly magic that any of them possessed—yet what purpose had it served?

Uneasiness stole through him like a thief, draining his elation at having both Quickening and the Stone.

Something was wrong and he didn't know what it was. He should feel in control of things and he did not.

They passed back onto a roadway leading south, winding their way down between the buildings, passing through the haze, two furtive shadows fleeing into light. Pe Ell slowed now, beginning to tire. He peered through the thin curtain of rain that hung before him, blinking uncertainly. Was this the way he had intended to come? Somehow, he didn't think so. He glanced right, then left. Wasn't this street the one he had been trying to avoid? Confusion filled him. He felt Quickening's eyes on him but would not allow himself to meet her gaze.

He steered them down another sidestreet and crossed to a broad plaza dominated by a tiered basin encircled by benches, some crumbling and split, and the remains of poles from which flags had once flown. He was working his way left toward an arched passageway between the buildings, intent on gaining the open street beyond, a street that would take him directly to the isthmus, when he heard his name called. He whirled, pulling the girl close, the blade of the Stiehl coming up to her throat.

Morgan Leah stood across the plaza from him, a lean and dangerous figure. Pe Ell stared. How had the Highlander found him? It was chance, he quickly decided. Nothing more. Dismay grappled with anger. Any misfortune that resulted from this encounter must not be his.

The Highlander did not appear to know what was happening. "What are you doing, Pe Ell?" he shouted through the forest of broken poles.

"What I wish!" Pe Ell responded, but there was a weariness in his voice that surprised him. "Get away, Highlander. I have no wish to hurt you. I have what I came for. Your one-armed friend has given me the Elfstone—here, in this pouch at my belt! I intend to keep it! If you wish the girl to go free, stand away!"

But Morgan Leah did not move. Haggard-looking and worn, just a boy really, he seemed both lost and unresolved. Yet he refused to give way. "Let her go, Pe Ell. Don't hurt her."

His plea was wasted, but Pe Ell managed a tired nod. "Go back, Highlander. Quickening comes with me."

Morgan Leah seemed to hesitate momentarily, then started forward. For the first time since he had seized her, Pe Ell felt Quickening tense. She was worried for the Highlander, he realized. Her concern enraged him. He pulled her back and brought the Stiehl against her throat, calling to the other man to stop.

And then suddenly Walker Boh appeared as well, materializing out of the gloom, close by Morgan Leah. He stepped forward unhurriedly and grasped the Highlander's arm, pulling him back. The Highlander struggled, but even with only one arm the other man was stronger.

"Think what you are doing, Pe Ell!" Walker Boh called out, and now there was anger in his voice.

How had the big man caught up to him so quickly? Pe Ell felt a twinge of uneasiness, a sense that for some unexplainable reason nothing was going right. He should have been clear of this madness by now, safely away. He should have had time to savor his victory, to speak with the girl before using the Stiehl, to see how much he could learn of her magic. Instead he was being harried unmercifully by the very men he had chosen to spare. Worse, he was in some danger of being trapped.

"Get away from me!" he shouted, his temper slipping, his control draining away. "You risk the girl's life by continuing this chase! Let me leave now or she dies!"

"Let her go!" the distraught Highlander screamed again. He had fallen to his knees, still firmly in the grip of the one-armed man.

Behind Pe Ell, still too far away to make any difference but closing on him steadily, came Horner Dees. The assassin was now ringed by his enemies. For the first time in his life he was trapped, and he sensed a hint of panic setting in. He jerked Quickening about to face the burly Tracker. "Out of my way, old man!" he bellowed.

But Horner Dees simply shook his head. "I don't think so, Pe Ell. I've backed away from you enough times. I've a stake in this business, too. I've given at least as much of myself as you. Besides, you've done nothing to earn what you claim. You simply seek to steal. We know who and what you are, all of us. Do as Morgan Leah says. Let the girl go."

Walker Boh's voice rose. "Pe Ell, if the Shadowen sent you to steal the Elfstone, take it and go. We won't stop you."

"The Shadowen!" Pe Ell laughed, fighting to contain his rage. "The Shadowen are nothing to me. I do for them what I wish and nothing more. Do you think I came all this way because of them? You are a fool!"

"Then take the Elfstone for yourself if you must."

The rage broke free. Caution disappeared in a red mist. "If I must! Of course, I must! But even the Elfstone isn't the real reason I came!"

"Then what is, Pe Ell?" Walker Boh asked tightly.

"She is!" Pe Ell yanked Quickening around once more, lifting her exquisite face above the point of his knife. "Look at her,

Walker Boh, and tell me that you don't desire her! You cannot, can you? Your feelings, mine, the Highlander's—they're all the same! We came on this journey because of her, because of the way she looked at us and made us feel, because of the way she wove her magic all about us! Think of the secrets she hides! Think of the magic she conceals! I came on this journey to discover what she is, to claim her. She has belonged to me from the first moment of her life, and when I am finished here she shall belong to me always! Yes, the Shadowen sent me, but it was my choice to come—my choice when I saw what she could give me! Don't you see? I came to Eldwist to kill her!"

The air went still suddenly, the tremors and the thunder fading into a vague and distant moan, leaving the assassin's words sharp and clear against the silence. The stone of the city caught their sound and held the echo within its walls, a long, endless reverberation of dismay.

"I have to discover what she is," Pe Ell whispered, trying vainly to explain now, unable to think what else to do, stunned that he had been foolish enough to reveal so much, knowing they would never let him go now. How had he managed to lose control of matters so completely? "I have to kill her," he repeated, the words sounding harsh and bitter. "That is how the magic works. It reveals all truths. In taking life, it gives life. To me. Once the killing is done, Quickening shall be mine forever."

For an instant no one spoke, stunned by the assassin's revelation. Then Horner Dees said slowly, deliberately, "Don't be stupid, Pe Ell. You can't get away from all of us. Let her go."

It was uncertain then exactly what happened next. There was an explosion of shattered rock as the Maw Grint broke free of the tunnels and reared skyward against the buildings of the city somewhere close to where the Stone King hid within his fortressed dome. The monster rose like a bloated snake, swaying against the shroud of mist and damp, huffing as if to catch its breath, as if the air were being sucked from it. Pe Ell started, feeling the earth begin to shudder so violently that it seemed Eldwist would be shaken apart.

Then Quickening broke free, slipping from his grasp as if she were made of air. She turned to him, disdaining to run, standing right against him, her hands gripping the arm that held the Stiehl, her black eyes shackling him as surely as if he were chained. He could not move; he just stood there, frozen in place. He saw the symmetry of her face and body as if seeing it for the first time; he marveled at the perfection of her, at beauty that lay not just upon the surface of her wondrous form, but ran deep within. He felt her press forward—or did he? Which was it? He saw her mouth open with surprise and pain and relief.

He glanced down then and saw that the handle of the Stiehl was flush against her stomach, the blade buried in her body. He could not remember stabbing her, yet somehow he had. Confusion and disbelief surged through him. How had this happened? What of his plan to kill her where and when he chose? What of his intention to savor the moment of her dying? He looked quickly into her eyes, desperate to snare what was trapped there and about to be set free, anxious to capture her magic. He looked, and what he saw filled him with rage.

Pe Ell screamed. As if seeking to hide what he had discovered, he stabbed her again and again, and each time it was a frantic, futile attempt to deny what he was seeing. Quickening's body jerked in response, but her gaze remained steady, and the visions shimmering in her eyes remained fixed.

Pe Ell understood at last, and with understanding came a horror against which he had no defense. His thoughts collapsed, tumbling into a quagmire of despair. He shoved himself free of the girl and watched her slump to the street in a slow, agonizing fall, her black eyes never leaving him. He was aware of Morgan Leah crying out in fury, of Walker Boh racing forward, and of Horner Dees charging at him from the rear. They did not matter. Only the girl did. He stepped away, shaking with a cold that threatened to freeze him in place. Everything he had hoped for had been stolen from him. Everything he had wanted was lost.

What have I done?

He wheeled about and began to run. His cold turned abruptly to fire, but the words buzzed within his mind, a nest of hornets with sharp and anxious stingers.

What have I done?

He darted past Horner Dees with a quickness born of fear

and despair, gone so fast that the old Tracker had no chance of stopping him. The stone street shuddered and quaked and was slick with rain, but nothing could slow his flight. Gloom shrouded him with its gray, friendless mantle, and he shrank to a tiny figure in the shadow of the city's ancient buildings, a speck of life caught up in a tangle of magic far older and harsher than his own. He saw Quickening's face before him. He felt her eyes watching as the Stiehl entered her body. He heard her sigh with relief.

Pe Ell fled through Eldwist as if possessed.

CHAPTER

31

ORGAN LEAH WAS the first to reach Quickening. He broke free of Walker with a strength that surprised the other, raced across the empty plaza as she tumbled to the stone, and caught her up almost before she was done falling. He knelt to hold her, turned her ashen face into his chest, and began whispering her name over and over again.

Walker Boh and Horner Dees hurried up from opposite sides, bent close momentarily, then exchanged a sober glance. The entire front of Quickening's shirt was soaked with her blood.

Walker straightened and peered through the gloom in the direction Pe Ell had gone. The assassin was already out of sight, gone into the maze of buildings and streets, fled back toward the isthmus and the cliffs beyond. Walker remembered the look he had seen on the other's face—a look filled with horror, disbelief, and rage. Killing Quickening clearly hadn't given him what he had been looking for.

"Walker!"

Morgan Leah's voice was a plea of desperation. Walker glanced down. "Help her! She's dying!"

Walker looked at the blood on her clothes, at the collapsed, broken body, at the face with its long hair spilled across the lovely features like a silver veil. *She's dying.* He whispered the words in the silence of his mind, marveling first that such a thing could be and second that he hadn't recognized much sooner its inevitability. He stared at the girl, as helpless and despairing as the Highlander, but beginning as well to catch a glimmer of understanding into the reason that it was happening.

"Walker, do something!" Morgan repeated, urgent, stricken.

"Highlander," Horner Dees said in response, taking hold of his shoulder gently. "What would you have him do?"

"What do you think I would have him do? Use his magic! Give her the same chance she gave him!"

Walker knelt. His voice was calm, low. "I can't, Morgan. I haven't the magic she needs." He reached out to touch the side of her throat, feeling for a pulse. It was there, faint, irregular. He could see her breathing. "She must do what she can to save herself."

Morgan stared at him momentarily, then began talking again to Quickening, urging her to wake, to speak to him. His words were jumbled, desperate, filled with need. The girl stirred sluggishly in response.

Walker looked again at Horner Dees. The old man shook his head slowly.

Then Quickening's eyes opened. They were clear and frightened, filled with pain. "Morgan," she whispered. "Pick me up. Carry me out of the city."

Morgan Leah, though he clearly thought to do otherwise, did not argue the matter. He lifted her effortlessly, carrying her as if she were weightless. He held her close against himself, infusing her with his warmth, whispering down to her as he went. Walker and Dees trailed after wordlessly. They moved across the plaza and into the street down which Pe Ell had fled.

"Stay back on the walkways," Walker cautioned hurriedly, and Morgan was quick to comply.

They had gone only a short distance when the earth began to rumble anew. All of Eldwist shook in response, the buildings cracking and splitting, shards of stone and clouds of dust tumbling down. Walker glanced back toward the heart of the city. The Maw Grint was moving again. Whatever the outcome of its confrontation with Uhl Belk, it had clearly decided on a new course of action. Perhaps it had put an end to its parent. Perhaps it had simply concluded that the Black Elfstone was more important. In any case, it was coming straight for them. Disdaining the use of its underground tunnels, it surged down the streets of Eldwist. Walls shattered and collapsed with its passing. The poison of its body spit wickedly. The air about it shimmered and steamed.

Those who remained of the company from Rampling Steep began to run southward toward the isthmus, fighting to keep their balance as the earth beneath them shuddered and quaked. Trapdoors sprang open all about, jarred loose by the tremors, and the debris of the crumbling buildings littered the pathway at every turn. Behind them, the Maw Grint huffed and grunted with the urgency of its movements and came on. Despite having to carry Quickening, Morgan set an exhausting pace, and neither Walker nor Horner Dees could maintain it. The old Tracker had already fallen fifty paces back by the time they broke clear of the city, his breathing short and labored, his bulky form lurching as he struggled to keep up. Walker was between the two, his own chest constricting with pain, his legs heavy and weak. He yelled once at Morgan to slow him down, but the Highlander was deaf to him, the whole of his attention focused on the girl. Walker glanced back at Dees, at the trembling of the buildings where the Maw Grint passed, closer to them now than before, at the shadow the monster cast against the graying light. He did not think they would escape. He could not help reflecting on how ironic it was that they were going to be killed for something they no longer even had.

The moments lengthened impossibly as they fled, receding into the pounding of their boots on the stone. The waves crashed against the shores of the isthmus to either side, the spray washing across their heated faces. The rocks grew slippery, and they stumbled and tripped as they ran. The clouds darkened, and it began to rain again. Walker thought again of the look on Pe Ell's face when he had stabbed Quickening. He revised his earlier assessment. What he had seen there was surprise. Pe Ell hadn't been ready for her to die. Had he even wanted to use the Stiehl? There was something in the movements of the two immediately before the stabbing that was troubling. Why hadn't Quickening simply run? She had been free of him for an instant, yet had turned back. Into the blade? Deliberately? Walker shivered. Had she done more than stand there and wait? Had she actually shoved herself against Pe Ell?

His jumbled thoughts seemed to crystallize, freezing to ice. Shades! Was that why Pe Ell had been summoned? Pe Ell, the assassin with magic in his weapon, magic that nothing could withstand—was that why he was there?

Ahead of him, Morgan Leah reached the base of the cliffs and the pathway leading up from the isthmus. Without slowing, he began to climb.

Behind them, the Maw Grint appeared, its monstrous head thrusting into view through the ruined buildings, lifting momentarily to test the air, then surging ahead. It oozed through the walls of the city like something without bones. It filled the whole of the isthmus with its bulk, hunching its way forward, a juggernaut of impossible size.

Walker scrambled up the pathway toward the summit of the cliffs, Horner Dees still lagging behind. He forced his thoughts of Quickening and Pe Ell aside. They made no sense. Why would Quickening want Pe Ell to kill her? Why would she want to die? There was no reason for any of it. He tried to concentrate on what he would do to slow the advance of the Maw Grint. He glanced back once more, watching the massive slug-thing work its way across the rock. Could he collapse the isthmus beneath it? No, the rock was too deep. The cliffs on top of it, then? No, again, it would simply tunnel its way free. Water would slow it, but all the water was behind them in the Tiderace. Nothing of Walker's magic or even Cogline's was strong enough to stop the Maw Grint. Running away was their only choice, and they could not run for long.

He reached the summit of the cliffs and found Morgan Leah waiting. The Highlander knelt gasping for breath on the ramp that overlooked the peninsula and Eldwist, his head lowered. Quickening was cradled in his arms, her eyes open and alert. Walker crossed to them and stopped. Quickening's face was chalk white.

Morgan Leah's eyes lifted. "She won't use her magic," he whispered in disbelief.

Walker knelt. "Save yourself, Quickening. You have the power."

She shook her head. Her black eyes glistened as they found Morgan's. "Listen to me," she said softly, her voice steady. "I love you. I will always love you and be with you. Remember that. Remember, too, that I would change things if I could. Now set me down and rise."

Morgan shook his head. "No, I want to stay with you . . ."

She touched him once on the cheek with her hand, and his voice trailed off, the sentence left hanging. Wordlessly, he laid her on the ground and backed away. There were tears running down his face.

"Take out your Sword, Morgan, and sheath it in the earth. Do so now."

Morgan drew out the Sword of Leah, gripped it in both hands, and jammed it into the rock. His hands remained tightly fixed about the hilt momentarily, then released.

He looked up slowly. "Don't die, Quickening," he said.

"Remember me," she whispered.

Horner Dees lumbered up beside Walker, panting. "What's going on?" he asked, bearded face close, rough voice hushed. "What's she doing?"

Walker shook his head. Her black eyes had shifted to find his. "Walker," she said, calling him.

He went to her, hearing the sounds of the Maw Grint advancing below, thinking they must run again, wondering like Dees what it was that she intended. He knelt beside her.

"Help me up," she said, her words quick and hurried, as if she sought to give voice to them while she still could. "Walk me to the edge of the cliffs."

Walker did not question what she asked. He put his arm about her waist and lifted her to her feet. She sagged against him weakly, her body shuddering. He heard Morgan cry out in protest, but a sudden glance from the girl silenced him. Walker held her up to keep her from falling as he maneuvered her slowly toward the drop. They reached the edge and stopped. Below, the Maw Grint hunched across the rock of the isthmus, an obscene cylinder of flesh, body rippling and poison oozing down. It was more than halfway to them now, its monstrous bulk steaming, the trail of its poison stretched back across the causeway to the city. Eldwist rose raggedly against the skyline, towers broken off, buildings split apart, walls crumbled and shattered. Dust and mist formed a screen against the dampness of the rain.

The dome where the Stone King made his lair stood intact.

Quickening turned and her face lifted. For an instant she was beautiful once more, as alive as she had been when she had brought Walker back from the dead, when she had restored his life and driven the poison of the Asphinx from his body. Walker caught his breath seeing her so, blinking against the momentary illusion. Her dark eyes fixed him.

"Dark Uncle," she whispered. "When you leave this place, when you go back into the world of the Four Lands, take with you the lessons you have learned here. Do not fight against yourself or what you might be. Simply consider your choices. Nothing is predetermined, Walker. We can always choose."

She reached up then and touched his face, her fingers cool against his cheek. Images flooded through him, her thoughts, her memories, and her knowledge. In an instant's time, she revealed herself completely, showing him the secrets she had kept hidden so carefully during the whole of their journey, the truth of who and what she was. He cried out as if he had been burned, staggered by what he saw. He clutched her tightly to him, and his pale face lowered into her hair in dismay.

Both Morgan and Horner Dees started forward, but Walker shouted for them to stand where they were. They stopped, hesitant, uncertain. Walker half-turned, still holding Quickening against him, his face an iron mask of concentration. He understood now; he understood everything.

"Walker." She spoke his name again. Her hand brushed him one final time, and a single image appeared.

It was the Grimpond's second vision.

Her eyes lifted to his. "Let me fall," she said softly.

He saw the vision clearly, himself standing at the summit of these cliffs with the Four Lands stretched out below and Quickening beside him, her black eyes beseeching as he shoved her away.

Here. Now. The vision come to pass.

He started to shake his head no, but her eyes stopped him, her gaze so intense it was threatening.

"Goodbye, Walker," she whispered.

He released her. He held her in the circle of his arm for just an instant more, then spun her away over the precipice. It was almost as if someone else was responsible, someone hidden inside himself, a being over which reason could not prevail. He heard Horner Dees gasp, horror-stricken. He heard Morgan scream out in disbelief. They rushed at him in a frenzy, grasped him roughly, and held him as Quickening tumbled away. They watched her fall, a small bundle of cloth with her silver hair streaming out behind her. They watched her shimmer.

Then, incredibly, she began to disintegrate. She came apart at the edges first, like fraying cloth, bits and pieces scattering away. Mute, awestruck, the three at the edge of the precipice stared downward as she disappeared. In seconds she was no more, her body turned to a dust that sparkled and shone as it was caught by the wind.

Below, the Maw Grint ceased its advance, its head lifting. Perhaps it knew what was about to happen; perhaps it even understood. It made no effort to escape, waiting patiently as the dust that had been Quickening settled over it. It shuddered then, cried out once, and began to shrink. It withered rapidly, its bulk shriveling away, disappearing back into the earth until nothing remained.

The dust blanketed the isthmus next and the rock began to change, turning green with grass and moss. Shoots sprang to life, vibrant and bright. The dust swept on, reaching the peninsula and Eldwist, and the transformation continued. Centuries of Uhl Belk's dark repression were undone in moments. The stone of the city crumbled—walls, towers, streets, and tunnels all collapsing. Everything gave way before the power of Quickening's magic, just as it had at the Meade Gardens in Culhaven. All that had existed before the Stone King had worked his change was brought to life again. Rocks shifted and reformed. Trees sprang up, gnarled limbs filled with summer leaves that shone against the gray skies and water. Patches of wildflowers bloomed, not in abundance as in Culhaven, for this had always been a rugged and unsettled place, but in isolated pockets, vibrant and rich. Sea grasses and scrub swept over the broken rock, changing the face of the land back into a coastal plain. The air came alive again, filled with the smell of growing things. The deadness of the land's stone armor faded into memory. Slowly, grudgingly, Eldwist sank from view, swallowed back into the earth, gone into the past that had given it birth.

When the transformation was complete, all that remained of Eldwist was the dome in which the Stone King had entombed himself—a solitary gray island amid the green of the land.

"THERE WAS NOTHING we could do to save her, Morgan," Walker Boh explained softly, bent close to the devastated Highlander to make certain he could hear. "Quickening came to Eldwist to die."

They were crouched down together at the edge of the cliffs, Horner Dees with them, speaking in hushed voices, as if the silence that had settled over the land in the aftermath of Quickening's transformation was glass that might shatter. Far distant, the roar of the Tiderace breaking against the shoreline and the cries of seabirds on the wing were faint and momentary. The magic had worked its way up the cliffs now and gone past them, cleansing the rock of the Maw Grint's poison, giving life back again to the land. Island breezes gusted at the clouds, forming breaks, and sunshine peeked through guardedly.

Morgan nodded wordlessly, his head purposefully lowered, his face taut.

Walker glanced at Horner Dees, who nodded encouragingly. "She let me see everything, Highlander, just before she died. She wanted me to know, so that I could tell you. She touched me on the cheek as we stood together looking down at Eldwist, and everything was revealed. All the secrets she kept hidden from us. All of her carefully guarded mysteries."

He shifted a few inches closer. "Her father created her to counteract the magic of Uhl Belk. He made her from the elements of the Gardens where he lived, from the strongest of his magic. He sent her to Eldwist to die. In a sense, he sent a part of himself. He really had no other choice. Nothing less would be sufficient to overcome the Stone King in his own domain. And Uhl Belk had to be overcome there because he would never leave Eldwist—could not leave, in fact, although he didn't know it. He was already a prisoner of his own magic. The Maw Grint had become Uhl Belk's surrogate, dispatched in his stead to turn the rest of the Four Lands to stone. But if the King of the Silver River waited for the monster to get close enough to confront, it would have grown too huge to stop."

His hand came up to rest on Morgan's shoulder. He felt the other flinch. "She selected each of us for a purpose, Highlander—just as she said. You and I were chosen to regain possession of the Black Elfstone, stolen by Belk from the Hall of Kings. The problem Quickening faced, of course, was that her magic would not work while Uhl Belk controlled the Elfstone. As long as he could wield the Druid magic, he could siphon off her own magic and prevent the necessary transformation from taking place. He would have done so instantly if he had discovered who she was. He would have turned her to stone. That was why she couldn't use her magic until the very last."

"But she changed the Meade Gardens simply by touching the earth!" Morgan protested, his voice angry, defiant.

"The Meade Gardens, yes. But Eldwist was far too monstrous to change so easily. She could not have done so with a simple touching. She needed to infuse herself into the rock, to make herself a part of the land." Walker sighed. "That was why she chose Pe Ell. The King of the Silver River must have known or at least sensed that the Shadowen would send someone to try to stop Quickening. It was no secret who she was or how she could change things. She was a very real threat. She had to be eliminated. A Shadowen, it appears now, would lack the necessary means. So Pe Ell was sent instead. Pe Ell believed that his purpose was a secret, that killing Quickening was his own idea. It wasn't. Not ever. It was hers, right from the beginning. It was the reason she sought him out, because her father had told her to do so, to take with her to Eldwist the man and the weapon that could penetrate the armor of her magic and allow her to transform."

"Why couldn't she simply change by willing it?"

"She was alive, Morgan—as human as you and I. She was an elemental, but an elemental in human guise. I don't think she could be anything else in life. It was necessary for her to die before she could work her magic on Eldwist. No ordinary weapon could kill her; her body would protect her against common metals. It required magic equal to her own, the magic of a weapon like the Stiehl—and the hands and mind of an assassin like Pe Ell."

Walker's smile was brief, tight. "She summoned us to help her—because she was told to and because we were needed to serve a purpose, yes—but because she believed in us, too. If we had failed her, any of us, even Pe Ell, if we had not done what she knew we could do, Uhl Belk would have won. There would have been no transformation of the land. The Maw Grint would have continued its advance and Uhl Belk's kingdom would have continued to expand. Combined with the onslaught of the Shadowen, everything would have been lost."

Morgan straightened perceptibly, and his eyes finally lifted. "She should have told us, Walker. She should have let us know what she had planned."

Walker shook his head gently. "No, Morgan. That was exactly what she couldn't do. We would not have acted as we did had we known the truth. Tell me. Wouldn't you have stopped her? You were in love with her, Highlander. She knew what that meant."

Morgan stared at him tight-lipped for a moment, then nodded reluctantly. "You're right. She knew."

"There wasn't any other way. She had to keep her purpose in coming here a secret."

"I know. I know." Morgan's breathing was ragged, strained. "But it hurts anyway. I can almost believe she isn't gone, that she will find a way to come back somehow." He took a deep breath. "I need her to come back."

They were silent then, staring off in separate directions, remembering. Walker wondered momentarily if he should tell the other of the Grimpond's vision, of how he had spoken of that vision with Quickening yet she had brought him anyway, of how she must have known from the first how it would end yet had come nevertheless so that her father's purpose in creating her could be fulfilled. He decided against it. The Highlander had heard enough of secrets and hidden plans. There was nothing to be gained by telling him any more.

"What's become of Belk, do you think?" Horner Dees' rough

voice broke the silence. "Is he still down there in that dome? Still alive?"

They looked as one over the cliff edge to where the last vestige of Eldwist sat amid the newborn green of the peninsula, closed about and secretive.

"I think a fairy creature like Uhl Belk does not die easily," Walker answered, his voice soft, introspective. "But Quickening holds him fast, a prisoner within a shell, and the land will not be changed to his liking again any time soon." He paused. "I think Uhl Belk might go mad when he understands that."

Morgan reached down tentatively and touched a patch of grass as if searching for something. His fingers brushed the blades gently. Walker watched him for a moment, then rose. His body ached, and his spirits were dark and mean. He was starved for real food, and his thirst seemed unquenchable. His own odyssey was just beginning, a trek back through the Four Lands in search of Pe Ell and the stolen Black Elfstone, a second confrontation to discover who should possess it, and if he survived all that, a journey to recover disappeared Paranor and the Druids . . .

His thoughts threatened to overwhelm him, to drain the last of his strength, and he shoved them away.

"Come, Highlander," Horner Dees urged, reaching down to take Morgan's shoulders. "She's gone. Be glad we had her for as long as we did. She was never meant to live in this world. She was meant for a better use. Take comfort in the fact that she loved you. That's no small thing."

The big hands gripped tight, and Morgan allowed himself to be pulled to his feet. He nodded without looking at the other. When his eyes finally lifted, they were hard and fixed. "I'm going after Pe Ell."

Horner Dees spat. "We're all going after him, Morgan Leah. All of us. He won't get away."

They took one final look down from the heights, then turned and began walking toward the defile that led back into the mountains. They had gone only a few steps when Morgan stopped suddenly, remembering, and looked over to where he had left the Sword of Leah. The sword was still jammed into the rocks, its shattered blade buried from sight. Morgan hesitated a moment, almost as if thinking to leave the weapon where it was, to abandon it once and for all. Then he stepped over and fastened his hands on the hilt. Slowly, he began to pull. And kept pulling, far longer than he should have needed to.

The blade slid free. Morgan Leah stared. The Sword of Leah was no longer broken. It was as perfect as it had been on the day it had been given to him by his father.

"Highlander!" Horner Dees breathed in astonishment.

"She spoke the truth," Morgan whispered, letting his fingers slide along the blade's gleaming surface. He looked at Walker, incredulous. "How?"

"Her magic," Walker answered, smiling at the look on the other's face. "She became again the elements of the earth that were used by her father to create her, among them the metals that forged the blade of the Sword of Leah. She remade your talisman in the same way she remade this land. It was her final act, Highlander. An act of love."

Morgan's gray eyes burned fiercely. "In a sense then, she's still with me, isn't she? And she'll stay with me as long as I keep possession of the Sword." He took a deep breath. "Do you think the Sword has its magic back again, Walker?"

"I think that the magic comes from you. I think it always has."

Morgan studied him wordlessly for a moment, then nodded slowly. He sheathed his weapon carefully in his belt. "I have my Sword back, but there is still the matter of your arm. What of that? She said that you, like the blade, would be made whole again."

Walker thought carefully a moment, then pursed his lips. "Indeed." With his good hand, he turned Morgan gently toward the defile. "I am beginning to think, Highlander," he said softly, "that when she spoke of becoming whole, she was not referring to my arm, but to something else altogether."

Behind them, sunlight spilled down across the Tiderace.

HER EYES!

They stared down at Pe Ell from the empty windows of the buildings of Eldwist, and when he was free of the city they peered up from the fissures and clefts of the isthmus rock, and when he was to the cliffs they peeked out from behind the misted boulders of the trail leading up. Everywhere he ran, the eyes followed.

What have I done?

He was consumed with despair. He had killed the girl, just as he had intended; he had gained possession of the Black Elfstone. Everything had gone exactly as planned. Except for the fact that the plan had never been his at all—it had been hers from the beginning. That was what he had seen in her eyes, the truth of why he was here and what he had been summoned to do. She had brought him to Eldwist not to face the Stone King and retrieve the Black Elfstone as he had believed; she had brought him to kill her.

Shades, to kill her!

He ran blindly, stumbling, sprawling, clawing his way back to his feet, torn by the realization of how she had used him.

He had never been in control. He had merely deluded himself into thinking he was. All of his efforts had been wasted. She had manipulated him from the first—seeking him out in Culhaven knowing who and what he was, persuading him to come with them while letting him think that he was coming because it was his choice, and keeping him carefully away from the others, turning him this way and that as her dictates required, using him! Why? Why had she done it? The question seared like fire. Why had she wanted to die?

The fire gave way to cold as he saw the eyes wink at him from left and right and all about. Had it even been his choice at the end to stab her? He couldn't remember making a conscious decision to do so. It had almost seemed as if she had impaled herself—or made his hand move forward those few necessary inches. Pe Ell had been a puppet for the daughter of the King of the Silver River all along; perhaps she had pulled the strings that moved him one final time—and then opened her eyes to him so that all her secrets could be his.

He TUMBLED TO THE GROUND when he reached the head of the cliff path, flinging himself into a cleft between the rocks, huddling down, burying his gaunt, ravaged face in his arms, wishing he could hide, could disappear. He clenched his teeth in fury. He hoped she was dead! He hoped they were all dead! Tears streaked his face, the anger and despair working through him, twisting him inside out. No one had ever done this to him. He could not stand what he was feeling! He could not tolerate it!

He looked up again, moments later, longer perhaps, aware suddenly that he was in danger, that the others would be coming in pursuit. Let them come! he thought savagely. But no, he was not ready to face them now. He could barely think. He needed time to recover himself.

He forced himself back to his feet. All he could think to do was run and keep running.

He reached the defile leading back through the cliffs, away from the ramp and any view of that hated city. He could feel tremors rock the earth and hear the rumble of the Maw Grint. Rain washed over him, and gray mist descended until it seemed the clouds were resting atop the land. Pe Ell clutched the leather bag with its rune markings and its precious contents close against his chest. The Stiehl rested once again in its sheath on his hip. He could feel the magic burning into his hands, against his thigh, hotter than he had ever felt it, fire that might never be quenched. What had the girl done to him? What had she done?

He fell, and for a moment was unable to rise. All the strength had left him. He looked down at his hands, seeing the blood that streaked them. Her blood.

Her face flashed before him out of the gloom, bright and vibrant, her silver hair flung back, her black eyes . . .

Quickening!

He managed to scramble back to his feet and ran faster still, slipping wildly, trying to fight against the visions, to regain his composure, his self-control. But nothing would settle into place, everything was jumbled and thrown about, madness loosed within him like a guard dog set free. He had killed her, yes. But she had made him do it, made him! All those feelings for her, false from the start, her creations, her twisting of him!

Bone Hollow opened before him, filled with rocks and emptiness. He did not slow. He ran on.

Something was happening behind him. He could feel a shifting of the tremors, a changing of the winds. He could feel something cold settling deep within. *Magic!* A voice whispered, teasing, insidious. *Quickening comes for you!* But Quickening was dead! He howled out loud, pursued by demons that all bore her face.

He stumbled and fell amid a scattering of bleached bones, shoved himself back to his knees, and realized suddenly where he was.

Time froze for Pe Ell, and a frightening moment of insight blossomed within.

The Koden!

Then, abruptly, it had him, its shaggy limbs enfolding him, its body smelling of age and decay. He could hear the whistle of its breath in his ear and could feel the heat of it on his face. The closeness of the beast was suffocating. He struggled to catch a glimpse of it and found he could not. It was there, and at the same time it wasn't. Had it somehow become invisible? He tried to reach for the handle of the Stiehl, but his fingers would not respond.

How could this be happening?

He knew suddenly that he was not going to escape. He was only mildly surprised to discover that he no longer cared.

An instant later, he was dead.

CHAPTER

32

ESS THAN AN HOUR LATER the last three survivors of the company from Rampling Steep made their way into Bone Hollow and found Pe Ell's body. It lay midway through, sprawled loose and uncaring upon the earth, lifeless gaze fixed upon the distant sky. One hand clutched the rune-marked leather bag that contained the Black Elfstone. The Stiehl was still in its sheath.

Walker Boh glanced about curiously. Quickening's magic had worked its way through Bone Hollow, changing it so that it was no longer recognizable. Saw grass and jump weed grew everywhere in tufts that shaded and softened the hard surface of the rock. Patches of yellow and purple wildflowers bent to find the sun, and the bones of the dead had faded back into the earth. Nothing remained of what had been.

"Not a mark on him," Horner Dees muttered, his rough face creased further by the frown that bent his mouth, his voice wondering. He moved forward, bent down to take a close look, then straightened. "Neck might be broke. Ribs crushed. Something like that. But nothing that I can see. A little blood on his hands, but that belongs to the girl. And look. Koden tracks all around, everywhere. It had to have caught him. Yet there's not a mark on his body. How do you like that?"

There was no sign of the Koden. It was gone, disappeared as if it had never been. Walker tested the air, probed the silence, closed his eyes to see if he could find the Koden in his mind.

No. Quickening's magic had set it free. As soon as the chains that bound it were broken, it had gone back into its old world, become itself again, a bear only, the memories of what had been done to it already fading. Walker felt a deep sense of satisfaction settle through him. He had managed to keep his promise after all.

"Look at his eyes, will you?" Horner Dees was saying. "Look at the fear in them. He didn't die a happy man, whatever it was that killed him. He died scared."

"It must have been the Koden," Morgan Leah insisted. He hung back from the body, unwilling to approach it.

Dees glanced pointedly at him. "You think so? How, then? What did it do, hug him to death? Must have done it pretty quick if it did. That knife of his isn't even out of its case. Take a look, Highlander. What do you see?"

Morgan stepped up hesitantly and stared down. "Nothing," he admitted.

"Just as I said." Dees sniffed. "You want me to turn him over, look there?"

Morgan shook his head. "No." He studied Pe Ell's face a moment without speaking. "It doesn't matter." Then his eyes lifted to find Walker's. "I don't know what to feel. Isn't that odd? I wanted him dead, but I wanted to be the one who killed him. I know it doesn't matter who did it or how it happened, but I feel cheated somehow. As if the chance to even things up had been taken away from me."

"I don't think that's the case, Morgan," the Dark Uncle replied softly. "I don't think the chance was ever yours in the first place."

The Highlander and the old Tracker stared at him in surprise. "What are you saying?" Dees snapped.

Walker shrugged. "If I were the King of the Silver River and it was necessary for me to sacrifice the life of my child to an assassin's blade, I would make certain her killer did not escape." He shifted his gaze from one face to the other and back again. "Perhaps the magic that Quickening carried in her body was meant to serve more than one purpose. Perhaps it did."

There was a long silence as the three contemplated the prospect. "The blood on his hands, you think?" Horner Dees said finally. "Like a poison?" He shook his head. "Makes as much sense as anything else."

Walker Boh reached down and carefully freed the bag with the Black Elfstone from Pe Ell's rigid fingers. He wiped it clean, then held it in his open palm for a moment, thinking to himself how ironic it was that the Elfstone would have been useless to the assassin. So much effort expended to gain possession of its magic and all for nothing. Quickening had known. The King of the Silver River had known. If Pe Ell had known as well, he would have killed the girl instantly and been done with the matter. Or would he have remained anyway, so captivated by her that even then he would not have been able to escape? Walker Boh wondered.

"What about this?" Horner Dees reached down and unstrapped the Stiehl from around Pe Ell's thigh. "What do we do with it?"

"Throw it into the ocean," Morgan said at once. "Or drop it into the deepest hole you can find."

It seemed to Walker that he could hear someone else speaking, that the words were unpleasantly familiar ones. Then he realized he was thinking of himself, remembering what he had said when Cogline had brought him the Druid History out of lost Paranor. Another time, another magic, he thought, but the dangers were always the same.

"Morgan," he said, and the other turned. "If we throw it away, we risk the possibility that it will be found again—perhaps by someone as twisted and evil as Pe Ell. Perhaps by someone worse. The blade needs to be locked away where no one can ever reach it again." He turned to Horner Dees. "If you give it to me, I will see that it is."

They stood there for a moment without moving, three worn and ragged figures in a field of broken stone and new green, measuring one another. Dees glanced once at Morgan, then handed the blade to Walker. "I guess we can trust you to keep your word as well as anyone," he offered.

Walker shoved the Stiehl and the Elfstone into the deep pockets of his cloak and hoped it was so.

THEY WALKED SOUTH the remainder of the day and spent their first night free of Eldwist on a barren, scrub-grown plain. A day earlier, the plain had been a part of Uhl Belk's kingdom, infected by the poison of the Maw Grint, a broken carpet of stone. Even with nothing more than the scrub to brighten its expanse, it felt lush and comforting after the deadness of the city. There was little to eat yet, a few roots and wild vegetables, but there was fresh water again, the skies were star filled, and the air was clean and new. They made a fire and sat up late, talking in low voices of what they were feeling, remembering in the long silences what had been.

When morning came they awoke with the sun on their faces, grateful simply to be alive.

They traveled down again through the high forests and crossed into the Charnals. Horner Dees took them a different way this time, carefully avoiding dead Carisman's tribe of Urdas, journeying east of the Spikes. The weather stayed mild, even in the mountains, and there were no storms or avalanches to cause them further grief. Food was plentiful again, and they began to regain their strength. A sense of well-being returned, and the harshest of their memories softened and faded.

Morgan Leah spoke often of Quickening. It seemed to help him to speak of her, and both Walker and Horner Dees encouraged him to do so. Sometimes the Highlander talked as if she were still alive, touching the Sword he carried, and gesturing back to the country they were leaving behind. She was there, he insisted, and better that she were there than gone completely. He could sense her presence at times; he was certain of it. He smiled and joked and slowly began to return to himself.

Horner Dees became his old self almost as quickly, the haunted look fading from his eyes, the tension disappearing from his face. The gruffness in his voice lost its edge, and for the first time in weeks the love he bore for his mountains began to work its way back into his conversation.

Walker Boh recovered more slowly. He was encased in an iron shell of fatalistic resignation that had stripped his feelings nearly bare. He had lost his arm in the Hall of Kings. He had lost Cogline and Rumor at Hearthstone. He had nearly lost his life any number of times. Carisman was dead. Quickening was dead. His vow to refuse the charge that Allanon had given him was dead. Quickening had been right. There were always choices. But sometimes the choices were made for you, whether you wanted it so or not. He might have thought not to be ensnared by Druid machinations, to turn his life away from Brin Ohmsford and her legacy of magic. But circumstances and conscience made that all but impossible. His was a destiny woven by threads that stretched back in time hundreds, perhaps thousands, of years, and he could not be free of them, not entirely, at least. He had thought the matter through since that night in Eldwist when he had agreed to return with Quickening to the lair of the Stone King in an effort to recover the Black Elfstone. He knew that by going he was agreeing that if they were successful he would carry the talisman back into the Four Lands and attempt to restore Paranor and the Druids—just as Allanon had charged him.

He knew without having to speak the words what that meant.

Make whatever choice you will, Quickening had advised.

But what choices were left to him? He had determined long ago to search out the Black Elfstone—perhaps from the moment he had first discovered its existence while reading the Druid History; certainly from the time of the death of Cogline. He had determined as well to discover what its magic would do— and that meant testing Allanon's charge that Paranor and the Druids could be restored. He might argue that he had been considering the matter right up until the moment Eldwist had met its end. But he knew the truth was otherwise. He knew as well that if the magic of the Black Elfstone was everything that had been promised, if it worked as he believed, then Paranor would be restored. And if that happened, then the Druids would come back into the Four Lands.

Through him.

Beginning with him.

And that reality provided the only choice left to him, the one he believed Quickening had wanted him to make—the choice of who he would be. If it was true that Paranor could be restored and that he must become the first of the Druids who would keep it, then he must make certain he did not lose himself in the process. He must make certain that Walker Boh sur-

vived—his heart, his ideas, his convictions, his misgivings—
everything he was and believed. He must not evolve into the
very thing he had struggled so hard to escape. He must not, in
other words, turn into Allanon. He must not become like the
Druids of old—manipulators, exploiters, dark and secretive con-
jurers, and hiders of truths. If the Druids must return in order
to preserve the Races, in order to ensure their survival against
the dark things of the world, Shadowen or whatever, then he
must make them as they should be—a better order of Men, of
teachers, and of givers of the power of magic.

That was the choice he could still make—a choice he must
make if he were to keep his sanity.

It took them almost two weeks to reach Rampling Steep, choosing the longer, safer routes, skirting any possibility of danger, sheltering when it was dark, and emerging to travel on when it was
light. They came on the mountainside town toward midday, the
skies washed with a gray, cloudy haze left by a summer shower
that suggested spun cotton pulled apart by too-anxious hands. The
day was warm and humid, and the buildings of the town glistened
like damp, squat toads hunched down against the rocks. The three
travelers approached as strangers, seeing the town anew, the first
since Eldwist. They slowed as one as they entered the solitary
street that navigated the gathering of taverns, stables, and trading
stores to either side, pausing to look back into the mountains they
had descended, watching momentarily as the runoff from the storm
churned down out of the cliffs into gullies and streams, the sound
a distant rush.

"Time to say goodbye," Horner Dees announced without
preliminaries and stuck out his hand to Morgan.

Morgan stared. There had been no talk of his leaving until
now. "You're not coming on with us?"

The old Tracker snorted. "I'm lucky to be alive, Highlander.
Now you want me to come south? How far do you expect me
to push things?"

Morgan stammered. "I didn't mean . . ."

"Fact is, I shouldn't have gone with you the first time." The
other cut him short with a wave of one big hand. "It was the
girl who talked me into it. Couldn't say no to her. And maybe
it was the sense of having left something behind when I fled the

Stone King and his monsters ten years ago. I had to go back to find it again. So here I am, the only man to have escaped Eldwist and Uhl Belk twice. Seems to me that's enough for one old man."

"You would be welcome to come with us, Horner Dees," Walker Boh assured him, taking Morgan's part. "You're not as old as you pretend and twice as able. The Highlander and his friends can use your experience."

"Yes, Horner," Morgan agreed hurriedly. "What about the Shadowen? We need you to help fight them. Come with us."

But the old Tracker shook his bearish head stubbornly. "Highlander, I'll miss you. I owe you my life. I look at you and see the son I might have had under other circumstances. Now isn't that something to admit? But I've had enough excitement in my life and I'm not anxious for any more. I need the dark quiet of the ale houses. I need the comforts of my own place." He stuck out his hand once again. "Who's to say that won't change though? So. Some other time, maybe?"

Morgan clasped the hand in his own. "Any time, Horner." Then, forsaking the hand, he embraced the old man. Horner Dees hugged him back.

The journey went swiftly after that, time slipping away almost magically, the days and nights passing like quicksilver. Walker and Morgan came down out of the Charnals into the foothills south and turned west along their threshold toward the Rabb. They forded the north branch of the river and the land opened into grasslands that stretched away toward the distant peaks of the Dragon's Teeth. The days were long and hot, the sun burning out of cloudless skies as the intemperate weather of the mountains was left behind. Sunrise came early, and daylight stayed late, and even the nights were warm and bright. The pair encountered few travelers and no Federation patrols. The land grew increasingly infected by the Shadowen sickness, dark patches that hinted at the spread of the disease, but there was no sign of the carriers.

At week's end, the Dark Uncle and the Highlander reached the south entrance to the Jannisson Pass. It was nearing noon, and the pass stretched away through the juncture of the cliffs of the Dragon's Teeth and the Charnals, a broad empty corridor leading north to the Streleheim. It was here that Padishar Creel had hoped to rally the forces of the Southland Movement, the Dwarf Resistance, and the Trolls of Axhind and his Kelktic Rock in an effort to confront and destroy the armies of the Federation. The wind blew gently across the flats and down through the pass, and no one stirred.

Morgan Leah cast about wearily, a resigned look on his face. Walker stood silently beside him for a moment, then put his hand on the other's shoulder. "Where to now, Highlander?" he asked softly.

Morgan shrugged and smiled bravely. "South, I suppose, to Varfleet. I'll try to make contact with Padishar, hope that he's found Par and Coll. If that fails, I'll go looking for the Valemen on my own." He paused, studying the other's hard, pale face. "I guess I know where you're going."

Walker nodded. "To find Paranor."

Morgan took a deep breath. "I know this isn't what you wanted, Walker."

"No, it isn't."

"I could come with you, if you'd like."

"No, Highlander, you've done enough for others. It is time to do something for yourself."

Morgan nodded. "Well, I'm not afraid, if that's what you're thinking. I have the magic of the Sword of Leah again. I might be of some use."

Walker's fingers tightened on the other's shoulder and then dropped away. "I don't think anyone can help me where I'm going. I think I have to help myself as best I can. The Elfstone will likely be my best protection." He sighed. "Strange how things work out. If not for Quickening, neither of us would be doing what he is or even be who he is, would he? She's given us both a new purpose, a new face, maybe even a new strength. Don't forget what she gave up for you, Morgan. She loved you. I think that in whatever way she is able she always will."

"I know."

"Horner Dees said you saved his life. You saved my life as well. If you hadn't used the sword, even broken as it was, Uhl Belk would have killed me. I think Par and Coll Ohmsford could ask for no better protector. Go after them. See that they are well. Help them in any way you can."

"I will."

They clasped hands and held tight for a moment, eyes locked.

"Be careful, Walker," Morgan said.

Walker's smile was faint and ironic. "Until we meet again, Morgan Leah."

Then Walker turned and walked into the pass, angling through sunlight into shadow as the rocks closed about. He did not look back.

FOR THE REMAINDER OF that day and the whole of the one following Walker Boh traveled west across the Streleheim, skirting the dark, ancient forests that lay south, cradled by the peaks of the Dragon's Teeth. On the third day he turned down, moving into the shadowed woods, leaving the plains and the sunshine behind. The trees were massive, towering sentinels set at watch like soldiers waiting to be sent forth into battle, thick trunks grown close in camaraderie, and limbs canopied against the light. These were the forests that for centuries past had sheltered the Druid's Keep against the world beyond. In the time of Shea Ohmsford there had been wolves set at watch. Even after, there had been a wall of thorns that none could penetrate but Allanon himself. The wolves were gone now, the wall of thorns as well, and even the Keep itself. Only the trees remained, wrapped in a deep, pervasive silence.

Walker navigated the trails as if he were a shadow, passing soundlessly through the sea of trunks, across the carpet of dead needles, lost in the roil of his increasing indecision. His thoughts of what he was about to do were jumbled and rough-edged, and whispers of uncertainty that he had thought safely put to rest had risen to haunt him once again. All his life he had fought to escape Brin Ohmsford's legacy; now he was rushing willingly to embrace it. His decision to do so had been long in coming and repeatedly questioned. It had resulted from an odd mix of circumstance, conscience, and deliberation. He had given it as much thought as he was capable of giving and he was convinced that he had chosen right. But the prospect of its consequences was terrifying nevertheless, and the closer he came to discovering them, the deeper grew his misgivings.

By the time he arrived at the heart of the forests and the bluff on which Paranor had once rested, he was in utter turmoil. He stood for a long time staring upward at the few stone blocks that remained of what had once been the outbuildings, at the streaking of red light across the bluff's crest where the sunset cast its heated, withering glow. In the shimmer of the dying light he could imagine it was possible to see Paranor rise up against the coming night, its parapets sharply defined and its towers piercing the sky's azure crown like spears. He could feel the immensity of the Keep's presence, the sullen bulk of its stone. He could touch the life of its magic, waiting to be reborn.

He built a fire and sat before it, awaiting the descent of night. When it was fully dark, he rose and walked again to the bluff's edge. The stars were pinpricks of brightness overhead, and the woods about him were anxious with night sounds. He felt foreign and alone. He stared upward once more at the crest of the rise, probing from within with his magic for some sign of what waited. Nothing revealed itself. Yet the Keep was there; he could sense its presence in a way that defied explanation. The fact that his magic failed to substantiate what he already knew made him even more uneasy. Bring back lost Paranor and the Druids, Allanon had said. What would it take to do so? What beyond possession of the Black Elfstone? There would be more, he knew. There would have to be.

He slept for a few hours, though sleep did not come easily, a frail need against the whisper of his fears. He lay awake at first, his resolve slipping away, eroded and breached. The trappings of a lifetime's mistrust ensnared him, working free of the restraints under which he had placed them, threatening to take control of him once again. He forced himself to think of Quickening. What must it have been like for her, knowing what she was expected to do? How frightened she must have been! Yet she had sacrificed herself because that was what was needed to give life back to the land. He took strength in remembering her courage, and after a time the whispers receded again, and he fell asleep.

It was already daybreak when he awoke, and he washed and ate quickly, woodenly, anxious in the shadow of what waited. When he was done he walked again to the base of the bluff and stared upward. The sun was behind him, and its light spilled down upon the bluff's barren summit. Nothing had changed. No hint of what had been or what might be revealed itself. Paranor remained lost in time and space and legend.

Walker stepped away, returning to the edge of the trees, safely back from the bluff. He reached into the deep pockets of his cloak and lifted free the pouch that contained the Black Elfstone. He stared blankly at it, feeling the weight of its power press against him. His body was stiff and sore; his missing arm ached. His throat was as dry as autumn leaves. He felt the insecurities, doubts, and fears begin to rise within him, massing in a wave that threatened to wash him away.

Quickly, he dumped the Elfstone into his open palm.

He closed his hand instantly, frightened to look into its dark light. His mind raced. One Stone, one for all, one for heart, mind, and body—made that way, he believed, because it was the antithesis of all the other Elfstones created by the creatures of the old world of faerie, a magic that devoured rather than expended, one that absorbed rather than released. The Elfstones that Allanon had given to Shea Ohmsford were a talisman to defend their holder against whatever dark magic threatened. But the Black Elfstone was created for another reason entirely—not to defend, but to enable. It was conceived for a single purpose— to counteract the magic that had been called forth to spirit away the Druid's Keep, to bring lost Paranor out of limbo again. It would do so by consuming that magic—and transferring it into the body of the Stone's holder—himself. What that would do to him, Walker could only imagine. He knew that the Stone's protection against misuse lay in the fact that it would work the same way no matter who wielded it and for what purpose. That was what had destroyed Uhl Belk. His absorption of the Maw Grint's magic had turned him to stone. Walker's own fate might be similar, he believed—yet it would also be more complex. But how? If use of the Black Elfstone restored Paranor, then what would be the consequence of transference to himself of the magic that bound the Keep?

Whosoever shall have cause and right shall wield it to its proper end.

Himself. Yet why? Because Allanon had decreed that it must be so? Had Allanon told the truth? Or simply a part of the truth? Or was he gamesplaying once more? What could Walker Boh believe?

He stood there, solitary, filled with indecision and dread, wondering what it was that had brought him to this end. He saw his hand begin to shake.

Then suddenly, unexpectedly, the whispers broke through his defenses in a torrent and turned to screams.

No!

He brought the Black Elfstone up almost without thinking, opened his hand, and thrust the dark gem forth.

Instantly the Elfstone flared to life, its magic a sharp tingling against his skin. Black light—the nonlight, the engulfing darkness. *Whosoever.* He watched the light gather before him, building on itself. *Shall have cause and right.* The backlash of the magic rushed through him, shredding doubt and fear, silencing whispers and screams, filling him with unimaginable power. *Shall wield it to its proper end.*

Now!

He sent the black light hurtling forth, a huge tunnel burrowing through the air, swallowing everything in its path, engulfing substance and space and time. It exploded against the crest of the empty bluff, and Walker was hammered back as if struck a blow by an invisible fist. Yet he did not fall. The magic rushed through him, bracing him, wrapping him in armor. The black light spread like ink against the sky, rising, broadening, angling first this way, then that, channeling itself as if there were runnels to be followed, gutters down which it must flow. It began to shape. Walker gasped. The light of the Black Elfstone was etching out the lines of a massive fortress, its parapets and battlements, and its towers and steeples. Walls rose and gates appeared. The light spread higher against the skies, and the sunlight was blocked away. Shadows cast down by the castle enveloped Walker Boh, and he felt himself disappear into them.

Something inside him began to change. He was draining away. No, rather he was filling up! Something, the magic, was washing through. *The other,* he thought, weak before its onslaught, helpless and suddenly terrified. It was the magic that encased lost Paranor being drawn down into the Elfstone!

And into him.

His jaw clenched, and his body went rigid. *I will not give way!*

The black light flooded the empty spaces of the image atop the bluff, coloring it, giving it first substance and then life— Paranor, the Druid's Keep, come back into the world of men, returned from the dark half-space that had concealed it all these years. It rose up against the sky, huge and forbidding. The Black Elfstone dimmed in Walker's hand; the nonlight softened and then disappeared.

Walker's hoarse cry ended in a groan. He fell to his knees, wracked with sensations he could not define and riddled with the magic he had absorbed, feeling it course through him as if it were his blood. His eyes closed and then slowly opened. He saw himself shimmering in a haze that stole away the definition of his features. He looked down in disbelief, then felt himself go cold. He wasn't really there anymore! He had become a wraith!

He forced his terror aside and climbed back to his feet, the Black Elfstone still clutched in his hand. He watched himself move as if he were someone else, watched the shimmer of his limbs and body and the shadings that overlapped and gave him the appearance of being fragmented. *Shades, what has been done to me!* He stumbled forward, scrambling to gain the bluff, to reach its crest, not knowing what else to do. He must gain Paranor, he sensed. He must get inside.

The climb was long and rugged, and he was gasping for breath by the time he reached the Keep's iron gates. His body reflected in a multitude of images, each a little outside of the others. But he could breathe and move as a normal man; he could feel as he had before. He took heart from that, and hastened to reach Paranor's gates. The stone of the Keep was real enough, hard and rough to his touch—yet forbidding, too, in a way he could not immediately identify. The gates opened when he leaned into them, as if he had the strength of a thousand men and could force anything that stood before him.

He entered cautiously. Shadows enfolded him. He stood in a well of darkness, and there was a whisper of death all about.

Then something moved within the gloom, detached, and took shape—a four-legged apparition, hulking and ominous. It was a moor cat, black as pitch with luminous gold eyes, there and not there, like Walker himself.

Walker froze. The moor cat looked exactly like . . .

Behind the cat, a man appeared, old and stooped, a translucent ghost, shimmering. As the man drew near, his features became recognizable.

"At last you've come, Walker," he whispered in an anxious, hollow voice.

The Dark Uncle felt the last vestiges of his resolve fade away.

The man was Cogline.

CHAPTER

33

THE KING OF THE SILVER RIVER sat in the Gardens that were his sanctuary and watched the sun melt into the western horizon. A stream of clear water trickled across the rocks at his feet and emptied into a pond from which a unicorn drank, and a breeze blew softly through the maidenhair, carrying the scent of lilacs and jonquils. The trees rustled, their leaves a shimmer of green, and birds sang contented day-end songs as they settled into place in preparation for the coming of night.

Beyond, in the world of Men, the heat was sullen and unyielding against the fall of darkness, and a pall of weariness draped the lives of the people of the Four Lands.

So must it be for now.

The eyes that could see everything had seen the death of his child and the transformation of the land of the Stone King. The Maw Grint was no more. The city of Eldwist had gone back into the earth, returned to the elements that had created it, and the land was green and fertile again. The magic of his child was rooted deep, a river that flowed invisibly about the solitary dome in which Uhl Belk was imprisoned. It would be long before his brother could emerge into the light again.

Iridescent dragonflies buzzed past him without slowing and disappeared into the twilight's glow.

Elsewhere, the battle against the Shadowen went on. Walker Boh had invoked the magic of the Black Elfstone, as Allanon had charged him, and the Druid's Keep had been summoned out of the mists that had hidden it for three centuries. What would the Dark Uncle make, the King of the Silver River wondered, of what he found there? West, where the Elves had once lived, Wren Ohmsford continued her search to discover what had become of them—and, more important, though she did not yet realize it, what would become of herself. North, the brothers Par and Coll Ohmsford struggled toward each other and the secrets of the Sword of Shannara and the Shadowen magic. There were those who would help and those who would betray, and all of the wheels of chance that Allanon had set in motion could yet be stopped.

The King of the Silver River rose and slipped into the waters of the pond momentarily, reveling in the cool wetness, letting himself become one with the flow. Then he emerged and passed down the Garden pathways, through stands of juniper and hemlock onto a hillock of centauries and bluebells that reflected gold about the edges of their petals with the day's fading light. He paused there, staring out again into the world beyond.

His daughter had done well, he reflected.

But the thought was strangely bleak and empty. He had created an elemental out of the life of his Gardens and sent that elemental forth to serve his needs. She had been nothing to him—a daughter in name only, a child merely by designation. She had been only a momentary reality, and he had never intended that she be anything more.

Yet he missed her. Shaping her as he did, breathing his life into her, he had brought himself too close. The human feelings they had shared would not dissolve as easily as their human forms. She should have meant nothing to him, now that she was gone. Instead, her absence formed a void he could not seem to fill.

Quickening.

A child of the elements and his magic, he repeated. He would do the same again—yet perhaps not so readily. There was something in the ways of the creatures of the mortal Races that endured beyond the leaving of the flesh. There was a residue of their emotions that lingered. He could still hear her voice, see her face, and feel the touch of her fingers against him. She was gone from him, yet remained.

Why should it be so?

He sat there as darkness cloaked the land and wondered at himself.

HERE ENDS BOOK TWO of *The Heritage of Shannara*. Book Three, *The Elf Queen of Shannara*, will reveal more of the mystery of Cogline and Paranor and chronicle the efforts of Wren Ohmsford to discover what has become of the missing Westland Elves.

ABOUT THE AUTHOR

A writer in high school, TERRY BROOKS published his first novel, *The Sword of Shannara*, in 1977. It was a New York Times bestseller for more than five months. He has published seventeen consecutive bestsellers since, including *The Voyage of the Jerle Shannara: Ilse Witch* and the novel based upon the screenplay and story by George Lucas: *Star Wars®: Episode I The Phantom Menace*. His novels *Running with the Demon* and *A Knight of the Word* were each selected by *The Rocky Mountain News* as among the best science fiction/fantasy novels of the twentieth century. The author was a practicing attorney for many years but now writes full-time. He lives with his wife, Judine, in the Pacific Northwest and Hawaii. Visit Terry Brooks online at www.shannara.com and at www.terrybrooks.net.